Praise for Peter Elbling's

"Loaded with humor and laced with fascinating period detail, this hilarious Renaissance romp also doubles as an enlightening microcosm of sixteenth-century society and customs." —*Booklist*

"A clever tale set in sixteenth-century Italy of a peasant turned food taster who survives by his wits, as well as by luck and a few twists of the incredible." —*Kirkus Reviews*

"An entertaining cast of characters, most notably the hapless but charismatic DiFonte, who somehow manages to keep his head above water as he stumbles from one palace conspiracy to the next. An enjoyable spin on the usual Renaissance comedy-of-manners formula." —*Publishers Weekly*

"Peter Elbling's first novel . . . offers a brutal, unromantic portrait of Renaissance life . . . funny, fast, visual, and gritty." —*The Portsmouth Herald*

"Elbling has penned in *The Food Taster* a bizarre and engaging tale in the tradition of Cervantes's *Don Quixote* . . . Fascinating details about love and death in sixteenth-century Italy form the substance of this ingenious fiction." —*The Independent*

Peter Elbling is a writer, actor, and director who has worked in television, film, and theater. He lives in Venice, California.

Visit www.peterelbling.com

The Food Taster

Peter Elbling

A PLUME BOOK

PLUME
Published by the Penguin Group
Penguin Group (USA) Inc., 375 Hudson Street, New York, New York 10014, U.S.A.
Penguin Books Ltd, 80 Strand, London WC2R 0RL, England
Penguin Books Australia Ltd, 250 Camberwell Road, Camberwell, Victoria 3124, Australia
Penguin Books Canada Ltd, 10 Alcorn Avenue, Toronto, Ontario, Canada M4V 3B2
Penguin Books (N.Z.) Ltd, Cnr Rosedale and Airborne Roads, Albany, Auckland 1310,
New Zealand

Penguin Books Ltd, Registered Offices: 80 Strand, London WC2R 0RL, England

Published by Plume, a member of Penguin Group (USA) Inc. This is an authorized
reprint of a hardcover edition published by The Permanent Press. For information
address The Permanent Press, 4170 Noyac Road, Sag Harbor, New York 11963.

First Plume Printing, June 2003
10 9 8 7 6 5 4 3 2 1

 REGISTERED TRADEMARK—MARCA REGISTRADA

The Library of Congress has catalogued the Permanent Press edition as follows:

Elbling, Peter.
    The food taster / Ugo DiFonte; translated by Peter Elbling.
        p.   cm.
    Fictional memoir of medieval Italy written by Peter Elbling and ostensibly translated
from Italian.
    ISBN 1-57962-047-7 (hc.)
    ISBN 0-452-28434-1 (pbk.)
    1. Father and daughters—Fiction. 2. Master and servant—Fiction. 3. Peasantry—
Fiction. 4. Poisoning—Fiction. 5. Nobility—Fiction. 6. Cookery—Fiction.
7. Italy—Fiction. I. Title.

PS35555 L19 F66 2002
813'.54—dc21   2001036618

Printed in the United States of America

PUBLISHER'S NOTE
This is a work of fiction. Names, characters, places, and incidents either are the products
of the author's imagination or are used fictitiously, and any resemblance to actual persons,
living or dead, business establishments, events, or locales is entirely coincidental.

for Dimitri and Simon

i

March 1534

For years after my mother hanged herself, I wished I had been older or stronger so that I could have stopped her. But since I was only a child who could not even reach her waist, I had to watch helplessly until it was over.

The day before, we had celebrated the feast of San Antony stuffing ourselves on roast pig, cabbage, beans, polenta, and dried chestnuts. We stuffed ourselves because the plague had been walking through the valley for weeks, striking whomever it pleased, and no one knew if they would live to see the sun rise.

Now it was evening and Mama and I were staring at the hilltops where my father and my older brother, Vittore, were lighting bonfires. I preferred to stay with my mother. I liked it when she scratched my head, put her arms around me, and called me "my little prince." Besides, that afternoon that bastard Vittore had banged my head against a tree and it still hurt.

It was dark, there was no moon, but I could hear my father's bellowing over everyone else's. The wind teased the fires this way and that as a man teases a dog by pulling on a stick in its mouth. Then the flames shot straight into the air, and for the blink of an eye I could see the men standing like ants on the top of the hills. Suddenly, one of the bonfires toppled over and bounced down the hill, a huge fiery ball, spinning over and over, faster and faster, leaping in the air, flattening bushes and crashing into trees as if the devil himself was guiding it.

"Holy Mother of God!" my mother cried. "It will eat us alive," and, grabbing my arm, she pulled me into our house. A moment later the flaming wheel passed right over the spot where we had been standing, and in the center of its fire I saw the face of Death staring straight at us. Then it disappeared down the hill leaving a trail of burning leaves and grasses behind it.

"Maria? Ugo? Are you all right?" my father shouted. "Are you hurt? Answer me!"

"*Stupido!*" my mother screamed, racing out of our house. "You could have killed us. *C'è uno bambino qui*. May the devil piss on your grave!"

"I missed," my father yelled to much laughter. My mother kept on shouting until she ran out of curses. They say I take after her because I use my tongue as others use a sword. Then my mother turned to me and said, "I am tired, I want to lie down."

When my father stumbled home, the sheepish expression on his face pulling his big curved nose even closer to his pointed chin, my mother had boils the size of eggs under her armpits. Her eyes had sunk into her head, her teeth were rising up from her gums. Everything I loved about her was slipping away in front of my eyes so I clasped her hand tightly so she would not vanish completely.

When the sun rose, Death was waiting in the doorway. My father sat on the floor by the bed, his big face in his hands, weeping silently.

"Vicente, lay me outside" my mother whispered. "Go. Take the boys with you."

I climbed up the chestnut tree outside our house and straddled one of the branches. My father lay my poor mama on the ground and placed a bowl of polenta and water next to her. My brother Vittore told me to come down to watch the sheep with him.

I shook my head.

"Come down!" my father yelled.

"Ugo, my angel, go with him," my mother pleaded.

But I would not. I knew that if I left I would never see her alive again. My father tried to climb up after me but he could not, and since Vittore was afraid of heights he threw stones at me instead. They hit my back and cracked my head, but though I cried bitterly, I stayed where I was.

"Go without him," my mother said.

So my father and Vittore climbed the hill, stopping every now and again to shout at me, but the wind twisted their words until they were no more than the cries of a distant animal. My mother coughed up blood. I told her I was praying for her and she would soon get better.

"*Mio piccolo principe*," she whispered. She winked at me and said she knew a secret cure. She took off her shift, tore it in half, threw one end up to me and told me to tie it round the branch. I was happy to help her. It was only when she wrapped the other end around her neck that I sensed something was wrong. "*Mamma, mi dispiace!*" I cried, "*Mi dispiace!*" I tried to untie the knot but my hands were too small and besides my mother was making it tighter by jumping into the air and pulling her knees up to her chest. I screamed for my father, but the wind threw my cries back in my face.

The third time my mother jumped there was a crack like a piece of wood snapping. Her tongue shot from her mouth and the smell of shit curled up to me.

I do not know how long I screamed. I only know that, unable to move, I stayed on the branch all night, whipped by the wind, ignored by the stars and engulfed by the stench of my mother's decaying body until my father and Vittore returned the following morning.

ii

Until the death of my mother, I had known only one sort of hunger, but now my heart was emptier than my stomach and only night brought my weeping mercifully to an end. Then I prayed to join her because after she died my father became more bitter than wormwood. Nothing I did pleased him. He said I burned the polenta. He said I let birds escape from his traps. Whatever I did or said made him angry. "You have your mother's tongue," he shouted at me. "You will come to a bad end."

To avoid his temper I spent my days minding our flock, sometimes taking Vittore's turn. Vittore was five years older than me and looked older still because he was tall and thin. He had a long nose like my father, but my mother's small flat chin which threatened to crumble under the weight of his face. When he boasted how he had won at cards or screwed some girl, my father clapped him on the back. When they went fishing I had to spend the night alone with the sheep. I did not mind. I knew them all by name. I talked to them. I sang to them. Christ! Later on I even fucked one of them. I am not proud of it, but it is the truth and what is the point of writing all this if I do not write the truth? Besides, *all* shepherds have fucked sheep and if they say they have not, then trust me, they are liars and they will burn in hell. Anyway, compared to Vittore, I was a saint. Whenever the sheep saw him coming, they would run the other way.

I built fires to warm myself at night, and if the sheep did not talk to me they did not beat me either, although I was nearly bitten by a wolf who snatched a lamb. I was blamed for that, too.

Five years after my mother died, famine struck our valley. Our crops died, our chickens were too thin to lay eggs, and since our sheep belonged to the lord of the valley, we were forbidden to even eat their turds. I had often prayed for sleep to forget my hunger, but now my stomach ached all the time and my knees were so weak I could not stand. My father made a pie out of chestnut flour and grass and baked it on the stones by the fire. He sang a song which went,

Cut the loaf of bread in half
The first half to eat,
The second to shove up my *culo*
To stop what I ate from coming out.

I dreamed my mother was making my favorite pies stuffed with figs and apples. The smell of the hot apples excited me and I asked her if I could have a small slice. She smiled and broke off a piece of crust for me. But as I reached out for it I woke up to find that my father and Vittore were already eating. "Where is mine?" I asked.

My father pointed to a small black glob of pie on one of the stones. "That is it?"

"You were asleep."

Tears welled in my eyes.

"Do you want it or not?" Vittore shouted at me. I grabbed it. His hand closed over my fist.

"It is mine," I screamed. The pie burned my palm but I would not let go. My father shouted "*Basta!*" and opened my fist up. The piece had been squeezed into a ball half its size. He broke it in two and gave half to Vittore. "He is bigger than you," he said. "Now eat before I give it all to him."

"One day I will have as much food as I like," I shouted. "You will be starving and I will not give you a crumb."

"You are no son of mine," my father said, and smacked me across the face. The pie flew out of my mouth. Vittore laughed and my father joined in. My father's words carved themselves into my heart even as the picture of the two of them laughing etched itself into my memory. No matter how many things have happened to me since then, I have never forgotten that moment. My mother used to say, "He who bears a grudge will be buried beneath it." But I thank God for giving me a grudge! I thought of it every single day and prayed for the time when I could have my revenge. Now God in His mercy has rewarded my patience.

iii

After my mother died, my father carried the weight of his sorrows on his back. In time they bent him double. When he could no longer walk to the pastures, Vittore inherited the flock. Since I had cared for them so often I asked Vittore for a few sheep to start my own farm somewhere else. He refused. That cursed, miserable *fallo!* (prick) I knew better than to ask him again, so the next morning before it was light, I bundled my clothes together, and without a word to Vittore or my father I left. I was about fourteen although I cannot be sure. I remember standing on top of the hills watching the clouds scurry across the skies as if they were late for church. I said, "They are blowing away my old life," and my spirits lifted immediately.

The sun was shining, the hills were dizzy with the smell of rosemary and fennel. God had blessed me! I began to sing and I would have sung all the way to Gubbio where I hoped to find work, had I not seen a girl on the path in front of me.

I noticed her hair first of all. It was as dark as the soil and tied in a plait which swayed down her back like a great horse's tail. I do not know why, but I wanted to grasp it in my hands. I wanted to bite it and rub its silky warmth against my face. Can you blame me? I was fourteen. I had spent all my life with sheep.

I did not know what to say to the girl so I crept behind a mulberry bush to see her better. She was about my own age with big dark eyebrows that matched her hair. Her lips were red and full, her nose straight and her cheeks as round as apples. She was wearing a loose blouse, but I could not see her breasts or if she had any. Her hands, which were quite small, were picking fennel and blue geraniums, lifting them up to her nose to smell before placing them in her basket. I had heard people talk and sing about love, but until that moment I did not know what it was. Now, as if I was suddenly bewitched, every part of me ached to be close to her.

The girl was singing to herself, a song about a woman waiting for her sweetheart to return from the war. At first, my heart was crushed because I thought she was singing about a real person. Then I remembered my mother used to sing about a woman waiting for her lover to come back from the sea, she had grown up in Bari, and I knew my father had never even seen the sea.

Although this gave me courage, I still did not say anything for the girl seemed so at peace and I did not want to frighten her. In truth, I feared she might be angry if she knew I had been watching her so I sat quite still as bees buzzed around my face and the stones cut into my thighs. A scorpion even crawled over my legs, but I hardly breathed.

I followed her back to her house, and all afternoon I hid in a nearby glade of oak trees, planning what I would say to her on the one hand, and on the other fighting with my feet, which wanted to run away. But as the sun sank behind the hills I was afraid that if I did not speak soon I never would. So I banged on her door and when she opened it, I asked her to marry me.

"If you had asked me on the hillside," she said slyly, "I might have said yes. But you waited too long." And she closed the door in my face!

Potta! I wanted to kill myself! But Elisabetta, for that was her name, had smiled before she closed the door so when her father, a small man with hands as large as cabbages, returned that evening, I told him I was looking for work. He asked me if I knew how to cut wood and I said I was the best woodcutter he had ever seen. He spat on the ground and said that if I was as good a woodcutter as I was a liar, he would never have to work again.

My days were filled with hard work, but Elisabetta's father had always wanted a son and he treated me kindly. If I did not eat well, at least I did not have to give my food to Vittore and my father. And in the summers, when we left off woodcutting and went to the plains north of Assisi to help with the wheat harvest, I ate like a pig. We were fed not once, but seven times in a day! There was as much pasta as we liked, bread shaped like *falli* and *bocche sdentate* (mouths without teeth), fried calves' liver, plenty of roast chicken and, of course, polenta. We drank and danced till we could not stand. A couple of the women lifted their dresses and showed off their *culi*. *Jesus in sancto!* That was it! The men leaped on them and screwed them in front of everyone.

The third summer, I took Elisabetta's hand and we walked to the trees on the edge of the field where the air was heavy with the scent of sage and thyme, and I asked her to marry me.

For a time we were happy. Then Elisabetta's father cut his thigh with a blow from his axe. It did not heal well and gangrene set in. Elisabetta became pregnant. Her father knew he was dying and wanted to live long enough to see his grandchild, but the good man passed away before that could happen.

One evening I came home to find Elisabetta screaming in pain. Her beautiful hair was matted with sweat. Her lips were black with dried blood where she had chewed them. She was in labor all day and all night. The midwife, a gnarled old woman said, "She is too thin. I can save one or the other."

"Save Elisabetta," I said, "we can always have more children."

When she heard that, Elisabetta lunged forward and grasped my arm. "Promise me you will take care of the child," she cried. "Promise!"

When I pleaded with her, she shook my arm and shrieked, "Promise!" so loudly that I did as she asked. No sooner had I done so than Elisabetta expelled the baby to the world and her soul to heaven. My Elisabetta for a blob of bloody, crying flesh.

I did not look at the suckling for two days. I blamed it for Elisabetta's death and, because I wanted to leave it for the wolves, the midwife hid it from me. On the third afternoon she put Miranda— that was the name Elisabetta had breathed before she died—in my arms. Oh, *miracolo!* What a miracle! That tiny life turned my sorrow to a joy I did not know existed! She was Elisabetta all over again. She had the same big, dark eyes, the same dimples in her cheeks, the same straight nose. She was already biting her bottom lip just as her mother used to! For months after, I prayed that God would forgive me for what I had said.

Miranda was a year old when I heard that Vittore's flock had died and that he had left the valley to become a soldier. I thought—my father will be lonely. This will be a good time to take Miranda to him, it is his first grandchild, he will be pleased to see her.

I got blisters upon blisters walking to my father's house and many times on the way I cursed myself for starting the journey. But when I saw his hunched-up figure sitting in the sun—he had become so much smaller—my pains were drowned in a sea of tenderness. Holding Miranda in my arms, I ran to him, crying, "Babbo! It is me, Ugo!"

He did not recognize me right away, his eyesight was failing, but when I came close and he knew who it was, he shouted at me for not coming to see him sooner! Even then it was my fault!

He was hungry and cold and had little money. "Where is Vittore?" I asked, pretending I did not know.

"Fighting for the Venetians," my father boasted. "He leads hundreds of men."

"Anyone who puts Vittore in charge of anything is a fool," I replied.

"You are jealous," my father shouted. "He has won honors. He will be a *condotierro*."

I was about to say, "You stupid ass! It is your own fault you are in this mess. Vittore ruined you and you know it. But instead you pretend he is a captain in the army. Screw you." But that is not really what I wanted to say.

In truth, I did not want to say anything. I wanted him to say something to show that he was glad to see me. I wanted him to cradle his only grandchild in his arms and kiss her face and squeeze her cheeks as other grandparents did. I wanted him to show Miranda off to his neighbors and proclaim that she was the most beautiful child in the whole world. But he did not. All he did was sniff at her and sneer, "A girl."

iv

After that I stopped cutting wood and raised vegetables in the valley of Corsoli. Most of them went to the palace, just as most of everything did. However, there was still enough left over to eat and sell in the market. I also had a goat, a sheep, some chickens, God's blessings, and Miranda, whom I loved more than life itself.

My Miranda! *Che bella raggazza!* A heavenly angel. Her lips were the color of rich red grapes and she had blushed apple cheeks just like her mother. Her skin was soft and she had light brown almond-shaped eyes that peeked out from beneath her thick, dark eyebrows. She often frowned even then, but this only endeared her to me even more. Her hair was thick like mine, but lighter in color. She loved to laugh and sing. And why not? She had the most beautiful voice even as a child. Clear and bright as a bird's in springtime. It was a mystery to me how she knew so many songs! Some, of course, she learned from me, but others must have been borne on the winds from churches in Assisi or festivals in Urbino. She only had to hear a melody once and I swear she could repeat it perfectly months later.

As they say, "He who makes himself laugh is never alone," and so she was never lonely. The animals adored her, sometimes knocking her to the ground in their eagerness to be near her. Then they would turn her cries to giggles by licking her tears away. When she was no more than three years old I saw her pretend to fall down just so they would do that. She could imitate all the birds and bleat so like our goat that it used to chase her round the farm. When she did this I would pick her up, squeeze her cheeks and say, "These are the prettiest apples in all of Corsoli," and tickle her till she begged me to stop.

When Miranda was eleven years old her breasts sprang up like young buds and she started her monthly courses. I used to take her to the market, but the boys would not leave her alone, so she often stayed at the Benedictine Convent, where the nuns stroked her hair and fought over who would teach her to read and write and spin wool.

One evening, as the sun was sinking behind the mountain, I was returning from the market with my friends Jacopo and Toro, when we were attacked by bandits. Jacopo fled, but Toro and I could not because we were sharing the same horse. Swearing loudly, Toro jumped down and drove his sword into the belly of one of the bandit's horses, causing it to rear up and fall on its rider. Since my knife was too small to fight against their swords, I threw my purse in the air, shouting, "Here is the money." I had tied another purse with most of the ducats to the horse's belly for safekeeping. Two bandits chased after it and I turned around to help Toro. But just then the fourth bandit was pulling his bloody sword from Toro's stomach. The effort made the bandit's hood jerk backward and I saw a thin gaunt face which, even though it had been over ten years since I had seen it, I recognized immediately. Vittore!

I shouted his name and he sprang toward me, but God sent an angel to protect me for I escaped his sword and rode into the forest as fast as I could. Suddenly I feared I might never see Miranda again, even as I had feared I would not see my mother the day she had fallen sick.

The nuns were at Vespers. The abbot Tottorini said it would be a sin to take Miranda from the convent, but I pushed him to the ground and ran through the convent opening every door until I found Miranda—in *his* room. Luckily for him, that fat bastard disappeared before I could find him.

"You brought me home to starve me," Miranda accused me a few weeks later. I had not planned it that way, but my traps were empty, our crops had withered, and our animals were too sick or thin to eat. We did not even have a few lousy chestnuts to make bread! "Sad is the person who is born poor and unfortunate," my mother used to say, "for he must have spit on his hands if he wants to eat and God knows how many times he will fast without a vow."

At dawn I led Miranda to the woods and told her to imitate a bird. When a finch perched on a tree close by, I killed it. I told her to do it again, but she shook her head.

I said, "What difference does it make how we catch them?"

She did not answer.

"If we do not eat we will die," I shouted at her.

She sang to please me, but the birds heard the tears in her voice and flew away.

I cooked the finch with some greens and told Miranda she could eat if she wanted, but if she was going to weep she had to go outside. She left. Despair overcame me. I thought of going to Corsoli to find work, but I was not a craftsman and I did not belong to a guild. I had no skills. I called Miranda to me. She looked fearfully at me from beneath her dark brown eyebrows. I held her in my arms—she was so thin I could put both my hands around her chest—and told her the story of how I met her mother, until she fell asleep.

I awoke as the sun's first rays were rising over the hills. I walked to our dried-up vegetables and fell on my knees saying, "Holy Mother, I ask your help not for me, but for my Miranda who will surely die unless she eats soon."

Before the words were out of my mouth the ground beneath me trembled. I could not see anything, but I could hear branches smashing and the yelping of hunting dogs. Suddenly, a most magnificent stag shot out of the trees, its eyes wild with fear, its black tongue hanging out of its mouth. It came so fast that before I could move, it leaped right over me and disappeared into the oaks on the other side. The next instant the air was filled with bloodthirsty cries and shouts that chilled my heart. I ran back to the hut just as a hundred hounds tore out of the forest, barking and snarling and howling, followed by a huge man on a black horse—Federico Basillione DiVincelli, Duke of Corsoli.

I had only seen Duke Federico once or twice and then from a distance, but that was the safest way to see him. Everyone knew he had killed his father and poisoned his brother Paolo to become duke. Before that he had been a *condotierro*—he had once slain thirty men single-handedly in battle—and had served princes all over Italy and Germany. It was also known that he had betrayed everyone he served. Because of this he had left Italy and spent five years in Turkey in the service of a sultan. Rumors swirled about him: he always wore silk, he feared the number seven because that was the day on which he had killed his brother, and he had once forced a woman to eat her own child. I did not know if any of this was true or not but *potta!* When I saw him face to face, I believed everything I had heard.

To begin with, his features were at war with one another. His face was round like a pie, but his nose, which cut his face in two, was as thin and as sharp as a sword. His eyes were small and fierce like a hawk's, but his bottom lip hung open like a dead fish. He had a thick bull neck but small hands.

But it was not just the way he looked that frightened me. I have seen stranger-looking men. There is a miller not far from Gubbio who has a third ear growing under his right one and a woman in Corsoli who has no nose. No, it was the arrogant way Duke Federico rode across my farm, as if not just the land but the very air itself belonged to him.

Do not ask me how, but the duke's horse nearly impaled himself on one of my bean stakes and reared so fiercely that Federico almost fell off. He drew his sword, cursing and yelling, and hacked the few shriveled beans I had left into a thousand pieces. Then he looked up and saw me standing in the doorway of my hut.

"*Avanzarsi!*" he shouted, his voice like two knives scraping together.

Sono fottuto, I thought, I am as good as dead. I whispered to Miranda, "Do not come out till after they have gone," and then I walked across my dusty, trampled plot to the duke. By this time the other hunters—there must have been a dozen or so—had ridden up and they sat on their prancing horses, in their dark green hunting jackets and big black boots, staring down their noses at me. The dogs bared their teeth and barked as I walked past them. A huge mastiff wearing a ruby-studded collar leaped up and would have bitten me if Duke Federico had not shouted, "Nero!"

I knelt in front of the duke, but as his sword was in his hand I decided it was better not to bow my head.

"Who told you to put your farm in the middle of my hunt?" Duke Federico demanded.

"No one, Your Honor. Begging a thousand pardons—"

"I lost a stag because of you," Federico said, and raised the sword above his head. I heard a scream and Miranda came running out of our hut and threw herself about my neck. Since the duke had served with the Turks, I knew he would not think twice about killing children, so I tore her arms from me and shouted, "Go away! Go away!"

A hunter with a long gray beard and a sad face said, "He could be useful."

"Useful?" Federico asked. "How?"

"He could take Lucca's place, Your Excellency."

"Yes," I said, rising to my feet. "I will take Lucca's place."

Federico's eyes opened wide and he laughed in a high shrill voice. The hunters immediately joined in, while I stood there, Federico's sword poised above me, Miranda's arms around my waist, thinking that must have been God speaking since I did not know what I was talking about! "Take him," Federico said, and looking at Miranda, he added, "And take her, too."

V

Since the hunter with the long gray beard sat Miranda in front of him on his horse, I did not mind running uphill with a rope tied around my neck for several hours. Each moment I stayed alive was a gift from God. He had performed a miracle. I was going to take Lucca's place. As I have written, I often went to Corsoli for market, but this time I saw things I had not noticed before or did not remember: the huge, gray stone wall of the West Gate, the houses huddled together along the streets winding their way to the top of the city, the sound of horses' hooves ringing on the cobblestones. We rode through the Piazza Del Vedura with its splashing fountain, through the Piazza San Giulio, and more winding streets, and then up the Weeping Steps to the Palazzo Fizzi. The palace stood on our right and, facing us across the piazza, the Duomo Santa Caterina with its beautiful golden Madonna above the door, to whom I whispered a prayer for Miranda's safety.

From the outside, the Palazzo Fizzi looked like a castle, but the inner courtyard was lined on three sides with columns and arches. That is what little I could see of it. Christ on a cross! It was as if the usual market had been moved inside. There was food everywhere! More food than I had ever seen in my whole life. Here women were tending to bubbling cauldrons and roasting spits; over there young girls sorted baskets of fruits and vegetables; and in the middle a group of men were carving up animal carcasses.

"What saint's day is this?" I asked a hunter. He said San Michele and the duke's birthday and then cuffed me on the head for not knowing. *Potta!* How was I to supposed know? There had been so many new saints in the past few years that I did not even know there was a San Michele.

We had just reached the stables when two soldiers dragged a man in front of Duke Federico.

"Did he confess?" The duke roared.

The soldiers nodded. But the man sobbed, "Your Excellency, it is not so."

The duke swung down from his horse and told the man to stick out his tongue. The courtyard had become silent, and glancing about me

I saw that every window had filled with faces. The man slowly, timidly stuck out his tongue. Duke Federico gripped it in his left hand, pulled his dagger with his right, sliced it off, and threw it to Nero.

Blood shot out of the man's mouth and onto Duke Federico's boots. Duke Federico turned to the other hunters. "First, he lies to me, then he bloodies my boots."

The man wailed piteously, his hands reaching to Nero, who, having eaten his tongue, was now busily lapping up his blood. Federico kicked the man. "Be quiet," he yelled and walked away.

But the man could not be quiet. As if they sympathized with his sorrow, the cauldrons, the spits, the prancing horses, and barking dogs all stilled so that his cries bounced off them and off the walls of the palazzo. Federico stopped, his back to the man.

I muttered, "Please God, make him be still."

But the man's good sense was captive to his terror. Tears streamed down his face, blood poured from his mouth, and agonized sobs continued to burst from his lips. Federico pulled his sword and, without looking, whirled about and stabbed the man through the back so that the point of his sword went right through his heart and came out blood red on the other side. All the hunters applauded. I felt Miranda's body stiffen and I pressed her face into me so she would not scream. A curly-haired youth—who I had noticed was staring at Miranda—nodded his head as if to say I had acted wisely.

Duke Federico pulled his sword from the man's back, wiped it on his body, and strode into the palace. The same soldiers who had brought the man out now dragged his body to the wall at the back of the courtyard and threw it down to the valley below. I could feel it bouncing off the cliffs, hear the bones crunching on its way to the bottom. In another moment the servants were back at work as if nothing had happened, but as we entered the palace I felt a great wind of hatred snap at the back of my neck.

Miranda and I were locked in the tower on the other side of the palace. The cell had iron doors with large locks, a tiny window near the ceiling, and a few wisps of soiled straw.

"Where are we, Babbo?" Miranda whispered. She was still trembling from what she had seen.

"In Duke Federico's palace."

"But this is not the palace."

"That is because they are preparing a grand room with beds and servants for each of us," I said as gaily as I could.

"But why?"

"Why? Because I am to take Lucca's place. Did you not hear the man?"

She thought for a moment and then said, "But who is Lucca?"

I did not know and when I did not answer I feared she would start weeping. I gathered her to me and looking in those soft dark eyes I promised her that God had not made us only to abandon us. I told her to recite all the prayers she had been taught, and while she did that I asked God if perhaps He had not mistaken us for someone else, and that if He had, could He not correct His mistake before it was too late.

Eventually, we ran out of prayers and so we huddled together in the corner of the cell and became so still that all I could hear was the beating of our hearts and at one moment I swear they stopped too.

"Please," I begged the guards when they came to take me away, "do not leave my daughter alone here."

A guard said, "We will do whatever we want." But the captain, who had a good heart said, "I have a daughter, too. I will take her upstairs."

I was led to a room with a large tub of sweet-smelling water and told to scrub myself and wash my hair. Other servants hurried by preparing for the banquet. The curly-haired youth passed by carrying a basket of apples. "Hey!" I called out, "Where's Lucca?" but he ignored me. The gray-bearded hunter looked in and said to the servants, "Make sure his hands are clean." The stupid idiots scrubbed my hands till they were raw and would have drawn blood had I not threatened to pull them into the tub with me. I was dried off and my hair brushed. Then I was shaved and given a pair of red hose, a white shirt, a jerkin, and a pair of shoes. When I had dressed, the servants held a mirror in front of me. They laughed, saying, "He does not recognize himself."

They were almost right. I recognized myself not because I knew what I looked like, but because I looked so much like my mother. My hair was straight like hers, I had her almond eyes, the left one slightly larger than the right. I do not remember what my nostrils looked like. Miranda says they are fleshy, but only my mother could have known if they were that way when I was born or if they became that way because of what I do. And yet, I was not that different from the men around me, thinner certainly, but no bigger or smaller. And so from appearances only, I did not know why I had been allowed to take Lucca's place. "Whose clothes are these?" I asked.

"Lucca's," the servants replied, and told me angrily I had no business asking questions.

Except for the shoes, which fit me perfectly, Lucca was bigger than me in every way. I was lost in his jerkin, the sleeves of the shirt were too long and so were the hose. Despite this I was pleased. It was still better than my shift. A guard took me to Miranda who was now in a pleasant room overlooking a garden of flowers.

"Babbo," she gasped, "you look like a prince!"

"This Lucca must have been somebody," I said. "Who knows, perhaps he has a daughter. Then you will get some new clothes too."

The sun had long stopped shining when the guards came for me again. I kissed Miranda and told her I loved her and to trust in God. I was led upstairs along silent stone hallways lit with fiery sconces. I heard noises followed by smells of food, both of them growing stronger and stronger till we turned a corner and then, O blessed saints! What a sight! A corridor crowded with servants, all handsomely dressed in red and white, holding platters of the very food I had seen earlier, but now cooked and roasted and boiled and stewed and fried in a hundred different ways.

In front of me, servants held more platters and upon each one was a swan with a silver crown on its head, its eyes so bright, its plumage so alive, that I said to myself—These are the best-trained birds in all of Italy. Holy Mother! What an innocent I was! They were not alive at all, but as I later found out, each one had been flayed so carefully that the feathers remained on the skin. Then after the insides were removed and the stomach stuffed with egg whites and finely chopped meats, the birds were roasted to perfection. Then the feathers, the feet, and the beak were cleverly gilded back on with saffron-colored paste. A miracle all of its own!

More servants carried aloft spit-roasted legs of goat, tender slices of veal, quail with eggplants, and still more platters of fish covered in parsley and dill. *Oi me!* I felt weak. The smells invaded my nose, they captured my brain, they seduced my stomach. Years of hunger which had become part of my flesh, pangs of starvation which had burned into my bones awakened with so great a cry that I had to clutch the wall or I would have thrown myself at a servant who was carrying a leg of mutton.

A short fierce man with bushy eyebrows and a goiter by his left ear angrily pushed past me and ran from one dish to another sniffing, tasting, and stirring. This was Cristoforo, the chief cook at that time. Then came the whistling of pipes, the beating of drums followed by laughter and barking and the frantic bleating of a sheep! The bleating stopped and a great roar rang through the halls.

The curly-haired youth walked by with a bowl filled with lettuce. "You *saw* Lucca," he said. "He was the one who had his tongue cut out."

I thought I would faint. My miracle had turned into a disaster. When he passed again I grabbed his arm. "But why?"

"For trying to poison Federico. He was the food taster."

"The food taster!" And I was taking his place! I wanted to rip my clothes off, jump through a window, and run until I reached my farm. But there were guards everywhere and now someone was shouting, "*Adesso!* We go. Now!" Trumpets blared and then we were marching toward the great hall and I was fourth in the line!

O my soul. That morning I thought I was at Death's door and now I was entering paradise. The smell of orris and rosemary was everywhere. Colorful banners and beautiful tapestries hung from the walls. There were long tables covered in white tablecloths and vases of flowers arranged so artfully as to make nature herself jealous. Seated at the tables were guests dressed in the finest silks and linens and velvets all trimmed with beaten gold. Jewels of every kind hung from necks and wrists, and sparkled against snow-white bosoms. Musicians played joyfully. Dogs rose from under the tables to watch us. A dwarf, covered in sweat, sat on top of a dead sheep. We stared straight ahead, our heads held high, although I was squeezing the cheeks of my *culo* together because of what I had just been told.

By this time we had reached Duke Federico's table at the far end of the hall. Dressed in a robe of red ermine with puffed sleeves, the duke was leaning back in an enormous chair watching us with his little beady eyes. A gold medallion with his face engraved upon it lay upon his chest. A servant placed the platter with the largest swan in front of him. The guests stopped their chatter. Nero yawned at the duke's feet. Cristoforo, the cook, stepped forward, a long knife in his right hand and a short spear with two points in the other. Squinting his eyes, he studied the swan, took a breath, and, stabbing it with the spear, lifted it into the air to the height of his chest. Then, first touching the bird with his knife to measure his aim, he cut six perfect slices off the right breast, zip, zip, zip, all while the swan was held by the spear and all so neatly that the pieces fell onto the duke's plate in one row as if they had been placed there by hand. "*Stupendo! Meraviglioso!*" everyone shouted. Cristoforo bowed.

Someone pushed me forward so that I was standing opposite Federico, the six slices of reddish brown meat wallowing in their own juices between us. Then Cristoforo picked up the platter and handing me a knife, said, "Taste it."

vi

"*Che bruta sorpresa,*" my mother would have said. "The unhappy surprise." Unhappy? *Oi me!* The slices of swan grew so big I could see nothing else. I thought I saw maggots feasting on them, worms slithering through them, green pus oozing from the sides. I looked at Federico. A river of saliva sat on his fat bottom lip. I could feel everyone's eyes on me—nobles, knights, wives, courtesans, servants. I remembered the hatred on the servants' faces earlier in the court-yard. Could one of them have poisoned the food? Miranda had already lost her mother and without me her life would be worthless. Although I did not wish to annoy Federico (God knows I wanted to do everything I could to please him), I put the knife down and said, "Thank you, Your Excellency, but I already ate."

The duke blinked, stared at me, then blinked again. His face quivered with rage. His teeth gnashed, his bottom lip fell to his chin.

"Taste it! For the love of God, taste it!" Cristoforo screamed.

Federico pushed back his chair, leaned over the table and snatched up the knife. All around me people cried, "Taste it! Taste it!"

I had no doubt that Federico was as good with a knife as he was with his sword, so I quickly picked up a slice of swan's breast and bit into it.

I had only eaten meat a few times in my life; pork on the feast of San Antony, a few chickens, and once a sheep that had become lame when we were driving the flock. Whenever my father ate meat he said, "This is the way meat should taste," just because it *was* meat. But the times I ate it were so far apart I could never remember what it tasted like from one time to the next. But this breast, this breast, I have never forgotten. When my teeth sank into it the flesh fell apart in my mouth. The juices trickled over my tongue like brooks in springtime. Someone groaned with pleasure. It was me!

Duke Federico slammed his fist onto the table. "Swallow it," he yelled. He did not have to tell me twice! I would have eaten the whole bird if I had had the chance. My throat opened, my stomach reached up to pull the food down, and yet the breast did not move. As much as one part of me yearned to swallow, another part did not. This other part of me said, "What if the breast *is* poisoned? How soon will I feel it? What will it feel like? Is it too late?" Something tickled my throat. Perhaps it was just my imagination, but when I felt that, I tried to pull the meat out of my mouth. Platters crashed to the floor, dogs barked, the guests rose in panic. Then my hands were grasped behind my back and the meat forced down my throat as if I was an animal.

I once saw a miller die from drinking bad water. He rolled over and over on the ground trying to tear his stomach out with his hands. His eyes bulged, his tongue grew thick in his mouth. He screamed he would leave his mill to the man who brought him a knife to end the fire in his belly, but his wretched wife forbade us. His cries lasted until morning and then he lay silent, his lips gnawed away by his frantic teeth.

But this meat did not burn my mouth, nor did it tear at my throat. My stomach did not feel as if it was being torn apart by a griffin's claws. I did not feel anything other than a wondrous sensation. Every part of my body sighed with satisfaction. Sconces flickered, flared up, and died down. Eyes darted from me to the duke and back again. When several moments had passed and still nothing had happened, the duke grunted, pulled the platter toward him, picked up the other slices with his hands, and ate them. That was the sign to the guests to begin eating. One moment every eye in the hall was on me, and the next I was invisible.

"Do you want to get me killed?" Cristoforo shouted when we returned to the kitchen. He was so angry his goiter had turned as red as his face. "Just do what you are told or I swear if Federico does not kill you *I* will."

I later found out being Federico's cook could be as precarious a position as a food taster, for when it came to food Federico was more suspicious than an old fool with a young bride, and would strike first and ask questions afterward. Cristoforo did not have time to continue his ranting, for the kitchen servants were busily preparing more dishes. Every now and then my stomach rumbled and I thought— This is it! This is the poison! But when I did not fall sick, I realized the rumbling was just my stomach getting used to having food inside it. The curly-haired boy, whose name was Tommaso said, "Stay close by. Federico will need you again."

I stayed by the serving table, where the meats and other foods were prepared, and watched as the guests nibbled at dainty little sausages, chewed on chicken legs, gobbled down slices of veal, and sucked the marrow out of bones. The color of their sleeves changed from red to mustard to brown as they dragged the food through a half-dozen different sauces. They spoke of politics and art and war. When someone sneezed, a hunchback with a big head, big ears, a black beard, and eyes that bulged beneath his spectacles began a discussion about table manners.

Just as I was walking behind him, he said, "In Venezia they get rid of snot like this," and holding his nose between his thumb and fore-finger, the little toad turned away from the table and blew a huge wad right onto my leg. Everyone laughed. I was furious because I had just been given this pair of hose and I did not know when I would get another.

Five more times I was called to taste the duke's food. I remember salted pork tongues cooked in a blood-red wine, fish galantine, vegetable ravioli delicately sprinkled with cheese, a farinata, a thick pudding of wheat grains with almond milk, and saffron for the venison. There were also capons. Capons with fritters, capons with lemon, capons with eggplants, capons cooked in their own juices. They loved it all! God in heaven! How could they *not* have loved it! As for me, each time I had to taste something I feared I would die. My stomach growled like an angry bear, but nothing happened.

So after tasting dish after dish without any ill effect, I said to myself—Ugo, perhaps the food is not poisoned. And since this might be the only time you taste food like this, why not enjoy it!

Just then Cristoforo served Federico a platter of flaky-crusted yellow pastries bursting with cream and sprinkled with sugar, called Neapolitan spice cakes, and best of all, pear tarts wrapped in marzipan. My mouth filled with enough saliva to drown an ox. I prayed Federico would choose the pear tart first. He did. Steadying myself not to show my excitement, I raised the tart to my mouth and bit into it.

O saints be praised! To those who say cooking is not as great an art as painting and sculpture, I say they have their head up their *culo*. It is far, far greater! A sculptor's work is eternal, but a cook's greatness is measured by how fast his creations disappear! A true master must produce great works every day. And that sniveling creep Cristoforo was a master. If you can imagine a warm doughy base crumbling against the sides of your palate, the sugary pulpiness of a soft brown pear lying on your tongue like a satisfied woman, Eden's succulent juices filling up the canals between your teeth, you would not even be close! You would think that I, who had never tasted such a delicacy, would have gladly surrendered myself to this pleasure, maybe even risked death and grabbed another bite. But I did not. Believe me, it was not because I did not want to, but because I *could* not! Something had changed in me. I received no pleasure from the tart at all. None. *Niente!* My taste buds had been robbed of all power of enjoyment. I left the table staring at the pear tarts and spice cakes with such disappointment that tears came to my eyes.

It is the same to this very day. Meals which have inspired men to poetry, women to open their legs, and ministers to reveal state secrets leave me unaffected. Even when I am not tasting for the duke, when I am here alone in my room, a single candle illuminating my solitude, with only bread and cheese for sustenance, I feel nothing. But it is a small price to pay. For if I had been allowed to enjoy food all these years, in time I would have become less vigilant, and the duke's enemies wait for such moments. No, much as I want to enjoy food, I love life even more.

It was now so late that the birds were awakening, but the banquet was still not finished. A thin man with yellow teeth, huge eyebrows, and a runny nose stood up to speak, and I noticed the servants slip quietly out of the hall. I tried to follow, but they closed the door in my face and I heard them giggling on the other side.

The thin man cleared his throat and began by saying, "Septivus, the lowest of all orators, gives you, Duke Federico Basillione DiVincelli, the greatest of all patrons, his warmest thanks."

I do not remember exactly what Septivus said that night, but I have heard so many of his speeches since then I could recite them in my sleep. First, he praised Duke Federico as if he was Jesus Christ and Julius Caesar rolled into one. Then he said that if Cicero had been here he would not have said, "We should eat to live," but, "Let us live to eat," because this was the most magnificent banquet he had ever seen. "It frees our senses and by eating the fruits which

God bestowed upon the Garden of Corsoli, we ingest paradise itself."

As if it was not bad enough that I could not enjoy the food, now I had to listen to this fool praising it! "This magnificent feast," Septivus cried, "not only puts us in harmony with nature, but also joins our hearts with those sitting beside us. Today, injuries are healed, quarrels are forgotten, for food is man's greatest healer."

I could hear my father shouting, "What the devil is that idiot talking about?"

Then Septivus went on to praise the mouth because in return for food it nurtured words. "These words, spiced by the food, celebrate the union between man and nature, man and society, and the body and the spirit. Did Christ not say, 'This is my body, this is my blood?' This blending of body and spirit leads us to another hunger which God alone can fulfill!"

He paused to sip some wine. "In the truly successful banquet the conversation is neither too stupid nor too intelligent, but flows so that everyone can join in." He waggled his finger. "For there is nothing worse than one person dominating the table with a long, boring speech which undoes all the pleasures the stomach has—"

"That is right. Nothing," Duke Federico said. "I am going to bed." He lurched to his feet and stomped out of the hall like a drunken ox. Within a minute the room was empty.

The pink fingers of dawn were already reaching over the hills when Tommaso said, "Now *we* eat," and led me to the servants' hall.

I wonder what Septivus would have said about the servants' meal. Meal? This was not a meal. Meals are prepared in a kitchen. This was prepared in a graveyard! For every breast of quail or capon served at the banquet, we were given a beak or a talon. For every goat leg, we were given a hoof. For every sausage, a horn or tail. No one spoke. No one made a speech or cracked a joke. Instead we crammed around the table, the pale yellow light of our candle of pigs' grease lighting our weary faces, and used what little strength we had to pretend that what we were eating was as delicious as what we had served. Suddenly, I remembered Miranda. "My daughter, I must find her—"

"She has already eaten," Tommaso said, sucking on a scorched black chicken's claw as if it was the tastiest morsel in the world. "Have some dessert." He dumped a bowl of figs, grapes, and plums onto the table, each piece so spoiled and rotten I could hardly tell one from the other. Then grabbing some bruises in the shape of an apple, he said, "Come, I will take you to her."

With a cocky stride, he led me through a maze of hallways and staircases, biting into his apple and spitting out the pips, until we came to a small room across from the stables in which three boys were fast asleep on their pallets. Miranda was curled up on another under a tattered blanket.

I grasped Tommaso's arm. "Thank you for your kindnesses."

He was looking at Miranda's face, which even in the ill-green light of the sconces was soft and beautiful. "*Buona notte,*" he replied and, cocking his head to one side, he left, whistling to himself.

I lay down next to Miranda and cradled her to me. Her fresh, strong smell enveloped me, and I pressed my face against hers and thanked God for keeping her safe from harm. But although I was exhausted I could not sleep.

Oi me! I have slept with sheep, goats, pigs, but all of them together were not as bad as the wretched stink in that room. Nor was it just the smell, but the yelling and arguing and weeping of the boys as they thrashed about, tossing from one side to another, kicking their legs backward and forward as they tried to outrun their nightmares.

But even if everything had been quiet and that pisshole had smelled like a Turkish harem, my mind refused to be silenced. I wanted to know how Lucca had tried to poison Federico. I wanted to know why, if I had to taste food, God did not allow me to enjoy it. I wanted to know, if someone did sprinkle poison over the meat or coated a pudding with it, how could I tell? *Potta!* How could I stop them?

However starved I had been on the farm, at least I was free. Now I was a bird trapped in a net waiting for Death, the eternal hunter, to collect me. And that day could be tomorrow! Or the day after. Or the one after that. Any meal could be my last. My heart beat so loudly it rang in my ears. I stood in the doorway to the courtyard to clear my head. The palace was silent. The moon was fading and the face in it barely visible. But then before my eyes, the face changed to that of my father and then my cursed brother Vittore. Vittore laughed. "Ugo's in the middle of all that food and he cannot taste it!" The food I had eaten welled up in my throat.

After I vomited, I picked Miranda up in my arms and carried her out of her room. People were sleeping everywhere, curled up against one another in the hallways and alcoves, and under benches. Every room was crowded with huddled forms, some under blankets, some without. Miranda opened her eyes and when I told her we were going back to our farm, she pulled my arm and said, "No, I like it here, Babbo. I had meat—"

"But Miranda," I whispered. "They have made me Duke Federico's new food taster. His old one, Lucca, was the man who had his tongue cut out."

The sleep fled from her eyes. I stood her up on her feet. "Babbo, I do not want you to be poisoned."

"No, nor do I. That is why we must—"

Suddenly, there was a growling and in the moonlight I saw Federico's dog, Nero, his teeth bared, his ears pricked back lumbering toward us. Miranda, who loved animals, was as scared of him as I was, and hid behind me.

"Nero!" said a voice from the shadows. My heart leaped out of the window. Duke Federico was limping toward us.

"*Scusi,* Your Honor," I bowed deeply. "My daughter had a dream—"

"You are the taster," the duke said.

33

"*Si*, Your Excellency."

"Come here." I hesitated and he repeated. "Come here! Do not worry, I try not to kill more than one person a day." Putting his weight on my shoulder he grimaced and lowered himself onto a nearby bench.

"Now pick up my foot." It was bandaged and swollen with gout and I did not know where or how to grasp it. "Underneath!" he snarled. "Underneath!"

Praying that I would not drop it, I picked up the foot as he instructed (it did not help that Nero's mouth was inches from my face), and raised it toward the bench.

"Careful!" Federico shouted and Nero barked loudly.

Sweating so much I could hardly see, I gently laid his foot down as if it was a newborn child. Federico leaned his head back against the wall and gave a great sigh. I did not know whether to leave or stay where I was. Then he said, "What are you doing?"

I realized he was not looking at me, but at Miranda who was stroking Nero's massive head. She immediately withdrew her hand.

"You like dogs?" the duke asked.

She nodded. "I like all animals," and she reached out her hand to Nero's face again. O blessed saints! Was there ever a braver child?

"I should have had a daughter," Federico grunted. "My eldest son will want to kill me soon enough."

I wanted to ask him if he thought his son might poison him, but just then Federico scratched his big toe and cursed with such anger I decided it best to remain silent. Then, as if he had forgotten we were there, he said harshly. "Go back to sleep!"

We hurried to our room.

Miranda was soon breathing quietly, but I lay awake thinking. Although it was true Federico was vicious and cruel, he had good reason to be so if people were trying to poison him. However, as they say, "A coin has two sides," and I had seen a glimpse of the other. He liked children, maybe not his own, but small girls anyway. Or at least he did not dislike them. Surely, this was a good omen. He also said he tried not to kill more than one person a day. It was a jest of course, but in every jest is a kernel of truth. *Potta!* There had to be or otherwise Corsoli would have long ceased to exist.

I marveled at the path God had led me on that day. He had given me the opportunity to serve a great duke; to rise to a better position than my father or my brother could have ever dreamed of. Surely that was why Federico had killed Lucca. Why the stag had run across my farm and why the man with the gray beard had spoken when he did. God had answered my prayer and saved Miranda from starving. I vowed to return His love by being the best food taster Federico had ever had.

I must have slept after all, for when Tommaso woke me the sun was shining and the guests were preparing to depart. "I have something for you," he said.

I left Miranda sleeping and followed him through the crowded hallways. He walked with the same cocky attitude he had the previous night, greeting everyone, be they footmen, courtiers, or servant girls, in a loud, high voice. It had not yet broken, which made his cockiness seem all the more ridiculous. After we passed them, he would say, "That washerwoman was a slave from Bosnia," or "He is a thief," "She is a gossip." According to Tommaso, everyone was a thief or a gossip except him.

Tommaso led me into the kitchen where the servants ran to and fro attending to the rows of ovens and cauldrons. Against the back wall were spits for small birds and another for larger animals. Knives and spoons stuck out from a bale of hay in the corner and on a nearby table lay tools for chopping, spearing, and mincing. There were also rows of pots for stewing and baking, ravioli wheels and sieves of all sizes, rolling pins, mortar and pestle, presses, jugs, whisks, graters, spoons, ladles, and a dozen different utensils which were a mystery to me.

Tommaso climbed to the top of a cabinet and threw a leather pouch down to me. I untied it and three stones and a piece of bone tumbled onto the table. The stones were small, dark, and round and looked like a thousand others I saw every day except these were smooth to the touch. "What are they?" I asked.

"Amulets. They belonged to Lucca."

A kitchen boy picked up the smallest black stone. "This is not an amulet. It is a sheep's turd."

The other boys laughed. At any other time I would have too, but because Tommaso had said they belonged to Lucca I could not even smile.

"It is a good-luck charm!" Tommaso said, snatching it from the boy. "This," he picked up the bone, "is a piece of unicorn's horn. If you dip it in wine and the wine is poisoned, the bone changes color."

"To what?"

He shrugged. "All I know is the unicorn has to be killed by a virgin so they are hard to find."

"No, they are not!" said a boy pointing to Tommaso, and the other boys burst into fits of laughter again.

Tommaso turned bright red. "Shut up!" he shouted, but the boys kept repeating *"vergine"* over and over.

I put my hand on his arm. "Take no notice of them."

He turned toward me, eyes blazing, and tried to compose himself. "Federico's goblet is made of gold and silver. If someone puts poison in it, it changes color and the wine bubbles like boiling pasta."

"Who is boiling pasta?" That cursed cook, Cristoforo, had returned flailing the air with a long wooden spoon. The boys tried to dodge his blows, but he was faster than he looked and beat several of them about the head and arms. Tommaso scooped up the amulets. "Come on, I have to piss." We slipped outside, passing a boy who was sitting on the ground tearfully rubbing his head. "I would have given you worse!" Tommaso said, and trod on his leg.

As we walked through the hallways, Tommaso again greeted whomever we met as if they were old friends.

"You know everyone," I said.

"And why not? I was born here."

I grasped his arm. "Do you know if Lucca really tried to poison Federico?"

He jerked himself free and did not answer. We reached a portion of the rampart which jutted out over the edge of the mountain. Men were pissing and shitting into a trough which ran through a wall and out into the valley. Some were talking about the banquet, boasting about what they had said or done; others walked about silently, still caught in the web of sleep.

We were surrounded on three sides by hills, and on top of each hill a tiny village glinted in the morning sunlight. Below us lay the town of Corsoli, the streets winding between the towers and then reappearing again like streams in springtime. Beyond the walls, the occasional traveler moved toward the city like a bustling ant. Yesterday I had looked just as small and unimportant, but today, God in His mercy had placed me on the roof of the world.

"Hey, *contadino*," Tommaso said. "If you want to take a shit, the straw is over there."

"My name is Ugo!" I said loudly. I had been called a peasant all my life, by the guards when I came to the city, by the merchants who cheated me, by tax collectors, even by the priests. Now that I was in the palace I wanted to be called by my right name.

"All right, *Ugo*." Tommaso pointed to the top floor of the palace. "That is where Duke Federico lives. Giovanni the hunchback, Federico's brother-in-law, lives below him."

"The one who spat on me?" I asked. Tommaso nodded. He told me that Giovanni was Corsoli's ambassador for the wool trade and without his contacts the valley would starve. "He wants to be a cardinal," Tommaso went on. "But Federico will not pay because every *scudo* he gives to the pope, the pope will use to attack Corsoli. So Federico hates the pope and everyone hates Federico."

"Perhaps Lucca and Giovanni—"

"Your nose is for sniffing, not poking," he warned me. "It does not concern you."

"But it does concern me. *Potta!* If some fool decides—"

"There is a ten *scudi* fine for swearing," Tommaso interrupted, holding out his hand. "Give me ten *scudi*."

"Ten *scudi!* I do not even have one."

Tommaso nibbled the nail of his little finger (all his nails were bitten to the quick), and his brown eyes stared at me from beneath his thatch of curly black hair. His eyes were a little too close together and his two front teeth too big for his mouth. His face had several pock-marks. My mother had warned me each mark was a lie the person had told. "You owe me then," he said. "Come on, this way."

Sometimes after the rains, when the grass sprouted up through the earth and the flowers burst into bloom, I had dreamed of a huge garden full of cauliflower, garlic bulbs, cabbages, rows of carrots like marching soldiers, and so on. Now Tommaso led me to a garden filled with every type of vegetable I had ever known and many I had only heard of. Beans, garlic, cabbages, carrots, onions, curly lettuces, eggplants, mint, fennel, anise, all neatly arranged in rows with little paths between them. "This is where I work," Tommaso boasted. "It is only for Federico and his family."

"You are in charge of all of this?"

"Me and an old woman. But I do all the work. Not even the pope has a garden like this. You have never seen anything like it, have you?"

I said I had not. He prattled on about how important his job was and would have gone on for hours had I not interrupted him saying, "Tommaso, you have lived in the palace all your life. You know everyone. I do not care what happens to me—I trust God will protect me—but my daughter, Miranda. She is young. She—"

"You want my help?"

"You work with the food. I wondered—"

"Do you want me to help you?" he repeated, folding his arms.

"Yes, but I cannot pay you. Whatever we agree—"

"How old is Miranda?"

"Ten, I believe."

Tommaso cocked his head to one side. "Marry her to me when she is thirteen and I will be your eyes and ears in the kitchen."

"Marry her?" I laughed.

His face turned red. "Do you not think I am good enough?"

"No, it is not that. It is just that she is a still a child."

"My mother was married when she was fourteen."

"Then when Miranda is fifteen," I said.

"Twat!" he spat on the ground. "I gave you amulets! I fed your daughter out of the goodness of my heart. You see how much I know about the palace. You ask for my help and this is how you repay me?"

In the blink of an eye he had worked himself into a rage, waving his arms about and turning as red as a beet so that I barely recognized him. Other people were looking over at us. I remembered my mother saying "Hot heads lead to cold graves." I said to myself—much can happen in four years—my whole life had changed in four minutes—so why not agree with him. "Fourteen then. When she is fourteen."

Tommaso stuck out his arm. I took hold of it. "We will not tell anyone now."

He shrugged. "As you will."

He started to pull away, but I held him fast. "You must be good to her because if you harm her, I will kill you."

"I will treat her as a princess," he said, "as long as she behaves like one."

Just then two serving boys called to us. They said Tommaso was wanted in the kitchen and I had to taste the duke's breakfast.

"What has Tommaso been telling you?" a serving boy asked as we climbed the stairs to Federico's chambers.

"About the palazzo and the people who live here."

"What have you been telling him?" asked the other.

"Nothing. I have nothing to tell."

"Just as well," he said, and the first one nodded his head in agreement.

Something gripped my insides. "Why?"

"*Niente*," they shrugged. "Nothing."

I wanted to know more, but guards were leading us through Federico's apartment to his bedroom.

After we had been searched for weapons, the serving boys knocked on Duke Federico's chamber. His doctor, Piero, answered. A short fat Jew, Piero was bald except for a few stray hairs on the top of his head. He smelled of fat, which he mixed with ground nuts and rubbed into his scalp to keep those same few hairs from falling out.

"Breakfast, My Lord," Piero laughed. He laughed after everything he said whether it was funny or not.

"Food!" roared the duke. "I have not shit for three days and you want me to eat more food?"

Piero's right cheek began to twitch. Another voice, lower and calmer, said something I did not hear.

"Oh, bring it in," came the duke's voice again.

We entered the duke's bedchamber. It was unlike any room I had ever seen. The floor was covered with thick carpets of many colors and tapestries hung from the walls showing men and women making love. In the center of the room stood a bed big enough for my whole family to have slept in. It was surrounded by deep red velvet curtains and covered with silken cushions and sheets that shone in the sunlight. The bed was raised up from the floor and when the duke sat up, as he was doing now, he was as tall as any man standing next to him. His thin, wispy hair lay like thin strands of wet pasta about his head, his eyes were runny and his face blotchy, and a great mass of hair poked out of his nightshirt. He did not look like a duke at all, but like a fishmonger I knew at the market.

The duke was listening to the solemn gray-bearded man, Cecchi, his lawyer and chief adviser, who was saying, "I told him since it was your birthday you assumed the horse was a gift, and it would not reflect well on your friendship if he were to ask for it back."

"Good," Federico said. "I will ride him later. Bernardo!" An untidy-faced man with scraggly hair and shifty pale blue eyes, Bernardo spat a mouthful of fennel seeds into his hands, scurried over to the bed and lay some charts in front of the duke. "Your Honor, Mars is on fire while Mercury and Saturn are cold. Now since Mars—"

"But is that good?" demanded the duke, slamming his hand on the chart.

"It is good for war," said Bernardo slowly. "Otherwise it is better not to do anything."

The duke sank back on his cushions. "If it were up to you, I would stay in bed all day."

Bernardo frowned and stuffed some more fennel seeds into his mouth as if this would prevent him from having to answer.

"Your Honor," said Piero, stepping forward on tiptoe, "I think—"

"You think?" said the duke. "You do not think. You do not know how to think. Leave me! All of you. Leave me!"

"Not you," the serving boy muttered to me. He gave me the bowl and followed everyone else out of the room, leaving me alone with Duke Federico.

Because we had spoken in the hallway during the night, I thought the duke would remember me, so I bowed and said, "Good morning, Your Excellency. I hope you slept well and that God brings you many blessings."

He stared at me as if he had never seen me before. "You are not here to talk to me," he yelled. "You are here to taste my food. Have you?"

"No, I—"

"What are you waiting for?"

I lifted the lid and saw a bowl of bubbling polenta covered with raisins. The steam sprang out, burning my face. There was only one spoon. As I raised my hand, the duke yelled, "Clean them," and pointed to a pitcher with a handle shaped like a naked woman.

Christ on a cross! Before last night I never washed my hands from one month to the next and now I was washing them twice in one day. I soon discovered Federico was so afraid of being poisoned that he insisted everything had to be clean. He changed clothes several times a day, and if he saw even a shadow of a spot on his clothing or a tablecloth or a curtain, it had to be washed again. I did not understand what that had to do with poisons, but no one was asking me, and if that is what he wanted who was I to tell him he was wrong?

I poured water into the bowl and rubbed my hands in it. Out of the corner of my eye, I saw the duke clamber out of bed and pull aside a beaded curtain. He raised his nightshirt and sat on a chair with a chamber pot underneath. He grunted and groaned and farted like a cannon. I pulled the amulet bone out of my pouch and dipped it into the porridge to see if it changed color. But I did not know how long to leave it in or if I should ask the duke's permission before I did so. What if he said no? He farted again, a great smelly fart all the perfumes of Arabia could not have hidden. I dipped the bone into the polenta.

The duke moaned. His back was toward me, his nightshirt raised above his waist. He was bending down staring at the chamber pot between his legs. I was so startled by his huge white *culo* that I dropped the bone into the porridge. I put my hand in to take it out, but the polenta was so hot I nearly screamed in pain.

"What are you doing?" asked the duke. I had stuffed my fingers into my mouth. "Tasting, Your Honor."

The duke climbed back into the bed. For the second his back was turned I dipped my hand into the water. "Give it to me," he said.

I gave him the bowl of polenta. The duke lifted a spoonful up to his mouth and swallowed it. I prayed he would not scoop up the bone.

"The last taster used amulets and stones and horns," he said. "Do not use any of them. I want you to taste EVERYTHING." He swallowed another mouthful and made a face. "Go. Take that with you." He pointed to the chamber pot. My thoughts were jumping around like a bat caught in the daylight. If the duke found the bone I would say that Cristoforo had put it there. I picked up the chamber pot. "Take this, too," he said, and handed me the bowl of porridge. By a blessed miracle, he had not seen the bone.

As soon as I was outside I pulled out the bone. It had not changed color so the porridge was not poisoned. But what color would it have changed to if it *had* been poisoned? And if the bone had changed color, what should I have done? Would Federico have made me taste it anyway? Each question led to another, and none of them led to an answer.

X

In the months that followed it became obvious that although many people feared and hated Federico, none were brave enough to kill him. Every moment of his life was protected either by a taster like myself or by guards who accompanied him wherever he went. They were posted outside his room and below his window. They listened for malicious gossip and wandered through the town looking for assassins. They looked under his bed before he slept. *Potta!* They would have looked up his *culo* if he suspected someone was hiding there. He also employed spies. Anyone could become a spy if they had useful information, and so even as the weather changed from one season to another, the climate of fear was always present in the palace.

The only people who did not fear Federico were Giovanni the hunchback and his sister Emilia, Federico's wife. Giovanni I have talked about so I will tell a little of Emilia, but only a little since she herself was no more than a small ball of fat with a voice of a crow and breasts which stuck out of her *camora* like pigs' bladders. She spent her time collecting paintings and sculptures, planning her flower garden, and writing letters to her relatives in Venezia and Germany, complaining how Federico consorted with the town whores. The whores claimed Emilia tried to poison them. Whether it was true or not I did not know, but I was glad I did not have to taste *her* food.

Even though Tommaso was now my eyes and ears in the kitchen, I still feared tasting the capons or kid or venison, asparagus, eggplant, peeled cucumbers dressed with salt and vinegar, fava beans, sweet-breads, pastas, almonds in milk, pies, tortes, and the thousand other dishes Federico ate.

Anyone reading this might think that I soon became fat, but since I only ate a little of every dish and many of them, such as apples and cherries, were for cleansing the bowels, added to which I did not enjoy what I was tasting, it is a wonder I did not starve to death. As it is, I am as thin now as when I first arrived in the palace five years ago. However, in two months' time when the wedding is over, I will sit down at the table and eat to my heart's content. Not just one helping either, but as many as I can. But to return to my story:

What eased my nervousness during the meals was listening to Septivus read. It was from Septivus that I heard of Julius Caesar, from whom Federico claimed he was descended, and also of Socrates, Homer, Cicero, Horace, as well as parts of the Bible. Or at least the beginnings of these stories; for if Federico became bored he would order Septivus to start a new tale. So it was not till Miranda taught me to read that I discovered that Odysseus arrived home safely or that Julius Caesar was assassinated!

Even if Federico was not bored he changed his mind so often that no one could tell what his mood would be from one moment to the next, except of course when he had not shit or when his gout flared up. Then he was more dangerous than a hungry wolf. For putting seven raisins in his polenta, a kitchen servant was flogged. For disagreeing with him, a kennel keeper was thrown down the mountain. It was best to avoid him, but as if he knew that he demanded that we stay close. We hopped from one leg to the other trying to guess which way to jump in case one of Federico's rages descended upon us.

Not that it was that different when he was in a good mood. Then he amused himself by throwing gold coins down into the streets of Corsoli to watch the peasants fight in the mud for them or he encouraged the courtiers to jostle for his favor. I remember one evening Federico had finished a new recipe of fried artichoke bottoms—I hated new recipes because I did not know what they were supposed to taste like—when instead of calling on Septivus to read, he pushed away his trencher and said, "I have been thinking that the world is shaped like a triangle. What say you?"

O my soul! I could hear the courtiers' brains clanging around in their heads as if a madman had been let loose in the campanile of Santa Caterina! They scrunched their faces up and stared at their half-eaten artichokes as if the answer lay among its leaves. Piero's tic started violently.

Septivus said, "To the immortal Dante, three is the highest number because it represents God the Father, Christ His Son, and the Holy Ghost. Thus it is only right that our world would reflect the Holy Trinity and be a triangle."

Federico nodded and bit into an orange.

Cecchi scratched his beard and furrowed his brow. (He always looked as if he had witnessed some tragedy that was forever replaying itself in front of his eyes.) "I must agree," he said. "Our lives are divided into three—past, present, and future. Since we are a mirror of the universe, it is only natural that the universe would also be in three. What I mean is, three sides, as in a triangle."

This was also clever for since Federico had not objected to Septivus's answer, Cecchi was wise to climb on its back.

"I too agree," Bernardo said, spitting some fennel seeds over his shoulder, "but for sounder reasons. In numerology, to which astrology is closely related, three is the highest power. Now it is well known that the stars, the moon, and the sun govern the earth; therefore, the earth reflects the wisdom of the heavens and thus the earth is unquestionably a triangle."

"Not just a triangle," Piero giggled, terrified he would be left out. "But a special triangle that has two long sides and one short side. And Corsoli," he said, when everything had become so quiet we could hear Federico's orange digesting, "is at the topmost point."

Federico stared at him as if he had spoken in Greek. Then he looked around the table, gobbled another piece of orange and said, "It was a stupid idea."

Again everyone was still. Then they burst out laughing, slapping their sides and wiping their eyes as if it was the funniest thing they had ever heard. Federico raised the tablecloth to wipe his chin, and I, who was standing behind him and a little to one side, saw him smile.

Piero said, "If my good friends will allow me to speak for them, let me say the duke has made us all feel very foolish. However, we do not hold this against him; indeed, we welcome this feeling of ridicule because of the skill with which the joke was delivered."

The others nodded. Federico swallowed the piece of orange. He snorted, coughed, his eyes bulged. His face turned purple and he made a harsh scraping noise at the back of his throat. He lurched to his feet, arms flailing. Bernardo ran toward him, but Federico's elbow struck his face and knocked him down. Drool dribbled from Federico's nose; his eyes were glazed over. He threw himself first one way and then the other while the courtiers watched paralyzed with fear.

I had been waiting for a moment whereby I could prove my loyalty and so as he whirled away from me, I hammered both my fists into the middle of his back as my mother had done to my father when he had choked on a chicken bone.

A piece of soggy, mangled orange flew out of Federico's mouth and he fell face forward onto the table. Everyone looked at me—some with fear, others with surprise. Raising himself up, Federico turned around, eyes and mouth wide open. I thought he would thank me, but Piero and Bernardo (whose nose was pouring with blood) ran in front of me crying, "It was necessary to save your life, Your Excellency. Please sit down. Drink this. Rest, lie down," and so on, as if they had been the ones to save him!

Federico pushed them aside and staggered from the hall, Piero, Bernardo, and other courtiers trailing behind. Only Septivus and Cecchi remained. Septivus looked at me, a half smile displaying his little ferret teeth. He sighed and shook his head.

I said, "Did I not—"

"Yes, you did," Cecchi said quickly and followed after the others.

"But since it was I who saved him," I said to Tommaso later when we were playing cards, "I should be the one who is rewarded. I will tell him at breakfast."

"Save your breath," Tommaso shrugged and dealt another hand of piquet.

I threw my cards down. "Why should Piero and Bernardo be praised for what I did?"

"Getting close to Federico is more of a curse than a blessing."

"How would you know?" I was annoyed that he did not care for my welfare.

He stared at me, his eyes flitting from side to side. "Oh, do what you will," he said, and throwing his cards in the air, he kicked over the table.

xi

It was not the first time Tommaso and I had argued. Christ! You could not ask him if the sun was out without getting into a fight with him. Not long after I had promised Miranda to him, he had complained to Cristoforo that he needed help in the garden. Cristoforo, who was only too pleased to do me ill, agreed Miranda would be a good helper. The days were growing shorter and the sun, having spent its summer strength, hid its weakened face behind a blanket of sullen clouds. Miranda often returned to our room muddy and cold. She did not complain, but at night when I held her shivering body close to me, her tears escaped under the cover of sleep. I told Tommaso she would get sick if she did not work inside the palace.

"Where? In the laundry?" he shouted. "So the lye can blind her?"

His shouting no longer had any effect on me, and besides I suspected the true reason he wanted Miranda to work in the garden was because he feared someone in the palazzo might steal her affection. I think it was for that same reason that he, who could not keep a secret any more than I could keep an ant on a string, did not tell anyone of their betrothal. I beseeched God, saying, "For all that You have given me, please take it away if it will ease Miranda's troubles."

God in His mercy answered my prayer.

One evening Septivus was reading the poetry of Catullus when Federico interrupted, saying, "I would rather be put on the rack than listen to this."

"A child would better understand," Septivus mumbled as we left the hall, to which I said, "I know such a child," and told him how Miranda had learned to read and write at the convent and could also sing and spin wool.

Despite his huge eyebrows which gave him a fierce expression, Septivus was gentle in nature for he said, "I only teach the children of courtiers. But if she is as you say, perhaps I can make an exception. Send her to me."

I ran to the garden and, without a word to Tommaso, pulled Miranda from her work and took her to the library. Before she went into Septivus's room I told her to remember everything the nuns had taught her and all would be well; then I pushed her inside. I pressed my ear to the door. I heard her speaking softly, reading perhaps, and then her small clear voice broke into song. Some moments later the door flew open and Septivus emerged, steering Miranda by the shoulder. "I will speak to Cecchi," he said. "She can start tomorrow."

In my haste I had not told Miranda why I had acted so and now she cried out, "Start what? What must I do?"

Septivus told her she would be studying with the other children.

"And not work in the garden?" she asked, her face lighting up like a candle in the darkness.

"Only for a little while each day," Septivus replied. "I will arrange it."

"You see how God protects those who serve Him," I said as I led her back to the garden. "Now you must honor Him by studying hard. It will also be good to meet the other children. One day you will become a maidservant. You will be seen by fine, wealthy men." I had not told her about my pledge to marry her to Tommaso, and if Tommaso said anything I would deny it. If Miranda could better herself then why should she not? As I had predicted, much could happen in four years.

Miranda, however, could not contain her excitement and, as I left, I heard her telling Tommaso that he would no longer be able to lord it over her since she would soon be a princess.

But the next day Miranda sat in the corner of the room picking at the scabs on her knees and refused to go to her class.

"But why? Yesterday you were so excited."

She would not answer. I said if she had not changed her mind after I had pissed I would drag her there myself. On my return I passed the garden where Tommaso was pulling up carrots and cabbages. I told him of Miranda's refusal to go to the class and asked him if he knew why.

He shrugged and opened his eyes wide to show his innocence. "But," he added, "she is right not to go. She will become vain and forget those who helped her."

I leaped across the path and jerked his head up by the neck. "Tell me what you told her or I will give you a blow your children will remember."

"I told her they will make fun of her because of her clothes," he stammered.

I boxed his ears and he ran away, swearing he would revenge himself. Then I found Miranda, pulled her dress from her shoulders, and took it to the laundry.

When my eyes got used to the sting of lye and the billowing clouds of steam, I saw that the dim shapes laboring over the boiling pots were mostly young girls no older than Miranda. There was also an older half-blind crone and the tall blonde woman whom Tommaso had told me was the slave from Bosnia. Their faces were red and sweaty, their arms and hands pink, rough, and wrinkled. I asked if one of them would be kind enough to wash Miranda's dress.

The tall blonde one, Agnese, who had a wide face and mouth, but a nose no larger than a button, raised her arm and pushed her hair out of her sad gray eyes in a way that moved something in me. Without saying a word, she took the dress from me and washed it. When she had finished I saw colors in it I had never seen before. I thanked her and returned it to Miranda. She kissed me over and over with delight, dancing around the room, holding the dress to her as if she was a princess. I lay on the bed, tears forming in my eyes, and resolved to do everything I could to make her happy even if it cost me my life.

The next day Miranda went to her classes. Except for Giulia, Cecchi's daughter, who was lame in one leg, the other children ignored her. This did not disturb Miranda for she enjoyed her lessons and practiced them in our room, especially the lyre, which she loved best of all. She still worked in the garden every day—Tommaso saved the dirtiest work for her—but since he often slipped away to his friends in the kitchen, Miranda did likewise, spending time in Giulia's apartment playing with her dolls.

Indeed, Tommaso seemed to have forgotten about Miranda altogether. The wind had whipped the peach fuzz from his face, hairs sprouted on his upper lip, and his voice no longer cracked. He swaggered around the palazzo in a new blue velvet jacket and matching blue hose, boasting how he would soon be a courtier. Of course, the kitchen boys teased him and threatened to cut up his jacket so he wore it all the time, even sleeping in it. It soon became shabby. He feared he would ruin it but was afraid to take it off. Eventually, he had to wash it and then hid it so it could dry. Someone must have been watching because when he returned, the jacket had been slashed into a thousand pieces. He fell into a maddened rage, weeping and threatening to kill whomever had destroyed it, which made the kitchen boys, who I am sure had cut it up, tease him even more.

I came upon him sitting by the stable. His face was puffy and red, and he was cradling the remains of his beloved jacket in his arms as if it was a dead child. I assured him he would soon get another but he burst into tears and fled from me.

The whole palace laughed at him, even Miranda, although when we were alone she surprised me by saying, "I wish I could buy him another because I cannot bear to see anyone so unhappy."

I still had not told her of her betrothal, and the longer I waited, the more difficult it became. But now that she felt so inclined toward him, I believed this might be the right time and was about to tell her so when she went on to say, "If only he did not boast so. I hate that." And the moment passed. I needed to ask someone's advice and so I sought out Agnese the laundrywoman.

In truth, I just wanted to talk to her. I had given her a ribbon for washing Miranda's dress, but one of the other washgirls had returned it to me, saying, "She still mourns her husband and her child."

"Tell her I will turn her mourning into dancing," I replied, but Agnese's ears were deaf to my words.

The underside of her arm and her pale sad eyes floated to me in my dreams and sometimes, when I walked past the laundry to glimpse her through the steaming white mist, my *fallo* got so hard I had to pull my shirt out to cover it. I spent hours thinking of ways to approach her and then one night, as I was carrying the remains of a platter of Federico's, I stuffed a piece of uneaten veal under my shirt, took it to the laundry, and offered it to her.

"*Non e velenoso*," I said, and took a small bite to show her that the meat was not poisoned. The other girls urged her to taste it. Agnese reached out her hand—her fingers and wrists had a muscular beauty to them—and put a small piece in her mouth. She chewed it, closing her eyes, moving her jaws slowly up and down as if she was not used to doing so. At last, when she had chewed all the juice out of it, she swallowed it and gave a little burp. Then she tore the rest of the meat into equal pieces and shared it with her friends. She made a space for me on the bench and I sat beside her in the dark, surrounded by the bubbling cauldrons and piles of laundry, watching the girls devour the veal. They did not talk and joke as the guests had done at the banquet. They savored each bite as if they might never have another, and when they had finished they said a prayer of thanks, kissed me on the cheek, and went back to their washing.

"*Grazie. Multo grazie*," Agnese said to me with such sincerity that my knees felt weak. I wanted to throw my arms around her and kiss the sadness from her eyes, but I simply nodded and said, "*Prego*."

In the weeks that followed, I snatched capon legs, slices of pork, a chicken neck, a wing of a bird, and small round cakes of dough with fennel seeds. I loved the way the girls stopped their washing the moment I arrived. I loved the way Agnese's eyes widened when she saw me. I loved the way she licked her lips to make sure she had not missed a crumb, how she patted her stomach when she had finished, leaned against the wall and pushed the hair off her forehead.

On the Feast of the Ascension I stole a fennel sausage, two roasted birds, and some roast lamb bathed in rosemary and garlic. "I could get hanged for this!" I said to myself, but I did not care. The girls shrieked and kept running to the door to see if someone was coming to arrest me. Agnese laid her hand on my arm (it was the first time she had touched me), and said "*Attenzione*."

"Do not worry about him," the old washerwoman laughed. "He could steal a halo from an angel."

Afterward, Agnese offered to wash my shirt because it was stained with sauce. Another girl offered to wash my hose, but Agnese would not let her. From then on she often washed my clothes and, no doubt because of her love for me, they fit me better than ever. I did not see how I could be any happier, but one morning at breakfast, Federico cuffed his serving man, saying, "Why can you not be clean and neat like Ugo?"

Jesus in sancto! Federico had noticed me not because I saved his life, but because my clothes were clean! I hurried to thank Agnese for my good fortune. No sooner had I started talking than she put her hand over my mouth and pointed to the girls who were taking their midday nap. Her hand was warm and I bit gently into the fleshy part of her palm. She gasped, but did not draw her hand away. I licked the part I had bitten. She looked at her palm and then into my eyes as if deciding something. Then, taking me by the hand, she led me through the sleeping forms, out past Emilia's garden, and we began climbing the hill behind the palace.

xii

Agnese did not tell me where we were going and I was glad for the silence, because I was overcome with such longing that my mouth would have made a fool of me had I spoken. God's almighty eye beat down on us, causing us to bow our heads and place our hands on our thighs to push us higher. A herd of goats sleeping beneath the outstretched arms of a fig tree barely glanced at us as we passed. A salamander darted across a rock and disappeared into a patch of purple geraniums. Finches and robins sang from the trees, and in the distance a small gray cloud sailed across the blue sky, pulled by an invisible breeze. The hill was steep so I offered Agnese my hand, but hers was as strong as mine, and when I slipped it was she who stopped me from falling. We climbed higher, our breathing joining us together until not only our breath, but our footsteps and our thoughts, became one; and when we came to a clearing among the trees we threw off our clothes, fell on the ground, and embraced so tightly that the air could not find any space between us.

I kissed her mouth and the underside of her arms—she smelled of lye—and pulled open her shift so that her small breasts could free themselves. She was as hungry as I was, biting my lips and making soft mewing noises. Then she pulled me roughly on top of her and wrapped her legs around me to draw me into her. When I looked into her eyes the sadness had disappeared.

Suddenly, Agnese pushed me off her and, sitting up naked in front of me, she turned to look at her two white moons. They were filled with small red bumps for we had, in our urgency, laid down on an insect nest and they were angrily repaying us. But we were both too overcome with lust to stop and, quickly crawling through the grass, found another spot where it was long and soft and, turning Agnese onto her hands and knees, I mounted her from behind.

O my soul! What pleasure we gave one another! It seemed as if, having taken so long for us to find each other, nothing could interrupt our joy. The cloud covered the sun but we did not notice. A wind sprang up and still we continued our cries. Drops of rain splattered onto us, slowly at first, and then as if no longer able to bear its own weight the cloud burst and the rain poured down, dripping from my face onto

Agnese's back and from her back onto the ground. We were still making love when the sun came out again and we exploded together like fireworks on Midsummer's Eve.

Later, Agnese lay in my arms and I spoke words of love to her. She furrowed her brow as if she did not understand. So I repeated them slowly one by one, and then it dawned on me that she was mocking me because she broke into a smile as wide as her face—it was the first time I had ever seen her smile—and kissed me with great passion. I caressed her breasts. I pressed my lips to her marks of childbirth.

"He would be seven," she said, the words chasing the smile from her face. Then she pulled me to my feet and made me dance round and round, trampling the memory beneath us.

She did a cartwheel. She squatted and pissed on the ground in front of me. She caught a butterfly and, showing me its beating wings, said, "That is my heart." Like a girl half her age, she climbed a tree, her strong arms and legs lifting her easily from one bough to the next. Then she sat on a branch and sang a sad song in a small, tuneless voice.

"Che c'è di male?" I asked.

"Niente," she said, and jumped into my arms. She took my face in her hands and said fiercely, "You must not tell anyone about us."

"But I want to tell the world."

She shook her head. "The world has taken my husband, my son, and my country. I do not want it to take you."

"What about Miranda?"

"Only Miranda."

I lay her on the ground for I wanted to put my head between her legs to taste her sweetness, for except for the freshly laid eggs I sometimes stole, she was the only thing that I knew would not be poisoned. But no sooner had I knelt between her knees than ants crawled all over my face. Agnese laughed, a great honking gooselike laugh that rang across the hillside. She curled up her legs and laughed until she was out of breath. Then she reached her arms out to me.

We had almost arrived back at the palace when a horse cantered past us. "It is Giovanni, the hunchback," Agnese said, and hid her face in my shoulder.

"He returned yesterday. We have nothing to fear from him."

"But no one must know," she cried, her eyes filled with worry.

"He did not see us," I assured her. "Without his spectacles he is as blind as a bat. You go first and I will follow in a while and then we will not be seen together."

I walked back to the kitchen lighter than the air itself, humming Agnese's tuneless little song. My blood trembled with delight. The serving boys immediately guessed that I had screwed someone but did not know who. "It was good, huh?" they laughed.

Because of my promise to Agnese I said nothing but, fearing that my good feelings would undo my lips, I left the kitchen and went to my room.

Miranda was standing by the window talking to the birds. When she saw me she twitched her face like Piero and stammered, "W-w-where have you been?" Then she growled like Federico, blustered like Tommaso and made me laugh till I cried. I wanted to tell her of Agnese, but since it was the first time she had been so playful in so long I was content to let her speak.

"Do you like my hair?" she asked. She had plucked the hairs from her forehead as was the fashion for girls at that time.

In truth, I did not like it, because it made her head look like an egg, but I said, "It makes you look very pretty."

"I want my hair to be blonder, too," she said, looking in her hand mirror. "I have been in the sun every day but it has not changed. Maybe I should get some false hair."

She would have gone on like this all evening had I not interrupted, saying, "Miranda, I have met a woman."

"A woman?"

"Agnese. The washerwoman. From Bosnia."

"Ah, with the blonde hair. I wonder if she—" her body stiffened. She put down the mirror and turned to face me. "Is she going to live with us?"

"I had not thought of that—"

"No! No, I do not want her to."

"But—"

"No."

"Miranda—"

"No!" she shouted and stamped her foot. Her outburst so annoyed me that I shouted back, "If I want her to and she wants to, then she will!"

She glared at me and turned away. I put my hand on her shoulder but she shook it off. I grasped both her shoulders, turned her around and forced her chin up to face me. "Do you think I will forget your mother?" I asked.

She nodded slowly.

"I will never forget your mother, I promise. But you must promise me something, too. You must not tell anyone about Agnese."

Her eyes opened wide. "I promise," she said.

For the rest of the afternoon I wondered why Miranda had lied to me, for even a blind man could have seen she was not thinking of her mother.

At dinner that same evening, Giovanni showered gifts on everyone to celebrate the wool contracts he had made. He gave Duke Federico a gold helmet encrusted with jewels, little trinkets to the servants, and showed off his new clothes, especially an English jacket which had been cleverly made to hide his hump.

"I could only stay a week in London," Giovanni sighed. "The ambassador in Paris was giving a dinner in my honor, *n'est-ce pas?* A countess in the Netherlands wanted to marry me, but *s'blood!* It is too cold there, *n'est-ce pas?*"

Every sentence began or ended with *"n'est-ce pas," "voilà!"* or *"s'blood!"* and for weeks after the servants called him "Miss Nesspa" behind his back. Giovanni again told Federico it was time to pay his indulgence for his cardinalship. Federico chewed his food and said nothing, but as the saying goes, "His silence spoke volumes," and as it pleased God, that was the beginning of my journey through hell. It began like this:

Whenever Giovanni returned from a trip he brought back a doll which was dressed in the latest fashion. His sister, Emilia, gave it to her dressmaker to copy and when he was finished with it, Emilia gave the doll to a daughter of a courtier. That was how Miranda's friend, Giulia, had received hers. However, this time Piero's child was the fortunate one.

"I will never get a doll," Miranda sulked.

"How do you know?"

"Because you are a food taster." She spat out the words as if they were poisonous.

"Ungrateful child," I shouted, grabbing her arm. "Because of me you eat two meals a day, you sleep in a bed under a sound roof. You have lessons three times a week. I face death every day! Is that why you do not want Agnese to live with us? Because she is a washer-woman?"

Miranda bit her lip. Tears leaped from her eyes. "My arm!" she whispered.

In my anger, I had gripped her so tightly that the bones were crying out. I let go and she fled from the room.

She did not speak to me for several days.

"You have no reason to be silent," I said. "I am the one who was insulted, not you!"

She still refused to speak to me. It was Agnese who came to my rescue. "Did you not tell me you were a woodcutter?" she said. "Why not carve her a doll?"

It was typical of Agnese's goodness that even though she was the reason for Miranda's anger, it was she who soothed it. Climbing the hill that afternoon with Agnese I found an old branch of an alder tree, and while she slept I carved a little doll. With berry juice from the kitchen, I painted a nose, a mouth, arms, legs, and hair. Agnese rouged its cheeks and when it was finished I lay it on Miranda's bed and hid myself close to our room. I heard Miranda enter and a moment later the door flew open and she ran out, shouting, "Babbo! Babbo! It is wonderful."

She cradled it in her arms, kissing it over and over. "Felicita! That is her name. Felicita!" Her eyes sparkled as she twirled around and around as she always did when she was happy.

I remember that day well because at dinner Giovanni began demanding yet again that Federico pay the indulgence for his cardi-nalship. His voice grew so insistent and his manner so impatient that his glasses fogged up. Taking them off to clean them, he peered at Federico, his big bulging eyes filled with anger. Federico chewed on a bone until he had finished and then, throwing the bone to Nero, said, "I am not paying that miserable goat one *scudo* and that is that!"

"You humiliate us," Emilia screamed. "If it were not for my brother, this palace would be a swamp."

Federico rose slowly, wiping the grease from his chin with his sleeve. I was standing behind him and, as he turned, he stuck his fist into my face and pushed me onto the floor. He would have trodden on me had I not rolled out of the way. The courtiers followed quickly, no one wishing to be seen with Giovanni, who remained at the table brooding, his sister Emilia whispering in his ear.

Potta! How long can you keep the lid on a pot before it boils over? Something had to happen. I did not know how, I did not know when, but I knew it would. Worse still, I felt in my bones it would affect me. I could not sleep. Little things—a hole in my hose, a platter being too hot, a sharp word—which would not have bothered me before now worried me. So when Miranda cried that Tommaso had thrown Felicita to the ground, breaking her arm, I went looking for him with murder in my heart.

I found him just before Vespers in the little chapel of the Duomo Santa Caterina. "Ugo," he said, swallowing a piece of apple, "I have been waiting for you." He moved into the middle of a pew so I could not reach him easily. "I have something to tell you." He wiped his mouth.

I did not answer. He looked around to make sure we were alone. "Federico refused to pay for Giovanni's indulgence again."

If he thought I would fall for his stupid tricks he was mistaken. "Wait!" he said, as I climbed over a pew. "Did you know Giovanni's mother Pia is coming from Venezia?"

"So?"

"Venezia!" He said it as if I had never heard of the place. "The city of poisoners." He went on, "They have a price list. Twenty gold pieces to kill a merchant, thirty for a soldier. A hundred for a duke."

"How do you know that?"

He shrugged as if it was common knowledge. "Lucca told me."

"Is this Pia bringing a poisoner with her?"

"Who knows? But if you were Giovanni and she was your mother—" he hissed. He did not need to continue.

"I think you are making this up to save yourself from a beating."

He clapped a hand to his forehead, then waved his arms in the air as if I had done him a terrible wrong. "You were the one who asked me to be your eyes and ears," he spluttered. "All right!" He made his way to the aisle. "On your head be it." He pointed to me as he walked out of the church. "And do not say I did not warn you." Whether his story was true or not, he had got out of a beating.

I did not follow him because part of what he had said, *was* true. Everyone knew there were more poisoners in Venezia than there were Romans in Roma. They spent their days concocting potions and were only too eager to try them out. Any lord, rich merchant, or person with money, which Pia was, could afford one. I closed my eyes to pray, but it was not the face of God, or Our Lord, or the Holy Mother who appeared to me, but the grinning mug of my brother, Vittore.

The evening meal was like the first banquet all over again. My mouth cracked like winter wheat. My stomach shrank. I suspected each dish more than the one before and became so afraid that when the milk custard was served, I sniffed at it, held it up closely to my eyes, turned the trencher around, sniffed at it again, scooped a tiny piece onto my finger, tasted it, and said, "The milk is off."

Federico's lower lip dropped to his chin. "Off?" he said. "What do you mean, off?"

"It is sour, Your Excellency, I fear it will upset your stomach."

I thought he would thank me, throw the custard away and eat some fruit, but he swept several platters off the table and called for Cristoforo the cook.

"Ugo says the milk is off."

"It is his head that should be off," Cristoforo replied, sniffing at the custard. "My Lord, Ugo is a fool who has grown too big for his breeches."

"I have tasted the duke's food for nearly a year," I yelled at him, "and I know the duke's stomach as well as my own. If I am a fool, then you are a villain and the truth will soon be obvious to everyone."

"Are you accusing me of doing something to the food?" Cristoforo said, waving a kitchen knife at me.

"I am neither accusing you nor not accusing you—"

"*Basta!*" Federico said. He passed the bowl to Cristoforo. "Eat it."

Cristoforo blinked. His goiter swelled up.

"Your Excellency, should Ugo not—"

"Eat it!" Federico roared.

Cristoforo ate a spoonful of pudding. "It is delicious!" he said, and ate two more spoonfuls. He burped. "Your Honor, if you wish me to finish—"

"No!" said Federico, and grabbed the custard from him.

"Shall I make some more?"

"Yes," Federico grunted.

I wanted to slip out of the hall while Federico was still eating, but I had barely moved when Federico said, "Where are you going?"

"He is going to eat some pudding," Cecchi said, to much laughter.

The servant boys told me that after I left they continued to talk about me, saying that for a servant to speak out of turn the way I did could only mean I had lost my mind for the moment. Piero said I was lucky the duke had not killed me for my rudeness and Bernardo added that if the chairs kept jumping up on the table the whole world would come to ruin. I did not care what they said because Federico had replied, "The more he wants to live, the better for me. But the next time he does something like this I will make him eat it just to be sure."

Cecchi gave Cristoforo some coins to ease his humiliation. Although I had been wrong about the pudding, it had turned out all the better for me. I was so relieved I wanted to take Agnese into the hills and screw her until my *fallo* fell off. But it was night, the gates were closed, and she would not let me touch her in the palace.

If Federico was concerned about Pia's arrival he did not show it. True, he killed a man in a joust, and confiscated a village and burned the houses, but he probably would have done those things anyway. He found a new whore called Bianca, who was pretty and well formed. For some reason she always wore a scarf or a hat which covered her forehead and in a certain light this made her look like an Arab.

"He uses her like an Arab, too," Emilia shrieked, as they left the table.

I understood why Federico preferred whores to Emilia. I could have understood if he preferred sheep, goats, or even chickens. There was nothing attractive about her form, her face, or her voice. I was told that when she was younger she had been slender, with a pretty face and a keen sense of humor. But living with Federico had soured her, and I did not doubt that she had tried to poison his other whores and would try to poison Bianca if she could—even Federico himself.

Thoughts of poison plagued me. Lying in the glade with Agnese, I dreamed everything I ate was green with decay and filled with maggots or that my stomach burst open and snakes and dragons crawled out. When I awoke, Agnese was sitting in her favorite tree.

"I can see Bosnia," she said. She told me what her son would be doing if he were alive. This talk had never bothered me before, but now my mind was crowded with Giovanni's sulking, Emilia's shrieking, and the arrival of their mother, Pia, from Venezia and I turned away from her.

But what could I do? For days I racked my brain until my head hurt and then suddenly it came to me. I could test my amulets! Why that had not occurred to me before I do not know, but God in His wisdom gave me the answer just when I needed it. To do so, however, I needed poisons.

As soon as I could I walked down the Weeping Steps to Corsoli. The steps had been built by Federico's brother, Paolo, and it was said that after Federico poisoned him, water trickled down the steps like tears even though it was midsummer. The night was warm, the last rays of autumn casting an orange glow over the city. The shouts of children echoed lazily through the streets, a lullaby wafted from a passing window. I turned a corner and there sat Piero dozing in a chair, his head bowed. I wondered if I should wake him when his eyes suddenly opened as if I had walked into his dream.

"Ugo," he said sharply. "What are you doing here?"

Without hesitation I asked him to instruct me in the effects of poisons and their antidotes.

"Poisons?" he laughed. "I know nothing about poisons." Rubbing his head as if he expected to find some new strands of hair there, he picked up his chair and entered his shop. I followed. Every shelf was filled with jars and bowls of herbs and spices, bones, dried plants, animal organs, and other things I did not recognize.

Piero nervously moved a pair of scales on the counter. "If the duke knew what you had just asked, there would be a new taster standing where you are in less than an hour," he said.

"Piero, what harm would it do to teach me a few things that could save my life and that of my daughter? Maybe yours as well someday. Or will you not tell me because you do not know anything?"

Before he could reply, I added, "Every week you bring new potions to the duke and he still complains he cannot shit. He cannot screw either." This last was not true.

"The duke said that?"

"No, Bianca did."

Outside, it had grown dark. The bell was ringing to warn everyone the gates were closing. The voices of the watch came toward us.

"You are lying," Piero laughed.

The watch were walking past the door.

"No, I am not!" I replied loudly.

There was a knock. "Piero? Is everything all right?"

Piero stared at me. If I was found in the shop it could be trouble for both of us. I opened my mouth as if to speak again and he blurted out, "Everything is good."

"*Buona notte.*"

"May God be with you."

We stood in the darkness till the voices had faded.

"I could be killed for this," Piero said, "If people see us together they will think we are plotting against Federico."

I told him I was a spy for Federico; how else would I have dared to speak to him like that? I swore I would keep my visit so secret I would not even tell myself.

He hemmed and hawed. "If you want to know about hemlock then read the death of Socrates. That is all I can tell you."

"Who was Socrates?"

"You do not know who Socrates was? He was a Greek who was ordered to drink poison because of crimes he committed against the state. But before he drank it he asked if he could propose a toast. Now *that* was a brave man." I nodded although it sounded foolish to me. "In the middle of dying, he told his friends to pay off one of his debts."

That sounded even more foolish, but for once I held my tongue. "What is this?" I picked up a jar full of pink petals from a shelf. "I have seen it before."

"Leave it, leave it!" He took it from me with his fat little hands. "It is meadow saffron. Deadly. Very deadly. One bite and your mouth burns like the flames of hell. You suffer violent stomach pains for precisely three days. And then you die."

So he *did* know about poisons, and I could tell that with a little flattery he would be only too happy to teach me everything he knew. "You must be very brave to live among so much death. I would be scared."

"Ugo," he said, allowing himself a small smile, "Neither of us is a fool, huh? As long as you know what you are doing there is no danger."

"But do poisons always take days before they—"

"Kill someone? No," he said, carefully replacing the jar. "Bitter almonds take just a few hours and are even more violent. I have never used them," he added hastily, "but I was told a woman in Gubbio poisoned her husband in this manner."

"Is that what Federico used to kill his brother?"

"No, that was aconite." He stopped. "I did not—" he began.

"What about Lucca?"

"Lucca? Lucca was filthy. He did not wash enough, there was dirt under his nails. Federico just told everyone he tried to poison him to scare—" he stopped. His cheek twitched. "I have spoken too much."

"I have seen this, too." I said, and quickly held up another jar.

"Yes, dandelion. That is nothing. But this," he picked up another jar, "this is wolfsbane. You must have seen it, it grows everywhere. It makes the body tingle and the hands feel furry like a wolf. Then you die. You always die. Sometimes you bleed, sometimes you shit, sometimes you do both. But you always die. And it is always painful. This is henbane," he said, showing me a smelly green plant. "It grows best in human shit." Now that his excitement had been unbound he wanted to show me every page of his knowledge. "You have heard of Cesare Borgia? He invented a concoction called *la tarantella*." He closed his eyes as if he was making the potion. "It is the saliva of a pig hung upside down and beaten until it goes mad."

I asked how long he thought that would take. He giggled. "No more than three days, because is that not how long it would take for you to go mad if you were hung upside down and beaten? But all the poisons together are not as deadly as this." He held up a small jar of silver-gray powder. "Arsenic. Just half a fingernail can kill a man. What is more, it is tasteless and odorless. There is immediate vomiting and uncontrollable diarrhea, as well as sharp blinding pains in the head as if someone had drilled nails into the skull. Oh, yes, and terrible itching, too. Some people also experience a giddiness and bleeding through the skin. Finally, complete and utter paralysis."

He licked his lips, nodding to himself as if he was making sure he had not left anything out. "In ancient Romagna, emperors would eat tiny amounts every day to build up a resistance to it."

"Did it work?"

"Who knows?" he tittered, as he returned the jar to the shelf. "They are all dead."

"What would a poisoner from Venezia use?"

"From Venezia?" He faced me. "Is someone coming from—?" His cheek twitched again. He dipped his hand into a jar of fat, absent-mindedly rubbing it on his head. "What have you heard?"

"Nothing. I was just asking. *Buona notte.*"

As I returned to the palace, clutching the small amount of arsenic I had stolen, I could not forget the look on Piero's face when I said Venezia. If only for a moment, a ray of hope crossed his eyes like a bird flying across a setting sun; a fleeting ray of hope which served to remind me that even as I was trying to protect Federico, no one would be sorry to see him dead.

Pia arrived on a crisp September afternoon with a train of courtiers and servants. She was wrinkled, plump, and even smaller than Emilia. From a distance she looked like a white raisin. She brought a horse for Federico, dresses for Emilia, and gifts for their sons, Giulio and Raffaello. She shared Giovanni's apartment, which she said was too small, and the first night demanded that Federico add a wing to the palace. "Use my architect. He is a student of Candocci. Everyone says my palazzo is the most beautiful in Venezia."

She wandered about talking to anyone she pleased, grabbing them by the elbow and asking them why they did what they did, and telling them how much better and easier it was done in Venezia. Her voice was as loud as a trumpet, twice as shrill, and could travel through walls. She played backgammon with Emilia and Giovanni or cards with Alessandro, her chief adviser. I studied her courtiers closely and was convinced that if any one of them was a poisoner it was Alessandro. He dressed in black from head to toe, had a huge forehead like a slab of white marble, and silver hair which swept back to his shoulders. There was always a golden toothpick stuck between his teeth like a twig of an unfinished nest. Once, when he, Giovanni, Emilia, and Pia were sitting together, I saw Death hovering about them.

Pia insisted her meals be cooked with butter instead of oil; she said it was fashionable in Germany where she had cousins, and she demanded nuts in everything. "They are good for the blood," she screeched. "Federico, why do you not eat calamari? Tell your cook to cut it into large pieces, boil it with some finely chopped parsley, fry it, and then squeeze a little orange juice over it. My cook, Pagolo—Oh, I so wish I had brought him—makes it twice a week without fail. I could live on it. Emilia tells me you do not eat peaches. Is that true?"

"He thinks they are poisonous," Emilia cackled.

"Just because an ancient king who could not overcome some Egyptians sent them all poisonous peaches," Giovanni said.

Federico's bottom lip fell to his chin. Pia, Emilia, and Giovanni did not notice or if they did they did not care.

Two days later, Tommaso told me he had seen Cristoforo whispering with Alessandro. "Christ! I knew in my bones that pig was treacherous," I said, and warned Tommaso to watch his vegetables carefully.

"You are the one who has to be careful," he replied.

He was right. I did not have the time to experiment with mad pigs. The days were passing swifter than a weaver's shuttle, and as the saying goes, "God helps those who help themselves."

I drank wine with Potero, the keeper of the duke's goblet, and when he fell asleep, I used his key to open Federico's cabinet. Federico's goblet was larger and more magnificent than any other. It had an elegant silver stem and a golden head upon which a lion, a unicorn, and a crab had been beautifully engraved. I filled it with wine and sprinkled in a pinch of arsenic. The arsenic dissolved and I waited for the rainbows to appear on the surface of the wine or for the wine to hiss and sparkle as if it was on fire. Nothing happened. I dipped the unicorn bone into it. According to Tommaso the wine was supposed to froth. Still nothing happened! Perhaps it was the arsenic. Maybe Piero did not know what he was talking about. More likely that fool Tommaso had misheard or misunderstood!

I found a half-starved tawny cat and offered her the wine. She lapped at it eagerly, stretched her front paws, and walked away, satisfied. She had not gone more than a few steps when she stumbled, her back legs crumbling beneath her. She looked up at me, her yellow eyes questioning me in the darkness. Then she lay down, whining pitifully, and her back stiffened into an ungodly shape. She gave a sigh, trembled, and then lay still. O blessed Jesus! There was nothing wrong with the arsenic. It was the amulets! The bone! The goblet! They were useless! They were worse than useless because they had filled me with false hope.

I held the goblet in my hand, uncertain what to do next. Then something occurred to me. What if I left a little arsenic in the goblet? And Federico drank it? How would my life change? If no one cared that Federico was killed, then I would be a hero. But if someone did, there would be a hunt for the poisoner. I wondered if anyone had seen me with Potero. Piero would say that I had asked him about poisons. I would be put on the rack. My limbs would be torn apart. I would be hanged or perhaps buried alive head first. Parts of my body would be cut off as Federico had cut out Lucca's tongue. Then I would be thrown over the mountain.

Fearful as these thoughts were, it was not they which deterred me. No, I did not leave arsenic in the goblet because Potero would surely be the first to die and he had never harmed me. Moreover, whatever ills Federico had brought on others, he had saved Miranda and me from starvation. Finally, I had promised to protect him and I could not betray my promise to God. So I washed and cleaned the goblet with the greatest care and replaced it.

I did not tell anyone what had happened. Instead, I told Tommaso I had taken the unicorn's bone to Santa Caterina during the full moon and offered it to the golden Madonna. I looked around, and after making sure we were alone, I whispered, "At the stroke of midnight it grew warm in my hands and glowed in the dark."

He looked up at me disbelievingly. "What happened?"

"The Madonna told me that she has made it so powerful that if someone even thinks of poisoning the food, the bone will crack in half all by itself."

He held out his hand. "Let me see this miracle."

"There is nothing to see," I said, showing him the dark brown bone.

"Then how do I know you are telling the truth?"

"Because God is my witness."

Like everyone in the palace, in Corsoli, in all of Italy, Tommaso loved to gossip. Even if he knew something was not true, even if he had been with me and seen that nothing I described had happened, he could not resist telling the story—unless he could make up a better one. Can any of us resist if the story is good enough? I was sure mine was good enough, just as I was sure that by the end of the day every servant would know about the bone and by tomorrow the rumor would reach Alessandro. Some of Federico's cunning had rubbed off on me.

That evening, Federico ate heated calves' brains mixed with eggs, salt, verjuice, and pepper and fried for a very short time with liquamen. He shared some with Bianca.

"You horse's *culo*," Pia shrieked. "You bring this whore to the table in front of my daughter!"

Federico lurched to his feet, snarling. Nero barked and Pia knew she had made a mistake. Federico pointed to her and, driving a knife into the table, roared in a voice that must have been heard in Urbino. "You dare to insult me, you ball of pig's fat! From now until you leave, you will live in the tower!"

Giovanni immediately stood up and pushed himself in front of his mother. Eager to make an impression, a young guard lunged at him, but quick as a snake, Giovanni drew a short thick dagger from his belt and stabbed him three times. The first blow went into his chest. He was already dead when the second blow struck his thigh. The third pierced his right eye, the ball spilling out onto the table. The man fell into a heap at Giovanni's feet. The other guards froze and looked at Federico, who, I believe, was as surprised as they were.

Speaking in very measured tones, his eyes never wavering from Federico's face, Giovanni said, "Duke Federico Basillione DiVincelli, I have served you faithfully for many years, but I cannot allow you to insult my mother and sister. It would be best for us to leave Corsoli as soon as possible. I ask only that you give us safe passage."

O my soul! Those are the moments by which men are remembered! The way Giovanni addressed Federico by his full title, the eloquent manner of his address. *Potta!* Who knew that little sodomite had such big balls! A most curious expression, almost a smile, came over Federico's face, as if he had finally found his match. He nodded to Giovanni, who, knife in hand, led his sister and his mother out of the hall.

We could not have been more shocked had an earthquake struck Corsoli. The palace talked of nothing else and everyone guessed as to what would happen next. One day Federico was going to burn them in the tower, the next he was going to massacre them in their beds. He did neither, but instructed Cecchi to arrange for Emilia's, Pia's, and Giovanni's departure. The children would have to stay to ensure that Giovanni would not harm the wool contracts. Emilia begged and wept but Federico would not change his mind. For their journey back to Venezia, Federico agreed to a train of twenty mules guarded by a battalion of soldiers as well as all the servants they needed.

"It is very generous," I said. "There must be some other reason."

"This is but a drop of Federico's gold," Tommaso replied. "He is just pleased to be rid of them."

The first storm of winter swept over the mountains tearing down trees, changing the course of rivers, and drowning animals where they stood. Soaking, starving peasants swarmed into Corsoli besieging the poorhouses and the churches because the hospital was already full of sick feverish people. It was impossible to keep warm. The fires were no use because the wood and the very air itself were damp. Winds whistled through the rooms and hailstones the size of a man's fist broke the windows. Rain poured through holes in the roof and Federico sent servants to fix them. Lightning struck one man, killing him.

After three days the courtyards were deep in mud. Federico could not hunt or joust, his gout pained him, and he cursed everyone. Bernardo said that according to the stars the rain would let up in two days' time on *Ognissanti* (All Saints' Day) and if Emilia left then she would have a safe journey home.

"There is to be a farewell meal," I told Agnese. "I will be glad when they have gone." We were standing in the courtyard, looking toward the hills where the bonfires spluttered weakly. Because of the rain, the parade for *Ognissanti* had been canceled.

Agnese took my hand and placed it on her stomach. "I am to have a baby," she said.

"A baby? O merciful God, what joy!" I pulled her to me and kissed her small button nose, her sad gray eyes, and wide mouth.

She pulled away from me and motioned her head to where Giovanni was watching us from a window in the tower.

"Why are you so afraid of him?" I asked.

She shrugged.

"Because he is a hunchback?"

She shrugged again, burying her head in my shoulder. "He is just a man. A little one. Screw him, he will be gone tomorrow." And to show that I did not care I made the sign of a fig at him, shouted "I am to be a father," and kissed Agnese again. "Now I must tell Miranda. Soon the whole world will know." I rushed off and passed someone slipping out of the kitchen. I was too busy thinking about my good fortune to notice who it was. I had to ask Cecchi if Agnese and I could have a room together. I had to ask Federico for a position other than food taster. It was only then that I realized the man coming out of the kitchen had been Alessandro, Pia's adviser. But surely, I thought, he was locked up with Giovanni? New fears so overcame my joys that I could not even remember what I wanted to tell Miranda.

Bernardo was wrong. It poured with rain on All Saints' Day, but the decision had already been made and Pia and her family were anxious to leave in case Federico changed his mind. All morning, servants loaded Emilia's and Giovanni's trunks into carts and onto horses. The soldiers polished their swords and festooned their horses with banners. At noon, looking pale but proud, Giovanni, Pia, and Emilia and their courtiers were led out of the tower. Some of Agnese's fear had rubbed off on me, so to be safe I told her to stay in the laundry until they had left. "Now we are to have a baby, you must be even more careful."

She smiled and kissed me. The other girls said I would be a good father because I truly loved her. I looked for Tommaso, but I did not see him until I entered the hall. He walked past me and, moving his lips silently, said, "Poison."

Are we ever more alive than when we are faced with danger? Every sense—seeing, hearing, smelling, touching, tasting—is heightened. Every nerve is on edge. We see nothing but what is important; everything else falls away like well-cooked meat from a bone. My mouth was dry, my armpits stuck to my sides. I had examined my amulets, experimented with poisons, but I was as helpless as a rat in a dog's mouth. I wanted to tell Federico of my fears, but he had said that the next time I suspected something was wrong I would have to taste all the dishes, so I remained silent. Bile rose in my stomach. My heart beat faster. My throat closed up. I could hardly breathe!

Federico sat next to Bianca at one end of the table while Emilia, Pia, Giovanni, and her advisers, who were dressed in their traveling clothes, sat at the other. First, in honor of the dead, came a white bean soup made in the Tuscan style with olive oil. Then Cristoforo laid a platter of capons in front of Federico. Federico passed his trencher to me and stuck his tongue into Bianca's ear. I watched Cristoforo leave the room. His goiter was its usual pink which meant he was unconcerned. The meal looked delicious and smelled even more so. Cristoforo had used more oil than usual. That was it! More oil would hide the poison. I sniffed at the trencher. Was that poison? I turned it to the side and sniffed at it again.

Federico's voice came at me from out of a mist. "Is something wrong?"

"Nothing, Your Excellency."

Even though I had made up the story about the unicorn bone breaking in two if the food was poisoned, I prayed it was true! As I bit into the bird I called on God, Christ, the Madonna, and every saint who ever existed. Then I tasted the capon on my tongue. O Lord be praised. I have said before that I had lost all enjoyment of food, and it was true, but when I sampled that first bite the pleasure which had been stored up for so long exploded into my mouth.

The meat fluttered, yes, it fluttered on my tongue. The olive oil had browned the bird to perfection and Cristoforo had added just a dash of mustard. The combination was so unexpected that my taste buds surrendered. I waited for an unfamiliar taste, for something to burn my palate. There was none. I passed the trencher to Federico. He picked up a breast and shared it with Bianca. Emilia looked away in disgust. I watched Giovanni, Emilia, and Pia picking at their food. Could I have heard wrong? Perhaps Tommaso was just amusing himself at my expense. I left the hall to look for him. He was not in the hallways or the kitchen. Thunder cracked, the rain beat down even harder. No wonder that cursed Socrates had been able to make a toast! He *knew* his cup was poisoned. But I could not go to Cristoforo and say, "You sniveling coward, tell me which dish you poisoned or I will cut your balls off, fry them in oil and make you eat them. And by the way, did you use hemlock or arsenic?"

"You are wanted," someone said. "They are going to serve the second course."

The second course consisted of fried veal sweetbreads with an eggplant sauce, cabbage soup, Federico's favorite sausages, and stuffed goose boiled Lombardy style—that is, covered with sliced almonds and served with cheese, sugar, and cinnamon. The goose liver was soaked in wine and sweetened with honey, and looked very appetizing.

"Hurry!" Federico groaned, handing me his trencher.

My hands were shaking. I tried some of the sweetbread and a little of the cabbage soup and the sausage. I felt no ill effects. The goose! It had to be the goose. Of *course* it was the goose! Federico loved goose, everyone knew that. I glanced again at Emilia and Pia. They used to be loud and raucous, but today they were silent. I thought— it is because they do not wish to attract attention to themselves!

The goose was placed in front of Federico. The hall was quiet except for the slurping of food and the rain beating against the window. Giovanni had hardly eaten anything. Thunder crashed over the hills.

"More wine," Federico shouted. I was afraid if he asked me to taste anything else I would die of fright. I nibbled at the goose and kept a small bit under my tongue ready to spit it out if I felt the slightest sensation. I handed the platter back to Federico. He did not even look at me. Bianca gobbled her food down.

It occurred to me that if I died right now I would never see Miranda again. This so disturbed me that I interrupted Federico, saying, "Honorable Duke—" and here I made a face that indicated I would piss on myself if I did not leave.

"No," Federico said, belching loudly. "Wait till after the dessert."

Cristoforo carried in the platter of cookies himself. And then I knew. It was the dessert. What better place to hide poison? Everyone knew Federico loved sugar ten times more than he loved goose, capons, or anything else. Each person was served several cookies shaped like beans and a skeleton made of almonds and sugar. "Ah, *ossi di morto*," Federico smiled.

He passed the platter to me. "Quick," he said, his big bruised lips salivating in anticipation. There was a flash of lightning. Thunder crashed again. Nero barked.

I picked up the skeleton. Oh, how clever of that little hunchback to use a skeleton. I thought—I will not bite the head because that was what Federico liked and anyone who had been in the palace for a while, as indeed Alessandro now had, would know that, and would therefore put the poison there. Instead, I raised the tiny feet to my mouth. Suddenly, I saw Tommaso looking at me from across the hall, his face a mask. I sniffed at the figure and could not part my lips.

"Come on!" Federico snapped.

"Your Excellency, I have reason to think Cristoforo—"

Federico looked at me with such anger I could not finish. "Eat it!" he snarled.

Pia and Emilia were looking at their figures. Giovanni was pouring himself some wine.

"To Miranda," I whispered and bit into the skeleton's feet.

I no longer have any memory of whether it was sugary or not. I swallowed. Lightning lit up the hall, illuminating the yellow teeth, the sharp little eyes and haughty noses. Thunder shook the foundations of the palace and now all the dogs started barking. I gulped. My throat! I grasped my throat! My hands trembled. My body shook and twisted. Something shot through my body. I raised my hand and pointed, "Giovanni!" Cursing, I fell back, crashing into a servant and onto the ground, my legs curling into my stomach, my back arched in the air as the cat's had done. I gasped. My tongue begged for water! Oh, water! Water! I could not control my cursed legs! They jerked backward and forward. I screamed. Chairs were pushed aside. Tables upended. I heard Federico roar, "Cristoforo!" I heard Emilia and Pia shouting above the thunder. Then came the clash of swords, and such bloodcurdling screams as I had never heard before.

Wind raced through the hall and mixed with the gurgles of the dying. Hands struggled to pick me up. I fell into a pool of blood. I was picked up again and carried out of the hall and into my room. The servants ran out. I could hear shouting and wailing and people running back and forth. The door opened again. I heard two people.

"God in heaven, have you ever seen anything like it?" I did not recognize Piero's voice at first because it was trembling so much. "He must have stabbed her six times in the face alone."

"Her mother, too." That was Bernardo.

"But why Cristoforo?"

"If Ugo was poisoned, then Cristoforo must have changed sides."

"But why?"

"It does not make sense. What about Alessandro?"

"He is pleading for his life even now."

"And Giovanni?"

"Who knows?"

Footsteps moved closer to my bed. Piero must have leaned over me for suddenly I smelled the fat of his hair. His hand felt my throat. "He is still breathing." He opened one of my eyes and then the other and stared at me. He leaned down to hear my heart and the fat on his balding head was right up against my nose. I thought I would throw up, but as I did not know whether it was safe yet, I pushed him away, sat up and, remembering the story of Socrates, pointed to Piero and said in a trembling voice, "Pay Tommaso the ten *scudi* I owe him," and sank back down again as if dead.

"What did he say?" Bernardo gasped.

At that moment the door opened and Miranda ran in and threw herself on my chest, wailing, "Babbo, Babbo!"

Her cries were so pitiful and heart-wrenching that even if I had really swallowed poison I would have roused myself from the dead to comfort her.

"The devil is fighting for his soul," Bernardo said, "and the devil has won."

"No, Babbo, no!" Miranda cried.

"Serves him right. He spoiled everything," Bernardo grunted and left the room.

I heard Piero whisper to Miranda. "Come with me. I will give you some olive oil. If you pour it down his throat you may still save him."

"Oh, please hurry," Miranda cried.

"Do not worry," Piero chuckled, "he will live."

I could still hear footsteps running along the corridors, and people shouting and yelling. Servants ran in to look at me and then ran out so as not to miss anything. Soon Miranda returned, lifted my head, and poured olive oil down my throat. Moments later, I was retching so hard I could have expelled Jonah himself. Miranda was overjoyed, weeping and kissing me at the same time.

"Babbo's alive," she kept saying.

Just then Tommaso came in wrinkling his nose at my vomit. "What happened?" he asked, suspiciously.

"What happened?" I gasped. "You fool! I was poisoned!"

Tommaso frowned. "Federico's food was not poisoned."

"Yes, it was," Miranda said angrily. "How can you say that? Babbo nearly died!" She would have beaten him with her fists if I had not whispered, "Miranda, please get me a piece of bread."

As soon as she left the room, I said, "What are you talking about? You said poison."

His eyes widened. "No! I would have told you if Federico's food was poisoned. He poisoned *their* food."

Christ on a cross! The puzzle had been upside down the whole time! Now I understood why Federico was so generous with the gifts, why he acted so surprised when I had fallen sick. He had planned to poison Giovanni, Emilia, and Pia and my pretending to be poisoned had confused everyone. But I still could not let anyone know the truth. "But why did Federico kill Cristoforo?" I asked.

"He must have thought Cristoforo had tricked him," Tommaso shrugged.

"But Alessandro—"

"Alessandro has been working for Federico since the moment he arrived."

How did Tommaso know this? To be sure I was not being trapped, I said, "But I *was* sick. The bone grew warm in my hand."

"You had better hope Federico believes you," Tommaso snorted.

Dressed in his armor, Federico was seated at his desk, his sword by his side. I had never seen him in his armor before, but I understood immediately how fearsome he must have looked on the battlefield. Bernardo, Cecchi, and Piero hovered behind him. Alessandro was not with them—Federico had imprisoned him until he knew exactly what had happened. I walked slowly toward Federico, for the retching had exhausted me. When I was in front of him he suddenly stood up, grasped my neck with both hands, and lifted me right off the floor.

"Why in the devil's name are you alive and my best cook is dead?" he roared.

The room spun around me. "Your Excellency—" My air was cut off. My heart beat in my ears and I could taste my own blood.

"My Lord," Cecchi exclaimed. "This is a blessing."

"A blessing? How?" Federico let me go and I fell to the floor coughing and spluttering.

"If Emilia and her mother had been poisoned, the pope would have blamed you," Cecchi explained. "But because Ugo fell sick everyone will know an attempt was made on your life. You were forced to take action against murderous assaults. Giovanni's leaving is proof of his guilt!"

I could have kissed Cecchi's feet. No wonder they called him "*Il Cicero di Corsoli*." It was a brilliant idea and for the second time in my life I praised God that this honorable and noble man had come to my aid.

"It is a pity Ugo was not killed," that pig Bernardo grumbled. "That would have been the best proof of Giovanni's intentions. We could still kill him."

"But if anyone asks him, he will say he was poisoned," Cecchi said.

"But I *was* poisoned," I said, and, struggling to my feet pulled out the bone which I had broken into two pieces. "The Virgin Mary said if I was poisoned my unicorn horn would break in two—"

Federico knocked the pieces out of my hand with one blow. "Leave me," he ordered. "All of you. Except Ugo." They hurried out.

It had stopped raining, but the wind was whipping around the castle to make sure that no one could escape. Federico leaned back in his chair and lowered his chin to his chest. His eyes became small and hard. "Cristoforo poisoned three skeletons. One each for Emilia, Pia, and Giovanni." He paused, waiting for me to speak.

"He must have poisoned yours as well, Your Excellency."

Federico reached across the desk. "You mean this one?" He lay the footless skeleton in front of me.

"Yes, Your Excellency," I said, indignantly. "That is the one."

"Are you telling the truth?" His eyebrows raised questioningly.

"The gospel truth, Your Excellency."

"Because if you are not, the rack will make you confess."

"My Lord, if you put me on the rack I will confess to killing Jesus Christ himself."

Federico scratched his nose and licked his lips. "There is only one way to find out." He pushed the skeleton toward me. "Eat it."

I stared at the cookie. "My Lord, if it *is* poisoned, then you will lose the best food taster you have ever had."

Federico's eyes did not waver from my face. "You are either very smart or very lucky. Which is it?"

"I am very lucky to serve you, Your Excellency."

Federico's face soured. "I was hoping you were smart. I am surrounded by idiots."

I cursed myself for not being braver. Federico rose from the desk, took out a key, went to a door, and opened it. Even as he unlocked it, part of the wall on my right moved slightly. I thought that Federico's key was moving this wall, but Federico did not look up. An eye peered into the room, saw me, and retreated into the darkness; and the wall moved silently back into place again. I was about to say something, but my words were stilled by the sight of thousands upon thousands of gold coins lying in a heap on the floor of the closet Duke Federico had opened.

He picked up two gold coins and threw them to me. "Have some new clothes made. Tell Cecchi I said you should have a new room."

"*Mille grazie*, Your Excellency, *mille grazie!*" He held out his right hand and allowed me to kiss it.

I left the duke's chambers as if I had been crowned pope. "Look at me now, Vittore! You poxy goat! And you too, Papa!" I shouted, "Look at me now!"

Miranda was rocking backward and forward on the bed, cradling Felicita to her bosom. I tossed a gold coin into her lap and cried, "We are to get a new room and new clothes. And you will have a brother for I am to be a father again!" I pulled her to her feet and swung her around the room. "I must find Agnese."

"No, Babbo," Miranda said.

"You do not want a brother? Very well, you shall have a sister."

She squeezed Felicita's neck as if it was just a piece of wood instead of her precious doll.

"What is it? Speak up."

"Agnese is dead," she whispered.

"Dead? No, she is in the laundry."

She shook her head.

"Tell me," I cried.

Tears poured down her face. The words burbled out in such confusion that I made her repeat them three times before I could understand what had happened. "Giovanni killed her! When Agnese heard the screaming she ran into the courtyard. He was coming out of the palace. The stable boys said he struck her down for no reason."

Oi me! How many times can a man's heart be broken without killing him? My mother. My best friend, Toro. Elisabetta. Agnese. My unborn child. All dead. Everyone I loved except Miranda. What was God telling me? That I must not love? Did that mean I would lose Miranda, too? I prayed to God but He did not answer me so I cursed Him. I cursed all the times I had prayed to Him and then, fearing He would avenge Himself, I wept, asking for His forgiveness, and begged Him to protect Miranda from me.

I have not written for several days because I ran out of paper. Septivus would not give me any more until his order arrived from Fabriano. It came today and so I will hurry and catch my story up to these present events.

The palace changed after the killings. After convincing Federico that he had not double-crossed him, Alessandro was rewarded with Giovanni's rooms and his role as ambassador. Tommaso was put to work in the kitchen and I was thrown into a pit of despair. The archbishop offered to bury Agnese in the graveyard, but I insisted that it be the glade where we had spent so many happy hours. I crawled on the ground weeping and tearing at my hair even as my father had done when my mother died. I sang Agnese's sad little song in words I did not understand. I climbed into the grave and held her close to me to remember her smell and the feel of her body. I cut off a lock of her hair. Then I wept all over again for the child I never knew. Cecchi came to fetch me, for Federico was soon to eat his evening meal.

I cursed Federico and said I did not care if he imprisoned me. Cecchi said Federico would most certainly do that and forced me to go with him. He warned me to hide my tears because it would upset Federico, but even as I tasted a capon bathed in lemon sauce, I was overcome with sorrow. Cecchi whispered something to Federico, who looked at me and said, "Ugo, I did not know Giovanni killed your *amorosa*. He is an evil man and you will be avenged."

"*Grazie*," I sobbed, "*mille grazie*."

Then Federico addressed everyone at the table, saying in a solemn voice, "There is no pain that time will not soften."

Everyone nodded and pleased with this morsel of wisdom, Federico turned to me again and said, "So stop crying!" and bit into his food.

Agnese's face appeared to me in my dreams and in my waking hours. Her voice called to me from behind every pillar and doorway. I lit candles in the Duomo Santa Caterina and begged God to forgive me for the part I had played in the killings of Pia and her family, for as sure as night followed day, I knew Agnese had been killed for my sins.

So drowned in grief were my senses that it was not until some time later that I realized servants I did not know were calling me "Ugo," and asking if I had slept well. They complimented me on my appearance, offered to do favors for me, and asked me to speak to Federico for them. One morning, the new cook Luigi, a man with stooped shoulders and a goatee, took me by the arm and whispered, "I swear on my life I will never do anything to harm Duke Federico or you."

"They think you were saved by a miracle," Tommaso snorted. "If they knew that you faked it—"

"But you are not going to tell them any different. If everyone is scared of me it will stop them from trying to poison Federico."

Tommaso folded and unfolded his arms—his tongue flapped like a banner in the wind for it was against his nature to keep a secret. It was in that moment that I recognized that it was his eye I had seen in the wall. He was a spy for Federico! That was why the serving boys had warned me about him my first day in the palace. That was why he warned me against getting too close to Federico. That was how he knew Giovanni's food had been poisoned. I did not tell him I recognized him. Even if he could not keep a secret, I could.

He was fifteen now and growing taller by the day. He did not like working in the kitchen—the spices made him sneeze—but I needed him there so I flattered him, saying, "One day you will be Federico's chef."

"And then Miranda will have to respect me," he said.

Oi me! I had hoped he had forgotten about Miranda, but she was growing prettier by the day, the other boys commented on it, and no doubt this fired his passion.

Miranda and I were given a new room with two beds, a beautifully painted chest, and a solid oak desk. Our windows overlooked Emilia's garden which, now that she was dead, was abandoned to the roses, daisies, and other wildflowers. At night their fragrances drifted up to our window and scented my dreams.

The biggest change of all came because of Bianca, Federico's new whore. She acted as if she had been born a princess. She looked haughtily at everyone, but issued her orders in a voice as soft as a kitten's purr, so no one knew which was the truer self. Perhaps because she had been a whore for so long (they say she had started at twelve), she knew exactly what men were thinking the moment they set eyes on her. Consequently, she could coax them into doing anything she wanted. Luigi inquired daily if there was a particular dish she liked. Bernardo hurried to consult the stars for her every morning, even making up excuses so that he might see her more often. Even Cecchi ordered special wines from Orvieto, Urbino, and Roma for her.

Bianca bought new clothes and jewelry, rearranged the furniture, and held little parties for her old friends. The sound of the whores gossiping made the wives of the courtiers jealous, but the men never said anything. She was careful never to offend Federico, but if, for some reason, his lip fell down to his chin, Bianca took him by the hand and led him back to her room. I do not know what they did behind those doors but sometimes he was too exhausted to leave for days. And when he did, he was smiling! It is the gospel truth! He hunted, he falconed, he played tricks to amuse himself—he ordered a lame woman to dance with a blind man—and insisted that I be with him at all times. Not that he spoke to me unless it was about food, as when after tasting Luigi's specialty of veal wrapped in bacon and toasted on bread, he turned to me and said, "This is excellent. I should have killed Cristoforo long ago."

To be respected by Federico eased the pain of Agnese's death and so I took my task with even greater seriousness. I spent time in the kitchen learning how different dishes were prepared, how long they had to be cooked, which sauces to use, and so on. I learned from Luigi that too many turnips brought on phlegm and that fava beans were good for men because they looked like testicles. I was so overflowing with knowledge that it spilled out before I could stop it.

One day I advised Federico the veal needed more pepper. Another time I said the chicken should have been marinated a little longer. And he agreed! Once, just by sniffing a venison sauce, I named all the ingredients: marjoram, basil, nutmeg, rosemary, cinnamon, celery, garlic, mustard, onion, summer savory, pepper, and parsley. Duke Federico was so impressed he often asked me to perform this trick in front of his guests.

Now I felt truly at home in the palazzo. Federico trusted me. True, it was only in small matters, but does the acorn not give birth to the oak tree? I was sure I would soon be promoted to a courtier and prayed for an opportunity to prove to Federico that I could be of greater use to him. However, God in His wisdom decided that I was not yet ready for such a post. But *potta!* Did He have to use that ungifted little dwarf, Ercole, to tell me?

The only thing Ercole and Giovanni had in common was their size. Ercole was as cowardly as Giovanni had been brave and as stupid as Giovanni had been clever. Where Giovanni had changed his clothes to suit his mood, Ercole wore the same brown jerkin and hose every day of his life. Had Giovanni been able to straighten his hump he would have been as tall as any man, whereas Ercole was a runt when he was born and will remain one till he dies.

I have hardly mentioned Ercole because, aside from wrestling a sheep to death at the first banquet, the little turd had never done anything worth mentioning; and, since Corsoli relied so much on its sheep, he could only perform that trick once a year. Most of the time, he hopped around in the corner of the hall trying to appear even smaller than he already was by bending his knees and bowing his head and banging softly on his little drum, praying Federico would not notice him.

One evening, Federico idly tossed away a half-eaten trencher which hit Ercole squarely on the head. Ercole rose up indignantly, the fury in his little lined face causing me to laugh louder than I had ever done at his tricks. He hissed at me because he thought I had thrown the trencher. Then, when he realized that it was Federico who had thrown it, he immediately picked it up. But as he did so something occurred to him. I could see the idea blossoming in his brain. He moved his head from side to side, examining the trencher as if he had never seen one before. He sniffed at it like a dog. He turned it upside down and sniffed it again. The little squirt, the little piece of shit was imitating me! Federico nudged Bianca. The diners stopped eating to watch. Aware of this, Ercole sniffed at the trencher some more and again turned it this way and that. Then he broke off a tiny piece and placed it on the tip of his tongue. He stood with his legs apart, hands on his hips, eyes pointed at the ceiling, his big wide mouth and thick lips pausing every other instant to chew and think, chew and think, until he swallowed it with a big gulp and traced its path with his finger down his throat and into his stomach.

I knew what he was going to do next. He clasped his throat, spluttered, and coughed. He sank to the ground, yelling and shrieking, thrusting first one part of his body into the air and then another, distorting his face, clawing at the ground and yelling, "My bone! My bone!" Then he arched his back and slumped to the floor, silent as if dead.

Bianca burst into laughter and could not stop. She covered her face with her hands, uncovered it, saw me and laughed again. Then Federico started snorting and laughing, and banging his fist on the table. Immediately, the rest of the court began braying like the asses they were. I wanted to plunge a knife into Ercole's neck and pull it down to his little balls. To have a dwarf mock me in front of everyone! After all I had been through?

Ercole bowed solemnly. The applause went on. He bowed again. He bowed four times. Good Christ! You would have thought he had conquered the French single-handedly! Federico wiped his eyes and said, "Bravo Ercole! Bravo! Do it again!"

The laughter and applause inspired Ercole. Contorting his face, he tried to imitate my haunted looks with his short squat body, making him look even more ridiculous.

"Do you not think he is funny?" Federico asked me.

"Since I have never seen myself eat," I said, "I cannot tell if it is accurate or not."

"Oh, it is accurate," Federico laughed. "Very accurate."

I left the hall, the laughter ringing in my ears. I found Miranda's mirror and watched myself eat in it. Ercole's moves were clumsy, but they were accurate. I wanted to kill him.

"You cannot," Tommaso warned. "Federico likes him. If something happens to Ercole, Federico will know it was you."

Soon Ercole was giving performances to anyone who would watch and the very same servants who had praised me the day before now sniggered when I passed. I tried different ways of eating, but how many ways can you chew a piece of food?

"Federico will forget, Babbo," Miranda said, trying to calm me.

But Federico did not forget and asked Ercole to perform his routine whenever he had guests. Once when I did not sniff the food, Federico said angrily in front of Duke Baglioni, "Do it the old way; otherwise it spoils Ercole's imitation."

So like the pet I had become, I had to sniff the food and then stand by while Ercole made a fool of me. Whenever Ercole did his imitation, Federico told the visitors about the killings of Pia and her family. They must have retold my story when they returned home, forgetting some things and adding others so that the tale became as varied as the roads they traveled. I became known in cities as far away as Roma and Venezia.

I cannot deny this pleased me and I told Septivus I would soon be the most famous food taster in Italy. He smiled, gnashing his little yellow teeth together. "Dante tells us that fame is like a breath of wind that is forgotten as soon as it dies."

"No doubt that is true. But while the wind blows everyone else is touched by it."

"Yes," he said, "some to praise and some to curse."

How right he was, but I am ahead of myself.

Of course, since I was *only* a food taster, none of the diners could believe *I* had thought of faking my death. No, they assumed Federico had told me to do it to justify his killing of his wife and mother-in-law. Soon Federico was convinced of it himself, and once, while I was standing right next to him, he boasted to the ambassador of Bologna that he not only had invented the plot, but also had shown me how to fake the death throes!

I remember thinking about this one winter's evening. The nights came with increasing swiftness and the rain turned the white walls of the palace gray in front of my eyes. Stories, it seemed to me, were like the walls in that someone seeing them for the first time would never have known they were once white, just as someone hearing my tale from Federico would have never known the true story. If the listeners enjoyed the story, they cared little for the truth. Perhaps, then, Jonah was not swallowed by a whale at all, but had eaten the large fish. Or maybe Jesus had never been killed, but had climbed down from the cross and hidden in the cave. Perhaps, too, Socrates had not joked before drinking the hemlock, but had begged and screamed for mercy.

This did little to comfort me. The rain beat down harder. I wondered where Miranda was; she had not returned from her classes, and so I searched for her. Outside a room where she sometimes played, I heard a voice say, "Oh, Miranda, do not be so upset."

I peered in. A few of her friends were huddled together in front of a large fire, their heads leaning against each other, their arms around one another's shoulders as girls will often do. They were laughing at Miranda, who was sitting a little way off, hugging her knees under her chin.

"Anyway," Miranda said sullenly, "you are not doing it right."

"*You* do it then," a girl teased and the others joined in. "You do it."

Miranda bit her lip. She stood up (my hand trembles as I write this), and imitated me tasting some food. Ercole was limited by his talent, but Miranda was gifted and knew things about me even I did not know. After she had mimicked me eating, which made the girls shriek with laughter, she pretended to examine her throat in a tiny mirror. She coughed and gargled and stuck her fingers inside her mouth as if a crumb had become stuck between her teeth, something I often did when I returned to our room after a meal. She did this with great earnestness, twisting her face, licking her lips, wiggling her tongue, and digging in her mouth as if she was mining for gold. One girl laughed so hard she wet herself.

Suddenly, Miranda looked in my direction, and when our eyes met she immediately ran out of the room. Her friends chased after her while I turned my face to the wall so they would not see me.

Later, I asked why she had made a fool of me.

"How do you think *I* feel?" she said. She did not say it, but I knew what she meant. It was because I was a food taster. "I will never have a dowry worth anything."

I wanted to laugh but I feared I would choke. I had done such a good job of raising Miranda to be a princess that she was now ashamed of me. I left her and went to Ercole's room.

"If you are asking me not to imitate you," he said, leaning back in the little chair he had made for himself, "I cannot. God has granted me a gift which Federico loves. If you were talented, you would be able to entertain him, too."

I put one foot on top of the other to prevent myself from kicking the chair out from under him. "Well then," I said, "You should do it correctly."

"I do do it correctly," he said hotly.

"Not according to Federico. From where I stand, I hear things."

"What things?" He frowned. "What have you been hearing?"

I pretended it was difficult for me to explain. I wanted him to get so interested that his eagerness would cloud his judgment. "Well, I overheard . . ."

"What?" he demanded in his squeaky voice.

"Federico thinks you are not as funny as you used to be. He thinks your movements should be bigger and grander."

Ercole raised the tip of his nose, which was already pointing straight up, and looked at me suspiciously. "Federico said I should make bigger movements?"

"That is what I heard. I wanted to tell you because you know if you do not please Federico . . ." I did not need to say anymore.

The next time Ercole imitated me he chewed and waved his arms as if he was having a fit. No one laughed. Federico's lower lip dropped to his chin. Ercole became so afraid he picked up his drum and started banging it for no reason.

"What are you doing?" Federico roared.

"Your Excellency," he stuttered. "You said—"

"What? Do it properly," Federico said.

By now, however, Ercole was so flustered he no longer knew what to do.

"Maybe this will help you remember," Federico roared and threw a bowl of soup at him, followed by several knives, spoons, and loaves of bread till Ercole was hunched up like a little ball on the floor.

"I think he should be hanged," I said loudly. "He was given a gift by God which he has abused."

"Shut up," Federico said. There was nothing more I wanted to say. I knew Ercole would never imitate me again and now others would think twice before they tried. But God had not finished with me, and worse was yet to come.

xvi

Our second winter in the palace, the winds drove the snow into huge piles which dotted the courtyard and the streets of the city. The boys made lions and birds out of snow and one morning Tommaso made a wolf sitting on its haunches. He used almonds coated with saffron for its eyes and a piece of leather for its tongue. He wanted Miranda to see it, but she refused, saying she was too busy reading the Bible.

"She is going to become a nun," Tommaso said, forming the wolf's paws. "She says she has no time for foolish things."

"She will have changed her mind by dinner."

He nibbled his nails. "She gives her food to the poor."

"How do you know? Have you been following her?"

He told me he had watched her kneeling in the rain in the Piazza Del Vedura and that had he not pulled her out of the way a soldier on horseback would have trampled her to death.

"Did she thank you?"

He shook his head. "She said I had no right to interfere in God's will."

Miranda was in the Duomo praying to a statue of the Virgin Mary. In between her entreaties I asked her gently why she was punishing herself so.

"I am preparing for the *privilegium paupertatis*," she answered, her voice filled with anguish and heartache as if she had just climbed down from the cross itself.

"Miranda, you do not have to have the *privilege* of being poor. You *are* poor. I am poor. This is because of the dowry, is it not?"

She turned away and went back to her prayers.

"You think because you will never get married you might as well devote your life to the church: am I right?" She did not answer. "Miranda, those nuns you admire so do not have to be poor either. They spend all day making things for free and then they beg for alms so they can eat. If they charged the churches just a little for their work, they would not have to beg from people like me who can ill afford to give them anything!"

"Begging reminds them to be humble," Miranda admonished me.

"Hunger reminds you how to be humble," I yelled. "*Basta!*"

But she did not stop. She continued to give her food away and would drop to her knees and pray wherever and whenever she felt like it. The old half-blind washerwoman said she was a saint. It did not matter whether I was angry or kind to her, Miranda would not listen to me.

"This will kill you and then what good will you be?" I pleaded, after I found her shivering in the snow. Her lips had turned blue and her teeth chattered. She recited Hail Marys and novenas to drown me out.

Two nights later I awoke to find her bed empty.

"She said God told her to go to the convent at San Verecondo," the guard at the gate said. I swear the gate guards are the most stupid of all God's creatures. It does not matter which city you go to, if the city has a gate and the gate has a guard, then the guard is bound to be stupid.

"This is madness! How could you have let her go in this weather?"

"She looked holy," he shrugged.

The sky was covered in a blanket of gray clouds. Soft, fat snowflakes fell silently like goose feathers from God's pillows. I ran as fast as I could, calling, "Miranda, Miranda!" A wolf's howl answered me. I prayed it had not found her and that I would soon catch her and if I did not it was because she had already reached the convent. The snow grew deeper. Every bush, each tree, each blade of grass was white. My shoes and hose were soaked through, my hands and face numb with cold. I called Miranda's name again, but the night swallowed my voice. I could not make out the hills and no longer knew if I was going in the right direction. Exhausted, I fell to my knees. As I knelt there I realized I was in the same position I had seen Miranda in. I wondered if this was God's way of punishing me for forbidding Miranda to do as He had wanted. I threw myself in the snow, weeping for forgiveness and promising God that if I found Miranda I would deliver her to the convent myself.

No sooner had I said this than a light came toward me through the trees. It was the Virgin Mary herself. She reached out her hand to me, saying in a soft, sweet voice, "Sleep. Rest. Then I will lead you to your daughter."

But another voice said, "This is not the Virgin Mary, this is Death." I rose to my feet and stumbled onward, plunging into the snow up to my waist, crying out to God to protect me. And when I was at my last breath I tripped over a body—Miranda.

I do not know how I returned to Corsoli for it was God alone who guided my footsteps. I knocked at Piero's house and though it was past midnight he woke his wife and children and ordered them to boil hot water while he covered Miranda in blankets. He bathed her hands and feet, gave her medicines, and, when I had to return to the palace to taste Federico's breakfast, watched over her as if she was his own daughter.

I spent every moment I could at Miranda's bedside, for Piero said her life was in danger. Tommaso brought soups and pastries—it was her illness that inspired him to become a cook—and I prayed and wiped the sweat from her brow.

I had never been inside a Jew's home and was surprised to see it was much like anyone else's. Since Federico was always complaining of some ailment, I asked Piero why he did not live in the palazzo.

"Duke Federico does not allow it because we are Hebrews. Besides, here," he smiled, "I am closer to the citizens of Corsoli."

Just then Miranda, whose face had turned from blue to white, gave out such a racking cough that it rattled the very bones in her body. She became feverish and cried out in her sleep. Piero said that although it did not seem so, it was in fact a good sign.

At last, through God's good graces and Piero's care—for which I could not thank him enough—Miranda was well enough to be taken back to the palazzo. She stayed in bed, and although Tommaso still brought her food and her friends inquired about her, she refused to see anyone. She did not say so, but I knew it was because the two smallest fingers of her right hand had withered as well as two of the toes on her right foot. She would never recover their use and wailed that she would never be able to walk again. I told her of soldiers who walked with only one leg and of an aunt of mine who walked all her life even though she had been born without a foot. I said she should give thanks to God and Piero that she was alive. This did little to comfort her. Indeed, she said I should have left her to die. "I have failed Santa Claire," she wept, "I have failed Our Lord."

I did not tell her of my promise to take her to a convent because, having found her, I could not bear to part with her again.

In the midst of her weeping there was a knock at our door. I opened it and there stood Bianca, dressed in furs, a hood studded with diamonds covering her forehead. "Is this where the little saint is hiding?" she asked.

I was so surprised to see her that she said, "Are you not going to ask me in?"

"Of course." And I stepped aside to allow her to enter.

She smelled of bergamot and musk and as she passed me she slid her tongue over her lower lip and smiled as if she knew secrets about me which even I did not know.

"Ah, here she is," she said playfully, and sat on Miranda's bed. She wiped away Miranda's tears and patted her cheeks. "We will fatten up these little beauties so they outshine the sun." Then she said to me, "Miranda and I have much to talk about so go away for a while. And do not listen outside the door. They all do," she winked to Miranda. "They are worse than women."

I walked into Corsoli and back again, wondering why Bianca had come to see Miranda. Was it simply out of the goodness of her heart? Beneath all her furs and jewels Bianca was still a whore; but, I reminded myself, many wives and mistresses of famous men had been whores. Certainly they knew the ways of men better than men did themselves. Bianca was no fool. She was Federico's mistress. She could help Miranda in many ways.

When I felt I had waited long enough I returned to our room. Miranda was alone, sitting up in bed, regarding herself in her hand mirror. A necklace of beautiful pearls hung around her neck. "Did Bianca give you those?" I asked.

"Yes," she said, trying to hide her excitement. "She invited me to her apartment."

"That is wonderful."

"But I cannot walk, Babbo. Even if I could, I could not go," she added earnestly, as only the righteous can. "She is a whore."

I was tempted to throw Miranda back into the snow, but instead I said, "Our Lord Jesus Christ turned away neither sinners nor prostitutes."

Miranda frowned, her big dark eyebrows knitting together in the center of her forehead, her teeth biting her bottom lip.

"What did you talk about?" I asked.

She tossed the hand mirror onto a nearby chair and held up her frozen fingers. "Bianca said they were not made for work and this was God's way of saying that I should not do any."

"I see. And what else?"

"She said I was the prettiest girl in the palazzo and that one day I would have a line of suitors waiting to court me."

"That is good news indeed."

"She said I must change my hair because this style is old." She reached for the hand mirror, but it was too far away so she threw off the covers, climbed out of bed, and picked it up. Then she realized what she had done. "Babbo," she breathed. "Babbo."

I took her in my arms. "If Bianca can make the lame walk, then maybe you should listen to her."

Miranda returned from Bianca's the next day wearing a beautiful bracelet and a red shawl made of the finest wool. Her face had been brushed faintly with powder and her lips were rouged to match her cheeks. The day after, her hair had been combed so that it curled softly around the edges of her face. She wore a little tiara and a dress that swirled about her when she turned. "How do I look?" she asked.

"Very beautiful." As indeed she did.

"I spent all afternoon at the dressmaker's." She held up her wrist to show off another bracelet. "Bianca says it is from the silver mines in Germany. They are the best in the world. Do you see these stones? You can only buy them in Firenze or Venezia. Now I have to practice my lyre."

The next week she returned, waving a little fan. "I danced, Babbo! I can almost dance as well as I could before. Alessandro said I danced as beautifully as anyone he had ever seen."

"Alessandro was in Bianca's apartment?"

"Yes, he showed me how to hold the fan so that no one would see my dead fingers."

"Bianca is turning Miranda into a whore," Tommaso complained.

He was jealous and angry that Miranda had not thanked him for the soup and pastries that he had brought her.

"Two weeks ago Miranda was starving herself to death. We should kiss Bianca's feet."

I did not kiss her feet, but thanked her for her kindnesses.

"Anything to get her away from those nuns," Bianca smiled. "She is a beautiful child."

"You are the mother she always wanted."

For a brief instant her face seemed older and sadder; and in a voice that was neither sultry nor haughty she said, wistfully, "She is the daughter I always wished for." Then she walked away, her furs twirling about her. "Make sure she practices her lyre and writes her poetry," she called over her shoulder.

The next day Miranda returned wearing a beautiful fur jacket Bianca had made for her. "Alessandro showed me how they dance in Venezia," she said, and demonstrated the steps he had taught her. In her fur jacket, her head held high, the girl disappeared into a woman.

Suddenly, Tommaso's warning came back to me.

"Miranda, please, do not wear that in the palazzo."

"Oh, I will not. I am saving it for Carnevale."

After Elisabetta died, I used to go to Corsoli every year for Carnevale with my friend Toro. Did we have fun then! We got there in time for the parades because right after the olive pickers, came men dressed as priests who blessed us with curses. Toro always walked in front because he could curse better than any ten men together. Some other friends and I would wait on the roof of a house by the West Gate and as Toro walked by, his face red with cursing and swearing, we pelted him with eggs and flour! I remember a crazy woman who tore off all her clothes; we chased her through the streets till we caught her and took turns screwing her. And the food! *Potta!* We stuffed ourselves so full of sausages and polenta we could hardly move. A grocer used to sell truffles marinated in olive oil that were so good Christ Himself would have risen again just to taste them.

The day Miranda spoke about Carnevale, Bianca also mentioned it at dinner. She told us that in Venezia, the noblemen held magnificent balls inviting hundreds of people including princes and princesses and ambassadors from Germany, France, and England as well as all over Italy. They dressed in costumes of Roman gods, some made out of gold. She said that once she had dressed as Venus, another time as a peacock. She told us her lover had spent half the profits from one of his ships for this costume; it was made of jewels, had taken two months to create, and the train was so long two boys had to carry it. She was proclaimed the most beautiful woman in Venezia and the doge himself had danced with her. But, she said, compared to some women even this was nothing.

We had never done anything like that in Corsoli and sat spellbound at these tales, even Federico, although I could see it was making him jealous.

As if she sensed this, Bianca turned to him and said, "Federico, you should throw a ball."

"A ball?" Federico frowned.

"You are right, who would come? But we must do something! She tugged gently at her scarf which had ridden up her brow in her excitement. "I know, we could switch places!"

At this everyone began to talk at once. When I was small my father wore breasts made of straw and cooked polenta while my mother put on his hose and spent the whole day swearing and farting. Vittore laughed so hard he was sick, but I was too small to understand and begged my mother to be herself. I had not seen anyone do it since then.

Cecchi said that he had once changed places with his servants. "They ate and drank and made a terrible mess because they knew I had to clean it up."

Alessandro admitted he had once dressed as a young girl and an old priest followed him around all day offering him gifts and money. It was not till Alessandro had taken several hundred ducats from him that he revealed he was really a boy.

Federico listened, gorging himself on pine kernels dipped in melted sugar and covered with thin gold leaf.

"Why do you not do it, Federico?" Bianca said.

"Do what?"

"Change places with someone."

"The duke should not lower himself," Cecchi said, rousing himself from his memories.

"But when men of great standing do it, it inspires love among their citizens," Alessandro said.

"But the duke *is* much loved," protested Piero. "Duke Federico is—"

"Let me consult the stars," Bernardo said. "If they—"

"Yes, why not?" said Federico, beaming at Bianca. "But who shall I change with?"

"Me!" Bianca laughed.

"You are not my servant," Federico cooed. "You are my delight."

He looked around the room. Everyone stared at the ceiling or the walls, anywhere, but at Federico.

"Why not Ugo?" said Alessandro, picking at his teeth with his little gold stick.

"Ugo?"

"He is loyal and trustworthy."

"That is an excellent choice," Bianca said.

"What do you say, Ugo?" Federico asked, turning his great bulk toward me.

Potta! What could I say? I thought I was done with people imitating me, but Alessandro was right. If a servant was to switch places with Federico, who among the court had proved themselves more loyal than me? So I said, "I would be honored, My Lord."

"Good. We will exchange roles for the last breakfast before Lent. In the servants' hall. Have it made ready," Federico said, and Bianca clapped her hands with delight.

"If you are going to change places why wait till tomorrow morning?" Luigi said when I told the kitchen help what had happened. "Start tonight, then you can sleep in Federico's bed."

"And he can sleep in mine."

"He would need yours *and* Miranda's," Luigi said to much laughter.

"But then," Tommaso said, with a frown, "the duke would be sleeping with Miranda."

"Yes, and Ugo likes doing that," a boy sniggered.

I drew my knife, but the servants came between us. "It was a joke," they shouted.

"Does everyone think that?" I asked Tommaso later.

"Well," he said, carefully measuring his words, "all the other girls have boys who like them, but Miranda keeps them away, so they think, perhaps . . ."

"I keep her away only because I do not want her to get with child," I said angrily.

"You asked me and I am telling you."

I was so upset that it chased away a thought that had been nagging me like a broken tooth. Now I could not remember what it was.

xvii

For once the clouds parted and a watery sun celebrated Carnevale with us. Laying in my bed I could hear the city filling with people. The fountains were already running red with wine and soon everyone would be drinking and carousing. I had no desire to join them. I could not stop thinking about changing places with Federico. It was supposed to be an amusement, but it felt like a death sentence. How would Federico act if I ordered him to do something?

"No," I said to Tommaso when he asked me if I was going to the *palio*. "My stomach hurts. There is bile in my throat. I am sick."

"Ugo! Federico will not go through with this. It is just talk. Come on, we will make some money on the horses." His words tripped over one another in excitement. "Even if you do get killed, at least you will have had a good time!" So I allowed him to persuade me.

The valley must have been deserted for the streets were so crowded I could not see the ground beneath my feet. Revelers hung out of windows and sat on rooftops. The families who owned the horses marched through the streets, singing, blowing their trumpets, and insulting one another.

By evening, it was raining and the cobblestones of the Piazza Del Vedura glistened in the flickering light of the sconces. When the horses surged by us the crowd screamed, yelling so loudly that I forgot my troubles. I saved my money for the last race which was riderless and always the most fun.

The first time the horses galloped through the piazza, a dark brown stallion was leading, a gray horse hanging on its shoulder. Tommaso had bet on the stallion and I on the gray. As soon as they had passed, the people on our side of the square rushed to the other side and those on that side ran to ours. There was much pushing and shoving as we banged into one another and then came the yells, "They are coming! They are coming!" and we flung ourselves against the walls to get out of the way of the trampling hooves.

The third time the horses swept by, the stallion was still leading. Tommaso turned to me, his eyes shining, and screamed, "Pay me!" Just then the stallion slipped and crashed into the crowd across from us, knocking the spectators down like blades of grass. A terrible wailing arose. The horse tried to stand, but could not because a bone was sticking out through the flesh of its foreleg. It fell backward, its terrified neighs and whinnies mixing with the pitiful cries of the people trapped beneath it. Everyone leaped on the horse, stabbing it and kicking it, trying to get it to move, but the poor beast just lay there, its legs kicking in the air, its white, panicked eyes looking straight at me. It reminded me of my own helplessness and I could not turn away.

Then it was pushed aside and the poor souls who had been crushed were carried off, some to the hospital, others to the graveyard. Tommaso went to the Palazzo Fizzi to see who had won, but I stared at the horse, watching the life drain out of its eyes. While it was still warm, it was cut into pieces and the pieces placed on spits for the poor. Within minutes it had gone from being a hero to a villain and now in death it was a hero again. Would that happen to me?

The next night—that is, the last one before Lent—Cecchi gave me one of Federico's old green robes. "He wants you to wear this."

"I will look like a fool."

"How do you think he will look in your clothes?"

Miranda climbed into the robe with me, but there was still room enough for another person. She stood in front of me and insisted on combing my hair forward like Federico's. She had dressed as a princess and Bianca had given her silver earrings to go with the fur jacket. Tears of pride flooded my eyes. I wanted the world to see her, yet I feared she was slipping away from me.

"Walk like this," Miranda said, pushing her chest out. She strode around the room like a bull with an ache in its *culo*. Although she weighed a quarter of Federico and barely came up to his stomach, she had caught the very essence of him.

"Do it again," I laughed.

Smiling and then frowning like Federico, she walked around the room, stopped in front of me, opened her mouth so that her bottom lip sat on her chin and, pretending to pull out a *fallo* said, "Ugo, taste this."

The laughter stilled in my mouth. "What did you say?"

Her face flushed.

"Where did you hear that?"

"From the boys," she whispered.

"Which boys? The kitchen boys?"

"The kitchen boys. The stable boys. All the boys. They all say it."

Fearing that I would become enraged, she hurried from the room. However, it was not rage that overcame me, but humiliation. Is this how people joked among themselves when I passed by? Would there never be any end to the shame I had to endure to stay alive?

When Miranda returned a short while later I was still sitting on the bed. She knelt at my feet and leaned her head against my knees. We sat like that until the darkness pulled a blanket over our shame.

The sun was barely awake and yet the servants' hall was alive with the colors of a thousand costumes. Grooms, chamberlains, seamstresses, ostlers, secretaries, even scribes had dressed up; stable boys as young girls, washerwomen like soldiers—the old, half-blind washerwoman had a mustache and kept pretending to scratch her balls. No one could remember the last time Federico had come into their hall. Christ! No one could remember the last time *any* duke had come into their hall.

No sooner did I enter than I tripped over the back of the robe and fell down. This caused much laughter, but so many hands helped me up and pushed me forward that, encouraged by their good spirits, I lost my fear and swaggered up to the grand table at which Piero, Bernardo, Bianca, and several others were already seated. Bianca was dressed like an Oriental slave girl, her bountiful breasts tumbling out of her bodice.

"He is coming," Cecchi said. "Remember, just do what he says."

A moment later Ercole the dwarf snuck in, grinning from ear to ear, followed by Federico. Federico was wearing a white shirt and a pair of red hose, though they must have sewn three pairs together just to cover his *culo*. Usually, he pounded his feet into the ground as if he was trying to leave his mark upon the earth, but today he moved his feet in little quick steps as if he was gliding on a set of wheels. As I did. Everyone applauded. Federico beamed. Bianca whispered, "Sit in his chair."

I had not expected that, but since Bianca nodded so eagerly I did as she suggested. Federico had sat in that chair for so long it was shaped to his body and I could only sit as Federico did, slouching to one side. Again everyone laughed. The laughter was as intoxicating as wine and gave me great confidence.

"Well," said Federico, who was now standing behind my chair. "Ask for the food!"

Perhaps it was the way I was sitting, perhaps it was the robe, certainly the laughter, but when he said that, I lifted the left cheek of my *culo*, and farted and belched just like he did. I said loudly, "Get that bean eater in here with my breakfast."

Cecchi tugged frantically at his beard, Piero clapped a hand over his mouth, Bianca and the servants shrieked. But the loudest laugh of all came from behind me.

"Bean eater!" Federico spluttered. "Bean eater! Luigi *is* a bean eater." He waddled in front of me. "Say it again."

I lay back in the seat, farted, belched, licked my lips, and said, "Tell that bean eater to bring me my breakfast. Now!" And turning to Federico, I said, "Get back to your place."

As soon as I said that, I thought—*Sono fottuto!* I am ruined! But God strike me dead, if Federico did not waddle back to his position! The hall could not stop laughing. And Federico did not mind at all! He thought they were laughing at his impression of me.

The trumpets blared, the doors opened, and Luigi entered carrying trays of breakfast foods. He laid down a silver platter with fresh apples, a bowl of polenta with raisins, and some grilled eggs sprinkled with sugar and cinnamon. Everyone waited to see what I would do. But I did not do anything. *Jesus in sancto!* How could I? This was the finest meal that had ever been placed in front of me! I just wanted to sit there and look at it. I wanted to take the platter back to my room and chew each piece slowly.

"Are you not going to make me taste it?" Federico hissed.

"Of course," I muttered. I looked over the hall. Miranda sat on a bench in the front, Tommaso behind her, dressed like a knight. The kitchen boys were sitting on one another's shoulders. I said loudly, "Where is my taster?"

"Here I am, My Lord," said Federico, stepping forward.

I could not believe my ears. Federico had called me "My Lord!" I waved my hand. "The apple first."

Federico nodded. He picked up an apple, rolled it in his hands and sniffed at it. The hall was silent. No one could have been more surprised had Federico grown wings and flown out of the window.

He lifted up one finger as if to see which way the wind was blowing. This was something I never did.

"Quite brilliant," said Piero.

"Yes," said Bernardo, "The duke is so amusing."

"Well?" I said to Federico.

He took a small bite. Screwing up his nose, he put his hands on his hips and looked thoughtfully at the ceiling. Now I understood why Ercole was grinning. He had coached Federico. At first people giggled, but Federico did it for too long and the laughter died away. I had to be careful. If it did not go well for Federico he might blame me so I said, "I do not feel like the apple after all."

"The polenta," Bianca whispered to me. She too sensed it was best to forget the apples.

"I want the polenta," I said, pushing the bowl toward Federico.

Federico pulled out a wishbone. He broke it in two and held it up to the light. This brought great laughter once again, for of course everyone knew the story of my bone. He dipped it into the bowl, pulled it out and made a great fuss over it.

"Just eat it," a voice shouted.

"Yes, eat it," came more voices. "Eat it."

"Well," I demanded, "What are you waiting for?"

Federico dipped a spoon into the polenta and slowly raised it up to his lips. Then he looked out over the crowd. They were staring at him. Slowly he put the spoon down and turned to me. "You eat it," he said.

"Me?" I dropped my lower lip onto my chin. People started to laugh, but then stopped.

Federico's eyes turned into little black dots. *Oi me!* He thought the polenta was poisoned! Now I remembered what had nagged me. It all fit like a key in a lock! Bianca had suggested switching places and Alessandro had suggested that Federico change places with me. Miranda had seen them together in Bianca's apartment and they were both from Venezia. Body of Christ! How could I have been so stupid!

"Go on," Federico said, tearing off the shift. "Taste it!"

"Of course," I answered. A thousand thoughts crowded my mind. If I said the polenta was poisoned, Federico would want to know why I had not spoken earlier. He would think I was part of the plot and force me to eat it. I raised the yellow steaming mush dotted with raisins to my lips when, just as the polenta touched my tongue, I cried out, "There are seven raisins, Luigi! How many times do I have to tell you! Not seven!" And picking up the bowl, I hurled it into the fire, smashing it into a hundred pieces. The flames leaped and hissed like a sleeping cat that had been trodden on.

No one laughed. No one made a sound. Federico's eyes narrowed and guards appeared from nowhere. They grasped my neck and shoulders and slammed my face on the table. Federico picked my head up in one hand, the knife in the other. My life came to a halt. I saw Ercole, his squat little body standing on one of the benches. I do not know if it was my mind playing tricks but there seemed to be a glow about him. At that moment I knew God was everywhere. Not just in what was beautiful and good, but also in what was ugly and crippled. For this had all come about because I had laughed at Ercole all those months ago when Federico had thrown the trencher at him, and since Ercole could never have foreseen something like this, it had to be God's hand.

At the same time as I was begging God's forgiveness I caught sight of Bianca's eyes. Her face turned white. I knew I was right. "My Lord—" I gasped.

"Oh, Federico!" Bianca squealed. "He did it just like you! Just like you!" She put her hand on Federico's arm, the one that held the dagger, and said, "Do not upset yourself, my pet. He is just a *cantadino!*" To Luigi she said, "Bring Duke Federico's garments and another bowl of polenta with lots of raisins. We will be eating in his room."

The hall applauded. Federico let go of my neck and I quietly slipped out of his reach. *Potta!* I thought, as they left the hall, she is a master.

After Federico and Bianca left, everyone crowded around telling me how lucky I was that Bianca had saved my life. Even Miranda said so. They kept on and on till I fled and walked up the hill to Agnese's resting place to be alone. It was not till that afternoon that I was able to return to the hall and search for the remains of the polenta which I had thrown in the fire.

Alas, it had vanished and all traces of the broken bowl had disappeared. I asked each of the boys if they had swept it away, but they denied it, thinking it might lead to trouble. When I said I would give ten ducats to whomever it was, they all claimed to have done it.

That evening, a boy a year or two younger than Miranda complained of a terrible bellyache. I hurried to his bedside. He was sweating and in such pain that his voice had become hoarse from screaming.

"He is pretending," Luigi said. "They all do it to get out of work."

The boy was holding his stomach. His eyes were sunken and peered fearfully out of their sockets. "Death waits for me by the door," he whispered. "Tell him to go away."

I gave him olive oil to drink, but it was too late. The poison was in his blood and the vomiting took away what little strength he had left. "Did you throw away the pieces of the bowl?" I asked.

He nodded.

"And the porridge? Did you taste it?"

He was about to answer when a wave of pain surged through him, shooting its claws into every part of his body, erasing his memory forever.

I waited for Bianca inside the doorway to the Duomo and as she entered I thanked her for turning Federico's anger away from me.

"Do not thank me. Thank God for your good fortune."

"As you are going to thank Him for yours?"

"I always do," she smiled.

Strangely, I no longer feared her or Alessandro. Soon after, Alessandro left for Germany where he was killed in a brawl. I could not blame Federico for his actions for he was right although he did not know it. Nor could I tell him without endangering myself or Bianca. As for me, it was neither the conspiracy nor my own cleverness that lingered in my memory, but the terrible face of the dying boy that appeared every time I closed my eyes.

After Carnevale, Bianca no longer entertained Miranda, saying that she had taught her everything she knew. Now, when Miranda practiced her lyre, I had to pretend to be a duke and clap and shout, "Brava!" when she finished.

She practiced the way Alessandro had taught her to walk and to dance. She practiced the art of kissing on her doll, Felicita. She wrote poems in writing as neat as Cecchi's.

"You try," she said, placing the quill in my hand. It is the same quill I am using now.

"But these are farmer's hands."

"So were mine."

I did it to please her and, by the end of the week, I could write the letters A and B as well as any scribe. Then I learned the other letters and as soon as I could I wrote my name. I had heard it so often, I wanted to see what it looked like and when I started writing it I could not stop.

"That is good, Babbo," Miranda said. "Now you will be a scribe as well as a taster."

If she had said that to me earlier the words might have stung, but not anymore. I had almost lost my life twice as a taster and as Miranda was becoming more beautiful every day, she deserved to have a real suitor and a dowry. Sometimes when I looked at her, thoughts came to me that I had to banish from my mind. Tommaso shared them, too.

Not long after, we were pissing when we saw Miranda walking in the courtyard below us, her pigtail bobbing gently on her behind. "In two years she will be fourteen and . . ." Tommaso grinned, and waved his *fallo* in the air.

"Perhaps," I said.

"What do you mean?"

"What I said."

"Those who break their word get their heads broken."

"Then watch your head. I was almost poisoned."

Someone was shouting to us from the courtyard. "Poisoned!" Tommaso exclaimed. "No one was trying to poison anyone. That was Federico! You know how he is."

"And what about the kitchen boy? You were supposed to be my eyes and ears in the kitchen."

"I was, and anyone who says I was not is a liar."

"*You* are the liar," I said calmly. "Because you were not there. You were in your room putting on your costume. Luigi said everyone was wearing costumes so anyone could have slipped poison in the porridge."

There was more shouting now. In the town below us people were running to and fro. One of the kitchen boys was running toward us.

"You just want to break our agreement," Tommaso said, pulling out his knife.

I pulled my knife out. "You already broke it. I am tired of your lying and boasting."

The boy ran up to us, panting. "The plague. The plague is coming."

xviii

The plague had already visited Genoa, Milano, Parma, and Bologna. The week before, the first cases had been discovered in Arezzo. The gates of Corsoli were closed, but what is a gate to the plague? A few days after my argument with Tommaso, a merchant sent his servant to the hospital with swellings in his groin and armpits. He died the next day. Three more people had died by the end of the week. At first, each death was given a burial, but then the gravedigger died and there was no one to do the burying so the corpses piled up in the streets. There was no wind to chase away the smell of death and it rose slowly until it reached the palace. Two kitchen boys fell ill. Giulio, Federico's youngest son, died, but his other, Raffaello, did not. Bernardo's wife perished. He did not shed a tear for her. Piero did what he could, running from one family to another, but after his eldest child died, he was so overcome with grief he could not go on.

Giulia, Miranda's friend and Cecchi's youngest daughter, died. Miranda wept, but the sight of Giulia's mother running through the halls screaming terrified her even more. A tall, thin woman, who until then hardly spoke to anyone, now could not stop talking to her dead daughter. Her hair turned white overnight and she shrieked when anyone, even Cecchi, came near her. She died a week later.

We were helpless. This was not an enemy we could fight or even see to run away from. Besides, where was there to go? Corsoli was the highest point in the valley.

"I am afraid," Miranda whispered, as she pulled the covers over her. She awoke in the night, tearing her clothes off, looking for boils. Fear overtook her modesty. She made me look under her arms, on her back, and on her buttocks. She imagined she saw marks and spots between her thighs and I had to comb away the soft hair and show her there was nothing there. Then she hunched into a ball and wept. I promised her she did not have to worry, but in truth I was as scared as she and when she slept I pulled down my hose and examined myself as closely as I had inspected her.

If a boil appeared on anyone in the city, they were driven out of doors, left to fend for themselves, and often starved to death. Houses which had been visited by the plague were boarded up and the tenants forced to stay inside, even those who were not sick. The markets were canceled, and so was the feast of San Giovanni. The archbishop and a few boys waved a burning torch over the fields to bless them, but they were afraid to carry the saint's head through the streets as was the custom. The same boys believed the cats and dogs were to blame so they hunted them down and burned them. Husbands deserted their wives, and wives their children. The screams of abandoned babies rose into the night air and hovered about the palace to remind us of their suffering.

In the third week, two boys in Miranda's class died. The archbishop said our wickedness was to blame and that we could only purge ourselves by fasting. Then he issued a proclamation forbidding blasphemy, games, sodomy, and prostitution. All the things that Federico liked best. Federico said nothing because he, too, was afraid. One night when the moon hovered above us, all of Corsoli's children paraded through the streets carrying pictures of the Holy Mother and San Sebastian. Even little ones who were too small and too sick to walk begged to join in. Some died even as they marched. Every day we flocked to the Duomo crying, *"Misericordia, misericordia!"* and begged God's forgiveness.

Women flogged themselves till the blood ran down their backs. It made no difference. The dying went on. The stench of death lodged in my nose even as the screams of the living rang in my ears.

Two weeks after his first sermon, the archbishop died. Now the fear of the plague was as bad as the plague itself. A servant whose master swore he was perfectly well was so afraid that he threw himself down a well. Miranda sat in the corner of our room wringing her hands. Her fingernails had been bitten to the quick and she had scratched the skin off her thighs and the underside of her arms. I feared she would lose her mind; and even though my mother had died of the plague in the country, I believed Miranda would be safer there.

"You can stay with my father. You are his grandchild. He will look after you."

"You are not coming with me?"

"No, Federico will not allow it." Cecchi had told me Federico asked every day if I was still well and would not eat otherwise. A surge of pride had rushed through me. Duke Federico Basillione DiVincelli *needed* me. He could not eat without me. He could not *live* without me!

"But I am your daughter," Miranda cried.

I asked a few courtiers, but they had their own lives to attend to and I knew their answers before the question left my mouth. It pained me more than having nails driven into my eyes, but I had to ask Tommaso.

Tommaso was making a cherry torte. Although he had not been in the kitchen very long, his hands already bore the nicks and burns of his new profession. His fingers were not thin and well formed like Miranda's, but they were quite skillful and it was a pleasure to witness them darting over the pots and pans like a bird weaving its nest.

He blended a bowl of ground-up cherries with crushed rose petals, added some finely grated cheese, a dash of pepper, a little ginger, some sugar, four beaten eggs and mixed them all together. Then he carefully poured the mixture into a crust and placed the pan over a small flame. I remembered that when he had made the snow wolf he said he wanted to be a sculptor and I said aloud, "You already are."

"Are what?" He whirled about. His cheeks were thinner and his eyes pained and sad.

"A sculptor. You said you wanted to be a sculptor. Now you are. Except you use food instead of marble."

He turned away to attend to the pan. "What do you want? I am busy."

"Miranda is not well." He looked up sharply. "She does not have the plague," I added quickly, "but she will go mad if she stays here. I want to send her to my father's house in Fonte."

"Why are you telling me?"

"She cannot go by herself and Federico will not let me go with her." I took a breath. "I want you to take her. I do not trust anyone else. I know we have had our differences, but I beg you to put them aside—if not for my sake, then for Miranda's. If you love her, you will do this."

He snorted. He snorted often now, thinking perhaps it made him more manly. A rat scurried past and he threw a pot at it which hit it on the head, stunning it.

"This means our agreement is on again?" He beat the rat to death and threw it into the courtyard.

"Yes."

"I want it in writing."

"You will have it so."

"Before we leave."

"Before you leave." He took off his apron. "Will you get into trouble with Federico?" I asked.

"Federico? Why?"

"Because you are his spy. I saw you in the doorway after the killings of Pia and Emilia."

"I do not do that anymore. Now I have this," he said, indicating the kitchen.

Septivus wrote the agreement, signed Tommaso's name for him, and then I signed mine. I packed a small bundle of Miranda's clothing, Tommaso brought some food, and we met by the stable at dawn.

"Tommaso will take care of you," I told Miranda as she mounted the horse I had bribed from the stable boys.

"With my life," Tommaso said, and swung himself up behind her. He unbound his sword and took the reins.

For a moment I felt jealous that I was not going. To be away from Corsoli, away from the plague. "Godspeed," I said. Miranda did not look at me. Tommaso jerked the reins and the horse moved toward the entranceway. I ran alongside, clutching at Miranda's foot. "May the Lord bless you and keep you. May He make His face to shine upon you and be gracious unto you. May the Lord lift up His countenance upon you and grant you peace."

She still did not look at me. "Miranda," I cried, "say something to me. We may never see one another again."

She looked down at me. "Take good care of Federico," she spat. Then she dug her heels in and the horse trotted through the entranceway to the palazzo, down the Weeping Steps, and disappeared into Corsoli.

I watched them ride through the streets, past the bodies of men and women, the piles of babies and children, until they reached the gate and passed through it. It came to me that my brother Vittore might be at my father's house and my heart froze. I wanted to ride after them and bring them back, but then I heard wailing from inside the palazzo and I was glad they had left.

That night I dreamed Tommaso had raped Miranda and I rose from my bed, shouting, "I will kill you," so loudly someone knocked on my door but did not come in for fear I had been stricken.

Cecchi said that a merchant in Firenze had told him that the scent of herbs such as fennel, mint, and basil, and spices like cardamom, cinnamon, saffron, cloves, aniseed, and nutmeg, prevented the evil odors from affecting the brain. The next day Emilia's garden was picked clean. Christ! The whole hillside behind the palace was picked clean. The spices in the kitchen were stolen. None of it helped. Potero, Federico's cup bearer, covered himself in spices and died the same day.

Spring slid into summer and the heat increased daily. Dogs and servants fought one another for shade. Federico and Bianca seldom left their chambers and I had to taste Federico's food while he watched me from the doorway. "You are still well?" he would say to me.

"Yes, My Lord. I am well."

He grunted, "Me and the food taster."

Another time when he opened the door, I could see all the way into his bedroom. Bianca was kneeling naked on the bed, her head bowed down, her *culo* in the air. She was wearing a mask and sobbing softly. Federico did not care if I saw or not. He just wanted to know if I had caught the plague.

One day Septivus wore a bag around his neck which contained snake venom. He had read in the *Decameron* that such bags had been worn to ward off the plague in earlier times so he had gone into the woods and killed a snake. He offered to sell other bags with snake venom. Those who were old or sick bought them, but everyone else went into the woods to hunt for snakes for themselves. Several people were bitten, including Raffaello, Federico's oldest son, and one man died in a fight with another over a snake that had no venom. Then Septivus was accused of putting ordinary ointment into the bags to make money.

Servants left the palace under cover of night for the countryside, but within days they returned, saying that wherever they had gone they had seen suffering and that it was the end of the world. I pleaded with God to forgive my sins and if He could not, not to avenge Himself by taking Miranda. I do not know why I bothered. God did not care who prayed and who did not! Most of the dead were children who had not lived long enough to harm a fly and did not know what a sin was. How can a merciful God snatch children from their mothers' arms?

One evening, Federico called some of us into the main hall. We were ragged and weary with fear, afraid of our shadows, afraid of ourselves. Federico said, "I never won a battle by being afraid. We have cowered too long and if I am going to die it will be on my feet."

He ordered food and drink and called whores from the city. He told the stable boys to paint their faces, Ercole to clown, and the musicians to bang drums and blow trumpets as loud as they liked. We cheered him as if he had delivered us. We ate and drank till we were sick, then ate and drank some more. Septivus leaped onto the table and recited obscene verses of Aretino. Federico told crude jokes and Bianca did a wild dance she had learned from a Turk. The Carnevale masks were brought out. I wore a bull's head. When Bernardo crept away with a whore, we threw open the door and cheered them on.

As the night came upon us, we pushed the food onto the floor and screwed on the tables. Soon we were all so drunk that men copulated with men, women with women, all of us grunting like wild beasts. Two boys were on their knees in front of Federico. I was crazed with drink and desire. I grabbed a woman with large breasts and a hawk's mask and pulled her into an empty room.

"Ugo," Bianca laughed.

Even though Federico was in the next room, I did not care. Bianca threw herself across the bed on her back and spread her legs. "Taste me," she yelled, and when I hesitated, she laughed, "I am not poisonous."

I was right, she *had* tried to kill Federico. But I liked her spirit. "I always wanted to fuck you," she said.

She had big lips the color of ripe cherries. She kissed my face, pulled my shirt off, and licked my body. I ripped open her bodice, and buried my face in her big breasts. One hour passed into another, one day into the next. Corpses rotted in the hallways while our love-making grew fiercer and fiercer as if it would help us outlast Death. The whores brought wooden *falli* and showed us how nuns enter-tained themselves. I wanted to sodomize Bianca, but she pleaded, "No, Federico makes me do it. I do not like it."

There were cries from the main hall. I ran in as the painted boys stumbled out weeping. The tables had been overturned and dogs were gobbling up the food. A boy lay bleeding on the ground, a sword stuck in his belly. Federico sat on the floor covered in sweat. His clothes were torn and in disarray, revealing his huge white belly. "Piss," he said, through parched, cracked lips. "We must drink piss. That will save us."

The few of us who were there looked at one another and laughed. Federico crawled across the table, overturned a bowl of food, took out his great fat snake, and pissed a dark yellow stream into it. He turned to me. "Taste it."

"But you just pissed it," I laughed. "How can anything be wrong?"

"You are my taster. Taste it."

"Duke Federico, why do you not taste Bianca's piss and then she can taste yours?"

Federico pulled the sword out of the dead boy. It dripped with blood and guts. "Are you forgetting who I am?" he said.

I *had* forgotten. In the madness which had seized us I no longer thought of him as our prince, but as just another man driven mad with fear. I picked up the bowl and looked at the dark yellow liquid. The odor was sharp and stung my nostrils. I said to myself—I need only drink a little and since I have trained myself not to taste anything, what harm can there be? I raised the bowl to my mouth, but my lips would not open.

What lies we tell ourselves! For over two years I had believed that although I could tell the ingredients of a meal, the taste meant nothing to me. But if that was true then why could I not drink this? Federico's sword pushed against my ribs. Big, fat bitter drops of Federico's urine sat on my lips. I wanted to swallow them quickly, but once inside my mouth they ran everywhere like a naughty child, between my teeth, up the sides of my mouth, under my gums, over my tongue. I was going to be sick, but then the point of Federico's sword broke my skin and blood trickled down my stomach. My throat had closed up. I could feel the piss burning on the back of my tongue, waiting to plunge into my stomach.

"Look at his face," Federico laughed. "Swallow it!"

Potta! The bastard! He knew his piss was not poisoned. I thought—if I am to die, then I will spit it in his face. I gathered the liquid in my mouth, when a scream froze me. A door swung open so hard it smashed against the wall and bounced back again. Bianca stood in the doorway. She was not wearing her mask. She was not wearing anything.

I thought she was going to tell Federico we had made love. I wanted to run, but something about her stopped me. It was not her full, heavy breasts with their huge pink nipples which I could still feel in my mouth. Nor was it her soft round belly, or her fleshy thighs, or dainty feet. Nor was it her eyes which were wide with fear, nor her mouth forever shaped by the agonizing scream which had been torn from it. Nor her hair which fell around her head like the pictures I had seen of Medusa.

It was the mole on her forehead. It looked like a large round plum, and far from being ugly, it was so big and beautiful, like everything else about her, that it was a shame she had hidden it for so long.

"Look!" she screamed. Her right hand was pointing to her groin and there, protruding from her blonde hair, was a huge black boil. She lifted one arm and then the other and in her armpits were two more boils as large as eggs. I swear had I not seen this I would not be writing it down, but as we looked more boils appeared on her body in front of our very eyes! First on her stomach. Now on her thighs, her ankle, her belly. An evil spirit had laid its eggs inside of her and its young were hatching all at once. More boils appeared. We backed away in horror. She opened her mouth and shouted in a strangled voice, as if something in her throat was growing there, "Help me!"

Federico stepped toward her—I thought to take her in his arms and comfort her. Instead, he stabbed her through the heart with his sword, the thrust pushing her back into the room and onto the floor. Then he closed the door, leaned on it and wept.

We tiptoed out of the hall and fled as far away as we could. I never saw Bianca again. Nor did I want to. I was terrified that because I had lain with her, I, too, had caught the plague. It was not till much, much later that I realized I had swallowed Federico's piss.

The deaths in the city slowed and when I had not fallen ill after two months I stopped worrying that I would die. The plague had spent itself out. Federico, Piero, Bernardo and his infernal fennel seeds, Cecchi, and Federico's son, Raffaello, were also spared although Raffaello was affected in the head and had to be looked after day and night from then on. Nearly a quarter of all those living in Corsoli died and many more in the palace. I feared I would never see Miranda again and I was planning to ride to my father's house when Tommaso entered the courtyard leading a lame horse on which Miranda was sitting.

I ran to her, but Tommaso, who had an angry wound across his right cheek, would not let me near until he had gently lifted her down. I covered her face with kisses and told her how much I missed her. Then I embraced Tommaso like a long-lost son and thanked him for returning Miranda safely to me. He listened, never taking his eyes from Miranda and, from his tender expression, I guessed that much had happened between them. I led Miranda to our room where I arranged water for her to bathe and oils and scents with which to freshen herself.

"Do you have a screen?" she asked.

"A screen? Why?" We did not have one and had never needed one even when she had her monthly courses. Bernardo saw his daughter naked and she was seventeen.

"I want a screen," she repeated.

I borrowed one from Cecchi, and while Miranda bathed I sat on the other side and told her of the sorrows that had overtaken the palace in her absence. She listened quietly, only interrupting once to ask about her friends. I told her that several of them had died, Bianca, too, although I did not say how. Miranda sobbed softly. I wanted to comfort her, but because of the screen I stayed where I was. The anguish of her weeping made me weep, too. Death had become so common I was sure my tears had dried up, but now we sat on either side of the screen mourning for all we had seen and for those we had lost.

Eventually, Miranda emerged, her dark brown hair resting gently on her shoulders. Her eyes seemed older, her lips fuller, her body more formed. In short, if she was not yet a woman, she was no longer a girl. I asked her if she had seen my father. She shook her head, showering droplets of water onto her shoulders like golden sunbeams. "He left with his neighbors." She screwed her face up with disgust. "We could not stay in his house. It was disgusting."

"Did you stay with the abbot Tottorini?"

She snorted, the same way Tommaso did. "With that fat pig? If all priests are like him, then God is in trouble!"

"God is good despite man, not because of him."

She stared at herself in her little mirror, examining her hair, her eyes, her mouth, first from one side and then the other. "All we wanted was some bread and cheese, but when we said we were from Corsoli he shut the door in our faces."

"The bastard!" I cried.

Miranda began to brush her hair. "So we kept on riding."

"To Gubbio?"

She shrugged. "I suppose. We just rode." She looked down at her feet. There was a scar across the top of her left foot. "A piece of burning wood fell on it," she said. "The plague was everywhere, Babbo. Men and women were lying in the fields, on the paths, in their houses. I saw a man and woman who had hanged themselves and their baby next to them. The birds had plucked their eyes out." She stopped brushing her hair as if the memory had suddenly appeared in front of her. "I did not know so many people could be dead at the same time." Her lips trembled and her body began to shake.

"What is it?"

"And then . . . then . . ."

I knelt beside her, grasping her hands.

"Two men . . ." she dissolved in tears. I stroked her hair and held her close. At last she sobbed, "Two men . . . raped me."

My heart tore in two. "Oh, my Miranda. My angel. My angel." I rocked her backward and forward. "Where was Tommaso?"

"They nearly killed him! If it were not for him I would be dead!" Again tears overcame her.

I did not question her any further. My ears, which hungered for the details, were at the same time reluctant to hear them. At last, Miranda continued. "Tommaso told them he was escorting me to die in my father's house."

"Where was this? In the valley?"

She furrowed her brow.

"At the bottom of the valley or on the way to Gubbio?"

She screwed her face up impatiently, "On the path going away from the house. What does it matter?"

I promised I would not interrupt her again.

"Tommaso said I had the plague and that he was escorting me to die in my father's house," she repeated. "They did not believe him. They wanted to see my boils. I told them that even in the time of a plague a lady must be respected. They said the plague did not care who was a lady and who was not and neither did they and if I did not show them the boils they would look for themselves."

"One attacked Tommaso, and the other—" She broke down, pressing her face into my chest. "Tommaso killed the first one and drove off my attacker, but not before . . ." The rest was lost in weeping.

I did not say anything. What was there to say? I had sent her away. "*Mi dispiace, mi dispiace*," I whispered.

I was blind with rage. I wanted to hunt down the criminals, scoop out their eyes, cut off their *falli*, and burn them at the stake. I dreaded what else I might hear, but I needed to put my mind at ease. "Are you . . . with child?"

"I do not know," she whispered.

"My angel, my Miranda. I will take care of you." I waited a moment longer and then I said, "What happened after that?"

"We found a hut. Just like the one we used to live in. Remember?" Her face brightened briefly. "Tommaso could not do anything because of his wounds. I was afraid he might die so I bathed them in urine."

I tried not to imagine what this had looked like. "What did you eat?"

"There was plenty of fruit—apples, peaches, and pomegranates— because no one had picked them. I swear I never want to see another pomegranate as long as I live," she laughed. "I made polenta and Tommaso killed a pig."

"He was better already?"

"No, when he got better. He is such a good cook, Babbo. One day he will be the chief chef. He is better than Luigi is even now, I swear it!"

She told me how they had eaten the pig for three days, how Tommaso had cut slices of ham and salted them and had even made a sausage. "He has wonderful hands, Babbo. Have you ever looked at them? They look so small and stubby and he is so tall and thin. But they are strong. He can crush a nut between his fingers!"

"Really!"

"Yes, it is true." Tommaso had also killed a chicken and a squirrel, built a fire, plucked a goose, and repaired part of the hut. It was a wonder he had not made the rains come.

Miranda held out her own hands and studied her long, thin fingers. "My hands are too long."

"You have the hands of an artist."

"But Tommaso's are tender." She rose and went behind the screen to dress.

I could not help myself. I said, "Where did you sleep?"

"In the hut."

"Did you sleep . . . ?" I could not finish.

"Of course not, Babbo! Tommaso said he could not betray your trust." She came out from behind the screen and placed her hand over her heart. "I swear by all that is holy." In that moment I knew as sure as sparks fly upward she was lying.

I stood up. "Where are you going?" she asked, alarm flickering in her eyes.

I did not answer.

She grabbed my arm. "You do not believe me?"

"I believe you."

"Babbo, if you hurt Tommaso, I will kill myself."

"Why would I hurt him?"

Her eyes filled with tears. "I love him, Babbo. I love him."

"I know. Now eat and sleep. And Miranda, do not tell anyone of this rape."

Tommaso was lying on his pallet. The wound on his right cheek made him appear older and, together with his hair, which had grown longer and curlier, he looked like the disciple Peter in a painting in the Duomo Santa Caterina.

"I want to thank you for saving Miranda's life."

"You asked me to take care of her and I did as you asked. It was nothing, *niente*."

"*Niente?*" I smiled. "The Tommaso I used to know would have bragged about it from the rooftops." I did not add "because you have never won a fight in your life." "What started it?"

He shrugged. "We met these men on the path. I told them to let us pass because Miranda had the plague but they wanted to see her boils. I said, no. I said . . . a lady . . . a lady . . ."

"Must be respected."

"Yes, yes. Exactly so. But they said if she did not show them the boils, they would force her! So I attacked them."

"That was very brave."

"But as I was fighting one, the other one ravished Miranda." He carried on as if he was afraid he would forget what he was supposed to say. "I killed the first one and drove the other one off."

"Miranda said you killed the second one."

"No. Maybe . . . no . . . I do not remember." He frowned, turning away. He was such a bad liar. "They cut me," he said. "I am lucky to be alive."

"I see." I had been looking at the wound on his cheek which was not as deep as it first appeared. Indeed, it seemed as if someone had inflicted it carefully so as not to cause too much pain. "Then you found a hut."

"If Miranda told you, why are you asking me?"

"She said that you cooked wonderful meals."

He tossed his hair out of his face and puffed his cheeks out. He was so easy to flatter. "I caught a pig if that is what you mean. I cooked it with some herbs and mushrooms. At night we prayed to God. And we prayed for you, too," he said earnestly.

"Me? Why?"

"Because Miranda missed you. We knew people in Corsoli were dying and that you had to look after Federico. She was worried about you."

"What else did you do?"

"We sang songs. We danced . . ." He stopped, the memory overtaking him. "It was . . . crazy."

"Crazy, why?"

"Why?" He waved his hands about, becoming excited like the old Tommaso. "All around us the world was dying, but we were living in this hut like . . ."

"Like what?"

"Do you not see?" he cried. "We were all alone . . . we could have been the only two people living . . . in the world—"

"Living like what?" I grasped his throat.

"Like man and wife!" His eyes stared into mine. Unafraid. "I cannot lie to you, Ugo. Kill me if you wish. I do not care. I love her. *E mio l'amor divino. L'amor divino*," he repeated.

She loves you too, I said to myself. So much so that she would pretend to be raped in case she got with child. How could I do anything to Tommaso? He had brought my Miranda back safely. I told him he could no longer sleep with her. "Our agreement is for one more year. If you love her you can wait."

Miranda woke each morning with Tommaso's name upon her lips. She whispered his name in her prayers. She wrote little poems to him and declared that they would get married and go to Roma so that Tommaso could cook for the pope. She swore she would be in love with him till the day she died.

Because Tommaso had won her heart, the other boys stopped teasing him. Now he walked around the palace with Miranda on his arm, as proud as a peacock. He worshiped her and brought her combs, ribbons, and other trinkets. He made pastries for her, little delicacies of sugar and fruits in the shapes of birds and flowers. Sometimes they sat for hours on the wall outside the palazzo entwined in one another's arms, caressing one another's faces, stroking each other's hair, saying nothing. She would take his short stubby hands in hers, kiss each nick and burn, press her face against his cheek, and sing to him.

Watching them, I sometimes wondered if there was not some invisible twine linking them together like the one Ariadne gave Theseus, for no sooner did they stray from one another's grasp than their fingers blindly searched for the other until they met again. I often overheard their conversations; most of them I do not recall, but this one I remember for it showed the gentleness of their nature. They were saying good night to one another when Miranda said, "You must sleep on your right side with your left arm extended like this. I will lie on my right side, too, and then I will know you are lying behind me and your arm is across my body and I will sleep well."

I smiled to myself and thought no more of it until I saw them together the next day. From the way they were standing I knew he had done as she asked. They were, in a word, as happy as doves who, having found a mate, remain together for the rest of their lives.

Miranda and Tommaso were not the only ones who embraced life after the plague. I could now read and write and took great pleasure in recording my experiments with plants and herbs. I also amused myself with a servant girl. In Corsoli, men took new wives and women found new husbands. I do not know where they all came from, but a few months later there seemed to be as many people in the city as there had ever been and all the women were with child.

I heard that after surviving the plague, some princes, like the duke of Ferrara, devoted themselves to the church or charitable works. Federico was the opposite. "We survived the worst God could send us," he said, stroking Nero, who now sat in Bianca's chair at the table. "Why should I believe in Him? Ugo does not believe in Him, do you, Ugo?"

Christ on a cross! Arguing and cursing God was something I did when I was alone, but Federico was asking me to denounce God with the new bishop of Santa Caterina sitting right there and everyone staring at me. I stumbled over my answer, afraid to speak and yet pleased that Federico had called upon me for my opinion. Fortunately, Federico did not wait for an answer, but said that from now on he was going to enjoy life even more.

He ate twice as much as he used to, took up with new whores, and increased the number of his hounds to a thousand—the dog shit around the palace was ankle deep. He spent huge sums on new silks, satin robes, rings, and other jewels. Sometimes when he dressed up he looked like an altar at a festival. But though he never mentioned Bianca's name again, her death affected him deeply. As the days grew shorter and the skies filled with melancholy clouds and angry, biting rains, he moped around the palace, Nero by his side.

"I want a wife!" he shouted at us one morning. He ordered Cecchi to write letters to the d'Este's, the Malatesta, the Medici and other courts stating his intentions. When the replies came, if they came at all, they said all the eligible women and girls were spoken for. Federico decided the only way to get a new wife would be to journey to Milano where he had once served Duke Sforza. Everyone in the palazzo was beside themselves with excitement. To leave Corsoli and go to Milano! They begged and lied, pleading with Cecchi for a place in the retinue. I did not have to raise my voice. I knew I would be going with Federico. He could not afford to go anywhere without me.

XX

Going on a journey with Federico was like going to war. Lists were drawn up of who should go and who should stay, then more lists were made of what to take. These lists changed every day, sometimes from hour to hour. Cecchi hardly slept for months and those parts of his beard which were gray turned white and those which were white fell out.

To begin with, there were to be no more than forty of us, but then three boys were required to look after the horses, and the cart master said he needed at least three servants and so did Federico's dressers. The number grew to eighty. The whole palace wanted to leave, but since few monasteries or palaces could house that number, carpenters, laborers, and sewers were added to build tents wherever we stayed. We were now a hundred. When Federico saw how much this would cost, he threatened to castrate Cecchi, burn his body, and then behead him. Cecchi reduced the number to sixty. By now Federico had grown so fat, and his gout so painful, that a special cart had to be built to carry him. It was lined with silken cushions and sheets, and pictures of jousting knights were painted on the sides. Federico tested it twice a day to make sure it was comfortable.

Since Miranda and Tommaso were not going to Milano, they paid little attention to the preparations. Besides, they were too much in love to care. Although Miranda had not been with child, I feared that could happen while I was away and since she often spoke of marrying Tommaso I was tempted to tell her of the pact I had made with him. In truth, I was surprised he had not mentioned it, but I guessed this was because he now loved her and wanted to respect me. This changed my feelings toward him and in this mood I went to the kitchen intending to say that although the four years were not yet up I would be happy to announce their marriage.

Tommaso was placing pieces of spit-roasted thrushes onto slices of toast. He had mixed up some spices, which by smelling the bowl I could tell included fennel, pepper, cinnamon, nutmeg, egg yolks, and vinegar. He poured the mix over the birds, placed the slices of toast in a pan, and put them over the flames. I told him it was fit for a duke and there was no doubt that he would one day be cooking for the pope.

"I could be a chef in Roma or Firenze right now if I wanted to," he boasted. He told me about new recipes he had invented, of special foods and spices from India he wanted to try, even ways of improving the kitchen. Never once did he mention Miranda. The longer I listened, the more uneasy I became. I thought—he has grown tired of Miranda, but does not know it yet. So I said nothing about the marriage contract.

Miranda spoke of him with as much love as ever and wandered about the kitchen wanting to be close to him, but where they had once walked side by side, now Tommaso walked a little ahead. He no longer brought her ribbons or combs and looked away when she spoke to him. He yawned when she sang and once when I was watching from the window, I saw her lead his hand to her breast. Laughing, he pulled away and strode off.

Septivus told me that Miranda had missed her lessons and had been seen weeping in Emilia's garden. I looked for her there and in the stables, but could not find her. I sought out her friends, asking them if they knew the cause of Miranda's distress.

"Tommaso," they answered, as if the whole world knew. "We warned her his word was not to be trusted."

I found Miranda in our room tearing at her hair, beating herself about the breast, and scratching her face like the shrieking harpies in Dante's *Inferno*. "He no longer loves me," she wept.

"No. It cannot be true."

"It is!" she screamed. "He told me. He told me!"

I sliced a mandrake root into tiny pieces, fed her a little, and she fell into a restless sleep. Then I sharpened my knife and went looking for Tommaso.

He was putting on a tight-fitting, green velvet jacket over some deep red silk hose. Rings twinkled on his fingers and the chains around his wrist glinted in the moonlight. I asked him where he was going at this late hour.

"What is it to you?" He pulled on a pair of black boots.

"You have upset my daughter."

"Your daughter." He shook his curls so that they sprayed out across his neck. "Your prisoner. She cannot pee without you watching over her."

"That is because I do not want her to become a whore like the girl you are going to see."

"I am not going to see a whore," he said hotly.

"You told me you loved her."

"I did not tell her of our betrothal so I did not break my promise to her."

"In the Bible, Jacob waited for Rachel for fourteen years."

"That was the Bible." He adjusted the feather in his hat. "This is Corsoli. My name is Tommaso, not Jacob. And tonight I am going to hunt the hare."

"What happened to your love?"

He shrugged as if he had lost a cheap coin. I threw myself at him, grasped his throat, and slammed him into the wall. I pulled my dagger and pressed the point into the crevice by his neck bone.

"I will teach you to taste the peach before you buy it." I drove my knee into his stomach. "You think I will carefully cut your face like Miranda did?" I pierced the skin and could feel his flesh quivering around the point of the knife. Blood spurted over the blade. "Tell me, what happened to your love?"

"I do not know," he begged, "I do not know."

"You do not know?" I pulled the knife across his neck. I wanted him to feel as much pain as Miranda felt.

"Who knows where love goes?" he gasped in bewilderment.

I was about to drive the knife into Tommaso's throat when a voice said, "No, Babbo!" with such power that I stopped.

Miranda was standing behind me, her head lifted high, her face as white as chalk. "He is not worth dying for."

"But he—"

"If you kill him and are hanged, what will happen to me?"

I lowered my knife. Tommaso pointed to Miranda and cried, "If you believe this will put me in your debt, then kill me now."

Miranda replied. "It is I who owe you. For you have closed my heart and opened my eyes." She reached her hand out to me, "Babbo, come. Anger shortens our lives and we have much to be grateful for."

I told her to come to Milano with me. "You will see wonderful palaces. There will be balls and parties and many fine young men."

"I do not want many fine young men."

I asked if there was any way I could be of comfort to her.

She said, "I am comforted by God. It is Tommaso who is restless.

He always has been and always will be. That is his nature. That is why he needs me."

"You still love him? After what he has done to you?"

"Does the shepherd stop loving the lamb who strays? I am his balm, Babbo. Without me he is lost."

Then she lay down on her bed and in a few moments was sleeping the sleep of the dead, while I stared out at the hillside wondering if I would ever be as wise as she.

Federico wanted to leave at the end of Lent, but Nero was sick and we had to wait three days. Then Federico would not leave on the seventh of the month, so it was not until the following Tuesday that the bishop blessed the journey and wished Federico "*buona ventura*" in his desire to find a wife.

As we emerged from the Duomo Santa Caterina into the bright spring morning, the bell rang joyfully and the most beautiful rainbow I had ever seen embraced the heavens, each color so clear and vibrant that we knew God was watching over us.

Twenty knights dressed in full armor climbed upon their horses, their red and white banners waving from their lances. Then came Federico's cart (pulled by eight horses), twenty more knights, carts containing Federico's clothing, and another cart bearing gifts. After that were the falconers, chamberlains, grooms, clerks, kitchen staff, dressers, whores, and more carts containing everything else.

Miranda watched from our window as we gathered in the courtyard. The night before I had urged her to practice her lyre, fulfill her duties cheerfully, and promise to take several drops of a potion for her humors before she went to bed. In truth, it was the juice of apple mixed with the powder of a dead frog and it dulled all feelings of romance. Although Tommaso was no longer in love with her, I feared that because she was a woman she might fall in love with someone else just to show him she no longer cared.

"Women are different than men," I counseled her. "They are weaker in the face of love, yet they are braver in their pursuit of it and I do not want you to get with child."

"Nor do I," she had yawned.

Now she suddenly ran out of the palace and threw herself into my arms. I held her close and whispered I was sorry she was not coming and that I would miss her. She said she was sorry for her rudeness and, putting on a brave smile, said that I had no need to worry on her behalf; she would discharge all of her duties faithfully and with good cheer.

There was a fanfare of trumpets, Federico's carriage stirred, and then we were moving out of the courtyard toward the Weeping Steps like a long colorful snake. All of Corsoli watched us leave. Federico threw a few gold coins to the cheering crowds though I swear the cheering became even louder after we passed through the city gates.

A brisk wind chased the puffy white clouds across the bright blue sky. The green hills were dotted with patches of yellow violas and blue lupines. Everywhere the sound of running water accompanied us, dripping from trees, spilling over rocks and rushing in little streams underfoot to the bottom of the valley. I felt the same as I did when I first left home: this journey would change my life!

Halfway down the valley, Federico's cart bounced over a boulder, the back left wheel snapped off, and the cart crashed to the ground. Federico emerged like a mad bull, tangled up in sheets and blankets, red in the face. "Who built this piece of shit?" he screamed.

Cecchi said they were Frenchmen who had been hired for the task, but who had since left Corsoli.

"Then we declare war on France," Federico shouted.

"Is that before or after the cart is fixed?" I muttered. A chamberlain next to me laughed. Federico ordered him killed. Instead, he was taken back to the palace and thrown into the dungeon. Cecchi said he knew some Italian workmen who could fix the cart and while Federico was carried back to the palace, Cecchi sent for the men who had built it—they were from Corsoli—and warned them if they did not repair the cart correctly they would be hanged. Two days later the procession started again. This time no one watched us leave.

The second day Federico complained that the path was too bumpy and any rock or stone larger than a ducat had to be removed before we could continue. Every servant, soldier, and minister—even Cecchi—had to get down on their hands and knees and clear them all away. By the end of the morning the road was so smooth you could have rolled an egg on it. Cecchi said at this rate it would take five years to get to Milano. Federico cursed and ordered all the geese from the nearby farms killed, and their feathers stuffed into his cushions. From then on many farmers drove their livestock into hiding when they heard we were coming. The abbeys were not so lucky.

At the bottom of the valley, we stopped at the abbey of Abbot Tottorini, the same one who had turned Miranda and Tommaso away during the plague. I remembered that he made his own wine and cheese and thought it only right to tell Federico how wonderful they were. Federico agreed with me. Indeed, he liked them so much we stayed for a whole week.

On the fifth day, I rode to my father's farm. Although my last visit had been a bitter one, I hoped that time had softened his heart toward me. I wanted him to see what I had made of myself. His house looked as if the slightest wind would blow it down. I looked about but could not see him, so I called out his name.

"In here," he cried out.

I no longer remembered if the house had always stunk like that or if it was because I was now used to the perfumes of the palace, but I could not enter and stood in the doorway. At last, my father's shrunken frame limped out of the darkness. He was bent over almost double now and he smelled of decay and death. He squinted at my new leather jerkin and brightly colored hose, but although I said my name I was not sure if he knew who I was. I put my arms around him and offered him a few coins. He could not open his hands properly so I pushed the coins into the spaces between his fingers. I told him I was accompanying Duke Federico to Milano and asked if he wanted to see the procession.

"What for?" he croaked.

"The knights, the duke's carriage. They are magnificent."

"Magnificent? Spain! Spain is magnificent."

"Spain? What do you know about Spain? You have never been out of the valley!"

"Vittore tells me," he said. "Spain is magnificent."

"Oh, so Vittore has fled to Spain."

"He is commanding a ship!"

"Yes, and I am the king of France."

He waved a finger at me. "Jealous," he shouted. "You are jealous. Jealous!"

"And you are a fool!" I said, climbing on my horse. "And I was a fool to come here."

He tried to throw the coins at me, but his hands could not let go of them.

The abbot Tottorini was waiting for me when I returned, his fat face sagging around his jowls. He hissed that all his wine had been drunk, and his cheese and fruit eaten. He said he prayed that all my children grew tails, my blood would boil, and that I caught the French disease. I told him he should wait until we had left before he insulted me or I would tell Federico about some of the tricks he liked to perform with the nuns. Then I made sure that whatever wine and cheese we had not drunk or eaten, we took with us.

I almost forgot! Just before we reached the abbey, we passed a peasant standing in his field. His skinny body was lost inside his shift and his naked legs protruded into the stony soil like sticks of wood which had been left out in the sun. When some of the soldiers laughed at him, the peasant ran alongside Federico's carriage, screaming that he had lost his children in the famine while Federico ate like a pig. He ran between the horses and before anyone could stop him, leaped onto Federico's cart just as Federico stuck his head out to discover the cause of the yelling.

Oi me! I do not know who was more surprised, the peasant or Federico. Before the peasant could harm Federico, the knights slashed him to pieces with their swords and he fell onto the ground where the knights continued to lance and slice him long after his soul had left the earth.

Federico was eager to reach Firenze and stay with Bento Verana, a wealthy wool merchant who traded with Corsoli. Most of the servants remained on Verana's estate in the country, but a few of us stayed in his palazzo overlooking the Arno. Verana was a thin-faced, stern-looking man who dressed as a priest and regarded his wealth as something to be hoarded and not enjoyed. But because he treated everyone with dignity and was said to be honest in his business dealings, he had no need of a food taster. He said at our first meal that since he considered Federico a friend he would be offended if Federico used a food taster in his house.

Federico licked his lips, not knowing what to say. I said, "My Lord, it is not that Duke Federico fears being poisoned. He has a tender digestion and as mine is the same as his, by tasting his food I am able to spare him any discomfort before it arises."

Federico nodded and said that was exactly so. Unfortunately, I could not soothe the other discomforts so easily. The Firenzani ate differently than we in Corsoli did. They liked more vegetables— pumpkins, leeks, broad beans—and less meat. They ate spinach with anchovies, baked fruit into their ravioli, and made desserts in the shapes of emblems. They used less seasoning and considered the uses of spices a gaudy display of wealth, employed squares of cloth called napkins to wipe their mouths, ate from gold plates instead of trenchers, and covered their mouths when they belched.

"There are so many things to remember," Federico complained at dinner. "I cannot enjoy the food!"

"But conversation is the real food, is it not?" Verana answered. "Too much food leads to gluttony, and gluttony slows the brain just as too much drink dulls the senses. Because the body is forced to expend energy to digest the meal, conversation is forgotten and the diners are reduced to animals who gorge themselves in silence. In my house, conversation is first on the menu."

Septivus chimed in. "The joy of eating is like the joy of learning, for each feast is like a book. The dishes are words to be savored, enjoyed, and digested. As Petrarch said, 'I ate in the morning what I would digest in the evening. I swallowed as a boy what I would ponder as a man!' "

"Indeed," cried Verana. "To be a slave to the stomach instead of acquiring knowledge at the table is, in my reckoning, to fail as a man." Verana must have seen Federico's face, for even from where I was standing I could see that Federico's bottom lip was now lower than his chin. "But come, let us eat. Forget the seasoning, Federico. Truly the best seasoning is the company of good friends."

O my soul! I prayed for his sake that Septivus would not say another word for as surely as there are stars in the sky, one of Federico's black moods was coming on. So when Verana recommended a thin pancake stuffed with liver called *fegatelli,* I took a small bite and suggested Federico not eat it because his stomach was too delicate. Federico loved that.

"Did you see Verana's face?" he roared afterward. "Well done, Ugo." I hoped he would instruct Cecchi to give me a gold coin but he did not.

Verana said much of what he learned came from a book by a Dutchman called Erasmus, which had just been translated into Italian, and after dinner he presented a copy to Federico. No one had ever given Federico a book before and he held it in his hand as if he did not know what to do with it. When he returned to his room he threw the book at Cecchi and told him to burn it. We left Verana's palazzo soon after because Federico said he would starve if he stayed another day.

I was sorry to leave Firenze. While it is true the Firenzani have "sharp eyes and bad tongues," they live in a beautiful city! I saw the blessed Duomo and the statues in the Piazza della Signoria and best of all, the stupendous David by Michelangelo next to City Hall. I wanted to kiss that magnificent sculptor's hands and kneel at his feet, but his servant said that unfortunately he had left for Roma that very morning. I saw many fine palaces built by wealthy princes and merchants, but the ones I liked best belonged to the guilds. As we journeyed on to Bologna, I could not stop thinking about them and soon an idea began forming in my head. I had never had an idea such as this one before and it thrilled and excited me. The hills on either side of us were covered in a rich tapestry of red, blue, and yellow flowers. I was sure that God Himself must live here since harmony and beauty are the truest aspects of His soul and my idea was in keeping with these surroundings. Thus I was sure my idea had been blessed by God. It was as follows:

Of all the servants, be they chamberlains, grooms, scribes, cooks or so on, surely the food taster is the bravest of all. What other servant risks his life not once, but two or three times a day just in the service of his work? In truth, we are as brave as the bravest knight for if a knight is outnumbered in battle he runs away—I have known many that fled before the battle even started—but does a food taster run away? No! Every day he does battle and every day he stays until the battle is ended. Why then, if there are guilds for goldsmiths, lawyers, spinners, weavers, bakers, and tailors, should there not be a guild for food tasters? Are we not as important as they? The very existence of our princes depends on us! Of course a food tasters' guild would be smaller, sometimes only one person to a city, but we could still meet, discuss new foods, poisons, antidotes, even assassins.

Thinking about this helped pass the hours of travel. Even as I was hunting for boar I was planning our initiation rites. I thought they should not only be severe, but useful. I listed them as follows.

1. An apprentice food taster should be starved for three days, after which he should be blindfolded and made to taste tiny amounts of poison which would be increased until he identified them correctly. If he survived he would have proven his ability. If he died, then he was obviously not suited for the task.

2. To make sure his heart was strong, he should be told after eating a meal that there was poison in it. If he immediately clutched an amulet and began praying to God, he should be thrown out the window, for if there had been poison in the meal, he would soon be dead anyway. But if he immediately found a woman and made sport with her, then he should be admitted with full honors. For a food taster must remain calm at all times: calmness will save a life, whereas a man who dabbles in superstition will act on the first thing that comes to his mind, which is usually wrong!

3. Most importantly, the examinations must be held in summer and in the open air since the emetics would cause such a foul odor in an enclosed room as to make a pig sick.

Having made these rules, I looked forward to meeting other food tasters to discuss my ideas with them.

But I met very few tasters on the way to Milano. A clown who claimed that he had faked his death was too stupid to change his story even after I told him who I was and so did not deserve to be in my guild. I also met a thin, nervous man with white hair, a pronounced nose, and thick lips. He sat in a chair in the sun and did not answer my questions, but every so often licked his lips with his tongue. When I asked him why, he said he was not aware he did so. Later, I saw other tasters do the same thing. They said they had been doing it ever since they could remember and were of the opinion that wet lips could better detect poisons.

In Piacenza, I met a taster who was convinced Federico had told me to fake my death; since *he*, the taster, was not capable of such cunning, how could *I* have done so?

Federico had planned to arrive in Milano in time for the feast of San Pietro. The guests included princes, merchants from Liguria, Genoa, and Savoy, as well as cardinals and an ambassador of the emperor. These many men of importance would ensure that many women would be there, too. However, we had traveled so slowly that the feast was already in progress the night we arrived. Federico was in a bad mood. Outside Parma, the cart had lurched unexpectedly while one of his whores was sitting on top of him. She had hit her head on a wooden beam, her eyes had become glassy, and she had muttered strange things. Fearing he would catch her madness, Federico left her on the side of the road. His gout had also been plaguing him badly. The gatekeepers allowed him and a few servants, including me, into the *castello*. The others were to follow in the morning.

I must say something in praise of Milano. If a finer city exists then they must invent new words to describe it. To begin with, the roads in the center of the city are not only as straight as gun barrels but also paved too, so that the carriages, of which there are many, may have a smoother ride! Is that not a miracle? And the castle! If a more magnificent one exists I have not seen it. It is almost as big as Corsoli itself and has an enormous moat around it. They told me the pig-swilling French stole many of its treasures, but *potta!* Everywhere I looked I saw the most beautiful paintings and the most exquisite sculptures! I remember a painting of Mary Magdalen by Il Giampietrino, which was so beautiful and tender it was no wonder Our Lord had reached out to her. By now I could write well enough to record things like this.

One staircase, designed by Leonardo da Vinci, was so magnificent I walked up and down it several times because it made me feel like a prince. Bold, colorful carpets of Oriental designs lined the hallways. A hundred scenes were painted on the ceilings and from the center of each room hung a chandelier with a thousand candles. Servants scurried to and fro, beautiful women entertained themselves, and from every room came the sound of laughter and music. If one is going to die in the service of a prince, I said to myself, then let it be for Duke Sforza.

Then I found the kitchen! Oh, what better sanctuary is there for a weary traveler than the hiss of boiling pots, the sight of steam curling up from the oven, and the warm smell of pies cooking? And what a kitchen! Compared to this, the kitchen in Corsoli was like a mousehole. There were three times as many ovens, five times the number of cauldrons, and more knives than in the Turkish army. I ate quickly because I wanted to visit the servants' quarters, for I was sure that such a magnificent prince would have extended his generosity to those who worked for him. I should have known better.

Just as in Corsoli, the servants' rooms were smaller and uncared for. Since French and Swiss soldiers had recently lived here, the stench was almost unbearable. As I wandered the hallways, my disappointment increasing with each step, the sound of voices pulled me to an open door. I peered in.

Six or seven men sat drinking and playing cards. One, a dandy with a careless attitude, wore a large feather in his hat and lounged with one leg over the arm of his chair. Another was a man with a bulbous onionlike face whose right eyelid was half closed from a knife wound. He was arguing with a fat man who looked as if he might have been a monk. "But if he sides with Venezia, then what?" the onion-faced man said fiercely.

The Fat One shrugged. "It depends on the pope."

The onion-faced man spat. "The pope changes sides more often than the weather."

"Who does not?" said the Fat One. "Besides I heard—" He saw me in the doorway. "What do you want?" he said brusquely.

"I have just arrived with Duke Federico Basillione DiVincelli," I said. "I am his food taster."

The others stopped their conversation to look at me. "Welcome," said the dandy in a smooth high voice. "We are all tasters here."

"Yes, come in," they cried.

At long last, I was home.

xxi

They sat me down at the table and a small, drunk man with bad teeth and a mouth that turned down at the corners like a frog poured a goblet of wine. I seldom drank wine, but since I was among friends I saw no reason not to enjoy myself. He handed me the goblet and said, "Mind the arsenic."

We laughed loudly. "*Salute!*" I said.

"*Salute!*" They cheered.

The wine swirled around my mouth like a spring river washing away the weary taste of my journey. "*Benissimo!*" I said. "*Benissimo!*"

"You do not have this in Corsoli?"

"We do not have anything in Corsoli."

"*We* do not have anything here either," the small man laughed, from which I gathered the flask had been stolen. They clapped me on the back and introduced themselves. Onionface served Duke Sforza, the small drunk a Cardinal of Ferrara, the Fat One a rich Genoese merchant. I believe the others were German and French.

"What is Federico like?" asked the drunk.

"Fat."

He laughed. "No, to work for."

"I have never worked for anyone else so I do not know."

Onionface jabbed me in the ribs. "Have you seen the food taster for the archbishop of Nîmes?"

"No," I said. "Is he here?"

"A he!" they laughed. "He is a she!"

"A woman?"

"As God is my witness," said the Fat One.

"I would like to dip my bone into her bush to see if it is poisoned," a German said, and we roared with laughter and drank again.

My heart soared. Here at last were men who risked their lives as I did. Who understood not the dangers of war, but the evil hidden in a leaf of lettuce. Here were men who would understand my guild! We spoke of which foods we liked and which we hated, which cooks we trusted and which to beware of. Oh, I could have talked like this forever and I would have done so had not the dandy suddenly slapped his thigh and said, "You are *that* Ugo DiFonte."

"Yes, that is me. Ugo DiFonte. Ugo, the magnificent!" I was a little drunk by now.

"Ugo the magnificent?" the Fat One said.

The dandy leaned across the table toward me. "Tell us what really happened."

"What happened when?" the Fat One asked.

"Yes, when?" I said.

"When Federico killed his wife and his mother-in-law because he thought the food was poisoned—"

"That was you?" said the drunk. The others murmured excitedly and crowded around me. They were younger than they had first appeared, some no more than boys. The drunk climbed onto a chair and, cupping his hands like a trumpet gave three loud blasts, shouted, "I salute you!"

Onionface knocked him to the floor.

"Why did you do that?" whined the drunk. "It is time one of us survived." I wanted to help him up, but Onionface stopped me.

"Never mind him," he said. "Tell us."

"Yes, tell us, tell us," the others pleaded, their faces desperate for any story of triumph.

"Ah, there will be time enough for that. Tonight, let us just drink and forget our cares."

No one moved. Perhaps I needed to be coaxed, one said, and called for more wine. They filled the goblets and shouted, "A long life."

"Tell us!" Onionface repeated. "We are all friends here." For all his bullying he seemed more anxious than the others.

"Wait," the drunk appealed, "he has just arrived. We cannot expect him to give away his secrets before we show him some of ours." He dug his hand into his pouch. "Ever seen one of these?" He held up a small, yellow stone dangling on the end of a chain. "It is a bezoar stone. From the belly of a cow. It saved my life."

"The only thing that saved your life," said Onionface, "was you were so drunk you threw up."

The drunk ignored him. "It gets hot in your hand if there is poison around."

"We all have them," said another, and, pushing the cards aside, spread a handful of stones on the table like a jeweler showing off his wares. The others did the same and in a moment the table was covered with objects of every size and color. As well as bezoar stones there were amulets of gold and silver, an earring which had belonged to John the Baptist, a stone from Jerusalem that threatened to crumble at the touch, a lock of Samson's hair, a fingernail of Saint Julian, a bee stinger locked in amber, finger rings of ivory. There were also ancient plants, the brain of a toad no bigger than my thumb, shells, pieces of ruby and topaz.

They picked up each piece in turn, told how it came into their possession, and boasted of its powers, each tale grander than the one before. Each time the owner swore to the Virgin Mary the tale was true—they had seen it with their own eyes or knew someone who had—and anyone who disputed them was a liar and should have their tongue cut out. No one doubted any of the stories and I saw for all their passions and boasts they were nothing more than ants, ants blindly marching forward without knowing why.

"I bet no one has one of these," said Onionface, holding out a dagger with a brown bone handle. "It is made from an African snake's fangs. It is the only one in the world."

"Then what is this?" said the Fat One, pulling out a knife with the same handle.

"This is the real one," Onionface said darkly, "I paid two hundred ducats for it."

"Then you were cheated," the Fat One smirked.

Onionface flicked the dagger around so the point was facing the fat man. The others hastily grabbed their stones and put them away.

"Neither of them are as good as a unicorn's bone, are they Ugo?" said the dandy, stepping between them.

"You have a unicorn bone?" Onionface asked.

They turned to me, the fight forgotten.

"I had one," I said, "but not anymore."

"What do you use, then?"

"Yes, show us," said the drunk.

"If you are hiding something—" The Fat One pushed me in the chest.

"I am not hiding anything."

"Then open your pouch," Onionface demanded.

I heard the door close behind me. Before I could pull my knife I was grabbed from behind and thrown to the floor. The Fat One sat on my chest. Onionface tore off my pouch, untied the string, and turned it upside down so the contents would spill out, but nothing did. It was empty.

xxii

A week earlier, just outside Cremona, it had rained for three days and three nights without stopping. The carts stuck in the mud and a child of a serving girl wailed so loudly that the knights wanted to kill her. I gave her my amulets to play with and told her stories of poisonings and hangings and other tragedies which befell noisy children. She listened quietly, hiding her face with her hair, so like Miranda when she was that age that I was about to tell her they were just tales when she suddenly snatched up my amulets and threw them into the darkness.

Although I had lost faith in them long ago, it had not occurred to me to throw them away so I jumped down into the pouring rain to search for them. By then, however, a dozen horses had already passed over that spot and unless the amulets themselves could have spoken I could never have separated them from the hundreds of stones beneath my feet. Since they did not mean anything to me I was not angry and I did not think of them again until the dandy turned my pouch upside down.

"Where are they?" Onionface said in bewilderment.

"I do not use them." I pushed the Fat One off my chest.

"You do not use talismans?" Onionface repeated. "But everyone uses them."

"Do they?" I brushed the dirt off my new, red velvet jacket.

They stared at me, waiting for me to explain myself.

I wanted to tell them that their charms and bones and stones were worthless, but they were too superstitious to give up their little shreds of hope. For the same reason, if I told them I relied only on my wits, they would not believe me and would accuse me of hiding something from them. No, they wanted me to give them a miraculous solution which would banish all their fears. So that is what I gave them.

"Magic," I said. "That is what I use." I was only half expecting they would believe me. Indeed, if only one of them had laughed I might have told them it was a joke.

But instead the Fat One said, "Only witches use magic."

As one they took a step backward, gaping at me as if I was the devil himself. Christ! What fools! What little respect I had for them vanished in that instant. In the end it mattered not. The word had fallen out of my mouth and I could not put it back.

"Then he must be a witch," Onionface said, pointing at me. His stupid bullying face annoyed me and I snapped at his finger with my teeth, catching one of the tips before he could pull it away. If they did not think I was a witch before, they did now. Some stumbled over themselves to get away from me, others pulled their daggers. I knew I must not show any fear so I bowed my head, wished them all "*Buona notte*," and very calmly walked into the hallway.

On the way back to Federico's quarters I could not help laughing at Onionface's stupidity. "*Ha il cervello di una gallina!*" as the saying goes. No, a chicken had *more* brains than he did, but as I lay down I was overcome with disappointment. No wonder there was no guild of food tasters. Nor, I saw now, was there any chance of there ever being one.

The next morning I cursed my mouth for running away with itself. Overnight my victory had become tarnished. I had never given any thought to the Inquisition, but now the word flew into my mind and nested there. I had not only said I knew magic, but also that I was a practitioner of it. If one of the tasters told his master or a priest, I could be hanged. I prayed that the tasters were as stupid as they looked and would believe that I would do them harm if they told anyone. And then, as quickly as my fears arose, they melted away for that evening I saw the woman the tasters had been talking about— Helene, food taster for the archbishop of Nîmes.

It had been nearly three years since the death of Agnese and during that time my heart had lain as dormant as a sleeping squirrel. Now it woke as if it was the first day of spring. O my soul. O blessed saints. The tasters had been far too modest in their praise. Helene was perfection itself. All of summer's flowers blended into one. She was slight of stature, yet there was a sense of sureness about her, like a young tree that bends in the wind but does not break. The French sun had tanned her skin to a light shade of brown, and her blonde hair was cut short in the French style. Everything about her—her hands, her feet, her breasts—was small and in perfect proportion, except for her nose, and her blue eyes, which were large and deep as spring pools. She dressed simply and did not paint her face, but when she smiled, her face seemed to light up from the inside and all the gold and jewelry in the world paled beside her. Not that she did anything to attract attention. And yet for that very reason I could not take my eyes off her.

Her movements were small and purposeful; she did not so much disturb the air as glide through it like a melody. All night long I repeated her name for it was the most beautiful I had ever heard. I borrowed paper, ink, and quill and wrote it over and over. I formed it out of stones, flowers, and leaves.

Helene remained closer to the archbishop than his shadow, assisting him in everything he did, whether it was arranging his platters, playing cards, or reading to him. I cursed him for condemning her to such a dangerous task, but it was hard to dislike him. He was filled with good humor and his big, red face creased in laughter when he told stories of the pope and other cardinals. At the serving table, I tried to tell Helene that she had slipped into my heart and I could not remove her. But I blushed when she looked at me and could not speak. I imagined her voice would be as musical as that of a thrush, but the sound which came out of her small pink mouth was low like a man's and sent shivers down my back. She caressed each word she spoke as if it was a precious child she hated to lose and, as I listened to her utter the most simple things, I suddenly wanted to hear her say my name more than anything in the world. I tried every trick that would give her reason to do so, but almost as if she knew what I wanted, she found ways of answering me—that is, if she answered me at all—by not saying it. To hear her say my name became my one desire. I could not sleep because of it.

I wrote her a sonnet. I had never written one before, but if Miranda could write poems to Tommaso why could I not write one, too? I rose early to be inspired by the beauty of the sunrise. At night I studied the mysteries of the moon. I remembered poems Septivus had read to Federico. I labored over my creation every waking moment, writing and rewriting it. Each hour I spent with it renewed my love for her. Thus, when at last I completed it I was both pleased and sad. It is as follows:

When first my eyes your radiance did behold
No breath, no sound, no movement could I make

Long had I slept, but now I was awake
Gazing on wonders no dream had foretold.
Your hair, ashine like summer's wheaten gold
Your eyes, twin pools of Como's blue lake
And oh, your cherried mouth my heart did break—
So soft it was, so kind, and yet so bold.
Then when you spoke, such music did cascade
As would make angels move from their addresses
To sail for Earth in Heaven's winged ships.
Life Eternal would I have given in trade
And all the bliss of Eden's sweet caresses
To hear my name drop once from your sweet lips.

    I wanted to give it to Helene right away, but I was afraid she might not like it. Then we would never speak and that would drive me to despair. "Courage," I said to myself. "Courage."

    When at last I did speak with her I did not have the poem with me so all my stored-up questions and desires burst forth in my eagerness to express myself. I spoke of the food, the wine, the ceiling, and then interrupted myself to praise her beauty. I talked of walking up and down the staircase da Vinci had built and of the straight roads in the city. I could not stop talking for I feared that if I did I might never be able to start again. And, when I could think of nothing more to say I told her that, too. She waited until I was out of breath and then said, "I must serve the archbishop." I had not realized she was holding a platter of food the whole time.

    In my dream that night, Helene was walking barefoot through a garden of yellow and blue flowers. Her dress was blood red and embroidered with gold. No matter how fast I ran I could not catch her. She did not look over her shoulder and yet I knew she wanted me to pursue her. After running through a bower of bushes she descended a flight of steps which led to a small piazza. Fearing she would escape me, I called her name. She stopped on the bottom stair, turned and looked as if she would speak, but instead of words, nightingales flew out of her mouth, all of them singing so sweetly that I was mesmerized by the beauty of their song. When I looked again, Helene had vanished.

I awoke with such longing and desire that I could not move. I prayed to God that Federico would find a woman so I might stay longer in Milano. I was drunk with love. So drunk that when the Fat One purposely jogged my arm I nearly dropped the platter of fruits I was carrying.

This was the second time the tasters had tried to hurt me. After our first meeting they avoided me. If I saw that lout Onionface in the hallways, I lowered my eyes and muttered, pretending to cast a spell. He shouted and pulled his knife, but he was too cowardly to do anything. The Fat One and the dandy were more dangerous. Before the Fat One jogged my arm, the dandy had tripped me and I had fallen into a German knight who beat me round the head for my pains. Now I would make them pay for their foolishness.

The next day as the dandy reached to pick up a bowl of meats, I poured a boat of steaming hot sauce over his hand. He screamed— not too loudly, for the banquet was starting—and accused me of burning him deliberately. I said he was lucky I was not holding a knife or I would have cut his hand off. After that I snuck up behind the Fat One and whispered, "If *you* try anything, I will carve your fat *culo* into more slices of bacon than you can count."

He gave a shriek and waddled away as fast as he could.

I learned that Helene and the archbishop walked the same path through the gardens every day at noon. I made it a practice to be there at the same time, my eyes half closed, as if writing poetry or studying the flowers, but all the while conspiring to bump into them as if by accident. Several days later I did just that, but because my eyes were half closed I trod on the archbishop's toe by mistake.

"A thousand pardons," I said. "I was consumed with my own thoughts."

"May I ask," said the archbishop, rubbing his injured foot, "What thoughts concern you on such a beautiful day?"

"I was thinking that all man has to do to be aware of God's grace is to look at the beauty around us." I said this to the archbishop although I was looking at Helene.

"Perhaps then," the archbishop snapped, "it would be better to keep your eyes open so you could *see* them!"

I did not mind that he was angry because this would give me reason to address him again. However, when that day came, I was again pretending to be deep in thought and so missed my path and tripped over that oaf Onionface and two other tasters who were hiding behind a bush. They were armed with cudgels and had obviously been waiting for me. It was only because they were as surprised as I that I avoided most of their blows. From then on I stopped walking in the garden and resolved to meet Helene in some other way.

While all this was going on, Federico was having no better luck than I in his pursuit of women. Every woman in Milano who was young or pretty or wealthy said she was betrothed. A few fat women with mustaches as thick as hairbrushes flounced around in front of him, but one look from Federico, or at him, and they left as quickly as they had come. He was sure the other dukes and princes, particularly Duke Sforza, were laughing behind his back, and so he avenged himself by beating them at cards. He soon amassed a small fortune and delighted in taunting Sforza, claiming the duke owed him enough to pay for his journey three times over. Cecchi pulled at his beard, urging Federico to leave before Duke Sforza regained his losses by force. Federico replied, "Did Caesar run? Did Marc Anthony run? Did Caligula run?"

I did not know Caligula played cards. *Potta!* I did not know who Caligula was. I did not care whether Federico won or lost as long as he stayed in Milano.

We had been in Milano for almost a month and the *castello* was again filled with dukes, princes, and rich merchants from Savoy, Piedmont, Genoa, and Bergamo who had come to celebrate Sforza's birthday.

"New blood," Federico muttered. His gout was causing him pain and he looked for anything that might take his mind off it.

I, too, was looking, not only for ways to speak with Helene, but also for ways to avoid the other tasters.

What a feast we had on Duke Sforza's birthday! Eel, lamprey, sole, trout, capon, quail, pheasant, boiled and roasted pork and veal, lamb, rabbit, venison, meat tart with cooked pears! Caviar and oranges fried with sugar and cinnamon, oysters with pepper and oranges, fried sparrows with oranges, rice with chopped sausage, boiled rice with calves' lungs, bacon, onion, and sage, a wonderful sausage called *cervellada* made of pork fat, cheese and spices, and pigs' brains. And that is just the food I remember!

At every banquet there had been a subject for discussion which had been decided upon beforehand. I did not listen to these any more than I listened to the speeches. Every orator thought he was the best in Italy, if not in what he said than in how long he took to say it, so after a few words my ears became deaf. I do remember that honor had been discussed as well as love, beauty, laughter, and wit. At this banquet the subject decided upon was trust.

There was talk about the treaty Venezia had signed with the emperor and how it would affect Milano. How Venezia could not be trusted any more than Firenze or Roma and that each state could only be concerned with its own interest and that was always changing. Someone said that the only true trust was between a man and his wife. This brought much laughter and everyone told of women who had deceived their husbands and the other way around. This talk went on for quite some time and then the archbishop said the only true trust was between God and man. A German soldier argued that God could not be trusted since no one knew what God was thinking. Someone else said that other than a dog, a prince could only place his trust in a faithful servant.

I was tasting some gorgonzola, cheese made from cows' milk which Federico loved, when a chill ran through me. It was not the cheese, but the conversation.

Duke Sforza said, "Federico places his greatest trust in his food taster, is that not so?"

Federico slowly moved his aching foot and replied that he did indeed place great trust in me.

"Would you sell him?" the duke of Savoy asked.

"Sell him? No. I need him. He advises me on the balance of humors and he anticipates poisons."

"Anticipates poisons?" said a Genoese merchant. "You exaggerate."

"I do not," Federico replied.

"He is the one who survived the poison that was meant for you, is he not, Federico?" Duke Sforza inquired.

Everyone craned their necks to see me. And that is when I noticed those traitorous, rat-shit dogs, Onionface, the dandy, and the Fat One, smirking and rubbing their greasy hands with glee.

"Yes," Federico said, "I can point to any dish and just by one taste he can tell me the ingredients in it."

"Then he must be able to identify every taste that exists," someone said.

"Every one I have come across," Federico answered.

"That is impossible," Sforza replied, gobbling a piece of veal shank covered in a gremalada sauce.

Federico's face turned red. "It is not," he said slowly.

"Well then," Sforza smiled, and, pointing to an uneaten platter in the middle of the table, said, "Will you wager he can tell us the ingredients in this dish?"

I tried to remember who had brought that platter to the table.

"What is it? Polpetta?"

"I do not know. But if he can identify all of the ingredients, I will double your winnings," said Duke Sforza. "If he cannot, you lose everything you have won."

My throat closed up.

"How shall we prove it?" Federico asked.

"My cook will write down exactly what he used."

The cook must have been waiting outside the door because he scuttled in like a cockroach. Someone magically produced some paper and a quill. The cook wrote down the list of ingredients and folded the paper, and it was placed on the table next to the polpetta. I looked to Cecchi for some guidance, but he was tugging at his beard. Everything had happened so fast we were taken unawares.

"I will join that wager," said the duke of Savoy, throwing several rings and medallions onto the table. They were joined quickly by golden earrings, goblets, silver necklaces, headbands, brooches.

The Fat One poured more wine for the duke of Savoy. Onionface licked his lips and I swore he winked at me. The dandy smiled coyly from behind Duke Sforza's chair. Suddenly, there in the midst of the magnificent paintings, the chandeliers with their thousand candles, the golden platters filled with delicious food, I saw myself writhing on the ground with Duke Sforza standing over me saying, "You lose, Federico. He guessed everything but the poison."

The polpetta was poisoned! I knew it! I wanted to tell Federico, but how could I? I could see the pile of jewels reflected in his eyes; he already possessed them! His determination spurred me on. If he wanted to win, then so did I! It was a moment in which the spirit of God spoke through me as it had when I rose from my dusty bean patch and said, "I will take Lucca's place." Now I turned to Duke Sforza, who was sitting at the table opposite Federico, and said, "I am willing, if your taster is."

"*My* taster?" said the duke.

"It would make the bet more exciting, if while I am tasting the polpetta, your taster could tell us," and here I pointed to a bowl of ripe blueberries, "what is in this bowl?"

Onionface's mouth dropped open.

"The bowl of berries?" Duke Sforza frowned.

I nodded. The dukes, merchants, knights, and princes looked at one another. Onionface looked to the dandy and the Fat One, but they were as stunned as he.

Duke Sforza laughed. "Yes, why not?"

I picked up the bowl and walked slowly toward Onionface. Halfway between the two tables, I stopped. Closing my eyes, I muttered something that sounded like a curse in Arabic just loud enough for Onionface to hear. In truth, I was praying silently to God, imploring Him that if He rewarded those who were righteous, brave, and honorable, to come to my aid.

Then I raised the bowl to my face and turned slowly in a circle. I pretended not to see the faces staring at me, some in bewilderment, others in surprise. The archbishop was frowning and Helene was looking at me with wide open eyes. I remember thinking, now she will know I exist.

When I had turned a full circle I blew slowly over the berries and then placed the bowl in Onionface's hands. Beads of sweat appeared on his brow. I could smell his fear. I turned my back on him and walked to my place. "Let us eat at the same time," I said, lifting a piece of veal from the platter.

Onionface looked at the berries and then at me. "He is a witch," he whimpered, pointing to me. Cecchi and Bernardo burst into laughter.

"He is scared," Septivus said. The others repeated, "He is scared!" The whole of Corsoli was behind me!

"Go on!" Federico suddenly roared. "Take one!" Others, too, added their voices, shouting, "Yes, take one."

It was as if Onionface had been challenged, and not me. I picked up a piece of veal. Sforza said something to Onionface. Onionface reached for one of the berries, then he withdrew his hand. Sweat trickled down his cheeks.

"Pick one!" The Genoese merchant shouted.

"No, do not touch it," someone said. "He has put a spell on it."

"By God! I will eat one," said a German knight.

"No," shouted Cecchi.

Federico rose to his feet, his face twisting with pain because of the weight on his gouty foot, and leaned his massive great body toward Onionface. This made everyone stand, even the archbishop. The dogs barked and a candle fell from the chandelier onto the pile of jewelry. No one was looking at me. Onionface reached into the bowl and picked up a berry.

"Taste it!" shouted Federico.

"Now!" I called out, and lifted the veal to my mouth.

Onionface raised the berry to his mouth. His hand seemed to be at war with itself, one force pushing it toward his lips, the other pulling it away. The berry touched his mouth and as soon as it did, he dropped the bowl. His eyes bulged out of his head as he staggered backward, lurching about like a ship in a storm, clutching at his heart. Then he crashed to the ground, spit drooling from his mouth. For an instant no one moved. Then the archbishop pushed his way to Onionface's side and, in the time it takes for a fly to beat its wings, someone behind me pulled my arm down and replaced the piece of veal with another.

"I am ready to taste," I said loudly, and bit into the veal. Everyone turned around.

Federico grabbed the paper in the middle of the table.

"I taste mozzarella cheese . . . raisins . . . parsley," I said loudly, "Garlic, salt, fennel, pepper, and, of course, veal."

"That is right," said Federico, reading off the paper, "although not in that order. But that does not matter, does it?"

Onionface was forgotten as Duke Sforza snatched the paper from Federico. The dandy and the Fat One were looking at me, waiting for me to scream, to shout out, to fall down. I knew I would not, but pretending I did not know they were watching, I took another bite, chewed it a little, furrowed my brow as if there was something wrong with it, coughed slightly, finished chewing, swallowed and belched loudly. "It is delicious!" I said, "I compliment the cook."

"I win!" Federico exclaimed, and scooped up as many jewels as he could in his fat, pudgy hands. Cecchi took the rest. Leaning on my arm, Federico walked out of the banquet hall, clenching his jaws, but refusing to acknowledge the pain his gout was causing him.

"Now," Federico said, as soon as we reached his quarters, "what was that about the polpetta?"

"My Lord, the polpetta was poisoned. I am sure of it."

"Poisoned!" His small eyes became like arrow points. "How do you know?"

"The other tasters have attacked me from the moment I arrived. Two weeks ago they lay in wait for me in the garden. They must have told Duke Sforza because if you recall he suggested the bet. They wanted to kill me and win back your winnings at the same time."

"Then why did you eat it if you knew it was poisoned?"

"Because you changed it, Your Honor."

"I changed nothing."

I looked to Cecchi. He shook his head, as did Piero, Bernardo, and Septivus.

Could I have imagined it?

"Triple the guards outside my door," Federico barked. "Cecchi, we leave in the morning."

The courtiers hurried to fulfill his commands. I wondered whether I had lost my senses and I tried to recall if I had touched the flesh of the hand that held the other piece of veal, but I could not.

"Ugo," Federico said.

"Yes, Excellency."

He ran his hands through the pile of jewels. "I do not know what happened. I do not care. But here." He tossed me a most beautiful silver ring sparkling with precious gems.

"*Mille grazie*, Your Excellency." I said, and kissed his hand.

"Be careful," he said roughly. "The Sforzas do not like to lose."

"*Mille grazie*, Duke Federico, *mille grazie*."

Septivus and Piero congratulated me as I entered the hallway, but Bernardo spat out some seeds and said, "You must have been born under the sign of the lion."

"Because of my boldness?"

"Because you have as many lives as a cat."

"To the winner go the spoils," Cecchi murmured, and told me to go to the bottom of the stairs.

Remembering what Federico had said, I took out my knife and slowly descended the steps, carefully looking all around me. The voices of other guests drifted toward me as I reached the bottom stair. But there was no one there except for the portraits staring at me from the walls. A voice whispered. "Ugo!"

I turned around and there she was, standing beside a column, her blue eyes shining in the light of the sconces. Helene. My Helene, calling my name.

"Are you all right?" She asked, raising her hand toward my throat.

"It was you! You switched—"

Footsteps came toward us. Helene pulled me behind the column and we waited until they passed. I would have been happy to remain there, feeling her warmth, smelling the sweetness of her hair. Motioning I should follow, she led me down staircases, through darkened hallways, and into the palace gardens. The stars were bright; the moon hung low over us.

"You saved my life, Helene." I needed to say her name aloud.

She shook her head so that her hair flew around her face. "Phppft! Those fools! What did you do to the berries?"

"Niente."

She smiled. "I did not think so. But he is dead."

"Onionface?"

"Onionface?"

"That is my name for him."

"Yes, Onionface." She smiled. "That was a good name for him. His heart stopped. I tried to explain to the archbishop, but he does not care."

"What concern is that of mine?"

"Because he investigates all suspicious activities for the Inquisition. He will not do anything tonight, but tomorrow . . . ?"

"But why?"

"You blew on the berries and Onionface died!" She shrugged as if no more explanation was necessary.

Oi me! How could I be thrust from heaven into hell so quickly? Helene paced in front of me, tapping her cheek with her finger. "How long are you staying in Milano?"

"We leave tomorrow."

"By which road?"

"I do not know—"

"Avoid Ferrara," she frowned. "The bishop has friends there."

"They do not ask me which way to go." I grasped her arms. "Why are you telling me this?"

She tucked her head to one side and looked at me. "I never believed those stories the other tasters said about you any more than I believed you poisoned the berries."

"How could you be so sure?"

She laughed. "If you knew magic you would not have said those stupid things in the garden or at the serving table."

I could not have stopped smiling had someone sewn my lips together. Every word from her mouth delighted me. I slid my hands down her arms till I felt her hands. They were soft and warm as I knew they would be. "But if the archbishop comes for me tonight—"

"He will sleep till morning. He drank a lot of wine."

Staring into her eyes I could see right into her heart; I saw myself walking beside her. I saw her bearing my children. I saw us old, unable to leave one another's side. I saw us in death, two branches of a tree entwined like Baucis and Philemon.

"Do you see our future?" she asked.

"You read minds, too?"

"Only yours, Ugo." She leaned forward and pressed her lips to mine.

Oh, Helene. Oh, my glorious Helene. My delight, my happiness, my Helene. To hear her call my name. Had any word ever sounded so sweet? l asked her to say it again and again. I wanted to memorize the sound of her voice in my heart. Joy surged through us, causing us to laugh for no other reason than we were alive. I could not keep from touching her, kissing her lips. I thought food was the sustenance for which I hungered, but again I was wrong. Holding her in my arms, I wept because I had found my strength, my rib, that part of me I did not know was missing. Even now I feel her skin upon mine. I smell her. Taste her sweat. I see her eyes, round and clear, I feel her breasts, her thighs, her small, strong feet. I hear her voice in my ears and in my heart. Oh, that my fingers could transfer her softness to this paper and my quill could capture her passion! The very thought of her illuminates my darkness even as the moon brightens this room. Everything I am cries out for her. O saints preserve me! To be overcome by such longing on the eve of the wedding. The past has reached into my present and captured my soul and I cannot write anymore.

xxiii

When Helene pressed her lips against mine I was lifted beyond the
skies to a place where all dreams are possible. I wanted to lie with
her, but the sky was growing lighter and the servants would soon be
rising to prepare our departure. I took Helene's hand and hurried to
the stable. We mounted a stallion, whose impatient snorting woke a
stable boy. He opened his mouth, as if to shout, but instead yelled,
"Courage!" and threw us a bundle of bread and cheese.

At the gates, Helene told the guards that we needed wild parsley to
soothe our princes' stomachs.

"Where are we going?" I asked as the *castello* faded from view
behind us.

"France," Helene said, as if this was something we had both
decided on.

I nodded. France. Why not? What was there here for me?

Our horse galloped with great speed. Soon the *castello* and Milano
were no more than memories. Everything aided us in our journey.
The grass lay down as we approached, the birds cheered us on, and
the green hills beckoned us forward.

I imagined how Federico would gnash his teeth when he discovered I was missing. At first he would think I had been killed. He
would surround himself with guards and leave hurriedly, clutching
his winnings. But perhaps a horse would be reported missing. Then
it would be known that I had left. I could be hanged just for taking a
horse. Christ! I could be hanged just for leaving! But when I felt
Helene's arms around my waist and her head against my back, I did
not care. O, God in heaven! The devil take Federico and Duke Sforza
and the whole lot of them. I was free! I could not contain my excitement and shouted with delight and wonder. For the third time in my
life I had been reborn.

The snowcapped mountains lined up on our right like northern kings.
Two travelers rode ahead of us and I called out to them, wanting to be
certain that this path led to France. But as we galloped toward them,
they grew frightened and raced away.

In the heat of the day we rested in a glade of beech trees and
gorged ourselves on the bread and cheese. How good it tasted, each

bite a blessing from heaven. I wanted to remember to tell Septivus that the most important thing about eating was not the food or the conversation but who you ate it with. We lay down amid the wild-flowers and loved one another until we fell asleep.

When we awoke, the setting sun had ignited the mountaintops. We rode swiftly for several more hours before we stopped at an inn. The first people we saw when we entered were the travelers we had seen on the path. I assured them we had not intended them any harm. The smaller one clapped his hand to his heart and said, "*Ecco!* I thought I would die of fright. You looked like the avenging angel the way you rode toward us."

Helene told the innkeeper she was employed by the archbishop of Nîmes and offered to cook his favorite meal in exchange for a bed. The innkeeper, a fellow with bushy eyebrows and a runny nose, happily agreed, in part I believe to annoy his wife, a large buxom woman with the arms of a blacksmith. We soaked two chickens in wine, added vinegar and spices, and while they baked, Helene made polenta *cocina*—a polenta sprinkled with grated cheese and truf-fles—a Sunday delight in Piedmont.

After the first mouthful, the innkeeper said, "If you cook like this every day, I will hire you as soon as my wife dies." To which his wife replied, "I promise you however long you live I will live one day longer."

It was in these good spirits that we ate and drank, surrounded by good company and good food. Suddenly, Helene started to laugh, softly at first, but soon louder and louder and with great abandon. She pointed to my trencher where my polenta lay half eaten. Hers was, too. Only then did I understand why she was laughing. Food tasters both of us, we had not tasted our food before eating it. We had not sniffed at it, nibbled it, or tested it in any way, but had enjoyed it just as our companions were doing.

I pulled Helene from the bench, held her tightly in my arms, and kissed her. Even tired and weary from our journey, she was the most beautiful woman I had ever seen. "This moment," I told her, "will be carved in my heart forever."

Our companions cheered and the smaller man said it was easy to see we were deeply in love. Thus, we were fulfilling God's most divine law, for He had sent love to ease man's path through life, and the sicknesses and wars which plagued us existed because man had forgotten this divine commandment.

Three soldiers entered the inn and for a moment my heart stopped, but since they were not wearing Federico's colors or those of the archbishop I thought no more about them. The innkeeper brought the soldiers some wine and when he returned to our table he said, "Those soldiers keep looking at you."

I said I did not know why they should, but even as I was speaking two of them approached our table. The captain, a man with broad shoulders and a rough beard, said, "What is your name and where are your passports?"

I said, "Ugo DiFonte. I am traveling with Duke Federico Basillione DiVincelli of Corsoli, but I have left him." I do not know what excuse I was about to give, but it did not matter for as soon as I said Corsoli the soldiers looked at one another and the other interrupted, asking, "Is that close to the Convent Verecondo?"

I replied it was no more than half a day's ride. He asked if I had heard of a Prince Garafalo. I said I had not, but only because I had never been in this part of Italy before. At this he eagerly laid a hand on my arm. "You must come with us right away to see our prince."

When I asked why, he said he could not tell me. Well, I had not left one prison to be thrown into another! I pushed his arm away, and leaping up, I knocked him backward over the bench with a blow to the head. Then I grabbed the carving knife and, pulling Helene behind me, shouted, "Though we are strangers here we hoped that we would be treated with respect. But if you or the prince are intent on harming us, then be prepared to die for I will not exchange the liberty God has given me for the chains of man."

He quickly rose up and said they were not here to harm us. The innkeeper cried out, "Prince Garafalo is a good man who loves every living thing. He often comes here to eat just to be with his subjects."

The soldier I had knocked down said they had simply been charged to take me to the prince, adding that if they had frightened me they were sorry. I wondered how this Prince Garafalo could have already known about me. However, trusting to God, I put down the knife and said that as their prince seemed to be a peace-loving man, I would be happy to accompany them. So without finishing the meal we had so lovingly prepared, Helene and I bid farewell to our gentle hosts and allowed ourselves to be led to Prince Garafalo's palace.

Fireflies lit our way through vineyards and orchards of perfumed orange trees till we arrived at the prince's palace. Peacocks roamed the grounds, their colors blending with the many beautiful flowers. We were given water to refresh ourselves and clean clothes to wear. Suddenly, I was overcome with fear and seeing me tremble, the servant asked the reason for it. "If this leads to another job like that of a food taster," I replied, "I would prefer to take the poison now."

Again I was assured that Prince Garafalo was a good man and intended neither of us any harm. I was led to a small room with beautifully carved chairs and a writing desk where Helene soon joined me. She had also bathed, washed her hair, and now wore a red gown exactly the same as she had worn in my dream. Not a moment later the door opened and a servant announced Prince Garafalo.

The first thing I noticed about him was his bowlegs which made him rock from side to side as he walked. The next was his good-natured spirit, for although he had a head of white hair like a sheep waiting to be shorn, he had the energy of a man half his age. I understood immediately why the soldiers and the innkeeper worshiped him so highly.

He came right up to me, staring into my face. Holding me at arm's length, he peered at me from head to toe, examining my hands and legs. Then he squinted at my face again. The soldier offered something to the prince, but the prince said, "I do not have to see it. I know. This is he! This is he!"

Although the prince had a manner about him which made me love him immediately, I disliked being prodded like a chicken so I said, "I am who?"

The prince laughed and, throwing his arms around me, cried, "My son! My son!"

You cannot imagine how I felt. The walls swirled around, the blood rushed to my head, and I fell to the floor as if I were dead.

Servants roused me by making me sniff pepper and when I had sneezed out all my brains, I assured the prince that although I was in the best of health, his news had rendered me helpless. However, if this was a jest he had performed it with great wit, but I begged him now to tell me the truth. The good prince insisted Helene and I join him at his table where he would explain the reasons for his belief. So we gave up a wonderful meal at the inn for an even greater one with the prince.

I hardly remember what we ate because I was so entranced by the prince's tale which I shall relate as best I can. He said that in his youth he had been a sergeant in the papal army of Pope Julius. They had been marching through Umbria on their way to attack Bologna when the pope instructed him to stop at the Convent Verecondo to make a donation. Close to the convent, he had met a young woman who was so distressed that the whole countryside could hear her weeping. Since the prince was then a young and handsome man and the girl was very beautiful, her tears touched him deeply. In answer to his questions, the girl said her husband had cruelly taken their small son with him to tend the sheep and she missed him terribly.

The prince continued to Verecondo where he spent the night, but the woman's weeping invaded his dreams. The following morning he went to her farm and declared his love for her. She had fallen in love with him the moment she saw him and so great was their passion they threw off their leaden shoes and danced the songs of love until the next day. The prince begged the woman to accompany him to Bologna, but she could not leave her child. With a heavy heart he left her and hurried to meet the pope. However, his absence had not gone unnoticed, and his enemies so maligned him to the pope that he was forced to flee to Firenze and then to Venezia for his safety.

Many years went by before he was able to return to the village, by which time the woman had died. The neighbors told him she had given birth to a second son, which he realized might be his own, but that child had since grown and left for Gubbio some years earlier.

I had been listening with astonishment to this tale and when the prince mentioned Gubbio I could contain myself no longer, throwing my arms around his neck and calling him my own dear father. I fell into such a weeping the like of which I had not done since my mother died. The prince did likewise and everyone at the table was so moved, the tears flowed like the sweet rain of spring, for beneath all of our sorrows, hope had blossomed again.

My father said he pursued a career trading olive oil which had made him very prosperous. He had never married, the remembrance of his love coming between him and every other woman, until one day it had burst forth into a painting which he held up for us to see. It showed with simple delicate lines a woman with dark hair and a somber face, with full lips just like mine and the left eye slightly larger than the right.

"Blessed be the Holy Virgin," I cried. "It is the mirror of my mother!"

The prince smiled. "When I was very young I studied with Leonardo da Vinci for a short while in Milano."

"You are a most worthy pupil," I said.

The prince said he had instructed his servants to remember my mother's likeness from the painting and to bring any man who resembled it to the palace. This they had done several times, but the prince had known immediately they were not his offspring. He despaired of ever finding his son until the moment he saw me. Now, as Death approached, he could die happy at last.

I pleaded with him not to speak in this manner ("God would not have waited so long to bring us together only to tear us apart"), and I told him the incredible journey that Helene and I had just undertaken had now resulted in our meeting. The prince said he would commission a new altar to be built on his grounds to celebrate our reunion. Thus with much rejoicing we continued until the chirping of the birds heralded the approaching dawn. Then my father led us to our bedroom whose walls and floors were covered in luxurious carpets and tapestries and to our bed covered with the finest linen sheets and pillows. I could not believe my good fortune. To have found my heart's desire and be reunited with my father all in the space of a few days! What had I done to deserve this? I reached out to Helene. Her softness, her goodness, her beauty and courage overwhelmed me. I see her even now as she bends her head toward me, her hand reaching for mine, her lips beckoning me. I see it as clearly as the day it happened.

Oh, but why go on with this? None of it happened. None of it. I did not run away with Helene. We did not stay at the inn, cook a meal, meet my real father or a thousand other fancies. I dreamed them all. I dreamed them by night and I dreamed them by day. I dreamed them so often they became servants to my desires and so real that I remember the food we ate, the clothes we wore, the words we spoke with greater passion than the things which really did happen. And now it is written down which makes it true. I do not know why that is so, but it is.

All my life I believed the stories of the Bible or of Greece or Roma were true just because they were written down. Now, as I read over what I have written, I see how easy it is to make up a story where none existed. To stir the humors, to make the reader weep, laugh, or clutch his heart—surely that is a gift more valuable than all the gold and silver that exist. Truly the man who succeeds in this is god of his own world.

In truth, Helene and I clung to one another every moment of the few hours we had together. Sometimes the words poured out and at other moments there was no need to speak. I recited my poem and she kissed me, repeating my name a hundred times so that whenever I heard it from then on, it was her voice I heard saying it. We loved one another standing against the walls of the *castello*, not caring if anyone saw us. Then I had to leave for the sun was beginning to rise and the servants were packing the mule carts.

When I returned from tasting Federico's breakfast, Helene was weeping and cursing her pride for the time she had wasted by not speaking to me. I kissed her again and again and told her to return to the archbishop because I was afraid she would get into trouble if she was seen with me. She refused to leave my side.

Then Federico was climbing into his carriage and the knights and ministers were mounting their horses. The mule carts were led out of the courtyard. Helene tore at her hair and began wailing loudly. I climbed down to comfort her while behind us the procession rode through the gates. The dandy and several other tasters had gathered by the stables, and were watching us.

"Go," Helene said, wiping her tears. "Go, before they harm you."

The guards were closing the gates, but I did not want to leave

Helene—had I not lost Agnese in a similar way?—but she assured me they would not dare to hurt her because she was the archbishop's taster and there were guards everywhere.

I told her that one day I would come back for her. It did not matter if she was in Nîmes, Milano, or Paris—I would find her. It might take the rest of my life, but without her my life was not worth living. She clung to me, laid her soft, small finger against my lips and said, "If God wills it, so it will be. But go now, please, Ugo. Go."

I mounted my horse. The tasters rushed at me, swinging their swords and clubs. I reared my horse, scattering them, and galloped out of the *castello* grounds just before the gates closed.

It was during our return to Corsoli that Cecchi named me *Il miracolo vivente*—a living miracle. But I was hardly living and my life was far from miraculous. Although I had every reason to rejoice, I was filled with melancholy. It was not just that I had found the love of my life only to have lost her again, but I was weary in mind and body. My bones ached, my blood was sluggish, and I did not sleep well. And when I did, my sleep was invaded by dreams of death and deception. I was given to looking over my shoulder and licking my lips like the food tasters I had met. Yes, I had triumphed over Onionface, but he had made a ghost of me. I finally understood what Tommaso had meant when he had warned me about becoming too close to Federico. I had taken on all of his fears as well as my own.

Thus, when on the third day of our journey Cecchi said that Federico had invited me into his carriage, I did not wish to go. Cecchi said although he was sure my reasons were good, he could not think of one that was good enough to disobey Federico's command.

The others were already there listening to Septivus read about a Roman emperor who had defeated the French and German hordes.

"And he was loved, too?" Federico asked.

"He was a stoic."

Federico's mouth puckered up. "A stoic."

"To a stoic, virtue was the highest good," Septivus explained. "They believed that to attain freedom, true freedom over their own lives, they had to set aside all passion."

"I can do that," Federico said, biting into a peach.

We nodded in agreement.

"And also put aside unjust thoughts," Septivus continued.

"I never have unjust thoughts," Federico said, wiping the juice from his chin.

Again we nodded.

"And live with nature and give up all indulgences," finished Septivus.

Federico swallowed the last of the peach. "*Basta.* We will read again tomorrow."

Septivus hastily closed the book and left, quickly followed by

Piero and Cecchi. Bernardo grasped my shirt and tried to pull me with him.

"Go," Federico said to him, and as Bernardo left, Federico hurled the peach stone at the back of his head.

"*Scusi*," Federico said, when Bernardo turned around. "An unjust thought." Then he turned to me and said, "Did you know Marcus Aurelius persecuted Christians? I wish they would have had popes then." He rearranged the cushions behind him and bit into another peach. "Did you like Milano?"

I replied that I had, although not as much as Firenze.

"Do you like the paintings and sculptures better in Firenze or Milano?"

I had to be careful how I replied because I did not know the reason for his questions. "I liked the painting of Mary Magdalen."

"With the book in her hand? Yes, I liked that one, too. Who painted that?"

"Il Giampietrino."

"Giampietrino." Federico nodded his head. "Did you see the da Vinci in the tower hall? The tree with all those golden ropes? Magnificent. Just magnificent. But you should see the paintings and the mosaics in Istanbul." He told me of the magnificent mosques, mosaics, and jewelry he had seen while he was employed by the sultan. I was surprised, not only that he remembered, but also that he was confiding in me. "I want to do something like that." He parted the curtains. "Look at the clouds. Do they not look like sculptures?"

I sat next to him and peered through the curtains. It was most peculiar talking to him as if he was just another man. "Yes," I said, "That one reminds me of the head of the David in Firenze.

"So it does." Christ on a cross! He was agreeing with me! I added, "I liked the Duomo in Firenze, and especially the statue of David. It has an unearthly beauty."

Federico stared at the clouds for a long moment and then closed the curtain. "You mentioned Milano, Firenze, but not Corsoli. Not even once."

"Your Excellency, that is because it is—"

"A shit hole," he said angrily.

"If I may beg to differ—"

"You may not. But I will change that." His eyes squinted with ambition. "I am going to build an altar to the Virgin Mary in the Duomo Santa Caterina."

"To echo the golden Madonna on the front?"

He must have forgotten about the golden Madonna. "Yes," he snapped, as if the idea now disappointed him. "I want to add something to the palace, too."

"A tower?"

"No. A new wing to go across the back to hold a library. A place for scribes to translate my manuscripts."

I did not know he had any manuscripts. I said, "To make a square out of the palace courtyard."

"Exactly. Make a square out of it."

"It is a bold and excellent idea, My Lord."

"Yes, it is bold. And excellent. The courtyard will be enclosed and the scribes can look upon it while they work. I spoke to a student of Bramantino while we were in Milano." He began to plump up his cushions and then looked at me, which meant that I should do it for him. I have since taken on that task whenever I see him. "But I do not wish to lose the garden," he continued. "A palace must have gardens. They are good for contemplation."

"Maybe if it were planted into the hillside."

He looked at me as a hawk does when it spies a rabbit. I was about to apologize when he said, "You mean like the Hanging Gardens of Babylon?"

Since I had never heard of the Hanging Gardens of Babylon, I said, "Yes. But bigger."

"Bigger! Of course, bigger." He rubbed his hands together. "I want to wake up and see the hillside covered in flowers. The Hanging Gardens of Corsoli. That would make those fools in Milano sit up! Do you know what they said about Corsoli?"

I shook my head although I could have guessed.

"Backward! They called it backward!"

I could see the storm brewing, and, as I was the only one in the carriage with him, I knew I would be the one to suffer, so I said, "But, My Lord, that just shows their own foolishness because when it comes to cleanliness and neatness they do not compare to Corsoli."

"You noticed that?" he cried.

"They were like pigs. The servants' quarters would have horrified you."

"I knew it! That is because of the Germans! And the Swiss. And the French. They are all pigs! I will build Corsoli to be the envy of Romagna and it will be clean. And neat, too!" He was excited again.

As soon as I emerged from Federico's carriage the others hissed at me. "What did he say? What did he want?"

I told them Federico had spoken to me as a trusted servant and I could not betray that trust.

Later, Cecchi took my arm and we walked a little ahead of the carriage where the clopping of hooves would bury our words. "Federico cannot rebuild Corsoli—"

"But why not? Some new buildings and statues will be good for the city."

Cecchi tugged at his beard. "But the *contadini* are already starving. If we raise the taxes again they will die. Then there will be no one to feed the palace."

The next day, Federico called me to his carriage again. I had been warned by Cecchi not to encourage his ideas, but when an idea seized Federico nothing could change his mind. Septivus sat in a corner trying to write as the carriage jolted up and down.

"I am inviting sculptors and painters to Corsoli," Federico said. "They will compete to design the back wing, the Hanging Gardens, a statue of me, and some paintings." He snatched a piece of paper from Septivus and read it with his thick bruised lips.

"To the most modern of ancients, my illustrious brother and Lord, Michelangelo Buonarroti, I thank the Virgin Mother that those of us who look upon your wonders are not required to be as gifted as you since then you would only have God Himself for company. For a man such as I, whose hands unfortunately have been *immerse in sangue,* it is not only a revelation, but also an absolution to know that man is capable of such magnificent deeds. Your statue of David, which I recently saw on my way to Bologna, so overwhelmed me that I was rooted to the spot, unable to eat or drink, unable to do anything but gaze upon this vision and give thanks to Almighty God that I was allowed to witness such unearthly beauty."

Those last were *my* words! There was another page of praise until, finally, Federico invited Michelangelo to paint Federico in one of three poses which he believed would be a challenge worthy of Michelangelo's talent. The first was Federico as Hercules strangling the lion of Nemea, the second as Alexander cutting the Gordian knot, and the third as Caesar crossing the Rubicon. Federico was prepared to pay a thousand gold coins and added that, knowing how promptly the pope paid his artists, he thought Michelangelo could use the money. When he finished reading he looked up at me.

"I cannot see how he will fail to come," I said.

He grunted and read another letter—this one to Titian—promising exactly the same amount, except he changed Hercules to Perseus slaying the minotaur.

"Federico as the minotaur is something I would pay to see," Cecchi growled after I told him.

Letters were also written to Piero Bembo and Matteo Bandello, inviting them to Corsoli, which Federico claimed was like the Garden of Eden and where inspiration was as common as dirt. He also wrote to Lorenzo Lotto, Marco D'Oggiono, and to the sculptor Agostino Busti, whose works he had admired in the cathedral in Milano. "I would like a statue of me on a horse," he wrote.

The third time I went into the carriage, Septivus was reading aloud from Verana's book. Fortunately, Septivus had not thrown it away as he had been instructed, for now Federico made him read from it every day. Septivus was reading a passage which said that after blowing one's nose it was not wise to look into the piece of cloth as if it contained the pope's jewels, but to place the piece of cloth in a pocket.

"That's easily solved," Federico boasted. "I always use my fingers."

Federico now ordered me to play backgammon with him while Septivus read from *The Odyssey*. Every now and then Federico would look up and say something like, "Who got turned into hogs?"

"Circe turned Eurylocus's men into hogs."

"Why?"

"Because she hated men."

"And where was Odysseus?"

"By the ship."

"Which ship?"

"The ship they were on when they left Laestrygones, no I mean . . . Aeolus . . . no . . . no . . . Telepylus."

"No wonder I am confused," Federico said. "Start again."

"From the beginning?" Septivus squeaked.

"Where else?"

Although it was often difficult to follow Septivus's reedy voice reciting the journeys of Odysseus or Dante, I found it pleasing to rock backward and forward as the rain drizzled lightly on the carriage roof and the wheels crushed the stones beneath us. Sometimes Federico fell asleep, sometimes I did, and once, Septivus himself began to snore even as he was reading.

It was only when Septivus explained that Beatrice had only been fourteen when Dante had fallen in love with her that I thought of Miranda. I wondered how she was, if she had fallen in love with another boy, if she had taken her potions, if she was with child. My heart ached to see her and I felt such a weariness that I said to Federico, "Your Excellency, I am so grateful for the many honors you have given me. As you must know my sole desire on earth is to serve you faithfully as Our Lord wills me to."

"I can always tell when someone wants something," Federico said. "They praise me as if I was Jesus Christ Himself. But you, Ugo? You disappoint me."

"It is only because I wish to serve you in an even greater way that I ask you to consider my request."

"What is it?"

"As a food taster I serve you twice a day. If, however, I were a courtier I could serve you every moment of the day."

"But what would you do?" Federico replied. "Piero's my doctor, Bernardo is my astrologer, Cecchi my chief administrator, Septivus my scribe and tutor."

"Perhaps I might assist Cecchi—"

"He does not need assisting. And besides," he frowned, "who would be my food taster?"

"I could train someone. It would not—"

"No," he laughed. "*Tu sei il mio gustatore.* You will *always* be my food taster. Let us hear no more about it."

"But, My Lord—"

"No!"

I could not stop myself and after a moment I said, "Your Excellency—"

"No," he roared. "Leave me!" I was never invited into his carriage again.

We had just passed the village of Arraggio, south of Bologna. A fine mist covered the hills and the smell of rain was in the air. A wind slipped through the trees, disrobing them of their red and brown leaves. Chestnuts clothed in their green, bristly armor stabbed at my feet. Across the valley a flock of sheep clung to the hillside. A shepherd and a girl huddled together beneath a tree. Michelangelo can have his thousand florins, I said to myself, all I want is to live here on a small farm with a flock of sheep and my Helene. I will love her. I will take care of her. We will sleep together at night and together we will wake in the morning. I made this promise to Helene, to myself, and to God, and I carved our names in a tree as a sacred covenant.

It was cold and wet when we entered the valley of Corsoli, but when I saw the jagged hills, the trees bunched together like broccoli tops, the palace rising like a sepulcher from the mist, I was so overcome that I kissed the ground, thanking God for returning us safely. Halfway up the valley the Duomo bell began to ring. We sang to encourage our weary feet, boys rode out to greet us, and no sooner had we entered the city than we were besieged by wives, husbands, and children. I wondered where Miranda was when suddenly, as I climbed the Weeping Steps, a woman shrieked, ran out of the crowd, and threw her arms around me, crying, "Babbo, Babbo!"

Oh, what joy to feel her in my arms again! "Mia Miranda, mia Miranda!" I barely recognized her. Her hair was in a coif, revealing her elegant swanlike neck. She wore earrings and a necklace lay on her soft white bosom. When I left she was a girl and now she was woman!

"Is that your *amorosa?*" said a voice behind me. I turned around. It was Federico. His carriage had stopped and he was looking out of the window at us.

"No, My Lord," I bowed. "This is my daughter, Miranda."

Federico stared at her in a way that made me feel uncomfortable. Miranda blushed, bowed her head, and said, "Welcome back to Corsoli, Your Excellency. Each day without you has been like a summer without a harvest."

Federico raised an eyebrow. "Did you hear that, Septivus?"

Septivus poked his head out of the carriage. "A summer without a harvest." Federico repeated. "Write that down. I like that."

The carriage moved on. I took Miranda's hand and we followed into the palace. As Federico climbed out of the carriage I saw him turn around as if looking for us.

I gave Miranda a comb, some rose water, and false hair made of blonde silk I had bought in Firenze. I did not tell her about the ring Federico had given me for I had given it to Helene. Miranda sat on my lap as she had done when she was a child, and I told her all that had happened to me. She looked at me with horror. "But Babbo, what if Onionface had eaten the berries and nothing had happened to him?"

"I trust God would have taken care of me."

She put a finger to her chin thoughtfully and asked, "Since I am your daughter, will God take care of me, too?"

"Of course," I cried, "of course." I told her about Helene and how one day I would marry her and that we would all live together in Arraggio.

Miranda pursed her lips. "I would not marry a food taster."

"And why not?"

"Because I would always fear for his life."

This thought had never occurred to me and after my disagreement with Federico I did not wish to think about it, so I said, "And who would you marry?"

"A prince."

"A prince, indeed. Is he anyone I know?"

"In Corsoli?" she said with wide eyes.

I smiled. "But it is good to aim high, Miranda. Birds that fly too close to the ground are the first to be shot out of the sky. How is Tommaso?"

"I neither know nor care," she shrugged, but I could hear mischief in her voice.

It was more complicated than that, which I discovered when I went to the kitchen. Tommaso, who was skinning some eels to put into a torta, barely nodded his head, but Luigi and the other boys crowded round, wanting to hear about the journey, and especially the story of Onionface, from my own lips. When I had finished I looked about for

Tommaso, but he had slipped away. Luigi said that two weeks after I had left, Tommaso had suffered a change of fortune.

Not content with seducing a merchant's wife (it was his first such conquest), Tommaso had boasted about to it his friends. Knowing how easy he was to tease, and also because he sometimes stretched the truth from here to Roma, they pretended to disbelieve him. "*È un impetuoso!*" Luigi said to much laughter.

So Tommaso had insisted the boys follow him the next time his lover's husband was in Arezzo to prove he was not lying. Unfortunately, he had not warned the woman's chambermaid that he was coming and so was unaware that the husband had returned. When Tommaso arrived in the dead of night, the husband and his brother were waiting with cudgels. They beat him, stripped him naked, locked Tommaso's balls in a chest and placed a razor in his hand. The husband said that if Tommaso was still in the house when he returned in an hour he would kill him. Fortunately, Tommaso's friends had heard the commotion, and when they saw the husband leave, they broke in and rescued him.

"He was in the hospital for more than a month. By the time he came out everyone in the valley knew what had happened."

Tommaso returned to his duties in the kitchen but when he was not working he sulked in his room. He refused to go outside because he could not stand to see the other boys pursuing Miranda through the palace. Since the four years to their betrothal passed without Miranda knowing, I saw no reason to tell her, and after what had happened even Tommaso could not insist upon it. As I had foreseen all along, God in His wisdom had known what was best.

As indeed God had known what was best for me. I turned my disappointment at not being given another position into good use, gathering herbs, mixing them, and taking small amounts to see what effect they had on me. Indeed, recording those effects was how my writing improved, and, watching Cecchi scurrying about at Federico's bidding, I was glad I had not been rewarded. I spent so much time with my experiments I resented each moment away from them. I did not tell anyone about them, and although Miranda and I shared the same room, she was too concerned with making her lips redder, her hair straighter, and her skin softer to notice. She cried when she thought boys did not look at her and acted aloof when they did. She practiced her lyre one day and the next refused to leave her bed. Within the space of a sentence she could be as sweet as sugar or as bitter as wormwood and many were the times I was glad there was a screen between us.

Federico's invitations to the painters and sculptors went unheeded, but *potta!* Some wit must have posted them in every piazza in Italy, for that summer artists swarmed over Corsoli like mosquitoes! They came from Roma, Venezia, and every town in between: students thrown out by their masters for laziness or thievery, beggars looking for free meals, debtors running from creditors. Half of them had never heard of a poem, did not know which way to hold a brush, and the only thing they had ever carved was a piece of bread. They got drunk, fought one another, and pestered the women.

Miranda and her friends walked arm in arm around Corsoli while these idiots wrestled one another to walk beside her. Sometimes she sat in the window, remaining there all morning, neglecting her lessons and duties, while the louts stood below serenading her. "They are like cats in heat," I said, and pissed out the window on them.

When Federico was told the artists were living for free he said, "Have them killed."

Instead Cecchi ordered the gatekeepers to forbid any more artists from entering Corsoli. He also announced a competition to design a new crest for Federico; the winner could stay but the rest had to leave. The first drawing showed Federico holding two cheetahs on a leash. He dismissed it with a wave of his hand: "It is too tame."

I was there when the second drawing was submitted. This time Federico's lip dropped to his chin. "Why," he asked the mealy-mouthed artist from Ravenna, "am I sitting next to a cow?"

"That is not a cow," the artist said, a little too haughtily. "It is a bear."

Federico had the man tied to a cow for a week to show him how mistaken he was. The competition was interrupted when a caravan arrived from Levantine carrying a lion and a giraffe—a gift from the sultan Federico had served. All of Corsoli thronged the streets singing and dancing. A great feast was held to which I wore my first silk shirt.

"Even the Medici did not have a lion *and* a giraffe," Federico boasted at the table.

Finally, another painter, Grazzari from Spoleto, designed a crest of Federico strangling a lion with his bare hands. Federico loved it. He ordered the other painters to leave before nightfall and commissioned Grazzari to paint a fresco of him. The fresco, which is in the main hall, shows Federico, as handsome and young as Michelangelo's David, sitting astride a white horse in the middle of battle. The horse is rearing on its hind legs while Federico, his black armor shining in the sunlight, leans over the horse's left flank to plunge a sword into a soldier's breast.

"Grazzari is a master," Federico said. "He captured me in my youth."

Federico took an interest in everything. He complimented Tommaso on a castle he was making out of sugar and marzipan. "Make a drawbridge," Federico said. "And make the turrets a little bit bigger." Like the fool he was, Tommaso resented Federico's suggestions.

One evening, I was standing in the courtyard before the evening meal. I had tasted a little too much juice of henbane and my head was spinning. I swore the clouds lying on the horizon were really sleeping dogs and I was about to warn everyone in the palace not to wake them, for fear they might attack us, when Tommaso came and stood next to me. He was almost eighteen in years and as tall as I. His hair, which had been cut into bangs, still refused to obey his comb, but his mouth had grown and his teeth now looked as if they belonged there rather than as if some devil had switched them with someone else's while he was asleep. But it was his eyes that had changed the most. They were melancholy and made him appear even older than he really was.

He said he knew that God had punished him for the way he had treated Miranda and that he was more sorry than words could say. "I still love her," he said quietly. These were the most words he had spoken to me since I had returned and very unlike the old Tommaso. He raised his head and, looking me boldly in the eye, said, "I beg you to find it in your heart to forgive me."

I said I forgave him. "Then please, speak to Miranda for me."

"You must speak to her yourself."

He shook his head. "I cannot."

"Then you should find yourself another girl. There are plenty in Corsoli. You are a fine young man—"

"No. I love her more than life itself."

Perhaps it was the henbane, but his sorrow reminded me of the loss of my Helene. "I cannot promise you anything," I replied, "but if the time is right and the occasion presents itself, I will press your suit with her."

He thanked me and wanted to kiss my hand, which I might have allowed him to do except that I felt, because of the henbane no doubt, that my hand would float away if I gave it to him. He said although we no longer had a contract, he would look out for me in the kitchen again. He was now assisting Luigi, and if I ever wanted any special food he would be happy to make it for me. Then he started boasting how he knew better than anyone else what was going on in the kitchen, and even though he was no longer a spy, he was in Federico's favor once again, and so on and so forth till I had to tell him to shut up! He was the same Tommaso after all!

The artists, the wild animals, the promise of new buildings gave Corsoli a festive air. Each day brought some new surprise, and so when Tommaso came to my door waving his arms in excitement, saying, "Come quick, there is someone you must see," I pulled my robe over my silk shirt, put on my new hat since it was raining, and followed him out of the palace.

"He has been to the Indies," Tommaso said breathlessly, as we hurried to the Piazza Del Vedura, "and seen men with three heads!"

The day was gray and the wind and rain spattered their marks all over it. As we entered the piazza I was surprised at the number of servants who were silently standing in a circle. Pushing my way to the front, I saw a tall thin man, with long gray matted hair covering the right half of his face. The part of his face I could see was deep brown and wrinkled like well-worn leather. His clothes were rags, his feet encased in old boots. A mass of charms and amulets hung from his neck and I could smell him from where I stood.

He dug his long grimy fingers into a pouch hanging from his waist and pulled out a piece of dark root. He raised it in the air, the rags falling away to reveal a thin, muscular arm. He lifted his face to the rain and cried out strange words in a hoarse, raspy voice. Then he opened his left eye and, looking us over, said, "Whoever places this root beneath their pillow will capture their heart's desire as surely as the fox captures the hare."

He walked to the half-blind washerwoman, placed the root in her hand, covered it with his own, and muttered in her ear. She clutched at his chest crying, "*Mille grazie, mille grazie.*"

"I want some," Tommaso blurted.

Ignoring the driving rain which was beating down, the magician placed his hand on Tommaso's brow. "I have more powerful potions for you." He pulled out a dove from inside his shirt. "Give this to Duke Federico and he will reward you with a long life; for this bird is descended from the one which brought the olive branch to Noah."

Tommaso thanked him over and over and promised to feed him and arrange for an introduction with Federico. "I will take you now," he said eagerly.

The magician smiled. In a moment he had gathered up his charms and potions and was striding toward the Weeping Steps.

"Are you not coming?" someone asked me.

I shook my head. Bile had risen in my stomach, phlegm had formed in my mouth. My knees trembled. I stood in the rain clenching my fists and asking God why He had yet again raised me up only to tear me down. Blood of the Antichrist! Just when my life was floating like a feather in a breeze, my brother, Vittore, had to show up!

xxvi

"I thought about you often, little brother," Vittore said. He had not been granted an audience with Federico yet, but he had been fed, and bathed, and given new clothes and was now lying on my bed eating an apple and stinking of perfumes. Even though I was the one who lived in the palazzo, who worked for Duke Federico, dressed in velvet, and was admired and respected all over Italy, and Vittore was just a thieving, lying tramp, the old fears still welled up in me.

"What do you want?" I snapped.

"Me?" he said, with the innocence of Christ. "Nothing. A roof over my head. A meal."

"I could have you hanged."

"Oh, Ugo. Is this still about those sheep?" In the light of the candle it was difficult to see his face—his hair still covered most of it, except for his one good eye. "Ah, my poor little brother."

He rose like a snake from the bed and began snooping about my room. "You should thank me. If it were not for me you would have spent your life running up and down Abbruzi chasing your flock. Now look at you. A silk shirt, a dagger with a bone handle. A fine room. A reputation. What is this?" He poked his finger into a cabinet. "Henbane?"

I snatched the leaves from him.

"And aconite? Who else knows about this, little brother?"

"No one," I said, pulling my knife.

"Ugo." He raised an eyebrow in mock surprise. "You would kill me for this?"

"No, but for killing my best friend Toro on the way back from the market."

Vittore sank to the floor in front of me. "Ugo, please!"

"Please what?" said a voice. The screen was moved aside and there stood Miranda, her dark brown hair mussed up, her small white teeth shining in the pale light of the candle, her soft plump feet sticking out of the bottom of her nightshirt.

"Miranda?" Vittore said, rising immediately. "*Che bella donzella!* Remember me? Your uncle Vittore?" He opened his arms as if to hold her and the thought of that bastard just touching her made me crazy. I stepped between them.

"Go to bed. Go to bed!"

"Ugo, let her stay! Aside from our father there are only us three DiFontes in the world. We should cherish these moments. Tomorrow we may part forever."

"Are you Vittore, my father's brother?"

Vittore bowed. "At your service, my princess."

Miranda saw the knife in my hand and her eyes widened in alarm. "What are you doing, Babbo?"

"He was showing me his knife," Vittore smiled. "As I was showing him mine." A long thin dagger appeared in his hand from out of nowhere. He smiled. "Two brothers showing one another how they keep the devil away. Nothing more."

I put my knife away and his dagger disappeared up his sleeve. Miranda sat on my bed.

"She is as beautiful as Elisabetta," Vittore smiled.

"You never knew her mother."

"Well, she does not get her looks from you." He winked at Miranda. "I remember when Ugo used to hide in his mother's skirts whenever there was a thunderstorm."

"You told me not to be afraid," Miranda accused me.

Vittore laughed. "We used to cut down long sticks and fence with them as if we were knights. Did Ugo not tell you?"

"Babbo hardly ever mentioned you. Where have you come from?"

"Everywhere." Vittore sat beside her.

Miranda stared at the twinkling amulets hanging from his neck. "Have you been to Venezia?" she asked.

"For a year I lived in a palazzo on the Grand Canal, one of the best years of my life."

"I wish I could go," Miranda sighed, hugging her knees to her chin. "Somebody once wanted to take me there."

"I have been to France, Germany, England too!"

"Is it true the English have tails? Papa said so."

"I did not!"

"Yes, you did!"

Vittore roared with laughter, and turning to me, said, "She is delightful. No, Miranda, they do not have tails. At least not the women I met. And I looked very carefully."

Miranda blushed.

"I have even been to the Indies."

"The Indies?" Miranda gasped.

"Yes, where men eat other men."

Miranda's eyes opened so wide I feared her pupils would pop out. "You saw them eat men?"

Vittore nodded. "They also smoke fire through their noses and walk naked all day long." He reached into a pouch and took out a tube with a small bowl at one end and which split into two small tubes at the other. From another pouch he withdrew some brown flakes which he placed into the bowl and then he put the two thin tubes into his nostrils. Using a taper, he lit the flakes and sucked in through his nose. Miranda and I watched as a second later, a long stream of smoke came out of his mouth. Miranda gasped in horror. "Is your stomach on fire?"

Vittore shook his head.

"What is it then?" I asked.

"They call it tabac. It cures whatever ails man. The stomach, the head, melancholy. Every illness known to man. In the Indies men and women smoke it all day long."

He puffed several more times until the bowl was empty and then put it away. "I have seen so many wondrous things. Countries where the sun shines every day and it rains only long enough to water the flowers. And flowers! Oh, Miranda! Flowers larger than a man's hands and all the colors of the rainbow!" He pointed a long arm toward the ceiling. "Trees that reach to the very top of the heavens and bear more fruit than in all of Eden." He sighed. "And yet wherever I am, I always come back to Corsoli."

"Why?" Miranda asked. "It is so boring here."

"Corsoli is my home. I want to die here." He crossed himself.

"Are you going to die?"

"We are all going to die someday."

"How true," I said. "Vittore, tell us what happened after you became a bandit."

"You were a bandit?" Miranda gasped.

Vittore shrugged. "Only to eat. Then they started paying me to rob people."

"Who did?" Miranda frowned.

"The duke of Ferrara, the Swiss, the emperor, the French. I became a soldier and I fought for whoever paid me." He leaned forward, his raspy voice dropping to a whisper. "I have seen horrors such as no man should ever witness." He shook his head as if a nightmare had suddenly risen in front of him. "After I stopped fighting I wanted to become a priest and devote myself to God."

"What stopped you?" I asked.

"I have a greater gift."

"Selling love potions?"

"Babbo, what is wrong with bringing love to people?"

"Exactly," said Vittore, gently patting her knee. "What higher calling can there be than spreading love?"

"Is that how you got the pox?"

"Babbo, why are you so mean?"

Vittore put his fingers to his lips. "Do not be angry with your father. He was trying to shield you from the bitterness of life. I only wish someone had done it for me." He turned to me. "I got it from a woman. I forgave her."

Slowly he moved his hair covering the one side of his face. Miranda cried out. Vittore's eye socket had fallen and twisted so that his eye peeked out between mounds of rotting flesh. The cheek was puckered and marked by deep lesions and his jaw had crumpled as if some spirit was eating his face from the inside. "I do not have long to live. I only ask to spend the rest of my days with those I love and those who love me."

"I think I am going to cry," I said.

"Two of my fingers are useless," Miranda said, holding out her right hand to Vittore, "and two of my toes."

With great solemnity Vittore took her hand in his, murmured a prayer and gently kissed the limp, withered fingers. Then he knelt on the floor and kissed her toes. Miranda watched him as if he was the pope himself. Still kneeling, he lifted a silver amulet from around his neck and placed it over Miranda's head so that it fell between her breasts. It was shaped as a hand in which the thumb and first two fingers were open and upright and the last two fingers were closed.

"For me?" Miranda exclaimed. "What is it?"

"The hand of Fatima. To ward off the evil eye."

"It does not appear to have done you any good," I said.

"It is so beautiful," Miranda breathed.

"Now it will protect both of us."

"I shall always wear it," she said.

I might as well have not been in the room!

"Is that rue?" Miranda pointed to a silver wildflower also hanging from Vittore's neck.

"Yes, rue and vervain, the flowers of Diana."

"And this one?"

Vittore caressed the silver, winged *fallo* softly between his fingers. "My love charm," he said.

What is it that makes evil so attractive? The uglier it is, the greater the mystery, the more attractive it becomes. I know people who would not dream of entering a lion's den and yet they think nothing of talking to the devil. Do they think they can overcome evil? That it will not touch them? Do they not see it is their very goodness that evil feeds on?

So it was with Miranda. "How can you be so cold to your brother?" she asked, after Vittore had left. "Can you not see the suffering he has endured?"

Christ on a cross! I thought I would pull my hair out! I told her of the times Vittore had beaten me when we were young. Of the lies he had told to get me in trouble with our father. How he refused to give me a few sheep to start my flock after I had looked after them in winter and in summer day and night, night and day, while he had been drinking and whoring. I told her how he had killed my best friend.

She nodded as if she understood, but then said, "Are we always to be judged on what we did yesterday? Did Christ not forgive those who had sinned?"

"A wolf is always a wolf, Miranda."

"But you are his brother and he is yours. I never had a brother or a sister. Or a mother."

She seemed to have forgotten everything I had just told her! I opened her hands, wanting to know if he had slipped her a potion. I pulled the necklace off her neck to make sure he had not rubbed something on it. How could he have turned her against me in a few short minutes? I became so enraged I said, "If I ever see you speaking to Vittore again I will beat you!"

Whenever the courtiers emerged from Federico's chamber they usually could not wait to speak ill of each other, but after Vittore's audience with Federico they were united in their fury.

"He said," Bernardo spluttered, "according to the stars Federico will have a new wife. He drew a circle on the ground, blabbed something in Latin, consulted a chicken leg, stared into Federico's eyes, and said, 'in two months and no longer than three!' "

"He gave him potions, too," Piero twitched. For once he was not laughing.

"Surely Federico did not believe him?" I asked.

"Not believe him? He has appointed him the court magician," Bernardo spat. "He will sit next to him at the table."

"When Federico does not get what he wants," I told Vittore, "he kills people."

"That will be my problem," he answered.

"Not just you. He will kill others—"

"Then pretend you do not know me. We are not brothers. We are not related at all."

"I will remember that," I replied.

From the day Vittore arrived the valley was covered with black clouds. The rain lashed the palace walls; the winds howled through the courtyard, shaking stones loose and uprooting trees older than time itself. In Corsoli, the peasants said that at night demons flew from the palace into the clouds and back again. An evil fungus spread through the hallways. I awoke with the smell of rot buried in my nose and I could not rid myself of it no matter how many perfumes I put on. I knew it was all because of Vittore.

At first, women were afraid of him, but I saw him take them softly by the wrist and pull them behind a pillar. When they emerged a moment later they were smiling and calm. It was not what he said because whenever I asked them to repeat it they could not. "It is the *way* he speaks," a woman shrugged, "his voice is like cream."

"He holds me with his eye," the old washerwoman sighed.

Holy Mother of God! To me his voice was like the bray of an ass mixed with the hiss of a serpent's tongue. Could they not see the evil riding on the back of his words? No, they shrugged, they could not. Or would not! Stupid, ignorant cows! It made no difference whether they were young or old, unmarried or married. Nor was it just the women, but the men, too! Only for them his voice lost its creamy softness and rang with the sounds of battle against the French or Germans. He told of sailing to the Indies and seeing nothing but sea for months on end. He spoke of whales as tall as ships and twice as long. Of a wave that rose out of the ocean and roared over the ship, swallowing all the men and disappearing again in less time than it took to tell it. He told of native women who went without clothes and were happy to do nothing but sport with sailors. He spoke of kings richer than the pope but who lived like peasants. Of brown men to whom gold was as common as grass. The servants listened to his tales and begged for more.

"They are in need of love," Vittore said.

I do not know what Vittore told Federico—he was careful not to speak when I was close by—but it must have been what Federico wanted to hear. Sometimes Vittore whispered something to make Federico laugh aloud. Then everyone else sat in silence, their eyes on the table for fear they were the objects of Vittore's ridicule.

Vittore advised Federico to eat ginger with every meal. My poor tongue hung out like a thirsty dog and I could taste nothing else. I wondered if Vittore was doing this so I would not be able to detect poisons. I woke up in the dead of night convinced he was working for Pia's relations in Venezia or perhaps Duke Sforza in Milano or some other prince Federico had injured. But I had not protected Federico with my life to have that sheep fucker kill him!

I asked Tommaso if Vittore ever came to the kitchen. "Why should he?" he said, annoyed that I had disturbed his sleep. I shook him angrily. "Does he give you anything to put in Federico's food?"

"No," he said indignantly. "He is *helping* Duke Federico."

That was all I needed to hear. Ever since Vittore had given Tommaso the dove, Tommaso worshiped Vittore because he hoped Vittore could help him win Miranda back.

"He will not," I said.

"Have *you* spoken to her?"

"The time has not been right."

He snorted and I must admit that even to my own ears my words were not convincing.

That evening, as Miranda was playing her lyre, I asked her if she ever thought of Tommaso. "No," she answered lightly, but the tremor in her voice betrayed her.

Within a few weeks, Vittore became as important to Federico as his cane, which he always used now because of his gout. I heard Vittore urging against the plans Federico had made on his way back from Milano.

"I think it would be more fitting for you to have another palace," Vittore said.

"Another palace," Federico mused as he chewed on a capon leg smothered in ginger.

"With your permission, Your Excellency," I said, "this excess of ginger is not good for your humors."

"Oh, Ugo," Federico said, "What do you know? What have you seen of the world? How many times have you been out of the valley? Once? And going to Milano does not count."

I stepped back as if I had been struck by lightning. Federico nudged Vittore and laughed, not seeing the rage welling in me. But Vittore did, and from the look in his eye, I realized he was afraid I would tell Federico we were brothers. The world had turned upside down! A few weeks ago, I was the one who did not want anyone to know, but now it was Vittore who felt I was a burden to him! I knew then he would not feel safe until he had killed me.

The morning after the full moon, the old washerwoman was found wandering naked in the yard muttering about Diana. No one knew which Diana she was talking about, and although there were several among the servants, they all denied it was them. Piero bled her and gave her some ointments but she would not say what had happened and kept falling to her knees, begging everyone's forgiveness. It was only one of many things which disturbed me. Miranda often fell asleep during her lessons. She was lax in her duties to Isabella, a courtier's wife. When I tried to speak to her she answered in a dull voice that she was doing as she always did. Tommaso refused to look me in the eye. Cecchi sulked about the palace. Bernardo did not leave his bed, claiming he was ill, and Piero was so afraid that he jumped at his own shadow. The palace was falling down around me, and it was all Vittore's doing.

Two boys stopped me at the stable entrance demanding to know what business I wanted. I was about to crack their heads when Vittore called out, "Let him in."

The horses looked at me with drowsy eyes as I walked past them. Vittore had made a home for himself at the back of the stable among the straw. Strange objects hung from the rafters—a jawbone of an ass, a lock of hair, a broken piece of a sculpture. The stony, gray palazzo was cold and drafty, but here the warm smell of horses and hay mingled in a pleasant manner and the odor of a sickly perfume made me want to lie down and sleep.

Vittore was sitting on a pile of straw. His hair was still matted, amulets and charms still hung from his neck, but his black robe was new as well as his boots and cape. It had taken me months to get new clothes and years before I had a new robe and boots. "You have done well for yourself," I said.

He leaned back, sucked on his *tabacca* and blew the smoke toward me. "God has been kind."

I was annoyed at the way I had to stand in front of him as if I was in his court. "What have you been giving Miranda?"

"Ah, Miranda, *mia angelica,*" he smiled.

"What have you been giving her?"

"What I give everyone, Ugo." He paused to suck his *tabacca*. "Love."

"Do not give her anything. I forbid it."

"Are you threatening me?"

"Yes, I am threatening you."

"It is too late for that."

"It is not too late," I said. I heard a noise and glanced around. The stable boys were approaching me, knives in hand.

"But it is, Ugo," Vittore said. His voice had changed. He sprang to his feet and pulled his dagger. "It is much too late."

The boys looked at one another, unsure of what to do. "He is the taster," one said stupidly.

I yelled loudly, and fortunately someone in the courtyard shouted back. As the boys turned I knocked them down and ran out of the stable, not stopping till I reached my room. With a pounding heart I sat by the window. From now on I had to be more careful; the next time I might not be so lucky.

It rained for seven days and seven nights. Clouds filled the sky until the day was as dark as night. A blanket of moss climbed the palace walls and a thin gray mist slipped through the corridors. Puddles formed in the dining hall, in the kitchen, and in my room. Fevers struck. Cecchi took to his bed, Bernardo moaned all day, and Federico had bad attacks of phlegm. I, too, caught a cold and could not shake it. Only Vittore did not fall ill. He had less than a month to fulfill his promise to Federico, but he did not seem concerned. Every night I prayed he would fail and that Federico would drive him out of the valley or throw him down the mountain.

Miranda ate little and stared at the rain for hours. She was no longer interested in boys and did not comb her hair. Sometimes when I was not experimenting with my herbs—I took small doses of arsenic every day as well as meadow saffron—I tried to follow her, but she slipped away from me and my head would grow so heavy I had to lie down. I asked Bernardo if the stars were affecting her.

"When was she born?"

"Three days after Corpus Christi." I remembered because Elisabetta had picked wild roses to throw in the procession, but the petals had caught in her hair and she had looked so pretty I had begged her to leave them there.

Bernardo grunted. "The crab. Behavior like that is to be expected. She will probably live to be at least seventy years old. Then again she might not."

Piero said it was probably her monthly courses and that he would know better when the moon was full in three days' time. He said he would be happy to bleed her.

"I will die before that pig touches me!" Miranda shouted.

"He saved you when you almost died from the cold."

Whatever I said caused her to be angry, even little things. When I remarked I had seen her talking to Tommaso, she cried, "You are spying on me!" Her voice trailed off and she averted her eyes from the window. Below us in Emilia's garden, Vittore was talking to the old washerwoman.

"It has to do with Vittore, has it not?" I said.

"No."

"It has!"

"No!" she screamed. "No! NO! NO! NO!"

Just then Vittore looked up at me and smiled.

The night of the next full moon, I slipped away from the table while Septivus was reading Dante's *Purgatory*, and into the stable. The stable boys were still eating in the servants' hall. At the back, where Vittore had made a space for himself, I climbed to the top of a pile of straw near the roof and waited. Amulets and charms hung everywhere, and that strange scent which had made me drowsy was there again.

I must have fallen asleep for I was awoken by muttered voices. It was dark except for the dim light of a candle. Several people sat on the ground with their backs to me sipping from a bowl which they passed to one another. Vittore sat facing them, stroking something in his lap. He spoke to it in a low voice and rubbed its back as one might pet a kitten. Then he held it up for all to see. It was not a kitten, but a toad! He *was* an *incantatore*. A witch! And this was a witch's sabbat. I wanted to tell Federico right away, but I stayed, for I had never seen a sabbat before.

One by one the men and women leaned forward and licked the toad. I have done some things that God will judge me for, like screwing a sheep, but I have never ever licked a toad. After a moment or two, a man stood up and jumped around as if the devil had entered his soul. It was Tommaso! That fool! Then the others rose to their feet stumbling about like newborn calves. They tried to walk, but the space was so small that they all bumped into one another. One woman turned around and around till she fell down, her eyes wide open, her mouth in a twisted smile. Another man raised his arms above his head and cried out. Vittore clapped his hand over his mouth with such force the man sank to the ground and did not speak another word. The woman lying on the ground turned her head and was staring straight at me. She raised her arm and pointed, but no one noticed.

I do not know how long they stumbled about like this till Vittore, who had turned his back on them, raised his arms in the air, and hissed, "I renounce Jesus Christ!"

"I renounce Jesus Christ!" they repeated. Then Vittore said, "The Madonna is a whore! Christ is a liar. I deny God!"

Potta! Even if God had not spoken to me, I had never denied Him. I prayed that if He was looking down on us that He would see that although I was here in the stable I was not part of this. Vittore said other blasphemies and each time they repeated his words with more fervor. A woman giggled and sang, "The Madonna is a whore. The Madonna is a whore."

Vittore called out softly, "*Diana, bella Diana.* Bring your horse."

Was this the Diana the old washerwoman had talked about? I wondered who she was and how she was going to get a horse in there because it was already so crowded.

Then Vittore asked them if they saw his mighty head. They said they did, but how could they? No one had left and the horses were still on the other side of the straw. They were under his spell!

"Obey him!" Vittore said and turned around. *Jesus in sancto!* He was wearing goats' horns on his head! I wanted to laugh, but then he lifted his shirt and showed himself. "*Sarete tutti nudi,*" he said, and they began to take off their clothes! Suddenly I saw that one of the women was Miranda! I am ashamed to say I could not look away. She was so young, so beautiful. Her breasts small and upturned, her stomach so flat, her thighs fully formed and her buttocks round and full. I was seized with rage. Yet I waited.

The old washerwoman with sagging breasts and thighs like tree trunks knelt in front of Vittore and kissed his *fallo.* He turned around and presented his *culo* to her. She pulled his cheeks apart and gave him the "*Osculum infame.*" Vittore turned around and laid his hand on her brow. She moaned and fell to the ground. I could not believe my eyes! Could this be happening here? Here in Duke Federico's stables while the rest of the palace was fast asleep a few yards away? But there was more.

Tommaso knelt in front of Vittore, kissed his *fallo* too, and then paid homage to Vittore's *culo.* Six of them did this and when they had finished they fell on one another and made love like wild beasts. Then it was Miranda's turn and there was no one for her to make love to except Vittore. He put his hand on the back of her head. I had seen enough and no longer cared if he conjured up demons or if he was the devil himself. Shouting the names of God, Jesus Christ, and the Holy Ghost, I threw myself down from the straw and ran at Vittore with my knife aiming for his good eye. The others screamed when they saw me, but I was past them before they could stop me. Vittore spat and raised his arm. His eye was completely black. He *was* the devil! My hand stopped as if some force was pushing against it! Vittore grasped my wrist, but I stabbed him! I stabbed him in the chest!

We fell on the ground. Other men threw themselves on top of me and I slashed at them with my knife. Someone pulled my clothes, another bit my wrist. The candles must have fallen over for suddenly flames were licking at the wet straw and smoke filled the stable. I caught hold of Miranda, but she fought me with the strength of a man so I was forced to crack her about the face and bang her head into the wall. I threw her over my shoulder. Now the flames were arching toward the roof. The horses—whinnying, bucking, and shrieking with fear—broke from their ties. Everyone was fighting to get past the flames and the horses. The fire shot through the roof, leaped over us, and now we were in hell itself! A man was trampled by a horse in front of me and I tripped over him. Miranda fell out of my arms. Part of the roof collapsed and the burning embers fell on the panicked horses. I pulled Miranda up, knifed another man in my way (I prayed it was Vittore), and staggered out of the stable, imps of flame clinging to my hose and Miranda's hair.

The air was filled with wailing, the crying of men and women, and the neighing of horses. The hounds were howling and barking, the fire bells chimed, and the great bell of the Duomo Santa Caterina added its frantic voice to the noise. Servants poured out of the palace. I carried Miranda through Emilia's garden to the back entrance of the palazzo and up the stairs to our room. Her eyes were clouded over; she was calling to Diana and singing songs to the devil. I stuffed rags in her mouth, tied her down to the bed, and hurried back to the courtyard where the fire roared, its flames fanned by a black wind.

Cecchi organized the servants to throw water onto the blaze, but Federico kept forcing them into the stable to rescue his horses. Then just when it appeared that the stable would be destroyed, lightning struck the palace, the thunder rolled, and the rain poured down. The flames hissed and sizzled till at last they shrank and withered into sodden defeat.

More than half the stable was destroyed as well as ten horses. Their pitiful cries and the smell of their burning flesh lingered for days.

When guards had not arrested me or Miranda by early morning, I decided to tell Federico what I had seen. He was already awake in his chamber and to my surprise Vittore was there as well. One of his hands was bandaged, but otherwise he appeared unharmed. Even more confusing, Federico was in a good mood.

"My Lord," I began, "permit me to say what a terrible trial you have been through—"

"Ugo, horses can be replaced. The Jew Piero will pay. Vittore says he was conducting sabbats in the stables."

"Piero?"

"Yes, he is on the rack. He will confess." I wanted to laugh; Piero conducting sabbats? "But, I have good news," Federico went on. "Vittore said the woman I have been looking for has been living here the whole time."

"Here in the palace?" I repeated. Each new pronouncement was crazier than the last. "Who is it?"

"Your daughter," Federico smiled, "Miranda."

"You are not pleased?"

"Pleased? I am honored. Heaven has blessed me," I cried.

"Her moon complements the duke's perfectly," Vittore smiled. "I want her to sit at my table tonight," Federico said.

"Yes, Your Honor."

"Make sure she rests well," Vittore added.

I walked back to my room, my head whirling as if I had ingested meadow saffron, belladonna, and henbane all at the same time. Miranda, my daughter, Miranda my child, was to sit at Federico's table. I knew why Vittore had done this. He had promised to find Federico a bride in two months and now those two months were almost up. If he could not have Miranda then he would give her to Federico. But would Federico really take my precious Miranda for his mistress? Surely not. She is too young, I said to myself, but what did that matter to Federico? She was no longer a virgin, but he did not know that, nor would he care. How would Miranda feel? What if she disappointed him or said something rude or screamed or laughed at the wrong time? The man who had laughed at my joke on the way to Milano was still in prison. The whore who had banged her head in Federico's carriage was dead in a ditch for all I knew. A peasant who had sung obscene verses at Carnevale had been beheaded. And what about me? Was I going to have to taste Federico's food while my daughter sat at his table? Surely, Federico would not allow that to happen.

Miranda had fallen into such a deep sleep that instead of waking her I walked through the palace and listened to the rumors of magic and witchcraft. Two stable boys and the old washerwoman had burned to death. Another body had been burned so badly no one could tell if it was a man or a woman. I passed by the kitchen where Tommaso was baking bread. So he had also escaped. He caught my eye and started to say something, but there were servants everywhere. Instead he followed me down the hallway, whispering, "Ugo, I must speak with you." I did not stop to listen. There was nothing he could say that was of interest to me.

Later in the day, Vittore advised Federico to spare Piero from more torture. "It is because Vittore does not know how to cure Federico's gout or any of his other diseases," Cecchi said. I heard that with bleeding fingers, the nails of his right hand had been removed, and, jabbering like a fool, Piero knelt in front of Vittore, kissed the hem of his robe, and swore allegiance to him.

I wanted to convince Miranda once and for all of Vittore's wickedness, but when she woke she remembered nothing! *Niente!* She stared at me, her pupils huge and round, as if she did not know me. She chewed on her lips, complaining of a metal taste in her mouth. I poured a basin of water and washed her face.

"What is that smell?" she asked.

She was still so young, so innocent. "It is nothing. Do not trouble yourself."

"What is it?" she said impatiently, and, pushing my hand away, went to the window.

"There was a fire in the stable. Some horses were—"

Her body stiffened. Her memory was wakening. She looked at me fiercely. "Vittore? I must—"

"Miranda—"

She pulled away. "Is he well? I must find him!"

I followed her to the door. "Forget Vittore."

She whirled around. "Is he dead?"

Christ on a cross! It was my father all over again!

She flew at me and beat me with her fists. "I hate you," she screamed, "I hate you."

"Vittore does not care about you!" I cried.

"He is alive then?" And seeing my face, she laughed. "He is alive!"

"He sold you," I said, grasping her arms. She did not understand. "He said you would make a perfect wife for Federico!"

Who knows the mind of a woman? In Castiglione's *The Courtier*, which Septivus sometimes read to Federico, the ideal woman is gracious, knowledgeable, prudent, generous, virtuous, remaining free from gossip, and is beautiful and talented as well. *Potta!* Are they talking about women made of flesh and blood? Did those women work in the fields like Elisabetta until the hour Miranda was born?

Did any of them witness the joy of a naked woman turning cart-wheels like Agnese? Did any of their women have Helene's courage or Miranda's strength? No, they lived in a different world.

All afternoon Miranda studied her hair in the mirror. It had always been a source of great pride, but because of the fire, the ends were ragged and of different lengths. Here and there were bald patches where an ember had singed her. Something had to be done, but I feared saying anything lest I upset her even more. At last I could not stand it and I said, "Perhaps you could wear a wig or maybe a scarf the way Bianca—"

As if to silence me, Miranda took a knife and began hacking away at her hair as if she was possessed by a devil. I tried to stop her and after a struggle she allowed me to wrest the knife away.

"Are you mad?" I cried. "You are to sit at Federico's table tonight."

She was not upset at all; indeed, she smiled at me as if I was a child and said, "Tell Lavinia and Beatrice to come here quickly."

These were her closest friends, who, when they heard what was going to happen, came at once. They were horrified at the sight of her hair, but Miranda cheerfully said that she had tried to cut it herself, but had made some mistakes and needed their help. They were only too happy to do so and, laughing and giggling, they cut it quite short except for a small curl that hung down over one eye. Then they painted her face and rouged her mouth. Miranda cleverly questioned them to see if they knew she had been part of the sabbat—they did not. Beatrice lent her an exquisite blue *camora* with pictures of colored birds woven into the sleeves. Miranda borrowed a necklace from Isabella and when she laid it against the top of her breasts I would have defied any man in Italy not to want to place his head there.

In the midst of this, Tommaso came to the door. "You cut your hair," he said, unable to hide his surprise.

Miranda turned from her dressing table. "You do not like it?"

"No. Yes, I—I am not used to it," he stammered. "Forgive me."

"And my dress?" She stood up and turned around for him. Tommaso grew red in the face. He said he had never seen anything so beautiful. But she was not finished. "What about my shoes?" And as her friends giggled, she stretched her foot toward him, displaying one of her slender ankles. Fearing the poor boy would faint, I asked him why he had come.

"Luigi wants to know if there are any particular dishes Miranda would like this evening."

"Mangiabianco," Miranda replied without hesitation.

"There is not time enough," Tommaso said.

"Hmm . . ." she frowned. "Then . . . some . . . veal . . ."

He nodded. "Sprinkled with salt and fennel?"

"Yes," Miranda replied.

"With marjoram and parsley and herbs," Lavinia laughed.

"Yes. Yes, like that," Miranda said, clapping her hands with delight.

"And rolled and put on the spit," Beatrice added.

Tommaso stood in the middle of the room staring at the floor. "And for dessert?" he asked.

Miranda raised her head, showing off her long white neck. "Cheesecake. And prosciutto."

"With the cheesecake?"

"No," she said, with disdain. "Before the cheesecake."

Tommaso nodded again and was about to leave when Miranda added, "With melon."

Tommaso stopped. "Prosciutto with melon?"

"Yes," she said. "With melon," as if everyone knew that was the way it should be. Then she turned back to the mirror as the girls burst into laughter once again.

Even though she was ready in time for dinner, Miranda arrived just late enough so that everyone would see her entrance. She apologized to Federico but offered no explanation, sat opposite him and adjusted the front of her *camora* bringing attention to her breasts as Bianca used to do. Then she smiled at Federico. I had seen her practice that smile in the mirror—her lips parted slightly, her eyebrows furrowed, and the dimples in her cheeks revealed themselves like two soft pearls.

Federico beamed. "A little princess."

The dinner continued as all dinners did. Federico was consumed with his food. Every now and then he glanced at Miranda, but did not say anything. The courtiers spoke to one another, but since Federico did not speak to Miranda, nor did they. I had been afraid that she might say something out of turn; now I worried that she might cry out of neglect. However Miranda felt, her face remained calm as if she had attended dinners like this all her life. Then Tommaso served the prosciutto with melon.

"An excellent combination," Cecchi said.

"Yes," Federico agreed, sucking on his fingers. "Luigi is a far better cook than Cristoforo ever was," he said, and called Luigi to the table.

Miranda's face still did not change. Luigi must have thought something was wrong—that was the only reason the chef was ever called—and, rushing to the table, said, "Your Excellency, if the prosciutto with melon does not please you I can easily change it. It was not a dish of mine and I—"

"Whose was it then, Tommaso's?"

"No, My Lord. Your Illustrious Highness, it would not be seemly to betray one whose beauty cannot compete with her experience—"

"It was your idea?" Federico asked Miranda.

She bowed her head modestly. "Yes, Your Excellency."

"Forgive her ignorance," Luigi chuckled, "I will prepare—"

"You will prepare nothing," said Federico. "It was excellent. Make some more."

For the rest of the meal Miranda was included in the conversation and her opinion asked on every subject. Most of the time she said she had no knowledge of such things, but once she quoted from Dante and another time from Polizian. Septivus had taught her well. She said she preferred the poetry of the people to that of the courts.

"Could you favor us with such a poem?" Federico asked.

"If it would please the duke."

"Yes," Federico said, "it would please me."

Carefully laying her spoon next to her trencher, Miranda closed her eyes and folded her hands. "My favorite poem in all the world goes like this." She cleared her throat and recited.

> Although the sun burns hot above
> I shake and shiver with the chill of love.

The table was quiet. "Is that it?" Bernardo laughed.

"It does not take many words to win a lover's heart," Miranda replied lightly. "Just the right ones."

"*Brava!*" Federico applauded, and, pointing to Septivus, added, "That is true of everything."

Miranda blushed, "Excuse me, honored duke, if I have spoken too much on a subject which women have no place—"

"No, no, no," said Federico. "Please honor us with your presence whenever we dine," and farted loudly to seal his announcement. Miranda thanked everyone, especially Duke Federico, patted Nero on the head, and left the table. She had not glanced even once at Vittore throughout the meal.

Federico followed her with his eyes until she had left the room. "I traveled all the way to Milano to look for a princess and she has been here the whole time."

Afterward, Miranda rushed up to me asking, "Babbo, what did Duke Federico say?"

I assured her that he had spoken highly of her and that she had conducted herself well. She was delighted and chitter-chatted with her friends, discussing what she had said, what had been said to her, what she had said back and so on and so on, the telling of which took three times longer than the event itself. When at last they left, she said, "Babbo, when I become a rich woman in the court, I will take care of you."

I held her in my arms and wondered what Federico had in mind for her. So much had happened in one day—the sabbat and the fire were already distant memories—that my thoughts were as jumbled as leaves in a storm. Later that evening, I stood in the courtyard looking up at the stars when Tommaso came to my side. We leaned over the wall looking down at the huddled houses of Corsoli bathing in the light of the moon. He said, "I swear I did not tell Miranda to go to the sabbat."

It amused me to think that he thought that he could convince Miranda to do something. "No," I laughed, "you cannot make Miranda do anything she does not want to do." He nibbled his nails. "Then why did you give Miranda to Federico?"

"I did not give her to Federico. Vittore did."

"What will you do about it?"

"Nothing. Why?"

His eyes became as round as the moon. "But Miranda cannot be with Federico!"

"Why not?"

"But she is—" His eyes closed, he gripped the wall.

"You may not have told her to go to the sabbat," I said, "but you did not stop her."

He hung his head. "It was she who made *me* go," he replied.

That night I had bad dreams. I do not know if it was because of the pinches of arsenic I had been taking, but I dreamed Corsoli was drenched in blood. No matter how many times I awoke I always fell back into the same dream. Blood flowed from everywhere. From every mouth, from every vessel, from the pores of my skin, and from the walls of the palazzo.

"We must leave," I said to Miranda the next morning. "I can find work in Firenze or Bologna. Maybe we could go to Roma."

She looked at me as if I had lost my senses. "Why, Babbo?"

"Something terrible is going to happen. I feel it."

"Babbo, you were dreaming again."

"Yes, but I dreamed it in the morning when the truth speaks clearer because it is farther away from the body."

"Then you must pray that you do not have bad dreams, Babbo."

"No, we must leave."

"But how can I?" she cried. "Duke Federico has ordered the dressmaker to make some new dresses for me." She stood up and danced around the room. "I am going to be a princess!"

"You are doing this to make Vittore jealous."

"Vittore?" she answered. "Who is Vittore?"

From then on Miranda ate at Federico's table every night. On the third meal, Federico pushed Nero off the seat so that Miranda could sit next to him. Soon she was imitating birds and animals, even some of the courtiers. Within a week, she was the life of the dinners and I could not have been happier. Even so, I was not prepared when a servant knocked on my door while Miranda was taking her lessons and said, "Federico is on his way to see you."

I did not have time to ask why. Like a madman, I pulled the large chest over to my table and in one sweep pushed every potion, herb, poison, antidote, all my experiments and all my writings into it. I had just lit some incense and spices and piled up the cushions on the bed when Federico entered.

I bowed. "I am honored, My Lord."

Federico coughed and waved his hat at the wisps of smoke. I snuffed out the candles and opened the window. He sat down on the chest. In my haste I had not closed it properly and part of my writing was sticking out.

"What does Miranda like?" Federico asked. "Vittore said you would know."

I might have known that bastard was behind this. "She likes to sing and play the lyre."

"I know that."

"When she was younger she used to stand in the window when the sun was setting and sing."

"What else?"

I could not think of anything because I was so worried that he might see the writing sticking out of the chest. I said on the farm she spoke to the animals as if they were her friends, and that she liked to ride on my back.

"I do not want to know what she liked when she was three! I want to know what she likes now! What sort of jewelry? What kind of perfumes? What styles of dress?"

"She likes all manner of jewelry and perfumes."

"She does not like rose water."

"All except rose water," I agreed.

He said, "You have known her all your life and I only a few days, yet I know her better than you do."

He stood up, sniffed the air, put on his hat and left. I opened my chest and rescued my experiments, but I could not work on them. Something Federico had said disturbed me. How could he know Miranda better than I? It was not possible. *I* knew Miranda's moods. I knew how she jumped up and down when she was happy. How she sang to stop her loneliness. How she bit her bottom lip when she was upset. What else was there to know? What father knew more about his daughter than I did? Did Cecchi know more about Giulia? Did Federico know more about his sons? No! Miranda would like any perfume because she had never had any of her own. She had never owned jewelry and her dresses had always belonged to someone else. She would be pleased with anything Federico gave her.

The next day Federico gave Miranda a gold bracelet and a peacock feather. The day after a statue and a tiara. The day after that a diamond-studded hand mirror. By the end of the week, we were so flooded with gifts we had no room to sleep. Federico evicted three clerks from the room next to ours and gave it to Miranda. A door was made between our rooms. Federico told Miranda to decorate her room however she pleased. She wanted the ceiling painted with stars, the floors covered with carpets, and on the wall opposite her bed, she told Grazzari to paint a picture of the Madonna and child.

"Ask her if I can paint something different," Grazzari complained. "I have painted the baby Jesus sitting in the Madonna's lap, standing on her knee, and lying in her arms. I have painted him with blond hair, black hair, curly hair, and no hair. I've drawn him asleep and awake, smiling at the sky, pointing in a book, and blessing a lion. I am tired of painting the Madonna, too. I want to paint something else."

Miranda insisted on a Madonna and child and so that is what Grazzari painted.

Miranda rose late and spent hours arranging her new furniture. She ignored her lessons. Federico said, "She does not need any more schooling. She is already cleverer than the rest of the court put together."

I hoped he would continue to think so because even though I loved Miranda more than life itself, sometimes she had no idea what she was talking about and when she became upset, her voice squeaked. Federico did not care. "She has the neck of a swan," he said at the table. "Her hair is like a dark river. Her eyes glow like fireflies." He asked me if her pee smelled like bergamot.

"Her pee? I do not know."

"You are her father. How can you not know what her pee smells like?"

And do you know, I wanted to ask him what his son's turds smell like? But I said nothing. It did not matter what I or anyone said. *Completamente in adorazione!* He worshiped her. He hid behind columns to watch her walk by while the servants carried on as if he was not there. He ordered his barbers to tease his wispy hairs into different shapes to please her. Piero made sweet-smelling potions for his skin, and two tailors worked day and night sewing him new robes and hose and hats.

"Federico is in love," the palace tittered. Just how deeply in love I saw one evening at dinner when Miranda related how she used to serenade her goats. Federico had just lifted a heaping spoon of finely chopped salted tongue mixed with spices and vinegar to his mouth when Miranda stayed his arm and began to sing.

Oi me! I thought, she is separating Federico from his food! But Federico did not say a word. He sat there, the spoon inches from his gaping cave while Miranda sang three verses of her little song. Then, when she had finished, she let go of his arm.

"Wonderful," Federico clapped.

"She has a voice," Septivus mused, "which is not so much like a bird, but an angel."

"Yes, but not any angel," Bernardo chimed in, "an angel who has been close to God."

"Surely all angels are close to God," said Vittore. "That is why they are angels." He was wearing a handsome green velvet jacket and matching hose, although his hair was still unkempt and his chest still covered with charms and talismans.

"That is it, Vittore," Federico said. "She *is* an angel."

Every day for a week Federico ate a soup of cloves, laurel, celery, and artichoke followed by a baked pie of layered ham and mince lambs' kidney doused in wine. There was something else in it, too.

"Sliced goats' balls," Tommaso said, as we stood in the courtyard watching the sunset. "Sprinkled with salt, cinnamon, and pepper."

That was all he had time to say because just then Federico rushed up to us and, pointing at the band of fire scorching the mountaintops, cried, "Do you see? The sun!" He took a deep breath and spouted:

> My heart is like the sun
> For when you leave the room
> Then I am filled with gloom
> And . . . and . . .

We waited. He took a breath, closed his eyes. Tommaso was standing next to me, and Federico was standing slightly in front of us. Tommaso's hand moved to his dagger.

"My heart is like the sun," Federico said again.

The dagger was halfway out of its sheath.

"For when you leave the room—"

I put my hand on Tommaso's arm to prevent him from pulling the dagger out any farther.

"A sonnet," Federico roared. "I want to write a sonnet."

He whirled around. My hand was back in its place and so was Tommaso's dagger. "I think it will be a wonderful expression of love, Your Excellency."

"So do I. I must find Septivus." And he rushed off.

Tommaso's face was white with rage. "I could have—" he began.

I inclined my head to the three guards standing in the doorway of the palace. "We would have both been killed and I will not die for your foolishness!"

"And I will not let Miranda die because of your selfishness," he cried, with such determination that for the first time I believed him.

Later that evening, I walked by Septivus's room. He was working by candlelight, his hair in disarray, muttering those same lines over and over again:

> My heart is like the sun
> For when you leave the room
> Then I am filled with gloom. . . .

Septivus has not slept since Federico fell in love. No one has. Love has changed Federico so much that even those who know him well do not know what to expect. He pulled Cecchi's beard and made fun of Piero's giggling. He no longer believed the world was in the shape of a triangle, but in the shape of a heart. He surprised us by saying,

"Surely, it is as Cicero said: 'There is nothing that cannot be achieved with a little kindness. Dare I say love?'"

We cheered and applauded. Federico quoting Cicero! He neither raped Miranda nor forced himself on her in any other way. He wanted her to love him. Love had bloomed in him, and although the walls of anger and cruelty were hardly collapsing in the face of its power, here and there a small hole appeared. As if she knew this, Miranda did her best to open them wider. "I want to go to Venezia, ride a camel, and meet the Holy Father," she announced, during a game of backgammon.

Federico's eyes crinkled with delight and disappeared between the fat folds on his face. "I will take you to Venezia next year and I will buy you a camel."

"And the pope?" Miranda asked. She removed several of Federico's pieces and clapped her hands with glee.

"Not the pope," Federico answered.

"Why not?" Miranda demanded.

"Because I said so!" Federico snarled. Miranda continued to play as if she had not heard him. Then she looked up and, smiling innocently, said, "The Federico I heard about as a child used to spit out popes as if they were fennel seeds. Oh, look," she said, moving a piece on the board. "I win. Again. Now can we go to Roma?"

Federico stared at her. I could see he wanted to smile, but his anger would not allow him. "We will see," he said gruffly.

He doted on Miranda's every word and sometimes found meanings in them she did not intend. When she said in passing that the other girls had mocked her when she first came to the palace, Federico ordered them into the hall—some were now married with children— and threatened to cut out their tongues if they ever spoke badly to Miranda again.

I pleaded with her to be cautious. Federico had once given jewels to a whore only to accuse her the next day of stealing them. "Are you comparing me to a whore?" Miranda asked.

"Of course not. I just beg you to be careful."

She rolled her eyes. "You worry too much."

Because Federico was in love with my daughter, women wanted to seduce me. *Potta!* It had been a long time since I had been with a woman, but by keeping the vision of Helene in front of me, I was able to resist them.

One night I saw Federico and Vittore standing beneath a tree in Emilia's garden. As I watched, Vittore raised his arms to the moon and uttered a prayer which Federico repeated. Then Vittore uncovered a bowl he was carrying, and Federico, after first looking around to make sure no one was watching, dipped his hand into the bowl, took out some paste, and rubbed it on his testes. I hurried to the kitchen maid and told her what I had seen.

"What is Federico eating?" she asked.

I told her about the soup with cloves, the pie of layered ham, and the sliced goats' balls.

"Aphrodisiacs," she giggled.

But they cannot be working, I thought to myself. Now I knew why Federico had not tried to rape Miranda or force himself upon her. He could not get it up. I prayed that this would not alter his love for her or change his good humor.

There was still reason to fear Federico. At breakfast, Miranda mentioned that roses were her favorite flower. Federico ordered twenty servants to gather all the roses in the valley and present them to Miranda at dinner. "I want to surprise her."

But roses were no longer in bloom. Enraged, Federico ordered the servants imprisoned and the eldest one put on the rack.

"Ask Federico to release them," I said to Miranda. "It is not their fault."

Miranda refused. "I cannot. He is doing it for me. To show how much he loves me."

"You will make enemies."

"Me?" She picked up a hand mirror and brushed her hair. "But I have done nothing."

"You have forgotten where you came from."

"Why should I want to remember?" she laughed.

"This is not how I raised you."

"Really?" She held up the mirror so I could see my face in it next to hers. "You think you are so different from me? Everything I am, I have learned from you. For the first time in my life someone is giving me everything I want and you are jealous."

"I am trying to protect you."

"Who from?"

"Yourself," I answered.

She laid the mirror down. "I did not think you would say who you really meant."

I grasped her shoulders. She glanced at my hands as if they were not worthy to touch her. I struck her and she fell to the ground holding her cheek. Picking her up, I begged her forgiveness. She got up slowly, her eyes cold, her cheek red from the mark of my hand.

"If you ever do that again, I will tell Federico."

I walked out and closed the door between us.

Every day the world changed a little more. Miranda spent her time becoming a princess, Federico spent his chasing Miranda and left the running of the palazzo to Vittore. Vittore supervised the wool contracts. He banned Bernardo from giving astrological readings and forced Piero to show him how he made his potions. He forbade Septivus from reading to Federico and argued with Cecchi. Guards accompanied him wherever he went. First two, then four.

Not long after, I heard a shuffling outside my door. When I opened it, Cecchi and Septivus entered quickly. "Candles are hard to come by," Checchi said, and snuffed mine out. We stood in the darkness, the moonlight casting our faces in shadow. Cecchi cleared his throat as he always did before he said something important. "We are concerned about the fate of Corsoli. We feel because Duke Federico is preoccupied, he is not listening to the best advice."

"Whose advice is he listening to?"

"Vittore's." Cecchi tugged at his beard.

"He has made friends with the soldiers," Septivus said. In other words, he was too well guarded for an ordinary assassination.

"Why are you telling me this?"

"You have served the duke well," Cecchi said carefully. "He is marrying your daughter. You are close to him. Maybe you can think of some way to save Corsoli."

A bat flew in the window and around the room, its wings beating frantically in the darkness. "An omen!" Septivus said.

But what sort of omen? I wondered, when the bat flew out again. "If I did something to help Corsoli—"

"We will be forever in your debt." Cecchi replied. We grasped one another's arms.

After they had gone I sat by the window. It was not raining as it is at this moment, but the stars were low enough for me to touch and the hills cutting into the dark, velvet sky looked more like a painting of nature than nature itself. Indeed, nothing was real anymore. Something had just happened that I was only just grasping. I, Ugo DiFonte, food taster to Duke Federico Basillione DiVincelli, was being treated like a courtier.

xxviii

I had always tried to *save* lives, be it Miranda's, my own, or
Federico's. Now I was being asked to become an assassin. Even
though I had tried to kill Vittore in the stable, planning his death
disturbed me. I wondered if God was watching. I found myself
looking over my shoulder, smiling for no reason other than I was
afraid that my face would betray my thoughts. Then, I remembered
how Vittore had killed Toro, my best friend, how he had almost
raped Miranda and . . . things, roused me . . . to . . . a passi—

I cannot write after I have drunk henbane juice. My eyes become
confused, things grow bigger and smaller, and nothing is what it
appears to be. My head aches. I will continue later.

The abbot Tottorini used to say God sees everything, but if that is
so then why had He allowed Vittore to curse Him and not avenge
Himself? Is He waiting, and if so, for what? He could avenge Himself
at any time. But, if it was as I thought, that God does *not* see everything, then surely it is the duty of those who *do* see, to take up arms
on His behalf. If Vittore was the devil, as he said he was, then I was
a soldier of Christ. Besides, if Vittore was planning to kill me, I knew
he did not concern himself if God saw him or not! Vittore did not care
if there was a God. So whenever the scepter of doubt hovered above
me, I contemplated the worthiness of my task and was filled with
pride that God had selected me to achieve it, and I swore I would not
abandon my effort unless I died doing so.

As we had agreed, ambushing Vittore was impossible because of
his guards, and to poison him would have been equally difficult. So
I watched and waited and asked questions of the servants, some of
whom were so in love with him that they told me far more than I ever
wanted to know. *Jesus in sancto!* What stupid women they were! But
it was through them that I discovered that Vittore never allowed
anyone in his room and whenever he left it, he not only locked the
door, but also posted a guard outside until he returned. That had to be
because there was something he wanted to hide and I was determined
to see what it was.

I dared not bribe a guard because the guard might take the money and tell Vittore, so for two weeks I plotted, and at the end of them I was no closer to a plan than I was at the beginning. I had fallen into despair when God Almighty blessed my mission by providing me the answer. It came about in this manner:

Federico could not shit and Piero, who was taking care of him again, ordered an extra plate of fruit with the juice of several lemons squeezed over it to relax Federico's bowels. It worked so well Federico barely had time to get out of bed before he shit like a horse. When I heard that, I asked Cecchi to have a key made which would fit Vittore's room and once he had given it to me, I instructed Luigi to give Vittore's guards the same breakfast as Piero had given Federico. They ate it greedily and all I had to do was wait. It took several days, but, when the guard outside Vittore's door had to relieve himself, I slipped inside the room.

Potta! May I never see another room like that one. It smelled as if a flock of bats had died in there. Nor was it just the smell. Vittore must have prowled the streets of Corsoli, Venezia, and Roma, collecting every piece of refuse he could find. The floor was littered with battered chests, soiled pallets, cracked vases, torn baskets, and cleaved helmets with the dried tissue of brain still clinging to them. Bloodied clothing lay piled on the floor beside worn-out saddles, crippled chairs, and broken swords. Where he had found all this I did not know. Nor why he had kept it. Perhaps being a soldier and a bandit had caused my brother to lose his senses.

A large desk cluttered with books stood on one side of the door and three full spittoons on the other. I tried to move the books, but they fell apart at my touch. The spittoons were so heavy the slop slipped over the sides, and the stench made me sick. I crawled under the desk, then climbed over mounds of clothing and broken furniture until I came to the far wall close to the bed. I stood up and opened a shutter. A thousand wretched smells flew out and fresh air rushed in. I closed my eyes and breathed deeply for several moments. And then I smelled it! An odor so faint that only a food taster such as myself would have noticed it. I traced its path to the back of the bed and there, hidden under the sheets, were six small bottles of ginger, crushed beetles, cinnamon, and mercury. No wonder Federico was acting strangely. They were aphrodisiacs and probably no more useful than my amulets, but ten times as deadly.

I put tiny amounts of arsenic into each bottle and placed them back where I had found them, all except for one. Then I raced out of the room, knocking over chairs, armor, and books. The guard, who had since returned, was so startled that I rushed by him before he could stop me. Running down the stairs, I shouted, "*Salvate il Duca!* Save the duke!"

Doors opened as if I had announced the second coming of Christ. I kept running and shouting, "*Salvate il Duca. Salvate il Duca!*" I passed through the courtyard and rang the stable bell. Guards came, their swords drawn.

"Is Federico dead?" they yelled. They grabbed my arms, but I pulled away and ran up the marble steps to the palace, through the hallways, past the kitchen, up a flight of stairs and down another, through the garden, gathering people like monks to money. And all the time I cried out, "Save the duke! Save the duke!"

Those following me joined in even though they did not know why. Their faces flushed, their blood surged, their cries echoed off the palace walls. I saw Cecchi. "Save the duke!" I shouted. Immediately, he ran behind me urging on the others. "Save the duke! Save the duke!"

Now there were guards, washerwomen, scribes, footmen, kitchen help, and grooms all following me. More than fifty voices and twice as many arms. I led them up the stairs to Federico's chambers. The guards outside his apartment drew their swords, but they were confused for we were not coming to attack the prince, but to save him. I had not been running and yelling like a fool all this time for my health—running is *not* good for the health—but because I prayed that Federico would hear us, and God granted my prayers. Federico opened the door himself.

"Save the duke! Save the duke!" I gasped.

"Save me from what?" Federico asked. He carried a sword in his hand and he pulled his nightgown around him as he pushed his way through the guards.

"From being poisoned!" I held up the tiny bottle. "By him!"

I pointed to Vittore, who was standing in the doorway behind

Federico. Until then no one knew what I had been shouting about. Now Vittore's guards drew their swords and knives. Vittore ran at me, but could not reach me because the passageway was too narrow and the guards were in the way.

"He is mixing arsenic in your aphrodisiacs," I said, and whiffed the bottle under Federico's nose. He jerked his head back as if he had been stung.

"Someone stole arsenic from my apothecary!" Piero exclaimed.

"Kill him!" Cecchi said.

"Burn him!" Bernardo spat.

"This is a conspiracy," Vittore shouted. "I do not have any arsenic. Ugo is the one who has poisons in his room."

The blood drained from my face as Federico whirled on me. "You have poisons in your room?"

Time crawled. So many things rushed through my head, each crying to be recognized. "My Lord," I said calmly. "You have seen my room. You came at a moment's notice. You sat there, we talked, you saw no poisons."

"He is lying," Vittore cried.

"It is a trick to divert your mind. Look first in his room. Then look in mine." I prayed Federico would listen to me because if he went into mine first he would see enough poisons to kill Caesar's army!

Cecchi said, "Ugo has served you loyally. You can always look in his room afterward."

Vittore tried to protest but the servants, whose loyalty changed as quickly as a summer breeze, shouted, "Look in his room!"

Federico marched to Vittore's room with everyone crushed behind him, pushing, shoving, and yelling. Vittore's guard disappeared the moment he saw Federico. I unlocked the door. Federico did not crawl under the table or over the soiled clothing. He did not move a spittoon. Just the sight of the room enraged him as I knew it would.

"My Lord—" Vittore began.

Federico ignored him and said to me, "How did you know about this?"

"With due respect, Your Excellency, since you have appointed Vittore as your adviser you have sometimes said and done things which are not always in your best interest."

"What have I done?" Federico's eyes narrowed.

"You have been eating fish which, if one eats too much of it, brings about black bile."

"That is not true," Vittore snarled.

"It is!" Piero answered.

Cecchi interrupted, "You have allowed a man who has no experience in finances to become involved with the wool trade. We have been losing money."

"That is not true!" Vittore shouted.

"The people of Corsoli have long loved you for your wisdom, your fairness, and your goodness, My Lord—"

"Is that also not true?" Federico turned to Vittore.

"But we hardly know you anymore," I continued.

"*La cospirazione,*" Vittore snarled.

Federico struck him so hard with the handle of his sword that Vittore fell to the ground. "Imprison him," he roared.

As I watched the soldiers take Vittore away I marveled how easy it had been. Just like that Vittore had been imprisoned and would likely be put to death. I did not feel sorry for him in the least. That he was my brother made no difference to me. Perhaps I was a better assassin than a food taster.

Piero bled Federico, examined his phlegm and his shit, and said since we had stopped the poisoning, he thought Federico would live till the next century. Federico pushed him away and rolled out of the bed.

"I am going to boil Vittore in oil," he said, pulling on his hose. "Then I will put him on the rack." As he was pulling on his shirt he said, "I will make him eat his poison and cut his heart out." By the time his shoes were on he wanted to cut out Vittore's heart, feed him poison, and *then* put him on the rack. I glanced at the others and knew what they were thinking—this is the Federico of old. Suddenly, a smile spread slowly across his face. "Did you hear that?" he asked.

All I could hear was the lion roaring.

Federico smiled. "We will have a *caccia* at my wedding. We will throw Vittore to the lion."

We stared at Federico. "Your wedding?" Cecchi said, tugging at his beard.

"Yes, my wedding," Federico replied, as if he had just decided to go hunting. "I will marry Miranda."

Marry Miranda!

"That is a brilliant idea!" the others cried. "A decision inspired by God! It will produce male children. She will make a worthy mate." The compliments came faster than a hailstorm.

"And you, Ugo?" Federico asked. "What do you say?"

"I am speechless, Your Excellency. You do me too great an honor. How can I ever repay you?"

"Your service to me is enough."

"But surely I shall not have to wait on my own daughter?"

"And why not?"

"And if I refuse?" I said, before I knew what I was saying.

"Refuse?" Rising like Neptune from the sea, he lurched to the fire and pulled out the poker. He had completely forgotten that I had just saved his life! Guards grasped my arms and turned me around so that my *culo* was pointing to Federico.

"My Lord," Cecchi cried, "If you kill Ugo you will have lost the very reason you wanted to keep him as a taster. Let Ugo have his own taster, but he will still taste your food. That would be enough, would it not, Ugo?"

I could feel the heat of the poker, smell my hose burning. My bunghole tightened up so much I did not void for three days.

"Yes," I gasped.

"Let him go," Federico ordered.

I fell to the floor, drained of all senses.

Federico kicked me with his foot. "His own taster," he laughed and, turning to the rest of the room he said, "He has the courage of a lion."

If God Himself had praised me, I could not have been in greater bliss. Federico had finally recognized my worth. I kissed the hem of his robe muttering, *"Mille grazie, mille grazie."*

"You must want to die," Cecchi said, shaking his head when we were outside Federico's chambers.

"No, I want to live! Vittore is imprisoned, my daughter is marrying the duke, and now, after almost five years, I will enjoy food again."

How could he understand how I felt? How could anyone understand? Now at long last, I would be able eat again. No, not just eat, but chew, gobble, suck all without fear of being poisoned! I could nibble as quickly as a rabbit or as slowly as a tortoise. I could munch as silently as a dormouse or chomp as noisily as a hog. Oh, what joy! What joy! I danced through the palace even though everyone could see my *culo*, but I did not care! Oh, that my father could see this. I could not wait to tell Vittore.

That was the night I began writing this manuscript. God had answered my prayers and it seemed as if all my tribulations were finally over. Now I will write what has happened since the announcement of the marriage three months ago, for just as a heavy rain will change the course of a river, so God in His wisdom saw fit to change the course of my life yet again.

I wanted to be the one to tell Miranda. She would be the princess she had always dreamed of becoming and have everything she wanted. But the news of the wedding had spread so fast that even as I was making my way to our room, courtiers and washerwomen and stable boys ran to congratulate me. Everyone was happy except Tommaso.

"This is what you always wanted," he accused me.

"You had your chance."

"And I will have it again."

I wanted to know what he meant, but first I had to tell Miranda of her good fortune. As it was she already knew. Her girlfriends were brushing her hair, kissing her cheeks, and reading her fortune. "Federico will invite all of Italy to the wedding. He will take you to Venezia. He will build you a new palace," they predicted. They claimed the wedding would take place next mont^ ....id. summer's festival. There would be two hundred hundred, then six.

That evening, Bernardo consulted his charts a for the wedding would be when Jupiter and Ven the sun, which would be on the last week of J time. Federico decided the wedding should las banquets, a play, a pageant, and the *caccia*. It would be the most expensive and greatest wedding Corsoli had ever seen.

What power there is in words! I had seen their effect on the palazzo when Federico had said, "I am going to Milano to find a wife." But when he said, "I will make Miranda my wife," *oi me!* The whole valley was transformed. Each house was to be cleaned, painted, and hung with banners. Four matrimonial arches flanked with statues of Harmony, Love, Beauty, and Fertility were to be built leading from the Main Gate through the town to the Palazzo Fizzi. All the cracked marble in the palace was to be replaced, Emilia's flower garden uprooted, and the hillside behind the palace re-created as the Hanging Gardens of Corsoli!

"I want a fresco of Miranda opposite mine," Federico told Grazzari. Grazzari was also instructed to design the pageant.

I cannot express how important I felt to sit at the same table with Duke Federico, Septivus, Cecchi, and Grazzari and make plans for Miranda's wedding. At the first meeting, an argument broke out between Bernardo and Septivus. Bernardo thought Federico should be portrayed as Justice because he was born in late September, but Septivus said, "A wise man is *master* of the stars," and that Hercules would be a better choice because of Federico's strength. "We could show Hercules and the twelve labors."

"Cleaning the stables?" Bernardo sneered.

"Hercules also captured a deer," Septivus retorted. "He killed a lion, and a monster, and captured a bull and a boar. In the tenth labor he captured four savage horses, in the eleventh—"

"*Basta!*" Federico said, "This is a wedding, not a zoo."

"Or a hunt!" Bernardo added.

"But it could be a hunt." Grazzari thought for a moment. "Miranda is a virgin, is she not?"

"Of course," I replied.

Grazzari leaned back, stroked his beard, and stared at the ceiling. "Since a unicorn symbolizes virginity, why not have a dance through ⟨th⟩e trees in which Hercules captures the unicorn."

"⟨He⟩rcules captures the unicorn," Federico mused.

"⟨no⟩t think it becoming," Bernardo said.

"I do," said Federico. "It is a marriage of strength and beauty. We can use the same piazza for the *caccia*."

"That is an excellent suggestion," Cecchi smiled.

"And then she turns into Venus," said Septivus.

"Venus?" Federico turned to Septivus.

"Whose only duty was to make love," he explained.

"Perfect," said Federico. "Hercules hunts the unicorn, he captures her, she changes into Venus, and they make love."

"But Venus comes ashore naked in a scallop shell," Grazzari said. Again Federico turned to Septivus.

"Well then," Septivus said, biting his little yellow teeth together, "Hercules comes upon a lion about to ravage a unicorn. While Hercules kills the lion, the unicorn flees into the sea. We think for a moment she has drowned, but she emerges naked in a shell and comes ashore into his arms."

Federico loved it, even though it meant building a cave where the unicorn would change into Venus and damming up a mountain stream to create a small flood.

As soon as the plans were announced, peasants from all over the valley poured into the city. Grazzari and Cecchi set them to work, building, painting, digging, planting, sewing, and polishing. Actors were hired from Padua, singers from Naples. Every moment of the day was devoted to the wedding, and everyone, whether they were courtiers or peasants, strove to fulfill Federico's dream and make Corsoli the envy of Gubbio, Parma, Arezzo, Perugia, and every other city in all of Italy.

Nor was Miranda left out of the preparations. Federico sought her opinions on everything. At first she delighted in making suggestions and was amazed to see her words transformed into colorful costumes or dresses. But one morning she came back to the room stamping her feet and cursing Septivus. "He still tr͏   ͏f I was one of his students! He smiles when I sa͏   yesterday he patted me on the head! If he does   Federico." Because of this she threw herself into ͏   greater urgency.

I discussed the menu with Luigi, for since I v   taster I wanted all the dishes I had ever longed veal in garlic sauce, and a dessert shaped like the Fizzi palace made out of marzipan, sugar, and many kinds of fruits.

At mealtimes, Federico instructed Septivus to read aloud passages from the book Verana of Firenze had given him so that we might uplift our behavior. Septivus read a passage which said that even though breaking wind was rude, to hold it in could be bad for the stomach.

"So what should we do?" asked Federico, drowning out Septivus's next sentence with a fart.

"Muffle it with a cough," Septivus repeated.

As the wedding drew closer, Federico rose early and checked on the progress of the fresco or watched the laborers replacing the marble. He inspected the costumes for the pageant and wanted to know which desserts Tommaso was planning for the banquets.

I prayed Tommaso would accept the marriage, but his eyes became haunted and he started biting his nails again. When I tried to talk to him, he turned away. He hated me as much as he hated Federico, but as long as he kept away from Miranda I did not care.

In the midst of the preparations, I heard that my father was dying. Duke Federico gave me permission to visit him, which I did one morning after breakfast. It was a relief to be out of the city and all of its activity, riding through the long grass, smelling the flowers, and the trees, and the freshness of spring.

When I was a child my father's house was as tall as a tower, but every time I had returned it appeared smaller. Now it was but a rude bump on the landscape that would soon be ground into the earth again. My father, who had also stood tall and proud, now lay on a bed of soiled straw, blind, barely able to move, crippled with pain, and covered in sores. A racking cough tore from his ribs and the smell of death was everywhere.

All my anger disappeared and I knelt beside his bed and took his hands in mine. "Babbo," I whispered, wishing that, if only for a moment, I could do something to relieve his agony. His mouth trem-
led, and his foul stinking breath covered my face.

"ittore?" he whispered.

! Christ! Would he never think of anyone else? But when

had he ever? When the flock died because Vittore had not taken care of it, my father blamed it on a neighbor. When Vittore was accused of rape, my father said the girl lied because he would not marry her. When Vittore became a bandit and stalked the highways, my father pretended he was a courier. When he fled to Spain, my father said he was a general in the army. My father worked in pouring rain, in burning heat, in swarms of mosquitoes, when he was well and when he was sick. He was robbed by his neighbors and deceived by those he served. Vittore avoided work, cheated, robbed, and raped, and my father loved him for it. What should I tell him?

"He prospers," I said.

My father raised his head a little from the bed. Parting his thin lips that revealed two sorry black stubs against the pale pink inside of his mouth, he croaked, "I knew, I knew." Then he sank back into silence.

"He asks about Vittore every day," the villagers told me, bringing me a bowl of *minestra* and some bread. They stared at me while I ate, feeling my clothing, especially my new hat with the feather. They wanted to know about my life in the palace. "Are the women as beautiful as they say?" the men asked. "Do you have your own bed? How many sleep in a room?"

"Do not let my clothes mislead you; I am no better off than you are."

A man said loudly to another, "It is not enough that he leads a better life, but he lies about it, too."

So I told them the beds were cool in summer and warm in winter. "Not only can we eat as much as we like, but we drink wine with every meal," I boasted.

"I knew it!" the man said.

I told them Federico gave jewels to his favorite servants at Easter and that I only worked enough to keep the blood moving. I bragged that Federico often asked my opinion on different matters. I made up stories about princes from India and strange animals from Africa. "We have a unicorn which is both male and female."

When they had brought the *minestra* to me, the muscles in my neck had tensed and my throat narrowed as it always did when I ate. But I became so swept up in my lies that it was not till I had eaten half the broth of grains, broccoli, fennel, and basil—the same broth my mother had fed me when I was young, the same broth which had left a gnawing in my stomach—that I sighed with satisfaction. When I realized that the sigh had come from my own lips, I burst into tears. The villagers, who had been staring in amazement, now looked at me with bewilderment, and the woman who had made the broth protested that she had made it with love; if I was crying it was not her fault.

My father coughed and I turned to him, my cheeks wet with memories, my heart overflowing with forgiveness. "Babbo," I cried, thinking perhaps that we might even now become friends and be kind to one another as all families should be, but he did not see me. He was staring past the empty nests tucked into the ceiling beams, past the cracks in the roof, to a paradise in the sky.

Ever since the wedding was announced I had desired to bring my father to the palace so that he might see how Vittore was awaiting death while I was giving my daughter in marriage. But God did not grant me that wish. My father withheld his eyes from me and this time they remained closed forever.

I sobbed as I dug his grave. Despite the day's warmth my body was frozen as if my soul was already in that ice reserved for traitors. My father was dead and I had triumphed over Vittore, but my victories were small and I even smaller for thinking them victories. How many hours, weeks, months, years had I wasted in hatred?

After I poured the last of the earth onto my father's body I rode home, weeping until there were no tears left inside me. It was only then that I saw how great was God's infinite mercy. At last I understood why He had given me Helene only to take her from me again. Had I never met Helene, then my mother's words—those who carry a grudge will be buried beneath it—would have come true. But now a millstone had been lifted from my neck. Since my anger for my father and brother was all spent, I was cleansed. From now on I could be inspired not by hatred, but by love, my love for Helene. Even as Dante had been inspired by Beatrice, Helene would be my inspiration. I would lead my life so that I might be worthy of her. Tears of joy replaced my sorrow and I dismounted and knelt in the sweet-smelling grass, praising God for showing me the way.

As soon as I returned I went to Miranda's room, intending to tell her of my father's death and of the miracle that had happened to me.

Her friends were there talking excitedly. One of the girls told me breathlessly that the actors from Padua had arrived that afternoon and Federico had told the leader that Miranda was to sing with them.

The leader had laughed and said, "The bride? It has never been done. People will talk."

"That is why I want it!" Federico said, poking a fat finger into his chest.

Miranda was seated on the bed in the midst of all this merry-making, smiling and laughing with the others, but I could tell from the way she was biting her lip that something had frightened her. Until now, bewitched by all the gifts and attention, she had thought it was all a game she could stop whenever she wanted. Even after the marriage was announced she was so flattered that she was to become a princess, and Federico had been so nice to her, that she had not considered it could be any other way. But now I suspected she was not so sure.

Suddenly, I remembered things about her I wanted to tell Federico. She had been raised without a mother. Although she laughed easily she was often scared. True, she was wise beyond her years, but she was still a girl. I wanted to silence the silly laughter that surrounded her. I wanted time to march backward. To when she first started bleeding. To when her hands were as plump as her cheeks. To when I told her stories of her mother. To when she sang to the sun and played with the goats. To when I carried her on my shoulders and wiped the sleep from her eyes. To when she was no bigger than a loaf of bread and could fit into both of my hands. I wanted to cross the room to her bedside and hold her in my arms and tell her that I would always care for her, but the way had become so crowded with our ambition that I could not get through.

That night I dreamed that Miranda and I and Helene were living in Arraggio; the rain was falling and the sheep were grazing on the hillside. When I awoke in the morning I saw I was still in Corsoli and my pillow was soaked with tears. I rose, dressed, and knocked on Miranda's door. It was open as it always was between us, and there, sitting on her bed, was Tommaso! He did not even stand up when I came in. "What are you doing here?" I said to him.

Miranda sprang out of bed and pushed Tommaso out the door.

"Do you want to get us all killed?" I hissed.

She said, "How could you betroth me to Tommaso without telling me?"

"Miranda, that was five years ago. We had just arrived in the palace. I was trying to protect you. I—"

"What else have you been keeping from me?"

"Nothing."

"You told Federico I was a virgin."

"Yes, of course."

"And when were you going to tell me Federico has the pox?"

"Who told you that? That fool Tommaso?"

"Vittore told him."

"And you believe Vittore?"

"Tommaso is willing to lay down his life for me!"

As if I had not! "Miranda, you encouraged Federico—"

"You should have stopped me. You should have spoken for me."

Oi me! Now *I* was being blamed? A banging interrupted us.

All day long Corsoli echoed with the sound of workmen sealing the marriage contract. They have finished the arches by the Main Gate, the Piazza Del Vedura, the Palazzo Ascati, and the last one leading to the entrance of the Palazzo Fizzi. They have decked statues of Diana with olive branches and doves. Every building, no matter how small, has been cleaned and decorated with banners. The fountains are being filled with wine.

And then, just as a soldier collapses with weariness once the battle is over, so did Miranda fall into my arms, weeping, "I cannot marry Duke Federico, Babbo. I cannot. I love Tommaso. I have always loved him. I will always love him."

My heart tore into pieces, each breath coming like fire. The moment I had long dreaded was upon me and I was no more prepared for it than when Federico had asked me, "What do you say, Ugo?"

I bathed Miranda's head with water, pressed a sponge dipped in mandrake root boiled in wine with crushed poppy seeds against her nose, and held her in my arms.

"What shall I do?" she wailed. "What will become of me?"

She sobbed until she fell asleep. What could I do? How could I tell Federico, five days before the wedding, when hundreds of animals are being slaughtered, music composed, actors rehearsed, poems written, and frescoes completed? When thousands of yards of cloth have been made into gowns and jackets, pantaloons, hats, and dresses? When princes are traveling for days with their retainers and servants, cavaliers and footmen? When an emissary of the pope is expected, and the lion has been starved to make him more savage and Federico has spent every penny so that the rest of Italy, if only for one week, will sit up and take notice of him? If I were to tell Federico now that Miranda does not wish to marry him, he would behead her, burn her body, cut her into pieces, and parade the parts around the city. I remembered the new poem Federico had ordered Septivus to finish:

> Your voice so soft so filled with pain
> Your looks so wounding to my eyes
> Your heart it breathes a thousand sighs
> Your soul—

He knows—the words screamed in my head—he knows about Miranda and Tommaso.

"You must be careful," I pleaded with Miranda.

But the next day I found Tommaso in Miranda's room again. I was so incensed at his boldness that I drew my knife, but Miranda said, "Federico ordered him to be here."

"It is true," Tommaso smiled. "He suspects Miranda has a secret lover so I am to guard her."

"You fools! It's a trick."

"I will tell him we are in love," Tommaso said boldly.

"You will not say a word!" I said, and forced him out the door.

Now I have caught up with my story, for this happened this very same evening. I have been sitting in my room ever since. Just now a star shot across the sky. It is a favorable omen. But for whom? Federico? Miranda? Tommaso? Me? Alas, it streaked with so much speed that I did not see a name attached to it. I will drink some mandrake juice. It helps me sleep and I must sleep to think clearly about what must be done. Not only that, but the guests began arriving two days ago, for tomorrow is the first day of the wedding.

xxix

The first day.

The first day is over but there are still six more! Thank God for henbane, although it plays tricks on me, for I can only hope that what I recall did happen and is not what I wanted to happen, because, if that is so, then I do not know what happened, and my life, which is already confusing, will become even more so.

Even though my eyes were weary after I had finished writing last night, they refused to close and so I wandered around the darkened palace. All day long, laborers and servants had been making sure that every detail had been attended to, but now all was silent except for the snoring and farting of those same weary servants sleeping in the shadows.

The kitchen was empty, the stoves glowing softly. Pots and cauldrons were lined up like soldiers' helmets. Vegetables were piled in every corner along with mounds of cheese, vats of milk, oil from Lucca, wine from Orvieto, Sienna, and Firenze, all of them waiting, like everything else in the palace—indeed in all of Corsoli—for the wedding to begin. From the kitchen I entered the inner courtyard. On three sides the marbled, white columns gleamed in the moonlight and facing me was the hillside which had been transformed into the Hanging Gardens. O blessed saints, as long as men can speak they will talk of it. For two months, fifty men stripped the hillside of its weeds and scrubs and planted flowers and bushes, trusting to God that He would smile on their plans. In His infinite mercy He heard their prayers and now the hillside is a flowered tapestry of blue, yellow, white, red—a painting sprung to life. "We have improved on nature herself," Grazzari said.

Oh, Helene, how I wish you could see this. I asked Duke Federico to invite the archbishop of Nîmes, but he refused, saying that he did not like Frenchmen. Where are you, Helene? Does your blood run faster at the thought of me as mine does of yours? Do you stretch your hand out at night hoping I might be by your side?

I walked through the palace to the Piazza Fizzi and the last of the four matrimonial arches. What a wonder! It stands three times the height of a man and is flanked on either side by statues carrying garlands of flowers. The figures of Virtuosa and Fortuna look so real they could spring to life.

From there it was but a short walk down the Weeping Steps to Corsoli. Like the palace, the town was silent except for the lazy flapping of red and white banners from the rooftops. Even the most decrepit house has been cleaned and repaired and the Piazza San Giulio is so changed with trees and bushes and flowers that it is hard to believe that during the plague you could not see the ground for dead bodies. It is from here that we will watch the pageant and the *caccia*.

Truly love, Federico's love for Miranda, has changed him. On our return from Milano, he wanted to build statues and sculptures of himself. Now he sees the beauty of a sunset, he wrestles with poetry, he appreciates Tommaso's artistry in the kitchen. The thought of Tommaso pierced me like an arrow and, whereas a moment before I had wanted to bang on every door and shout in every window, "This is all for my daughter, Miranda!" now I hurried back to the palace to be certain Tommaso was asleep in his bed and Miranda was in hers.

Tommaso lay on his side, his mouth open, his face frowning slightly. He murmured something and stretched his head forward as if trying to reach someone lying next to him. I hurried to Miranda's room. She was also asleep, lying on her side, her face pale against her black hair, her lips parted, and her hand pressed against her breast as if she was holding someone's hand there. Anger rose in me because of the foolish way their love refused to be cowed. I could have cut off their offending hands but what good would it have done? Their passion mocks every obstacle between them. I returned to my room and, exhausted by the heaviness of my heart, fell into a restless sleep.

This morning, Duke Federico was sitting on the side of his bed—his feet in a bowl of vinegar, his gout had returned unexpectedly—yelling at Bernardo, "But what does it mean?"

Bernardo looked at me sharply, as if my entrance had disturbed him, when we both knew that he was grateful for it. "Miranda is running away," Bernardo said slowly, "and she wishes you to pursue her even as the hunter pursues the game."

Federico must have been dreaming again. "But whenever I caught her," Federico said, "she slipped through my hands."

"If I may interrupt, Your Excellency, it means that her spirit can never be captured. Everyone knows that just as dreams are not real, the people in them are only spirits." As I had no idea what I was saying, I went on quickly, "I have apples and figs with honey for your breakfast, My Lord."

"Her spirit cannot be captured," Federico repeated to himself.

Relieved that he was off the hook, Bernardo hurried from the room. I shifted the cushions behind Federico. He lay back and asked, "How is Miranda this morning?"

"Resting," I said, and carefully lifted his gouty foot onto the bed. I reached for the bowl of figs and honey. Federico's head was turned away from me, looking out at the Hanging Gardens. His eyes darted toward me, then turned away again. I thought perhaps he wished to be alone, but he waved his paw and said, "*Reste!*"

Once more he looked out at the gardens and back at me. His mouth opened, words formed, but he did not speak. His eyes were wounded, not from the fiery pain of gout, but from a deeper, more powerful ache.

I had never seen Federico weep; indeed, until then I did not think he was *capable* of weeping, but I swore I could see tears in his eyes. Then, as if I had spied upon the sacred ark itself, a veil descended and he sat up, dipped a fig in honey, and ate it. "The night before a battle," he licked his lips, "my senses are sharper than my sword. I can see in the dark. I can hear grasshoppers fucking in the next field. I can smell the fear of the enemy."

I waited, certain he would ask about Miranda, but he did not. Instead he asked, "Has Princess Marguerite of Rimini arrived?"

"She is expected this morning."

He nodded. Gritting his teeth, he threw the covers off the bed and lurched his full weight onto his good leg and the rest onto my shoulder. Sweat formed on his brow, but as in Milano, he would not admit he was in pain. "The Hanging Gardens are beautiful," he grunted.

"Yes, Your Excellency. They are magnificent."

He stared at me. I did not blink or turn my head away even though his breath was fouler than a sewer on a hot day. I helped him to the chair so he could shit. Then I waited until he had finished and gave him my arm so he could return to his bed. He sat down and waved me away. I wanted to say something to ease his mind, but I was afraid that whatever I said would only arouse his suspicions further.

When I returned to my room I could hear Miranda's handmaidens giggling as they helped her dress. "As thick as my arm and twice as long," a girl tittered.

A moment later, Miranda knocked on my door. She was wearing a gown of blue silk and velvet. Precious jewels had been sewn into the design to compliment her necklace of rubies and emeralds. She seemed thinner and moved slowly as if her head might fall off her neck. Her pupils were still large from the potion I had given her earlier, but the paleness of her face set against the darkness of her hair only enhanced its beauty. "I need some more potion." Her voice cracked when she spoke.

"Your lips will bleed if you do not stop biting them."

"Give it to me!"

"Only a sip."

Her huge, dark eyes looked at me over the edge of the bowl.

"Miranda, you must not listen to stories about Federico. He loves you, deeply. For your own sake, I beg you—"

She swallowed the potion in one gulp, wiped her mouth with her hand, and then threw the empty bowl against the wall. She pretended to stagger as if she had suddenly become drunk, laughed too loudly, went back to her ladies, and together they walked down the hallway. I followed, fearing the potion might make her say something she would regret, but I lost her in the courtyard amid the colorful confusion of the carriages of the arriving guests.

The women were dressed in traveling clothes, but the men paraded around like peacocks, admiring themselves and congratulating one another on the safety of the journey. They wore goatees—it is now the fashion in Venezia—and two-colored hose. They had slits in the back of their jackets as if their tailors had forgotten to sew up the seams.

No sooner did their feet touch the ground than their tongues started wagging. "Federico has spent a fortune." "Not as much as the Estes in Ferrara." "But more than the Carpuchis!" "Corsoli looks splendid!"

"The matrimonial arches are wonderful!" "To have spent all this money, he must truly be in love!" "But with the daughter of a food taster?" a prince from Piacenza sniggered, as if food tasters had six legs or a *fallo* where their nose should be. I mentioned to the prince that it was my daughter, Miranda, the duke was marrying. He looked at me as if I was an idiot. Christ on a cross! He insulted food tasters and then he did not believe I was one! What did he think food tasters looked like? Oh, but he would soon find out, I would make sure of that. Indeed, they all did later that afternoon.

We had gathered in the entrance hall for the unveiling of Miranda's fresco. By now the palazzo was so crowded with guests and their servants that the very air tingled with excitement. Grazzari made a speech in which he praised Federico for being the sun from which he had drawn his strength, and Miranda the moon from which he had taken his inspiration. Then he pulled the curtain aside. I had watched Miranda pose several times and each time I had been astounded as Grazzari transferred her beauty to the wall. But now that the fresco was finished I was astounded all over again. The fresco is as tall as I am and twice as wide. In it, Miranda flies through the air from left to right, her dark black hair streaming behind her. She is dressed as an angel and the sun's rays form a halo around her head. Her face, which is turned toward us, is aglow, the ends of her mouth turned up as if she carried within it the secret to happiness. Grazzari had finished it that very afternoon—the colors were not yet dry—and it seemed so alive that I was sure that if I had pressed my head against the wall I could have heard the beat of her heart. I had always known she was beautiful, but to see every mole, every eyelash, every dimple larger than life was to behold the very essence of beauty itself.

I thought everyone would cheer, but no one said a word. "Are you all blind?" I wanted to shout. "This is the best painting I have ever seen! Better even than the Mary Magdalen in Milano!" Then I saw it was not that they did not wish to speak, but that they could not. The loveliness of the painting had stolen their breath away.

"Magnifico!" someone sighed at last, and then, like a damn bursting its sides, the praise poured out. *"Stupendo! Meraviglioso!"* over and over again, as if only a mountain of words could express their admiration. They surrounded Miranda, heaping praises upon her.

"But it is Grazzari you must applaud," Miranda said. "He has improved upon nature a second time."

"No," Grazzari replied. "When God saw how ill prepared I was to complete this task, He assisted me Himself."

He explained how the doves flying next to Miranda symbolized peace which could be seen by the lion and lamb lying together in the grassy foreground. "The necklace around Miranda's neck is the same one Aphrodite gave Harmonia at her wedding. It gives the wearer irresistible beauty."

"Maybe she needs it in the painting," Federico said, "but not in real life."

The guests agreed heartily. Miranda blushed. I did not hear what she said because just then I saw Tommaso in the doorway.

"I came to see the fresco," he said. His eyes were red from weeping, his face drawn from lack of sleep.

"If you do anything foolish," I whispered, "you will be killed!"

"I have nothing to live for!" he cried, and dashed away.

I could not follow because just then Federico led the guests into the main hall for a small dinner. Because many of them were weary from their journeys they went to bed soon after and I returned to look at the vision of Miranda once more.

I remembered that Grazzari had begun painting Miranda's face the day after the marriage was announced, when it was all still a game to her, which was why her face appeared so playful. Gazing at it again, I understood the madness of Tommaso's desire. Did I not feel the same for Helene? Did my heart not ache when I thought that I might never see her again?

Behind me, someone whispered, "Who is that?"

I turned around. Miranda was pointing to the fresco. "Why is she smiling when her heart is breaking in two?"

I reached out to comfort her, but she brushed my hand away. What could I say? It has been decided she will marry Federico. The wedding can only be canceled if something were to happen to him. But nothing will. Tommaso cannot stop it. What could he do? Stab Federico? He would never get through his guards. Poison him? Not as long as I am Federico's food taster. He had his chance. As Miranda had hers. Time marches forward not backward. What is done is done.

Federico will marry Miranda and I will no longer be a food taster. That is the way it is and that is the way it will be and if Tommaso even thinks of doing something about it, by the beard of Christ, I will cut his balls off!

The second day.

I do not know if it is the potions I have been taking, my anger toward Tommaso, or the excitement of the wedding, but I woke this morning wearier than when I had closed my eyes. I went to the kitchen, intending to speak with Tommaso. It was already crowded with servants chopping and mixing and boiling and frying, each one inspired to best the other. Luigi confided to me that over the next week two hundred sheep, fifty cattle, and fifty deer will be eaten, as well as two thousand doves, capons, and woodcocks. No wonder so many peasants have flocked to work here: there is no food anywhere else.

Tommaso was pouring cinnamon, verjuice, and ginger onto a bowl of berries. The berries reminded me of that oaf Onionface and I became furious that berries, which had once saved my life, could now bring about my death. "A perfect place," I said, as Tommaso poured them into a crust.

He jumped. "What do you want?" he shouted. I wanted to talk to him quietly, but he yelled again, "What do you want?" as if I was a peasant who had just wandered in from the country. I picked up a heavy ladle and would have cracked him over the head had Luigi not pushed me out of the kitchen, chiding, "What devil has got into you? We have work to do."

In the courtyard servants were lighting fires beneath vats and cauldrons. The smell of roasting meat filled the air. Giggling girls hurried past, clutching garlands of flowers. I should have been happy, but I was nervous and the roaring of the lion only agitated me further. The lion has not been fed for over a week to prepare him for the *caccia* and the smell of fresh meat has excited him. I was suddenly reminded of Vittore, for with so much going on I had forgotten about him.

When he heard my footsteps descending the steps to his cell, he stood up eagerly like a child expecting a treat. Then he saw who I was and sat back against the wall as if he had not a care in the world. His nails had grown and were thick with dirt, his clothes were black with filth, his hair was more matted than ever.

"Are you going to let Federico put me in the piazza with the lion?" he said, rubbing his poxy eye.

"I cannot stop him."

"Tell him I am your brother."

"But you did not want me to tell him, remember?"

He leaped up and clutched hold of the bars as if he could tear them apart. "You will not be satisfied until Papa and I are dead, will you?"

"Papa is already dead," I said.

He stared at me. "You are lying."

"A week ago, I heard he was sick so I went to see him. He died while I was there."

"Why did you not tell me?"

Why had I not told him? "I am sorry. I forgot. I—"

"You did not forget!" he yelled. "You are jealous. You have always been jealous." He spat out the last word as if it could hurt me.

"If you had truly loved him you would have visited him yourself or brought him to the palace," I answered.

"You . . . ass shit!!" He was no longer listening. "ASS SHIT!" He banged his forehead against the bars.

"He asked after you," I said. He stopped his pounding. "I told him you prospered."

He looked at me, and after a moment sneered, "Am I supposed to thank you?"

"No."

The air seemed to leave his body. He had always been taller than me, but now, standing in the middle of the cell, tugging at his hair, muttering to himself, he reminded me of that thin, feeble peasant who had attacked Federico's carriage on the way to Milano. He leaned his head on the bars again. "*Grazie*," he whispered. "*Grazie*."

A small ball of light glowed between us. It was filled with memories of what might have been—two boys playing together, two young men, their arms linked in friendship, two brothers, companions in life. Then it was gone and an emptiness overcame me. "I have to go. Cardinal Sevinelli is arriving from Roma."

As I reached the top of the stairs I heard a cry like the tearing of a soul. I crouched down and could just see into Vittore's cell. He was lying on the floor, his face in the muck, his hands grasping at the soiled straw, sobbing, "Babbo! Babbo!"

I took my place on the balcony behind Federico and Miranda and next to guests from Perugia and Spoleto. Below us, the crowd was singing and dancing around the matrimonial arch. Trumpets sounded some way off and a whisper spread through the crowd, "Here he is! Here he is!" and then twelve knights dressed in shining armor and green and white sashes rode into the piazza. They carried olive branches in their right hands and sat tall in the saddle as if their heads were attached to heaven. Behind them came twenty magnificent white horses without riders, each outfitted with golden saddles and bridles. Then came three nobles, each carrying a banner. One bore the sign of a cross, the next the keys of the church, and the third, the five crescents—the imperial flag of the Holy Church of Roma. Then came knights wearing papal robes and between them servants carried a canopy of blazing gold.

The procession stopped in front of the balcony and a figure stepped out from under the canopy. Holy Christ! I could not believe my eyes. It was not Cardinal Sevinelli, but that damned hunchback, Giovanni! I could tell those ears a mile away! My stomach heaved into my throat. I looked again to make sure I had not been mistaken. But no, it was him! He was wearing a robe of beaten gold and that dammed little red hat on the top of his head! The piazza fell silent! Everyone looked to Federico. I thought he would throw himself off the balcony and attack Giovanni, but instead he stood up and said, in a strong clear voice, "We welcome Cardinal Giovanni to Corsoli and pray that his stay finds us all in God's good graces." The crowd cheered; the procession moved into the palace.

The guests hurried away, buzzing like a thousand bees. I could not move, my *culo* was rooted to the chair, my legs as solid as a stone sculpture. Perhaps I am dreaming, I said to myself. I asked Cecchi if he had known that Giovanni was coming but he shook his head. Septivus swore he had not written to invite him. Who else could it have been then?

The guests gossiped about nothing else all afternoon. "Surely Giovanni would not have come unless he was invited!" they said. "Even so, one cannot deny he has the balls of a giant!" "And the dick of a horse, so I hear," someone joked. Rumor fell upon rumor until they piled so high they blotted out the sun.

That evening, we gathered in the courtyard for the first performance by the actors from Padua. The air was heavy with the scent of roses. Fireflies darted here and there, eager to play their part in the celebration. The chairs were lined up so that they faced two columns of scenery depicting clouds and birds and flowers which blended perfectly with the Hanging Gardens behind them. Miranda was dressed all in white except for a necklace of dazzling emeralds and a dainty golden crown. Whatever she was feeling, maybe even because of it, she had never appeared more lovely. As she took her place next to Federico, the sconces were lit and we beheld the most sparkling sight we had ever seen. There were so many exquisite women, so many shimmering jewels, so many handsome men all enhanced by the magnificence and splendor of nature, that we were not the pale imitators of heaven, but its very inspiration! Everyone sighed, honored to be part of such a wondrous spectacle.

I leaned back in my chair, drunk with the wine of goodness, and saw Tommaso's face staring down from a palace window. I was so startled I almost lost my balance. Just then, the flutes and drums commenced to play and I wrenched my eyes away from him to watch the stage. First a huge cloud suspended between the two columns slowly descended to the stage. When at last it came to rest, actors dressed as gods stepped out from it and called upon nature to show her pleasure. Thereupon more actors dressed as lions, lambs, cats, and dogs ran onto the stage and danced together. They sang love songs to Federico and Miranda and beseeched the gods for a fruitful union.

Then they left the stage and the columns of scenery were turned, displaying a series of paintings which would unfold throughout the evening. This one showed a convent's cell for a performance of a Boccaccio story about a nun who lost her wimple or something, I do not remember exactly. My mind was so distracted. I could not stop wondering why Giovanni had come or if Tommaso was planning something foolish. More dancing followed, another comedy, and, finally, two huge griffins pulled a golden chariot onto the stage in which Miranda was seated. It had all been planned so smoothly that I had not seen her leave her seat. She was seated in front of a painting of a hillside filled with trees which blended so well with the Hanging Gardens that it was perfection itself.

I looked to see if Tommaso was still watching; he was not and I cursed him for spoiling my enjoyment. Good God in heaven! Magnificence such as this only happenes once in a lifetime and I wanted to remember every detail. I wished my father and my dear mother could have seen it! *Potta!* I WANTED THE WORLD TO SEE IT! I would have even released Vittore just to show him how his poisonous words had been turned into gold.

Miranda strummed her lyre and notes spilled out like a gentle stream. She closed her eyes and sang of a love so great it could not be contained by the human heart. It burned so fiercely that it consumed not only the poet, but also her *amoroso*, and only in death, unhindered by flesh, could the lovers unite. As the last notes rose into the night, she opened her eyes and raised her head slightly, as if she could see the souls escaping into the starry blackness above us. Then she dropped her head, the griffins pulled the carriage off the stage, and the last thing we saw was the ghostly pale of Miranda's neck. I looked up at the window. Tommaso was weeping.

The guests cheered and shouted as Federico rose from his throne and turned to face us. "She is better than all the actors from Padua!" he beamed. Everyone cheered again. Federico shouted, "*Mangiamo!*" and with Miranda by his side, led the way into the banquet hall. No one mentioned the song.

If I had not seen the hall every day for the past five years I would never have recognized it. Chandeliers bearing hundreds of candles hung from the ceiling. Fine linen cloths covered the tables and at every place setting there were gold plates instead of trenchers. Grazzari had designed everything, even ensuring that the napkins were folded like delicate flowers. No sooner had the guests seated themselves than trumpets announced the serving of the food. I have already mentioned the first course. The second course consisted of fried veal sweetbreads, liver covered with the sauce of eggplant and served with slices of prosciutto and melon, as well as hot foods from the kitchen. Since it was early summer, the meat was tender, especially the rabbits, which had been raised for the occasion, and were served with pine nuts. The slices of spit-roasted veal were bathed in a sauce of its own juices. Of course, Septivus had to make a speech.

"Keep it short," Federico said.

Septivus said that although Corsoli could not boast of the grandeur of Roma or the splendor of Venezia, the three cities were sisters in spirit. Each had their virtues and, since Corsoli was situated midway between them, it benefited from both. If Corsoli's reputation in art or commerce was lacking, that was due to its geography for which only God Himself could be faulted, and who would fault God for placing Corsoli where it was? This made no sense to me, nor anyone else or perhaps even to Septivus, because he stammered and said that Corsoli would make amends for its geography by being the first city in Romagna to use the fork! Then the servants presented each guest with a silver fork. *Oi me!* You would have thought they were nuggets of gold! Luigi had to stand on a table to get the guests' attention.

"Grasp the fork like this," he said, holding the fork in his left hand. "Now spear the meat on the platter and carry it to your plate."

Everyone immediately stabbed at the bowls of meat. "Be firm," I heard Giovanni say.

"Now," continued Luigi, "holding the meat securely on the plate with the fork, and picking up the knife in the right hand, cut off a slice."

He cut a small piece of veal to demonstrate, stuck it on a fork, and offered it to me as if I was a dog! I tasted it, pronounced it free of poison, and returned the plate to Federico. Federico immediately stabbed the veal as if there was still life in it and cut it into three slices. "It is easy," he boasted.

Everyone did as they had been instructed. The women giggled and shrieked, "Blessed Holy Mother! The fork is a gift from heaven. Oh, how could we have lived without it."

Septivus, who as usual was talking as he ate, stabbed himself twice in the mouth. The stabbing reminded me of Tommaso and I wondered if he had tampered with the berry torte. All around me guests laughed and joked. Even Miranda! What was she laughing at? Unless it was because she KNEW the berries were poisoned and did not care.

"My pastry chef," Federico said, as Tommaso entered, carrying Federico's torte on a golden plate. Federico spooned out some torte, but instead of giving it to me, he gave it to Miranda! Why did he do that? Did he know something was wrong? Should I shout aloud? Throw myself at her? Tear the food from her mouth? I looked at Tommaso. His face was as blank as a stone wall.

"Your Excellency," I said, "should I not try the berries first?"

"There is no need, is there?" Federico asked, holding the spoon in the air.

"No, but as I will not be your taster much longer—"

Miranda calmly took the spoon from Federico and, before I could do anything, swallowed the torte and sighed with pleasure. Tommaso walked out, looking at me with such disgust that I trembled with rage. Actors sang, clowns juggled, musicians played. My shirt was soaking with sweat, my knees would not stop shaking. There was a hole in my stomach. I wanted to die.

I have just come back to my room. The first rays of dawn are sliding over the mountains. Some of the guests walked into the garden to watch the sunrise but I am wearier than Job and need to sleep. As I crossed the courtyard, Cardinal Giovanni passed me with four of his guards. I bowed and said, *"Bouna notte,* Cardinal Giovanni."

Giovanni stepped in front of me, blocking my path. "Ugo DiFonte, Duke Federico's food taster." He looked me up and down as if I was a piece of meat he might wish to buy. "Tell me Ugo, will you still be Duke Federico's taster after your daughter becomes Duke Federico's wife?"

"No. I am to have my own taster."

"Your own taster?" The little twat turned to his guards. "Did you hear that? Ugo is going to have his own taster." The guards smirked and Giovanni turned back to me. "When will that be?"

"At the last banquet."

"In five days' time?" His eyes bulged from behind his spectacles.

"Yes." I could hardly believe it myself.

"Well, we will see," he smirked, and strode off without a backward glance.

What did he mean by that? Who cares what he means. He can think what he likes. He cannot harm me. Not here in Corsoli. This is Federico's court and Federico is marrying my daughter and even if Giovanni is an emissary of the pope and Jesus Christ Himself, he cannot do anything to me here.

*   *   *

The third day.

Oi me! Sono fottuto! My life has been overturned! The jaws of hell gape below me and devils grasp at my heels. How can this have happened? I was sitting in my room . . . no, no. I must start at the beginning. This morning in the Duomo Santa Caterina, Giovanni gave a sermon in which he talked about rendering to Caesar what was Caesar's and to God what was God's. I was sure Giovanni was talking to me because of the conversation we had last night and this afternoon I knew I was right! As soon as mass was over I came here to write the very words I have just written, when there was a knock at the door.

"Un momento!" I called out, because I wanted to hide this manuscript. A voice said if I did not open the door it would be broken down. I was outraged that someone would talk to me like that. Me! A courtier! The father of the bride! In the middle of the wedding! "I will give whoever it is a good thrashing for disturbing me," I shouted, as I opened the door. There standing before me were the same four soldiers I had seen with Cardinal Giovanni the night before. The captain said Cardinal Giovanni wanted to see me. I replied that Cardinal Giovanni must have forgotten that my daughter was getting married and that I had many things to do and if Cardinal Giovanni wanted to see me could he please come to my room. The captain warned me that if I did not come immediately I could be thrown in prison. *Potta!* What could I do?

Giovanni was bending over his desk writing when I entered. His hair had been cut short and without his hat his head looked like a big pot and his ears handles to pick it up with. I waited for a moment and then said, "Cardinal Giovanni, if you will pardon me for interrupt—"

"No, I will not," he snapped, and went on writing.

The fool was acting like the pope himself! After a few moments, he put down his quill, sat back in his chair and said, "Do you know why I am here?"

He was obviously playing a game, but since I did not know the rules I replied quite innocently, "Surely, it is to give the pope's blessing to this holy marriage."

He said, "I am here by authority of Pope Clement to investigate anyone who has sinned against the church."

"What has that to do with me?" I shrugged.

He did not answer but continued to look straight at me.

I said, "Cardinal Giovanni, I swear by la Santa Madre Vergine, *I* have never said anything against our Lord Jesus Christ, the Lord God, the church, or a saint. Not even the pope!"

Giovanni picked up a piece of paper from the desk, adjusted his spectacles, and read, "The Imperial Church of Roma hereby accuses Ugo DiFonte of Corsoli of practicing witchcraft."

"Me?" I laughed. "A witch?"

"This is a serious charge! The penalty is death!"

"Cardinal Giovanni, you have the wrong DiFonte! My brother Vittore held sabbats in the stable. He cursed Christ. He made his followers kiss his *culo*—"

"It would be better if you confessed."

"To what?" I replied hotly.

Someone hit me in the back of my head and I fell to the ground. I was kicked in the ribs, then picked up, and stood in front of Giovanni again as if I was nothing more than a doll. My head was ringing and blood flowed from my mouth, for a tooth had come loose.

"You should control your temper. We have a witness."

"I would like to see who it is," I shouted.

Cardinal Giovanni nodded to a guard who opened a side door— *Jesus in sancto!* O my soul!—in stepped the dandy from Milano! "Perhaps you remember Battista Girolamo," Giovanni went on. "He used to be the food taster to the Duke of Savoy. He says he saw you perform witchcraft at a banquet last year given by Francesco Sforza."

"He put a spell over a bowl of berries that killed Antonio DeGenoa," the dandy said slyly.

"I never killed him—"

"Quiet! You saw this happen, Battista?"

"Yes, Cardinal Giovanni."

"Had you ever met Ugo DiFonte before?"

"Yes, Your Excellency, Cardinal Giovanni. The night he arrived a group of us food tasters were drinking and talking about amulets."

"What did he say?"

"He said he did not use any amulets."

"What *did* he use?"

"He said he used magic."

"*Magic?*"

"Yes, Cardinal Giovanni, magic!"

Potta! They were even better rehearsed than the actors from Padua!

"You may go," Giovanni smiled. The guard opened the side door. The dandy walked through it but paused in the doorway, turned to me, and drew his hand across his throat.

"Now what do you say?" asked Giovanni, adjusting his spectacles once more.

What could I say? If I told him that no one was more surprised than I when Onionface had died he would not believe me. If I told him I could not perform magic if my life depended on it he would not believe me. It did not matter what I said. He wanted revenge for the killing of his sister and mother.

"Cardinal Giovanni, if I could really do magic, why would I have remained a food taster here in Corsoli risking my life twice a day, every day of the week, for all these years? Would I not have gone to Roma or Milano or Venezia and made a fortune? Indeed, if I knew magic why would I be standing here right now?"

Giovanni's face turned as red as a beet. "How dare you mock this court," he shouted. "You could be beheaded for your insolence. That is all. Until I call you again."

The guards marched me back to my room, telling me I was lucky to be alive because Giovanni had ordered other men to prison and some to death on far less evidence. Now here I sit, trembling. Why did Giovanni not put me to death? Or at least in prison? Why is he taunting me? Is he afraid of Federico? Perhaps he is waiting till after the wedding. O merciful God, what shall I do? Where can I go? For the moment I must remain calm. Above all I must not let Giovanni see I am afraid. Oh, why did you have to come now, you little bastard, hunchback sodomite dwarf! Ugo, calm yourself. Courage! Something will come to me.

Whenever there was something I did not understand in the Bible, such as why God allowed saints to be killed and sinners to live, the abbot Tottorini said that God's ways were mysterious and not to be questioned. The more I thought about this, the more it seemed that what people thought were God's mysteries were really mistakes. When I told this to the abbot he replied angrily, "God does not make mistakes!"

"If they are not mistakes, then he must not care," I answered.

This made the abbot angrier still. He said God had sacrificed His only Son for the sins of mankind, which showed how much He cared. And because we are His children He watches over all of us.

"Then His eyes are bad," I replied. How can He watch over me and also watch over everyone else in Corsoli? As well as everyone in Venezia and Roma and Milano and France and all at the same time? We pray and beg Him to favor us, praising Him when He does and blaming ourselves when He does not. The truth is I do not think He sees us. And if He does, I do not think He cares. I remember the first time I looked down from the palace walls and saw the villagers making their way to market. They appeared no bigger than ants and I could not tell one from the other. Surely that is how we must look to God. Thousands upon thousands of ants, each struggling to overcome the twigs and stones in their lives. But for what? If there is some reason why I must overcome these twigs and stones, why does God not give me a sign? Does He think I am too stupid to understand? I, who have overcome Onionface and my father and Vittore? Does He think I have no more brains than an ant? Why give me a brain at all? I would rather be an ant and not think. Then I would be at peace.

Truly, the world has gone mad. Guests stand below my window watching the rain—it started earlier today—while just above them I burn in hell. I must speak to Federico. I have served him well. I have saved his life. He is marrying my daughter. He will protect me against Giovanni. He must. It would not look well if the father of the bride was arrested for witchcraft at Federico's wedding.

I have just returned from Federico's chamber. The guard said Federico was resting and did not wish to be disturbed. I swear if Giovanni locks me up in the same cell as Vittore I will go mad! Now I must prepare for the jousting.

I have returned from the jousting. Miranda was cheering and laughing as if she did not have a care in the world. I wanted to ask her why, but I did not feel well. The walls of my room sway up and down like a boat at sea. My paper refuses to lie still on the desk even after I threatened to tear it into pieces. Ugo, Ugo, Ugo. U U U U. The quill has sharp claws. Giovanni has claws. Everyone has claws. Even I. I cannot scratch my face unless I am very careful so my face does not see. Someone is standing by the door. They are calling me. They have the mouth of a rat. I shall ignore them because I cannot be seen with a rat. I cannot go to the banquet with a rat. I do not care how many times it calls me, I am not going. I am not . . .

The fourth day—midafternoon.

My senses have deserted me! I *am* mad! It is the afternoon of the fourth day and I am a bowstring pulled to its tautest point. Federico did not go on the hunt—what horse could carry him?—and neither did Giovanni. As we prepared to leave I saw them talking together. What were they talking about? I asked Cecchi but he did not know. The hunt was abandoned because of rain. I am going to see Federico again.

Early evening.

Federico was still resting. Why? He never rested before. Perhaps he does not wish to see me. But how would he know why I was coming to see him? I wandered around the palace. The guests were gossiping about Federico marrying a peasant girl and not just taking her as he had done with so many others. "I would kill myself," a woman said. Another man wondered how I could have allowed Miranda to marry the duke, for he would never have agreed to such a match. It is jealousy. I see it in their faces. I hear it in their voices.

Thunder clapped just now, lightning rent the sky and the rain falls with a vengeance. Some moments ago the actors returned from the Piazza San Giulio. The actress playing the unicorn said if the ground became any muddier Hercules would not be chasing a unicorn but an elephant.

After Federico refused to see me I went to the kitchen to make sure Luigi was making my favorite little rolls of tame game as he had promised. The game is finely cut, mixed with fat of veal and spices, wrapped in a crust, and baked. Then the yolks of two eggs are beaten together with a little verjuice and dripped gently over four rolls. It was just as well I went, for when I arrived Luigi was not making the rolls, but mixing ground-up breast of chicken with ground almonds and soft bread.

"We are having *mangiabianco* instead," he said, looking at me as if I should have been cleaning out the cesspool. Christ on a cross! Three years ago he did not know pork from chicken and now he thinks he has invented cooking! "I changed it because after so much feasting the stomach is saturated with food and it is necessary to tease it."

"But we have not had that much feasting."

"What did we do two nights ago?" he asked indignantly.

I looked at Tommaso but he pretended not to see me.

"As a taster you are not acquainted with the many different types of appetite," Luigi said.

I, Ugo, the food taster, not acquainted with different types of appetite?

"The appetite of an empty stomach is not the same as one which has enjoyed a meal." He added a handful of ginger and sugar, mixing it with the chicken and almonds. "Once the appetite has been aroused, it is not so curious. It says, 'Surprise me.' "

I will surprise you, I thought, taking out my knife. "Whose idea was this?"

"Tommaso's."

So that was why he had ignored me.

"I cannot talk now," he shouted, waving his arms in the air. He was making a chariot and horses out of sugar and marzipan. I wanted to smash it into pieces. He must have sensed this because he stood in front of it. "What do you want?" he yelled.

Everyone in the kitchen stared at me. Luigi said, "You cannot keep coming in here while we have work to do!"

"I will come in whenever I like!" I shouted.

I found Miranda, but she would not listen to me either. Now my head hurts and my skin prickles. I have scratched it till it bleeds but it will not stop. Why does it not stop? I must prepare for the banquet.

*   *   *

Dawn.

I am barely alive. There is no reason for me to go to hell for I am already there. O God in heaven, what are you preparing me for?

After the banquet, which I can no longer remember for I have aged a thousand years since then, I fell into a deep sleep. I do not know how long I slept, but suddenly I was dreaming of Federico. He was walking along a corridor, his cane in one hand, his sword in the other. He was walking slowly at first, but then faster, down one corridor and along the next. I knew he was coming to my room. I knew I had to hide something, but I did not know what it was. I ran around the room, searching under the bed, behind the chairs, all the time knowing that Federico was coming closer and closer. I tore the curtains from the windows, tears streaming down my face, crying for my mother to help me, when all of a sudden I knew what I was looking for. I shot up out of my sleep, sprang to the door Miranda and I shared, and banged on it.

"Who is it?" she answered.

"Your father!" I hissed. I could hear the shuffling of feet. "Open the door! For the love of God, open the door!" The door opened and there stood Miranda and Tommaso, clutching sheets to their nakedness. "Are you mad? Federico is coming!"

Miranda said, "I will have Tommaso's child."

"I will tell him we are betrothed," Tommaso said. They stood there, grains of sand before an onrushing tide.

"He will kill you both!"

"Then we will be together in heaven," Tommaso replied. *Oi me!* I could hear Federico's three-footed walk in the hallway! Tommaso ran toward the door as if to confront Federico himself. With a cry, I flung Miranda back into her bed and with a strength I did not know I had, pulled Tommaso by the back of his head into my room, closed the door and leaned against it. He tried to pull me away. I put my hands over his mouth and wrestled him to the ground. We heard Miranda scream, the clanking feet of Federico's guard and then Federico's harsh voice, demanding, "Where is he?"

Only then did Tommaso emerge from his dream state. I let him go, pointed to the window, and threw myself against the door of

Miranda's room as it opened. I was pushed to the ground as the guard strode past me and in the doorway stood Federico as I had pictured him in my dream. "Who are you?" he roared, his face twisted with rage, his sword at my neck.

"Ugo DiFonte, Your Excellency. Your food taster. Your faithful servant. I heard Miranda scream—"

Behind me the guard tore my room apart, searching through the bedclothes and overturning my desk.

"I smell it!" Federico hissed. "I smell it." He slashed the air with his sword and stabbed my bedclothes over and over.

I wanted to say, "Your Excellency, it is not Miranda's fault but that ass, Tommaso. Kill him and your worries will be over!" But as I raised my head I saw Miranda's pleading, terrified eyes—so I said nothing. Besides I could not say anything without implicating her.

Federico hobbled into the hall, his footsteps echoing on the stone floor. When I could hear them no longer I went into Miranda's room. She was sitting up, trembling and shaking. She reached out her arms to me. "Babbo," she wept, "Babbo."

I told her that God has plans for all of us and that we must trust in Him. Even when the world is against us, when darkness and evil overtake us, we must have faith in Him. For the blackest clouds disperse in time, revealing the sun. So it is with God. For those who believe in Him, He is the sun and like the sun He will heal us when the clouds of dismay have vanished.

Miranda did not say anything; she did not have to, for she knew, that it was not her I was trying to convince, but myself.

The fifth day.

Dear God, why do you not listen to me? I pray for your guidance but YOU GIVE ME NONE! My world is shattered. Giovanni's guards came for me again. This time they just burst into my room and dragged me to Giovanni. As soon as I stood before him, Giovanni asked, "Ugo DiFonte, do you believe in God?"

"Of course," I made the sign of the cross. "God the Father, the Son, the Holy Ghost. Our creator. Our Father."

"Our Father?"

"Yes. Our Father, that is to say, we are made in His image."

Giovanni chewed the end of his quill. "If we are made in His image, ipso facto, He must reflect us, *n'est-ce pas?*"

"I am sorry, Cardinal Giovanni, but I do not know what you mean."

"If we are made in His image then He must be like us," he repeated. "Our strengths are His strengths and our weaknesses His weaknesses."

"Cardinal Giovanni, your words are sharper than your sword. I am just a peasant—"

"If you were a peasant you would not be wearing those clothes and be sitting at Duke Federico's table tomorrow night with your own taster," he snapped. "So," he carried on, "according to you, God can be caring and yet uncaring. Merciful, but cruel—"

"Cardinal Giovanni—"

"Selfish, arrogant, a thief, a murderer—"

"We are made in God's image, but our failings come because we stray from His teachings."

"What is the worst failing?"

I was afraid to answer for no matter what I said I knew it would be wrong.

"Pride, Ugo."

"It is as you say then."

"Are you not proud of your daughter?"

"But is that a sin?"

He ignored me. "You are proud of your daughter. You are proud you have risen from a food taster to a courtier. You are proud you have cheated death. Your pride is like a stench around you. You walk about in your fancy silks, but you are still a peasant. And a witch. That is all."

He waved a hand and I was thrown out of the room. Still he did not arrest me. Why? On the way back I saw Miranda talking to Tommaso in Emilia's garden.

"This is madness," I said to them. "You were nearly killed last night and now today—"

"We were discussing the dessert for the banquet," Miranda said coldly, and walked away.

Tommaso followed her with his eyes and I stepped in front so no one might see. "There are guests everywhere! I cannot believe you would sacrifice her life so."

"I?" he cried. "You have already done so," and he too walked away.

They lie. They are planning something. That is why they stopped talking when they saw me. They plan to poison Federico, and me, too. I know it. I know it. I, who persuaded Tommaso to become a chef, am going to be poisoned by him. And my daughter is going to help him. That is a comedy even Boccaccio would envy.

I wanted to tell Duke Federico about Cardinal Giovanni and Tommaso, but after last night I no longer know if he will listen to me. Besides, whenever he eats or wherever he goes he is surrounded by guests. Even when I taste his food in the morning there are people around him. This time he was playing cards with the duke of Perugia and Marguerite of Rimini. I waited for the game to finish, but he started another immediately. I know he saw me, but he avoided me. Is it because of Cardinal Giovanni? I do not care anymore. I will speak with him at the banquet even if I have to yell.

The actors will perform more plays tonight because the pageant has been canceled because of rain. It is a shame. I looked forward to seeing Hercules chasing the unicorn and the unicorn changing into Venus. Now the Piazza San Giulio will only be used for the *caccia*. I pray that will not be canceled. Now I must dress. I tried to talk to Miranda, but she was surrounded by guests and friends. There is no banquet tonight. After everything we ate last night, it is a wonder anyone will ever want to eat again.

The fifth night.
Tommaso! That stupid, hot-headed ignorant fool! If he wants to kill himself, then let him do so, but he will cause Miranda's death, too. I knew they were planning something. Miranda was smiling and talking with the guests and clutching Federico's hand, but I did not believe her for an instant. Then, while the actors were performing the piece about the nun again, I suddenly thought of Vittore. Perhaps it was the nun's cell which alerted me, I do not know. Whatever it was, I slipped away from the performance and looked for Tommaso. He was not in the kitchen nor in his room. Like a madman I ran all over the palace. Then suddenly I knew. I raced to the prison. The guard was not at the top of the stairs, and as fate should have it when I came to the bottom I saw someone struggling with the lock of Vittore's cell. I called out. "In the name of Duke Federico, stop what you are doing."

Tommaso turned round. He was trembling and panting, his mouth open, his hair in disarray.

"Open it!" Vittore commanded. Tommaso fumbled with the key again.

I pulled out my dagger. "Do not make me kill you, Tommaso."

"He does not have the balls," Vittore hissed.

"He will take Miranda and murder you. Remember what happened after the sabbats," I pleaded.

"I cannot live without her," Tommaso cried.

He turned the key. I ran at him and that bastard Vittore pushed the cell door open so violently that Tommaso fell backward onto my knife. He screamed as the blade sank into his thigh. I staggered back. "Ugo!" he cried.

I collapsed under his weight and he fell on top of me. His cry brought the guards. I pushed Tommaso off me and as he rolled over, blood poured from the wound. His hand grasped my shirt.

"Why did you not listen to me?" I pleaded.

"I will try . . ." His eyes rolled to the back of his head and he fainted.

"Ugo killed him!" Vittore shouted. He had slipped back into his cell and was holding the door closed. The guards tried to arrest me, but I fought them, yelling that it was Vittore who had stabbed him.

"But he is locked in his cell," said the guard. "And this is your knife?"

"Put him in here," Vittore shouted.

I tried to explain what I had seen, but in my anger and despair I made no sense.

"Where is the key to the cell?" the guard demanded.

"Vittore must have it."

"He is in the cell," the stupid guard repeated and started to drag me up the stairs. "He will escape!" I shouted.

Fortunately, Cecchi had become alarmed at my disappearance and came by at that moment. He ordered the guards to search the cell and they found the key buried beneath the straw. Tommaso was carried away and Piero attended to him. Shaking, I went to my room and waited for Miranda.

She arrived, pale and trembling, with Cecchi by her side. "What is it?" she kept saying, "what is it?"

Cecchi said, "Tommaso was stabbed trying to release Vittore."

Miranda would have fallen to the floor had Cecchi not caught her and slapped her about the face. He said if Federico discovered that she had been involved trying to free Vittore he would kill her himself. He said she had endangered not only herself, but me and others in the palace. He told her to put away all memory of Tommaso and never think of him again. Then he took her by the hand and led her away.

I think now, finally, she has grasped that there is nothing she can do. I pray the wound in Tommaso's thigh will remind him, too.

The sixth day—midday.

I have not slept. I look at my hands and do not recognize them. Although I tell myself that it was Vittore who pushed Tommaso onto me, I would have stabbed him to death in the next moment. Although the wound is deep, Tommaso will live. Even now he is making the pastry for the last banquet. I remember hearing that brown eyes mean that their owner is clever and wise, but Tommaso has brown eyes and he is foolish. Brave but foolish. Is he brave *because* he is foolish? How could he have believed Vittore would help him?

Miranda dressed in a gown which showed her breasts to the nipples. She painted her face with so much rouge that a fly would have left a mark had it landed there.

"Why are you doing this?"

"Since I am a whore, I am dressing like one."

"Miranda, listen to me!"

"Or what? You will kill me?"

I walked toward her but she clutched a knife and screamed "Guard! Guard!" so loudly that I left.

It is astonishing how this tragedy unfolds unnoticed amid all the festivities. Even now the bell of Santa Caterina leaps out of the vestry, its chimes joyfully tumbling into one another. The golden Madonna glimmers in the sunlight. Banners hang from every window and loggia, people sing and dance. They know nothing of this. Even if they did, it would not stop their merrymaking. Nothing can prevent today's celebration. The wedding *will* take place. I wish my mother could see it. My father, too. But both are dead. Soon my brother

Vittore will join them. He, above all, deserves to die, but this afternoon I was filled with remorse. I wanted to ask Federico that since the rain has stopped and death is not a good omen for the marriage, perhaps the *caccia* should be postponed till after the wedding. But Federico will not listen to me.

Night.

It was a shame the pageant was canceled because by the light of the sconces the Piazza San Giulio was more beautiful than anyone could have imagined. When Miranda appeared the crowd embraced her, calling her an angel and the queen of Corsoli. They praised Federico for choosing her and wished them many children. It was such an outpouring of love that even Miranda was surprised and moved. A man shouted that our patron saint, Santa Caterina, could be seen in the stars smiling down upon us. The bishop prayed that we would always be worthy to be held in the palm of God's hand. Then cats and dogs were thrown into the piazza and immediately there was barking and mewling as they bit and scratched one another to death.

The crowd shouted and yelled for the next event. After a flourish of trumpets a cart carrying a cage was pushed into the garden. It held three men: the first, a thief who had scraped gold leaf from the Madonna on the Duomo Santa Caterina; the second, the prison guard Tommaso had bribed when he tried to free Vittore; and the third was Vittore. More trumpet blasts announced another cage bearing the lion. The keepers freed the lion and then hurriedly clambered onto a platform. The thief tried to climb up after them, but the crowd pushed him back into the mud. The guard fell to his knees and prayed. Vittore stood next to a tree, his jacket and hose as torn and dirty as the day he arrived.

The lion walked slowly out of the cage, its knotty tail flicking back and forth. It had a large head and a huge mane, but it was so thin you could see its ribs. "It must be from Corsoli," a woman shouted to much laughter. I wondered if the lion thought it was at home in Africa. Did it know all these trees and bushes had been brought in for its benefit? The crowd cheered and whistled. A star shot across the sky.

Suddenly, Vittore shouted, "*Io sono vittima di una cospirazione! Cospirazione! Cospirazione!*" He said it over and over, turning round and round and beating his chest with his long thin arms.

The crowd mocked him, beating their chests and wailing, *"Cospirazione! Cospirazione!"*

The lion stood quite still, patiently waiting for his cue to begin.

"Yes, I gave Federico a potion," Vittore shouted, "but not arsenic."

"No one is interested in your lies," I cried.

The lion padded behind a bush. Vittore pointed at me and said, "He does not want you to know the truth."

"You would not know the truth if you spoke it," I shouted, and the crowd laughed.

"I gave Federico mercury," Vittore shouted. "Do you know why?"

Cristo in croce! Why was the lion taking so long?

Pulling his hair away from his face, Vittore ran toward the balcony where Federico was sitting with Miranda. "This will be your fate—"

Even as it occurred to me that Vittore had been telling the truth about Federico, the lion leaped over the bush, caught Vittore's back leg in his jaw and pulled him to the wet ground. Vittore screamed. The lion clubbed Vittore's head with his paw. Vittore's legs jerked violently and his cry was silenced.

Miranda collapsed and Federico lifted her up in his arms and carried her away, her handmaidens running after him. The crowd did not notice for they were too busy watching the lion. It tore Vittore's left shoulder from his body and bit into his chest. Blood shot into the air, covering the lion's face. Vittore's bones snapped like twigs and with each bite a part of me snapped until I wondered if I was not dying, too.

"Tell all witches to come to Corsoli," someone shouted. "We have a hungry lion."

The crowd cheered. I was silent. Exhausted. Weighed down by the blood on my hands.

As soon as the *caccia* was over I went to Federico's chambers, telling the guards that Federico had summoned me to tell him of Miranda's condition. Federico was standing by the window when I entered. "How is Miranda?" he asked. His face was pale and worried.

"She is recovering, Your Excellency."

He sighed deeply. "Good. Good!" He clapped his hands together in a praying motion and then blew a kiss to heaven.

I did not wait for permission to speak. "Your Excellency, Cardinal

Giovanni has accused me twice of witchcraft in Milano." As if he had not heard, Federico turned his back on me to look out at the hillside. I did not let that stop me. "He is talking about the time I blew on the berries. But I did not use any magic. As you know it was only by the grace of God that Onionface died."

Federico did not answer. Was he still thinking about Miranda? Perhaps he was hoping I would go away.

"Your Honor—"

"Ugo." He turned toward me, and with a smile such as a parent uses to calm an anxious child, said, "How long have you been my taster?"

"Five years, My Lord."

"And you have served me faithfully."

"It has been my honor, Your Excellency."

"And now you are giving your daughter to me in marriage." He laid a heavy hand upon my shoulder and stared straight into my eyes. "Do you really think I would allow anything to happen to you?"

"But—"

"Think no more about it."

"Your Honor—"

"And say no more about it."

I knew then, as sure as my name is Ugo DiFonte, that he was lying. But I had not served him for five years without learning anything, so I heaved a sigh of relief and said "Your Excellency, you have given me new life and made me eternally grateful." I kissed his hand. Then I hurried out of the room before I vomited.

The poxy bastard has deserted me! Me! Who serves him faithfully. Who eats his food and saves him from poison! Who gently lifts his gouty foul-smelling leg! Who fluffs his pillows. Who stands by his chair when he shits! It has to do with Giovanni. But what is it?

Night.

I have found out why Federico lied to me! At the banquet I was as close to him as my quill is to this paper and yet he refused to look at me. Miranda also refused, but I do not blame her. I would beg her forgiveness for I have wronged her terribly, but I do not have time.

Halfway through the banquet, as golden platters stacked high with crests of hen and roast pigeon were being served, Cardinal Giovanni made a speech.

"Love is the seed of life," he said. "There is love for one's family, love for mankind, and love for God. When one inspires the other, the windfall of happiness knows no bounds. Because of his great love for Miranda, Duke Federico has agreed to take his new bride on a pilgrimage to Roma to receive a blessing from the pope!"

Everyone cheered Federico, who was beaming proudly! I looked at Miranda, who seemed as mystified as I was. And now, finally, I understood why Federico had not spoken to me! He has betrayed me! Betrayed me to satisfy a whim of Miranda's that she cannot even remember! Federico thinks by taking her to Roma as she had asked months ago, she will love him. And in return for safe passage Federico will allow Giovanni to arrest me. And I thought Federico would protect me! What a fool I have been! Federico will not protect me! Why should he? He no longer needs me. He will be married to Miranda who is loved by everyone. The peasants love him. The guests praise him!

Giovanni sat down and everyone congratulated him for making peace with Federico. It was then that I lost control of all of my senses. What need had I for them anymore? Voices echoed inside my head like the shouting of giants. My eyes glazed over and I could not see. The power of my nose, which I used to control as finely as Grazzari controlled his paintbrush, no longer obeyed me. Suddenly, I could smell not only the garlic, the lemon, the smoked cheeses, and the fennel, but also the perfumes of ambergris, musk, and rosemary. I could detect the whiff of velvet in the robes of the guests, their woolen shirts, the beaten gold trimming on the dresses. While everyone around me was talking about Miranda meeting the pope, I was overcome by the stink of their unwashed hair, the damp sweat under their arms, the dirt between their toes, the shit in their *culo*. My eyes watered at the overpowering aroma of Federico's lust. I gagged on Giovanni's choking smugness. I was overcome by the stench of Miranda's despair. Holy Mother of God! What have I done to my daughter? I have sacrificed her so that I might eat again.

There rose then still one more odor. One which had lain buried beneath the others but now snaked its way out of the bile of my stomach and up into my throat. It was my fear. My betrayal. My cowardice.

I sat there suffocating while all around me the guests celebrated. I prayed to God and He spoke to me, saying, "I help those who help themselves." No sooner had I heard those words than I knew what I had to do. I turned to Miranda, but she was not at the table.

"She left the hall," Duke Orsino said.

Miranda was in the courtyard standing on the ledge where the bodies are thrown down the mountain. In the moonlight she looked so like my mother that at first I thought it was her ghost. "Miranda!" I called.

She did not answer.

"Miranda, it is not over yet."

She looked down the mountain. "Not quite. But soon."

"Where there is life, there is hope."

She turned to me. "My champions have all been beaten."

"I am your champion."

"You?" she sneered.

"We have been in difficult times before. Miranda, I promised your mother I would always take care of you."

"Please . . ."

"I have a plan. As soon as you marry Federico, you must complain of an ache in your stomach." I moved closer as I was talking. "You must tell Federico that I have a potion that will cure it." I moved closer still. "Then you will come to my room and drink a potion I have prepared."

"What will it do?"

"You know I have been experimenting with potions—"

"What will it do?" she repeated angrily.

"It will make you appear as if you are dead." I did not have such a potion but I could not tell her that.

"How will that help?"

"Like this." And grasping her hand, I pulled her off the ledge.

"You tricked me," she hissed. She spat in my face and tried to scratch me. "Oh, why will you not let me die!" she wailed.

"Because I am your father and you will do whatever I tell you!" I led her back to the hall. I had to do that. I could not stop my mother from killing herself, but I would die before I let Miranda do the same.

*   *   *

Soon I have to taste Federico's breakfast and prepare for mass. Today is the day Miranda will be married and I will enjoy food again. I must do that at least once, otherwise this has all been for nothing.

The last day—morning.

Tommaso was fast asleep so I put my knife to his *fallo* and my hand over his mouth and when he woke I whispered, "Lie still or by God you will die here and now." Then I said, "Do you still love Miranda?"

His eyes flitted from side to side as if he was hoping to wake one of the other boys sleeping in the room.

"Will you marry her and take care of her for the rest of your life? Answer me!"

One of the boys raised his head, grunted and went back to sleep.

"Answer me!" Tommaso nodded. "Then get up. We have little time."

Outside the room I said, "You must make three cookies. One of Miranda, one of the duke, and one of me. The figures must be good but not great, for it must be as if I made them. Miranda's will be only marzipan and sugar, but in the duke's you must mix in the contents of this bag." I held it up. "Place the figures on the turret of the cake. This is the only way you and Miranda will be free."

He frowned angrily. "But they will know that *I*—"

"That is why they must be clumsy. Then everyone will believe me when I say *I* made them."

Questions dashed to the front of his mouth only to be overtaken by more pressing ones.

"Tommaso, I have inflicted great wrongs on you and Miranda. Allow me to heal them. I have but a few hours."

He was so confused that it was easy to lead him to the kitchen. There I persuaded him to make three small piles of dough and flavored them with sugar and marzipan. I poured the contents of my bag into two of the piles. "Make this one look like Federico and the other look like me."

Tommaso's head jerked up. "But—"

"Giovanni is going to kill me anyway for what happened to his sister and mother. That is why he is here."

He stared at me in disbelief. "Does Miranda know?"

"Of course," I lied. He had stopped working and I had to jog his arm. "Hurry!"

"I will put less in yours."

"No, Tommaso. You will put *more* in mine."

He stopped.

"Do what I say! I have my reasons."

He rubbed the poisons into the dough and began to shape the figures. In no time they took on the forms of Federico, Miranda, and myself. "Do not make them perfect," I warned him.

He placed them on the fire. There were voices in the hallway. "Go," he said. "I will finish them."

"You will take care of Miranda?"

"With my life. You have my word." We grasped arms and kissed one another on the cheek.

I prayed all day though I realize that my praying has made little difference to what has followed. That is not to say that I doubt God's existence. When I look out of my window and see the valley in springtime, when I see Miranda's face when she sleeps, when I close my eyes and imagine my Helene, I know that God exists. I believe He watches me. Not over me. But watches me. He leaves omens for me. For instance, I thought that I had overcome so many obstacles to Miranda's happiness when the biggest obstacle was myself. I am grateful to Him for allowing me to understand this.

Now I am going to the wedding feast. I am wearing a white silk shirt, a doublet of blue velvet trimmed with gold brocade puffed at the wrists, and my velvet hat with a jeweled brooch in its center. A medallion of pure gold, a gift Cecchi gave me, hangs around my neck. I have silver rings on three of my fingers. When I look in the mirror I see a courtier who would be at home in the palazzos of Firenze or Venezia. A man who was once afraid of Death, but is no longer, for in facing Death he has given purpose to his life.

Night.

I will try to complete this in the time I have left to live. Tonight, I was seated at the table between Miranda and Princess Marguerite of Rimini. I laughed and joked with everyone and even ate with a silver fork. Septivus could not finish Federico's poem, so I offered him the one I had written for Helene. I am glad to say everyone loved it.

The trumpets sounded—I am tired of trumpets, they are shrill and noisy and I am glad I will never have to hear them anymore. The servants marched in carrying platters of food. O my soul! Has it truly been five years since I was in that line? On each platter sat a swan wearing a golden crown, its eyes shining brightly, its wings spread out in flight, its beak casting out fiery sparks. Luigi placed the largest platter in front of me! Me! Ugo the food taster! He raised the long fork.

"Where is your taster?" Federico asked me.

I told him I did not want one.

"You are not going to use a taster?" He turned to the guests. "I told him he could have his own taster. Why do you not want one?"

I stood up. Septivus had given a speech, so had Giovanni, the bishop and nobles from Urbino and Spoleto, so why not I? Everyone quieted down. I cleared my throat. "Magnificent Prince," I began. "On this day, Christ in His Glory, the Holy Mother, and God Himself have all blessed Corsoli and all who dwell within her gates. In such a sacred house, the spirits will not allow anyone to harbor thoughts or deeds against you, Miranda, or anyone else." Then I sat down.

"Amen," the bishop said, and everyone echoed his blessing.

Federico leaned across Miranda (he was holding her hand as if she might escape) and whispered to me, "You are still going to taste my food."

"Your Excellency," I said looking into his eyes, "I am still your taster."

Luigi stuck the fork into the swan, raised it to the height of his chest, cut six slices off its breast, and poured the juices over it. I speared a piece with my fork and lifted it to my mouth. The odor made me dizzy. Luigi had used just the right amount of fennel. I opened my mouth and placed it on my tongue. It was warm, rich, tender.

"Ugo is weeping," Federico shouted, and the hall rocked with laughter.

"They are tears of joy," Cecchi said.

"It is not only free of all poison," I declared, "but it is delicious!"

"Now *you* must eat!" Federico said.

The evening I had been waiting for was here at last. I began with the spit-roasted quails. They were heavenly. The skylarks and pheasants were even better. The kid cooked in garlic sauce, superb. I ran out of words of praise before the first course had ended. There were also eggplants, capons in lemon sauce, platters of pasta, and sausages browned to perfection. The salted pork was succulent, if a little salty, but the fried broad beans were crisp as spring frost. I ate an entire plateful of calves' brains and had not one, but two helpings of Turkish rice with almonds.

I chewed over every bite, savoring every morsel, making up for all the meals I had missed.

"He is eating as if it was his last meal," Bernardo grumbled. Cecchi looked at me and raised his glass in my honor. I drank many goblets of wine and even smiled at Cardinal Giovanni, addressing several remarks to him. Miranda flashed her eyes and adjusted her dress so that more of her breasts showed.

I seized a moment when Federico was not looking at her and, squeezing her arm, whispered that although she hated me I loved her more than life itself. "If I could suffer a *thousand* deaths in your place, I would do so. I beg you, do not judge me. It is not over yet." She pulled away as more trumpets announced the wedding cake— Tommaso's sugar and marzipan extravaganza.

It was so large that two servants had to carry it on a tray. They held it aloft and walked around the hall as everyone marveled at how brilliantly Tommaso had copied the palazzo. Then they placed it in front of Federico. I prayed Tommaso had done as I asked and I was not disappointed. On the turret were the three figures of Miranda, Duke Federico, and myself.

"It is better than anything Bramante ever built," Federico said. The windows and columns were made out of cheeses, sweets, and nuts, the marble courtyard out of pieces of glazed orange and lemon.

"But what are these figures?" Marguerite of Rimini asked.

"Your Excellency." I stood up again. Everyone quieted again to listen to me. "I prepared these three figures myself. They are of Your Honor, Miranda, and myself.

"You are becoming a cook now?" Federico said, as everyone laughed.

"Why not? Who knows more about food than me?"

I could see Miranda looking at me, trying to shake off the effects of the wine.

"Why did you make them?" Federico said, his eyes narrowing.

I had spent so much time planning this that I had not thought that

Federico would question me, but once again God put the words into my mouth.

"My Lord, you have everything a duke could wish for. The valley of Corsoli is known for its beauty. Your city is prosperous and wealthy. Your reputation as a fearless *condotierro* is well known. As a lord you are admired, feared, and loved. You have distinguished friends and loyal citizens. Your walls are decorated with the finest works of art, your stables blessed with magnificent horses. Now you have the love of my daughter, the most beautiful woman in Corsoli. You do me the greatest honor of my life by allowing my family to join yours. Since there is nothing I can give you which can compare to all that I have mentioned, these cookies are simple tokens of the sweetness and the undying love which will now exist between our two families."

"He should be an orator," Septivus announced. The guests applauded loudly. Federico said nothing. He was thinking, as I knew he would, of the cookies of the Day of the Dead.

"Therefore," I went on, "let us partake of this symbol and so be united forever."

Again the guests applauded loudly. I reached for the three cookies and gave Miranda hers, Federico his, and I took mine. The hall was silent, waiting to see what Federico would do. He looked at Tommaso. I feared Tommaso would say something, but for the first time in his life, he remained silent. Ah, I thought, he has grown up at last. Then Federico turned to me and said, "Since I am taking over the responsibility of Miranda's protection, would it not be right for me to eat *your* cookie and for you to eat mine?"

I acted as if I was surprised, but I replied cheerfully, "If the duke wishes, he can exchange his cookie with mine or Miranda's."

Federico looked at Miranda, and then at the cookie in her hand. I prayed I was right and that he loved her as much as I thought he did.

Patting her hand gently, Federico turned to me and said, "No, I will exchange my cookie with yours."

"Then let it be so," I said. I gave him my cookie and took his. "Now let us eat." I bit down hard into my cookie to show everyone how much I enjoyed it. Miranda, thinking perhaps that I had poisoned hers, ate it greedily. Federico did the same.

Ah, now comes the fire. I did not think the poisons would take effect so quickly. I must hurry.

After the cookies and the cake were eaten, the bishop led Federico and Miranda through the palazzo to his bedchamber. The guests walked behind singing hymns of praise. Men sighed and women wept. At Federico's bedchamber, the bishop said a prayer. I kissed Miranda and placed her hand into Federico's. They went inside and closed the door.

Oh, but it hurts. I was blind but now the veil is lifted, the mist disappears. Septivus, you were right. Food together with the spirit creates a hunger only God can satisfy.

Ah, *potta!* But this is quick! Oh, my stomach! Claws of fire. The griffin's beak rips my flesh. It spreads through my bowels like a flaming sword.

Cardinal Giovanni, you think I am a coward for taking my own life, but my mother was not a coward.

O God! It comes again. Oh, . . . Oh, *potta!* I have shit myself! Oh, Helene. My darling, Helene, love of my life. We will not meet in this world, but I will wait for you.

My door is open, I must hear Federico fall! DEATH CANNOT TAKE ME FIRST.

My hands itch. My face bleeds.

Oh, fire! Helene, forgive me.

O my God,

Purify

Your servant.

I did not die. Cecchi once called me "*Il miracolo vivente*," and now I deserve the name. Truly it is a miracle that I am alive. I did not plan to live. Indeed, I was prepared to die, but God in His wisdom has spared me.

I did not hear what happened in the duke's chamber because after he closed the door I returned to my room. Cecchi told me that soon after the door closed, the guests, who were waiting outside for Federico to declare that he had taken Miranda's virginity, heard strange noises. At first, they thought it was the duke making love, but Miranda came running out crying that the duke was vomiting and complaining of burning in his throat and palpitations round his heart.

The courtiers, Cardinal Giovanni, and the bishop immediately went inside. Federico was crying, screaming, throwing himself around the room, smashing into the walls and furniture as though possessed by a thousand demons. Blood and vomit spilled from his mouth. He was shitting blood and feces. He tried to stab himself but his hands kept dropping the dagger. Teeth fell from his mouth. Howling like a madman, he rolled on the bed and tried to strangle himself. The courtiers threw themselves on top of him and after much fighting he sank to the floor, clutching Miranda to him. She screamed but he would not let go. He tried to bite her, but could not close his mouth. Afraid that he might squeeze her to death and distressed at seeing the duke in such agony, Cardinal Giovanni thrust his sword through the duke's heart to end his suffering. Federico shuddered, heaved like a huge dying whale, and then was still. Nero lay beside him, licking his face. They were forced to cut Federico's fingers off to release Miranda.

Then they came running to my room. By this time I was also screaming, bleeding, and shitting. I could only see shapes but I remember Cardinal Giovanni waving his bloody sword. Miranda knelt down and picked up my head in her hands. There was confusion and fear in her eyes. She was remembering the cookies of the Day of the Dead, the breakfast at Carnevale, the stories I had told her of Onionface. She wanted to embrace me, but I could not let her do that, for Giovanni was waiting to kill me and I could not let anyone think that she was part of the plan, so I spat in her face.

She jerked away and dropped my head to the ground. Turning to Giovanni, she said, "No, Cardinal Giovanni. Do not kill him. Let him suffer! Let him suffer a *thousand* deaths for the crimes he has committed this day."

Oh, bless her. Bless her! All the actors in Padua should take lessons from her! Cardinal Giovanni hesitated, but there was no question that I was poisoned, and in great pain. He put his sword away and agreed that I deserved the slowest of deaths. So did the courtiers. By this time I no longer knew what was going on. All I know is that they must have left the room because someone raised my head (I was told later it was Piero) and poured olive oil down my throat. I threw up, retching everything up that I had ever eaten, but it did no good. The poison was in me. I fell violently ill and was expected to die.

All of the guests, including Giovanni, left the palazzo as soon as it was light. Federico was buried the day after. Only a few courtiers attended his funeral. The city took a holiday. I was too ill to know any of this and lay like a dead person. Sometimes I slept and sometimes I was awake. It made no difference. Although I could hear people I could not speak or move any part of my body, nor could I see them. I was sure I was in purgatory and that God had not yet decided whether I should go to heaven or hell.

Tommaso was the soul of kindness, for every day he brought fresh cakes for me in case I should wake. On the other hand, Bernardo said my illness was a bad omen and I should be buried immediately even though I was not yet dead! Fortunately, Cecchi insisted on waiting.

Miranda spent hours by my bedside praying and singing. She imitated her birds and animals, put her arms around me, and whispered she loved me. I wanted to cry out, but could not. I tried to move my fingers the width of a fly. I could not and wept from exhaustion. Luckily, Miranda saw my tears and told the others.

One morning several weeks later, I awoke hungrier than I had ever been in my life. Piero said I had survived because of all the poisons I had taken for so many months. My recovery was cause for celebration, but in the middle of the festivities, Cecchi said that as soon as I was strong enough it would be best for Miranda, Tommaso, and me to leave before Giovanni found out that I had recovered. Bernardo had been seen riding out of the city and it was known he intended to tell him.

The following week everyone bid us farewell. I embraced Cecchi, Piero, and Septivus; truer friends I have never had. Tommaso, Miranda, and I mounted our horses and with the Duomo bell ringing joyfully in our ears, and tears in our eyes, we rode out of the courtyard, down the Weeping Steps through the Piazza Del Vedura and the West Gate, and out of Corsoli forever.

Miranda is truly a woman now—beautiful, brave, and wiser than many twice her age. I could not be more proud of her. With my blessing, she and Tommaso have ridden on to Venezia where Tommaso intends to find work as a cook. Before she left, I kissed her apple cheeks over and over and held her close to me. Although it broke my heart to see her leave, I am comforted knowing that Tommaso is ready to take care of her.

I have purchased a small piece of land here in Arraggio. The soil is rich and perfect for grazing. I am still thin, I suffer from cramps and throw up for no reason. I have lost some teeth and others have become loose. I am not as strong as I once was. Perhaps I will never be again, I do not know. I *do* know that God has given me one more chance to change my life.

My clothes are bundled beside me. My horse waits by the door. As soon as the sun rises I will ride to France. To Nîmes. To Helene. No matter how long it takes, no matter where she is, I will find her. And I will bring her here, to Arraggio, to be my love.

Renaissance Recipes

Rafioli Commun de Herbe Vanzati
(Mint and Spinach Ravioli)

This is plain old spinach ravioli, but with exotic flavorings. The pinches of spice at the end are important. From the fourteenth-century anonymous work *Libro per Cuoco*.

1 (10-ounce) bag spinach leaves, chopped, about 6 cups,
    loosely packed
¼ cup chopped fresh mint
¼ cup chopped parsley
2 tablespoons olive oil
1 egg, lightly beaten
½ cup shredded mozzarella cheese
Ground cinnamon
Ground ginger
Ground cumin
Salt, pepper
Ravioli dough
Boiling salted water
Parmesan cheese, grated

Sauté spinach, mint, and parsley in olive oil until spinach is wilted. Let cool. Stir in egg, mozzarella, ⅛ teaspoon cinnamon, ⅛ teaspoon ginger, and ⅛ teaspoon cumin, and salt and pepper to taste.

Divide ravioli dough into 8 portions. Roll each piece through pasta machine on successively finer settings into thin sheets, about 4 inches wide and 16 to 18 inches long. Spread 1 pasta sheet on floured work surface. Place filling by teaspoons at 8 regular intervals about 2 inches apart, 1 inch from right-hand long edge of sheet. Lightly moisten pasta around fillings. Fold left half of pasta over filling, carefully squeezing out all air pockets. Seal between fillings by pressing firmly with sides of hands. Cut into

8 (2-inch) squares with filling in center of each. Transfer to floured cloth. Repeat with remaining sheets of dough.

Cook ravioli in boiling salted water until they float to surface, about 5 minutes. Remove with slotted spoon and drain in colander. Serve sprinkled with cinnamon, ginger, cumin, and grated Parmesan cheese to taste. Makes 8 servings.

Ravioli Dough

2 cups unbleached flour
2 extra-large eggs
1 tablespoon olive oil

Place flour in food-processor bowl fitted with metal blade. Beat eggs and olive oil in small bowl until blended, then add to food processor with motor running. Process until dough forms ball and is very smooth. Turn dough out onto lightly floured work surface. Knead well, adding small amounts of flour as needed to keep from sticking to hands and surface, until dough is smooth and very elastic. Let dough stand 20 to 30 minutes before rolling out.

Each serving contains about 224 calories, 137 mg sodium, 110 mg cholesterol, 9 grams of fat, 26 grams carbohydrates, 9 grams protein, 0.5 gram fiber.

Torta Bononiensis (Chard Pie)

Taken from the famous 1446 *De Honesta Voluptate* (*Dishes of Lawful Pleasure*) by Bartolommeo Sacchi. Better known as Platina (Dish) because of the cookbook, Bartolommeo wrote it to impress two cardinals he had run afoul of. He was a librarian and a scholar, but not a cook; this was one of the dishes that he lifted unchanged from Maestro Martino, who *was* a cook. Martino called it plain old Torta Bolognese.

6 tablespoons butter
1½ cups flour
¼ teaspoon salt
4 to 5 tablespoons ice water
Chard filling
1 egg
1 teaspoon water
⅛ teaspoon saffron threads

Cut butter into flour and salt until particles are size of small peas. Sprinkle with ice water and quickly stir with fork until dough is evenly moistened and will form into a ball. On lightly floured board, roll out about ¾ of dough to fit bottom and sides of 9-inch tart pan. Trim edges. Roll out remaining dough and cut into about ½-inch-wide lattice strips. Fill tart with chard filling. Arrange lattice strips crisscross on top. Blend egg with 1 teaspoon water and saffron threads and brush on pastry.

Bake at 350 degrees 30 to 35 minutes or until filling is puffed and crust is browned. Remove tart from pan to baking sheet during last 5 minutes. Brush sides with remaining saffron-egg mixture and finish baking. Makes 6 servings.

Chard Filling

1 bunch Swiss chard, tough stems removed, chopped, about 5
   cups
2 tablespoons butter
1 teaspoon saffron threads, loosely packed
¼ cup chopped parsley
2 tablespoons minced fresh marjoram leaves
Salt, pepper
3 eggs, lightly beaten
½ cup ricotta cheese
½ cup mozzarella cheese, shredded

Sauté chard in butter until tender. Crush saffron and stir in. Stir in parsley and marjoram. Season to taste with salt and pepper. Let stand until just warm. Mix with eggs, ricotta and mozzarella cheeses.

Each serving contains about 371 calories, 491 mg sodium, 230 mg cholesterol, 23 grams fat, 27 grams carbohydrates, 14 grams protein, 0.4 gram fiber.

Polpette Grigliate (Spiced Scaloppine)

To the modern taste, the most appealing part of this recipe is probably the pan juices fragrant with garlic and fennel. Use the Salsa Camelino sparingly; it's very sweet. This recipe comes from *Libro Novo nel Qual s'Insegna a Far d'Ogni Sorte di Vivande,* by Cristofaro Messisbugo, published in 1557.

12 thin slices veal for scaloppine
3 cloves garlic, crushed
1½ teaspoons fennel seeds, ground
Salt, pepper
6 tablespoons white wine vinegar
6 tablespoons butter
Salsa Camelino

Pound veal to flatten. Rub garlic, fennel, and salt and pepper to taste over all sides of meat. Place in shallow dish, sprinkle with vinegar, and marinate 30 minutes.

Heat butter in skillet until sizzling. Add meat and sauté quickly on both sides in several batches until lightly browned, about 1 minute per side.

Remove to platter. Spoon pan juices over meat. Spoon some Salsa Camelino on top, if desired, and serve remaining on side. Makes 4 servings.

Salsa Camelino

½ cup golden raisins
½ cup Marsala wine
2 to 3 tablespoons white wine vinegar
3 tablespoons fresh bread crumbs

1 tablespoon honey
⅛ teaspoon ground cinnamon
⅛ teaspoon black pepper
Dash ground ginger
Dash Ground cloves

Chop raisins coarsely. Add to small saucepan with wine and vinegar. Heat to boiling. Stir in bread crumbs, honey, cinnamon, pepper, ginger, and cloves. Simmer 1 to 2 minutes. Makes about ½ cup.

Each serving contains about 362 calories, 327 mg sodium, 124 mg cholesterol, 19 grams fat, 23 grams carbohydrates, 22 grams protein, 0.42 grams fiber.

Polpette Grigliate (Grilled Saltimbocca)

Another scaloppine recipe from Messisbugo, again sweetened with raisins and fragrant with fennel and garlic, but this time with a rich cheese filling.

8 thin slices veal for scaloppine
2 tablespoons white wine vinegar
Salt, pepper
Cheese filling

Marinate veal with vinegar and salt and pepper to taste 1 hour. Pat dry with paper towels. Spoon about 2 tablespoons cheese filing on each slice and roll up. Grill quickly over high heat, turning to cook evenly, until meat is browned and cheese filling is melted. Makes 8 appetizer servings.

Cheese Filling

1 cup shredded mozzarella cheese
½ cup seedless raisins, chopped
2 tablespoons chopped parsley
1 clove garlic, minced
1 teaspoon fennel seeds, crushed
2 egg yolks, lightly beaten
Salt, pepper

Mix mozzarella, raisins, parsley, garlic, fennel, and egg yolks. Season to taste with salt and pepper.

Each serving contains about 119 calories, 164 mg sodium, 102 mg cholesterol, 4 grams fat, 9 grams carbohydrates, 12 grams protein, 0.2 gram fiber.

Pollo Fricto con Limone
(Chicken Fried with Diced Lemon)

A strange but surprisingly tasty dish. Mentioned in a banquet menu recorded by Messisbugo.

1 chicken, cut up
Salt
3 tablespoons olive oil
4½ lemons
3 tablespoons sugar
1 tablespoon peppercorns, freshly ground

Rub chicken with salt to taste and brown in olive oil. Drain off excess oil.

Squeeze juice of 3 lemons and cut remaining 1½ lemons into ½-inch dice. Add lemon juice and diced lemons to pan, cover and simmer 15 minutes. Uncover and simmer 5 to 10 minutes longer, turning chicken to glaze all sides.

Combine sugar and ground peppercorns and pass with chicken for diners to season to taste. Makes 4 servings.

Each serving contains about 393 calories, 158 mg sodium, 90 mg cholesterol, 28 grams fat, 13 grams carbohydrates, 22 grams protein, 0 fiber.

Verze Piene (Cabbage Stuffed with Walnuts)

Not your ordinary stuffed cabbage—here, only meat is in the sauce. From Messisbugo 1557.

2 cups ground walnuts
½ cup grated Parmesan cheese
2 cloves garlic, minced
1 teaspoon ground ginger
1 teaspoon minced fresh sage
¼ teaspoon crushed saffron threads
⅛ teaspoon ground cloves
½ teaspoon black pepper
3 eggs, lightly beaten
6 large cabbage leaves
5 cups chicken broth
1 cup diced cooked ham
¼ cup minced parsley

Combine walnuts, Parmesan cheese, garlic, ginger, sage, saffron, cloves, pepper, and eggs. Blanch cabbage leaves until tender in boiling water. Drain leaves. Spoon about ¼ cup filling into each leaf and roll up.

Combine chicken broth, ham, and parsley in large pot. Bring to boil, reduce heat, and add cabbage rolls. Cover and simmer 30 minutes. Serve in shallow bowls with broth and ham. Makes 6 servings.

Each serving contains about 413 calories, 1,143 mg sodium, 127 mg cholesterol, 33 grams fat, 11 grams carbohydrates, 21 grams protein, 2 grams fiber.

Torta de Cerase (Cherry Cheesecake)

Cheesecakes have been made in Italy since Roman times. This one seems almost modern. From Maestro Martino's *Libro di Arte Coquinaria,* mid-fifteenth century.

2¼ cups flour
¼ cup sugar
½ teaspoon salt
¾ cup butter, cut up
3 egg yolks, lightly beaten
¼ cup Marsala wine
Cherry-cheese filling
Fresh Bing cherries for garnish, optional

Combine flour, sugar, and salt. Cut in butter until particles are size of small peas. Combine egg yolks and Marsala wine. Stir in quickly with fork until dough is evenly moistened and will form into ball.

On lightly floured board, roll out dough to fit bottom and sides of 9-inch springform pan. Place in pan, bringing sides up to about 1 inch below top edge. Chill until dough is firm.

Spread cherry-cheese filling evenly into crust and smooth top. Bake at 350 degrees 50 to 60 minutes or until center is set. Remove and allow to cool. Remove from springform pan. Garnish with fresh cherries. Makes 20 servings.

Cherry-Cheese Filling

5 cups ricotta cheese
½ cup grated Parmesan cheese
½ cup sugar
3 eggs

2 tablespoons minced crystallized ginger
¼ teaspoon ground cinnamon
¼ teaspoon white pepper
1 (1-pound) can dark sweet pitted cherries, drained and
 halved

Beat together ricotta cheese, Parmesan cheese, and sugar in large mixer bowl or food processor. Beat in eggs, 1 at a time, until blended. Beat in ginger, cinnamon, and white pepper. Fold in drained cherries.

Each serving contains about 274 calories, 263 mg sodium, 112 mg cholesterol, 14 grams fat, 25 grams carbohydrates, 11 grams protein, trace fiber.

Suppa Dorata (Saffron "French Toast")

The luxurious ancestor of the French *pain perdu* or *pain doree*; really quite golden in color when you add the saffron-colored syrup. From Maestro Martino, mid-fifteenth-century.

3 eggs, lightly beaten
2 tablespoons sugar
½ teaspoon rose water
4 slices bread (½ inch thick), crusts removed and quartered
1½ to 2 tablespoons butter
Saffron syrup

Combine eggs, sugar, and rose water. Soak slices in mixture just until absorbed. Heat butter in skillet. Fry toast until golden brown on both sides. Serve with saffron syrup. Makes 4 servings.

Saffron Syrup

1 cup water
1 cup sugar
Dash saffron threads
¼ teaspoon rose water

Cook water, sugar, and saffron to syrup stage, 230 to 234 degrees. Let cool and stir in rose water. Makes 1¼ cups.

Each serving contains about 366 calories, 218 mg sodium, 172 mg cholesterol, 9 grams fat, 66 grams carbohydrates, 7 grams protein, trace fiber.

Recipes used by permission of Charles Perry.

ACKNOWLEDGMENTS

Many people contributed to this book, but none more than Bill Berensmann and Dulcie Apgar. For their suggestions and guidance, I am deeply grateful. I must also thank Charles Perry for his advice on Italian cuisine, Carla Balatresi for correcting my Italian, and Garry Goodrow for his knowledge of all things poetic.

The book was started in Jim Krusoe's writing class at Santa Monica City College, and without his continual encouragement and criticism, and that of his class, it would never have been completed.

Finally, it might never have seen the light of day had it not been for the faith, persistence, and enthusiasm of my agent, Julia Lord, and my first publisher, Martin Shepard. To all, my deepest thanks.

Discarded
Legacy

Politics and Poetics in the
Life of Frances E. W. Harper
1825–1911

Melba Joyce Boyd

 Wayne State University Press   Detroit

African American Life Series

A complete listing of the books in this series can be found at the back of this volume.

General Editors

Toni Cade Bambara
Author and Filmmaker

Wilbur C. Rich
Wellesley College

Geneva Smitherman
Michigan State University

Ronald W. Walters
Howard University

99 98 97 96 95 94   5 4 3 2 1

Library of Congress Cataloging-in-Publication Data

Boyd, Melba Joyce.
    Discarded legacy : politics and poetics in the life of Frances
E. W. Harper, 1825–1911 / by Melba Joyce Boyd.
       p.   cm.—(African American life series)
    Includes bibliographical references and index.
    ISBN 0-8143-2488-6 (alk. paper).—ISBN 0-8143-2489-4 (pbk./alk. paper)
    1. Harper, Frances Ellen Watkins, 1825–1911. 2. Feminism and
literature—United States—History—19th century. 3. Afro-American
women authors—19th century—Biography. 4. Women abolitionists—
United States—Biography. 5. Feminists—United States—Biography.
6. Afro-American women in literature. 7. Afro-Americans in
literature. I. Title. II. Series.
PS1799.H7Z59   1994
811'.3—dc20
[B]   93-36922
                                                    CIP

Designer: Elizabeth Pilon

Special Acknowledgment: Portions of this book have appeared in "The Radical Vision of Frances E. W. Harper," in *The Garland Companion to American Nineteenth Century Verse,* ed. Eric Haralson, New York: Garland Press, 1994; and in "The Critical Mistreatment of Frances E. W. Harper," *Drumvoices Review: A Confluence of Literary, Cultural & Vision Arts,* ed. Eugene B. Redmond, vol. 3, nos. 1 & 2 (Fall/Winter 1993–4).

Dedicated to the living legacy of
Frances Ellen Watkins Harper
and all writers
engaged in the struggle
to free our humanity.

If our talents are to be recognized we must write less of issues that are particular and more of feelings that are general. We are blessed with hearts and brains that encompass more than ourselves in our present plight. . . . We must look to the future which, God willing, will be better than the present or the past, and delve into the heart of the world.

Frances E. W. Harper, 1861
In Jay Saunders Redding,
To Make a Poet Black

Contents

Acknowledgments

Though in concept and in delivery I am solely responsible for *Discarded Legacy: Politics and Poetics in the Life of Frances E. W. Harper,* this work is also an outgrowth of my interaction with many others. In particular, I would like to recognize those who were graduate researchers for the Afro-American Studies Program at the University of Iowa when I began this effort: Jay Berry, Deirdre Cross, Eygirba High, and especially Peter Thornton. I highly value and appreciate the enthusiasm and investment in Frances Harper's legacy. Likewise, my colleagues, the late Darwin T. Turner and the late Jonathan Walton, who have since passed and left their creative and scholarly legacies of the Afroamerican experience, are inherently part of these pages. Peter Nazareth, Florence Boos, and Albert Stone deserve special mention. Conversations with them about conceptual approach and literary history were invaluable.

Support for this project from friends and colleagues who read manuscripts versions and/or listened to difficulties with politics in the discipline and with publishing is truly valued. I deeply appreciate Ursula Bauer, William Bryce, Carolyn Campbell, Robert Chrisman, Verna Cole, Maria Dietrich, Nora Faires, Maryemma Graham, Dieter Herms, Sybil Kein, Kamala Kempadoo, Naomi Long Madgett, Manning Marable, Dudley Randall, John Sayles, Judith Schonburg, Steve Sobel and Geneva Smitherman. Their shared interest was invaluable when academics, readers, or publishers were insensitive or indifferent to my interests.

Libraries, the mainstays of history and culture, are the storehouses for scholars. The raw materials of Frances Harper's legacy have been contained and maintained by the quiet and unheralded efforts of librarians at the Library of Congress, the Detroit Public Library, the University of Iowa Library, the Moorland-Spingarn Research Center at Howard University, the Philadelphia Historical Society, and the Schomburg Library of African American History and Culture of the New York City Libraries. The librarians at these institutions were generous and nothing short of wonderful. I especially remember Betty M. Culpepper, bibliographer and Head of Reference at the Moorland-Spingarn Research Center. This library has the most extensive primary materials by and about Harper.

Without time and money, *Discarded Legacy* would still be in its primary stages. This work has been made possible by an Old Gold Summer Fellowship from the University of Iowa and research support from the Dean's Office, College of Liberal Arts, the University of Iowa. Likewise, Ohio State University, and the University of Michigan—Flint have been

8

especially generous in support for this project. I am grateful to my staff at the University of Michigan—Flint, including my secretary, Jeanne Clark, and my research assistant, Sharetha Smith.

Without mental space I would not have been able to complete the writing. The support of my family was critical in this regard. The patience of my children, John and Maya, was appreciated. During those periods when I needed to retreat and write, my family provided space for me to work. As usual, I am especially indebted to them.

As I was completing the last revisions of the manuscript, my grand aunt, Inez Boyd Foston, died at the age of ninety-five. I realized that she represented the legacy of education and culture in my extended family, as she had been an English professor at Tennessee State University during the 1920s and 1930s and had worked in education formally and informally all of her life. This legacy emanates from a vision that sees the descendents of American slaves appreciated for the special genius that is ours to claim and to seek. In many ways this book emulates that tradition and celebrates her passing as life-affirming.

Prelude

If all the wealthy and influential honored were men as the Bible teaches, would they ever throw their lives between God's sunshine and the shivering poor, and fence in leagues of land by bonds and chains and title deeds, when land and water, air and light are God's own gifts and heritage to man? Should they not remember that the humblest and poorest human being who enters the threshold of life comes as the child of a King, and at the feast of life be received as the guest of the living God? Would not the vision of Christians grow clearer to see, beneath the darkened skin and shaded countenance, poverty of condition, or the dust and grime of labor, the human soul all written over with the handmarks of Divinity, and the common chains of humanity?

Frances Ellen Watkins Harper,
Philadelphia, 1898

Like the crocuses, we awaken every spring, the sun still calling our color, the rain refilling the rivers. The Afroamerican spiral of history has no clear opening or closing. It should not be flattened by innocuous memory or inflated by postured revisions. Superimposing the resiliency of Frances Harper's path, I encountered the ongoing conflicts of human despair and defiant resistance. The shouting sidewalks tell us what is too obvious—we are running out of time. The people fill their shrinking space with blasting music. Their faces, hung-heavy, lifted by liquor and the death crack of cocaine, contour a known fact nearly nobody notices. The quagmire of hopelessness steals more grandchildren in a week than Harriet "Moses" Tubman ever delivered. This retrieval of Harper's inscription is a resonance of resistance, confronting the cryptic irony of human history.

Melba Joyce Boyd,
Detroit, 1994

Introduction: Discarded Legacy

Frances Ellen Watkins Harper (1825–1911) published her first book of poetry, *Forest Leaves*, in 1846. Subsequently, several of her poems appeared in abolitionist periodicals. But Harper did not achieve a literary reputation until the publication of her second book, *Poems on Miscellaneous Subjects* (1854). The first edition was published by a Boston printing company, J. B. Yerrinton and Son, with an introduction by William Lloyd Garrison. At this time Harper was secured as an antislavery lecturer and delivered her first speech, "Education and the Elevation of the Coloured Race," in New Bedford.

The second edition of *Poems on Miscellaneous Subjects* was published in 1857 in Philadelphia by the antislavery publishers, Merrihew and Thompson. In 1858, Merrihew and Thompson became Merrihew and Son and published most of Harper's ten books of poetry. But "when that company retired from the business the stereotype plates were sold to the firm of Ferguson and Co. In the late 1950s Ferguson sold out their business and some of Mrs. Harper's remaining stock, manuscripts and correspondence were discarded as rubbish."[1]

Obviously, it is impossible to retrieve that which has been materially discarded, but this book is a contribution to the reconstruction of the fragmented and obscured legacy of Frances Harper. This particular reading of Harper's life, as artist-activist, emerges from the intersection of her poetry with her political and cultural stature as an abolitionist and as a feminist. It demonstrates the integral presence of a black woman on the axis of democratic challenges of the nineteenth century and the unique perspective she cultivated through her work.

Harper's insight, developed during an era rife with violent enforcement of racism, sexism, and classism, constitutes a viable ideological framework for contemporary radical thought. Her vision evolved from complex multifaceted oppression and her relentless intellectual and political involvement with the black American dilemma and progressive human rights movements. In *Woman's Legacy*, Bettina Aptheker aptly capsulates the dynamics of compounded oppression in a society dichotomized by white over black, male over female:

By focusing attention on the female experience we begin to understand the way in which racial oppression of a people intersects with the patriarchal and capitalist structure in a definitive way. The black female experience, by the very nature of its extremity, illuminates the subjugation of all women. In the United States, at least, we may project the conclusion that emancipation of woman is inseparable from the liberation of Afro-American people in general, and the Afro-American woman in particular.[2]

Harper's legacy brings attention to the black female experience through the individual experience of a black woman writer engaged with the crucial issues of her times and anticipating the concerns of the future. She published the first of ten books of poetry in 1846, the first short story by a black woman in 1859, three serialized novels in 1859, 1877, and 1887–88, and the first reputable novel by an American black woman in 1892. At the same time she was involved in lecturing tours that took her throughout the United States and Canada. As lecturer, educator, poet, essayist, and novelist, she championed abolitionist and feminist causes in the radical, Christian tradition, and she was widely recognized as the foremost poet of the "free colored community." And yet, neither her art nor her political insight was preserved by subsequent generations until the most recent resurgence of the women's movement.

Frances Harper was neither the first nor the only black woman orator, but her fame and acclaim heightened black feminist presence in American politics and culture. Maria W. Stewart, the first black woman to speak at a public lectern in 1832, published essays in Garrison's *Liberator* and introduced a black feminist consciousness to liberationist ideology. Undoubtedly, Stewart's visibility in public and in print provided a precedent and a premise for Harper's immersion into activism.

Concurrently, other black women activists like Charlotte, Harriet, and Sarah Forten, who founded the Philadelphia Female Anti-Slavery Society in 1833; Clarissa C. Lawrence, the vice-president of the Salem Anti-Slavery Society, founded in 1832; and Mary Shadd, the editor-publisher of the *Provincial Freedman* (1854–59) in Ontario, represent the prominence and zeal black women activists brought to the abolitionist movement. Notwithstanding, the collective consciousness of Harper and her contemporaries constituted a legacy distinguished by a faith determined to defy and defeat legal and social denial.

To a larger extent, this study of Harper is concerned with her as a creative writer of poetry, prose, and political essays. Her writing was published in newspapers and journals, including: *The Anglo-African Weekly, The African Methodist Review, Frederick Douglass' Paper, The Englishwoman's Review, The Liberator, The New National Era, The New York Independent, The Philadelphia Tribune, The Provincial Freeman, The Christian Recorder,* and others. This appraisal of Harper's poetry and prose is considered within her aesthetic context, which is explicitly and implicitly political.

Even though a comparative analysis of all her literary peers would be counterproductive in this bio-critical treatment of Harper, some literary references and allusions have been incorporated to demonstrate obvious influences and parallels. In particular, Sarah Forten, who published her poetry in *The Liberator* under the pseudonyms Ada and Magawesca, probably best represents the black abolitionist-feminist aesthetic that emerged and merged with Harper's poetic perspective. "Lines, Suggested on Reading 'An Appeal to Christian Women of the South' by A. E. Grimke" by Ada (Sarah Forten) was originally published in 1836. The biblical references to Israel and Christ are key Afroamerican cultural symbols, but the pronouncement of women's involvement in public political issues as "women's work" in poetic verse is a political and an artistic statement.

> One may not 'cry aloud' as they are bid,
> And lift our voices in the public ear;
> Nor yet be mute. The pen is ours to wield,
> The heart to will, and hands to execute.
> And more the gracious promise gives to all
> Ask, says the saviour, and ye shall receive.
> In concert then, Father of love, we join,
> To wrestle with thy presence, as of old
> Did Israel, and will not let thee go
> Until them bless. The cause is thine—for tis
> Thy guiltless poor who are oppressed, on whom
> The sun of Freedom may not cast his beams,
> Now dew of heavenly knowledge e'er descend.
> And for their fearless advocates we ask
> The wisdom of the serpent—above all,
> Our heavenly Father, clothe, oh clothe them with
> The dove-like spirit of thine own dear Son.
> Then they are safe; tho' persecution's waves
> Dash o'er their backs, and furious winds assail—
> Still they are safe.
>   Yes, this is woman's work, Her
> own appropriate sphere; and nought should drive Her
> from the mercy seat, til mercy's work be finished.[3]

To engage political themes is an American literary tradition as evidenced by Harper's contemporaries, i.e. Harriet Forten, John Greenleaf

INTRODUCTION

Whittier, Herman Melville, Mark Twain, Ida B. Wells, Henry David Thoreau, William Wells Brown, and Ralph Waldo Emerson. About her work, the black novelist William Wells Brown wrote in *The Black Man: His Antecedents, His Genius, and His Achievements* (1863): "All of Mrs. Harper's writings are characterized by chaste language, much thought and a soul-stirring ring that are refreshing to the reader."[4]

The thematic range of Harper's second book, *Poems on Miscellaneous Subjects* (1854) which appeared in the same season she began lecturing for the abolitionist cause, includes poems about religion, slavery, gender, temperance, and poverty. It also contains two essays, "Christianity" and "The Colored People in America." For the most part, this book embodies the nucleus of Harper's literary tributaries. Subsequent publications—poetry and prose—extend, accentuate, and elaborate the themes constituted in this book.

What distinguishes Harper's poetic voice is her capacity to demonstrate how racism, sexism, and classism are intricately intertwined in American culture. Her focus on the slave woman in her abolitionist poetry is an examination of sexism in a racist institution to the benefit of a privileged aristocracy. Likewise, poems about the inequities of gender roles, rights, and relationships reveal how "free" social values manifest second-class citizenship for women on both sides of the color line.

Moreover, the practical application of her art to her activism rendered an aesthetic and political integrity that was consistent and prophetic. She incorporated abolitionist poetry into her antislavery lectures, and her feminist poems reflect her integrative work with women's organizations. Likewise, later poems addressed to her white sisters convey the subliminal and overt racism that circumvented the feminist movement, while poems addressed to her black brothers reflect their emulation of Euroamerican patriarchal beliefs and practices which contradicted the principles of the racial struggle for equal rights.

Harper's third book, *Moses: A Story of the Nile* (1869) includes a long blank-verse poem of the same title. This publication highlights the pinnacle of her poetic craft. She meticulously sustains a most eloquent work of more than seven hundred lines. The poem extends the biblical tale by presenting the perspectives of Moses' Egyptian mother and his Hebrew mother. The poem is culturally significant for Afroamericans because it articulates in literary form the biblical story that cultivated a radical Christianity promoting the upheaval of slavery. Harper's inclusion of Christ imagery within the narrative of the Old Testament story clearly exemplifies the intertwining of the two most significant biblical characters in Afroamerican Christian culture, Moses and Jesus.

Harper's fourth book, *Poems* (1871), is a collection of miscellaneous poems written since *Poems on Miscellaneous Subjects*. Shortly after the printing of this volume, the number of Harper books sold exceeded fifty thousand, which was accredited to her stature and visibility at the antislavery lectern. *Poems* was reprinted several times and appeared in 1895 with additional poems under the title *Atlanta Offering Poems*. Another edition was published in 1898 and in 1900 with six new poems.

Sketches of Southern Life (1872), Harper's fifth book, is tantamount and comparable to *Moses* because it also marks a zenith in her literary career. *Sketches* (in this poet's opinion) is the first successful transcription of Afroamerican dialect into literature. Unlike her contemporaries and her immediate predecessors, Harper evaded the pitfalls of apostrophic dialect and the constrictions of fixed meter in her adaptation of black American language to literary text. She adjusted the ballad with varied meters in each line to accommodate the nuances of black language. Again, one must consider cultural imperialism when assessing critical perceptions of *Sketches*, as the persona's perspective is radical and feminist. Even today, this dynamic still intimidates some critics.

Other more obscure books of poetry (of which subsequent publications of *Poems* did to some extent collect) like *The Martyr of Alabama and Other Poems* (ca. 1894), *The Sparrow's Fall* (no date), *Light Beyond the Darkness* (no date), and her first publication, *Forest Leaves* (1846), have disappeared from the public domain, with the exception of a few copies preserved in rare collections. *Forest Leaves* has not been located, but references to the work in other publications confirm its publication and significance in Harper's literary reputation. Fortunately, the bulk of her work has been preserved by the Library of Congress and Howard University, and most recently has been reprinted by Beacon Press, the Feminist Press, and Oxford University Press.

Minnie's Sacrifice (March 20, 1869–September 25, 1869), *Sowing and Reaping: A Temperance Story* (August 10, 1876–February 8, 1877), and *Trial and Triumph* (October 4, 1888–February 14, 1889) are three serialized novels that were published in *The Christian Recorder*, an A.M.E. journal. The publication dates listed in *The Pen Is Ours: A Listing of Writings by and about African-American Women before 1910 with Secondary Bibliography to the Present*, compiled by Jean Fagan Yellin and Cynthia D. Bond, reflect bimonthly printings. At the time of this writing Frances Foster was diligently searching for editions of *The Christian Recorder* which contain missing chapters of these works. These works will be reprinted by Beacon Press (forthcoming in 1994) with an introduction by Foster. Foster's efforts indicate the ongoing recovery of Harper's work and the difficulty involved in a search for materials that are often not privy to the protection of libraries or appropriate conservation in archives.

These serialized novels by Frances Harper appeared in ten-year intervals prior to the publication of *Iola Leroy, or Shadows Uplifted.* The publication of novels in periodicals was usual practice in the nineteenth century and the publication of a novel by Martin Delany, *Blake or the Huts of America* in *The Anglo-African Weekly* (1859–1862) demonstrates this development in Afroamerican publications. The recent recovery of these works alters the perception of the development of the Afroamerican novel and Harper's role in that history. In particular, it demonstrates that Harper's primary purpose was not an appeal for acceptance by the white reading audience, but rather for the political organizing of black people in the development of a wider reading audience. Harper includes a direct address to young black people at the end of *Minnie's Sacrifice* that explicitly states her literary purpose:

> *We have wealth among us, but how much of it is ever spent in building up the future of the race? in encouraging talent, and developing genius? We have intelligence, but how much do we add to the reservoir of the world's thought? We have genius among us, but how much can it rely upon the colored race for support?*
>
> *Take even the Christian Recorder; where are the graduates from college and high school whose pens and brains lend beauty, strength, grace and culture to its pages?*
>
> *If, when their school days are over, the last composition shall have been given at the examination, will not the disused faculties revenge themselves by rusting? If I could say it without being officious and intrusive, I would say to some who are about to graduate this year, do not feel that your education is finished, when the diploma of your institution is in your hands. Look upon the knowledge you have gained only as a stepping stone to a future, which you are determined shall grandly contrast with the past.*[5]

Likewise, the appeal at the end of *Iola Leroy* is a calling to black people to commit themselves to the struggle of institution-building and racial uplift in the face of white supremacist terrorism at the turn of the nineteenth century. However, historical ignorance and theoretical corruption of the intellectual imagination clouded past critical readings of *Iola Leroy.* To take a writer and her work out of historical context and then impose a twentieth-century perspective that is ignorant of that writer's particular presence and aesthetic agenda not only subverts the value of her work, but also disavows the need for a literary tradition that provides realistic presentations of the perils that still haunt the safety, welfare, and future of most black people in America today. The beating of Rodney King in Los Angeles and the killing of Malice Green in Detroit are modern-day lynchings that should be recalled in the memory of literature, music, and other modes of cultural expression.

For these reasons and others, Harper's novel, *Iola Leroy, or Shadows Uplifted* (1892) merits a serious study for its historical and cultural value. The novel utilizes a broad range of voices and perspectives to narrate and characterize the Afroamerican slave and "free" experiences. The novel critiques the concepts of race identity in America and reflects the compounded socioeconomic repression that subjugated nineteenth-century black women. *Iola Leroy* not only reveals the slaves' perspectives and their participation in the Civil War, it also provides political dialogue that encompasses the ideological dilemmas the black intelligentsia confronted during and after the Reconstruction.

Iola Leroy, Harper's protagonist, experiences racist sexism during enslavement and articulates many of the issues and concerns that black women and their organizations confronted including: discrimination in the work place, educational opportunities, suffrage, temperance, and the terrors of lynching. *Iola Leroy* appeared at a point when black feminism advanced into a new era, and Frances Harper was at the forefront of this movement.

At the Congress of Representative Women Conference held in connection with the World's Columbian Exposition in Chicago in 1893, Harper explained in one of her most famous speeches, "Woman's Political Future," that

> *If the fifteenth century discovered America to the Old World, the nineteenth is discovering woman to herself.*[6]

Subsequently the journal, *Woman's Era*, was founded in 1894 by the Woman's Club in Boston. In 1895, the first Congress of Colored Women convened in Boston, and in 1896, the National Federation of Colored Women and the National Association of Colored Women were founded. Harper was an elected officer in these organizations and her prominence as a writer embellished her political impact.

In her lectures, she constructs moral arguments for change by identifying irrefutable evidence, and also infusing her delivery with an urgent, forceful tone. Her language combines an Aristotelian rhetorical style with biblical references and the Afroamerican call-and-response pattern. Additionally, she weaves poetry into her lectures. The form and content of her poetry imprints disturbing imagery into the souls and imaginations of her audiences. In both genres, the author passionately challenges apathy and draws attention to the subjective realities of human oppression. In other instances, she enlists arguments to deconstruct social inequities, historical distortions, and vicious lies to confront adherence to the status quo. But in all instances, the ideas and words of Frances Ellen Watkins Harper call for a spiritual resurrection within people and in their actions as moral beings.

Harper was born "colored," female, and poor. From this position she experienced the complexity of American oppression and developed a political perspective that realized the multifaceted dynamics of social and cultural oppression. She used a variety of literary forms to express this understanding, but it is poetry which forms the foundation for all of her imagery.

Critical Displacement

For the most part, Afroamerican literature advocates a political aesthetic. Since the majority of Harper's work considers political subjects, a narrowness in critical perception has confused literary memory and thereby denied not only the validity of her work, but also the beauty of it.

As I was reading Houston A. Baker's critique of *Iola Leroy* (1892) in *Workings of the Spirit: The Poetics of Afro-American Women's Writing* (1991), a passage from Pablo Neruda's *Memoirs* converged with my response to Baker's treatment of nineteenth-century women's writing. Neruda relates an incident wherein he shared one of his poems with his father, who casually dismissed it. Neruda explains this as his first encounter with "irresponsible literary criticism." Assuming my colleague would not intentionally misrepresent a work of literature with an irresponsible reading of the text, I can only presume that Baker's critique is the consequence of the throes of an ongoing battle he has been waging with black women scholars in an intellectual turf war. I have often found the icy political grounds of criticism to be the antithesis of the temperate zones of poetry.

The introduction to Houston Baker's *Workings of the Spirit* includes Baker's claim of kinship with contemporary black women critics, and Baker dedicates the book to his mother. But despite our friendship and our kinship as poets, I find the gist of his critical discourse rather disturbing. Baker defends his alliance with deconstructionist theory by attacking historical readings of black literature. His aversion to history and radical feminist politics is reflected in the proliferation of errors in his historical, textual, and thematic references and allusions. Baker not only takes text out of context in his defensive "blackmale" (racial and gender) position, but he also revises plot and characterizations in order to accommodate his theoretical paradigm.

Baker condemns Frances Harper and Anna Julia Cooper for advocating the "uplift" of the "race," as if to suggest that peasantry and illiteracy represent true cultural identity and convey authentic imagery. He accuses them of embracing Victorian values in their literature, while he imposes postmodern French thought on their language. He applauds Frederick Douglass for not speaking in the vernacular as an abolitionist lecturer, but barely mentions Harper's prominence at antislavery podiums, and ignores her elocutionary precision and distinction.

He condemns the characterizations in *Iola Leroy* and argues that Harper engages class arrogance; he cites Aunt Linda's ignorance of basic geography as an example. He finds fault with Harper's honest portrayal of an illiterate ex-slave, even though a quick trip to North Philly today would reveal parallel instances of ignorance during our present illiteracy crisis. On the contrary, Harper conveys Aunt Linda's integrity, common sense, and visionary foresight, but not as a pretense that intuitive intelligence is enough to survive the advance of racism and sexism.

Baker says the character "spends most of her words condemning the tomfoolery of her people, whom she labels 'niggers.'" Again, Baker knows well that "nigger" has been and still is a key expression in the vernacular. He does not relate that the character Robert cautions Aunt Linda about "running down" the people. But Aunt Linda's hard-line position stems from the perspective of the disenfranchised black woman. Her complaint is not petty, but expresses a legitimate concern for the welfare of the entire black community, especially for the children.

Baker appears to be quite comfortable "running down" black women's literature, but whenever the women point out the internal manifestations of oppression, he condemns them for betraying the race. The fact is that "blackmale" opportunism was a contributing factor in the deconstruction of the black Reconstruction, as the ruling white aristocracy identified those men who could be bought off and would sell their people down the river for the illusion of political power and economic advantage. But Baker does not credit Aunt Linda, who also recognizes those men of integrity who did not sell their souls for liquor, sugar, or gold.

But the most absurd accusation Baker makes about Harper's thematic intentions in *Iola Leroy* is the establishment of a "mulatto utopia." Indeed, Iola and her mulatto husband consistently deny the illusion of caucasian supremacy and forthrightly embrace their black heritage.

Much attention is given in the dialogue (which Baker abhors even though it follows the slave narrative tradition of this literary period) to dismantle myths that support racial and caste supremacy.

Baker's blackmale is to accuse Harper of being overtly influenced by William Lloyd Garrison, a white abolitionist, and not enough under the influence of Marx, Freud, Du Bois, or Washington. This strange selection of men reflects Baker's own ideology, and reiterates his decision to ignore Harper's ideological framework. He expects her to adhere to his male hegemony in order to make sense to him.

Perhaps the real concern is that the resurrection of Harper, Cooper, Wells, and other nineteenth-century black women writers by black women scholars significantly alters black male domination of Afroamerican cultural and political thought. The danger in Baker's discourse is that it upholds the elitism of the current reactionaryism which belittles the validity of "minority" and gender studies. Furthermore, his practice of quoting text out of context and of rearranging historical memory and culture to create his own critical fiction is "irresponsible literary criticism." Baker has a right to his literary canon, but this attempt to maintain the patriarchy that has determined the black literary canon for the past one hundred years is a false projection and has brought us full circle to one of his literary forefathers, Benjamin Brawley.

For the most part, nineteenth-century literary critics ignored Frances Harper's work despite her obvious popularity and visibility. Understandably so, as the pervasive cultural perception of people of color was one of determined racism. Ironically, in the twentieth century, the supposition of the black critic, Benjamin Brawley—that "great" literature is that which conforms to the aesthetic of the ruling culture—undermined the literary stature of most nineteenth-century Afroamerican writers. Of course, the fundamental problem with Brawley's theory of "Negro genius," or genetic criticism, is that he attributes racial talent to the predominance of African blood. This inverted racial thesis, an unfortunate reaction to Caucasian supremacy, diametrically disqualifies an impure "mulatto" writer like Harper.

Another serious consideration when reading Brawley's criticism is his superficial treatment of text. Like Baker, his criticism provides little or no detailed structural analysis. His discussion is thematically rhetorical and unsubstantiated by textual analysis. Additionally, in "Three Negro Poets: Horton, Mrs. Harper, and Whitman," (1917) Brawley identifies only one book by Frances Harper, *Poems on Miscellaneous Subjects,* which demonstrates the inadequacy of his bibliography, while he dismisses her literary career with a snide generalization: "decidedly lacking

in technique." Brawley's conclusion about the inferiority of the three poets is reflective of his own "double consciousness"[7] emerging from white
supremacist subterfuge:

> Further, and this is the most important point, the work of those in
> question almost never exhibits imagination expressed in intense,
> condensed, vivid and suggestive phrase—such phrasing, for in-
> stance, as one will find in "The Eve of St. Agnes," which I am not
> alone in considering the most lavishly brilliant and successful brief
> effort in poetry in the language. To all of this might be added a re-
> fining of taste, something all too frequently lacking and something
> that can come only from the most arduous and diligent culture.
> When we further secure such things as these the race may indeed
> possess not only a Horton, a Harper or a Whitman, but a Tennyson,
> a Keats, and even a Shakespeare.[8]

Twenty years later, Brawley devoted more space to his critical assessment of Harper in *The Negro Genius* (1937). The inclusion of increased bibliographical information coincides with the completion of
Theodora Williams Daniel's M.A. thesis, "The Poems of Frances E. W.
Harper" at Howard University, where Brawley was on faculty. Brawley expands his discussion somewhat, but his critical analysis does not benefit
from the materials Daniels mined from libraries, as he restates the same
reductionism.

In the preface to *The Negro Author: His Development in America to 1900*
in 1931, Vernon Loggins acknowledges Benjamin Brawley for his assistance while Loggins did research at the Howard University Library. To
some extent, this intellectual connection with Brawley affected Loggins's
critical perspective, though Loggins's structural analysis of *Poems on Miscellaneous Subjects* is textually based and therefore more accurate. He recognizes "Rizpah, the Daughter of Ai," as one of the best in the volume,
indicating Harper's legitimate place in the nineteenth century: "Mrs.
Harper was in no sense the least skillful among them."[9]

Loggins's assessment of most of Harper's work reflects the limitations of the bourgeois aesthetic, as even he anticipates, "it is no doubt destined to receive far more study than I have been able to give it. Negro
scholars naturally will come more and more to regard the investigation
of it as their own peculiar duty. The greatest service which this book can
render is to suggest to them new avenues of approach."[10] But what Loggins did not realize was that it would take women scholars to retrieve old
legacies already inscribed.

Loggins certainly offers a more conscientious effort than Brawley, but they both perceive the literature through an imperialist prism of English language and literature. About "Sketches of Southern Life," Loggins states: "One regrets the "Sketches of Southern Life" contains pieces, mainly of reform topics, in which Aunt Chloe is not the narrator and in which Uncle Jacob, a pleasing old mystic, is not on hand to warn and exhort. In creating these two characters Mrs. Harper perhaps did more than any other Negro poet before Dunbar in getting close to the reality of primitive Negro life."[11]

The fundamental problem with the critical vision of Brawley and Loggins is the indictment that politics circumvents the aesthetic. It was neither the intention nor the practice of Frances Harper to write for or of the ruling culture. More important, the concepts of "high art" and "primitive Negro life" are antithetical to Harper's political and aesthetic perspective. Interestingly, neither Brawley nor Loggins attempted a serious study of *Moses: A Story of the Nile*, Harper's most ambitious and accomplished work.

Loggins, a white critic and author of *The Negro Author*, clearly misunderstands Harper's innovative adaptation of black dialect into literature. He acknowledges her skillful religious poetry, but belittles her work with a patronizing "nobility of purpose." Brawley's *The Negro Genius* relegates Harper to the stature of a minor literary figure. In contrast, Jay Saunders Redding's work, *To Make A Poet Black* (1939), gives Harper's poetry a more reasonable treatment with regard to thematic range and structural execution: "In all her verse Miss Watkins attempted to suit her language to her themes."[12] Redding recognizes Harper's aesthetic attitude from her perspective. About *Poems on Miscellaneous Subjects*, Redding explains that

> The title is significant, for it indicates a different trend in the creative urge of the Negro. Except for Jupiter Hammon and Phillis Wheatley, Negro writers up to this time were interested mainly in one theme of slavery and in one purpose of bringing about freedom. . . . It remained for Miss Watkins, with implications in the title of her volume, to attempt a redirection.[13]

Redding balances the criticism of Brawley and Loggins with a salient evaluation of Harper's aesthetic concerns and accomplishments, thereby providing an alternative to the short-sightedness of Brawley and the cultural myopia of Loggins. But even Redding does not fully understand the dynamics of Harper's aesthetic.

The Retrieval

Early discussions of Harper's poetry and prose pigeonholed her as an abolitionist poet, or as a "protest poet," critical misreadings that discredited her literary merit. Fortunately, more recent developments in women's readings of black women writers have rendered revelations and resurrections. Barbara Christian's *Black Women Novelists* (1980) contradicts some misreadings of *Iola Leroy*, and Erlene Stetson's work, *Black Sister: Poetry by Black American Women, 1746–1980* (1981), a comprehensive anthology of black women poets, reveals Harper's feminist themes, significantly expanding thematic and political perceptions of Harper. Additionally, historians such as Bettina Aptheker, Paula Giddings, Gerda Lerdner, Dorothy Sterling, and others, place Harper in the center of women's struggles.

This expansion cast a feminist revival for Harper's writing. *A Brighter Coming Day* (1990), edited by Frances Foster, and *The Complete Poems of Frances E. W. Harper* (1988), with an introduction by Maryemma Graham (the "Schomburg Library of Nineteenth-Century Black Women Writers series), are substantial retrievals of Frances Harper's work that reinstate her literature in libraries. The reprinting of *Iola Leroy* (1987) with an introduction by Hazel V. Carby, and the inclusion of excerpts from the novel in Mary Helen Washington's *Invented Lives* (1987) represent a resurgence of interest in Harper's work. Harper's three serialized novels, *Minnie's Sacrifice, Trial and Triumph,* and *Sowing and Reaping,* recently recovered by Foster will be published by Beacon Press in 1994. Frances Hope Bacon, a Philadelphia historian, keeps Harper's image alive in local and state publications. Only recently has the breadth of Harper's philosophical complexity and aesthetic range been comprehensively considered.

In her introduction to *The Pen Is Ours,* which contains one of the most extensive bibliographies of Harper's work and wherein all writings noted in this text can be referenced, Jean Fagan Yellin explains that nineteenth-century women writers knew each other more often than not. Likewise, the women writers writing on these women also know each other. The movement to retain, retrace, and reconfigure Harper's legacy has weaved a network of scholars and poets. In the introduction to *Black-Eyed Susans* (1976), Mary Helen Washington profoundly alters the reading of black women's literature. The essay is instrumental to the foundations of black feminist thought. Washington's voice remains in the foreground with the publication of *Invented Lives* (1987). Her comments on Carby's analysis of Harper's literary context demonstrates the concentration of scholarly efforts focused on Harper and the emerging canon developing around Harper's works:

> She [Carby] reminds us that the 1890s was a period of intense intellectual and political activity for black women and as one of these extraordinary intellectuals Harper crafted *Iola Leroy* "with the same political intensity that she gave her lectures, speeches and articles." Thus Harper's narrative strategy is not so much to defend the race against stereotypical portrayals as to represent a world in which a new social order, displacing a racist white patriarchal order, prevails.[14]

Washington and Carby question any critical reading that does not consider the historical circumstances of the novel or its author. The confines of traditional or postmodern critical theory render interpretations that remove the text and the writer from historical perspective. In the case of a historically grounded writer like Harper, the very essence of the literary experience disappears. This is a concern about past criticism on Harper's novel and her poetry as well, but it could also contribute to a backlash that would destabilize the restoration of Harper's work and the legacy of other women writers, past and present.

In her introduction to *Complete Poems*, Maryemma Graham discerns that the consistencies and complexities of Harper's subjects center around the issues of racism, sexism, and classism, but that these themes were envisioned through a radical Christian perspective advocating reform, revolution, and humanism.

> The thematic focus on women and gender-related issues has its source in Harper's political activism, which itself took on several manifestations—political reform, civil rights, and Christian humanism. To ignore or minimize the racial and class content of this activism, however, is to underestimate the degree of Harper's understanding of the social and economic structure of society.[15]

The publication of *Complete Poems*, a genteel, navy blue hardcover with gold lettering, contributes a more presentable library presence for Harper's poetry. But Graham reiterates the need and the reason for more work to be done on Harper, as a forerunner of Afroamerican literature.

> Even with this volume of Harper's published poetry and the reissue of *Iola Leroy* the canon is far from complete, and it is certainly too soon to consider a definitive assessment. In any case, Harper stands

at a critical juncture in the development of Afro-American poetry. By merging elements of the folk and the formal, and oral and written forms of discourse, she prefigured the work of Paul Laurence Dunbar, Charles Chesnutt, Langston Hughes, Sterling Brown, and Margaret Walker, as well as an entire generation of Black Arts Movement poets in the 1960s. It is this tradition—and Harper is its pioneering voice—that renounces "art for art's sake." Frances Harper's poetry is the intellectual endowment of an entire age; her life, a shared social vision imparted to us all.[16]

Frances Foster collected Harper's poetry, speeches, letters and prose in *A Brighter Coming Day*. This volume is especially significant because it contains Harper's voice in its myriad forms. It provides Harper's full range and reflects ten years of arduous research. The paperback edition makes Harper's work accessible and affordable for classrooms and for general audiences. With the exception of *Forest Leaves* (1846), which remains unrecovered, Harper's writings have now been substantially retrieved from obscurity.

The Legacy Experience

My first encounter with Frances Harper's voice was with the poems, "Bury Me In A Free Land" and "The Slave Auction." I read them in 1972 in Dudley Randall's comprehensive anthology, *The Black Poets*, when I was a graduate student engaged in an intense study of Afroamerican poetry. By inclusion, they had been established as major works in the literary tradition of black poetry. That same year I studied the art of editing and publishing as the assistant editor to Randall at the Broadside Press. Randall's editorial and poetic eye trained me to determine the nuances of poetry as an art and as a craft, and that "good" poetry is not constructed for literary critics but is only responsible to the truth as the poet sees it.

My engagement with Harper's poetry expanded with the publication of *Black Sister*, edited by Erlene Stetson, wherein the poetry of both Harper and me is collected. Her poetry is positioned in the beginning of the book and mine is included toward the end, as the anthology is arranged chronologically. Like Harper, I have often been identified as an activist poet, but the poetry Stetson selected is not overtly political. Perhaps, in light of Harper's literary destiny, this arbitrary decision by Stetson may better serve my literary longevity.

I became especially interested in Harper's life and work in 1984 when I was petitioned to write an article on nineteenth-century black women poets for *Gulliver*, a German scholarly journal. During my research, I found crude, but functional photocopies of five of Harper's poetry books of the original texts that are housed in the Library of Congress. These copies are bound in brown hardcovers, but to me they were like buried treasures on the library shelves. They opened the breadth and depth of Harper's voice and vision, encouraged me beyond the limitations of an essay, and inspired the writing of this book.

I discovered five major works, remarkable achievements, which at that point were rarely mentioned in literary conversations. I was amazed at the precision sustained in the book-length poems, *Sketches of Southern Life*, and *Moses: A Story of the Nile.* Having just published a long poem in 1983, *Song for Maya*, I was especially taken with these poems.

Poems on Miscellaneous Subjects (1854) and *Poems* (1871) reflect the complexity of Harper's thematic and philosophical range as well as her literary skill. The emotional content and stylistic precision of this writer's passion, commitment, and sense of humor reflect the tenacity of a zealot and the capacity of craftswoman. Hers is the heart of an artist who could contextualize a world that had too often been ignored, and personalize voices that had too long been silenced.

As a poet I approached Harper as a poet. The poetry was the prism through which I refracted her life. The concept of the study is constructed in a manner that likewise refracts my vision of Harper's vision. Therefore the experience of this book reveals as much about my creative attitude and my political and aesthetic motivations as it does about Harper's legacy. For that reason, there is an abundance of creative and political writing by Harper to provide her unedited thoughts and creative expression. It is almost impossible to reserve one's subjective beliefs and responses, even though I have carefully distinguished the difference between Harper's views and my inferences about those views. In effect, the book reflects how Harper's legacy has impact upon another artist-activist, which is how a legacy works.

A legacy is not static. It is not suspended in the time frame of the birth and death of the person. Rather, it is like a poem. It imparts to each person who encounters it an affirmation, a confrontation, or an indulgence. The conceptual framework of the book develops around the voice of Harper speaking directly to the reader, and my voice speaks over her shoulder in another verbal dimension. Like a voiceover in a documentary film, my writing is a commentary that supplies the information that fills the historical gaps and technical details about her work. My writing also formulates the transitions. The use of italic type provides a visual cue for the switching of voices and avoids the mechanical and disruptive interference of textual introductions, which makes the reading experience too stiff and staid.

Harper's inclusion of personal experiences and her use of first-person narrative in her essays provides ideal material for the biographical dimension of the book. Her correspondence throughout her life with William Still, the stationmaster of the Underground Railroad in Philadelphia also provided primary text for the biography. Fortunately, Still edited and incorporated much of Harper's correspondence in his comprehensive and massive historical account, *The Underground Rail Road* (1872). His book contains the most substantial biography on Harper and has preserved a critical layer of the legacy.

I wrote this book as a poet-scholar. Hence, my response to Harper's work is interactive and improvisational, maintaining Harper's voice as the precedent for reflection. My purpose is to explain the ellipses and to reconfigure context. When analyzing her language, my primary concern is to give insight into Harper's aesthetic by discussing the works thematically and structurally within a biographical framework. Whenever possible, Harper speaks about her work for herself.

My reading of her writing extends her perspective and presents it in an accessible format for a turn-of-the-twentieth-century audience. I was not interested in engaging contemporary critical theory or in adhering or reacting to academic arrogance; but rather, I designed this discussion to illuminate the beliefs and practices reflected in the literature and life of Frances Harper. Likewise, the creative format of the book is modeled by the needs of the subject. Hence, I found *I Love Myself When I Am Laughing . . . And Then Again When I Am Looking Mean and Impressive: Zora Neale Hurston Reader* (edited by Alice Walker); Dorothy Sterling's *We Are Your Sisters*; and Darwin T. Turner's *The Wayward and the Seeking: The Writings of Jean Toomer* especially helpful for the textual design.

Discarded Legacy comprises three parts: "The Abolitionist Years," "The Pursuit of the Promised Land," and "The Woman's Era." These divisions characterize the thrust of the historical periods which encompass her lifetime and the thematic focus of her writings. Though Harper's primary political focus is on slavery and the Reconstruction, she sustains a strong feminist voice throughout these times and in all of her writings. Likewise, during the woman's era, she maintains a strong anti-racist stance against lynching and strongly criticizes racism in white feminist politics.

Discarded Legacy weaves Harper's radical vision with the intuitive and analytical dimensions of her imagination and language. I approached Harper by absorbing all of her writing and distilling her thematic inclinations and political and social affiliations. I then determined how she crafted her subjects and how the literature and speeches interrelated in theme and historical experience.

The study was organized around publications of poetry, speeches, or letters which constitute a historical and literary series of concentric circles that reflect a progressive cycle of experience and expression. This arrangement reflects the evolution of the writing, just as a writer experiences and then responds. It is the interactive and organic nature of the creative process, and therefore the book assumes a format that simulates the life and the literature.

The criticism is presented within the historical and literary context in which Harper wrote. I discuss literary technique with regard to the praxis of cultural tradition, of biblical text, or in many instances, both. In almost all instances, I consider the related liberation movement as a part of the critical discussion. The literary discussions incorporate and overlap the historical chapters which precede and extend the poetry and the prose.

My search for Frances Ellen Watkins Harper was beset by difficulties, and yet, inspired by support and generosity. Many of Harper's books listed in the card catalog at the Library of Congress are missing. Several of the titles have completely disappeared from public libraries. In fact, when I searched the files of the Historical Society of Pennsylvania in Philadelphia, the librarians could not locate two broadsides, "Twenty Fifth Anniversary of Freedom" and "Enlightened Motherhood."

While the absence of materials is tragic, the insight and enthusiasm of collectors and librarians concerning the project made my task considerably easier. The librarians at Howard University's Moorland-Spingarn Research Center and at Temple University's Charles Blockson's Afro-American Collection were impressively organized and generous with their resources. Frances Foster was most generous with her resources. Unfortunately, due to time constraints, a discussion of two of the serialized novels will not appear in this text. Much of Harper's legacy has been retained through the inconspicuous dedication of these unassuming cultural workers. I greatly appreciate their diligence and generosity.

Conclusion: Writer to Writer

Some might read this work on Harper as a conversation between two poets, but the language between Harper and me is the unspoken and the understood. The affinity I feel for Harper is characteristic of the kind of creatures poets are. Robert Hayden best expressed it in an interview about two years before his death in 1980: "Any man or woman who dedicates his life to poetry is trying to get down to something very, very fundamental, trying to say what cannot be said."[17] Moreover, Dudley Randall explains, "Whatever good poetry is, it should move the audience."[18]

With the dilemmas of human experience reduced to racial, gender, and socio-economic categories, it is the ultimate purpose of the poet to inspire the reader to reach beyond the pain of personal difficulties, to aspire to resolve those contradictions which inhibit spiritual growth, and to defy those social confines which prohibit a universal oneness. For all the workings with words, it is the love for humanity that these poets aspire to instill.

My identification as black, female, poet, and born in the United States places me within a special proximity to Harper. I align my perspective with hers becuase of the familiarity of her radical politics. She is ever suspicious of government and persistent in her critique of individual or social domination over the human spirit for the purpose of material, political, or personal gain.

I have read many black women poets and when I have been moved by their script, it was not because of cultural or historical kinship but because of their skill and their vision. At the same time, I have known many Afroamerican women who couldn't care less about Harper's poetry or her political mission. Conversely, I have engaged in many literary and political discussions with communities of international scholars, female and male, in a range of cultural complexions, who have taken an avid and genuine interest in Harper's literature. Most recently I was invited to lecture on Harper to a group of black women in Amsterdam. Their intense interest in Harper and in me had to do with the special leadership role Afroamerican women writers have been thrust into because of their prolific literary history and political and creative vision. The independent spirit of the writing is a testament to an attitude that presupposes possibilities for an alternative and radical reading of freedom.

My task was to arrange the Harper materials in a manner that would connect our present to Harper's past—to re-envision her consciousness. But when a people's history has been white-washed and "blackmaled" in order to reinforce the illusions of those defining the past to the benefit of intellectual and cultural control, any discarded legacy is more readily restored via the spirit than by the alleged assumptions that have estranged it. In a single poetic instance or as a holistic encounter, Harper's writing chartered a cultural and political perspective needed for an American democracy.

INTRODUCTION

Since the writing of this book no buried diaries of Harper's have been uncovered in some attic. But because her writings include an honest personal investment, we can experience her personal voice. The Harper legacy has been resurrected and has become the subject of much critical and intellectual debate at the turn of the twenty-first century, almost a hundred and fifty years since her first public appearance. This book does not define nor confine her legacy; but fortunately, it has restored some glimmer of it. The political and poetic vision of Frances E. W. Harper can be realized.

The Abolitionist Years

CHAPTER 1

Orphaned and Exiled

Bury Me In A Free Land

Make me a grave where'er you will,
In a lowly plain, or a lofty hill;
Make it among earth's humblest graves,
But not in a land where men are slaves.

I could not rest if around my grave
I heard the steps of a trembling slave
His shadow above my silent tomb
Would make it a place of fearful gloom.

I could not rest if I heard the tread
Of a coffle gang to the shambles led,
And the mother's shriek of wild despair
Rise like a curse on the trembling air.

I could not sleep if I saw the lash
Drinking her blood at each fearful gash,
And I saw her babes torn from her breast,
Like trembling doves from their parent nest.

I'd shudder and start if I heard the bay
Of bloodhounds seizing their human prey,
And I heard the captive plead in vain
As they bound afresh his galling chain.

If I saw young girls from their mothers' arms
Bartered and sold for their youthful charms,
My eye would flash with a mournful flame,
My death-paled cheek grow red with shame.

I would sleep, dear friends, where bloated might
Can rob no man of his dearest right
My rest shall be calm in any grave
Where none can call his brother a slave.

I ask no monument, proud and high,
To arrest the gaze of the passers-by;
All that my yearning spirit craves,
Is bury me not in a land of slaves.

Frances E. W. Harper, 1858
in *Anti-Slavery Bugle*

My health is not very strong, and I may have to give up before long. I may have to yield on account of my voice, which I think, has become somewhat affected. I might be so glad if it was only so that I could go home among my own kindred and people, but slavery comes up like a dark shadow between me and the home of my childhood. Well, perhaps it is my lot to die from home and be buried among strangers; and yet I do not regret that I espoused this cause; perhaps I have been of some service to the cause of human rights, and I hope the consciousness that I have not lived in vain, will be a halo of peace around my dying bed, a heavenly sunshine lighting up the dark valley and shadow of death.
Make me a grave where'er you will
In a lowly plain, or a lofty hill,
Make it among earth's humblest graves,
But not in a land where men are slaves.
I have lived in the midst of oppression and wrong, and I am saddened by every captured fugitive in the North; a blow has been struck at my freedom; North and South have both been guilty, and they that sin must suffer.[1]

In 1988, when plans were made to restore Frances Harper's Philadelphia home, "Bury Me In a Free Land" was to be engraved on a bronze plaque and mounted next to the front door. As the bronze muse of the abolitionist movement, this was and is the most prominent of her antislavery poems. It has achieved beyond Harper's life and has assured her position in Afroamerican literature. The origin of this poem lies in a letter to William Still, the Philadelphia station master for the Underground Railroad and a lifelong friend of Harper. In the letter Harper expresses her estrangement from her birthplace (Baltimore), her failing health, her life, and the possibility of an early death.

Frances Ellen Watkins was born free on September 24, 1825, but before she was three years old, she was an orphan. On the most primal level, the early death of Harper's mother haunted the imagery of her poetry. An impelling undercurrent of loneliness resided in Harper's steadfast embrace of human suffering.

Oh, is it not a privilege, if you are sisterless and lonely, to be a sister to the human race, and to place your heart where it may throb close to down-trodden humanity.[2]

Have I yearned for a mother's love? The grave was my robber. Before I was three years death had won my mother from me. Would the strong arm of a brother have been welcomed? I was my mother's only child.[3]

Days of My Childhood

Days of my childhood I woo you not back,
With sunshine and shadow upon your track,
Far holier hopes in my soul have birth,
Than I learned in the days of my childish mirth.

Childhood may boast of its path of flowers
Missing all the thistles and thorns of ours,
But who that has gazed on the true and right,
Should exchange them for childhood's laughing light.

Though the glittering dews of my early life,
Have been pressed in the cup of care and strife,
Thy silver of age mid my locks is spread,
And the lightsome step of my youth has fled.

To the future I lift my earnest gaze,
Nor sigh for the bloom of my vanished days;
Far clearer I see through life's mellowed light,
Than the rosy flush of its morning bright.

Oh! childhood had laughter, song and mirth,
The freshness of life, the sunshine of earth;
But instead of its gilded dreams and toys,
I have loftier hopes and calmer joys.

Help me spotless Christ by a life of truth,
To keep round my soul the dew of its youth;
That loving and pure I may yield it thee,
When the angel of death shall set me free.[4]

This separation anxiety infuses her poetry with empathetic appeal as she compares the selling of slave children away from their mothers as akin to the death of loved ones severed from the family. It is her intention to instill moral responsibility into the political values of the American people. She appeals to their emotions while she argues against the pain and injustice of slavery.

"Bury Me In a Free Land," Harper's epitaph, has achieved beyond its age. Written in the first person, the perspective of the poem is the consciousness of a nineteenth-century black woman whose life was overcast by the institution of slavery and the social curse of caste and class. Her other abolitionist poems are tales of escaping and enduring slaves braving death for freedom and sacrificing life bound for the heavens. But in this poem, Harper reveals her political commitment from a deep personal level. If she were to die, slavery would be the hell that would haunt her grave.

Ironically, it was her uncle, William Watkins, the most influential person during Harper's early development, who died the same year the poem was written (1858). Shortly before his death, Watkins moved to Canada because he wanted to spend some years of his life on "free land." For Watkins, "free land" was crucial to the concept of a free society; and for these abolitionists, the repressive, second-class experience demonstrated the critical relationship between land and power.

Upon her mother's death Frances was raised by her maternal uncle, William Watkins, and his wife, Henrietta. Hence, her guardian-uncle became her father, her teacher, and her political mentor. Known for his radical, antislavery speeches and incendiary essays, William Watkins taught his outspoken racial pride and independence at his Academy for Negro Youth. "Almost entirely through independent study he mastered the English language and learned much of Greek, Latin and medicine. Although a shoemaker by trade and a local preacher of some popularity, he forsook both vocations to found the William Watkins Academy for Negro Youth."[5]

Compositions were required almost daily, "a subject in which Frances Ellen excelled, frequently visiting the woods where she listened to the birds and gathered leaves tinted by the sun in order to stimulate her imagination."[6] "Every example of etymology, syntax and prosody had to be given as correctly as a sound upon a keyboard," and "every rule had to be repeated and accurately applied—every peculiarity of declension, mood and tense readily borne in mind."[7] Daily study of the bible was required with a curriculum which included History, Geography, Mathematics, English, Natural Philosophy, Greek, Latin, Music, and Rhetoric. "His forte as a teacher, however, was an amazing command of the English language."[8]

The formation of the African Methodist Episcopal Church in 1816 profoundly affected the Watkinses. William Watkins became a leading member of the Sharp Street Methodist Church. For him, religion was a political point of view as well as a cosmic belief, and the A.M.E. church ascribed to a liberationist doctrine and strong black consciousness.

"Doing for oneself was first nature to William Watkins."[9] Noted for his opposition to the colonization of colored Americans by the U.S. government, whether it be Afroamericans shipped to Liberia or Cherokees removed to Oklahoma, this position identified him as a radical advocate for the disenfranchised. "In this regard, he urged blacks to contribute to the cause of the more destitute Indian,"[10] realizing the fundamental intentions of racial imperialism. Identifying himself as a "Colored Baltimorean," he wrote to the *Freedom's Journal* in 1827 that "a philanthropic slaveholder is as great a solecism as a sober drunkard," and, "why is it that they would have us yield, with implicit credulity, without the exercise of our own judgment to whatever they propose for our happiness."[11]

In 1831, he sardonically reiterated his opposition to the racist assumptions of the colonizationists stating, "we are not begging them to send us to Liberia. If we are begging them to do anything, it is to let us alone; . . . those who would elevate us to the dignity of men in the land of our birth, our veritable home."[12]

William Watkins was a foremost political figure during the early nineteenth century, and when William Lloyd Garrison "served an apprenticeship in the abolitionist movement and newspaper business under Benjamin Lundy in Baltimore," from 1829 to 1830, he "got to know Watkins, and was generally impressed and influenced by him, especially in the matter of the 'right way' of thinking with regard to colonizationists."[13] Thereafter, Watkins contributed essays to Garrison's *Liberator* published in Boston.

William Watkins's son, William J. Watkins, "would eventually become an associate of Frederick Douglass, assisting Douglass with his antislavery paper, *The North Star.* When Douglass was a slave, he lived several years in Baltimore, and undoubtedly was aware of William Watkins, Sr."[14] Ironically, in his early days as an abolitionist lecturer, "Douglass received help in his new calling from William Lloyd Garrison, the most feared white abolitionist amongst slaveholders after 1830."[15] In 1832, William Watkins wrote:

The God that rules on high,
That thunders when he pleases,
That rides upon the stormy sky,
And manages the seas is our
Father, Our Protector, our Defender.[16]

Also a poet, William Watkins's lyrics were motivated by his religious and political convictions. The thematic thrust of Harper's work clearly reflects his literary influence. But even more so, William Watkins's parental guidance constituted the foundation for Harper's ideological framework and her devotion to the radical movements. Though his historical significance has been obscured by his proximity to more visible and more renowned figures, he was axiomatic to the political origin of the radical abolitionist tradition and some of its key characters, including Frederick Douglass, William Lloyd Garrison, William Watkins Jr., and Frances Harper.

In 1839, Harper's studies at the academy ended. But since she fortunately found employment as a domestic and seamstress for a book merchant, she was able to develop her literary interests and to continue her studies. The proprietor, a Mr. Armstrong, opened his library to her, thereby encouraging and embellishing her writing. Her poetry first emerged during this period. "Some of her work which appeared in newspapers was of such surprising quality that the originality was doubted."[17] And in 1846, when she was twenty-one years of age, her first collection of poetry and prose, *Forest Leaves*, was published.[18] The title possibly refers to her inspirational relationship with nature when she was a student at her uncle's academy.

In 1850, Harper left Baltimore to live in a free state and teach sewing at Union Seminary in Wilberforce, Ohio. She was the first woman to teach at this school founded by the Ohio Conference of the African Methodist Episcopal Church in 1844, and there was considerable protest against her appointment. The curriculum was termed the "Manual Labor Plan" and during the time Harper taught there, the school served 217 students. The school experienced significant but limited success and was later resolved, but it was subsequently retrieved and transformed into Wilberforce University.

The principal, Reverend John M. Brown, blamed the initial failure of the school on the withdrawal of sponsors and supporters, but he exalted his faculty and their efforts. About Harper, he exclaimed:

> *Miss Watkins has taught a class in embroidery which numbers twelve; also a class in plain serving. . . . She has been faithful to her trust, and has manifested in every effort a commendable zeal for the cause of education; and a sacrificing spirit, so that it may be promoted. She has firmly braved the flood of opposition which has manifested itself from the beginning and I take great pleasure in commending her to the favorable notice of the brethren.[19]*

Quite possibly, Harper made her first acquaintance with her future husband, Fenton Harper, during this residence in Ohio; however, in 1852 she left Wilberforce for another teaching position in Little York, Pennsylvania. William Still explains, "Here, she not only had to encounter the trouble of dealing with unruly children, she was also sorely oppressed with the condition of her people in Maryland."[20] In a letter to Still, she contemplates her personal dilemma, and in an essay, "The Colored People in America," she resolves an activist upheaval in her life:

> *What would you do if you were in my place? Would you give up and go back and work at your trade (dress-making)? There are no people that need all the benefits resulting from a well-directed education more than we do. The condition of our people, the wants of our children, and the welfare of our own race demand the aid of every helping hand, the God-speed of every Christian heart.*
>
> *It is the work of time, a labour of patience, to become an effective school teacher; and it should be a work of love in which they who engage should not abate heart or hope until it is done. And after all, it is one of woman's most sacred rights to have the privilege of forming the symmetry and rightly adjusting the mental balance of an immortal mind.*[21]

> *Having been placed by a dominant race in circumstances over which we have had no control, we have been the butt of ridicule and the mark of oppression. Identified with a people over whom weary ages of degradation have passed, whatever concerns them, as a race, concerns me. I have noticed among our people a disposition to censure and upbraid each other, a disposition which has its foundation rather, perhaps, in a want of common sympathy and consideration, than mutual hatred, or other unholy passions. Born to an inheritance of misery, nurtured in degradation, and cradled in oppression, with the scorn of the white man upon their souls, his fetters upon their limbs, his scourge upon their flesh, what can be expected from their offspring, but a mournful reaction of that cursed system which spreads its baneful influence over body and soul; which dwarfs the intellect, stunts its development, debases the spirit, and degrades the soul? Place any nation in the same condition which has been our hapless lot, fetter their limbs and degrade their souls, debase their sons and corrupt their daughters, and when the restless yearnings for liberty shall burn through heart and brain—when, tortured by wrong and goaded by oppression, the hearts that would madden with misery, or break in despair, resolve to break their thrall, and escape from bondage, then let the bay of the bloodhound and the scent of the human tiger be upon their track;—let them feel that, from the ceaseless murmur of the Atlantic to the sullen roar of the Pacific, from the thunders of the rainbow-crowned Niagara to the swollen waters of the Mexican gulf, they have no*

39

shelter for their bleeding feet, or resting-place for their defenseless heads;—let prejudice assign them the lowest places and the humblest positions, and make them "hewers of wood and drawers of water;"—let their income be so small that they must from necessity bequeath to their children an inheritance of poverty and a limited education,—and tell me, reviler of our race! censurer of our people! if there is a nation in whose veins runs the purest Caucasian blood, upon whom the same causes would not produce the same effects; whose social condition, intellectual and moral character, would present a more favorable aspect than ours? But there is hope; yes, blessed be God! for our down-trodden and despised race. Public and private schools accommodate our children; and in my own southern home, I see women, whose lot is unremitted labor, saving a pittance from their scanty wages to defray the expense of learning to read. We have papers edited by colored editors, which we may consider it an honor to possess, and a credit to sustain. We have a church that is extending itself from east to west, from north to south, through poverty and reproach, persecution and pain. We have our faults, our want of union and concentration of purpose; but are there not extenuating circumstances around our darkest faults—palliating excuses for our most egregious errors? and shall we not hope, that the mental and moral aspect which we present is but the first step of a mighty advancement, the faintest coruscations of the day that will dawn with unclouded splendor upon our downtrodden and benighted race, and that ere long we may present to the admiring gaze of those who wish us well, a people to whom knowledge has given power, and righteousness exaltation?[22]

Exiled

In 1853, Maryland enacted a law whereby any person of color who entered via the northern border of the state could be sold into slavery. Consequently, any Maryland native who was a person of color and who resided in the North, such as Harper, was exiled. Harper heard about a "free" man who was captured and remanded to a slaveholder. He attempted to escape twice and subsequently died.

Upon that grave I pledged myself to the anti-slavery cause . . . . "It may be that God himself has written upon both my heart and brain a commission to use time, talent and energy in the cause of freedom."[23]

Harper left for Philadelphia where she "visited the Anti-Slavery office and read Anti-Slavery documents with great avidity; in the meantime making her home at the station of the Underground Rail Road, where she frequently saw passengers and heard their melting tales of suffering and wrong, which intensely increased her sympathy in their behalf."[24]

> *I have written a lecture on education, and I am also writing a small book.*[25]

During this brief stay in Philadelphia, she published the poem "Eliza Harris" in Garrison's *Liberator* and in *Frederick Douglass' Paper*, but she was unable to secure a publisher for her book. She left for Boston in the spring of 1854 and was warmly received by the Anti-Slavery Office and Y. B. Yerrinton and Sons, the printing company that published *Poems on Miscellaneous Subjects.*

The Mission and the Muse

The Slave Auction

The sale began—young girls were there,
  Defenseless in their wretchedness,
Whose stifled sobs of deep despair
  Revealed their anguish and distress.

And mothers stood with streaming eyes,
  And saw their dearest children sold;
Unheeded were their bitter cries,
  While tyrants bartered them for gold.

And woman, with her love and truth—
  For those in sable forms may dwell—
Gaz'd on the husband of her youth,
  With anguish none may paint or tell.

And men, whose sole crime was their hue,
  The impress of the Maker's hand,
And frail sad shrinking children, too,
  Were gathered in that mournful band.

Ye who have laid your love to rest,
  And wept above the lifeless clay,
Know not the anguish of that breast,
  Whose lov'd are rudely torn away.

Ye may not know how desolate
Are bosoms rudely forced to part,
And how a dull and heavy weight
Will press the life-drops from the heart.

Well, I am out lecturing. I have lectured every night this week; besides a Sunday-school, and I shall speak, if nothing prevents, to-night. My lectures have met with success. Last night I lectured in a white church in Providence. Mr. Gardener was present, and made the estimate of about six hundred persons. Never, perhaps, was a speaker, old or young, favored with a more attentive audience. My voice is not wanting in strength, as I am aware of, to reach well over the house. The church was the Roger Williams; the pastor, a Mr. Furnell, who appeared to be a kind and Christian man. My maiden lecture was Monday night in New Bedford on the Elevation and Education of our People. Perhaps as intellectual a place as any I was ever at of its size.[26]

In August, she delivered her first antislavery lecture in New Bedford, and on September 24, her twenty-ninth birthday, she began her activist work as a writer and an orator. Through the State Anti-Slavery Society of Maine she travelled throughout the northern states and into Canada.[27] In her correspondence with William Still, she reported a schedule during a six-week period wherein she appeared in twenty-one different towns or cities and delivered thirty-one lectures. Her elocutionary style, as taught and exemplified by her uncle, included biblical references and incorporated poetic verse. During these tours, she circulated and sold several thousand copies of her books, and contributed a generous portion of the proceeds to the Underground Railroad. Newspaper accounts portray her elocutionary skill and the powerful effect Harper had on audiences:

She spoke for nearly an hour and a half, her subject being "The Mission of the War and the Demands of the Colored Race in the Work of Reconstruction;" and we have seldom seen an audience more attentive, better pleased, or more enthusiastic. Mrs. Harper has a splendid articulation, uses chaste, pure language, has a pleasant voice, and allows no one to tire of hearing her. We shall attempt no abstract of her address; none that we could make would do her justice. It was one of which any lecturer might feel proud, and her reception by a Portland audience was all that could be desired. We have seen no praises of her that were overdrawn. We have heard Miss Dickinson, and do not hesitate to award the palm to her darker colored sister.[28]

One cannot but feel, while listening to the recital of the wrongs in-flicted upon her race, and to her fervent and eloquent appeals in their behalf that hers is a heavenly appointed mission. Although Miss Watkins is slender and graceful both in personal appearance and manners, and her voice soft and musical, yet the deep fervor of feeling and pathos that she manifests, together with the choice se-lection of language which she uses arm her elocution with almost superhuman force and power over her spellbound audience.[29]

An article by Grace Greenwood, a well-known poet and free-lance writer who became a personal friend of Harper, appeared in the *Philadel-phia Independent*. It depicts Frances Harper in Victorian detail highlighted by Greenwood's abolitionist consciousness and admiration for Harper.

Next on the course was Mrs. Harper, a colored woman; about as col-ored as some of the Cuban belles I have met with at Saratoga. She has a noble head, the bronze muse; a strong face, with a shadowed glow upon it, indicative of thoughtful fervor, and of a nature most femininely sensitive, but not in the least morbid. Her form is deli-cate, her hands daintily small. She stands quietly beside her desk, and speaks without notes, with gestures few and fitting. Her man-ner is marked by dignity and composure. She is never assuming, never theatrical. In the first part of her lecture she was most im-pressive in her pleading for the race with whom her lot is cast. There was something touching in her attitude as their representa-tive. The woe of two hundred years sighed through her tones. Every glance of her sad eyes was a mournful remonstrance against injus-tice and wrong. Feeling on her soul, as she must have felt it, the chilling weight of caste she seemed to say: "I lift my heavy heart up solemnly, / As once Electra her sepulchral urn." As I listened to her, there swept over me, in a chill wave of horror, the realization that this noble woman had she not been rescued from her mother's con-dition, might have been sold on the auction-block, to the highest bidder—her intellect, fancy, eloquence, the flashing wit, that might make the delight of a Parisian salon, and her pure, Christian char-acter all thrown in—the recollection that women like her could be dragged out of public conveyance in our own city, or frowned out of fashionable churches by Anglo-Saxon saints.[30]

This description of Frances Ellen Watkins Harper focuses on the subtle nuances of her physical features and her strong countenance, a complex portrait which sharply contrasts with the two-dimensional, and harsh black-and-white ink drawing that usually appears with contemporary discussions about her.

For many, the ambiguity of her physical appearance was perplexing. "We confess that we began to wonder, and we asked a fine-looking man near us, 'What is her color? Is she dark or light?' He answered, 'She is mulatto; what they call a red mulatto.' The 'red' was new to us."[31]

Red mulattos were considered the offspring of blacks and Amerindians. The Native American experience within the context of Afroamerican history has obscured the variations that emerged from this cross-cultural experience. Insofar as most persons of this blended heritage were ultimately identified, classified, and hence, acculturated as black Americans, the Native American identity was often subverted by a segregated society outlined in "black" and oversimplified by "white."

The likelihood that Frances Harper was of Amerindian descent is quite probable in lieu of descriptions of her and because many "free people of colour" in the United States prior to the end of the Civil War oftentimes achieved that status through intermarriage or linkage with Native Americans. In Maryland, the poet's home state, blacks, Amerindians, and mulattos were exempt from any legal or constitutional rights. An 1831–32 statute indicated that: "People of color" were classified as "free negro" and "mulatto," blacks and Amerindians inclusive. And according to the 1790 Maryland census, Piscataway Indians were all classified as "mulatto."[32] At the same time, Harper refers to the blood kinship of "colored" Americans to "whites" in a letter to William Still, which suggests another dynamic in her racial heritage:

> *Not that we have not a right to breathe the air as freely as anybody else, but we are treated worse than aliens among a people whose language we speak, whose religion we profess, and whose blood flows and mingles in our veins: Homeless in the land of our birth and worse off than strangers in the home of our nativity.*[33]

Three photographs of Frances Harper exist, each of them decidedly different. In one, she appears to be fair-complexioned. In another, she appears to be very dark-complexioned. And in the third, she appears to have a medium-brown shading. The camera exposure as well as the time of year in which she was photographed could have affected the outcome of these images. Persons of multiracial descent often possess a wide range of color variations depending on exposure to the sun. At any rate, it makes for an interesting interplay with the ambiguity of racial identity.

A more spontaneous appraisal of Harper's public presence and political impact is portrayed in a personal letter by Mary Shadd (Cary) to her husband, Thomas Cary. Shadd, one of the foremost black feminist abolitionists, was the editor and publisher of *The Provincial Freeman*, which was based originally in Chatham, Ontario. In September, 1858, from Detroit, Shadd wrote:

> Miss Watkins & Mr. Nell come back to Detroit and she is to go West a ways. Why the whites and colored people here are just crazy with excitement about her. She is the greatest female speaker ever was here, so wisdom obliges me to keep out of the way as with her prepared lectures there would be no chance of a favorable comparison. I puff her as strongly as any body in fact it is the very best policy for me to do so as otherwise it would be set down to jealousy. Please tell me in your letter if Dr. Watson said anything about Ann Arbor. Miss Watkins has been there so that I suspect they will have enough to digest for one while.[34]

Subsequent to Harper's visit to the Detroit area, the black abolitionist, William C. Nell, wrote to William Lloyd Garrison about her presentation to "a crowded meeting of Negroes in the Groghan Street Baptist Church, where Miss Watkins, in the course of one of her very best outbursts of eloquent indignation, protested the kidnapping of two fugitive slaves living in Detroit."[35]

Her first lecturing tour in 1854 from September 5 to October 20 included Portland, North Berwich, Limerick (twice), Springvale, Portsmouth, Elliott, Waterborough (four times), Lyman, Saccarappo, Moderation, Steep Falls (twice), North Buxton, Goram, Gardner, Litchfield (twice), Monmouth Ridge (twice), Monmouth Centre (three times), West Waterville, (twice), and Livermore Temple.[36]

Harper continued such rigorous lecturing schedules for the abolitionist cause until her marriage to Fenton Harper (a widower with three children) on November 22, 1860 and the birth of their daughter, Mary, in 1862. But despite her commitment to her family and their modest farm near Columbus, Ohio, Frances Harper intermittently gave abolitionist lectures up to and until the end of the Civil War.

On the Abolitionist Trail

The agent of the State Anti-Slavery Society of Maine travels with me, and she is a pleasant, dear, sweet lady. I do like her so. We travel together,

*eat together, and sleep together. (She is a white woman.) In fact I have not
been in one colored person's house since I left Massachusetts; but I have a
pleasant time. My life reminds me of a beautiful dream. What a difference
between this and York! I have met with some of the kindest treatment up here
that I have ever received. I have lectured three times this week. After I went
from Limerick, I went to Springvale; there I spoke on Sunday night at an
Anti-Slavery meeting. Some of the people are Anti-Slavery, Anti-rum and
Anti-Catholic; and if you could see our Maine ladies,—some of them among
the noblest types of womanhood you have ever seen! They are for putting men
of Anti-Slavery principles in office, to cleanse the corrupt fountains of our
government by sending men to Congress who will plead for our down-
trodden and oppressed brethren, our crushed and helpless sisters, whose tears
and blood bedew our soil, whose chains are clanking 'neath our proudest
banners, whose cries and groans amid our loudest paeans rise.[37]*

    *I spoke on Free Produce, and now by the way I believe in that kind of
Abolition. Oh, it does seem to strike at one of the principal roots of the matter. I have commenced since I read Solomon Northrup. Oh, if Mrs. Stowe has
clothed American slavery in the graceful garb of fiction, Solomon Northrup
comes up from the dark habitation of Southern cruelty where slavery fattens
and feasts on human blood with such mournful revelations that one might
almost wish for the sake of humanity that the tales of horror which he reveals
were not so. Oh, how can we pamper our appetites upon luxuries drawn from
reluctant fingers? Oh, could slavery exist long it if did not sit on a commercial throne? I have read somewhere, if I remember aright, of a Hindoo being
loth to cut a tree because being a believer in the transmigration of souls, he
thought the soul of his father had passed into it. Oh, friend, beneath the most
delicate preparations of the cane can you not see the stinging lash and clot-
ted whip? I have reason to be thankful that I am able to give a little more for
a Free Labor dress, if it is coarser. I can thank God that upon its warp and
wool I see no stain of blood and tears; that to procure a little finer muslin for
my limbs no crushed and broken heart went out in sighs, and that from the
field where it was raised went up no wild and startling cry unto the throne
of God to witness there in language deep and strong, that in demanding that
cotton I was nerving oppression's hand for deeds of guilt and crime. If the liberation of the slave demanded it, I could consent to part with a portion of the
blood from my own veins if that would do him any good.[38]*

    *I see by the Cincinnati papers that you have had an attempted rescue
and a failure. That is sad! Can you not give me the particulars? and if there
is anything that I can do for them in money or works, call upon me. . . . This
is a common cause; and if there is any burden to be borne in the Anti-Slavery cause—anything to be done to weaken our hateful claims or assert our*

46

manhood and womanhood, I have a right to do my share of the work. The humblest and feeblest of us can do something; and though I may be deficient in many of the conventionalisms of city life, and be considered as a person of good impulses, but unfinished, yet if there is common rough work to be done, call on me.[39]

I send you to-day two dollars for the Underground Rail Road. It is only a part of what I subscribed at your meeting. May God speed the flight of the slave as he speeds through our Republic to gain his liberty in a monarchical land. I am still in the lecturing field, though not very strong physically. Send me word what I can do for the fugitive.[40]

Yesterday I sent you thirty dollars. Take five of it for the rescuers [who were in prison], and the rest to pay away on the books. My offering is not large; but if you need more, send me word. Also how comes on the Underground Rail Road? Do you need anything for that? You have probably heard of the shameful outrage of a colored man or boy named Wagner who was kidnapped in Ohio and carried across the river and sold for a slave. Ohio has become a kind of a negro hunting ground, a new Congo's coast and Guinea's shore. A man was kidnapped almost under the shadow of our capital. Oh, was it not dreadful?[41]

How fared the girl who came robed in male attire? Do write me every time you write how many come to your house; and, my dear friend, if you have that much in hand of mine from my books, will you please pay the Vigilance Committee two or three dollars for me to help carry on the glorious enterprise. Now, please do not write back that you are not going to do any such thing. Let me explain a few matters to you. In the first place, I am able to give something. In the second place, I am willing to do so. Oh, life is fading away, and we have but an hour of time! Should we not, therefore, endeavor to let its history gladden the earth? The nearer we ally ourselves to the wants and woes of humanity and the spirit of Christ, the closer we get to the great heart of God; the nearer we stand by the beating of the pulse of universal love . . . . Oh, may the living God prepare me for an earnest and faithful advocacy of the cause of justice and right![42]

I never saw so clearly the nature and intent of the Constitution before. Oh, was it not strangely inconsistent that men fresh, so fresh, from

the baptism of the Revolution should make such concessions to the foul spirit of Despotism! that, when fresh from gaining their own liberty, they could permit the African slave trade—could let their national flag hang a sigh of death on Guinea's coast and Congo's shore! Twenty-one years the slave-ships of the new Republic could gorge the sea monsters with their prey; twenty-one years of mourning and desolation for the children of the tropics, to gratify the avarice and cupidity of men styling themselves free! And then the dark intent of the fugitive clause veiled under worlds so specious that a stranger unacquainted with our nefarious government would not know that such a thing was meant by it. Alas for these fatal concessions. They remind me of the fabulous teeth sown by Cadmus—they rise, armed men, to smite. It is a great mystery to you why these things are permitted? Wait, my brother, awhile; the end is not yet. The Psalmist was rather puzzled when he saw the wicked in power and spreading like a Bay tree; but how soon their end! Rest assured that, as nations and individuals, God will do right by us, and we should not ask of either God or man to do less than that. In the freedom of man's will I read the philosophy of his crimes, and the impossibility of his actions having a responsible moral character without it; and hence the continuance of slavery does not strike me as being so very mysterious.[43]

I have just returned from Canada. . . . I gave one lecture at Toronto, which was well attended. Well, I have gazed for the first time upon Free Land! And would you believe it, tears sprang to my eyes and I wept. Oh! it was a glorious sight to gaze for the first time on a land where a poor slave, flying from our glorious land of liberty(!), would in a moment find his fetters broken, his shackles loosed, and whatever he was in the land of Washington, beneath the shadow of Bunker Hill Monument, or even Plymouth Rock, here he becomes "a man and a brother."

I had gazed on Harper's Ferry, or rather the Rock at the Ferry, towering up in simple grandeur with the gentle Potomac gliding peacefully by its feet, and felt that that was God's Masonry; and my soul had expanded in gazing on its sublimity. I had seen the Ocean singing its wild chorus of sounding waves, and ecstasy had thrilled upon the living chords of my heart. I have since then seen the rainbow-crowned Niagara, girdled with grandeur, and robed with glory, chanting the choral hymn of Omnipotence, but none of the sights have melted me as the first sight of Free Land.

Towering mountains, lifting their hoary summits to catch the first faint flush of day when the sunbeams kiss the shadows from morning's drowsy face, may expand and exalt your soul. The first view of the ocean may fill you with strange ecstasy and delight. Niagara, the great, the glorious Niagara, may hush your spirit with its ceaseless thunder; it may charm

you with its robe of crested spray and rainbow crown; but the land of Free-
dom has a lesson of deeper significance than foaming waves or towering
mountains.

    It carries the heart back to that heroic struggle for emancipation,
in Great Britain, in which the great heart of the people throbbed for liberty,
and the mighty pulse of the nation beat for freedom till nearly 800,000
men, women and children arose redeemed from bondage and freed from
chains.[44]

Frances Harper and Harpers Ferry

Frances Harper was a close friend of John and Mary Brown, and after the failed raid at Harpers Ferry by Brown and his militia in 1859,
Harper wrote him a letter via William Still, in which she proclaims slavery "the giant sin of our country" and metaphorically correlates Brown's
supreme sacrifice to that of Christ at Mount Calvary.

    Dear Friend: Although the hands of Slavery throw a barrier between
you and me, and it may not be my privilege to see you in your prison-house,
Virginia has no bolts or bars through which I dread to send you my sympa-
thy. In the name of the young girl sold from the warm clasp of a mother's
arms to the clutches of a libertine or a profligate,—in the name of the slave
mother, her heart rocked to and fro by the agony of her mournful separa-
tions,—I thank you, that you have been brave enough to reach out your
hands to the crushed and blighted of my race. You have rocked the bloody
Bastille; and I hope that from your sad fate great good may arise to the cause
of freedom. Already from our prison has come a shout of triumph against the
giant sin of our country. The hemlock is distilled with victory when it is
pressed to the lips of Socrates. The Cross becomes a glorious ensign when Cal-
vary's page-browed sufferer yields up his life upon it. And, if Universal Free-
dom is ever to be the dominant power of the land, your bodies may be only
her first stepping stones to dominion. I would prefer to see Slavery go down
peaceably by men breaking off their sins by righteousness and their inequities
by showing justice and mercy to the poor; but we cannot tell what the future
may bring forth. God writes national judgements upon national sins; and
what may be slumbering in the storehouse of divine justice we do not know.
We may earnestly hope that your fate will not be a vain lesson, that it will
intensify our hatred of Slavery and love of freedom, and that your martyr
grave will be a sacred altar upon which men will record their vows of un-
dying hatred to that system which tramples on man and bids defiance to God.
I have written to your dear wife, and sent her a few dollars, and I pledge my-
self to you that I will continue to assist her. May the ever-blessed God shield
you and your fellow-prisoners; tell them to be of good courage; to seek a refuge

in the Eternal God, and lean upon His everlasting arms for a sure support. If any of them, like you, have a wife or children that I can help, let them send me word.

Yours in the cause of freedom,

F.E.W.[45]

In a "Letter to John Brown's Wife," Harper not only reiterates the image of John Brown as a martyr, but in a sisterly gesture, she also confirms Mary Brown's role, congratulating her bravery and nobility:

My dear madam:—In an hour like this the common words of sympathy may seem like idle words, and yet I want to say something to you, the noble wife of the hero of the nineteenth century. Belonging to the race your dear husband reached forth his hand to assist, I need not tell you that my sympathies are with you. I thank you for the brave words you have spoken. A republic that produces such a wife and mother may hope for better days. Our heart may grow more hopeful for humanity when it sees the sublime sacrifice it is about to receive from his hands. Not in vain has your dear husband periled all, if the martyrdom of one hero is worth more than the life of a million cowards. From the prison comes forth a shout of triumph over that power whose ethics are robbery of the feeble and oppression of the weak, the trophies of whose chivalry are a plundered cradle and a scourged and bleeding woman. Dear sister, I thank you for the brave and noble words that you have spoken. Enclosed I send you a few dollars as a token of my gratitude, reverence and love.

Yours respectfully, Frances Ellen Watkins

Post Office address: care of William Still, 107 Fifth St., Philadelphia, Penn.

May God, our own God, sustain you in the hour of trial. If there is one thing on earth I can do for you or yours, let me be apprised. I am at your service.[46]

Harper returned to Philadelphia shortly thereafter, to be with John Brown's wife and daughter who were residing at Still's home for the duration of the trial and the impending execution. Also taking refuge at Still's home were several of Brown's men who managed to escape, returning via Harriet Tubman's Underground Railroad passage. Harper remained with Mary Brown and assisted in the financial and emotional needs of this critical moment in freedom's wake. During these two weeks, she wrote letters of support and faith to the other men awaiting trial and execution.

You see Brown towered up so bravely that these doomed and fated men may have been almost overlooked, and just think that I am able to send one ray through the night around them.[47]

Enclosed with a letter, Harper sent the poem, "Bury Me In A Free Land," to Aaron A. Stevens, who was convicted for treason for his participation in John Brown's raid on Harpers Ferry. In reply Stevens thanked Harper "for those beautiful verses which go to the inmost parts of my soul."[48] And "before his execution he copied the poem; it was found in his trunk among his most precious possessions afterwards."[49]

Marriage during the War Years

Well, what think you of the war? To me one of the most interesting features is Fremont's Proclamation freeing the slaves of the rebels. Is there no ray of hope in that? I should not wonder if Edward M. Davis breathed that into his ear. His proclamation looks like real earnestness; no mincing the matter with the rebels. Death to the traitors and confiscation of their slaves is no child's play. I hope that the boldness of his stand will inspire others to look the real cause of the war in the face and inspire the government with uncompromising earnestness to remove the festering curse. And yet I am not uneasy about the result of this war. We may look upon it as God's controversy with the nation; His arising to plead by fire and blood the cause of His poor and needy people. Some time since Breckinridge, in writing to Sumner, asks, if I rightly remember, What is the fate of a few negroes to me or mine? Bound up in one great bundle of humanity our fates seem linked together, our destiny entwined with theirs, and our rights are interwoven together.[50]

Frances Ellen Watkins married Fenton Harper of Ohio in 1860, one year before the beginning of the Civil War. This union refocused Harper's primary activities inside the domestic sphere as she and her husband bought a small farm outside of Columbus, Ohio, reportedly from the earnings from her royalities and lectures. Though no romantic lyrics have been recovered, "The Mother's Blessing" gives thanks to God for their daughter Mary. It is a very simple poem, revealing no effort on the author's part to delve into deep symbolism. But on the other hand, it reveals a strong sense of isolation, and a prevailing loneliness that was not abated through marriage.

The opening lines explain the weariness of the soul, *With its many cares opprest*, and her *heart's high aspirations*. She continues by considering herself *a lonely stranger*,

. . . whose language is a jargon
Past her skill, and past her art.

The frustration and the depression in these lines indicates a yearning for her literary and political pursuits. The birth of her daughter re-
lieves some of this frustration and her personal desolation *That had
gathered there for years.* Likewise, the poem, "To a Babe Smiling in Her
Sleep," rejoices in the tiny wonder of a baby's smile, speculating on the
angelic delight of the infant's dreams. But despite the joys of motherhood, she wrote to William Still that she was most unhappy in Ohio because of the oppressive political conditions:

> *Rome had her altars where the trembling criminal, and the worn and
> weary slave might fly for an asylum—Judea her cities of refuge, but Ohio,
> with her Bibles and churches, her baptisms and prayers, had not one temple
> so dedicated to human rights, one altar so consecrated to human liberty, that
> trampled upon and down-trodden innocence knew that it could find protec-
> tion for a night or shelter for a day.*[51]

To the Cleveland Union-Savers:
An Appeal from One of the Fugitive's Own Race

Men of Cleveland, had a vulture
Clutched a timid dove for prey,
Would ye not, with human pity,
Drive the gory bird away?

Had you seen a feeble lambkin
Shrinking from a wolf so bold,
Would ye not, to shield the trembler,
In your arms have made its fold?

But when she, a hunted sister,
Stretched her hands that ye might save,
colder far then Zembla's regions
Was the answer that ye gave.[52]

As the bronze muse of the abolitionist movement Harper wrote
many poems to commemorate particular occasions and historical events.
"President Lincoln's Proclamation of Freedom" was written to record the
significance of the 1863 Emancipation Proclamation. Other inspirational
verses, such as "Words for the Home," which recruits soldiers for the war

and "The Freedom Bill," celebrating the proclamation making the nation free, served such momentous occasions.

I spoke in Columbus on the President's Proclamations. But was not such an event worthy the awakening of every power—the congratulation of every faculty? What hath God wrought! We may well exclaim how event after event has paved the way for freedom. In the crucible of disaster and defeat God has stirred the nation, and permitted no permanent victory to crown her banners while she kept her hand upon the trembling slave and held him back from freedom. And even now the scale may still seem to oscillate between the contending parties, and some may say, Why does not God give us full and quick victory? My friend, do not despair if even deeper shadows gather around the fate of the nation, that truth will not ultimately triumph, and the right be established and vindicated; but the deadly gangrene has taken such deep and almost fatal hold upon the nation that the very centres of its life seem to be involved in its eradication. Just look, after all the trials deep and fiery through which the nation has waded, how mournfully suggestive was the response the proclamation received from the democratic triumphs which followed so close upon its footsteps. Well, thank God that the President did not fail us, that the fierce rumbling of democratic thunder did not shake from his hand the bolt he leveled against slavery. Oh, it would have been so sad if, after all the desolation and carnage that have dyed our plains with blood and crimsoned our borders with warfare, the pale young corpses trodden down by the hoofs of war, the dim eyes that have looked their last upon the loved and lost, had the arm of Executive power failed us in the nation's fearful crisis! For how mournful it is when the unrighted wrongs and fearful agonies of ages reach their culminating point, and events solemn, terrible and sublime marshal themselves in dread array to mould the destiny of nations, the hands appointed to hold the helm of affairs, instead of grasping the mighty occasions and stamping them with the great seals of duty and right, permit them to float along with current of circumstances without comprehending the hour of visitation of the momentous day of opportunity. Yes, we may thank God that in the hour when the nation's life was convulsed, and fearful gloom had shed its shadows over the land, the President reached out his hand through the darkness to break the chains on which the rust of centuries had gathered. Well, did you ever expect to see this day? I know that all is not accomplished; but we may rejoice in what has already been wrought,—the wondrous change in so short a time. Just a little while since the American flag to the flying bondman was an ensign of bondage; now it has become a symbol of protection and freedom. Once the slave was a despised and trampled on pariah; now he has become a useful ally to the American Government. From the crimson folds of war springs the white flower of freedom, and songs of deliverance mingle with the crash and roar of war. The shadow of the American army becomes a covert for the slave, and beneath the American Eagle he grasps the key of knowledge and is lifted to a higher destiny.[53]

Frances Harper's marriage ended suddenly on May 23, 1864 when Fenton Harper died, leaving the poet with their daughter and his three children from a previous marriage. Unfortunate circumstances surrounding the death of her husband shortened Harper's stay in Ohio. Their home, a small farm, was interned by the courts.

> *I tried to keep my children together. But my husband died in debt, and before he had been in his grave three months, the administration had swept the very milk-crocks and wash tubs from my hands. I was a farmer's wife and made butter for the Columbus market, but what could I do, when they had swept all away? They left me one thing—and that was a looking glass!*[54]

Reflecting on her disenfranchised position, she left her stepchildren with her in-laws in Ohio and returned to the East with her daughter, Mary. Ironically, the state of Maryland had abolished slavery with the ratification of its new constitution in October 1864. In January 1865, Harper returned to her birthplace after eleven years in exile. Enroute, she celebrated with Henry Highland Garnett at the Cooper Institute in New York City on November 28, 1864. In Baltimore, she was reunited with the Watkinses and Frederick Douglass, a former Maryland slave who saw his newly emancipated sister for the first time in thirty years.

Shortly thereafter, the Civil War ended and so did slavery. But this triumphant ending to a long and difficult fight against injustice was eclipsed by the assassination of President Lincoln.

> *Sorrow treads on the footsteps of the nation's joy. A few days since the telegraph thrilled and throbbed with a nation's joy. To-day a nation sits down beneath the shadow of its mournful grief. Oh, what a terrible lesson does this event read to us! A few years since slavery tortured, burned, hung and outraged us, and the nation passed by and said, they had nothing to do with slavery where it was, slavery would have something to do with them where they were. Oh, how fearfully the judgments of Ichabod have pressed upon the nation's life! Well, it may be in the providence of God this blow was needed to intensify the nation's hatred of slavery, to show the utter fallacy of basing national reconstruction upon the votes of returned rebels, and rejecting loyal black men; making (after all the blood poured out like water, and wheat scattered like chaff) a return to the old idea that a white rebel is better or of more account in the body politic than a loyal black man.*

Moses, the meekest man on earth, let the children of Israel over the Red Sea, but was not permitted to see them settled in Canaan. Mr. Lincoln has led up through another Red Sea to the table land of triumphant victory, and God has seen fit to summon for the new era another man. It is ours then to bow to the Chastener and let our honored and loved chieftain go. Surely the everlasting arms that have hushed him so strangely to sleep are able to guide the nation through its untrod future; but in vain should be this fearful baptism of blood if from the dark bosom of slavery springs such terrible crimes. Let the whole nation resolve that the whole virus shall be eliminated from its body; the past that shall never have the faintest hope of a resurrection.[55]

'Neath Sheltering Vines and Stately Palms: The Radical Vision of Frances Ellen Watkins Harper

Ethiopia

"Let bronze be brought to Egypt, let Ethiopia
hasten to stretch out her hands to God," Psalm 68:31

Yĕs! Ethiopia yet shall stretch
   Her bleeding hands abroad;
Her cry of agony shall reach
   The burning throne of God.

The tyrant's yoke from off her neck,
   His fetters from her soul,
The mighty hand of God shall break,
   And spurn the base control.

Redeemed from dust and freed from chains
   Her sons shall lift their eyes;
From cloud-capt hills and verdant plains
   Shall shouts of triumph rise.

Upon her dark, despairing brow,
   Shall play a smile of peace;
For God shall bend unto her wo,
   And bid her sorrows cease.

'Neath sheltering vines and stately palms
   Shall laughing children play,
And aged sires with joyous psalms
   Shall gladden every day.

Secure by night, and blest by day,
   Shall pass her happy hours;
Nor human tigers hunt for prey
   Within her peaceful bowers.

Then Ethiopia! stretch, oh! stretch
   Thy bleeding hands abroad;
Thy cry of agony shall reach
   And find redress from God

    Frances E.W. Harper, 1854
    Poems on Miscellaneous Subjects

One month after Frances Harper delivered her first lecture on behalf of the antislavery cause, her second book of poetry and essays, *Poems and Miscellaneous Subjects,* was published by J. B. Yerrinton & Son in Boston. In 1857, the second edition was published by Merrihew & Thompson in Philadelphia with an introduction by William Lloyd Garrison. Many of these poems appeared in her first book, *Forest Leaves,* as well as in abolitionist periodicals. She had already acquired some literary notice, but this second book dramatically expanded her reputation. She emerged as the bronze muse of the abolitionist movement.

While confirming her talent and her artistic future, William Lloyd Garrison's introduction insinuates limitations in Harper's poetry. In a patronizing tone, he qualifies her poetry by asking the audience to consider her circumstances.

> Hence, in reviewing the following *Poems,* the critic will remember that they are written by one young in years, and identified in complexion and destiny with a depressed and outcast race, and who has had to contend with a thousand disadvantages from earliest life. They certainly are very credible to her, both in literary and moral point of view, and indicate the possession of a talent which, if carefully cultivated and properly encouraged, cannot fail to secure for herself a poetic reputation, and to deepen the interest always so extensively felt in the liberation and enfranchisement of the entire colored race.[1]

On September 2, 1854, a similar review of Harper's work by William Still of Philadelphia appeared in the Canadian "colored" newspaper, *The Provincial Freeman.* But Still's statements are more enthusiastic than

Garrison's. Still's article contains the emerging Afroamerican cultural perspective. His critique considers Harper's poetry an achievement for a literary tradition outside of the leisure class:

> It may not be amiss to state here, that Miss Watkins has been constantly engaged as school teacher and seamstress during the time of writing this book, and consequently has only had the privilege for study of such leisure hours as fall the lot of those in her calling. But according to the judgment of several able critics who have examined the manuscript, I think I may take the liberty to predict that it may rank as high, if not higher, than any production of the kind ever published in this country by a colored person.[2]

Though Garrison and Still respectfully promote Harper's work, the implications of this book are more profound than either of them realized. The thematic range of *Poems on Miscellaneous Subjects* challenges repressive cultural and political practices by attacking racist and sexist beliefs. Harper confronts American social, political, and cultural systems of repression. The "miscellaneous" format of the book centers around human suffering; and when the holistic context of that format is considered, one can more appropriately perceive and appreciate the poet's complexity. *Poems on Miscellaneous Subjects* refracts Harper's radical vision, and these themes determine her political and literary direction.

Poems on Miscellaneous Subjects is a "colored" prism. Through graphic portrayals, Harper conveys the traumatic feelings of the enslaved. Her imagery focuses on the experience rather than the issue of slavery. This shift in poetic perspective is extremely important because it engages slavery as a concrete reality rather than as an intellectual abstraction. At the same time, Harper's abolitionist poetry reveals how racism and sexism interact. Focusing on the perspective of the slave woman exposes the oppressive nature of the white patriarchal slave society. Many of these abolitionist poems emanate from the destruction of the family, whereby the slave mother is physically and emotionally abused, and her children are destined for debased servitude.

Poetry about poverty in Charles Dickens's England and about alcoholism throughout American society extend beyond the boundaries of social segregation and provide contexts for shared human experiences. Poems about male/female relationships and gender attitudes extend common, tragic themes that affect most western women. These social themes consider realities that cross racial and class lines. Still's decision to showcase Harper's "Died of Starvation" as part of his review of *Poems on Miscellaneous Subjects* demonstrates Harper's literary influences and her influence on the reading interests of the abolitionist audience. The epigraph reads, "See this case, as touchingly related in *Oliver Twist* by Dickens."

> *Sadly crouching by the embers,*
> *Her famished children lay;*
> *And she longed to gaze upon them,*
> *As her spirit passed away.*
>
> *But the embers were too feeble,*
> *She could not see each face,*
> *So she clasped her arms around them—*
> *'Twas their mother's last embrace.*

This parallels the desolate experience found in another poem in *Poems on Miscellaneous Subjects*, "The Slave Mother:"

> *They tear him from her circling arms,*
> *Her vast and fond embrace:*
> *Oh! never more may her sad eyes*
> *Gaze on his mournful face.*
>
> *No marvel, then, these bitter shrieks*
> *Disturb the listening air:*
> *She is the mother, and her heart*
> *Is breaking in despair.*

The reading of a book of poetry, like the reading of a poem, is not a linear experience. The collective consciousness of the book renders relationships capable of transforming past perceptions of reality by revealing patterns and parallels that are imperceptible to most people because of social and cultural conditioning. These two poems associate women in the lower class of Victorian England with women in the slave class in nineteenth-century America. Conversely, this parallel demonstrates Harper's continental consciousness. America's social investment in economic disparity is directly related to its postcolonial inheritance of British class values. Both portrayals of the disenfranchised are qualitatively and definitively class-associated experiences from the perspective of lower-class women.

Derived from the oral folk tradition, the ballad was the poetic form Frances Harper preferred for most of her abolitionist poems. They are folk poems, poetic slave narratives adapted from Underground Railroad stories about runaways, from reports she heard from escaped slaves, or from scenes she witnessed with her own eyes. The narrative voice of the black slave woman characterizes the poems "The Slave Mother," "Eliza Harris," and "The Slave Mother: A Tale of Ohio." Dialogue personalizes and provides an opportunity for the slave to testify.

"Eliza Harris," a poetic abstraction of Harriet Beecher Stowe's novel *Uncle Tom's Cabin,* was first published in William Lloyd Garrison's *Liberator* (1853). It reappeared in *Frederick Douglass' Paper* on December 23 of the same year.

> Like a fawn from the arrow, startled and wild,
> A woman swept by us, bearing a child;
> In her eye was the night of a settled despair,
> And her brow was o'ershaded with anguish and care.
>
> She was nearing the river—in reaching the brink,
> She heeded no danger, she paused not to think;
> For she is a mother—her child is a slave—
> And she'll give him his freedom, or find him a grave!

The publication of this poem in both papers aggravated an already existing antagonism between the two abolitionist camps. A stern letter from the Garrisonians to the *Frederick Douglass' Paper* charged the poem "Eliza Harris" had been presented in *Frederick Douglass' Paper* as if the poem had been especially written for the publication. The letter argued that the poem had originally appeared in the *Liberator.* The *Frederick Douglass' Paper* responded by admitting to a technical error. The response also includes an apology to Harper and an appeal that she continue to submit literature to their publication.[3]

Despite this debate and the differences between Douglass and Garrison, Harper remained unaffected by their disputes and was able to work politically with them both. Undoubtedly, her prominence as a political figure prevented any unreasonable appeal from either of them. Most certainly, their reserve and respect for Harper's uncle, William Watkins, protected the poet from an exclusive alignment with either editor.

Significant changes occurred in "Eliza Harris" from the time it was first published in the 1853 antislavery publications. In the first version the rhyme and rhythm are not thematically coordinated or tightly metered. Additionally, the point of view shifts, which conflicts with the narrative and disrupts the visual development of the imagery. The graphic depiction of plot in the second version is more succinctly synchronized with the rhythm and rhyming techniques, producing a smoother and more subtle interplay of poetic devices. The political statement is entwined to heighten dramatic tension and to underscore social horror. The critical difference between the two versions lies in the endings. The second version is extended with an additional stanza that cyclically completes and unifies the poem by focusing on the mother and the child in both the first and last stanzas.

> *But she's free! —yes free from the land where the slaves*
> *From the hand of oppression must rest in the grave.*
> *Where bondage and blood, where scourges and chains,*
> *Have placed on our banner indelible stains.*
>
> *Did a fever ever burning through bosom and brain,*
> *Send a love-like flood through every vein,*
> *Till it suddenly encoded 'neath a healing spell,*
> *And you know, oh! the joy, you know you were well.*

The revised version reads:

> *But she's free!—yes, free from the land where the slave*
> *From the hand of oppression must rest in the grave;*
> *Where bondage and torture, where scourges and chains*
> *Have plac'd on our banner indelible stains.*
>
> *The bloodhounds have miss'd the scent of her way;*
> *The hunter is rifled and foil'd of his prey;*
> *Fierce jargon and cursing, with clanking chains,*
> *Make sounds of strange discord on Liberty's plains.*
>
> *With rapture of love and fullness of bliss,*
> *She plac'd on his brow a mother's fond kiss:—*
> *Oh! poverty, danger and death she can brave,*
> *For the child of her love is no longer a slave!*

This poem underwent another structural transition when it was anthologized in 1981 in *Black Sister* under the title, "She's Free." The poem was transformed into a sonnet by deleting some lines and rearranging others. Hence, the narrative was edited into an alien form, creating a visual disruption in the imagery and an aural disorientation in the sound. There is no historical indication that the poet made these alterations because the poem was not published or collected in this form during the poet's lifetime.

Admiration for Stowe's political contribution to abolitionism is enshrined in a poem entitled, "To Mrs. Harriet Beecher Stowe." It applauds the power of the novel that is credited for raising the consciousness of thousands of Americans. The ending lines are indicative of a prevailing radical Christian reception of Stowe's novel:

> *The halo that surrounds thy name*
> *Hath reached from shore to shore*
> *But thy best and brightest fame*
> *Is the blessing of the poor.*

This poem appeared in *Frederick Douglass' Paper* (February 3, 1854), but was not later collected. In the same issue, a review of Dickens's "Christmas Number of Household Words" appeared. The reviewer notes: "Some we have read; but all we mean to read, for we always expect great things of Mr. Dickens, and are rarely disappointed."[4] The presence of Harper, Stowe, and Dickens on the same page exemplifies the cross-cultural influences on and of abolitionist literature. Reportedly, Dickens praised Stowe's *Uncle Tom's Cabin* and was very critical of American slavery.

"The Slave Mother: A Tale of Ohio" is based on a real slave narrative, a famous case which brought attention to the severity of slavery and to what ends a mother would go to save her children from that fate. But unlike "Eliza Harris," a fictional character who escapes, the unnamed slave mother of Ohio is captured after she kills one of her children. The poem begins with the mother's voice, but an omniscient narrator weaves the persona's thoughts with foreboding anticipation of bounty hunters tracking her trail. Resigned to her inevitable capture, as foreshadowed by warnings and flashing visions, the slave mother is persuaded by her desperation to deliver her children from slavery through death.

> *I will save my precious children*
> *From their darkly threatened doom,*
> *I will hew their path to freedom*
> *Through the portals of the tomb.*

But the poet does not trust the audience's logic and does not simply conclude with the tale's deadly ending. The last lines define the mother's action as a *deed of fearful daring*, and then raises the rhetorical question, and through call and response challenges the audience to join the fight against the true cause of the crime:

> *Do the icy hands of slavery*
> *Every pure emotion chill?*

Toni Morrison's novel, *Beloved*, invokes the ghost of this child, who returns, not to haunt the community, but to obtain understanding for the meaning of her death. Frances Harper's poem blames the inhumanity of slavery for the death and supplies this alternative perspective for compassionate understanding.

> *They snatched away the fatal knife,*
> *Her boys shrieked wild with dread;*
> *The baby girl was pale and cold,*
> *They raised it up, the child was dead.*
>
> *Sends this deed of fearful daring*
> *Through my country's heart no thrill,*
> *Do the icy hands of slavery*
> *Every pure emotion chill?*
>
> *Oh! if there is any honor,*
> *Truth or justice in the land,*
> *Will ye not, us men and Christians,*
> *On the side of freedom stand?*

"The Slave Auction," one of Harper's most famous poems, begins with stanzas that present slavery as an extension of an inhumane economic system. The moral disgrace of dealing human life directs attention to the emotional humiliation and devastation of those being bartered. This imagery conveys the harshness and inhumanity of slave dealers. In direct and chilling language the poem describes and accuses:

> *The sale began—young girls were there,*
> *Defenseless in their wretchedness,*
> *Those stifled sobs of deep despair*
> *Revealed their anguish and distress.*
>
> *And mothers stood with streaming eyes,*
> *And saw their dearest daughters sold;*

Unheeded rose their bitter cries,
  While tyrants bartered them for gold.

And woman, with her love and truth—
  For those in sable forms may dwell—
Gaz'd on the husband of her youth,
  With anguish none may paint of tell.

And men, whose sole crime was their hue,
  The impress of the Maker's hand,
And frail sad shrinking children, too,
  Were gathered in that mournful band.

"The Slave Auction" evokes an emotional response via graphic description and elicits the trauma of being sold at a slave auction. The interplay between low pitch and elongated syllables creates a slow rhythm which produces a haunting echo. The poem revolves around the image of the "sable" woman as the first stanza opens with African women internalizing the sexist dehumanization of their nakedness in the human marketplace. The second stanza expands the image with anguished children being abducted from their screaming mothers. This terrorizing destruction of the family is further dramatized as the husbands of these women are divorced from them by a bill of sale. The fourth stanza, the climax, shifts the perspective of the poem to the *shrinking children* who foreshadow the future. This image foregrounds the end of the poem, which is a direct appeal to the audience. She attempts to engage their empathy by connecting a death in the family to their emotional response to "The Slave Auction." Through such comparison, the poem establishes a parallel between the two situations and depicts slavery as an agonizing existence, grimmer than grief and crueler than death.

Ye who have laid your love to rest,
  And wept above the lifeless clay,
Know not the anguish of that breast,
  Whose lov'd are rudely torn away.

Ye may not know how desolate
  Are bosoms rudely forced to part,
And how dull and heavy weight
  Will press the life-drops from the heart.

This poem appeared simultaneously in *Frederick Douglass' Paper* (September 22, 1854) and in *Poems on Miscellaneous Subjects.* It is one of the most often referenced abolitionist poems, and the one from this collection that has been repeatedly anthologized. It is considered a classic and has managed to maintain a position for the poet in Afroamerican poetry.

Poems that focus on enslaved men praise heroic acts of resistance, rebellion, and escape, thereby contradicting prevailing propaganda about the "contented slave" and preordained stereotypes of the "docile" negro. These poems advocate the defiance of black men and the innate spirit of freedom. In concurrence with egalitarian feminist views, Harper advocated strong convictions about male character. While she confronted woman's sexual oppression and maternal agony during slavery, she praised bondmen defying punishment and death in order to maintain their integrity or to acquire freedom.

"The Tennessee Hero," based on *an actual incident in 1856*, evokes the voice of a dead slave, an unheralded hero. The poem's epigraph reads: *He had heard his comrades plotting to obtain their liberty, and rather than betray them he received 750 lashes and died.* "The Tennessee Hero" champions one man's resistance against sanctioned tyranny, and at the same time it counters the racist perception that black men do not inherently possess ethical principles.

It is an inspirational poem written to remember and herald such character. An imagined dialogue between the slave and his assailants creates drama and tension in the poem. The hero's defiance defines resistance to tyranny as natural, necessary, and spiritual:

> *"I know the men who would be free;*
> *They are the heroes of your land,*
> *But death and torture I defy,*
> *Ere I betray that band.*
>
> *And what! oh, what is life to one,*
> *Beneath your base control?*
> *Nay! do your worst. Ye have no chains*
> *To bind my free-born soul."*
>
> *They brought the hateful lash and scourge,*
> *With murder in each eye.*
> *But a solemn vow was on his lips—*
> *He had resolved to die.*
>
> *Yes, rather than betray his trust,*
> *He'd meet a death of pain;*
> *T'was sweeter far to meet it thus*
> *Than wear a treason stain!*

Like storms of wrath, of hate and pain,
*   The blows rained thick and fast;*
But the monarch soul kept true
*   Till the gates of life were past.*

And the martyr spirit fled
*   To the throne of God on high,*
And showed his gaping wounds
*   Before unslumbering eye.*

Likewise, "A Mother's Heroism" exalts political activism as commensurate with individual integrity. This poems salutes the white abolitionist Elijah P. Lovejoy, editor and publisher of an antislavery newspaper, as a martyr. Killed in 1837 by a proslavery mob in Alton, Illinois, his mother is quoted in the epigraph: "When the mother of Lovejoy heard of her son's death, she said, 'It is well! I had rather he should die so than desert his principles.' "

From lip and brow the color fled—
*   But light flashed to her eye:*
" 'Tis well! 'tis well!" the mother said,
*   "That thus my child should die."*

" 'Tis well that, to his latest breath,
*   He pleaded for liberty;*
Truth nerved him for the hour of death,
*   And taught him how to die."*

"It taught him how to cast aside
*   Earth's honors and renown;*
To trample on her fame and pride,
*   And win a martyr's crown."*

The paradoxical "The Fugitive's Wife," considers the conflicting response to a freedom tale. A slave woman simultaneously mourns and rejoices her husband's escape from slavery. Like an early blues poem, a countertheme of bitter abandonment undercuts this ballad of celebration. A heavy, forlorn rhythm that rises and then falls on a down beat at the end of each stanza develops this contrast. The woman bemoans the loss of her husband, whose *manly pride* was too frail to sustain the *grief and pain* of enslavement. But the ambivalent slave woman consoles her heartbreak with compassion for his motivations, and confirms his right to take flight:

He strained me to his heaving heart—
  My own beat wild with fear;
I knew not, but I sadly felt
  There must be evil near.

He vainly strove to cast aside
  The tears that fell like rain:—
Too frail, indeed, is manly pride,
  To strive with grief and pain.

Again he clasped me to his breast,
  And said that we must part:
I tried to speak—but, oh! it seemed
  An arrow reached my heart.

"Bear not," I cried, "unto your grave,
  The yoke you've borne from birth;
No longer live a helpless slave,
  The meanest thing on earth!"

Harper's preference for the ballad form had direct bearing on the practicality of her art. She was not a poet removed from her work as political activist, but rather, her poetry was inclusive of her activism, an integral part of her lectures and writing. The overriding purpose of her poetry was to challenge the power of evil and greed.

The ballad form embraces the natural lyrical patterns of nineteenth-century mass culture, and with its flexible meter, it coincides well with the elocutionary format. Weaving her poems into the context of her lectures, she adhered to the elocutionary style of William Watkins, whose beliefs and praxis she emulated and improvised. The abolitionist platform amplified her stature as a nationally recognized intellectual and poet. Moreover, her activism intensified her poetic themes. "The Dying Bondman" demonstrates this development in her poetic craft. The subtle ambience is achieved through a more complex rhythm and a more subtle manipulation of diction, while the dramatic tension transcends simplistic romanticism by juxtaposing irony and pathos.

By his bedside stood the master
Gazing on the dying one,
Knowing by the dull grey shadows
That life's sands were almost run.

"Master," said the dying bondman,
"Home and friends I soon shall see;
But before I reach my country,
Master write that I am free;

Give to me the precious token,
That my kindred dead may see—
Master! Write it, write it quickly!
Master write that I am free!"

Eagerly he grasped the writing;
"I am free!" at least he said.
Backward fell upon the pillow
He was free among the dead.

Such imagery intends to disturb audiences by supplanting benign abstract perceptions of slavery with horrifying concrete experiences. By focusing on personal experiences of slaves, Harper's poetry humanizes the appeal for justice. The physical and cultural distance that contributed to northern indifference to southern slavery was bridged by such storytelling. Harper ingrains memory with this imagery, and reinforces these images with subliminal sound devices and the power of rhyme.

Feminist Poetry

The abolitionist movement gave impetus to the feminist movement, and as an abolitionist-feminist, Harper's poetry bonds the two movements through the compounded oppression of black women in slavery. But sexist repression is pervasive, and Harper's feminist poems addressed to the "free public" extend and educate the black and white communities. The poem, "Report," advises young men, *wed not for beauty* for it will *fade in your eyes*. But rather, select a woman with *actions discreet, manners refined*, and who is *free from deceit*. In the poem "Advice to the Girls," Harper cautions,

Wed not a man whose merit lies
In things of outward show,

but one who is *free from all pretense* and *at least has common sense*.

This "light verse" is tuned by precise, taut phrasing which complements the fundamental common sense and tried truths conveyed in the

lines. The regularity and simplicity of rhythm and the even, *a b a b* terminal rhyme scheme encase these poetic thoughts for easy memorization,
recall, and reflection. But "The Contrast" offers a more serious lesson.

This poem criticizes the hypocrisy of sexism. It tells the story of a
woman disgraced for her involvement in a love affair, while the man, a
person of position and wealth, is assured impunity and marries another
in a proper ceremony.

> *None scorned him for his sinning,*
>   *Few saw it through his gold;*
> *His crimes were only foibles,*
>   *And these were gently told.*

The poem provides a typical Victorian twist to this all-too-common sce-
nario. In the second part of the poem, marked by a distinct break, the
man stands undaunted at the altar, when a vision of "the other woman's"
funeral flashes in his mind and shocks his consciousness. The scorned
woman is dead. The superimposition of the funeral over the wedding
provides contrasting imagery to emphasize the tragedy resulting from an
endorsed double standard society.

Harper revises this theme and plot in a later poem, "A Double Standard," which replaces tragic resignation with a transcendent, feminist
consciousness.[5] Instead of committing suicide, the shunned woman testifies against the privileged position of the man, repudiates social con-
demnation, and chooses life renewed through spiritual redemption. Like
Eve, she was tempted by the *adder's hiss.* Like the Samaritan woman, condemned for her alleged infidelity, her lips were pressed to stone. Harper
engages the image of Jesus Christ, who defended the Samaritan woman,
as the persona's feminist advocate. The poem promotes forgiveness and
transcendence as a mechanism to reverse Victorian, patriarchal, and religious persecution. Additionally, the call-and-response pattern in the
repetition and the refrain of questions encourages the audience to affirm
the poem's position against injustice and to speak out against hypocrisy.

> *Would you blame him, when you drew from me*
>   *Your dainty robes aside,*
> *If he with gilded baits should claim*
>   *Your fairest as his bride?*
>
> *Would you blame the world if it should press*
>   *On him a civic crown;*

And see me struggling in the depth,
Then harshly press me down?

Crime has no sex and yet today
I wear the brand of shame;
Whilst he amid the gay and proud
Still bears an honored name.

Can you blame me if I've learned to think
Your hate of vice a sham,
When you so coldly crushed me down,
And then excused the man?

Religious Poetry

To man, guilty, fallen and degraded man, she shows a fountain drawn from Redeemer's veins; there she bids him wash and be clean. She points to Mount Zion, the city of the living God, to an innumerable company of angels, to the spirits of just men made perfect and to Jesus, the mediator of the new Covenant, and urges him to rise from the denigration of sin, renew his nature, and join with them.[6]

Harper's essay, "Christianity," ridicules the material and intellectual arrogance of man's civilized history and denotes the frivolity of illusion and the pitfalls of power while emphasizing the living presence and vision of God. Harper's spiritual beliefs underlined her feminist and abolitionist convictions. Radical Christianity constituted a spiritual system and defined a cosmic order that facilitated her political principles. Since the spirituality of orthodox Christianity had more often than not been corrupted by the economic and social designs of the white patriarchal culture, the poet used her writing to reveal the philosophical contradictions in theological dogma and its impact on everyday experience.

Published in *Poems on Miscellaneous Subjects*, "Christianity" articulates a theoretical Christian premise similarly espoused by the African Methodist Episcopal church. It does not represent the doctrine of this church, but it does articulate Harper's early religious views and a belief similar to that of most radical abolitionists. She envisions Christianity as the only infallible system for spiritual survival in man's contrived and debased society.

Likewise, the poem, "Bible Defense of Slavery," evidences the difference between *Mount Zion, the city of the living God* and the New Egypt, in the United States. The poem attacks a book of the same title that distorts biblical text in order to support the institution of slavery. Published in 1851, the book employs pseudoscientific logic to prove Caucasian supremacy. It conversely promotes "a plan of national colonization to the entire removal of the free blacks."[7] Like William Watkins, Harper strongly opposed the colonizationists and advocated civil rights for people of color in the United States.

The poem aptly indicts the book's racist, religious appeal by identifying the contradictions and explaining that such thoughts and proposals endanger the moral and social integrity of the country. Through comparison, Harper references Sodom and Gomorrah (Genesis 13:10) whose wicked citizens were destroyed by God, concluding that denigration will be answered on Judgment Day (Matthew 10:15). The poem forewarns of the treachery of church and state:

> A "reverend" man, whose light should be
> The guide of age and youth,
> Brings to the shrine of Slavery
> The sacrifice of truth!
>
> For the direst wrong by men imposed,
> Since Sodom's fearful cry,
> The word of life has been unclosed,
> To give your God the lie.
>
> Oh! when ye pray for heathen lands,
> And plead for their dark shores,
> Remember Slavery's cruel hands
> Make heathens at your doors!

"Ethiopia" is drawn from Psalms 68:31, "Let bronze be brought to Egypt; let Ethiopia hasten to stretch out her hands to God." This biblical epigraph, the theological foundation of the African Methodist Episcopal church, becomes the symbolic connection between American abolitionism with black Christianity. An inspirational poem, it is a finely woven ballad infused with Eden-like imagery and envisioned deliverance in the promised land.

Other religious poems, like "Saved by Faith," "The Dying Christian," "The Syrophenician Woman" (based on Mark 7:24–30), "That Blessed Hope," "Eva's Farewell," and "The Prodigal's Return" (Luke 15:11–32) are based on or related to biblical text and render a more modern interpretation of these stories. Harper's poetry emphasizes the spirit of Jesus as a soothing source of peace and transcendence as a favored theme in her religious poetry; but again, the feminist dimension expands the presentation of biblical text in order to recenter gender in religious belief and practice.

Of her religious poems in *Poems on Miscellaneous Subjects*, "Ruth and Naomi" and "Rizpah, The Daughter of Ai" contain the most impressive adaptations of biblical texts. Based on Ruth, one of two books in the Bible by and about women, "Ruth and Naomi" flows with a delicate lyricism characterized by subtle, oblique rhyme affecting the soft end rhymes. In this poem, Harper demonstrates her adeptness with rhythm and internal structural devices. Almost all of the vowel sounds in the following stanzas are short and light, except during the lowering of mood with words like "fell," "pale," and "farewell."

> Like rain upon a blighted tree,
>   The tears of Orpah fell,
> Kissing the pale and quivering lip,
>   She breathed her sad farewell.
>
> But Ruth stood up, on her brow
>   There lay a heavenly calm;
> And from her lips came, soft and low,
>   Words like a holy charm.
>
> I will not leave thee, on thy brow
>   Are lines of sorrow, age and care;
> Thy form is bent, thy step is slow,
>   Thy bosom stricken, lone and scar.

"Rizpah, The Daughter of Ai" (2 Samuel 3:7) demonstrates similar grace and lilt:

> She sprang from her sad and lowly seat,
> For a moment her heart forgot to beat,
> And the blood rushed up to her marble cheek
> And a flash to her eye so sad and meek.
>
> The vulture paused in his downward flight,
> As she raised her form to its queenly height,
> The hyena's eye had a horrid glare
> As he turned to his desert lair.

The jackal slunk back with a quickened tread,
From his cowardly search of Rizpah's dead;
Unsated he turned from the noble prey,
Subdued by a glance of the daughter of Ai.

Oh grief! that a mother's heart should know,
Such a weary weight of consuming wo,
For seldom if ever earth has known
Such love as the daughter of Ai has known.

"Vashti" from *Poems*, 1871, one of Harper's later and most exemplary religious poems, deserves attention. Characteristic of her feminist revisions of biblical interpretations and her views on intemperance, the poem focuses on the banishment of a queen of Persia because she refuses to be disgraced by her king's demand that she unveil before a drunken crowd of men. The king wishes to display her beauty as his prize possession. Defending her self-respect, she exclaims:

"I'll take the crown from off my head
And tread it 'neath my feet
Before their rude and careless gaze
My shrinking eyes shall meet.

"A queen unveil'd before the crowd!—
Upon each lip my name!—
Why, Persia's women all would blush
And weep for Vashti's shame!"

This act of resistance is met with patriarchal protest by the king's counselors:

"The women, restive 'neath our rule,
Would learn to scorn our name,
And from her deed to us would come
Reproach and burning shame."

The king is encouraged to dethrone and banish the queen *From distant Jud to Ethiop*, the massive expanse of this ancient kingdom. In addition to Harper's portrayal of this repressive patriarchal act fueled by drunkenness, the inclusion of geographical detail illuminates black

73

African historical presence, a critical contrast against the conscious exclusion of Africa from orthodox religious teachings and from some versions of the Bible.

"Vashti" further extends the poet's feminist Christian vision, as
"Ruth and Naomi" and "Rizpah, The Daughter of Ai" reflect in her earlier work. Structurally and thematically, "Vashti" expresses the poet's
best forum, as her visionary depth expands and enhances her skill. Her
religious poetic productions consistently reflect the poet's most impressive work.

On a more philosophical level, this poem attempts a simplification
of abstract religious concepts through poetic expression. In particular,
"Youth in Heaven" (from *Poems*) translates the metaphysics of Emanuel
Swedenborg (1688–1722), a Swedish physicist turned spiritualist, who
speculated on the spatial and temporal dimensions of heaven. He defined the universe as an organic hierarchy that could be mathematically
measured (or approximated) as the finite and the infinite. The all-en-
compassing God, according to Swedenborg, is composed of "three degrees of being," that is, love, wisdom, and creative energy. This poem also
relates to Harper's conversion to Unitarianism, as the Swedenborgians
held ideological beliefs similar to those of the Unitarian church. In the
United States the Unitarians were staunch supporters of the Underground Railroad and the abolitionist movement. Harper's involvement
with Unitarianism developed through her political affiliations.

In "Youth in Heaven," Harper explains very plainly, that life is a procession, whereby death is the passage or entry into eternal life. The poem
suggests a reversal of the aging process as the planet evolves in darkness
toward death; the motion of the heavens reverses that rotation, moving
towards light. Hence, in heaven,

> *the eldest of the angels*
> *Seems the youngest brother there.*

Likewise, Harper images Goethe's death around a similar theme
that dominated his work. In her poem, "Let the Light Enter! The dying
words of Goethe" (*Poems*), Goethe identifies *light* as the energy by which
life enters into heaven:

> *Gracious Savior when our day dreams*
> *Melt and vanish from the sight,*
> *May our dim and longing vision*
> *Then be blessed with light, more light.*

Light energizes the motion of death that moves the spirit through the dark, finite, four-dimensional sphere into the infinite, ethereal realm. The spiritual world interfaces the physical, mortal planet, whereby death provides a transition into the afterlife.

These poems were useful to Harper as a Sunday school teacher because they demystify the concept of eternal life. Harper's aesthetic strategy is the application of poetics to inspire faith, and to access the obscure and abstract. Unlike most nineteenth-century black poets who inundated their poetry with Greek references for a select audience, Harper used simple language and lucid imagery to explain and to clarify.

Temperance Poetry

> *If mind is more than matter, if the destiny of the human soul reaches out into the eternities, and as we sow so must we reap, then bad as was American slavery the slavery of intemperance is worse. Slavery was the enemy of one section, the oppressor of one race, but intemperance is the curse of every land and the deadly foe of every kindred, tribe and race which falls beneath its influence.*[8]

Frances Harper wrote essays and lectures against alcoholism, which she considered another form of slavery and a serious social issue that affected all classes. Temperance was a key issue of Christian abolitionists and radical feminists, and it found favor with Harper's poetry. Like her Dickensian poem concerning class repression in England, her dedication to the temperance movement relates to her broader social vision. Before the end of the nineteenth century, alcoholism had become one of the most destructive forces in oppressed communities of color in the United States, preying on their desperate conditions.

"The Drunkard's Child" dramatizes a pathetic scene in order to accentuate the devastating impact of alcoholism on the family:

> *He stood beside his dying child,*
> *With dim and bloodshot eye;*
> *They'd won him from the haunts of vice*
> *To see his first born die.*
>
> *He came with a slow and staggering tread,*
> *A vague, unmeaning stare,*

And, reeling, clasped the clammy hand,
  So deathly pale and fair.

Like "Died of Starvation" and "The Slave Mother: A Tale of Ohio," "The Drunkard's Child" ends with death. The dramatic pursuit of the poem is to capture audience imagination, to engage its empathy, and to enlist its moral outrage. Aesthetic dismissal of a poem often uses resistance to sentimentality as a common excuse. It is a response to tragedy, which is more characteristic of women's writing. Apparently this affronts aesthetic distance or male "objectivity." But as evidenced in Stowe's *Uncle Tom's Cabin* and many other nineteenth-century women's writing, the purpose of the literature is to instigate a compassionate response in thought and action. Harper conveyed this romanticism from the lectern to sway the subjective receptivity of the audience. Death offers deliverance until an indifferent society changes.

He clasped him to his throbbing heart,
  "I will! I will!" he said;
His pleading ceased—the father held
  His first born and his dead.

Bibliographical Commentary

During the abolitionist tour, several poems by Frances Harper appeared in antislavery publications. Undoubtedly, this promoted her visibility on the lecture circuit. "Be Active" was published in *Frederick Douglass' Paper* (January 11, 1856), and in and in *The Weekly Anglo-African* (July 30, 1859); "To Charles Sumner" appeared in *The Liberator* (1860) and in *The Weekly Anglo-African* (June 30, 1860); "The Dismissal of Tyng" was printed in *The National Anti-Slavery Standard* (November 29, 1856) *Frederick Douglass' Paper* (December 5, 1856). "The Drunkard's Child" was published in *Frederick Douglass' Paper* on March 14, 1856. "The Dying Fugitive" appeared in *The Anglo-African* on August 20, 1859, with "Gone to God." "Youth in Heaven" appeared in *Anglo-African Magazine* in 1860. *Frederick Douglass' Paper* published "The Slave Auction" on September 22, 1854, shortly after *Poems on Miscellaneous Subjects* was published. And on September 12, 1856, "Ruth and Naomi" appeared in *Frederick Douglass' Paper*. Harper's poems were reprinted in many publications even after her death.

By 1858, *Poems on Miscellaneous Subjects* had reached twelve thousand copies in print, and by 1874 it had been reprinted several times. This significant publication embodies a thematic labyrinth that had not heretofore been engaged in American poetry. Harper articulates a holistic and transcendent perspective. The book thematically encompasses the complexity of compounded, interconnected oppression as it impacts, interacts, and manifests injustice in a class-stratified society.

Those poems written after 1854 were later collected in the volume *Poems* (1871), an elegant hardcover that was reprinted in different colors, with additons and deletions until the final 1901 edition. But in the first edition, evidence of Harper's internationalist perspective is readily apparent especially in poems like, "Let The Light Enter! The dying words of Goethe," "Youth in Heaven." Within a political framework, "Death of Zombi, the Chief of a Negro Kingdom in South America," celebrates black liberation in South America, while the "The Czar of Russia" sardonically condemns the tyranny of an imperial despot and foreshadows the Bolshevik Revolution.

Poems contains obvious inspirational verses, like "Words for the Hour" which recruits for the Civil War against slavery; "The Freedom Bill," proclaiming all the nation free; as well as the salutatory "President Lincoln's Proclamation of Freedom" anticipating *the glorious dawn of freedom*. Repeated publications of *Poems* included new and selected poems from 1871 until 1901. Likewise, many of these poems appeared in periodicals (see bibliography).

Other, more obscure titles of slender volumes, such as *The Sparrow's Fall and Other Poems* (no date), *The Martyr of Alabama and Other Poems* (1894), and *Light Beyond the Darkness* (no date), appear to be self-published. The absence of dates and the appearance of the poet's Philadelphia address on the title page suggest practical printings, possibly for Sunday schools. More often than not, these poems are included in the collected *Poems* (1871), *Atlanta Offering Poems* (1895), *Poems* (1898 and 1900). But *Moses: A Story of the Nile* (1869) represents her most ambitious achievement, and *Sketches of Southern Life* (1872) demonstrates her most innovative performance. According to William Still, fifty thousand of her first four books were in print by 1872.

Like the struggle, her poetry persisted, flourished, and expanded with the demands of activism. Harper's involvement in the human rights struggle diversified and intensified with the efforts of the Reconstruction era and the suffrage movement. Conversely, her poetry expresses and engages the directions and conflicts emanating from the radical context of these movements. Notwithstanding, " 'Neath sheltering vines and stately palms," Harper's radical vision advocated deliverance and helped to sustain and shape the quest for "the Promised Land."

> Yes! Ethiopia yet shall stretch
>   Her bleeding hands abroad;
> Her cry of agony shall reach
>   The burning throne of God.

Mosaic Legacy: Frances Harper and the Afroamerican Quest for the Promised Land

I like the character of Moses. He is the first disunionist we read of in the Jewish Scriptures. The magnificence of Pharaoh's throne loomed up before his vision, its oriental splendors glittered before his eyes; but he turned from them all and chose rather to suffer with the enslaved than rejoice with the free. He would have no union with the slave power in Egypt. When we have a race of men whom this blood stained government cannot tempt or flatter, who would sternly refuse every office in the nation's gift, from a president down to a tide-waiter, until she shook her hands from complicity in the guilt of cradle plundering and man stealing, then for us the foundations of an historic character will have been laid. We need men and women whose hearts are the homes of a high and lofty enthusiasm, and a noble devotion to the cause of emancipation, who are ready and willing to lay time, talent and money on the altar of universal freedom. We have money among us, but how much of it is spent to bring deliverance to our captive brethren? Are our wealthiest men the most liberal sustainers of the Anti-slavery enterprise? Or does the bare fact of their having money, really help mold public opinion and reverse its sentiments? We need what money cannot buy and what affluence is too beggarly to purchase. Earnest self sacrificing souls that will stamp themselves not only on the present but the future. Let us not then defer all our noble opportunities till we get rich. And here I am, not aiming to enlist a fanatical crusade against the desire for riches, but I do protest against chaining down the soul, with its Heaven endowed faculties and God given attributes to the one idea of getting money as stepping into power or even gaining our rights in common with others. The respect that is only bought by gold is not worth much. It is no honor to shake hands politically with men who whip women and steal babies. If this government has no call for our services, no aim for your children, we have the greater need of them to build up a true manhood and womanhood for ourselves. The important lesson we should hear and be able to teach, is how to make every gift, whether gold or talent, fortune or genius, subserve the cause of crushed

humanity and carry out the greatest idea of the present age, the glorious idea of human brotherhood.[1]

"Our Greatest Want" appeared in *The Anglo-African Magazine* (1859), five years after Harper had embarked on her mission as an abolitionist lecturer with her second book of poetry, *Poems on Miscellaneous Subjects* (1854). In her writing and speeches, Frances Harper encourages an allegorical connection between the repression and enslavement of the Hebrew people and the Afroamerican dilemma. This parallel provides a context for historical insight, spiritual fortification, and revolutionary action. More specifically, she extends this comparison in order to construct a "Moses" model for radical, Christian character. Moses first appears in Harper's script with "Our Greatest Want" in 1859, then reemerges as a metaphor for President Lincoln in a letter to Still upon Lincoln's death in 1865. He is the primary persona in *Moses: A Story of the Nile* in 1869, and a recurring image in Harper's lectures. Moses is also a major reference in her novel, *Iola Leroy*. Ostensibly, this biblical character evolves into Harper's visionary motif.

An overview of Harper's work reveals a steadfast embrace of this Old Testament story about the liberation of the Hebrews from the oppressive Egyptian kingdom. He serves as the quintessential model for Afroamerican character, male and female, and the Hebrew exodus from slavery is considered a parallel path for Afroamerican aspirations. The poem, *Moses: A Story of the Nile*, is Harper's ultimate testament to Moses and this liberation movement. But in keeping with Harper's feminist perspective, her poetic interpretation of Exodus includes a radical presentation of Moses' mother as the key molder of his political and religious consciousness.

David Walker's Appeal

Even though the exact time of Moses' emergence as a symbolic figure in Afroamerican liberation is unclear, we can ascertain that the adaptation of Christianity to the social and political circumstances of the slave experience rendered a more radical interpretation and application of biblical mythology than the slave-holding class intended or anticipated. At the same time, David Walker's *An Appeal to the Coloured Citizens of the World* was the literature most effective in advancing this religious vision into political action. The *Appeal* challenged and affected the political direction of Christian abolitionists and the slave community. Like the spirituals "Go Down Moses" and "Steal Away to Jesus," this incendiary decree identified Moses as the force of deliverance, and Christ as the spirit of freedom.

The conceptual underpinning of Frances Harper's poetic vision literarily and autobiographically connects to David Walker's *Appeal*, wherein her uncle, William Watkins, is quoted. After David Walker was mysteriously murdered in 1830, William Lloyd Garrison reprinted the *Appeal* in the *Liberator* that same year, which William Watkins circulated throughout Maryland. Since the *Appeal* advocated religiously inspired violence, it was considered the most dangerous indictment against slavery yet written. After Nat Turner's rebellion in Southhampton County, Virginia in 1831, David Walker's *Appeal* and slave spirituals about Israel and Moses became verboten in some slave states.

In particular, lines from one of Harper's early poems, "Ethiopia," coincide with Walker's philosophical "Preamble" to the *Appeal:*

> Let them remember, that though our cruel oppressors and murderers, may (if possible) treat us more cruel as Pharaoh did the children of Israel, yet God of the Ethiopians, has been pleased to hear our means in consequence of oppression; and the day of our redemption from abject wretchedness draweth near, when we shall be enabled, in the most extended sense of the word, to stretch forth our hands to the Lord our God but there must be a willingness on our part, for God to do these things for us, for we may be assured that he will not take us by the hairs of our head against our will and desire and drag us from our very, mean, low and abject condition.[2]

Both Walker and Harper identify God as the Lord of the Ethiopians, a critical departure from the southern aristocratic presentation of the Bible as justification of white supremacy and black subjugation. Moses acts as the revolutionary metaphor for Afroamerican character, an example for individual guidance out of the depths of complicity with the forces of slavery. Whereas Harper's essay, "Our Greatest Want," published in *The Anglo-African Magazine* thirty years later (1859), addresses the free "colored" Americans, Walker's *Appeal* (1829), self-published and smuggled by sailors behind the legal boundaries of slavery, addresses the slaves:

> In all probability, Moses would have become Prince Regent to the throne, and no doubt, in process of time but he would have been seated on the throne of Egypt. But he would rather suffer shame,

with the people of God, then to enjoy pleasures with that wicked people for a season. O! that the coloured people were long since of Moses' excellent disposition, instead of courting favour with, and telling news and lies to our natural enemies, against each other— aiding them to keep their hellish chains of slavery upon us.[3]

Walker's influence on Harper can be detailed in "Our Greatest Want" as both writers contrast Great Britain's abolition of slavery with America's democratic hypocrisy. In a more aggressive vein, Henry Highland Garnett published an 1848 edition of the *Appeal*, calling for the overthrow of slavery by the slaves: "You had far better die—die *immediately*, than live slaves, and entail your wretchedness upon your posterity."[4]

Likewise, Harper's *Moses: A Story of the Nile* intersects with the thematic flow of Walker's *Appeal*. The convergence of Moses and Jesus Christ as liberating spirituality occurs in both texts, as it does in the emerging tradition of Afroamerican Christianity in the slave quarters and in the A.M.E. church. Harper conveys Christ as a redemptive source, while Walker instructs the slaves to hold their tongues and to trust their prayers and rebellion to the liberatory force of Christ:

> Remember, also to lay humble at the feet of our Lord and Master Jesus Christ, with prayers and fastings. Let our enemies go on with their butcheries, and at once fill up their cup. Never make an attempt to gain our freedom or natural right, from under our cruel oppressors and murderers, until you see your way clear—when that hour arrives and you move, be not afraid or dismayed; for be you assured that Jesus Christ the king of heaven and of earth who is God of justice and of armies, will surely go before you. And those enemies who have for hundreds of years, stolen our rights, and kept us ignorant of Him and His divine worship, he will remove.[5]

Harper's Moses adheres to the biblical narrative as he parts the Nile and drowns Pharaoh's army:

> *Then arose*
> *A cry of terror, baffled hate and hopeless dread,*
> *A gurgling sound of horror, as "the waves*
> *Come madly dashing, wildly crashing, sucking*
> *Out their place again," and the flower and pride*
> *Of Egypt sank as lead within the sea*

Till the waves threw back their corpses cold and stark
Upon the shore, and the song of Israel's
Triumph was the requiem of their foes.

And chapter 7 follows with Christ, an inclusion that extends the violent deliverance with a vision of Christ in the promised land, the icon of universal peace and brotherhood.

> *Only one God,—*
> *This truth received into the world's great life,*
> *Not as an idle dream nor speculative thing,*
> *But as a living, vitalizing thought,*
> *Should bind us closer to our God and link us*
> *With our fellow man, the brothers and co-heirs*
> *With Christ, the elder brother of our race.*
> *Before this truth let every blade of war*
> *Grow dull, and slavery, cowering at the light,*
> *Skulk from the homes of men; instead*
> *Of war bring peace and freedom, love and joy.*
> *And light for man, instead of bondage, whips*
> *And chains.*

This improvisation distinguishes the poem from Exodus, and her character developments differ slightly from Walker's perspective. But these distinctions are appropriate for the circumstances of Afroamericans, especially during the Reconstruction when *Moses: A Story of the Nile* appeared, four years after deliverance. Afroamerican liberationist theology is based on Exodus and the New Testament. Moses and Jesus Christ are viewed in a similar light, as forces of God and as symbols of physical and spiritual liberation. While the spirituals sang "Go Down Moses" and "Steal Away to Jesus," Harper's Moses delivers the Hebrews to a River Jordan where Jesus resides, then Moses lies down in an indiscernible grave.

> *None saw their chosen grave;*
> *It was the angels secret*
> *Where Moses should be laid*

Moses' angelic burial is strikingly similar to Jesus' disappearance from the tomb. Moses' unmarked grave parallels Jesus' resurrection. Like the crocuses that appear at Easter,

the fairest flowers
Sprang up beneath their angels tread.

Nor broken turf, nor hillock
Did e'er reveal that grave,
And truthful lips have never said
We know where he is laid.

Both Walker and Harper embrace Christianity as the spiritual and cultural context for American "Ethiopians" (blacks). Walker's *Appeal* and Harper's essay, "Our Greatest Want," were written in anticipation of emancipation. At the same time, Harper's book-length poem, *Moses*, demonstrates a more deliberate literary effort to cultivate a religious cultural work about the passage from bondage into Canaan. But unlike Exodus, there is nowhere to go. In this historical instance, the promised land must be pursued within the hostile boundaries of the New Egypt, the United States. These intense circumstances benefit from the compounded power of Moses *and* Jesus.

At the same time, a point of contrast with the more resigned religious and literary posture of some black American writers was ever present. George Moses Horton's poem, "Slavery" (*Liberator*, March 29, 1834) is a tragic, ironic vision of a Moses held in bondage. This slave-poet-in-residence at the University of North Carolina published his first book, *Hope for Freedom* (1845) in an attempt to raise enough money to purchase his freedom. Unable to acquiesce to the legacy of his name or the desire in his theme, his dispirited imagery conveys a slave waiting and resigning, instead of acting and engaging.

When first my bosom glowed with hope,
I gaze as from a mountain top
On some delightful plain;
But oh! how transient was the scene—
It fled as though it had not been
And all my hopes were vain.

Is it because my skin is black,
That thou shoul'st be so dull and slack,
And scorn to set me free?
Then let me hasten to the grave,
The only refuge for the slave,
Who mourns for liberty.

Harriet Tubman, John Brown, and Abraham Lincoln: Moses and Christ in America

We have a woman in our country who has received the name of "Moses," not by lying about it, but by acting it out—a woman who has gone down into the Egypt of slavery and brought out hundreds of our people into liberty. The last time I saw that woman, her hands were swollen. That woman who had led one of Montgomery's most successful expeditions, who was brave enough and secretive enough to act as a scout for the American army, had her hands all swollen from a conflict with a brutal conductor, who undertook to eject her from her place. That woman, whose courage and bravery won a recognition from our army and from every black man in the land, is excluded from every thoroughfare of travel.[6]

Frances Harper and Harriet Tubman were political allies connected through the Underground Railroad and the radical network. Harper lectured on the abolitionist circuit, calling for the end of slavery, while she channeled funds to William Still's headquarters in Philadelphia, a critical stop on Tubman's deliverance route. Harper's admiration for Tubman as a female Moses figure reinforces the role of women in the struggle for freedom. Inasmuch as the Walker legacy influenced Harper's developing political and literary activism, the political deeds of Harriet Tubman and John Brown serve as the author's historical reference for biblical intersection; and inasmuch as Tubman was endowed the "Black Moses," the living legend, John Brown was revered as a Christ-like martyr of Harpers Ferry.

Tubman was a cohort of Brown and provided him with demographic information about the plantations and descriptive details of the Virginia terrain for his raid on Harpers Ferry. Bad health presumably prevented Tubman from accompanying Brown during the raid. Perhaps the absence of the black Moses was a prophetic sign. Hence, the attempt at deliverance was transformed into another crucifixion. In his own words, John Brown characterized his commitment to freedom as appropriate Christian action. Jesus was his supreme model: "Did not my Master Jesus Christ come down from Heaven and sacrifice Himself upon the altar for the salvation of the race, and should I, a worm, not worthy to crawl under His feet, refuse to sacrifice myself?"[7]

In a letter to John Brown, Harper identifies Brown as a Christ figure. She envisions him and his men as martyrs and writes:

And, if Universal Freedom is ever to be the dominant power of the land, your bodies may be only her first stepping stones to dominion.[8]

This image is later immortalized in "John Brown's Body," a song sung by Union soldiers during the Civil War to inspire them in battle.

John Brown inspires the image of the spirit of Agitation, a character in Harper's short story, "The Triumph of Freedom—A Dream" in 1860. His description and fate are derived from Brown:

> Then I saw an aged man standing before her altars; his gray hair floated in the air, a solemn radiance lit upon his eye, and a lofty purpose sat enthroned upon his brow. He fixed his eye upon the goddess, and she cowered beneath his unfaltering gaze. He laid his aged hands upon her blood-cemented throne, and it shook and trembled to its base; her cheeks blanched with dread, her hands fell nerveless by her side. It seemed as if his very gaze would have almost annihilated her; but just then I saw, bristling with bayonets, a blood-stained ruffian, named the General Government, and he caught the hands of the aged man and fettered them, and he was then led to prison.[9]

As part of the story Harper extracts sentences from her condolence letters written to John and Mary Brown during his imprisonment and trial.

> In the name of the young girl sold from the clutches of a libertine or a profligate—[10]

is transformed into dialogue for the

> blood stained goddess: are the hearts of young girls, sold from the warm clasp of their mothers' arms to the brutal clutches of a libertine or a profligate—from the temples of Christ to the altars of shame.[11]

Likewise, Harper incorporates a line from her letter to Mary Brown, that images a female crucifixion:

> From the prison comes forth a shout of triumph over that power whose ethics are robbery of the feeble and oppression of the weak, the trophies of whose chivalry are a plundered cradle and a scourged and bleeding woman.[12]

This sentence precedes the Christlike imagery of the old man in the story:

> I saw the green sword stained with his blood, but every drop of it was like the terrible teeth sown by Cadmus; they woke up armed men to smite the terror-striken power that had invaded his life. It seemed as if his blood had

been instilled into the veins of freemen and given them fresh vigor to battle against the hoary forms of gigantic Error and colossal Theory, who stood as sentinels around the throne of the goddess. His blood was a new baptism of Liberty.[13]

Harper sustains her inspired a verse throughout the historical moment of the event and her emotional relationship to that moment. Her admiration for John Brown does not reflect the perception of a naive woman or a sheltered poet. This story and her characterization of Brown convey the expression of a personal friend and political comrade. He represents her ideal of the revolutionary Christ inside the human being.

Abraham Lincoln

Moses, the meekest man on earth, led the children of Israel over the Red Sea, but was not permitted to see them settled in Canaan. Mr. Lincoln has led us through another Red Sea to the land of triumphant victory, and God has seen fit to summon for the new era another man.[14]

Both blacks and whites largely regarded Lincoln as an American Moses, and in this letter to William Still, Harper heralds Lincoln as such. But the practices of segregation were still intact, and blacks were not permitted to pay their respects to Lincoln while he lay in state at the White House. According to one of Harper's descendents, Frances Ellen Fattah, Harper wrote a moving letter to the administrators of Lincoln's funeral requesting that blacks be permitted to view the president's body. Her appeal and possibly others convinced the authorities that such a barring against blacks was a gross impropriety. Consequently, they relented.

Tubman, Brown, and Lincoln are the most dynamic historical personalities that prefigured Harper's literary Mosaic. As Harper identifies them as beacons for liberation in her letters, speeches, poetry, and prose, her language functions as a source for inspiration. Moreover, *Moses: A Story of the Nile*, is also a religiously inspired work.

Harper's Religion and Religious Verse

What I ask of American Christianity is not to show us more creeds, but more of Christ; not more rites and ceremonies, but more religion glowing with love and replete with life—religion which will be to all weaker races an uplifting power, and not a degrading influence.[15]

Frances Harper wrote about Christianity as a dissident and a scholar. In her poetry she challenges racist and sexist religious dogma with renewed faith and biblical knowledge. "The Dying Christian" is derived from a favorite hymn, and "That Blessed Hope," "The River," "The Syrophenician Woman," "Saved by Faith," "The Prodigal's Return," "Eva's Farewell," "The Dismissal of Tyng," "Rizpah, The Daughter of Ai," and "Ruth and Naomi" are based on either specific biblical passages or are infused with biblical verses and a feminist interpretation of text.

Beyond "The Bible Defense of Slavery," which refutes a pseudo-scientific argument for racism, *Moses: A Story of the Nile*, represents an alternative theological interpretation of the origins of Christianity. The poem criticizes the morality of the ancient slave society and thereby makes allusions to America's ruling social and economic order. It is a cultural expression of abolitionist activism during the Reconstruction and a spiritual vision for the future of a new people.

Moses: A Story of the Nile is a book-length poem consisting of eight chapters. This division into chapters instead of parts, suggests biblical text and context. The use of blank verse is also consistent with biblical style. The poem contains metaphors, allusions, and syntax reflective of biblical verse, and represents a distinct departure from Harper's ballads. As in other works, Harper demonstrates a stylistic preference for voice. In particular, "Eliza Harris," "The Dying Bondman," as well as "Ruth and Naomi" and "Vashti," employ narrative to characterize and dramatize the creative experience. Likewise, the feminist perspective, another key feature of Harper's secular and religious verse, illuminates the power and presence of women. *Moses: A Story of the Nile* is Frances Harper's most intricate and most accomplished poem.

Literary Legacy

Harper's adaptation of Exodus contributed to the acculturation of this biblical mythology into the Afroamerican consciousness. During slavery, "bible preachers" were often distrusted because of duplicitous relationships with the slaveholding class. Therefore, the recitation and the circulation of this poem through Harper's involvement with the Reconstruction of the post-war South connected the radical, Christian abolitionists with the political tradition of the slave spirituals. At the same time, *Moses: A Story of the Nile*, provided a biblical context that could repair the damaged reputation of the Bible. Often lecturing for the A.M.E. church, she recruited for religious and secular convergence, promoting the legacy of Moses as a model for a liberated consciousness. She cited the "living God of Zion" as a vision to be cultivated according to the natural order and the doctrine of the New Testament, while she emphasized the urgency to acquire land.

Harper was engaged with Reconstruction work after the Civil War, but she lectured in the northern states as well. *Moses*, a literary tribute to the mythological underpinnings of Afroamerican culture, received impressive reviews from northern journalists:

> Mrs. F. E. W. Harper delivered a poem upon 'Moses' in Wilbraham to a large and delighted audience. She is a woman of high moral tone, with superior native powers highly cultivated, and a captivating eloquence that hold her audience in rapt attention from the beginning to the close. She will delight any intelligent audience, and those who wish first-class lecturers cannot do better than to secure her services.[16]

> Mrs. Frances E. W. Harper read her poem of "Moses" last evening at Rev. Mr. Harrison's church to a good audience. It deals with the story of the Hebrew Moses from his finding in the wicker basket on the Nile to his death on Mount Nebo and his burial in an unknown grave; following closely the Scripture account. It contains about 700 lines, beginning with blank verse of the common measure, and changing to other measures, but always without rhyme; and is a pathetic and well-sustained piece. Mrs. Harper recited it with good effect, and it was well received. She is a lady of much talent, and always speaks well, particularly when her subject relates to the condition of her own people, in whose welfare, before and since the war, she has taken the deepest interest. As a lecturer Mrs. Harper is more effective than most of those who come before our lyceums: with a natural eloquence that is very moving.[17]

An Embryonic Possibility

In 1856, Harper visited fugitive slaves in Ontario, Canada. "While in Toronto she lectured, and was listened to with serious consideration; but she only made a brief visit (approximately from August 30th to September 12th) then returning to Philadelphia her adopted home."[18] Shortly preceding this Canadian tour, a poem, "The Burial of Moses," appeared in the May 24, 1856 issue of the *Provincial Freeman*. This newspaper, founded and edited by Mary Shadd, was the noted publication of the Canadian black communities, printed intermittently in Chatham, Windsor, and Toronto from March 24, 1853 to September 15, 1857, with some issues appearing as late as 1859.

"The Burial of Moses," is unsigned, an oversight on the part of the copyeditor. However, Harper's contact with Chatham and Toronto "colored" communities and the coincidental appearance of this poem in the *Provincial Freeman* deserves some scrutiny, if only to indicate cultural consistency. "The Burial of Moses," is prefaced with the biblical scripture: "And He buried him in a valley in the land of Moab, over against Bethpeor; but no man knoweth of his sepulchre unto this day," (Deut. 34:6). The poem extends and elaborates the biblical imagery, exceeding the biblical description of Moses' death by imaging a funeral for him in heaven and by infusing it with a celebration of his victories as a warrior-poet struggling against nineteenth-century slavery.

The poetic structure is strikingly and characteristically Harperean. The ballad form and the descriptive, didactic narrative echo the stylistic devices of her earlier poetry. In particular, the gesture of the last two stanzas of the poem, connecting the historical to contemporary nineteenth-century circumstances, remains consistent with all of Harper's antislavery poems, a point noted in my analysis of "Eliza Harris" (1853), and in the quintessential "Bury Me In A Free Land" (1860). "The Burial of Moses" relates:

> *In that deep grave without a name,*
> *Whence his uncoffin'd clay*
> *Shall break again, most wondrous thought*
> *Before the Judgement Day;*
> *And stand with glory wrapped around*
> *On the hills has never trod,*
> *And speak of the strife that won our life*
> *With the Incarnate Son of God.*
>
> *O lonely tomb in Moab's lan;*
> *O dark Bethpeor' hell,*
> *Speak to these curious hearts of ours,*
> *And teach them to be still.*
> *God hath his mysteries of grace,*
> *Ways that we cannot tell;*
> *He hides them deep like the secret sleep*
> *Of him He loved so well.*

The connection between "The Burial of Moses" and Harper's work is even more of a point for consideration when one compares the ending of the anonymous work to the last section of Harper's poem, "The Death of Moses." Unlike the rest of *Moses*, this last section rounds into metered lines with occasional terminal rhyme, ending with rhyming couplets. This section does not conclude with the cyclical implications of "The Burial of Moses," but rather, the descriptive language of the heavenly funeral parallels the scene conveyed in "The Death of Moses." "The Burial of Moses" portrays:

> *By Nebo's lonely mountain*
> *On this side Jordan's wave,*
> *In a vale in the land of Moab*
> *There lies a lonely grave.*
> *And no man saw it e'er;*
> *For the angels of God upturned the soil,*
> *And laid the dead man there.*

In "The Death of Moses," Harper relays:

> *Oh never on that mountain*
> *Was seen a lovelier sight*
> *Than the troupe of fair young angels*
> *That gathered 'round the dead.*
> *With gentle hands they bore him*
> *That bright and shiny train,*
> *From Nebo's lonely mountain*
> *To sleep in Moab's vale.*

Juxtaposing *By Nebo's lonely mountain* with *From Nebo's lonely mountain*; and aligning *In a vale in the land of Moab* with *To sleep in Moab's vale* demonstrates probable evidence of authorship. Both poems emphasize the angels selecting and preparing the grave:

> *For the angels of God upturned the soil,*
> *And laid the dead man there* ("Burial of Moses").

> *It was the angels secret*
> *Where Moses should be laid,"* ("Death of Moses").

"The Burial of Moses" may be a found Harper poem which could have been the germinating nucleus for the long poem. On the other hand, others may argue that an unsigned poem can only be credited to that great poet, Anonymous. But more important, Harper's presence in Canada when the poem appeared suggests that she at least read it.

91

Therefore, at the very least, this argument about origin and influence is an intriguing parallel and prelude to Harper's later, more elaborate, and most ambitious poetic production, *Moses: A Story of the Nile*."

Moses: A Story of the Nile

Entitled "The Parting," chapter 1 consists of a dialogue between Moses and the Egyptian princess, Charmean, who adopts Moses (an Egyptian name which means "to draw out of the water") who was floating in a basket in the Nile. Moses tells his foster mother that he must leave the palace

> *to join*
> *The fortunes of my race.*

In amazement, the princess protests with a series of questions, wondering how he could leave the advantages of the royal court for *The badge of servitude and toil?* Moses explains that he has a purpose that binds him to the Hebrew people and their God, who will lead the slaves to freedom. As the first "disunionist," Moses commits class suicide. From her privileged perspective, the princess does not understand why Moses will not accept a king's destiny over a slave's tragedy:

> *Bright dreams and glowing hopes; could'st thou not live*
> *Them out as well beneath the radiance*
> *Of our throne as in the shadow of those*
> *Bondage-darkened huts?*

The subtle, oblique rhyme interfacing the imagery sustains a subdued sound pattern that structures the poem. This pattern occurs throughout the poem as exemplified in the carriage of alliteration in *thou, Them, the, throne,* and *those;* the modulation of *o*'s in *glowing hopes,* and *thou;* and the interplay between iambic meter and hyphenated alliteration in *Bondage-darkened huts.* These aural features form the underpinnings of the poem's strength. The asymmetrical sound patterns are understated and never upstage the imagery. Harper's poetic movement into blank verse underscores her versatility as an artist and craftsperson. The following scene, wherein Moses rejects Egypt, exemplifies the effects of Harper's blank verse style:

And then thy richest viands pall upon my taste,
And discord jars in every tone of song.
I cannot live in pleasure while they faint
In pain.

Similar subtlety appears in Harper's essays, which are technically precise, and yet infused with oblique rhyme and alliteration. Likewise, this long poem pulls from the blank verse found in the Book of Exodus. But at the same time, the imagery compares and contrasts by juxtaposing the roots of injustice with human suffering, representing the two class extremes.

The poem continues as the princess reminisces about her discovery of Moses in the river, where she went to bathe and *to weave a crown of lotus leaves.* The princess explains how Moses eased her loneliness like the soothing of the river itself. Harper envisions the maternal need of the princess, who received Moses and rescued him from her father's decree, which condemned male Hebrew babies to death. This variation on theme provides a sensitive portrayal of characterization, whereby the feelings of Charmean are presented relative to her role as fostermother. Her defiance of her father's death decree is a woman's bravery, whereby she defended Moses upon her father's discovery of him one day in the palace.

Pharaoh's response incorporates Egyptian lore, which predicted the birth of the Hebrew deliverer. The irony of Pharaoh's act of mercy stems from his recognition of Charmean's mother, Apenath, flashing from the light of his daughter's eyes,

To darkness, grief and pain, and for her sake,
Not thine, I'll spare the child.

A double entendre follows this scene when the princess claims she has saved Moses twice,—*once from the angry sword and once from the devouring flood,* for it will be the flood of the Nile that will devour Pharaoh's army.

Charmean appeals to Moses through her maternal longing, evoking *a painful silence* and

the quick
Throbbing of the other's heart.

This response reflects the emotional ties between the privileged house slave and the benevolent slave mistress. If Moses would "pass" for an Egyptian and deny his race, he could acquire power and position in the empire. But he repels her offer with another mother's love, the umbilical connection that explains the radicalization of Moses. Harper deviates from the biblical plot, suggesting that Moses' Hebrew mother played a critical role in his subversive religious and political acculturation. Likewise, Harriet Tubman, the black woman Moses, explained how her mother told her about Nat Turner's prophecy, and how God would deliver his children from bondage.

Charmean's hand slave, who was sent to secure a nurse for Moses, was Moses' sister and the nurse she sought was their mother. Moses tells the princess of his tradition as taught to him, his brother, Aaron, and his sister, Miriam. These lines reference Genesis and the story of Abraham's test of faith by God on Mount Moriah. Because of Abraham's faith, God promised

> *a great Deliverance, Beneath our vines and palms,*
> *our flocks and herds.*
> *Increase, and joyful children crowd our streets.*

These lines entail the imagery of a new Eden, of the promised land, imagery that first emerged in Harper's poem, "Ethiopia," a biblical cross-reference to Psalms 68:31.

It is important to note this inclusion of the Psalms reference, for it reiterates Harper's belief in the African frame of reference for biblical interpretation. The suggestion that Hebrews were descendents of Africans contradicts nineteenth-century distortion of biblical text that dismissed the overwhelming influence of Ethiopian presence on Egyptian civilization and on Hebrew history. The paling of biblical characters belonged to Euroamerican Christian dogma that denied and justified enslavement of dark peoples through historical exclusion and cultural denial. Hence, Harper's direct and indirect approach to this story of the Nile renders a recoloring of history.

The princess is described as having *dark prophetic eyes*, and the

> *bright tropical blood sent its quick*
> *Flushes o'er the life of her cheek.*

David Walker explains in his *Appeal* that the Egyptians were a dark-skinned people, an Ethiopian mixture. Harper's physical description of the princess reinforces this claim. Additionally, the poem does not indicate any significant physical distinctions between the Hebrews, who are enslaved, and the Egyptians, who rule. The pharaoh does not realize Moses is a Hebrew until his daughter discloses his racial difference, which is cultural, not physical.

> *She had hoped to see*
> *The crown of Egypt on his brow, the sacred*
> *Leopard skin adorn his shoulders, and his seat*
> *The throne of the proud Pharaoh's.*

The chapter ends with Moses leaving the palace, which was *Bought by sin and gilded o'er with vice.* The ending imagery is of a baptism, or rebirth, as Moses enters Christlike into a new era:

> *And he had chosen well, for on his brow*
> *God poured the chrism of a holy work.*
> *And thus anointed he has stood a bright*
> *Ensample through the changing centuries of time.*

Chapter 2 opens with Moses' exit from the palace, pivoting on contrasted imagery of royal splendor against dispirited oppression. *Those regal halls* under the *lofty grandeur* of the magnificent obelisks fade into the background, *like a shadow o'er his mind,* as he enters the *lowly homes of Goshen,* where

> *he saw the women of his race kneading*
> *Their tale of bricks; the sons of Abraham*
> *Crouching beneath their heavy burdens.*

His dark eyes reflect the enchanted memories of wealth, like the black woman Moses, his spiritual vision, is guided by a *tender light . . . with lofty purposes and faith.* Harper contrasts the splendor of the palace with the *quaint* and *grim* expression of the sphinxes against Moses' entry into the desolate slave quarters.

Throughout the poem, Harper engages a cosmic context for color coding. While *ashen* and *pale* are connected with *fear,* and *blanched* and *grey* are connected with physical death, *white* is associated with *sin,* indicating spiritual death. *Dark* and *shadow* relate to depression, and mourning, but *black* is reserved for anger. In contrast to the linear abstraction that typified most nineteenth-century symbolism, whereby skin color is

95

equated with ingrained human character as well as spiritual value, Harper's symbolism operates on a cosmic plane, reflecting nature's symbolic systems to characterize human feelings, thoughts, and actions.

The pervasive gloom of his people crystallizes lucidly as Moses returns home, where he notes the *increasing pallor on his sister's cheek,* the *deepening shadows on his mother's brow,* and the restless light *glowing in his brother's eye* that characterize the consequences of *servitude and toil.* Moses tells his mother that he has left the pharaoh's palace to share the fate of their race. She lets him know of a rumor that he had sworn his allegiance to the Egyptian god and kingdom at the temple of the sun. The dialogue between Moses and his mother is not taken from Exodus; again Harper empowers the woman's voice to qualify and to extend the possibilities of the unreported and the unexplained.

Harper uses the refrain *by faith* taken from the Book of Hebrews to constitute the perspective of Moses' mother. While Amram, Moses' father, had submitted to rumor, his mother *had stronger faith than that.* The implications of her refrain make an indelible statement about the spirituality of women, whose faith seems stronger than men in the face of tragedy and treachery. She says:

> *By faith I hid thee, . . .*
> *by faith I wove*
> *The rushes of thine ark, and laid thee 'mid*
> *The answer to that faith when Pharaoh's daughter*
> *Placed thee in my arms, and bade me nurse the child*
> *For her: and by that faith sustained, I heard*
> *As idle words the cruel news that stabbed*
> *Thy father like a sword.*

Moses reverses the rumor by describing the festivities of an Egyptian holiday, when the idols of Isis and Osiris were unveiled and Pharaoh and Charmean were seated on their thrones. The priests of Or requested his pledge to Egypt and Isis so he could become

> *enrafted*
> *Into Pharaoh's royal love, and be called*
> *The son of Pharaoh's daughter.*

Moses explains that his mother's teachings resounded in his memory when he was faced with the appeal of Egyptian power that would have caused him to disown his Hebrew heritage:

Again I heard
Thee tell the grand traditions of our race,
The blessed hopes and glorious promises
That weave their golden threads among the
    sombre
Tissues of our lives, and shimmer still amid
The gloom and shadows of our lot.

Moses' narrative details the legacy of faith and the dilemmas that have beset his people, from Abraham to Isaac to Jacob. When a vision of angels descends and delivers Moses, it parallels Joseph's resistance to temptation, *the soft white hand that beckoned him to sin.* This predates and transcends twentieth-century Afroamerican literary inversions of racist symbolism, whereby white replaces black as the color of evil. Instead, in Harper's poem, white is the color of death, the loss of spirit paled by cruelty and selfishness, or in this case through sexual seduction. Joseph who, like Moses, was tested by Egypt's material benefits, remained steadfast in his dedication to faith and the promise of Canaan. Moses compares the humble grave of Joseph in Machpelah's cave to

the proudest tomb amid
The princely dead of Egypt

Moses' mother sustains his cultural identity while he resides under the influence of Pharaoh's earthly power. Moses claims her words

as messengers of light to guide
My steps.

He refuses the princely crown and

the priests of Or
Grow pale with fear, an ashen terror creeping
O'er the princess' face

while the pharaoh becomes as angry as a thunderstorm. The political ramifications of this chapter of the poem are endemic to Egyptian and American slavery and emblematic of Harper's appeal for a Mosaic consciousness.

The role of Moses' mother as a subversive force, generating a cultural offensive inside the home, is a reasonable explanation for Moses' resistance to Egypt's appeal. Such a resolution also suggests a strategy for the development of a Moses character in Afroamerican communities. Certainly, reference to the essay, "Our Greatest Want," explains Harper's belief in the need to develop a community based on Moses' character. Likewise, Harper's expansion of Exodus endows Moses' mother as a political example servicing the subversive decrees of a spiritual legacy.

This correlation between poetic text and contemporary history was undoubtedly made more directly when Harper recited the poem within the context of lectures given before black audiences during the Reconstruction era. Similarly, Harriet Tubman's steadfast faith in God protected her by way of visions that warned and guided her past certain dangers and blind junctions along the Underground Railroad. At these moments, Tubman would drop into sleep, whereby vision-dreams would intervene and prophesy. The value of the vision dreams depended upon faith.

Chapter 3, "Flight to Midian," is a point of convergence with biblical text. Whereas chapter 2 explains the revolutionary consciousness of Moses, chapter 3 delineates the more abrupt depiction of Moses' assassination of an Egyptian officer in the biblical passage. The scene opens with Pharaoh's preconceived fear of Israel, and his oppressive obsession to build a pyramid in an attempt to acquire immortality. The Israelites must build this monument *as cold / And hard, and heartless as* the pharaoh. Moses hears about the horrors perpetrated on the slaves—the excessive toil and brutal whippings.

The contemplative expressions crouched in the downcast eyes of the slaves

> *seemed to say, today we bide our time*
> *And hide our wrath in every nerve, and only*
> *Wait a fitting hour to strike the hands that press*
> *us down.*

As Moses leaves the oppressive scene, he encounters an Egyptian officer beating an old man. Moses cries out:

> *Stay thy hand; seest thou*
> *That aged man? His head is whiter than our*
> *Desert sands; his limbs refuse to do thy*
> *Bidding because thy cruel tasks have drained*
> *Away their strength.*

98

The slave driver's reply

> *back*
> *To thy task base slave, nor dare resist the will*
> *Of Pharaoh,*

infuriates Moses, who kills the overseer with one blow.

This rebellious action endangers Moses, and when he interrupts an argument between two Hebrews and appeals for brotherhood and peace, they challenge his interference by asking if he would *Mete to them the fate of the Egyptian?* Realizing his secret is not safe, not even under the tongues of his brethren, Moses flees Goshen into the Arabian desert where he becomes a shepherd, *For the priest of Midian.*

One contradictory response to repression is self-denial. Oftentimes misguided, internalized strife ferments until it explodes. Moses, unlike the two self-destructive Hebrews attacking each other, has been politicized to defend his people and to despise injustice. But his defense of the old man is not respected by all slaves who hear of it; instead, many feel threatened by his radical action. The spread of spiritual degeneration undermines the oppressed, within and without. Tubman was sensitive to the treachery of the frightened slave, and therefore she never disclosed the routes of the Underground Railroad.

> *Men grow strong in action, but in solitude*
> *Their thoughts are ripened.*

In Midian, Moses grows grey with the years, but stronger in faith. The gleam in his dark eyes *had deepened / To a calm and steady light,* simmering with patience and insight. During this passage of the poem, Moses encounters *the burning bush: and Jehovah's command to lead the Hebrews out of bondage.* Harper's description of the burning bush offers more detail than the biblical version of the vision. And in contrast to the inclusion of character dialogue, God's decree does not appear in quotations, indicating a difference in the nature of voice. Harper has condensed chapters three and four of Exodus into one. The interaction between Moses and the God of Abraham and his reunion with Aaron, are integrated into the flow of the story's narrative:

> *And as he paused and turned, he saw a bush with fire*
> *Aglow; from root to stem a latent flame*
> *Sent up its jets and sprays of purest light,*

And yet the bush, with leaves uncrisped, uncurled.
Was just as green and fresh as if the breath
Of early spring were kissing every leaf.
Then Moses said I'll turn aside to see
This sight, and as he turned he heard a voice
Bidding him lay his sandals by, for Lo! he
Stood on holy ground. Then Moses bowed his head
Upon his staff and spread his mantle o'er
His face, lest he should see the dreadful majesty
Of God' and there, upon that lonely spot,
By Horeb's mount, his shrinking hands received
The burden of his God, which bade him go
To Egypt's guilty king, and bid him let
The oppressed go free.

The American Moses had vision-dreams of her family being sold away. Unable to live as a free person while her family remained enslaved, Tubman returned again and again to deliver them and others. Likewise, Moses leaves his Midian refuge with Jethro, his father-in-law, his wife, Zipporah, and his sons. Again, the story deviates from the patriarchal perspective of the Old Testament as Zipporah reflects on *precious memories* about her earlier life. Her regret contrasts against Moses' anticipation *to see the long-lost faces of his distant home.* Enroute they encounter Aaron, who has been sent by God to meet Moses in the wilderness. As it was for Tubman, such a reunion is a rejoice of family and the resolution of destiny.

And then they talked of Israel's bondage,
And the great deliverance about to dawn.

Moses approaches the throne of Pharaoh and delivers God's message. The pharaoh retorts *in cold and scornful tones,* about the absence of Israel's God, claiming the power of Isis, the goddess of Egypt, *who has endowed the fertile flourishes of Egypt.* The pharaoh dismisses Moses' appeal and,

yet he felt
Strangely awed before their presence.

Chapter 5 of this story of the Nile progresses with heightened dramatic tension as Egypt is cursed by plagues and death. Pharaoh's dismissal of Moses' appeal is reiterated through an intensification of labor

100

subjugation of the Hebrew slaves. Like the Nat Turner rebellion, the slaveholder meets the threat of slave insurrection with intensified repression in an attempt to quell dissent. His consort, Amorphil, advises Pharoah to increase the Hebrew burden so

> *they will have less time to plot sedition*
> *And revolt.*

Rhadma, another lord of the court, identifies Moses as Charmean's adopted prince and the *base slave* who *slew an Egyptian* and escaped to Arabia.

Pharaoh pressures the Hebrews who

> *fainted 'neath*
> *Their added tasks, then cried unto the king,*
> *That he would ease their burdens; but he hissed,*
> *   like an evil serpent in the garden, "ye are*
> *Idle, and your minds are filled with vain*
> *And foolish thoughts; get you unto your tasks,*
> *And ye shall not 'minish of your tale of bricks."*

The trauma of persecution rarely encourages clarity, and the slaves blame Moses and Aaron for Pharaoh's anger and the severity of his retribution.

This misplaced projection crucifies Moses and Aaron. Conversely, the Christlike imagery in the following lines characterize Moses and Aaron as saviors. The predominance of the long *e* sound extends the imagery of *bleeding feet, pierced with cruel nail, beneath* God and *the thorny crowns of earth.* Their crucifixion is the consequence of the fear and confusion of the oppressed, which coincides with faithless human frailty.

> *how God's anointed ones*
> *Must walk with bleeding feet the paths that turn*
> *To lines of living light; how hands that buy*
> *Salvation in their palms are pierced with cruel*
> *Nails, and lips that quiver first with some great truth*
> *Are steeped in bitterness and tears, and brows*
> *Now bright beneath the aureole of God,*
> *Have bent beneath the thorny crowns of earth.*

The intersection of this New Testament symbolism with the Old Testament figure is consistent with Walker's and Harper's perception and projection of biblical scripture. At the same time, Harper's Unitarianism encourages the humanization of Jesus. Moses, the deliverer, is elevated to the spirit of Jesus, the savior; that is, Jesus Christ symbolizes freedom on earth and in heaven. Jesus died because of our sins, not for them.

Moses moves from the grey gloom of Hebrew despair to confront the dark anger of Pharaoh's court. There, Moses demonstrates the power of Jehovah by turning his staff into a serpent. Pharaoh's magicians enlist the *powers of night*, and likewise, turn their rods into serpents. But Moses' serpent swallows these in one *angry gulp*. God turns the waters of Egypt's silver fountains into blood, symbolic of the source of life by which the empire prospered. The bloody fountains spout forth a drought. A million frogs emerge from the Nile and menace the kitchens and bedrooms of the court, an amphibian warning for the Egyptian soldiers, soon to be consumed by the sea. The abhorrent appearance of a dark cloud of vermin, grey and infectious, transfers diseased flies that kill Egypt's cattle. Hail hatchets the fruit from the harvests and swarms of locusts devour ensuing crops. Egypt becomes *brown and bare* and its citizens are covered with boils, as God *lengthened night lay like a / burden.*

Then, the angels of death descend, kissing the first-born dead; the ironic tragedy that once jeopardized Moses, when the pharaoh executed the Hebrew male children. Broken by the wrath of God as manifested by the horror of plagues, the physical devastation of his nation, and the slaying of his children, Pharaoh relents and releases the Hebrew slaves. The portrayal of Egypt's demise is contained in one long stanza. The short lines and semicolons contract the rhythm which intensifies it and produces an accolade of nightmarish images more terrible than slavery. The depletion of Egyptian wealth and power is shrouded with grey tones and lifeless abstractions. The contraction of sound and the compilation of tragic images accelerates and accentuates the dramatic fall of the empire.

> *Then came another plague, of loathsome vermin;*
> *They were gray and creeping things, that made*
> *Their very clothes alive with dark and sombre*
> *Spots—things so loathsome in the land they did*
> *Suspend the service of the temple; for no priest*
> *Dared to lift his hand to any god with one*
> *Of these upon him. And then the sky grew*
> *Dark, as if a cloud were passing o'er its*
> *Changeless blue; a buzzing sound broke o'er*
> *The city, and the land was swarmed with flies.*
> *The murrain laid their cattle low; the hail*
> *Cut off the first fruits of the Nile; the locusts,*

With their hungry jaws, destroyed the later crops,
And left the ground as brown and bare as if a fire
Had scorched it through,
                    Then angry blains

And fiery boils did blur the flesh of man
And beast; and then for three long days, nor saffron
Tint, nor crimson flush, nor soft and silvery light
Divided day from morn, nor told the passage
Of the hours; men rose not from their seats, but sat
In silent awe.
. . . . . .

But Pharaoh was strangely blind, and turning
From his first born and his dead, with Egypt's wail
Scarce still upon his ear, he asked which way had
Israel gone? They told him that they journeyed
Towards the mighty sea, and were encamped
Near Baalzephn.
Then Pharaoh said, "the wilderness will hem them in,
The mighty sea will roll its barriers in front,
And with my chariots and my warlike men
I'll bring them back, or mete them out their graves."

With his *proud escutcheons blazoned to the sun,* the king of Egypt gathers his troops and pursues the Hebrews. Again, confronted with Pharaoh's tyranny, the weak and the faithless question Moses. The climactic parting of the Red Sea and the drowning of Pharaoh's army parallel the parting of the nation into the Union and the Confederacy, and the bloody red battles of the Civil War. Tubman, a spy for the Union, led one of Montgomery's most successful expeditions against the Confederacy.

                    And Moses smote
The restless sea; the waves stood up in heaps,
Then lay as calm and still as lips that just
had tasted death. The secret-loving sea
Laid bare her coral caves and iris tinted
Floor; that wall of flood which lined the people's
Way was God's own wondrous masonry.

The Israelites escape across the sea floor as God's masonry is contrasted against the bricked pyramids they, as slaves, were forced to build. The Confederate army was likewise destroyed in the civil conflict. But unlike the slow grind of centuries of servitude, Pharaoh's army is crushed by the powerful sea. The Red Sea spews *their corpses cold and stark / Upon the shore,* while Israel celebrates triumphantly.

Miriam reminisces about the life and fate of her brother, Moses, recollecting the planted basket among the lotus leaves in the Nile, the favored adoption by the princess, and the subversive return of the child to their mother. Embracing his fate and his people's pain, Moses had delivered them from bondage. Inspired by this miracle of faith and magnificence, she rejoices in a spiritual of jubilee.

"Miriam's Song" reclaims the regularity, rhythm, and rhyme found in Harper's ballad style. The easy iambic meter and *a b c b* rhyme scheme celebrate the destruction of Egypt's evil and the power of God's wrath as well as the form of the slave spirituals. It ends the heightened excitement of this chapter with a finality about Egyptian history repudiated by the intervention of divine justice:

> *As a monument blasted and blighted by God*
> *Through the ages proud Pharaoh shall stand,*
> *All seamed with the vengeance and scarred with the wrath*
> *That leaped from God's terrible hand.*

The Israelites journey to Mount Sinai, where

> *The central and the primal truth of all*
> *The Universe—the unity of God*

is received *as a living, vitalizing thought.* This section ascends the momentum of the Red Sea miracle and connects the vision to the messiah, with Christ, *the elder brother of our race.* This explicit inclusion of New Testament doctrine intersects with the earlier reference in chapter 5, and provides an extension for a peaceful vision contrasted against the tragedy of war and bondage.

> *Before this truth let every blade of war*
> *Grow dull, and slavery, cowering at the light,*
> *Skulk from the homes of men; instead*
> *Of war bring peace and freedom, love and joy,*
> *And light for man, instead of bondage, whips*
> *And chains.*

This chapter reproaches the arrogance of the aristocracy and validates the sanctity of birth and the legitimacy of earthly citizenry as God's law. The four natural elements, *land and water,* and *air and light* are cited as God's gifts and human inheritance, forbidding the only infringement of this order as a defiance of the natural law that binds man to God, and earth to heaven. This sequence ends with the fury of thunder and lightning succumbing to the gentleness of the setting sun,

> *and Sinai stood a bare*
> *And rugged thing among the sacred scenes*
> *of Earth.*

Chapter 8 ends the journey of the failed Hebrews, who could not bear the hardships of freedom and confused faith, replacing it with a golden idol and embracing the decadence of materialistic seduction.

> *Born slaves, they did not love*
> *The freedom of the wild more than their pots of flesh.*

The impact of enslavement meted out consequences unforeseen by Moses.

> *For when the chains were shaken from their limits*
> *They failed to strike the impress from their souls.*

Moses sadly realizes the failure of the nonbelievers to accept their spirituality and the challenges of freedom. The idolators and the dispirited join forces, resigning their spiritual legacy. They attempt a return to Egypt prepared to resubmit to servitude. But their retreat leaves their bones *to bleach beneath Arabia's desert sands.* Similarly, for the survival of the group and the Underground Railroad, the black woman Moses threatened death for those slaves who wanted to desert and return to the plantation.

This chapter of the poem sadly explains the long-term ramifications of severe oppression on the human spirit. The difficulties that beset the Reconstruction, including political and moral corruption, adversely affected the developing freed community. Harper's campaign against intemperance, domestic violence, and illiteracy was critical to survival and transcendence. Deliverance does not promise material wealth, nor does it accommodate the debased expectations of the newly liberated. Any people who aspire to embrace the destructive facets of civilization are doomed to dissipate in the blanched deserts of history. The poem corresponds with the American historical experience, whereby a democracy contradicts its theoretical principles and thereby undermines the nation's spirit. At the same time, the American freedmen and women are encouraged to build a promised land on the character of Moses and in the spirit of Jesus, or they too, will vanish into the blanched memory of dust and stone.

The correlation between Egypt and the United States and between the pharaohs and the slavemasters allegorically identifies parallel historical cycles of a cosmic order. Harper's devout belief in reciprocity, a spiritual foundation for the building of a sharing character, and an egalitarian society offers an alternative to a pyramidal, patriarchal civilization. *Moses: A Story of the Nile* is a parable for an American culture and a statement about Afroamerican destiny. The poem conveys that the responsibility of the delivered is to construct an alternative vision, which will form the foundation of a true promised land for all people.

The challenge of the Reconstruction era was met with the resistance and terror of dethroned pharaohs, trying to divert the liberated to sharecropping and a Jim Crow order. Though many of the liberated fought with guns and persevered through faith, too many others were corrupted by power, or faltered under alcohol, or submitted to Klan tyranny, or succumbed to the economic oppression of sharecropping. Unfortunately, the struggle to reach the River Jordan is ongoing.

"The Death of Moses" is the ninth and final chapter in *Moses: A Story of the Nile*. It marks the end of Moses' mission and the beginning of Joshua's mission to lead the people across the River Jordan. Moses' vision of Canaan retrieves Harper's earlier imagery in "Ethiopia":

> *The sheltering vines and stately palms of that*
> *Fair land.*

The deliverer does not enter the promised land. His family has since perished: his brother Aaron, his sister Miriam, Moses' first and second wives, and children.

> *And yet he was not all alone,*
> *For God's great presence flowed around his path*
> *And stayed him in that solemn hour.*

106

From atop Mount Moab, Moses views the banks of the Jordan

bright by scarlet blooms
  . . . and purple blossoms.

The compelling landscape of milk and honey is richly laced with nature's beauty, emanating an ethereal calm.

The placid lakes
And emerald meadows, the snowy crest
Of distant mountains, the ancient rocks
That dripped with honey, the hills all bathed
In light and beauty; the shady graves
And peaceful vistas, the vines opprest
With purple arches, the fig trees fruit crowned
Green and golden, the pomegranates with crimson
Blushes, the olives with their darker clusters,
Rose before him like a vision, full of beauty
And delight.

This scene is shadowed by

. . . the wing
Of death's sweet anger hovered o'er the mountain's crest.

The winds shift the vision of Canaan and replace it with uplifting imagery:

Then another vision
Broke upon his longing gaze; 'twas the land
Of crystal fountains, love and beauty, joy
And light, for the pearly gates flew open,
And his ransomed soul went in.

Moses' cold body is buried by angels. His burial crypt forms the ending of the long poem. These lines are shorter and so are the words. The type size of the ending text is significantly reduced, evoking a sense of distance and forming a visual coffin. End rhyme encloses the more open style of blank verse that typifies the poem's overall narrative flow. The original text possibly had these last lines on the same page to visually simulate the crypt. The poem rounds into rhyming couplets and then ends. These structural considerations also support the idea that "The Burial of

Moses" was the conceptual beginning for this longer work. It certainly co-incides with the evolutionary process of long poems.

In historical terms, the martyrdom of John Brown and Abraham Lincoln both converge as the crucifixion and the resurrection—the ending is the beginning, the beginning is the ending.

> *Oh never on that mountain*
> *Was seen a lovelier sight*
> *Than the troupe of fair young angels*
> *That gathered 'round the dead,*
> *With gentle hands they bore him,*
> *That bright and shining train,*
> *From Nebo's lonely mountain*
> *To sleep in Moab's vale.*
> *But they sung no mournful dirges,*
> *No solemn requiems said,*
> *And the soft wave of their pinions*
> *Made music as they trod.*
> *But no one heard them passing,*
> *None saw their chosen grave;*
> *It was the angels secret*
> *Where Moses should be laid.*
> *And when the grave was finished,*
> *They trod with golden sandals*
> *Above the sacred spot,*
> *And the brightest, fairest flowers*
> *Sprang up beneath their tread.*
> *Nor broken turf, nor hillock*
> *Did e'er reveal that grave,*
> *And truthful lips have never said*
> *We know where he is laid.*

Conclusion

Within a biblical context, Harper's *Moses* embraces and articulates the Afroamerican cultural presence in human history. Harper's text is expanded by woman's presence. The poem is infused with woman's faith, and it presents woman's political consciousness and influence as axiomatic to a people's vision and future. Her inclusion of New Testament doctrine distinguishes the Afroamerican spiritual difference as well as Harper's religious, radical vision.

Ironically, or appropriately, Moses' second wife was black, "for he had married an Ethiopian woman."[19] This historical marriage is resurrected when the American Ethiopians enlisted Moses' spiritual legacy in their quest for freedom. The rise of a new people searching for the unmarked grave of Moses, calls upon the God of slaves to send Moses, the deliverer. Moses arises in Harriet Tubman as well as in Stewart, Garrison, Still, Douglass, and in the voice of Harper calling for support for the Underground Railroad and in the building of the promised land.

For the ex-slaves, who called "Go Down Moses" and "Steal Away to Jesus" with a crescendo that inspired the poet's activism and words, *Moses: A Story of the Nile,* was the most appropriate response for a shared legacy of spirituality and struggle.

The Pursuit of the
Promised Land

CHAPTER 4

The Legacy of the Daughters of Ishmael: To Be Black and Female

Peace

Welcome Peace! thou blest evangel—
Welcome to this war-cursed land;
O'er the weary waiting millions
Let thy banner be unfurled.
On the burning brow of anger
Lay thy gentle, soothing hand;
Say to Carnage and Destruction,
Ye shall cease to blight the land.

Plead in tones of love and mercy,
'Mid the battle's crash and roar;
'Till the nations new created
Learn the art of war no more.
On the brow of martial Glory
Bid the people place their ban;
Nothing in the world is sacred
Like the sacredness of man.

Heroes grasping fame and laurels
On the bloody fields of crime;
'Tis a fearful path to glory,
Over human hearts to climb.
God for man did light each planet,
Warmed the sun, and bade it shine;
And upon each human spirit
Left his finger prints divine.

Bury deep your proud ambitions.
Cease your struggles, fierce and wild;
Oh,'tis higher bliss to rescue,

Than to trample down God's child.
Better far to aid the feeble,
Raise the groveler from the clod;
Lives are only great and noble
When they clasp both man and God.
                    Frances Harper, 1873
                    in *Christian Recorder*

I am feeling something of a novice upon this platform. Born of a race whose inheritance has been outrage and wrong, most of my life had been spent in battling against those wrongs. But I did not feel as keenly as others, that I had these rights, in common with other women, which are now demanded. About two years ago, I stood within the shadows of my home. A great sorrow had fallen upon my life. My husband had died suddenly, leaving me a widow, with four children, one my own, and the others stepchildren. I tried to keep my children together. But my husband died in debt; and before he had been in his grave three months, the administrator had swept the very milk-crocks and wash tubs from my hands. I was a farmer's wife and had made butter for the Columbus market; but what could I do, when they had swept all away? They left me one thing—and that was a looking-glass! Had I died instead of my husband, how different would have been the result! By this time he would have had another wife, it is likely; and no administrator would have gone into his house, broken up his home, and sold his bed, and taken away his means of support.

I took my children in my arms, and went out to seek my living. While I was gone; a neighbor to whom I had once lent five dollars, went before a magistrate and swore that he believed I was a non-resident, and laid an attachment on my very bed. And I went back to Ohio with my orphan children in my arms, without a single feather bed in this wide world, that was not in the custody of the law. I say, then, that justice is not fulfilled so long as woman is unequal before the law.

We are all bound up together in one great bundle of humanity, and society cannot trample on the weakest and feeblest of its members without receiving the curse in its own soul. You tried that in the case of the negro. You pressed him down for two centuries; and in so doing you crippled the moral strength and paralyzed the spiritual energies of the white men of the country. When the hands of the black were fettered, white men were deprived of the liberty of speech and the freedom of the press. Society cannot afford to neglect the enlightenment of any class of its members. At the South, the legislation of the country was in behalf of the rich slaveholders, while the poor white man was neglected. What is the consequence to-day? From that very class of neglected poor white men, comes the man who stands to-day with his hand across the helm of the nation. He fails to catch the watchword of the hour, and throws himself, the incarnation of meanness, across the pathway

114

of the nation. My objection to Andrew Johnson is not that he has been a poor white man; my objection is that he keeps "poor whits" all the way through. That is the trouble with him.

This grand and glorious revolution which has commenced, will fail to reach its climax of success, until throughout the length and breadth of the American Republic, the nation shall be so color-blind, as to know no man in the color of his skin or the curl of his hair. It will then have no privileged class, trampling upon and outraging the unprivileged classes, but will be then one great privileged nation, whose privilege will be to produce the loftiest manhood and womanhood that humanity can attain.

I do not believe that giving the woman the ballot is immediately going to cure all the ills of life. I do not believe that white women are dewdrops just exhaled from the skies. I think that like men they may be divided into three classes, the good, the bad, and the indifferent. The good would vote according to their convictions and principles; the bad, as dictated by prejudice or malice; and the indifferent will vote on the strongest side of the question, with the winning party.

You white women speak here of rights. I speak of wrongs. I, as a colored woman, have had in this country an education which has made me feel as if I were in the situation of Ishmael, my hand against every man, and every man's hand against me. Let me go to-morrow morning and take my seat in one of your street cars—I do not know that they will do it in New York, but they will in Philadelphia—and the conductor will put up his hand and stop the car rather than let me ride.

Going from Washington to Baltimore this Spring, they put me in the smoking car. Aye, in the capital of the nation, where the black man consecrated himself to the nation's defense, faithful when the white man was faithless, they put me in the smoking car! They did it once; but the next time they tried it, they failed; for I would not go in. I felt the fight in me; but I don't want to have to fight all the time. To-day I am puzzled where to make my home. I would like to make it in Philadelphia, near my own friends and relations. But if I want to ride in the streets of Philadelphia, they send me to ride on the platform with the driver. Have women nothing to do with this? Not long since, a colored woman took her seat in an Eleventh Street car in Philadelphia, and the conductor stopped the car, and told the rest of the passengers to get out, and left the car with her in it alone, then they took it back to the station. One day I took my seat in a car, and the conductor came to me and told me to take another seat. I just screamed "murder." The man said if I was black I ought to behave myself. I know that if he was white he was not behaving himself. Are there not wrongs to be righted?

In advocating the cause of the colored man, since the Dred Scott decision, I have sometimes said I thought the nation had touched bottom. But let me tell you there is a depth of infamy lower than that. It is when the nation, standing upon the threshold of a great peril, reached out its hands to a feebler race, and asked that race to help it, and when the peril was over, said, you are good enough for soldiers, but not good enough for citizens. When Judge Taney said that the men of my race had no rights which the white man was bound to respect, he had not seen the bones of the black man bleaching outside of Richmond. He had not seen the thinned ranks and the thickened graves of the Louisiana Second, a regiment which went into battle nine hundred strong, and came out with three hundred. He had not stood at Olustee and seen defeat and disaster crushing down the pride of our banner, until word was bright to Col. Hallowell, "The day is lost; go in and save it;" and black men stood in the gap, beat back the enemy, and saved your army.

We have a woman in our country who has received the name of "Moses," not by lying about it, but by acting it out—a woman who has gone down into the Egypt of slavery and brought out hundreds of our people into liberty. The last time I saw that woman, her hands were swollen. That woman who had led one of Montgomery's most successful expeditions, who was brave enough and secretive enough to act as a scout for the American army, had her hands all swollen from a conflict with a brutal conductor, who undertook to eject her from her place. That woman, whose courage and bravery won a recognition from our army and from every black man in the land, is excluded from every thoroughfare of travel. Talk of giving women the ballot-box? Go on. It is a normal school, and the white woman of this country need it. While there exists this brutal element in society which tramples upon the feeble and treads down the weak, I tell you that if there is any class of people who need to be lifted out of their airy nothings and selfishness, it is the white women of America.[1]

Frances Harper delivered this speech before the 1866 National Woman's Rights Convention in New York, one year after the blood of the Civil War had extinguished slavery from the formal structure of American society. But as her personal reality reflects, deliverance had been circumvented by Jim Crow laws that reassured the advantages for the privileged classes and demeaned the possibilities for the newly liberated. The necessity for suffrage and representation was impressed intently upon Harper through her widowed circumstances and through her interactions with racist and sexist public policies—the compounded reality of black women's second-class citizenship.

The present challenge was to acquire equal rights and to seek a substantial shift in quality of life. The attitude and spirit of the Equal Rights Association attempted to channel this political vision by advocating a solidified effort for suffrage for women and blacks, which included the particular class of black women. In her opening address at this, the Eleventh

National Woman's Rights Convention held at the Church of the Puritans in New York City, Elizabeth Cady Stanton said: "The question now is, have we the wisdom and consequence, from the present upheavings of our political system, to reconstruct a government on the one and enduring basis that has never yet been tried—'Equal Rights to All.' "[2]

Frances Harper's presence and speech contributed significantly to the ideological position established at this convention. Following Harper's speech, Susan B. Anthony, the secretary of the organization, proposed this resolution:

> Whereas, By the act of Emancipation and the Civil Rights bill, the negro and woman now hold the same civil and political status alike, needing only the ballot; and whereas the same arguments apply equally to both classes, proving all partial legislation fatal to republican institutions, therefore
> Resolved, that the time has come for an organization that shall demand Universal Suffrage, and that hereafter we shall be known as the "American Equal Rights Association.[3]

Anthony explained that the theoretical basis for this ideological expansion of the organization belonged to Lucretia Mott, the first president of the National Woman's Rights Convention and the beacon for women's enlightenment since its inception in 1850. Mott had pursued "the claims of woman to the right of representation in this government." Identifying the spirit of their movement "—a Human Rights Platform," Anthony stated, "As women we can no longer *seem* to claim for ourselves what we do not for others—nor can we work in separate movements to get the ballot for the two disfranchised classes—the negro and woman— since to do so must be at double cost of time, energy and money."[4]

Mott, suffering from a severe cold, hoarseness, and bruises resulting from a fall from a streetcar, represented a beleaguered veteran foreshadowing an impending breakdown in the human rights movement. The abolitionist-feminist delivered her departing speech, wherein she identified Harper, thereby incorporating race as an integral aspect of feminist ideology and endorsing Harper as a leader in the organization: "I am sorry to come before you with so impaired a voice, and with a face so scarred; but I rejoice that as we who have labored in the cause become less able to work the younger ones, the Tiltons and the Harpers, come forward to fill our places. It is no loss, but the proper order of things, that the mothers should depart and give place to the children."[5]

Feminist Prose

Harper's early prose reflects this feminist solidarity. "Two Offers" appeared in 1859 and is still considered the first published short story by an Afroamerican woman. She gives no racial dimension to the characters which provides a cross-cultural thematic latitude for the story despite its appearance in the *Anglo-African Magazine*. The story concerns two cousins, Laura and Jane, who contemplate two offers of marriage extended to Laura. The two women represent different class experiences, one of privilege and the other of poverty. Such class juxtaposition is very Dickensian, and Harper's story contrasts these economic differences and influences on women's lives and consciousness.

Laura feels she must marry or face the fate of becoming an old maid. Conversely, Jane is unmarried and has gained economic independence through her career as a writer, paralleling Harper's life. In 1859, Harper was still unmarried and pursuing her writing and lecturing career. But a year later she married Fenton Harper and gave birth to her daughter. During the marriage, however, Harper continued to write and lecture, demonstrating an alternative marriage. Jane, on the other hand, has completely rejected the conventional role of the woman as wife and mother, and her name, Jane Alston, alludes to Jane Austen. Jane advises Laura to refuse both proposals because indecision on Laura's part indicates a deficiency in love and dedication to either of the men. Jane also says that for Laura to marry for economic reasons relegates the bond to a business arrangement, which defiles the sanctity of the union.

But Laura decides to marry and ten years later when the cousins reunite, Laura is gazing into death's gaping mouth, having suffered a possessive, repressive husband, who has violated their vows and acted as if the marriage contract were a bill of sale. The omniscient narrative voice reflects the feminist politics of Harper and the movement. It criticizes society's denial of *the true woman.*

> *Her conscience should be enlightened, her faith in the true and right established, and scope given to her Heaven-endowed and God-given faculties.*[6]

Harper's rejection of romantic illusions and her advocacy of women's independent spirit is not a wholesale rejection of marriage. Her intent is to dispel romantic attraction and emotional manipulation as determinants for marriage. Inequitable unions lead to spiritual demise, and in some cases a heartbreak that leads to physical death. Harper's early literature often ends with death as typified by Victorian literature. But the contrast between the two women offers autonomy and economic independence as the alternative to social repression and despair.

Harper and the Radical Reconstruction

Realization of the especial plight of "colored" women necessitated enlightenment inside and outside the black community. Harper maintained her established leadership role within the feminist framework of the radical movement, while she worked diligently with domestic issues concerning sexism in the black community. In both contexts Harper's political perspective argued against the causes of repression, while highlighting the Mosaic ideal as a model for transcendent human values. She promoted literacy, self-determination, women's rights, and human dignity for all Americans, while she lambasted Klan terrorism, chastised domestic violence, condemned intemperance, and reprimanded the federal government for its indifference to the black citizenry.

Harper's activism encompassed the immediate and pragmatic needs of the free men and women in the South and in the North. William Still advertised her Philadelphia appearance for the Social, Civil and Statistical Association of the Colored People of Pennsylvania on February 27, 1866 and on March 1, 1867. Frederick Douglass and William Lloyd Garrison also spoke for the organization's lecture series to raise funds for the "freedmen" and the "colored" soldiers. Despite Harper's stature, Still, chairman of the organization, anticipated gender prejudice. A broadside circulated prior to the event qualified Harper's exceptional credentials as a "colored lady" in the company of eminent, "gentlemen speakers": "A few extracts from newspaper notices of Mrs. Harper's lectures in different parts of the country; to apprize those who may have no knowledge of her extraordinary abilities we hope will help to enlighten such as may be curious to know how a colored lady is to sustain herself in connection with such eminent talent on the part of the gentlemen speakers in this course."[7]

Harper's lectures were sometimes sponsored by the Quakers, who had also supported the religious and political work of her uncle, William Watkins.[8] During the Reconstruction, Harper was a lecturer for the African Methodist Episcopal church. Harper travelled throughout the South, lived in struggling black communities, and lectured to freedmen's schools and in Sunday schools. Whereas her abolitionist work contributed to the deliverance from the American Egypt, her embarkment on a Reconstruction lecturing tour was symbolic of a desert trek throughout the South in pursuit of the promised land. From 1867 to 1869 she travelled and lectured in South Carolina, Georgia, Alabama, and Tennessee. This experience expanded and reinforced her appeal for moral courage and political integrity.

"Literacy, Land and Liberation" was Harper's theme for her lectures, and her writings often preceded her appearances. Harper's "Ethiopia," "Bury Me in a Free Land," "The Dying Christian," "Thank God for Little Children," "President Lincoln's Proclamation of Emancipation," and the essay, "The Air of Freedom," were collected in *The Freedman's Book* (1865), which was widely distributed throughout the North and South. Lydia Maria Child, a noted abolitionist, feminist, writer, and editor of Linda Brent's slave narrative, *Incidents in the Life of a Slave Girl* (1846), conceptualized *The Freedman's Book* as a reading text for freedmen's schools and Sunday schools. Some of the other writers included in the book are Phillis Wheatley, George Moses Horton, John Greenleaf Whittier, Harriet Beecher Stowe, William Lloyd Garrison, and Charlotte L. Forten. Slave narratives and creative works by other noted abolitionist writers complete this text. This book, as well as other works by Harper and these authors reflected radical Republicans' insistence on literacy for freedmen and women during the Reconstruction era.

Harper's Reconstruction lectures promote a historical understanding of the social and economic ramifications of slavery, still impacting and infecting race progress. Her analysis and advice do not adhere to the opinion or the actions of the conservative white political position. In letters to William Still, her observations about the conditions of the South and the dynamics of Reconstruction reveal both enthusiasm and resentment, reflecting the antagonistic resistance of the defeated defying the hopeful aspirations of the liberated. At the same time, the personal dimension of these letters reveals Harper's inner strength and selfless humility. Like her pre-war tour in the North, newspaper accounts of her lectures reveal impressive, pensive responses to her presentations. The following article from a South Carolina newspaper provides a journalistic appraisal of Harper's presence and an introduction for her reflections:

> We received a polite invitation from the trustees of the State-Street African Methodist Episcopal Zion Church to attend a lecture in that edifice on Thursday evening. Being told that the discourse would be delivered by a female colored lecturer from Maryland, curiosity, as well as an interest to see how the colored citizens were managing their own institutions, led us at once to accept the in-vitations. We found a very spacious church, gas-light, and the balustrades of the galleries copiously hung with wreaths

and festoons of flowers, and a large audience of both sexes, which, both in appearance and behavior, were respectable and decorously observant of the proprieties of the place. The services were opened, as usual, with prayer and a hymn, the latter inspired by powerful lungs and in which the musical ear at once caught the negro talent for melody. The lecturer was then introduced as Mrs. F. E. W. Harper, from Maryland. Without a moment's hesitation she started off in the flow of her discourse, which rolled smoothly and uninterruptedly on for nearly two hours. It was very apparent that it was not a cut and dried speech, for she was as fluent and as felicitous in her allusions to circumstances immediately around her as she was when she rose to a more exalted pitch of laudation of the "Union," or of execration of the old slavery system. Her voice was remarkable—as sweet as any woman's voice we ever heard, and so clear and distinct as to pass every syllable to the most distant ear in the house.

Without any effort at attentive listening we followed the speaker to the end, not discerning a single grammatical inaccuracy of speech, or the slightest violation of good taste in manner or matter. At times the current of thoughts flowed in eloquent and poetic expression, and often her quaint humor would expose the ivory in half a thousand mouths. We confess that we began to wonder, and we asked a fine-looking man before us, "What is her color? Is she dark or light?" He answered, "She is mulatto; what they call a red mulatto." The "red" was new to us. Our neighbor asked, "How do you like her?" We replied, "She is giving your people the best kind and the very wisest of advice." He rejoined, "I wish I had her education." To which we added, "That's just what she tells you is your great duty and your need, and if you are too old to get it yourselves, you must give it to your children."

The speaker left the impression on our mind that she was not only intelligent and educated, but—the great end of education—she was enlightened. She comprehends perfectly the situations of her people, to whose interests she seems ardently devoted. The main theme of her discourse, the one strung to the harmony of which all the others were attuned, was the grand opportunity that emancipation had afforded to the black race to lift itself to the level of the duties and responsibilities enjoined by it. *"You have muscle power and brain power,"* she said; *"you must utilize them, or be content to remain forever the inferior race. Get land, every one that can, and as fast as you can. A landless people must be dependent upon the landed people. A few acres to till for food and a roof, however humble, over your head, are the castle of your independence, and when you have it you are fortified to act and vote independently whenever your intrests are at stake,"* That part of her lecture (and there was much of it) that dwelt on the moral duties and domestic relations of the colored people was pitched on the highest key of sound morality. She urged the cultivation of the "home life," the sanctity of the marriage state (a happy contrast to her strong-minded, free-love, white sisters of the North), and the duties of mothers to their daughters. *"Why,"* said she in a voice of much surprise, *"I have actually heard since I have been South that sometimes colored husbands positively beat their wives! I do not mean to insinuate for a moment that such things can possibly happen in Mobile. The very appearance of this congregation forbids it; but I did hear of one terrible husband defending himself for the unmanly practice with 'Well, I have got to whip her or leave her.'"*

There were parts of the lecturer's discourse that grated a little on a white Southern ear, but it was lost and forgiven in the genuine earnestness and profound good sense with which the woman spoke to her kind in words of sound advice.

On the whole, we are very glad we accepted the [A.M.E.] Zion's invitation. It gave us much food for new thought. It reminded us, perhaps, of neglected duties to these people, and it impressed strongly on our minds that these people are getting along, getting onward, and progress was a star becoming familiar to their gaze and their desires. Whatever the negroes have done in the path of advancement, they have done largely without white aid. But politics and white pride have kept the white people aloof from offering that earnest and moral assistance which would be so useful to a people just starting from infancy into a life of self-dependence.[9]

You will see by this that I am in the sunny South. I here read and see human nature under new lights and phases. I meet with a people eager to hear, ready to listen, as if they felt that the slumber of the ages had been broken, and that they were to sleep no more. I am glad that the colored man gets his freedom and suffrage together; that he is not forced to go through the same condition of things here, that has inclined him so much to apathy, isolation, and indifference, in the North. You, perhaps, wonder why I have been so slow in writing to you, but if you knew how busy I am, just working up to or past the limit of my strength. Traveling, conversing, addressing day and Sunday-schools (picking up scraps of information, takes up a large portion of my time), besides what I give to reading. For my audiences I have both white and colored. On the cars, some find out that I am a lecturer, and then, again, I am drawn into conversation. "What are you lecturing about?" the question comes up, and if I say, among other topics, politics, then I may look for an onset. There is a sensitiveness on this subject, a dread, it may be, that some one will "put the devil in the nigger's head," or exert some influence inimical to them; still, I get along somewhat pleasantly. Last week I had a small congregation of listeners in the cars, where I sat. I got in conversation with a former slave dealer, and we had rather an exciting time. I was traveling alone, but it is not worth while to show any signs of fear.

Last Saturday I spoke in Sumter; a number of white persons were present, and I had been invited to speak there by the Mayor and editor of the paper. There had been some violence in the district, and some of my friends did not wish me to go, but I had promised, and, of course, I went. I am in Darlington, and spoke yesterday, but my congregation was so large, that I stood near the door of the church, so that I might be heard both inside and out, for a large portion, perhaps nearly half my congregation were on the outside; and this, in Darlington, where, about two years ago, a girl was hung for making a childish and indiscreet speech. Victory was perched on our banners. Our army had been through, and this poor, ill-fated girl, almost a child in years, about seventeen years of age, rejoiced over the event, and said that she was going to marry a Yankee and set up housekeeping. She was reported as having made an incendiary speech and arrested, cruelly scourged, and then brutally hung. Poor child! she had been a faithful servant—her master tried to save her, but the tide of fury swept away his efforts.

Oh, friend, perhaps, sometimes your heart would ache, if you were only here and heard of the wrongs and abuses to which these people have been subjected. Things, I believe, are a little more hopeful; at least, I believe, some of the colored people are getting better contracts, and, I understand, that there's less murdering. While I am writing, a colored man stands here, with a tale of wrong—he has worked a whole year, year before last, and now he has been put off with fifteen bushels of corn and his food; yesterday he went to see about getting his money, and the person to whom he went, threatened to kick him off, and accused him of stealing. I don't know how the colored man will vote, but perhaps many of them will be intimidated at the polls.[10]

Well, Carolina is an interesting place. There is not a state in the Union I prefer to Carolina. Kinder, more hospitable, warmer-hearted people perhaps you will not find anywhere. I have been to Georgia; but Carolina is my preference. The South is to be a great theatre for the colored man's development and progress. There is brain-power here. If any doubt it, let him come into our schools, or even converse with some of our Freedmen either in their homes or by the way-side.[11]

Now, in reference to being bought by rebels and becoming a Johnsonite I hold that between the white people and the colored there is a community of interests, and the sooner they find it out, the better it will be for both parties; but the community of interests does not consist of increasing the privileges of one class and curtailing the rights of the other, but in getting every citizen interested in the welfare, progress and durability of the state. I do not in lecturing confine myself to the political side of the question. While I am in fa-

vor of Universal suffrage, yet I know that the colored man needs something more than a vote in his hand: he needs to know the value of a home life; to rightly appreciate the value of the marriage relation; to know how and to be incited to leave behind him the old shards and shells of slavery and to rise in the scale of character, wealth and influence. Like the Nautilus outgrowing his home to build for himself more "stately temples" of social condition. A man landless, ignorant and poor may use the vote against his interests; but with intelligence and land he holds in his hand the basis of power and elements of strength.[12]

Thank God for the wonderful change! I have lectured several nights this week, and the weather is quite warm; but I do like South Carolina. No state in the Union as far as colored people are concerned, do I like better— the land of warm welcomes and friendly hearts. God bless her and give her great peace![13]

A fearful catastrophe had just occurred [Kingstree, S.C., July 11th, 1867], the burning of the jail with a number of colored prisoners in it. It was a very sad affair. There was only one white prisoner and he got out. I believe there was some effort made to release some of the prisoners; but the smoke was such that the effort proved ineffectual. Well, for the credit of our common human nature we may hope that it was so. Last night I had some of the "rebs" to hear me (part of the time some of the white folks come out). Our meetings are just as quiet and as orderly on the whole in Carolina as one might desire. I like General Sickles as a Military Governor. "Massa Daniel, the King of the Carolinas." I like his Mastership. Under him we ride in the City Cars, and get first-class passage on the railroad. At this place a colored man was in prison under sentence of death for "participating in a riot;" and the next day was fixed for his execution.[14]

Still further explains, "with some others, Mrs. Harper called at General Sickles' Head Quarters, hoping to elicit his sympathies whereby the poor fellow's life might be saved; but he was not in. Hence they were not able to do anything."[15]

Next week, I am to speak in a place where one of our teachers was struck and a colored man shot, who, I believe, gave offense by some words spoke at a public meeting. I do not feel any particular fear.[16]

Subsequent to her lecture tour Harper wrote a letter of appeal to
Colonel Hinton on behalf of Jeff Ghee, a black man sentenced to death
for aiding the escape of two Yankee prisoners. Harper relates observations about the disparaged conditions of poor whites and the horrible
racial tyranny against blacks. She makes a poignant point about the danger that lurks inside impoverished ignorance. This letter reflects
Harper's class sensitivity as she identifies the racial interconnections of
America's destiny and the bases of her decision to support the black male
vote and the Fifteenth Amendment.

> *Col. Hinton: Dear Sir—I am about leaving the unreconstructed
> States. The South is a sad place, it is so rife with mournful memories and
> sad revelations of the past. Here you listen to heart-saddening stories of griev-
> ous old wrongs, for the shadows of the past have not been fully lifted from
> the minds of the former victims of slavery. We have had a mournful past in
> this country, enslaved in the South and proscribed in the North; still it is not
> the best to dwell too mournfully upon "by-gones." If we have had no past, it
> is well for us to look hopefully to the future—for the shadows bear the promise
> of a brighter coming day; and in fact, so far as the colored man is concerned,
> I do not feel particularly uneasy about his future. With his breadth of phys-
> ical organization, his fund of mental endurance, and his former discipline
> in the school of toil and privation, I think he will be able to force his way up-
> ward and win his recognition even in the South. To me one of the saddest
> features in the South is not even the old rebel class. It is said they are or have
> been dying "powerful fast." Perhaps the best thing for them and their coun-
> try will be "short lives and happy deaths;" but the most puzzling feature of
> Southern social life is, what shall become of the poorer white classes? Free-
> dom comes to the colored man with new hopes, advantages and opportuni-
> ties. He stands on the threshold of a new era, with the tides of a new
> dispensation coursing through his veins; but this poor "cracker class," what
> is there for them? They were the dregs of society before the war, and their sta-
> tus is unchanged. I have seen them in my travels, and I do not remember
> ever to have noticed a face among a certain class of them that seemed lighted
> up with any ambition, hope of lofty aspirations. The victims and partisans
> of slavery, they have stood by and seen their brother outraged and wronged;
> have consented to the crime and received the curse into their souls.
>
> *I don't know what you all think of Gen. Sickle's letter about a more
> general amnesty; but I think the former ruling class in the South have proved
> that they are not fit to be trusted with the welfare of the whites nor the liberty
> of the blacks. Mr. Whitemore, of Darlington, who is perhaps as heartily dis-
> liked by the rebels as any man in eastern South Carolina, has been holding,
> in company with myself, some interesting meetings in the State. Our last
> meeting was in Marion. I spoke there on Monday evening, and then for
> North Carolina. You may judge of my work when I tell you that in two weeks*

I have spoken twelve times. Thank God! the work goes bravely on. Freedom of speech, which has been an outlaw in the South, has found a welcome and home among those whose lips were once sealed by the iron gags of slavery. But to return to Marion. While there I visited Jeff Ghee. Do you know about Jeff Ghee? He is a young man, under sentence of death, as an accomplice in a murder committed by two Union soldiers, escaping from that charnel house of death, Florence stockade. I have seen that place, where our men burrowed in the earth, and I have been a little further, where I have seen the thickened graves of the men whose lives went out in that modern Golgotha. This colored man hid these men several weeks. Was not that a deed to endear him to every Northern heart? to every woman, whose son's, husband's or brother's life was drained away by hunger, cold, want and misery? He says that he is not guilty; that the man killed "would be living to-day, if he'd had his way." The soldiers escaped, and this man is under sentence of death, and was to have been executed the third Friday in July, and now the jailor tells me it is to be the second Friday in August. Shall this be? Shall Lee, with tens of thousands of murders clinging to his skirts, escape the full dessert of his crimes, and this man, who aided his victims, die a felon's death? Shall Jefferson Davis, with his hands dripping with the blood of Andersonville, and Libby, and Florence, breathe the air of freedom, and this man, who probably risked his life in defense of our soldiers, be choked to death? Oh! friend, you are acquainted in Washington. For God's and humanity's sake lay this case before the men who have the power to change this decree of death, and try for, the honor of our country, to have his life saved.[17]

The ERA and the Fifteenth Amendment

Frances Harper joined Susan B. Anthony, Frederick Douglass, and Elizabeth Cady Stanton at the 1869 American Equal Rights Association meeting in a debate over the proposed Fifteenth Amendment to the United States Constitution, which would grant suffrage to black men. This debate determined the issues of a divisive argument which severed the abolitionist-feminist alliance and split the human rights movement. In the absence of a more defined class analysis, the argument was reduced to a confrontation between "black" and "white." Unfortunately, the limitations of this two-dimensional argument did not render a resolution capable of salvaging the movement or the moment.[18]

Douglass confronted Stanton, an editor of the feminist publication, *The Revolution*, about an article that argued white racial supremacy to promote women's suffrage. He said:

With us, the matter is a question of life and death, at least, in fifteen States of the union. When women, because they are women, are hunted down through the cities of New York and New Orleans; when they are dragged from their houses and hung upon lamp-posts; when their children are torn from their arms, and their brains dashed upon the pavement; when they are objects of insult and outrage at every turn; when they are in danger of having their homes burnt down over their heads; when their children are not allowed to enter schools; then they will have an urgency to obtain the ballot equal to our own. . . . Yes, yes, yes; it is true of the black woman, but not because she is a woman, but because she is black.[19]

Douglass, sensitive to the dialectics of the dilemma and the ambiguity of human actions, took caution by acknowledging Stanton's demonstrated commitment and courage as an abolitionist: "Let me tell you that when there were few houses in which the black man could have put his head, this wooly head of mine found a refuge in the house of Mrs. Elizabeth Cady Stanton, and if I had been blacker than sixteen midnights, without a single star, it would have been the same."[20]

But Stanton was unimpressed by Douglass's courtesy. In rebuttal she charged, "if Black women weren't given the ballot, they would be fated to a triple bondage that man never knows." However, she took her analysis to the absurd when she concluded, "It would be better to be the slave of an educated white man than an ignorant black one."[21] But *educated wickedness,* as Harper later called it, had proven no solace for the slave woman.

Likewise, Susan B. Anthony, who has been much maligned by contemporary theorists for her racist revisionism during the debate, should also be considered relative to her holistic political history: "Escaping slaves were secreted in the Anthony home and, with the guidance of Frederick Douglass and others, led on to Canada. Susan B. Anthony participated in all these activities . . . [and] her brother Merritt fought with John Brown during the Kansas Civil War in 1856."[22]

According to *The Revolution,* Susan B. Anthony said:

The old anti-slavery school and others have said that the women must stand back and wait until the other class shall be recognized. But we say that if you will not give the whole loaf and justice and suffrage to an entire people, give it to the most intelligent first. If intelligence, justice and morality are to be placed in the Government, then let the question of woman be brought up first and that of the negro last. . . . When Mr. Douglass mentioned the black man first and the woman last, if he had noticed he would have seen that it was the men that clapped and not the women.[23]

In the position of Ishmael, Frances Harper responded:

> *When it was a question of race, I let the lesser question of sex go. But the white women all go for sex, letting race occupy a minor position.* [I'd like] *to know if it was broad enough to take colored women.* Miss Anthony and several others answered, "Yes, yes." [24]

Within the context of this argument, granting suffrage to white women instead of black men could not benefit black women, but it would cater to race privilege.

Therefore Harper rebutted with:

> *when I was at Boston there were sixty women who left work because one colored woman went to gain a livelihood in their midst. If the nation could handle one question, I would not have the black woman put a single straw in the way, if only the men of the race could obtain what they wanted.* [25]

Harper, who had most recently returned from the "unreconstructed South," offered the black female support for the black male vote—a survivalist position. As reported in her letters to Still, black women were as much victimized by racial terrorism as black men. Despite the domestic repression many black women encountered in the home and in the social practice of the culture, some component of the Afroamerican community had to procure a political defense against lynching and obtain the assurance of some legal rights. For the most part, the white women who comprised the radical leadership of the feminist movement at this time did not typify the racial consciousness of most white American women. White women at large were not dependable allies. And as the proceedings reflected, the political ambition of Anthony and Stanton—to secure electoral power—adversely affected their racial consciousness to the point at which they voiced the racism of the old slaveholding class they had most recently opposed.

Harper's assessment of white women's *airy nothingness* and white men's *educated wickedness* was too often confirmed through their complicity to maintain race privilege. Harper's poem, "To My Country-women," compares white women's dubious social status to white male society: *Sin is the consort of Woe.* Most white women were bound to the vortex of their own repression as the focus of white male supremacy. The peculiar dilemma of the black woman, from Harper's point of view, was that she would not acquire direct power from the Fifteenth Amendment, but the probable defeat of the amendment, with the inclusion for woman's suffrage, was a gamble too dangerous to risk.[26] The vote to support the Fifteenth Amendment carried the majority, and Stanton and Anthony resigned from the Equal Rights Association.

The Mission of the Flowers

"The Mission of the Flowers," a short story by Harper, was published in *Moses: A Story of the Nile* in 1869, and by virtue of the theme, seems to have been written with the critical debate of the Equal Rights Association in mind and as a literary nod in the direction of Anthony and Stanton. On the surface, there do not seem to be any racial references in the story, but the implicit meaning of this floral fable intersects with the issue of diversity and difference, which still colors American feminist politics.

Complexity, variety, and individuality are sacrificed to the vanity of the rose. The lesson imparted in this story applies both to white feminists who are ignorant of the especial problem of racism that women of color face, and to elite black women who are ignorant of the cultural difference and intelligence of freedwomen. And as the moral explains:

> But an important lesson had been taught; she had learned to respect the individuality of her sister flowers, and began to see that they, as well as herself, had their own missions . . . and of those whose mission she did not understand, she wisely concluded there must be some object in their creation, and resolved to be true to her own earth-mission, and lay their fairest buds and flowers upon the altars of love and truth.[27]

A most interesting feature of the story is Harper's symbolic manipulation of the rose's sexuality. The intoxicating allure of the rose—which throughout Western literature has been symbolic of woman's sexual power—entices, seduces, and even rapes some of the flowers until they all agree to become roses:

> A modest lily that grew near the rose tree shrank instinctively from her; but it was in vain, and with tearful eyes and trembling limbs she yielded, while a quiver of agony convulsed her frame.[28]

This should also be related to the objectification of sex. Consequently, the *men grew tired of roses, for they were everywhere.* When women are valued only as propagators or for sexual pleasure, they are at best, two-dimensional beings. Hence, on a metaphorical level, sexuality and individuality are also related to the essence of complexity and depth in person and in community.

Minnie's Sacrifice, Harper's serialized novel, also appeared in 1869. Written with a focus on the pressing political issues of the day, including suffrage, lynching, and acquisition of land and education for the ex-slaves, it was published bimonthly in the A.M.E. *Christian Recorder* (March 20, 1869 through September 25, 1869). Harper's Reconstruction work and organizational involvement provided the context for realistic settings and characters. As a lecturer in the South from 1866 to 1869 she derived literary material from material reality. The lynching of her feminist protagonist by the Ku Klux Klan was a literary strategy that radically challenged the pristine aesthetic of nineteenth-century literature and the political apathy of the black reading public.

This death is not glorified in the novel for dramatic entertainment. It is unglamorous and tragic, and the purpose of the ending is to confirm the horrible reality of racial terrorism during the Reconstruction era. Minnie's death is fictional, but Harper includes a reference to an actual lynching that occurred in Darlington, South Carolina, just before Harper's arrival there. Minnie's death is explained by a character whose daughter's death reflects this historical account of a lynching.

What is especially significant about *Minnie's Sacrifice* is that this work explicitly espouses and reiterates the proletarian thesis of Harper's literature. Harper integrates her experiential knowledge with a literary style that predates social realism. This novel does not graphically depict the horrors of the lynching, but relays it through dialogue in the tradition of the slave narrative. The absence of graphic details leaves the reader suspended with a desire to resolve this emotional conflict with tragedy. But Harper does not allow the reader to reconcile this dilemma. Instead, in a conclusion outside of the text, after the ending of the story, she addresses the complacent reader in a structural design that deals with a reality beyond the fiction:

> *And now, in conclusion, may I not ask the indulgence of my readers for a few moments simply to say that Louis and Minnie are only ideal beings, touched here and there with a coloring from real life?*
>
> *But while I confess (not wishing to misrepresent the most lawless of the Ku-Klux) that Minnie has only lived and died in my imagination, may I not modestly ask that the lesson of Minnie shall have its place among the educational ideas for the advancement of our race?*

The greatest want of our people, if I understand our wants aright, is not simply wealth, nor genius, nor mere intelligence, but live men, and earnest, lovely women, whose lives shall represent not a "stagnant mass, but a living force.

Harper's characters exemplify the kind of advocacy she espouses in this statement, which is reflective of her essay, "Our Greatest Want." While the two main characters, Minnie and Louis, are actually "born again black people," having been raised ignorant of their racial heritage, they rise to the challenge and through this realization come to refocus their perspective on race and humanity. Moreover, these characters realize there is much to be learned from the former slaves whose valiant underground activities during the Civil War have gone unheralded and unappreciated.

Harper's characters evolve a radical consciousness, and through the dialogue and the narrative their words and deeds reiterate her speeches and essays during the Reconstruction. Harper's position on the Fifteenth Amendment is articulated in the novel, but at the same time, extended beyond that position when Minnie voices the need for women's suffrage:

But I cannot recognize that the negro man is the only one who has pressing claims at this hour. Today our government needs woman's conscience as well as man's judgment. And while I would not throw a straw in the way of the colored man, even though I know that he would vote against me as soon as he gets his vote, yet I do think that woman should have some power to defend herself from oppression, and equal laws as if she were a man.

This analysis coincides with the class analysis Bettina Aptheker relates on the subject in *Woman's Legacy*, wherein the long-range vision for the human rights struggle necessitated a compromise on the part of the women's movement at that time in order to waylay racial terrorism in the South. Minnie's statement is broader than Harper's statement at the Equal Rights Association debate that same year. Here, within the format of the *Christian Recorder*, Harper presents women's rights as important as black male suffrage. Such a statement would have strengthened Susan B. Anthony and Elizabeth Cady Stanton's position for women's suffrage and thereby weakened Harper's racial alignment with Frederick Douglass. But in this cultural context Harper clarifies her feminist convictions as advocacy for human rights and to the benefit of black male and female enlightenment. Minnie explains:

131

I think, Louis, that basing our rights on the ground of our common humanity is the only true foundation for national peace and durability. If you would have the government strong and enduring you should entrench it in the hearts of both the men and women of the land.

Another important historical parallel between the novel and radical activism is that Minnie's foster parents, the Carpenters, are Quakers and avid abolitionists. Quakers are prominently displayed in Harper's literature as a consequence of her political relationship with that community throughout her life. In this work they represent the humanistic values of their religious convictions. Minnie's belief in nonviolence was nurtured by her white foster parents, but when she comes to live as a black person, she modifies this position when the abolition of slavery becomes a part of the Civil War. Additionally, Louis advocates self-defense against Klan terrorism as a part of his political platform.

Louis Le Croix, Minnie's husband, also displays the class consciousness Harper promoted in her lectures in his strategy for political organizing:

He attended their political meetings, not to array class against class, nor to inflame the passions of either side. He wanted the vote of the colored people not to express the old hates and animosities of the plantation, but the new community of interests arising from freedom.

Minnie's Sacrifice appeared during Harper's brief stay in her new home in Philadelphia between southern lecture tours. Thematically, her characters fictionally represent her work in reality and the overall struggle of the radical community in the South. Minnie is an educator of the intellect and of the aspects of feminine domestic culture, the latter of which Harper taught at Union Seminary in Ohio. This seemingly traditional characterization of "true womanhood" is radicalized by Minnie's political views, in her advocacy of women's rights, and in her belief in the insight and strength of her gender. But this feminist dimension is related as an anticipated goal to be retained but not to supplant the urgency of the moment—racial terrorism. To reiterate this urgency, Minnie and Louis do not live happily ever after in romantic bliss. Minnie is killed by the Klan and Louis must gain spiritual strength from this Christlike sacrifice and persevere.

The End of the Abolitionist Era

One year later, Frances Harper joined the Pennsylvania Anti-Slavery Society to celebrate the end of the abolitionist movement. Even though detailed public discussions about the subversive activities of the Underground Railroad were still considered verboten, the participants were heralded for their heroism. Frederick Douglass's *The New National Era* printed the proceedings:

> Yesterday, too, with the society, expired that corporation—"The Underground Railroad"—in which the society was the chief stockholder. Its work, too, has ended—no mails, no messages; and so yesterday it wound up its business, closed its books, and disappeared. No wonder that the anti-slavists were jubilant as they sat in the hall and recalled their toils and perils, and above all, their triumphs. . . . In the dark days of the fugitive slave law, it is scarcely necessary to add, in the opinion of almost everybody, the less said or written on the subject of the Underground Railroad the safer were all concerned. . . . Thousands of narratives have been listened to with the deepest interest by individuals who have hardly felt at liberty to let their left hand know what their right hand had been doing.[29]

Dr. Charles B. Purvis referenced the Fifteenth Amendment as evidence of achievement, but reminded these comrades of future struggles to extend the triumphs of the moment: "We have the fifteenth, the next step will be the sixteenth, woman's suffrage, and I hope within ten years a seventeenth, that will protect the Indian on his reservations. If any class has a right to rejoice after the colored man, it is the Anti-Slavery Society."[30] Though not in attendance, Garrison, Anthony, and Stanton received ceremonial nods. Near the end of the program, Frances Harper, having interrupted her Reconstructionist work in the South to attend the occasion, "was introduced and varied the evening's exercises by the reading of the following original poem":

Fifteenth Amendment

Beneath the burden of our joy
Tremble, O wires, from East to West!
Fashion with words your tongues of fire,
To tell the nation's high behest.

Outstrip the winds, and leave behind
  The murmur of the restless waves;
Nor tarry with your glorious news,
  Amid the ocean's coral caves.

Ring out! ring out! your sweetest chimes,
  Ye bells, that call to prayer;
Let every heart with gladness thrill,
  And songs of joyful triumph raise.

Shake off the dust, O rising race!
  Crowned as a brother and a man;
Justice to-day asserts her claim,
  And from thy brow fades out the ban.

With freedom's chrism upon thy head,
  Her precious ensign in thy hand,
Go place thy once despised name
  Amid the noblest of the land.

O ransomed race! give God the praise,
  Who led thee through a crimson sea,
And 'mid the storm of fire and blood,
  Turned out the war-cloud's light to thee.[31]

The passage of the Fifteenth Amendment had been accomplished, and black men had allegedly acquired suffrage; and Harper, a devout feminist, had subscribed her moral support to the strategical advantage of the "race." Subsequently, her words and influence sacrificed no criticisms nor excused any irresponsibilities on the part of black men in public or private life. At the same time, she consistently indicted the U.S. government for its silent acceptance of Klan terrorism, mocking democracy and deconstructing the Reconstruction. But remaining true to the ethics of her religion, her uncle's philosophy of self-determination, and the Mosaic ideal, she insisted this was *no time to be discouraged*. The evidence of progress despite active adversity and internalized contradictions, are the *lights and shades* of affairs.

Concurrently, Harper's long poem, *Moses: A Story of the Nile* was published by Merrihew and Son in Philadelphia (1869); she was appointed head of the Colored Division by the National Woman's Christian Temperance Union; and Frederick Douglass' paper, *The New National Era*, advertised that she was "prepared to accept calls from Lyceums and Lecturing Committees for the 1870 lecturing season then commencing."[32] In a lecture given at the Centennial Anniversary of the Pennsylvania Society for Promoting the Abolition of Slavery on April 14, 1875, Harper addressed the challenges of the Reconstruction era for the nation. Expressing the necessity for education and equity of the race, her speech is a call for Christian character, and a challenge to women to put meaning in their lives by engaging political and social issues of the times.

> *The great problem to be solved by the American people, if I understand it, is this: Whether or not there is strength enough in democracy, virtue enough in our civilization, and power enough in our religion to have mercy and deal justly with four millions of people but lately translated from the old oligarchy of slavery to the new commonwealth of freedom; and upon the right solution of this question depends in a large measure the future strength, progress, and durability of our nation. The most important question before us colored people is not simply what the Democratic party may do against us or the Republican party do for us; but what are we going to do for ourselves? What shall we do towards developing our character, adding our quota to the civilization and strength of the country, diversifying our industry, and practising those lordly virtues that conquer success, and turn the world's dread laugh into admiring recognition? The white race has yet work to do in making practical the political axiom of equal rights, and the Christian idea of human brotherhood; but while I lift mine eyes to the future I would not ungratefully ignore the past.*
>
> *One hundred years ago and Africa was the privileged hunting-ground of Europe and America, and the flag of different nations hung a sign of death on the coasts of Congo and Guinea, and for years unbroken silence had hung around the horrors of the African slave-trade. Since then Great Britain and other nations have wiped the bloody traffic from their hands, and shaken the gory merchandise from their fingers, and the brand of piracy has been placed upon the African slave-trade. Less than fifty years ago mob violence belched out its wrath against the men who dared to arraign the slaveholder before the bar of conscience and Christendom. Instead of golden showers upon his head, he who garrisoned the front had a halter around his neck. Since, if I may borrow the idea, the nation has caught the old inspiration from his lips and written it in the new organic world. Less than twenty-five years ago slavery clasped hands with King Cotton, and said slavery fights and cotton conquers for American slavery. Since then slavery is dead, the colored man has exchanged the fetters on his wrist for the ballot in his hand. Freedom is king, and Cotton a subject.*
>
> *It may not seem to be a gracious thing to mingle complaint in a season of general rejoicing. It may appear like the ancient Egyptians seating a corpse at their festal board to avenge the Americans for their shortcomings when so much has been accomplished. And yet with all the victories and triumphs which freedom and justice have won in this country, I do not believe*

135

there is another civilized nation under Heaven where there are half so many people who have been brutally and shamefully murdered, with or without impunity, as in this Republic within the last yen years. And who cares? Where is the public opinion that has scorched with red-hot indignation the cowardly murderers of Vicksburg and Louisiana? Sheridan lifts up the veil from Southern society, and behind it is the smell of blood, and our bones scattered at the grave's mouth; murdered people in a White League with its "covenant of death and agreement with hell." And who cares? What city pauses one hour to drop a pitying tear over these mangled corpses, or has forged against the perpetrator one thunderbolt of furious protest? But let there be a supposed or real invasion of Southern rights by our soldiers, and our great commercial emporium will rally its forces from the old man in his classic shades, to clasp hands with "dead rabbits" and "plug-uglies" in protesting against military interference.

What we need to-day in the onward march of humanity is a public sentiment in favor of common justice and simple mercy. We have a civilization which has produced grand and magnificent results, diffused knowledge, overthrown slavery, made constant conquests over nature, and built up a wonderful material prosperity. But two things are wanting in American civilization—a keener and deeper, broader and tenderer sense of justice—a sense of humanity, which shall crystalize into the life of the nation the sentiment that justice, simple justice, is the right, not simply of the strong and powerful, but of the weakest and feeblest of all God's children; a deeper and broader humanity, which will teach men to look upon their feeble brethren not as vermin to be crushed out, or beasts of burden to be bridled and bitten, but as the children of the living God; of that God whom we can earnestly hope is in perfect wisdom and in perfect love working for the best good of all.

Ethnologists may differ about the origin of the human race. Huxley may search for it in protoplasms, and Darwin send for the missing links, but there is one thing of which we may rest assured,—that we all come from the living God and that He is the common Father. The nation that has no reverence for man is also lacking in reverence for God and needs to be instructed.

As fellow citizens, leaving out all humanitarian views—as a mere matter of political economy it is better to have the colored race a living force animated and strengthened by self-reliance and self-respect, than a stagnant mass, degraded and self-condemned. Instead of the North relaxing its efforts to diffuse education in the South, it behooves us for our national life, to throw into the South all the healthful reconstructing influences we can command. Our work in this country is grandly constructive. Some races have come into this world and overthrown and destroyed. But if it is glory to destroy, it is happiness to save; and Oh! what a noble work there is before our nation! Where is there a young man who would consent to lead an aimless life when there are such glorious opportunities before him? Before our young man is another battle—not a battle of flashing swords and clashing steel—but a moral warfare, a battle against ignorance, poverty, and low social condition. In physical warfare the keenest swords may be blunted and the loudest batteries hushed; but in the great conflict of moral and spiritual progress your weapons shall be brighter for their service and better for their use. In fighting truly and nobly for others you win the victory for yourselves.

Give power and significance to your own life, and in the great work of upbuilding there is room for woman's work and woman's heart. Oh, that our hearts were alive and our vision quickened, to see the grandeur of the work that lies before. We have some culture among us, but I think our culture lacks enthusiasm. We need a deep earnestness and a lofty unselfishness to round out our lives. It is the inner life that develops the outer, and if we are in earnest the precious things lie all around our feet, and we need not waste our strength in striving after the dim and unattainable. Women, in your golden youth; mother, binding around your heart all the precious ties of life,—let no magnificence of culture, or amplitude of fortune, or refinement of sensibilities, repel you from helping the weaker and less favored. If you have ampler gifts, hold them as larger opportunities with which you can benefit others. Oh, it is better to feel that the weaker and feebler our race the closer we will cling to them, than it is to isolate ourselves from them in selfish, or careless unconcern, saying there is a lion without. Inviting you to this work I do not promise you fair sailing and unclouded skies. You may meet with coolness where you expect sympathy; disappointment where you feel sure of success; isolation and loneliness instead of heart-support and cooperation. But if your lives are based and built upon these divine certitudes, which are the only enduring strength of humanity, then whatever defeat and discomfiture may overshadow your plans or frustrate your schemes, for a life that is in harmony with God and sympathy for man there is no such word as fail. And in conclusion, permit me to say, let no misfortunes crush you; no hostility of enemies or failure of friends discourage you. Apparent failure may hold in its rough shell the germs of a success that will blossom in time, and bear fruit throughout eternity. What seemed to be a failure around the Cross of Calvary and in the garden has been the grandest recorded success.[33]

Harper resumed an even more rigorous lecturing schedule, which moved the poet through Georgia into Florida, Alabama, Mississippi, Louisiana, North Carolina, Virginia, Kentucky, Tennessee, Missouri, Delaware, and Maryland (1869–71). When Harper settled in Philadelphia in February 1871, she and her daughter Mary secured a modest, but impressive row house on 1006 Bainbridge Street within walking distance of her close friend, William Still. The attic contained a secret passage to the adjoining brownstone, a connection to the retired network of secret routes of the Underground Railroad. The home of William Still was only a few streets north, at 413 Lombard. During lecturing tours and political meetings that Harper and her daughter attended, Still and his family managed the Harper home. The intricacies of their familial involvements are reflected in Still's letter to Harper, as he describes the mundane, day-to-day details of property management and responds to Harper's worry over oppressive subtleties, like taxes.

Nov. 3, 18—

Mrs. Harper:

Dear friend:

Your letter enclosed with Tweety's came to us on Saturday and contents were duly noted. With regard to your taxes, give your self no further anxiety about them as they have been paid. I had attended to them before your letter came to hand. $65.80 was the assessment paid. For the luxury of a 3 story house this is not so bad.

Now I am not sure whether you asked me to look after anything else or not—Tweety has the letter. I called for the rent today, and got it, and also was notified that a light was needed in the front somewhere, and likewise that a covering is needed for the entrance to the Basement. I suppose I may have these matters attended to. 35 copies of the U.G.R.R. [*Underground Rail Road*] called for by this morning's mail—25 for Syracuse and 10 for Mobile. Why don't you speak to some of our smart men or women and urge them to take agencies. The time may come when you may want me to publish a great book for yourself. Several have offered me their works.

Tweety was here this afternoon and she is quite well.

Yours Truly,
W. Still[34]

But Harper's letters to Still also reveal the intense political climate of the old South resisting the newly enfranchised black citizenry. The letters also inscribe the personality of an activist veteran whose tenacity was prepared to confront not only the adversity of white hostility, but was also willing to endure personal hardship. Often lecturing without pay, Harper was undaunted by the imposing poverty or the looming possibility of attack by Rebel violence. She remained encouraged by the energy, kindness and resourcefulness of the freedmen and women, but at the same time, she remained firmly critical of spouse abuse, especially in the wake of the present turmoil, with the slash of the overseer's whip still raw in racial memory.

Reconstruction Lecture Tour II

If those who can benefit our people will hang around places where they are not needed, they may expect to be discouraged. Here is ignorance to be instructed; a race who needs to be helped up to higher planes of thought and action; and whether we are hindered or helped, we should try to be true to the commission God has written upon our souls. As far as the colored people are concerned, they are beginning to get homes for themselves and depositing money in banks. They have hundreds of homes in Kentucky. There is progress in Tennessee, and even in this state [Georgia] while a number have been leaving, some who stay seem to be getting along prosperously. In Augusta colored persons are in the Revenue Office and Post Office. I have just been having some good meetings there. Some of my meetings pay me poorly; but I have a chance to instruct and visit among the people and talk to their Sunday-schools and day schools also. Of course I do not pretend that all are saving money or getting homes. I rather think from what I hear that the interest of the grown-up people in getting education has somewhat subsided, owing perhaps, in a measure, to the novelty having worn off and the absorption or rather direction of the mind to other matters. Still I don't think that I have visited scarcely a place since last August where there was no desire for a teacher; and Mr. Fidler, who is a Captain or Colonel, thought some time since that there were more colored than white who were learning or had learned to read. There has been quite an amount of violence and trouble in the State; but we have the military here, and if they can keep Georgia out of the Union about a year or two longer, and the colored people continue to live as they have been doing, from what I hear, perhaps these rebels will learn a little more sense. I have been in Atlanta for some time, but did not stay until the Legislature was organized; but I was there when colored members returned and took their seats. It was rather a stormy time in the House; but no blood was shed. Since then there has been some "sticking;" but I don't think any of the colored ones were in it.[35]

Last evening I visited one of the plantations and had an interesting time. Oh, how warm was the welcome! I went out near dark, and between that time and attending my lecture, I was out to supper in two homes. The people are living in the old cabins of slavery; some of them have no windows, at all, that I see; in fact, I don't remember of having seen a pane of window-

glass in the settlement. But, humble as their homes were, I was kindly treated, and well received; and what a chance one has for observation among these people, if one takes with her a manner that unlocks other hearts. I had quite a little gathering after less, perhaps, than a day's notice; the minister did not know that I was coming, till he met me in the afternoon. There was no fire in the church, and so they lit fires outside, and we gathered, or at least a number of us, around the fire. To-night I am going over to Georgia to lecture. In consequence of the low price of cotton, the people may not be able to pay much, and I am giving all my lectures free. You speak of things looking dark in the South; there is no trouble here that I know of—cotton is low, but the people do not seem to be particularly depressed about it; this emigration question has been on the carpet, and I do not wonder if some of them, with their limited knowledge, lose hope in seeing full justice done to them, among their life-long oppressors; Congress has been agitating the St. Domingo question; a legitimate theme for discussion, and one that comes nearer home, is how they can give more security and strength to the government which we have established in the South—for there has been a miserable weakness in the security to human life. The man with whom I stopped, had a son who married a white woman, or girl, and was shot down, and there was, as I understand, no investigation by the jury; and a number of cases have occurred of murders, for which the punishment has been very lax, or not at all, and it may be, never will be; however, I rather think things are somewhat quieter. A few days ago a shameful outrage occurred at this place—some men had been out fox hunting, and came to the door of a colored woman and demanded entrance, making out they wanted fire; she replied that she had none, and refused to open the door; the miserable cowards broke open the door, and shamefully beat her. I am going to see her this afternoon. It is remarkable, however, in spite of circumstances, how some of these people are getting along. Here is a woman who, with her husband, at the surrender, had a single dollar; and now they have a home of their own, and several acres attached—five altogether; but, as that was rather small, her husband has contracted for two hundred and forty acres more, and has now gone out and commenced operations.[36]

I am almost constantly either traveling or speaking. I do not think that I have missed more than one Sunday that I have not addressed some Sunday-school, and I have not missed many day-schools either. And as I am giving all my lectures free the proceeds of the collections are not often very large; still as ignorant as part of the people are perhaps a number of them would not hear at all, and may prejudice others if I charged even ten cents, and so perhaps in the long run, even if my work is wearing, I may be of some real benefit to my race. I don't know but that you would laugh if you were to hear some of the remarks which my lectures call forth: "She is a man," again "She is not colored, she is painted." Both white and colored come out to hear me, and I have very fine meetings; and then part of the time I am talking in between times, and how tired I am some of the time. Still I am standing with my race on the threshold of a new era, and though some be far past me in the learning of the schools, yet to-day, with my limited and fragmentary knowledge, I may help the race forward a little. Some of our people remind me of sheep without a shepherd.[37]

But really my hands are almost constantly full of work; sometimes I speak twice a day. Part of my lectures are given privately to women, and for them I never make any charge, or take up any collection. But this part of the country reminds me of heathen ground, and though my work may not be recognized as part of it used to be in the North, yet never perhaps were my services more needed; and according to their intelligence and means perhaps never better appreciated than here among these lowly people. I am now going to have a private meeting with the women of this place if they will come out. I am going to talk with them about their daughters, and about things connected with the welfare of the race. Now is the time for our women to begin to try to lift up their heads and plant the roots of progress under the hearthstone. Last night I spoke in a school-house, where there was not, to my knowledge, a single window glass; to-day I write to you in a lowly cabin, where the windows in the room are formed by two apertures in the wall. There is a wide-spread and almost universal appearance of poverty in this State where I have been, but thus far I have seen no, or scarcely any, pauperism. I am not sure than I have seen any. The climate is so fine, so little cold that poor people can live off of less than they can in the North. Last night my table was adorned with roses, although I did not get one cent for my lecture.

The political heavens are getting somewhat overcast. Some of this old rebel element, I think, are in favor of taking away the colored man's vote, and if he loses it now it may be generations before he gets it again. Well, after all perhaps the colored man generally is not really developed enough to value his vote and equality with other races, so he gets enough to eat and drink, and be comfortable, perhaps the loss of his vote would not be a serious grievance to many; but his children differently educated and trained by circumstance might feel political inferiority rather a bitter cup.

After all whether they encourage or discourage me, I belong to this race, and when it is down I belong to a down race; when it is up I belong to a risen race.[38]

Did you ever read a little poem commencing, I think, with these words:
A mother cried, Oh give me joy,
For I have born a darling boy!
A darling boy! why the world is full
Of the men who play at push and pull.

Well, as full as the room was of beds and tenants, on the morning of the twenty-second, there arose a wail upon the air, and this mundane sphere had another inhabitant, and my room another occupant. I left after that, and when I came back the house was fuller than it was before, and my hostess gave me to understand that she would rather I should be somewhere else, and I left again. How did I fare? Well, I had been stopping with one of our teachers and went back; but the room in which I stopped was one of those southern shells through which both light and cold enter at the same time; it had one window and perhaps more than half or one half of the panes gone. I don't know that I was ever more conquered by the cold than I had been at that house, and I have lived parts of winter after winter amid the snows of New England; but if it was cold out of doors, there was warmth and light within doors; but here, if you opened the door for light, the cold would also enter, and so part of the time I sat by the fire, and that and the crevices in the house supplied me with light in one room, and we had the deficient window sash, or perhaps it never had any lights in it. You could put your finger through some of the apertures in the house; at least I could mine, and the water froze down to the bottom of the tumbler. From another such domicile may kind fate save me. And then the man asked me four dollars and a half a week board.

One of the nights there was no fire in the stove, and the next time we had fires, one stove might have been a second-hand chamber stove. Now perhaps you think these people very poor, but the man with whom I stopped has no family that I saw, but himself and wife, and he would make two dollars and a half a day, and she worked out and kept a boarder. And yet, except the beds and bed clothing, I wouldn't have given fifteen dollars for all their house furniture. I should think that his has been one of the lowest down States in the South [Alabama], as far as civilization has been concerned. In the future, until these people are educated, look out for Democratic victories, for here are two materials with which Democracy can work, ignorance and poverty. Men talk about missionary work among the heathen, but if any lover of Christ wants a field for civilizing work, here is a field. Part of the time I am preaching against men ill-treating their wives. I have heard though, that often during the war men hired out their wives and drew their pay.

And then there is another trouble, some of our Northern men have been down this way and by some means they have not made the best impression on every mind here. One woman here has been expressing her mind very freely to me about some of our Northerners, and we are not all considered here as saints and angels, and of course in their minds I get associated with some or all the humbugs that have been before me. But I am not discouraged, my race needs me, if I will only be faithful, and in spite of suspicion and distrust, I will work on; the deeper our degradation, the louder our call for redemption. If they have little or no faith in goodness and earnestness, that is only one reason why we should be more faithful and earnest, and so I shall probably stay here in the South all winter. I am not making much money,

and perhaps will hardly clear expenses this winter; but after all what mat-
ters it when I am in my grave whether I have been rich or poor, loved or hated,
despised or respected, if Christ will only own me to His Father, and I be per-
mitted a place in one of the mansions of rest.[39]

Colonel J. W. Tourney, editor of *The Press*, introduced Harper's letter (published July 12, 1871) with the following:

The following letter, written by Mrs. F.E.W. Harper, the well-known
colored orator, to a friend, Mr. Wm. Still, of Philadelphia, will be
read with surprise and pleasure by all classes; especially supple-
mented as it is by an article from the *Mobile Register*, referring to one
of her addresses in that city. The *Register* is the organ of the fire-
eaters of the South, conducted by John Forsyth, heretofore one of
the most intolerant of that school. Mrs. Harper describes the manner in which the old plantation of Jefferson Davis in Mississippi was
cultivated by his brother's former slave, having been a guest in the
Davis mansion, now occupied by Mr. Montgomery, the aforesaid
slave. She also draws a graphic picture of her own marvelous advancement from utter obscurity to the platform of a public lecturer,
honored by her own race and applauded by their oppressors. While
we regret, as she says, that her experience and that of Mr. Montgomery is exceptional, it is easy to anticipate the harvest of such a
sowing. The same culture—the same courage on the part of the men
and women who undertake to advocate Republican doctrines in the
South—the same perseverance and intelligence on the part of those
who are earning their bread by the cultivation of the soil, will be
crowned with the same success. Violence, bloodshed, and murder
cannot rule long in communities where these restless elements are
allowed to work. No scene in the unparalleled tragedy of the rebellion, or in the drama which succeeded that tragedy, can be compared to the picture outlined by Mrs. Harper herself, and filled in
by the ready pen of the rebel editor of the *Mobile Register*.
  My Dear Friend: —It is said that truth is stranger than fiction; and
if ten years since some one had entered my humble log house and seen me
kneading bread and making butter, and said that in less than ten years you
will be in the lecture field, you will be a welcome guest under the roof of the
President of the Confederacy [Jefferson Davis], though not by special invi-
tation from him, that you will see his brother's former slave a man of busi-
ness and influence, that hundreds of colored men will congregate on the old
baronial possessions, that a school will spring up there like a well in the
desert dust, that this former slave will be a magistrate upon the plantation,

that labor will be organized upon a new basis, and that under the sole aus-pices and molding hands of this man and his sons will be developed a busi-ness whose transactions will be numbered in hundreds of thousands of dollars, would you not have smiled incredulously? And I have lived to see the day when the plantation was passed into new hands, and these hands once wore the fetters of slavery. Mr. Montgomery, the present proprietor by contract of between five and six thousand acres of land, has one of the most interesting families that I have ever seen in the South. They are building up a future which if exceptional now I hope will become more general hereafter. Every hand of his family is adding its quota to the success of this experiment of a colored man both trading and farming on an extensive scale. Last year his wife too had on her hands about 130 acres of land, and with her force she raised about 107 bales of cotton. She has a number of orphan children employed, and not only does she supervise their labor, but she works herself. One daughter, an intelligent young lady, is postmistress and I believe assis-tant book-keeper. One son attends to the planting interest, and another daughter attends to one of the stores. The business of this firm of Montgomery & Sons has amounted, I understand, to between three and four hundred thousand dollars in a year. I stayed on the place several days and was hos-pitably entertained and kindly treated. When I come, if nothing prevents, I will tell you more about them. Now for the next strange truth. Enclosed I send you a notice from one of the leading and representative papers of rebel-dom. The editor has been, or is considered, one of the representative men of the South. I have given a lecture since this notice, which brought out some of the most noted rebels, among whom was Admiral Semmes. In my speech I referred to the Alabama sweeping away our commerce and his son sat near him and seemed to receive it with much good humor. I don't know what the papers will say to-day; perhaps they will think that I dwelt upon the past too much. Oh, if you had seen the rebs I had out last night, perhaps you would have felt a little nervous for me. However, I lived through it, and gave them more gospel truth than perhaps some of them have heard for some time.[40]

Oh, what a field there is here in this region! Let me give you a short ac-count of this week's work. Sunday I addressed a Sunday-school in Talladega; on Monday afternoon a day-school. On Monday I rode several miles to a meeting; addressed it, and came back the same night. Got back about or af-ter twelve o'clock. The next day I had a meeting of women and addressed them, and then lectured in the evening in the Court-House to both colored and white. Last night I spoke again, about ten miles from where I am now stopping, and returned the same night, and to-morrow evening probably I shall speak again. I grow quite tired part of the time. And now let me give you an anecdote or two of some of our new citizens. While in Talladega I was entertained and well entertained, at the house of one of our new citizens. He

is living in the house of his former master. He is a brick-maker by trade, and I rather think mason also. He was worth to his owner, it was reckoned, fifteen hundred or about that a year. He worked with him seven years; and in that seven years he remembers receiving from him fifty cents. Now mark the contrast! That man is now free, owns the home of his former master, has I think more than sixty acres of land, and his master is in the poor house. I heard of another such case not long since: A woman was cruelly treated once or more than once. She escaped and ran naked into town. The villain in whose clutch she found herself was trying to drag her downward to his own low level of impurity, and at last she fell. She was poorly fed, so that she was tempted to sell her person. Even scraps thrown to the dog she was hunger-bitten enough to aim for. Poor thing, was there anything in the future for her? Had not hunger and cruelty and prostitution done their work, and left her an entire wreck for life? It seems not. Freedom came, and with it dawned a new era upon that poor, overshadowed, and sin-darkened life. Freedom brought opportunity for work and wages combined. She went to work, and got ten dollars a month. She has contrived to get some education, and has since been teaching school. While her former mistress has been to her for help.

Do not the mills of God grind exceedingly fine? And she has helped that mistress, and so has the colored man given money, from what I heard, to his former master. After all, friend, do we not belong to one of the best branches of the human race? And yet, how have our people been murdered in the South, and their bones scattered at the grave's mouth! Oh, when will we have a government strong enough to make human life safe? Only yesterday I heard of a murder committed on a man for an old grudge of several years' standing. I have visited the place, but had just got away. Last summer a Mr. Luke was hung, and several other men also, I heard.[41]

Can you spare a little time from your book [The Underground Rail Road] to just take a peep at some of our Alabama people? If you would see some instances of apparent poverty and ignorance that I have seen perhaps you would not wonder very much at the conservative voting in the State. A few days since I was about to pay a woman a dollar and a quarter for some washing in ten cent (currency) notes, when she informed me that she could not count it; she must trust to my honesty—she could count forty cents. Since I left Eufala I have seen something of the plantation life. The first plantation I visited was about five or six miles from Eufala, and I should think that the improvement in some of the cabins was not very much in advance of what it was in Slavery. The cabins are made with doors, but not, to my recollection, a single window pane or speck of plastering; and yet even in some of those lowly homes I met with hospitality. A room to myself is a luxury that I do not always enjoy. Still I live through it, and find life rather interesting. The people have much to learn. The condition of the women is not very enviable in some cases. They have had some of them a terribly hard time

145

in Slavery, and their subjection has not ceased in freedom. One man said of some women, that a man must leave them or whip them.

Let me introduce you to another scene: here is a gathering; a large fire is burning out of doors, and here are one or two boys with hats on. Here is a little girl with her bonnet on, and there a little boy moves off and commences to climb a tree. Do you know what the gathering means? It is a school, and the teacher, I believe, is paid from the school fund. He says he is from New Hampshire. That may be. But to look at him and to hear him teach, you would perhaps think him not very lately from the North; at least I do not think he is a model teacher. They have a church; but somehow they have burnt a hole, I understand, in the top, and so I lectured inside, and they gathered around the fire outside. Here is another—what shall I call it?— meeting-place. It is a brush arbor. And what pray is that? Shall I call it an edifice or an impoverished meeting-house? Well, it is called a brush arbor. It is a kind of brush house with seats, and a kind of covering made partly, I rather think, of branches of trees, and a humble place for pulpit. I lectured in a place where they seemed to have no other church; but I spoke at a house. In Glenville, a little out-of-the-way place, I spent part of a week. There they have two unfinished churches. One has not a single pane of glass and the same aperture that admits the light also give ingress to the air; and the other one, I rather think, is less finished than that. I spoke in one, and then the white people gave me a hall, and quite a number attended. I am now at Union Springs, where I shall probably room with three women. But amid all this roughing it in the bush, I find a field of work where kindness and hospitality have thrown their sunshine around my way. And Oh what a field of work is here! How much one needs the Spirit of our dear Master to make one's life a living, loving force to help men to higher places of thought and action. I am giving all my lectures with free admission; but still I get along, and the way has been opening for me almost ever since I have been South. Oh, if some more of our young women would only consecrate their lives to the work of upbuilding the race! Oh, if I could only see our young men and women aiming to build up a future for themselves which would grandly contrast with the past—with its pain, ignorance and low social condition.[42]

CHAPTER 5

The Dialectics of Dialect Poetry: Frances Harper's *Sketches of Southern Life*

Aunt Chloe's Politics

Of course, I don't know very much
   About these politics,
But I think that some who run 'em,
   Do mighty ugly tricks.

I've seen 'em honey-fugle round,
   And talk so awful sweet,
That you'd think them full of kindness,
   As an egg is full of meat.

Now I don't believe in looking
   Honest people in the face,
In saying when you're doing wrong,
   That " I haven't sold my race."

When we want to school our children,
   If the money isn't there,
Whether black or white have took it,
   The loss we all must share.

And this buying up each other
   Is something worse than mean,
Though I thinks a heap of voting,
   I go for voting clean.
            Frances Harper, 1872
            Sketches of Southern Life

The women as a class are quite equal to the men in energy and executive ability. In fact I find by close observation, that the mothers are the levers which move in education. The men talk about it, especially about election time, if they want an office for self or their candidate, but the women work most for it. They labour in many ways to support the family, while the children attend school. They make great sacrifices to spare their own children during school hours. I know of girls from sixteen to twenty-two who iron till midnight that they may come to school in the day. Some of our scholars, aged about nineteen, living about thirty miles off, rented land, ploughed, planted, and sold their cotton, in order to come to us. A woman near me, urged her husband to in debt 500 dollars for a home, as the titles to the land they had built on were insecure, and she said to me, "We have five years to pay it in, and I shall begin to-day to do it, if life is spared. I will make a hundred dollars at washing, for I have done it." Yet they have seven little children to feed, clothe, and educate. In the field the women receive the same wages as the men, and are often preferred, clearing land, hoeing, or picking cotton, with equal ability.

In different departments of business, coloured women have not only been enabled to keep the wolf from the door, but also to acquire property, and in some cases the coloured woman is the mainstay of the family, and when work fails the men in large cities, the money which the wife can obtain by washing, ironing, and other services, often keeps pauperism at bay. I do not suppose, considering the state of her industrial lore and her limited advantages, that there is among the poorer classes a more helpful woman than the coloured woman as a labourer. When I was in Mississippi, I stopped with Mr. Montgomery, a former slave of Jefferson Davis's brother. His wife was a woman capable of taking on her hands 130 acres of land, and raising one hundred and seven bales of cotton by the force which she could organize. Since then I have received a very interesting letter from her daughter, who for years has held the position of Assistant Postmistress. In her letter she says: "There are many women around me who would serve as models of executiveness anywhere. They do double duty, a man's share in the field, and a woman's part at home. They do any kind of field work, even ploughing, and at home the cooking, washing, milking, and gardening. but these have husbands; let me tell you of some widows and unaided women:—

1st. Mrs. Hill, a widow, has rented, cultivated, and solely managed a farm of five acres for five years. She makes her garden, raises poultry, and cultivates enough corn and cotton to live comfortably, and keep a surplus in the bank. She saves somthing every year, and this is much, considering the low price of cotton and unfavorable seasons.

2nd. Another woman, whose husband died in the service during the war, cultivated one acre, making vegetables for sale, besides a little cotton. She raises poultry, spins thread, and knits hose for a living. She supports herself comfortably, never having to ask credit or to borrow.

Mrs. Jane Brown and Mrs. Halsey formed a partnership about ten years ago, leased nine acres and a horse, and have cultivated the land all that time, just the same as men would have done. They have saved considerable money from year to year, and are living independently. They have never had any expenses for labour, making and gathering the crops themselves.

4th. Mrs. Henry, by farming and peddling cakes, has the last seven years laid up seven hundred dollars. She is an invalid, and unable to work at all times. Since then she has been engaged in planting sweet potatoes and raising poultry and hogs. Last year she succeeded in raising 250 hogs, but lost two-thirds by diseases. She furnished eggs and chickens, say fifty dozen chickens. On nine acres she made 600 bushels of sweet potatoes. The present year she has planted ten acres of potatoes. She has 100 hogs, thirty dozen chickens, a small lot of ducks and turkeys, and also a few sheep and goats. She has also a large garden under her supervision, which is planted in cabbages. She has two women and a boy to assist. Miss Montgomery, a coloured lady, says: "I have constantly been engaged in bookkeeping for eight years, and for ten years as assistant postmistress, doing all the work of the office. Now, instead of bookkeeping, I manage a school of 133 pupils, and I have an assistant, and I am still attending to the post-office." Of her sister she says, she is a better and swifter worker than herself; that she generally sews, but that last year she made 100 dozen jars of preserved fruit for sale. An acquaintance of mine, who lives in South Carolina, and has been engaged in mission work, reports that, in supporting the family, women are the mainstay; that two-thirds of the truck gardening is done by them in South Carolina; that in the city they are more industrious than the men; that when the men lose their work through their political affiliations, the women stand by them, and say, "stand by your principles." And I have been informed by the same person that a number of women have homes of their own, bought by their hard earnings since freedom. Mr. Steward, who was employed in the Freedmen's bank, says he has seen scores of coloured women in the South working and managing plantations of from twenty to 100 acres. They and their boys and girls doing all the labour, and marketing the fall from ten to fifty bales of cotton. He speaks of a mulatto woman who rented land, which she and her children worked until they had made enough to purchase a farm of 130 acres. She then lived alone upon it, hiring help and working it herself, making a comfortable living, and assisting her sons in the purchase of land. The best sugar maker, he observes, he ever saw was a stupid looking coloured woman, apparently twenty-five years old. With a score or more of labourers, she was the "boss," and it was her eye which detected the exact consistency to which the syrup had boiled, and, while tossing it in the air, she told with certainty the point of granulation.[1]

Frances Harper lectured and lived with ex-slaves during the Reconstruction period, listening to their stories, learning about their culture and assisting their struggles for the building of a promised land. Her spiritual intimacy with the newly liberated infused her language and confirmed her mission. *Sketches of Southern Life* is a long poem tantamount to Harper's *Moses: A Story of the Nile.* But insofar as *Moses* was composed in blank verse, like the biblical text it emulates, *Sketches* assumes the ballad form for its oral tradition. In demeanor and style, *Sketches of Southern Life* is characteristic of the folk poetry that developed during slavery. Voiced in the first person, the poem is the poetic slave narrative of Aunt Chloe, who reflects her slave history and "free" accomplishments.

Harper's respect for the intelligence, perseverance, and accomplishments of the freedmen and women encouraged her to craft an alternative to written black dialect that did not compromise their identity or their integrity. This long poem captures the mother wit, the sense of humor, the tenacity, and the progressive outlook of black women. This perspective and voice are infused with Frances Harper's activist agenda and with the radical politics of the Reconstruction.

Harper developed a broader language facility for her poetic voice and a new realm for Afroamerican literature that revealed the poetic grace of black English. This literary development was a particularly useful pedagogical strategy. Because most black folks were illiterate or in the process of pursuing literacy, the invention of a characteristic voice was needed to carry Harper's message and to bridge the cultural distance between standard English and black dialect. Hence, *Sketches of Southern Life* was composed in the language of the people as reflected in the slave narrative of a newly literate woman with similar experiences and a familiar voice.

When Harper returned to Philadelphia in 1871 after several trips back and forth between the North and South, she reached her publishing zenith. *Moses: A Story of the Nile* (1869), *Poems* (1871) and *Sketches of Southern Life* (1872), were published by Merrihew and Thompson, and the serialized novel, *Minnie's Sacrifice,* appeared in *The Christian Recorder.* These works were read and circulated throughout Sunday schools and freedmen's schools as cultural and educational texts. Written in accessible language, *Sketches* assisted literacy programs because personal indentificaion with the poem encouraged a positive psychological response to learning. Harper, a teacher, viewed her literature as "Songs for the People," and the application of her poetry for teaching was a practical function of her literacy campaign and of her political aesthetic.

Sketches, her fifth book of poetry, was published in soft-cover, making it easier to transport and inexpensive to print. The beige covers were simply, but attractively embroidered around the borders, accented by an elegant, but unpretentious design in each corner. It displays three variations of typefaces which emphasize "Southern Life," in the largest and darkest letters as the thematic focus of the collection.

Other poems in the collection, *Sketches of Southern Life,* include "The Jewish Grandfather's Story," "I Thirst," "The Dying Queen," "Save the Boys," "Nothing and Something," "Signing the Pledge," "Fishers of Men," and a short story, "Shalmanezer, The Prince of Cosman." "The Jewish Grandfather's Story," another long poem, begins with references to the story of Moses but extends the Hebrew legacy, with short stanzas about other key figures, like Jepthath, Gideon, Deborah, and David. These poems constitute the thematic range of Harper, including temperance and spiritual transcendence. Hence, the book embodies a contextual range that interrelates social struggles to reconstitute human worth and to refocus vision.

By avoiding existing examples of dialect, as exemplified by Stowe and other popular writers, Harper evaded the pitfalls of an over-apostrophied dialect with stilted articulations. Harper's personae speak fluidly and intelligently about enslavement, the Civil War, literacy, religion, and electoral politics. Speaking their own consciousness, their tongues are rounded from injustice and embellished with insightful imagery. Their souls have not suffered through slavery for the sake of literary acceptance, but rather for the possibility of self-determination and cultural integrity.

Ironically, Harper, who spoke nearly perfect standard English—having been strictly educated in grammar, etymology, and syntax, and whose diction was trained for elocutionary delivery from public lecterns—revolutionized the presentation and adaptation of black American English. Unlike many of her contemporaries, she ignored the prejudices of the bourgeois imagination and thereby transcended the cultural and class contradictions of traditional writing. Her aesthetic motivations determined an oral approach for the written language for the benefit of culture rather than exploiting the experience of the culture for the benefit of the literature. Hence, her dialect poetry, written for the historicization of a people and to promote a positive vision for their future, advanced the democratic tradition of American literature and envisioned the dialect achievements of twentieth-century writers.

The dialectics of dialect poetry operates within a cultural and a linguistic framework, and the nineteenth-century American writer who strove to authenticate indigenous speech had to abandon imperialist perceptions of the English language and consider the American language as a departure in cultural values and expression. Harper conceptualized her orientation to the written word and its spatial relationship to the page. She violated aesthetic and political conventions to achieve the poem. At the same time, dialect is also individual. In the novel, *Iola Leroy*, Harper's characters speak within a broad range of dialects, depending on education and situation. But within that relative framework, she maintains a consistency in syntax, vocabulary, and enunciation. Moreover, all of her characters convey intelligence and personality via attitudes, witticisms, and poetic phrasings. These distinctions in their language configure them as persons with a culture and thereby defy caricature.

Sketches of Iola Leroy

"Sketches of Southern Life" also appears to be a sketch for Harper's subsequent novel, *Iola Leroy* (1892). *Iola Leroy* evidences an even broader range in slave and "free" speech, as Harper's skill and preference for voice, as seen in her earlier ballads, is further extended through her experimentation with language in both the long poem and the novel. The persona in "Sketches," Aunt Chloe, whose name alludes to Harriet Beecher Stowe's character in *Uncle Tom's Cabin*, bears some similarity to Aunt Linda, a minor character in *Iola Leroy* who outlives slavery and provides a critical assessment of the state of affairs in the black community during Reconstruction. In this regard, the two women represent the same political vantage point, though their individuality is distinct.

Aunt Chloe is far more progressive in her pursuit for knowledge. She lives alone until her children return, unlike Aunt Linda, who drinks on occasion and feels she is too old to learn to read. Additionally, the long poem appears to be a silhouette, or a poetic abstraction that is later expanded in the novel with an elaborate plot and a range of characters who represent the caste and class of postbellum southern life.

There are obvious parallels in the format of "Sketches of Southern Life" that outline the plot for Harper's novel, *Iola Leroy*. These similarities adhere to Harper's framework of history and themes and are better indicated in my discussion in chapter 6. But, in particular, Harper's dexterity with dialect is better considered by recognizing the range and implications of her system. The novel includes many more voices, which demonstrates personality through variety as well as how literacy and physical mobility affect language.

The novel supplies slave characters who are literate. Robert Johnson, a subversive leader who coordinates the escape to the Yankee troops and who becomes an army officer and businessman, is literate. He was taught to read by his mistress and had access to her library. Because he speaks and reads standard English, he can report information from newspapers to the slave community and can explain words and technical terms related to the Civil War that are sometimes incomprehensible to illiterate ears. But at the same time, when he speaks about religion, he testifies in black English. Robert's dual dialect is similar to Harper's cross-over literacy strategy. His capacity to communicate in both languages is essential to maintain identity and to preserve strong cultural affiliation with the community.

Robert knows the language of his origin. And as he explains whence he received his religion, he quotes Aunt Kizzy inclusively and appropriately by code switching:

> *"Many a time," continued Robert, "have I heard her humming to herself in the kitchen and saying, 'I has my trials, ups and downs, but it won't allers be so. I specs one day to wing and wing wid de angels, Hallelujah! Den I specs to hear a voice sayin', "Poor ole Kizzy, she's done de bes' she kin. Go down, Gabriel, an' tote her in." De I specs to put on my golden slippers, my long white robe, an' my starry crown, an' walk dem golden streets, Hallelujah!' I've known that dear old soul to travel going on two miles, after her work was done, to have some one to read to her."[2]*

For the most part, the dialect spoken is easy to translate. It is consistent in its use of certain sounds, such as "dat," "dem," and "de," wherein the "th" sound is replaced with the "d" and with the clipped endings, like "las'" and "happen'," whereby the *t*'s and the *d*'s are dropped to produce a more lyrical transition between words. "Ob" instead of "of" and "war" instead of "was" are combined with words using standard spelling to evoke a tonal rather than phonetic dialect system. This dialect, as it is in the oral tradition of its speakers, is more dependent on rhythm and intonation than on the misperception of standard speech. Here, apostrophies are used to indicate inflection rather than deficiency, for example: *But, Uncle Dan'il, you won't say nothin' 'bout our going, will you?*

Aunt Linda, who reflects the political consciousness of Aunt Chloe in "Sketches," speaks a more distinct dialect. Her voice affects the inherent, poetic beauty of the language. This prose form, approaching free verse, expands the possibilities for the unrestrained, natural, rhythmic flow of black English. Since Aunt Linda is not literate, her language is

distinctly accented by "der," "den," "ter," "hab," and "ef," and to what extent the reader is willing to concede to the code in order to comprehend
the intelligence of the speaker is relative. Certainly, the inclusion of these
dialect narratives provides a sense of cultural identity for the text and a
sense of respect for those blacks who cannot read, but who sustain the
voice of integrity in the community. The individuality of voice defies caricature, as even the loyalty of Uncle Daniel to his master who had gone to
fight for the Confederacy is understandable within his contextual experience and reasoning.

Aunt Linda tells some of the same tales Aunt Chloe relates about
those black men who sold their votes, and how their women harangued
them for being so cheap. The names are different but the scenes are the
same. She explains a dialogue between a man who sold his vote and his
wife who argued with him about his actions:

> "Wen 'lection time 'rived, he com'd home bringing some flour an' meat; an'
> he says ter Aunt Polly, 'Ole woman, I got dis fer de wote.' She jis' picked up
> dat meat an' flour an' sent it sailin' outer doors, an' den com'd back an' gib
> him a good tongue-lashin'. 'Oder people,' she said, 'a wotin' ter lib good, an'
> you a sellin' yore wote! Ain't you got 'nuff ob ole Marster, an' ole Marster
> bin cuttin' you up? It shan't stay yere.' And so she wouldn't let de things
> stay in de house"[3]

But even more radical statements are transferred through the
novel's narrative as the young liberated suggest the need for a community militia for self-defense.

> "No," said Salters, "fer one night arter some ob our pore people had
> been killed, an' some ob our women had run'd away 'bout seventeen miles,
> my gran'son, looking me square in de face, said: 'Ain't you got five fingers?
> Can't you pull a trigger as well as a white man?' I tell yer, Cap, dat jis' got
> te me, an' I made up my mine dat my boy should neber call me a coward."[4]

Harper uses literacy as a symbol of empowerment. This empowerment can be abused and misused, but in most instances she associates it
with a liberated consciousness. Robert Johnson and Salter's grandson are
not intimidated by white terrorism, as their literacy has dispelled the
overpowering illusions of white supremacy by breaking the code that defines and confuses the subjugated community. This enlightenment, like
the movement toward knowledge and self-determination, advocates a de-

mythification of white culture and power. The variations in dialect as well as in the linguistic ability of Harper's characters to interact intelligently with two American languages demonstrates the breadth of Harper's creativity.

Dialect Poetry

Harper's adaptation of natural speech patterns does not rely on the excessive use of apostrophes to convey sound differences. The thrust of the rhythm provides an authentic musical quality inherent in the syntax. The poetic line is used as a gauge of rhythmic variations, expanding or contracting the meter in order to facilitate the natural inclination of the expression. The line responds to the sound rather than to a rigid metrical formula. Expressions like, *honey-fugle round* and *like an egg is full of meat,* determine a rhythm that is more reflexive relative to the syntax of the dialect than it is to the poetic line. The rhythm of the oral speech pattern takes precedence, resonating in an improvisational response to the ballad structure that contains the overall thrust of the poem's aural impact. Hence, when Harper uses conventional spellings, the words do not resound as standard voice pronunciations.

Particular syntactical features germane to black dialect, even today, like subject-verb agreement, colloquial expressions, and biblically coded symbolism, contribute to structural and thematic cohesion. The impetus of the energy is affected through the thematic frame of imagery, and its rhythmic resonance is amplified by an authentic voice. Harper's poem transcends the technical technique of nineteenth-century literature by activating a synergistic plane of aural intersection. This intersection is dependent on the convergence of sound patterns that interact beyond any single word or syllable; hence, Harper's critical departure from conventional dialect.

Harper's personae speak fluidly and critically about enslavement, the Civil War, literacy, religion, and electoral politics. "Sketches of Southern Life" speaks to the people in their memory and about their especial American identity. For these and other reasons, Aunt Chloe of "Sketches" constitutes an indelible character. She speaks a fusion of the standard and the dialect. Her literacy has modified her dialect, but since her purpose was to learn to read the Bible and not to master the King's English, her narrative represents a natural adjustment. Her diction is less affected, and her syntax to an even lesser extent. Unlike the slave narratives that were tightly edited for the benefit of white readers, Harper's "Sketches of

Southern Life" is a fresh and marvelous expression that stands independently without the intimidation of cultural imperialist considerations.

The Poem

"Sketches of Southern Life" is the slave narrative of Aunt Chloe, an elderly ex-slave woman who explains her trials during bondage, exclaims the joys of deliverance, and reveals the political conflicts that arise during Reconstruction. She relays her determination to learn to read, and the community's efforts to build a church. The poem ends cyclically and appropriately with the first reunion of Chloe's family since her sons were sold away from her during slavery.

The long poem begins with the tension of tragedy and the promise of peace. The experience expressed by Aunt Chloe's language and point of view determines the tone and setting. While the ballad provides a flexible framework wherein variations in Chloe's speech pattern are modulated by the drama in the imagery and the *a b c b* rhyme pattern, the consistency of the subject-verb conjugation combined with the vernacular dialect assure a folk pronunciation. The first section of the poem is subtitled, "Aunt Chloe," and it begins with reflections of her most traumatic slave experience and a typical Harper theme, the selling of her children away from the plantation. The first-person pronoun and the capitalization of all the letters in "REMEMBER" emphasize the influence of oral history.

> *I REMEMBER, well remember,*
> *That dark and dreadful day,*
> *When they whispered to me, "Chloe,*
> *Your children's sold away!"*

The dialogue between Aunt Chloe and her cousin Milly explains the nature and cause of this disaster, as the master of the plantation has died and left his wife in debt. Milly empathizes with Chloe, explaining how her son Saul was likewise sold away by the old master. Pinioned by depression, Chloe *waste*[s] into a *shadow,* and turns *to skin and bone,* until Uncle Jacob advises her to take her troubles to the Lord, who lightens her load and redeems her soul:

> *"You'll get justice in the kingdom,*
> *If you do not get it here."*

156

The reiteration of the image of the heart appears in the second stanza,

> *And I felt as if my heart-strings*
> *Was breaking right in two.*

Likewise the Mistus is crying in the big house *like her heart would break,* and Uncle Jacob warns Chloe *your poor heart is in the fire.* In folk culture there is an integral connection between the heart and the spirit. The "old folks" believe the spirit lives in the heart. Hence, Chloe's sorrow had emaciated her body and her soul, until she was lingering on the edge of death.

When Uncle Jacob speaks, the imagery of the poem becomes Christlike:

> *And he told me of the Savior,*
> *And the fountain in His side.*

It should also be noted that "master" when used to reference the slave-holder, is not capitalized, unlike when referencing Jesus, *the blessed Master's feet.* After Chloe prays, the biblical reference to the stone being rolled from Jesus' tomb is used to symbolize the uplifting of her spirit and the salvation of her soul:

> *And I felt my heavy burden*
> *Rolling like a stone away.*

Resurrected, her new consciousness elevates her to a higher cosmic plane, one of spiritual enlightenment.

Chloe's rebirth demonstrates how spirituality contributed to the survival of the slave. Religion was a source of replenishment, relieving the agony of suffering through transcendence, but not through resignation to maltreatment. Chloe is sustained by the God of justice during her plight, but her understanding of that does not preclude justice on earth. The biblical and folk references reflected in names and in the dialogue are culturally characteristic and enhance the folk diction.

"The Deliverance," the second part of "Sketches", carries Chloe's narrative through the Civil War, the abolition of slavery, the death of Lincoln, the retrenchment of Reconstruction, and the enactment of the Fifteenth Amendment. It is the longest section in the poem. Chloe discusses several historical events intertwined with personal experiences and

157

political convictions. But Chloe's portrayal of plantation life is not particularly gruesome. In fact, the new master, Mister Thomas, is described as *kind at heart,* with a judicious disposition. The contrast between the cruel master and the benevolent slaveholder suggests that the "kind" master profited because his slaves were more cooperative.

> *He kept right on that very way*
> *Till he got big and tall,*
> *And ole Mistus used to chide him,*
> *And say he'd spile us all.*

> *But somehow the farm did prosper*
> *When he took things in hand;*
> *And though all the servants liked him,*
> *He made them understand.*

The ambiguity of the slave/master relationship, as Harper portrays it here, avoids a simplistic, didactic reduction of "white" as completely bad and "black" as completely helpless. With regards to the consistency of diction, words like *spile* and *mistus* as opposed to "spoil" and "mistress" contribute to the presence of dialect and to the subtle underplay of oblique rhyme, as in the case of *chide* and *spile.* Likewise, the dynamic imagery inherent in the dialect contributes to the imaginative expressions.

The war intervenes and Mister Thomas, no matter how kind at heart, is still a Confederate advocate. He explains to his mother, who

> *looked on Mister Thomas*
> *With a face as pale as death,*

that he wished he had been at the battle at Fort Sumter. Now, the *mistus* must contend with the same pain imposed on the slave mother.

> *"I was thinking, dearest Thomas,*
> *'Twould break my very heart*
> *If a fierce and dreadful battle*
> *Should tear our lives apart."*

Aunt Chloe expresses sympathy for old Mistus as she relays Mister Thomas's departure, but the encroaching agony of this mother and son, is intuitively scrutinized:

> *But somehow I couldn't help thinking*
>   *His fighting must be wrong.*

and that,

> *For I felt somehow or other*
>   *We was mixed up in that fight.*

Chloe recognizes the pendulum of reciprocity:

> *How old Mistres feels the sting,*
> *For this parting with your children*
>   *Is a mighty dreadful thing.*

Uncle Jacob tells Chloe that slavery is doomed, and that the war will be the slave's retribution. Like his biblical antecedent, Jacob symbolizes persistence and endurance. While Mistress *prayed up in the parlor,* the slaves

> *were praying in the cabins,*
> *Wanting freedom to begin,*

and when the Yankee troops arrived,

> *the word ran through the village*
>   *The colored folks are free—*
> *In the kitchens and the cabins*
>   *We held a jubilee.*

The dramatic tension of these stanzas is constructed by a progressive upbeat that moves toward the climax of the last lines, and the last word, *jubilee.*

> *And he often used to tell us,*
>   *"Children, don't forget to pray;*
> *For the darkest time of morning*
>   *Is just 'fore the break of day."*

> *Well, one morning bright and early*
>   *We heard the fife and drum,*

And the booming of the cannon—
  The Yankee troops had come.

When the word ran through the village,
  The colored folks are free—
In the kitchens and the cabins
  We held a jubilee.

The high spirit of the jubilee sequence is eclipsed by the death of President Lincoln, and the dismal failure of his successor, Andrew Johnson, who they hoped would be *the Moses / Of all the colored race.* Again the Mosaic motif surfaces in Harper's script. But Johnson fails to acquiesce to the biblical allusion while the Rebels resist black, postwar independence.

The elliptical curve of Afroamerican language is characteristic of Chloe's narrative. She rarely speaks directly to describe or to delineate the literal, but rather she alludes to effects and ramifications. Concerning Johnson's alleged attempt to address Rebel tyranny, Chloe says:

Cause I heard 'em talking 'bout a circle
  That he was swinging round.

But subsequently, Johnson loses the election, and Chloe elicits a common Afroamerican expression (that is still vividly active in contemporary speech) to reference Johnson's electoral defeat: *They let poor Andy slide.*

Chloe praises President Grant

  for breaking up
The wicked Ku-Klux Klan.

and the narrative proceeds with a series of critical observations about suffrage and the black vote. She explains that selling one's vote is a treacherous act, and relates three examples of men selling out. She also includes the political attitudes and actions of the women, responding to such selfish irresponsibility. Notwithstanding, Harper's position on the Fifteenth Amendment renders some disappointment with the irresponsible voting practices of some black men.

When John Thomas Reeder sold his vote to buy some flour and meat, his wife, Aunt Kitty, threw them away and scolded him for being so cheap, and likewise *voting for the wrong side*. David Rand's treachery was highlighted by his stupidity, when he sold his vote for sugar that turned out to be sand. The superficial level of white sugar is associated with Rands' shallow intelligence. In both instances, the vote is considered priceless by the wives; both of these images reemerge in *Iola Leroy*.

Lucinda Grange harassed her husband, Joe, when she discovered he had sold his vote, and told him to either take the *rations* back or if he voted wrong, *To take his rags and go*. Such volatile reactions on the part of the women are intensified in the ensuing stanza, whereby the election is crucial to the defeat of the rebel candidate and the possibilities for the radical party. The inclusion of the pronoun "we" is collective and inclusive as the political perspective of the poet and the community.

> *I think that Curnel Johnson said*
> *His side had won the day,*
> *Had not we women radicals*
> *Just got right in the way.*

In contrast to the travesties of Reeder, Rand, and Grange, John Slade is exemplified as a man of integrity,

> *And we've got lots of other men*
> *Who rally round the cause.*

Chloe concludes the section of the story on an encouraging note for the transcendent black man:

> *And yet I would not have you think*
> *That all our men are shabby;*
> *But 'tis said in every flock of sheep*
> *There will be one that's scabby.*
>
> *I've heard, before election came*
> *They tried to buy John Slade;*
> *But he gave them all to understand*
> *That he wasn't in that trade.*
>
> *And we've got lots of other men*
> *Who rally round the cause,*
> *And go for holding up the hands*
> *That gave us equal laws.*

Who know their freedom cost too much
 Of blood and pain and treasure,
For them to fool away their votes
 For profit or for pleasure.

"Aunt Chloe's Politics" is the third part of the poem and is the short-est—only five stanzas. Speaking metaphorically, Chloe's expressions sustain the aural consistency of the poem. She cuts critically into the diabolical motives of politicians with sardonic similes, the latter of which can be found in Shakespeare:

I've seen 'em honey-fugle round,
 And talk so awful sweet,
That you'd think them full of kindness,
 As an egg is full of meat

Her political concern is for the future, in particular, *we want to school our children.* This active concern and sacrifice on the part of the freedwomen was observed and reported by Harper in her letters and essays. Likewise, Chloe's politics do not accept or exempt responsibility according to color. She states matter-of-factly that:

When we want to school our children
 If money isn't there,
Whether black or white have took it,
 The loss we all must share.

And this buying up each other
 Is something worse than mean,
Though I thinks a heap of voting,
 I go for voting clean.

The pragmatic vision of Aunt Chloe, like many freedwomen, coincides with Harper's black feminist perspective. These women do not have the vote but many realize that the value of electoral politics is the power and protection it could give. This sequence of "Sketches" does not include the historical action, but rather intersects thematically with the progressive thrust of Chloe's story.

The sequence, "Church Building" exemplifies the apex of spiritual confirmation and engages the social, political, and religious convergence of Christianity for the Afroamerican community. Uncle Jacob, the

162

religious leader of the community, advises them to build *a meeting place.* This opening stanza indicates the historical experience of the church during slavery, a place where the slaves met under the auspices of spiritual and political communion.

The poor but conscientious community manages to salvage savings from their wages until the church becomes a reality. Uncle Jacob's death is forecasted with greying anticipation, *But his voice rang like a trumpet,* the sound of Gabriel calling him home to heaven. The rolling of the *o*'s inside the internal and terminal rhyme pattern reinforces the musical simile, while the dialect modulates the rhythm. Uncle Jacob's passing into *the promised land,* has a deliberate ring. After the deliverance from slavery the people never crossed the River Jordan, as they were beset by the tyranny of the Ku Klux Klan and unkept promises from the federal government. Uncle Jacob tells them to keep the faith,

> *"Children you meet me*
> *Right in the promised land,*

which unfortunately still resides only in heaven.

> *"For when I'm done a moiling*
> *And toiling here below,*
> *Through the gate into the city*
> *Straightway I hope to go."*

"Learning to Read" addresses the quest for literacy during and after slavery. Slave illiteracy was often enforced through legislation, and for the most part, nineteenth-century Americans as a whole were illiterate. Harper's advocacy of Afroamerican education was an extension of her own specialized preparation by her abolitionist uncle for survival in a hostile society. Harper's strenuous academic training was regarded as a political weapon against the confabulations of the American power brokers advocating racist/sexist legislation, cultivating cultural chauvinism, distorting biblical text, and thereby undermining the possibilities of a participatory democracy.

Chloe conveys the historical connection between slave society and Confederate resistance to Freedman schools even after slavery:

> *Our masters always tried to hide*
> *Book learning from our eyes.*

The popular belief of the slave holding class was that an educated slave was a discontented slave, which was not an especially astute observation since literate slaves were not dependent on plantation propaganda for insight or information. In fact, the impact of David Walker's *Appeal* on Nat Turner encouraged the enactment of antiliteracy legislation. But intellectual isolation did not necessarily obstruct visionary possibilities for escape through the labyrinth of lies that strengthened the mental chains of slavery, as well as the vicissitudes of national politics that veiled the self-determination of the newly freed during Reconstruction.

Aunt Chloe relays the tales of Uncle Caldwell and Ben Turner who pursued reading during slavery despite the threat of punishment. Caldwell

> *took pot liquor fat*
> *And greased the pages of his book*
> *And hid it in his hat.*

This maneuver deluded his overseers who would not suspect that these *greasy papers* were part of a library.

Turner, like Tom in *Iola Leroy*, who one also associates with Nat Turner, had *heard the children spell*, memorized their words, and learned to read through aural association. A point to observe here is how the oral orientation of the culture can become a pedagogical technique for literacy. Sound identification internalized before visual recognition of written transcription, to some extent disrupts dialect interference because tonal distinctions are differentiated before the visual symbol is cognitively processed. "Sketches" is a text that benefits this learning strategy, with the infusion of dialect interrelating with a predominance of standard spelling in folk rhythms.

Chloe also says, *I longed to read my Bible,* but because she is *rising sixty,* most folks say it is too late. But Chloe considers her age as an incentive and does not stop studying until she can read the *hymns and Testament.* After she learns to read, she acquires her own place, thereby connecting literacy to self-sufficiency, as well as to spiritual independence. The feminist attitude about education, work, and autonomy is conveyed in the following image:

> *Then I got a little cabin*
> *A place to call my own—*
> *And I felt as independent*
> *As a queen upon her throne.*

The last section of "Sketches" is "The Reunion." The ending cyclically rounds the long poem into its resolution with the reunion of Chloe and her son Jake. The reunion fulfills Uncle Jacob's prophecy and demonstrates Harper's belief in the cosmic justice. The thematic thrust of the ending invigorates vision, sustained by faith, focused on family. Chloe's son returns asking for *Missis Chloe Fleet*. She recognizes his voice and turns to embrace Jake. Her metaphor for joy is derived from the Twenty-third Psalm, as she exclaims:

> *What gladness filled my cup!*
> *And I laughed, and just rolled over.*

Jake explains how he, like so many other freed slaves, was determined to find his family. Likewise, he reports the circumstances of his brother Ben, Chloe's second son:

> *"Why, mammy, I've been on your hunt*
> *Since ever I've been free,*
> *And I have heard from brother Ben,—*
> *He's down in Tennessee.*
>
> *"He wrote me that he had a wife,"*
> *"And children?" "Yes, he's three."*
> *"You married, too?" "Oh no, indeed,*
> *I thought I'd first get free."*

The intense dialogue between mother and son in the preceding stanzas contains tight, lyrical control through brevity, drama, and dense imagery. In only two stanzas we come to understand how, where, and why Chloe's family is alive and prospering. The following lines contrast her good fortune with the demise of the *"Mistus"* and the death of *"Mister Thomas."*

> *I'm richer now then Mistus*
> *Because I have got my son;*
> *And Mister Thomas he is dead,*
> *And she's got nary one.*

Chloe culminates the denouement with a suggestion to *write to brother Benny* and to tell him *he must come this fall*. She declares they will make her cabin big enough to *hold us all*. The poem ends with a final request to collect her entire family before she dies, thus the encircling of the children, a necessary ritual before the passage through death into heaven. Chloe compares her spirit to Simeon, who helped Jesus bear the burden of the cross on the road to Mount Calvary. But she must reunite with her offspring before she can pass into peace.

> *Tell him I want to see 'em all*
> *Before my life do cease.*
> *And then, like good old Simeon,*
> *I hope to die in peace.*

Conclusion

"Sketches of Southern Life" is one of the first works of American literature that appreciates the dynamics of Afroamerican folk language and culture. More than any other Harper poem, "Sketches" embodies the source and force of slave resistance. Harper's class sensitivity, which was an outgrowth of her own experiences with economic uncertainty and social strife, and her expansive perspective, which was the consequence of her ongoing interactions with grass roots activists and radical political activity, developed the creative insight necessary to write a poem reflective of the strength and beauty of the people she served and the complexity and dynamics of the history they prevailed.

The Woman's Era

CHAPTER 6

Iola Leroy, or Shadows Uplifted: A Novel by a Black Nazarene

"And is there," continued Iola, "a path which we have trodden in this country, unless it be the path of sin, into which Jesus Christ has not put His feet and left it luminous with the light of His steps? Has the negro been poor and homeless? The birds of the air had nests and the foxes had holes, but the Son of man had not where to lay his head. Has our name been a synonym for contempt? 'He shall be called a Nazarene.' Have we been despised and trodden under foot? Christ was despised and rejected of men. Have we been ignorant and unlearned? It was said of Jesus Christ, 'How knoweth this man letters, never having learned?' Have we been beaten and bruised in the prison-house of bondage? 'They took Jesus and scourged Him.' Have we been slaughtered, our bones scattered at the graves' mouth? He was spit upon by the mob, smitten and mocked by the rabble, and died as died Rome's meanest criminal slave. To-day that cross of shame is a throne of power. Those robes of scorn have changed to habiliments of light, and that crown of mockery to a diadem of glory. And never, while the agony of Gethsemane and the suffering of Calvary have their hold upon my heart, will I recognize any religion as His which despises the least of His brethren."[1]

In this key scene in *Iola Leroy*, the protagonist converges with the spirit of Christ to personify and to politicize religious characterization:

"The tones of her voice are like benedictions of peace; her words a call to a higher service and a nobler life" (p. 257).

Harper's Christ is the light and the way. He is not impaled on a cross or trapped in a trinity, but is humanly attainable because His essence is a realizable spirit. Because the plight of Afroamericans reflected the persecution of Christ, Harper believed His path was their spiritual destiny. In the aftermath of the war of deliverance, Harper's mission was to convince the newly liberated that they must construct a nation with a spiritual foundation. As a black woman Nazarene, Frances Harper gave a calling to this higher mission through this novel.

Harper's first piece of fiction, "The Two Offers," appeared in 1859 in the *Anglo-African Magazine* the same year Harriet Wilson published the first novel by a black American woman, *Our Nig*. Considered the first published short story by a black American woman, "The Two Offers" challenges women's repressed role in marriage and offers an alternative viewpoint on progressive lifestyles. In "The Mission of the Flowers" (1869), Harper crafts a thematic appeal for a holistic, female self and the need for tolerance and acceptance of difference. The garden comprises a range of characterizations that color the intonations of women's character and community. Harper inverts the metaphor of woman as rose through a flower fable that engages sexual seduction as a force that can negatively transform consciousness and repress individual will.

"Fancy Etchings" (1873–74) deals directly and explicitly with the challenges of sexism in the black community. Unlike "The Two Offers," which does not distinguish race as a consideration in the women's lives, "Fancy Etchings" very specifically relates sexism to the prejudices of black men. "Shalmanezer, Prince of Cosman," in the 1891 edition of *Sketches of Southern Life*, on the other hand, has a more religious context. This short story is concerned with the pitfalls of man's materialism. The Christian moral of the story promotes peace as a higher ideal, as the plot exposes the destructive illusions offered by the abstract characters Desire, Pleasure, Wealth, and Fame. The story especially promotes class consciousness and spiritual redemption.

These pieces evidence Harper's early interest in short prose. Her long poems, *Moses: A Story of the Nile* and *Sketches of Southern Life*, which are also composed of parts, demonstrate Harper's capacity to sustain longer literary works. Likewise, the serialized novels, *Minnie's Sacrifice, Sowing and Reaping: A Temperance Story*, and *Trial and Triumph*, demonstrate Harper's prolific capacity and expansion. The novel, *Iola Leroy, or Shadows Uplifted*, is Harper's last major literary work.

In the introduction to the novel, William Still proclaims: "The previous books from her pen, which have been so widely circulated and admired, North and South—"Forest Leaves," Miscellaneous Poems," "Moses: A Story of the Nile," "Poems," and "Sketches of Southern Life"— these, I predict, will be eclipsed by this last effort, which will, in all probability, be the crowning effort of her long and valuable services in the cause of humanity."[2]

The novel has not necessarily "eclipsed" Harper's poetry, and it most certainly has benefited from its poetic forerunners. The novel borrows heavily from imagery and voices inscribed in Harper's poetry, lyrics, fiction, letters, and essays. The characters manifest historical accounts portrayed in the long poem, "Sketches of Southern Life," and they aspire for the political ideals argued in "Our Greatest Want." The novel contextualizes the ideological appeal of her essays and speeches. It also enhances the descriptions and reflections contained in correspondence between Harper and Still. Even more so, there is a strong kinship between *Minnie's Sacrifice* and *Iola Leroy*.

Minnie's Sacrifice is clearly a precursor of *Iola Leroy*. In many ways the two works complement each other. *Minnie's Sacrifice* focuses on the Reconstruction era in the South even though the early chapters begin during the Civil War in Philadelphia and carry the characters south. *Iola Leroy* begins during the Civil War in the South and the characters migrate north. The ending of *Iola Leroy* returns the characters to the South to build a future but that future is not a part of the enacted plot. In this regard, *Minnie's Sacrifice* is based in the contemporary history of 1869, and is parallel to the setting of *Iola Leroy* which reflects on the past in hopes for the future.

In both novels the major characters are black people who look "white" and have been raised with that self-perception. These characters acquiesce to their identity as black people and commit to the struggle against racial injustice. As Harper states in the conclusion of *Minnie's Sacrifice*:

> *While some of the authors of the present day have been weaving their stories about white men marrying beautiful quadroon girls, who, in so doing were lost to us socially, I conceived of one of that same class to whom I gave a higher, holier destiny; a life of lofty self-sacrifice and beautiful self-consecration, finished a post of duty, and rounded off with the fiery crown of martyrdom, a circlet which ever changes into a diadem of glory.*

Minnie's Sacrifice and *Iola Leroy* demonstrate Harper's activist aesthetic and her focus on racial identity as a key thematic challenge to political injustice and oppression. While her characters must struggle with the ambiguity of their identities the resolution to the dilemma lies in political involvement to alter the socio-economic structure that advocates and benefits from such confusion and class divisions. Harper's characters are designed to embody the dichotomy of race and gender, but unlike the tragic mulattos of nineteenth-century literature, her characters transcend these cultural contradictions by adhering to a higher calling in the liberation movements. Without this political insight her characters would have to resign themselves to the popular fiction of law and custom, which valued caste and gender as class positions determined relative to the power of white supremacy. Hence, Harper's literary thesis is an anti-thesis confronting literary and social tradition:

> *The lesson of Minnie's sacrifice is this, that it is braver to suffer with one's own branch of the human race,—to feel, that the weaker and the more despised they are, the closer we will cling to them, for the sake of helping them, than to attempt to creep out of all identity with them in their feebleness, for the sake of mere personal advantages, and to do this at the expense of self-respect, and a true manhood, and a truly dignified womanhood, that with whatever gifts we possess, whether they be genius, culture, wealth or social position, we can best serve the interests of our race by a generous and loving diffusion, than by a narrow and selfish isolation which, after all, is only one type of the barbarous and antisocial state.*

The political themes Harper pursues in *Iola Leroy* are consistent with those presented in *Minnie's Sacrifice*. But in the later novel, Harper more readily engages the perspectives and the resistance of the enslaved during the Civil War. Whereas in *Minnie's Sacrifice*, the slaves are often unnamed references in related events, character development of the slaves in *Iola Leroy* is more detailed. This attention to personality and political resistance in the 1892 novel is a reminder for an apathetic and frightened audience that may be confused by the conservative leadership of men like Booker T. Washington. These novels provide a connection between the past horrors of slavery and the present terror of lynching.

The radical history Harper preserves in both novels is a time continuum essential to a liberated vision in the future. In both instances, the works are written for the black reading audience and she attaches a final comment, a calling to uphold the radical Christian tradition of resistance and self-defense as political action and spiritual upliftment.

In form, this novel is considerably dependent upon the interplay of dialogue to advance its thematic complexity, which is typical of nineteenth-century prose. At the same time, the work further demonstrates Harper's talent for capturing and contextualizing voice. A range of perspectives are employed to avoid a monolithic view of the slave experience. *Iola Leroy* combines the politicized slave narrative (as in the case of Linda Brent's *Incidents in the Life of a Slave Girl*) with the episodic romanticism of the Victorian utopian novel to produce a unique prose form.

Oftentimes, Harper intersperses descriptions of the historical settings with didactic political commentary, which disrupts the creative flow of the plot. This technique is typical of proletarian editors and writers, as evidenced in Harper's poetry and prose as well as in Brent's slave narrative. The interjection of narrative commentary diffuses any extended idealizing of the protagonist, thereby indicating an explicit distrust of the audience to associate the fiction with reality. As this novel marks the climax of Harper's literary career, it is compacted by the beliefs and activisms that have driven the author's life.

But this remark is not intended to discount the literary or ideological value of the novel. The novel accomplishes an honesty that many writers never achieve. Indeed, Harper rebelled against Victorian pretentiousness. As the novel unravels the confabulations of social fiction it also unveils the illusions of literary tradition while inventing an alternative aesthetic for a society that has unknowingly perpetuated its own psychological enslavement to bourgeois myopia.

The novel's purpose is multifaceted, and the unevenness of the author's stylistic techniques accomplishes her objectives. In particular, her unprecedented dexterity with dialect patterns extends the literary experience of the slave narrative into an active voice in another genre. Arranged in dramatic settings, the narratives comprise an interactive dialogue. These settings reflect the inhumanity of chattel slavery, but at the same time reveal the range of and the degrees of its severity. They also provide the communal survival network of the slaves and their indisputable desire for freedom, as the slave narratives are delivered in both standard English and dialect. But more important, in all instances the characters display intelligence and spirit, thereby refuting prevailing myths of racial inferiority. Throughout the novel, individually and collectively, the black characters confront, engage, and dispel illusions in order to free their minds.

The plot of the novel evolves cyclically around Iola Leroy, the feminist protagonist, and the emancipation of American slaves. At the same time, the Moses motif underpins the thematic framework of the novel. In addition to the main characters, who exemplify the Mosaic ethics of sacrifice and leadership, the novel can be conceptually divided into "Deliverance" and the "Quest for the Promised Land." The novel opens during the Civil War with flashback chapters expanding the character development and the historical insight of the audience. As the novel progresses into the Reconstruction era (which hindsight can otherwise identify as the deconstruction dilemma) the perceptual view of the audience requires a dialectical understanding of the problems which the newly liberated must confront and contend.

The novel bridges the antislavery era and the Reconstruction era as well as the social and political issues and events of the 1890s. In the novel, education, temperance, women's rights, political resistance, and spiritual faith are proposed as the critical elements in the formation of a new vision to build the promised land. There is a direct call for the newly liberated to create their own promised land and for others to assist them in this endeavor. Obviously, Harper's novel is a major effort to convince her audience that America will continue to be an unrealized democracy as long as it inflicts injustice and disenfranchises its women and darker citizens.

Deliverance

The slaves who had lived in the shadow of slavery are revealed in the novel as participants in the struggle for liberation. The novel identifies the subversive network of slave intelligence aiding the military efforts of the Union army. In addition to the "colored" troops fighting in battle, some enslaved are spies. Despite their restricted mobility, they convey messages to Yankee troops. They also use their intuitive sense to determine a general sense of the war winds. Linda, an illiterate house servant, reads the face of her mistress like an open book:

> *"Ef her face is long an' she walks kine a' droopy den I think things is gwine wrong for dem. But ef she comes out yere looking mighty pleased, an' larffin all ober her face, an' steppin' so frisky, den I knows de Secesh is gittin' de bes' ob de Yankees"* (pp. 9–10).

Introduced as a person with clairvoyant insight, Linda foretells the future:

> *"Mark my words, Bobby, we's all gwine to git free. I seed it all in a vision, as plain as de nose on yer face"* (p. 14).

Harper's introduction of Robert Johnson contains a commentary on the character's benevolent slave mistress and the ambiguity of their peculiar relationship. Though

> *reared by his mistress as a favorite slave. She had fondled him as a pet animal, and even taught him to read. Notwithstanding their relation as mistress and slave, they had strong personal likings for each other* (p. 7).

174

Since Robert can read, he is a vital source of knowledge for the slave community, who often communicate through coded conversation.

The same repression that enforces a need to encode language, forces the slaves to meet in secret. These prayer meetings are planned for political as well as spiritual purposes. At these prayer meetings, the slaves combine their information and perception to decipher their circumstances. The black dialect spoken by most of the characters is monitored and balanced by the standard English spoken by Robert. Likewise, Robert's literacy supplies the community with unfamiliar terms and dispels Confederate propaganda. Robert facilitates the reader in much the same way he facilitates the other slaves. He provides details that clarify and broaden perspective.

The setting of the prayer meeting provides the context for the inclusion of slave narratives. These conversations exemplify not only the conditions of the slaves, but also the spirit of the culture, which counters the stereotypes of the "sloven slave" and "loyal servant." Tom Anderson reports that his master supposes that the slaves will support the South in battle because they are incapable and unwilling to take care of themselves—a popular proslavery argument. Several of them protest.

> *"Only let 'em try it," chorused a half dozen voices, "An dey'll soon see who'll git de bes' ob de guns; an' as to taking keer ob ourselves, I specs we kin take keer ob ourselves as well as we take keer ob dem"* (p. 16.)

Tom calls the first line of the folk song, "We Raise de Wheat" and the others respond in refrain:

> *"They eat the meat and give use the bones,*
> *Eat the cherries and give us the stones."*

The call-and-response pattern reflects community resentment and by content and function, the folk poem preserves a class consciousness. Robert explains that despite his relatively congenial enslavement, he will never forget that his mistress sold his mother away from the plantation, and even

> *"if she were the best woman on earth I would rather have my freedom than belong to her"* (p. 18).

Though Robert distinguishes the individual differences among slaveholders, he does not consider benevolent entrapment a desirable alternative to true freedom.

The complex dynamics that characterize the master/slave relationship are reflected in a sympathetic light by Uncle Daniel. He is one of the older slaves, and he explains that he cannot follow their plans to join the Union army because of his age and his peculiar duty to young master Robert. His decision is critical to the integrity of his word. Daniel contrasts the tyranny of master Robert's father—who terrorized the plantation until his death—with the kindness of his wife and son.

> *"When he died, Miss Anna used to keep me 'bout her jes' like I war her shadder. I used to nuss Marse Robert jes' de same as ef I were his own fadder"* (pp. 20–21).

The bonding of Uncle Daniel to this family is metaphorically described as a shadow. The presence and purpose of his dark existence were in the light of his master and mistress's needs. His proximity to them rendered a peculiar, but understandable, loyalty. The shadow simile reflects the novel's subtitle, as the end of slavery would terminate such social staging.

Before Miss Anna dies, she appeals to Uncle Daniel to look after Master Robert.

> *"In a while she war gone—jis' faded away like a flower. I belieb ef dere's a saint in glory, Miss Anna's dere"* (p. 21).

But at the next meeting, Tom Anderson challenges Uncle Daniel's logic for maintaining his loyalty and scoffs at Master Robert's promise to free Uncle Daniel when he returns. Uncle Daniel explains why he believes his master will keep the promise of freedom—because Master Robert had rescued Daniel's wife from the Gundover plantation. This act gained Uncle Daniel's allegiance.

In contrast, Tom Anderson does not share Uncle Daniel's dedication or his religious faith.

> *"I think wen some of dem preachers brings de Bible 'round an tells us 'bout mindin' our marsters and not stealen' dere things, dat dey preach to please the white folks an dey frows coldness ober de meetin"* (pp. 21–22).

Tom compares the "bible preachers" with the Guinean man who refuses to be broken.

> *"Old Marse was trying to break him in, but dat fellow war spunk to de backbone, an' when he 'gin talkin' to him 'bout savin' his soul and gittin' to hebbin, he tole him ef he went to hebbin an' foun' he war dare, he wouldn't go in"* (p. 22).

The Guinean man, Potombra, begs for his freedom papers on his death bed. He believes his spirit would return to Africa.

> *"He thought if he did, his people would look down on him, an' he wanted to go back to Africa a free man"* (p. 23).

Like "The Dying Bondman" in Harper's poem, Potombra embraces his freedom papers and speaks the spiritual refrain, *"I'se free at las'."* Potombra's story acknowledges an African heritage and a persistent resistance in the slave community. Tom explains, *"I specs his was war some ole Guinea king."*

Ben Tunnel also decides against escaping to the Yankee camp because his mother is not strong enough to make the journey. Known for his brave defiance of the overseer's brutality, he denies his own chance for freedom in order to protect and support his mother.

> *"So while I love freedom more than a child loves its mother's milk, I've made up my mind to stay on the plantation"* (p. 31).

The reference to *mother's milk* is an ironic metaphor that aptly describes Ben's dilemma and reinforces Harper's thematic emphasis on the family. Though Ben does not trust the words of "white folks" like Uncle Daniel, he does share a strong sense of responsibility.

The narratives present the complexities and ambiguities of the known slave experiences. By providing the thoughts and motivations of those characters, Harper supplies insight to displace stereotypes. Southern mythology and social fiction romanticized and simplified the slave whereby northern prejudice against abolition was readily pacified. Harper's portrayals of the enslaved contradict popular opinion, manifesting vital, thriving voices of resistance. At the same time, Harper does not romanticize the slaves to benefit a counterargument. She reveals adverse effects of slavery, such as rumors the slaves have heard, for instance, that Yankees have tails and will poison them. The ignorance that slavery perpetuated is second only to the injustice it imposed. Robert's literacy enlightens their blind isolation as he dispels distortions which are intended to inflict fear and to enslave minds.

Blood and Skin Don't Think

American society defines the black race by maternal linkage to slavery. Conversely, this definition accommodated the economic interest of slaveholders and was culturally reinforced through religious dogma and social segregation. Therefore, the majority of Americans absorbed and contributed to the concept of Caucasian supremacy. Of course, more adequate refutations of racial theories have been demonstrated recently by enlightened anthropologists, but it is a subject that has concerned Afroamerican writers since Phillis Wheatley.

Frances Harper's novel is especially concerned with the "myth of blood and race," and contributes much of the text to argue against the absurdity of this social fiction. The mulatto represents the irony of this genetic reductionism of the human race, and Harper uses the ambiguity of physical presence and cultural experience to refute this racist premise. In particular, the rape of the black slave woman by white male privilege evidences the moral inferiority of the "superior" race. Consequently, the slave family became matrifocal as the father was oftentimes a white, hostile, external force.

Robert Johnson does not mention his father, but he has not forgotten his mother and has not forgiven his mistress for selling her. As the first Moses figure in the novel, Robert shuns the advantages of remaining a favored slave and leads the escape to the Union army. He becomes a commander of the colored troops, which further extends his Moses role in the deliverance. Because he is white-skinned and has inherited the physical features of his Anglo ancestors, he could easily pass for white. When a Yankee officer asks him why he doesn't transfer to the white regiment, Robert replies:

> "Well, Captain, when a man's been colored all his life it comes a little hard for him to get white all at once. Were I to try it, I would feel like a cat in a strange garret" (p. 43).

The captain feels that Robert should not have been a slave because of his white-likeness. But Robert reproaches the captain's selective anti-slavery position:

"I don't think it was any worse to have held me in slavery than the blackest man in the South" (p. 44).

Robert uses Tom Anderson's example to identify a man of solid character and resilient spirit. Like Uncle Caldwell in "Sketches of Southern Life," Tom secreted greased papers inside his hat to trick his master.

"Then if his master had ever knocked his hat off he would have thought them greasy papers, and not that Tom was carrying his library on his head"

Likewise, Robert identifies the ingenuity of another slave who had learned the alphabet by ear, and then carved the letters inside the bark of a tree and wrote words in the sand.

Robert's refusal to pass for white is also a resistance to the hypocrisy racism perpetuates. He places his faith in the religion of Aunt Kizzy, who, like Aunt Chloe in "Sketches," found religion at *the foot of the cross* when her children were sold away from her. From such suffering, the spirituals were birthed and souls were reborn.

"Let not your heart be troubled, ye believe in God, believe also in Me" (p. 48).

Though Robert explains in standard English, he testifies for Aunt Kizzy in black English, which demonstrates his dual dialect and the cultural origin of his religion:

" *'Troubles over, troubles over, and den my troubles will be over. We'll walk de golden streets all 'roun' in de New Jerusalem.' Now, Captain, that's the kind of religion that I want. Not that kind which could ride to church on Sundays, and talk so solemn with the minister about heaven and good things, then come home and light down on the servants like a thousand bricks"* (p. 48).

The captain agrees with Robert and reveals that his mother is a Quaker preacher. His racial perceptions reflect a liberal attitude about color and caste. The captain's pledge to fight in the war was expressively to *free the slaves* despite his mother's conscientious objection to war. His political openness is a feature of Quaker culture. Noted for their active support of the Underground Railroad, Quakers were the first religious sect to condemn slavery. In fact, William Watkins received support from the Quakers for his church activities, and Frances Harper was engaged by the Quakers as an abolitionist lecturer. She features them prominently in *Minnie's Sacrifice*.

Iola Leroy enters the novel during the escape of the Yankee troops. Tom Anderson desires to rescue her from the Gundover plantation, but she is too closely guarded. The Union commander arranges her release, and she becomes a nurse in the field hospital. Tom lauds her fiery spirit and her physical beauty.

> *"Why, dey say she was sole seben times in six weeks, 'cause she's so putty, but dat she war game to de las'"* (p. 42).

Here, the sexual plight of the "attractive" slave woman is revealed, as her market value is equated with her physical sexuality.

Iola's unusual and tragic experiences are designed to accentuate the absurdity of American racial beliefs. Ignorant of her ancestral connection to blacks, she was raised with the comfort and advantages afforded to her by her wealthy white father. Her "black awareness" was the consequence of a rude awakening after the death of her father whereupon she is disinherited by a cousin and sold into slavery. Thus, for the early years of her life she is white, but like in a Dickens tale, she is unjustly removed from her social status and enters into a lower-class experience. Her enslavement alters her class and caste perspective and radically changes her point of view.

Her "negro" identity is concealed from her because her father wished to shelter her from the shame and pain of association with a "cursed" race. Eugene Leroy is convinced that knowledge of their total identity would distort the children's self concept.

> *"The strongest men and women of a down-trodden race may have their bosoms to an adverse fate and develop courage in the midst of opposition, but we have no right to subject our children to such crucial tests before their characters are formed"* (p. 84).

He identifies famous men of African descent, including Ira Aldridge, Alexander Dumas, Alexander Sergevitch, as well as Harper's comrade, Frederick Douglass, to confirm his faith in the intelligence of the race.

But this silence, which is intended to protect them while they grow, actually serves to subvert their consciousness. In an argument with her fellow classmates, Iola defends the institution of slavery and unknowingly condones her tragic fate. Iola ignores the evidence offered to the contrary, when her classmate references the slave mother who crossed the frozen Ohio River and then killed one of her children rather than see it be reenslaved as recorded in Harper's poem "The Slave Mother: A Tale of Ohio". The student bolsters her argument with the thriving Underground Railroad and resistance to the Fugitive Slave Act as further evidence of the desire for freedom. Ironically, during the course of this argument, Iola is being appraised for the auction block by two slave catchers.

As an example of privileged arrogance, Iola's white frame of mind is incapable of understanding the slave perspective. After she is enslaved and undergoes the humiliation and degradation of a slave woman, she reemerges from the shadows of slavery reborn. The veil of illusion is removed, and Iola succumbs to a higher calling, and a transcendent vision.

Iola's physical ambiguity provides a pivotal point for perceptual and societal contradictions. When she is perceived as a white woman, her beauty is romanticized. For example, when she meets Dr. Gresham, Iola's sad countenance perplexes the doctor, but is understood by Tom Anderson who knew Iola on the Gundover plantation, where her beauty inspired sexual harassment. Gresham is shocked when he learns that the *great sorrow* that *overshadows* her life is slavery; *"It can't be so! A woman as white as she a slave?"* Because he

> *was a member of a wealthy and aristocratic family, proud of its lineage, which it could trace through generations of good blood to its ancestral isle,*

the doctor tries to repress his romantic attraction to Iola;

> *but his constant observation of her only increased his interest and admiration* (p. 58).

The reference to "good blood" is critical to understanding the American inheritance of European class values. In the structuring of the new society, the first families are identified by ancestral lineage, much like the royal families in England. This class distinction by blood intensifies when the element of a different race enters, as this constitutes an even greater taboo. In order to have the love of his passion, Gresham must convince Iola to deny her black identity and to live a white lie, literally and figuratively.

181

Iola's argument is an attack on the illusion of white supremacy, she refuses to join the Anglo-Saxon race and its civilization that continues to

> *"victimize feebler races and minister to a selfish greed of gold and a love of domination."*
> *"But, Iola,"* said Dr. Gresham, a little impatiently, *"What has all this to do with our marriage? Your complexion is as fair as mine"* (p. 116).

When Iola suggests the possibility of a brown offspring, the doctor lowers his head in capitulation. As a Moses figure, Iola refuses the proposal of the privileged, rich doctor, who wishes to shelter her in a traditional marriage, and focuses on her pledge to her dying sister, Grace, *"To stand by Mama."* Grace's death transfigures her into a Christ symbol; and by the grace of God, Iola perseveres until she is reunited with her family.

Flashbacks reflect the details of Iola's tragic history, but they also give insight into class perspectives of slaveholders. Iola's mother, Marie (a mulatto slave) had married her master, Eugene Leroy. This union, though not unprecedented, defied protocol and aristocratic demeanor. Eugene Leroy fell in love with Marie who saved his life, which he had almost lost because of alcoholism and excessive indulgence in sensual pleasures such as in the short story, "Shalmanezer, Prince of Cosman."

Eugene's liberal openness, though tainted and obscured by aristocratic advantage, is polemical to his cousin Alfred Lorraine's conservative rigidity, blinded and maligned by economic insecurity. Their dialogue demonstrates the rationalizations of genetic racism as a fiction of law and custom that preserves a social hierarchy based on race. Alfred's economic instability instigates his racism, which substantiates his subsequent opportunistic actions against Eugene's family. Eugene's marriage to a woman with *negro blood in her veins* infuriates Alfred who expresses the logic of his class and his gender: *"Are you not satisfied with the power and possession the law gives you?"* But Eugene wants Marie's love free.

> *"She is very beautiful,"* [he explains]. *"In the North no one would suspect that she has one drop of negro blood in her veins, but here, where I am known, to marry her is to lose caste"* (p. 66). [And Alfred reminds Eugene] *"one drop of negro blood in her veins curses the rest"* (p. 67).

In order to distinguish the subtleties of social fiction, perceptual variances must be identified. The more liberal view of Eugene, for example, argues that those of mixed blood are barely black, *not much of a negro;* and therefore they are closer to white, as their skin color indicates.

This analysis, though softer in tone than Alfred's one-drop-curses-the-rest theory, is still fundamentally racist because human value is determined in both instances relative to the alleged purity of Caucasians.

Marie's marriage to Eugene delivers her from loneliness. Sold away from her mother early in life, she is the typical slave character from a Frances Harper poem,

who nearly all her life, had been deprived of a parent's love and care (p. 76).

Marie is characterized as Esther, a Hebrew who marries the slaveholding King Ahasuerus of Persia. Before Marie and Eugene marry, he sends her north to school. At the commencement ceremony, Marie gives an anti-slavery speech (Esther 7: 3,4).

Though tightly bound to her husband's love and devotion, Marie does not acquiesce to the posture of plantation mistress. Conscious of her affiliation to a cursed race, Marie's lineage to an enslaved people divorces both her and her husband from "respectable" society. As the marriage ridicules the privileged status of white women,

none of his female friends ever entered his doors, when it became known that Marie held the position of mistress of his mansion and presided at his table (p. 76).

This reaction demonstrates the complicity between oppressed femininity and patriarchal racism.

Like Robert, who clarifies and extends the slave perspectives in the opening chapters, Marie Leroy also performs a similar function in contradiction to the slaveholder's perspective. Likewise, the dialogues between Marie and Eugene extend the debate on racism and sexism within the social context of slavery. Marie indicts the so-called "civilized" white man's indifference to his mulatto offspring.

Eugene offers an exception, whereby a slaveholder had promised his wife he would sell his illegitimate children and their mother to New Orleans to waylay his wife's jealousy and resentment.

"Instead, he was going to Ohio to give them freedom, and make provisions for their future" (p. 77).

Marie exclaims this compensation is a pathetic gesture relative to the grave injustice, which negatively impacted upon all persons involved:

183

"Your friend wronged himself by sinning against his own soul. He wronged his wife by arousing her hatred and jealousy through his unfaithfulness. He wronged those children by giving them the status of slaves and outcasts. He wronged their mother by imposing upon her the burdens and cares of maternity without the rights and privileges of a wife. He made her crown of motherhood a circlet of shame" (p. 77).

Marie's radical perspective raises the discussion to a level that goes to the root of the problem. The slaveholder, the progenitor of mulattoes and the executor of economics, is ultimately responsible for the social ills that proliferate.

"Slavery is a sword that cuts both ways. If it wrongs the negro, it also curses the white man," [Eugene observes]. *"But we are in it, and what can we do?'"* [Marie states simply:] *"Get out of it as quickly as possible"* (p. 79).

Unfortunately Eugene does not act as swiftly as his wife warns him he should, and his sudden death from yellow fever circumvents his family's fate. Alfred has the marriage annulled, seizes the estate, and relegates Marie and her two daughters to the status of slaves. Only her son, Harry, remains free in New England.

The compounded dilemma of racism, sexism, and classism within the context of southern society during slavery is presented in the first half of the novel from both black and white points of view. The range of opinions and social experiences relative to the prevailing rule of legal and social fiction of black inferiority and white supremacy demonstrate the dialectics of human interaction as well as illuminate the realities lurking behind the illusions. Since the arguments of the aristocracy are heard after the opinions of the oppressed class, the audience is more sympathetic to moral considerations than to economic interests.

The Deconstruction of the Reconstruction

The Reconstruction era constitutes the setting for the second half of the novel. In order for the delivered to reach the promised land, the veil must be further uplifted, and Harper proposes education and religion as the key features of enlightenment. But the adverse reactions of lynching, Ku Klux Klan terrorism, corruption in politics and the church, as well as alcoholism, undermine the vision of the future. Iola engages the Moses characterization as a teacher in a freedmen's school. As the significance of literacy was introduced through the intelligence of Robert Johnson, and through the persistence of Tom Anderson and Uncle Caldwell to learn to read during slavery, education underlines the author's belief in self-determination.

> *"Iola had found a school-room in the basement of a colored church, where the doors were willingly opened to her. Her pupils came from miles around, ready and anxious to get some 'book larnin'.' Some of the old folks were eager to learn, and it was touching to see the eyes which had grown dim under the shadows of slavery, donning spectacles and trying to make out the words"* (pp. 146).

The school is in the basement of the church because faith must not be blind, but sustained by insight. The symbolic reference to the dim vision *under the shadows of slavery* is a double entendre, as the "spectacles" correct the physical and intellectual impairment of the "old folks." But the joy of accomplishment is met with the vindictive rage of the Ku Klux Klan, who set fire to the church. But Iola is inspired by the resiliency of the people, replenishing their faith by singing a spiritual:

> *"Oh, do not be discouraged*
> *For Jesus is your friend."*

While the Reconstruction era focuses on building a future, much of this future depends upon the rebuilding of the family. Likewise, as the spirituals supply collective inspiration, they also encode memory. When Robert Johnson hears Iola singing a favorite Methodist hymn of her mother's, they suspect they are related. After the war, they encounter each other on a train headed for the old plantations in South Carolina, and during this meeting their suspicion is confirmed by the red birthmark above Robert's temple, a true "blood" sign. On discovering that Robert is her uncle, Iola joins him to find the rest of the family.

In the land of their old home, the tables have turned, the imagery is reversed. Robert's old mistress is *weighted down* by hard times and Iola's old master is dead and gone. Robert returns to where they *held their last prayer-meeting*. The liberated slaves now own the Gundover plantation, and a *school-house had taken the place of the slave pen and auction-block*. At the same time Aunt Linda's sound common sense and crafty meta-phors cut to the bone of their problems since freedom. She identifies alcoholism as a major issue, and the treachery of the carpetbaggers, who she believes are the same *white men who were northern slave catchers.*

> *"Dem Yankees set me free, an' I thinks a powerful heap ob dem. But it does rile me ter see dese mean white men comin' down yere an' settin' up dere grog-shops, tryin' to fedder dere nests sellin' licker to pore culled people. Deys de bery kine ob men dat used ter keep dorgs to ketch runaways. I'd be chokin' fer a drink 'fore I'd eber spen' a cent wid dem, a spreadin' dere traps to git de black folks' money. You jis' go down town 'fore sun up to-morrer mornin' an' you see ef dey don't hab dem bars open to sell dere drams to dem hard workin' culled people 'fore dey goes ter work. I thinks some niggers is mighty big fools"* (pp. 159–60).

Robert tries to get Aunt Linda not to cut her tongue so sharply, *"Oh, Aunt Linda, don't run down your race. Leave that for the white people."* But Aunt Linda's cold clarity is the basis of her radical perspective.

> *"I ain't runnin' down my people. But a fool's a fool, wether he's white or black. An I think de nigger who will spen' his hard-earned money in dese yere new grog-shops is de biggest kine ob a fool, an' I sticks ter dat. You know we didn't hab all dese low places in slave times. An' what is dey fere, but to get the people's money. An' its a shame how dey do sling de licker 'bout 'lection times"* (p. 160).

Her narrative is infused with imagery from *Sketches of Southern Life,* as Aunt Linda's voice echoes Aunt Chloe. But in the absence of regular rhyme, the more distinct dialect of Aunt Linda affects the inherent poetic beauty of the language. Aunt Linda talks about *ceitful* men trying to rule the women and the community losing its *'ligion* and its self-respect to *grog* and no-good politicians. But at the same time, she praises their accomplishments. And it is the Jews who help the people buy land, possibly another ironic, Mosaic intersection in human history.

Aunt Linda's narrative supplies the freedwoman's perspective. Her criticisms of freedmen are balanced by revelations about the deception of white men. Like the slave narratives in the beginning of the novel, her voice reveals unfair disadvantages imposed on the liberated, while dishonest white men and opportunistic black men exploit the community. She reminisces:

> *"Don't you 'member dem meetins we used to hab in de woods? We don't hab to hide like we did den. But it don't seem as ef de people had de same good 'li-*

gion we had den. 'Pears like folks is took up wid makin' money an' politics"
(p. 162).

Some of the most insightful moments in Aunt Linda's narrative concretely reveal the internal factors that undermined the Reconstruction. Tom Anderson's brother, John, is the height of hypocrisy, and yet, his quest for wealth and political power was achieved because he knew how to manipulate the masses by catering to and profiting from their weaknesses.

"He was down in de lower kentry wen de war war ober. He war mighty smart, an' had a good head-piece, an' a orful glib tongue. He set up store an' sole whisky, an' made a lot ob money. Den he wanted ter go to legislatur. Now what should he do but make out he'd got 'ligion, an' war called to preach. He had no more 'ligion dan my ole dorg. But he had money an' built a meetin' house, whar he could hole meeting, an hab funerals; an' you know cullud folks is mighty great on funerals. Well dat jis' tuck wid de people, an' he got 'lected to de legestatur. Den he got a fine house, an' his ole wife warn't good 'nuff for him. Den dere war a young school-teacher, an' he begun cuttin' his eyes at her. But she war as deep in de mud as he war in de mire, an' he jis' gib up his ole wife and married her, a fusty thing. He war a mean ole hypocrite, an' I wouldn't sen' fer him to bury my cat" (p. 161).

Robert learns that his mother was sold from the plantation because she refused to be whipped by the mistress. In fact, his mother disarmed the mistress and struck the mistress instead. Slave narratives about rebellion were rarely reported. After communing with Uncle Daniel, who was rewarded for his loyalty to his master and given a modest, comfortable home, Robert enjoys some days with his old friends. Robert and Iola join Aunt Linda and travel to the church meeting. When he begins to sing his mother's hymn, she rushes from her seat and begins to testify to her *"trials an' temptations."*

They match stories and plantations to confirm years of separation. The rest of the family is likewise united through the church, which was the focal point for the reunification of families after slavery. Iola's brother, Harry, is discovered by their mother during the war, and afterwards Harry searches for Iola at the Methodist (A.M.E.) conferences throughout the South. Here, Harper emphasizes the church as a holding force for the family. The symbolic use of the hymn as a signal is an extension of that faith, and by that faith that sustains them. Her vision of the promised land constitutes a familial focus.

Racism in the North

Iola, Robert, Marie, and Mrs. Johnson (the grandmother) move to the North where Robert has established himself in the hardware business. Iola attempts to secure work because she believes

> *"that every woman should have some skill or art which would insure her at least a comfortable support. I believe there would be less unhappy marriages if labor were more honored among women"* (p. 210).

This progressive feminist stance is disrupted by northern racism, particularly on the part of white women. When Iola's white women coworkers discover she is black, they express racist outrage. In all but one instance, the employers submit to popular dissent, and Iola loses her job. After repeated encounters with discrimination in the work place, Iola ventilates a reaction that invigorates her identity, but does not resolve the dilemma:

> *"The best blood in my veins is African blood, and I am not ashamed of it"* (p. 108).

Despite attempts to emphasize *Iola Leroy* as a mulatto novel, this particular statement disavows any illusions manifested by critics.

She is finally able to keep a job, when a store owner announces that he has hired

> *"Miss Iola,"* [who has] *"colored blood in her veins,"* [and] *"If any one objected to working with her, he or she could step to the cashier's desk and receive what was due"* (p. 211).

This sequence not only demonstrates the presence of racial prejudice, but also offers a solution to this injustice, which requires integrity on the part of employers who must stand up for fair labor practices. This sequence is also related to Harper's speech during the 1869 Equal Rights Association debate, wherein she challenged the racial convictions of white women before Susan B. Anthony and Elizabeth Cady Stanton. Incidents of racism by white women workers against black women convinced Harper that the severity of racism was as serious a contradiction among white women, as it was among white men.

Race and Intelligence

Debates on racism in the second half of the novel extend and resolve positions posed in the first half. Dr. Latrobe, a confirmed segregationist like Alfred Lorraine, represents the one-drop-of-black-blood-curses-the-rest theory. Latrobe is also the name of the American colonizationist who proposed the deportation of free blacks to Liberia in the 1830s, and against whom William Watkins argued. Dr. Gresham, the liberal New England doctor, reemerges in the second half of the novel to appeal for Iola's hand in marriage a second time, and to counter Dr. Latrobe's racist arguments.

Dr. Latrobe proclaims

> "*This is a white man's government, and a white man's country,*" [and that] "*there are niggers who are as white as I am, but the taint of blood is there and we will always exclude them*" (p. 229).

He mistakes Dr. Latimer for a white man and praises his intellect to the benefit of *heredity and environment*. When Latrobe is informed that Latimer "*belongs to that negro race both by blood and choice,*" Latrobe rationalizes that Latimer's intelligence is because of the white blood in his veins.

The one-drop rule not only affects those persons with African ancestry, but all nonwhite people living under the rule of this fiction. Jim Crow laws instituted after the Civil War were designed to divide the country into white and black. The mulatto characters in Harper's novel align themselves with their darker relatives, refusing to pass for white which could have benefited them. This position, by blood and choice, reflects the Mosaic ideal. Like Robert Johnson, who explains his choice as one of commitment, preference, and cultural identity, Dr. Latimer also swears his allegiance to the race of his mother. The insistence on integrity results in sacrifice and social disadvantages, but these acts of resistance to white supremacy reinforce a fundamental belief in equality. In the case of Rev. Carmicle who is not mixed, *every person of unmixed blood who succeeds is an argument for the capability which is in the race.* However, Dr. Latrobe downplays Carmicle's achievements with *the exception proves the rule.*

As black achievers cannot become obsessed by racist attitudes, the now more radicalized Dr. Gresham extends the problem of racism to address a critical question. Gresham continues:

189

"The problem of the nation is not what men will do with the negro, but what will they do with the reckless, lawless white men who murder, lynch, and burn their fellow-citizens" (p. 217).

This statement reiterates one of Harper's most insistent themes during the 1890s. Her speeches, "Duty to Dependent Races," and "Woman's Political Future," and the most pointed essay, "How to Stop Lynching" propose that it is the federal government's moral responsibility to stop lynching and white terrorism.

The *Conversazione*

Like the prayer meetings at Uncle Daniel's before emancipation, the *conversazione* at the Stillmans engages the social and political issues and decisions the free community must consider. The name, Stillman, is probably a symbolic gesture toward William Still, whose home was the headquarters for the Underground Railroad in Philadelphia during slavery, and was likewise the place where intellectuals congregated after the war to determine post–Civil War issues affecting the black community. These meetings reflected the variance of political attitudes and strategies proposed for the Reconstruction era, from conservative adherence to the economic system to radical resolutions for feminist rights.

This parlor colloquium is composed of

"a select company of earnest men and women deeply interested in the welfare of the race" (p. 246).

One such meeting involves discussion of Bishop Tunster's paper "Negro Emancipation," in which he advocates expatriation and missionary migration to Africa. Lucille Delany proposes that America *"is the best field for human development."*

American colonizationists like Latrobe initially proposed the back to Africa concept for the imperialist purposes of the United States. Harriet Beecher Stowe and even Abraham Lincoln considered this a more desirable alternative to racial integration. But, says Lucille:

"I do not believe that the Southern white people themselves desire any wholesale exodus of the colored from their labor fields. It would be suicidal to attempt their expatriation" (p. 248).

Iola agrees with Lucille and echoes the resistance of William Watkins:

190

"We did not," said Iola, "place the bounds of our habitation. And I believe we are to be fixtures in this country. But beyond the shadows I see the coruscation of a brighter day; and we can help usher it in, not by answering hate with hate, or giving scorn for scorn, but by striving to be more generous, noble, and just" (p. 249).

These intellectuals articulate the challenges of citizenship that will develop decided political differences in the twentieth century. Some will continue to look to Africa for identity and liberation, but Harper encourages others to invest their energies in America, building their promised land on a higher vision. Mrs. Watson's poem, "A Rallying Cry," calls the people to uplift their condition and invest their faith in God. This character's name probably alludes to Harper's maiden name, Watkins.

Iola's contribution is a paper entitled, "Education of Mothers," which references Harper's essay, "Enlightened Motherhood" (1892) given as a speech before the Brooklyn Literary Society. Her concern stimulates discussion about domestic relationships and parental responsibility. Lucille enjoins:

"If there is anything I chafe to see it is a strong, hearty man shirking his burdens, putting them on the shoulders of his wife, and taking life easy for himself."

"I do not think," said Mrs. Stillman, "that we can begin too early to teach our boys to be manly and self-respecting, and our girls to be useful and self-reliant" (p. 253).

In words from Harper's essay, "Christianity," Reverend Carmicle speaks about religion:

"For the evils of society there are no solvents as potent as love and justice, and our greatest need is not more wealth and learning, but a religion replete with life and glowing with love" (p. 260).

"And," said Dr. Latimer, "instead of narrowing our sympathies to mere racial questions, let us broaden them to humanity's wider issues,"

which echoes Harper's cosmic aesthetic expressed in her letter to Thomas Hamilton, the editor of the *Anglo-African* in 1861.

Harper arranged the discussion around the experiences of the characters, the thematic tributaries of the novel, and her activist concerns. Racism, temperance, feminism, education, culture, and religion are engaged and encouraged through the author's perspective. Some of the men and all of the women voice Harper's sentiments. These characters represent the leadership—doctors, professors, editors, writers, and clergymen. By contrasting the past with the present, Reverend Carmicle reports the remarkable achievements of the liberated diligently pursuing education and self-determination:

> *"Where toil-worn mothers bent beneath their heavy burdens their more favored daughters are enjoying the privileges of education. Young people are making recitations in Greek and Latin where it was once a crime to teach their parents to read. I also became acquainted with colored professors and presidents of colleges. Saw young ladies who had graduated as doctors. Comfortable homes have succeeded old cabins of slavery. Vast crops have been raised by free labor. I read with interest and pleasure a number of papers edited by colored men"* (p. 258).

When Iola equates the Negro fate with that of Christ, she envisions the black Nazarene. As a Unitarian, Harper's religious belief viewed the embodiment of Jesus' spirit as available to anyone who submitted to the spirit. The black Jesus symbolizes Afroamerican faith, which was established during the extreme repression of slavery, hence that suffering has led them to receive the spirit of Christ.

When Iola speaks about Christ and the plight of Afroamericans, her aura emanates. Energized by her words, she enraptures the others. Here, Iola's characterization has received inappropriate critical treatment through comparison with traditional Victorian symbolism. Iola's glow is not unattainable, unapproachable female purity, but rather, her "ethereal aura" is the spiritual presence of Christ. In this scene, through Iola, Moses' character converges with Jesus' spirit.

Conclusions and Resolutions: In Pursuit of the Promised Land

During slavery the North was metaphorically referred to as "the Promised Land" as runaways stole away to freedom. After the 1850 Fugitive Slave Act, another country, Canada, became the promised land. But after the Civil War and the Emancipation Proclamation, the vast majority of the liberated remained in the South, where they attempted to cultivate a free life on the soil enriched by their ancestors' sweat and bones.

Iola's brother, Harry, remains in the South, actively engaged in local politics. Their mother frets over his future because he *is so fearless and outspoken.* His commitment to struggle was the outgrowth of his black awakening and his dedication to his mother. He, too, represents the Moses ideal through this realization:

> *"I confess at first I felt a shrinking from taking the step, but love for my mother overcame all repugnance on my part. Now that I have linked my fortunes to the race I intend to do all I can for its elevation"* (p. 203).

When Harry visits Iola and Robert Johnson in the North he meets and marries Lucille Delany. Like Moses, who married a dark-skinned Ethiopian, Harry's marriage is another symbolic statement against caste and class. Lucille, is likewise identified as a Moses character and her name alludes to the "pure" African, Martin Delany (1812–85), an abolitionist, medical doctor, Army major, scientist, and judge. Another allusion could be to Lucy Delaney, an escaped slave and author of *From the Darkness Cometh the Light or Struggles for Freedom.* Lucille is introduced as a close friend of Iola's, and their relationship constitutes a female bond based on intelligence and industry directed to benefit the community rather than conflicted by jealousy and personal advantage.

> *There were no foolish rivalries and jealousies between them. Their lives were too full of zeal and earnestness for them to waste in selfishness their power to be moral and spiritual forces among a people who so much needed their helping hands* (p. 200).

Iola identifies the Mosaic ideal in Dr. Latimer's refusal of his family inheritance. In discussion with Uncle Robert, Iola says:

> *"The characters of the Old Testament I most admire are Moses and Nehemiah. They were willing to put aside their own advantages for their race and country. Dr. Latimer comes up to my ideal of a high, heroic manhood"* (p. 265).

Iola sees Latimer as a chivalric figure. Latimer's name may allude to George Latimer (a fugitive slave whose incarceration in Boston led to Frederick Douglass's first printed piece) or Lewis Latimer (an inventor and associate of Thomas Edison and Alexander Graham Bell). He sees himself as a worker who owes his enlightened consciousness to the teachings of his mother, and likewise, identifies the Moses in Iola:

"My mother," replied Dr. Latimer, "faithful and true, belongs to that race. Where else should I be?".... "But I know a young lady who could have cast her lot with the favored race, yet chose to take her place with the freed people, as their teacher, friend, and adviser. This young lady was alone in the world. She had been fearfully wronged, and to her stricken heart came a brilliant offer of love, home and social position. But she bound her heart to the mast of duty, closed her ears to the syren song, and could not be lured from her purpose" (p. 263).

In order for these two couples to fulfill their purpose and to extend their characterizations into the future, they return South to contribute to the new vision. Dr. Latimer proposes marriage to Iola. He is the man for which her heart can *be as open as the flowers to the sun*. Their marriage is bound by a shared history and character. Together, the two couples constitute a balance of gender and talent. This motif is further evidenced when Latimer conjures an exodus metaphor while repudiating attempts to demean and repress the future of the freed:

"I think," said Dr. Latimer, indignantly, "that the Israelites had just as much right to scatter flowers over the bodies of the Egyptians, when the waves threw back their corpses on the shore of the Red Sea, as these children had to strew the path of Jefferson Davis with flowers. We want our boys to grow up manly citizens, and not cringing sycophants" (p. 242).

This attitude is a position that considers no compromise of basic human principles.

Aunt Linda has foreseen the coming of Iola and her new husband in a vision dream. This spiritual symbol confirms providence.

"I seed it in a vision dat somebody fair war comin' to help us. An' wen I yered it war you, I larffed and jist rolled ober, and larffed and jist gib up" (p. 275).

In ironic denial, Iola's response is intended to reduce racial emphasis on skin color, Iola replies,

"But, Aunt Linda, I am not very fair" (p. 275).

The end of the novel is direct and matter-of-fact. The adventure and romanticism of the preceding chapters are leveled in the conclusion by the mundane, everyday existence that Iola and the other characters live. This kind of conclusion is typical of Victorian novels, and the technique serviced Harper's final thematic gesture. Now that the war had ended, the community must resign itself to the undramatic and the unglamorous. The author sets up the pivotal point in the preceding chapter for this realistic ending when Iola idealizes Dr. Latimer by saying he *"belongs to the days of chivalry."* Latimer refutes this romantic notion by saying that *"he only belongs to the days of hard-pan service."*

This opposition is significant. By contradicting this romantic, medieval metaphor which typified Victorian imagery, Harper refutes this patriarchal notion of manhood and offers an egalitarian alternative in reconsideration of it. At the same time, Harper demonstrates the need for another cultural aesthetic, one based on reality and guarded by spiritual faith. Latimer's statement brings Iola and the audience back down to earth.

The couple settles down in a modest cottage with the extended family living nearby. Lucille teaches school. Harry continues in politics. Latimer practices medicine and Iola teaches Sunday school. The older members of the family, including Aunt Linda and Uncle Daniel, live out the rest of their lives peacefully.

It is hoped that Iola will fulfill the legacy of her name, the nom de plume of the radical writer and activist, Ida B. Wells. When she expresses the desire to write a novel, Iola's characterization converges with the novel's aesthetic perspective and its educational function. Latimer encourages her to

"Write, out of the fullness of your heart, a book to inspire men and women with a deeper sense of justice and humanity" (p. 262).

As a Sunday school teacher, Iola is likewise aligned with Frances Harper's major activity during her latter years. As William Still explains in the introduction, "thousands of colored Sunday schools in the South, in casting about for an interesting, moral story-book, full of practical lessons, will not be content to be without *Iola Leroy, or Shadows Uplifted*" (p. 3).

Iola Leroy, or Shadows Uplifted has to be considered in the critical light the author intended. Harper very directly expresses her aesthetic and thematic intentions. The novel proselytizes the author's life long themes; and in style and form, it adheres and contextualizes those issues and endeavors. To what extent the novel transcends the deliberateness of the writer's intention to manifest a "splendid" work of art was of less concern to her. Most certainly, the novel did disrupt the critical community since

195

it did not attempt to emulate the aesthetic of its European predecessors. And in that regard, the author harbored no especial aspirations.

Iola Leroy is a proletarian work. It embodies the poet's person and fuses her political and literary spirit. Harper placed her poetry, prose, speeches, essays, and letters explicitly and implicitly in the novel, maintaining her thematic focus and ideological consistency. Her thematic quest for human rights and universal brotherhood and sisterhood has been considered "childish" and, certainly by bourgeois critical standards, naive and unsophisticated. But as these institutions and standards too often embody the insensitive cisterns of arrogant objectivity, such critical observations are too removed and too myopic to appreciate a literary effort designed for an alternative culture emanating from a spiritual vision.

The final statement concerning the novel is Harper's end "note," in which the author uplifts the conclusion with new idealism and rounds the prose into poetry for balance and an open closure.

> *There is light beyond the darkness,*
> *Joy beyond the present pain;*
> *There is hope in God's great justice*
> *And the negro's rising brain.*
> *Though the morning seems to linger*
> *O'er the hill-tops far away,*
> *Yet the shadows bear the promise*
> *Of a brighter coming day.*

CHAPTER 7

Frances E. W. Harper and the Legacy of Black Feminism

An Appeal to My Countrywomen

You can sigh o'er the sad-eyed Armenian
    Who weeps in her desolate home.
You can mourn o'er the exile of Russia.
    From kindred and friends doomed to roam.

You can pity the men who have woven
    From passion and appetite chains
To coil with a terrible tension
    Around their heartstrings and brains.

You can sorrow o'er little children
    Disinherited from their birth,
The wee waifs and toddlers neglected,
    Robbed of sunshine, music and mirth.

For beasts you have gentle compassion;
    Your mercy and pity they share.
For the wretched, outcast and fallen
    You have tenderness, love and care.

But hark! from our Southland are floating
    Sobs of anguish, murmurs of pain,
And women heart-stricken are weeping
    Over their tortured and their slain.

On their brows the sun has left traces;
    Shrink not from their sorrow in scorn.
When they entered the threshold of being
    The children of a King were born.

Each comes as a guest to the table
    The hand of our God has outspread,

To fountains that ever leap upward,
 To share in the soil we all tread.

When ye plead for the wrecked and fallen,
 The exile from far-distant shores,
Remember that men are still wasting
 Life's crimson around your own doors.

Have ye not, oh, my favored sisters,
 Just a plea, a prayer or a tear,
For mothers who dwell 'neath the shadows
 Of agony, hatred and fear?

Men may tread down the poor and lowly,
 May crush them in anger and hate,
But surely the mills of God's justice
 Will grind out the grist of their fate.

Oh, people sin-laden and guilty,
 So lusty and proud in your prime,
The sharp sickles of God's retribution
 Will gather your harvest of crime.

Weep not, oh my well-sheltered sisters,
 Weep not for the Negro alone,
But weep for your sons who must gather
 The crops which their fathers have sown.

Go read on the tombstones of nations
 Of chieftains who masterful trod,
The sentence which time has engraved,
 That they had forgotten their God.

'Tis the judgment of God that men reap
 The tares which in madness they sow,
Sorrow follows the footsteps of crime,
 And Sin is the consort of Woe.

Frances Harper, 1900,
Poems

Behind the facts of the present, is the history of the past. The present facts are a divided North and a solid South, a defeated Democracy grasping again the reins of Government, stronger in its representative basis than when it went out of power—the ballot in the hands of the colored man being an accession to their strength. Among the facts of the past is the history of a race who have behind them ages of heathenism, and the inferior civilization

198

of slavery, the deliverance that came through the Civil War, and the failures and crimes of the reconstruction period. To some the aspect may seem gloomy, but if we look beyond the present to the future possibilities of our race, we have no right to despair. Our better work is to organize victory out of defeat, and make friends of our calamities. Had slavery been abolished by the nation breaking off its sins by righteousness, and its iniquities by showing mercy to the poor, there would have been a moral adaptation in the country to the new conditions of freedom; but when it went down by a sudden wrench, it found master and slave facing a problem of which I know no parallel in history. Slavery and serfdom had existed in other ages and among other civilizations; but I know of no other country in which the enslaved and the enslavers were so physically different that the complexion of the one was a symbol of power and superiority, and that of the other an emblem of poverty, ignorance, and social abasement. I suppose the Jews differed in physical appearance from the Egyptians, but their disposition after freedom was different from ours. They left behind them the land of their oppressors, and turned their faces to a land made sacred by the grand traditions of their race and memories of their kindred dead.

But the negro, torn away ages since from Africa, having in many instances in his veins the blood of the dominant race, and being in physiological accord with America, has not grand historic memories or sacred traditions to impel him to Africa. The Israelites went into Egypt as a kindred race. The Africans came as the units of different tribes, differing in dialects, localities, and even complexions. If the ancient Israelite knew Egypt as the land of his exile, the expatriated African lost his native language, and in a generation knew America only as the land of his birth. After his emancipation, his enslavers had the need of his labor, and his deliverers a use for his ballot, and as he was freed partly as a military necessity, it may have been equally pertinent to have given him his vote a political necessity.

I shall not attempt to dwell on the failures of reconstruction. Let the man who is prepared to take an impartial view of the subject, read the volume on the Ku Klux conspiracy on one side, and the Prostrate State, and the history of Republican rule in the Southern State governments on the other, and it may be that he will justly conclude, that ages of oppression by one class, and the pliancy of submission by the other, unfitted both classes to develop and evolve a good, stable government out of the chaos, derangement and revolution, which the Civil War had created; and yet the rehabilitation and reconstruction of Southern governments, one of the most intricate and delicate things to rightly adjust and manage was, in a measure, placed in some of the most inexperienced hands in the country.

I visited the South soon after emancipation, and saw colored men as legislators and office-holders, but I scarcely remember having seen one colored man holding any important position, whom I had known, either by person or reputation, as having been either a leader, or very prominent in the anti-slavery agitation. They were, as far as I remember, generally new men. Was

199

it strange, that with their inexperience, and the sudden temptations which surrounded then, that some of them should make mistakes, fall into blunders, and even commit shameful crimes? In what school had they been trained to be noble patriots, or self-sacrificing lovers of their race? Were they not as much subject to the law of environments as any other people? And would they not have been a wonderful class, such a class as the world has never seen, if they had never made any mistakes?

"Ignorance of, and contempt and neglect for human rights," create wretched surroundings out of which to develop all the manly virtues and Christian graces. But we cannot recall the dead past; it is the living present which demands our attention. Two things remain for us to do: Trust in God and be patient. By patience, I do not mean a servile submission to wrong; an idle folding of hands and going to sleep, waiting for the good time coming, but that patience which, realizing that between the white and colored people of the country there is a community of interests, will base its action, not on the old animosities of the past, but on the new conditions of the present, and go earnestly to work and develop self-reliance, self-control, and self-respect in the race; and so build up worthy characters by planting the roots of progress under the hearthstone.

By faith in God, I do not mean an unreasoning waiting for God to do for us what we can and ought to do for ourselves, but that faith which will teach us to work on the same line with Him, with the assurance that the only true safety for a race or nation is to live in harmony with God's laws of moral and spiritual life. Man cannot live by politics alone, and if for the next ten years the national government shall be too weak or too vicious to place protection to human life at the basis of its civilization, let the colored man abate somewhat of his political zeal, and do all he can to shame the nation into a higher regard for human rights, and human life, than it now possesses. A government that can protect its citizens and will not, is a vicious government; a government that would protect its citizens and cannot is a weak government. Let the intellectuality in our race, which has been used in advocating the claims of the Republican party, grapple with the inherent weakness or viciousness in our government, which has power to tax men in peace and draft them in war, and yet fails to make their lives sacred under the shadow of its Constitution.

Let them expose to the gaze of Christendom the condition of Southern prisons, and the treatment colored men receive in them. Let no Hamburg or Danville massacre pass without earnest indignation meetings, and appeals to all that is highest and best in American civilization and Christianity. If for the next twenty years the colored people take no feverish interest in the success or failure of either party, but will do all they can to build up an intelligent and virtuous manhood, and a tender, strong and true womanhood, we can afford to wait for political strength while developing moral and spiritual power. We can better, if need be, postpone taking part in the next election, than we can neglect attending to the best interests of the next generation.

Power will naturally gravitate into the strongest hands, be they white or black; and to strengthen our hands, and base our race-life on those divine certitudes, which are the only safe foundations of either individuals or nations, is of more vital importance to us than being the appendages of any political party. Let the race which expends so much for pleasure, learn to expend more for strength. Let the young people all over the country form themselves into reading clubs, and gather information from ancient lore and modern learning, to throw light on the unsolved problems of our modern civilization. Let them learn to unite with the great moral and philanthropic movements of the day, and add to their quota the progress and development of the country.

I do not despair of the future of the colored race in this country. Perhaps the white race have just as much or more reason to be anxious about their future in the South as we have, just so long as it shall be written, "As ye sow, so shall ye reap." With his breadth of physical organization and fund of mental endurance, which enabled him to live through ages of slavery, with a vitality by which he increases faster than the white race by whom he is surrounded, with his adaption to soil and climate, and his liberated muscle and mind power, through which he has become the possessor, it is estimated, of millions of acres of land, and has put millions of dollars in his pocket, what is to hinder the colored man if he will only let his moral life keep pace with his physical advantages, from building up a future which will grandly contrast with the old sad past?

Let me say, in conclusion, to the men and women of my race, that this is not the time for inaction or discouragement. As a colored woman, I am not disheartened at the failure of Blaine, nor, as a temperance woman, at the non-election of St. John. As a race, we have a right to be interested in the success of the temperance movement. The liquor power is too strong and dangerous for us to give it aid or countenance. We are too poor to be moderate drinkers, and in part of the country too much of political nonentities to clasp hands with a power which can dictate its terms to the two great parties, and awe one into silence and entice the other into alliance. In the shell of apparent failure look for the germ of an ever-growing success. It has been said of Napoleon, "that he was not himself till the battle began to go against him, then when the dead began to fall in ranks around him, awoke his power of combination, and he put on terror and victory as a robe." Men of my race look at the dead who have fallen basely and brutally murdered since the war in Southern lands. See the liquor traffic, sending its floods of sorrow, shame and death to the habitations of men, and forget for the next four years that there is such a thing as ease or luxury in the world. Strive to outgrow the old shards and shells of the past, and build up such noble, good and useful characters, that if every man should hate you, no one could despise you.[1]

Just as this essay, "Temperance," extends the Mosaic motif into the woman's era, Frances Harper's vision and prominence as a national figure soared during the 1870s, 1880s and 1890s. Her work in education, temperance reform, and related radical activities included leadership roles in national and local (Philadelphia) organizations. She joined the American Association of Colored Youth and its affiliate, the Authors Association. She delivered lectures and read poetry for these organizations, addressing topics like "Environment," and "The Young Men's Christian Association as a Factor in Education." She was appointed to the board of directors in July 1894, and remained connected to the organization as late as 1898. Her interest in national literacy was based on her faith for an "intelligent and informed" democracy. Likewise, she perceived her temperance work as fundamental to the human rights struggle. Her serialized novel, *Trial and Triumph*, appeared in *The Christian Recorder* during the intense period dedicated to organizing women. Though a more detailed analysis of this story will appear in another publication, a particular concern Harper brings forth in this work is the domestic danger women risk when they wed men who drink.

Harper worked in an integrative capacity with the women's movement through the Woman's Christian Temperance Union (WCTU) and was appointed city, then state, and eventually national supervisor for its organizing efforts in the black communities. In 1883 she monitored the efforts of the membership to organize "colored" people, noting the integrative efforts of some members against the exclusionary practices of southern chapters. In this endeavor, she remained steadfast and crystalline in her social and religious indictment of institutional racism. Her lectures on behalf of the organization included her racial concerns and her feminist politics. As her earliest poetry and prose revealed, she advocated a strong resistance to alcoholism. The poem, "Signing the Pledge" (1883), reflects a human tragedy to recruit for this facet of political struggle.

> He stood beside his dying child,
>   With a dim and bloodshot eye;
> They'd won him from the haunts of vice
>   To see his first-born die.
> He came with a slow and staggering tread,
>   A vague, unmeaning stare,
> And, reeling, clasped the clammy hand,
>   So deathly pale and fair.
>
> In a dark and gloomy chamber,
>   Life ebbing fast away,

On a coarse and wretched pallet,
The dying sufferer lay:
A smile of recognition
Lit up the glazing eye;
"I'm very glad," it seemed to say,
"You've come to see me die."

That smile reached to his callous heart,
It scaled fountains stirred;
He tried to speak, but on his lips
Faltered and died each word.
And burning tears like rain
Poured down his bloated face,
Where guilt, remorse and shame
Had scathed, and left their trace.

"My father!" said the dying child,
(His voice was faint and low,)
"Oh! clasp me closely to your heart,
And kiss me ere I go.
Bright angels beckon me away,
To the holy city fair—
Oh! tell me, father, ere I go,
Say, will you meet me there?"

He clasped him to his throbbing heart,
"I will! I will!" he said;
His pleading ceased—the father held
His first-born and his dead!
The marble brow, with golden curls,
Lay lifeless on his breast;
Like sunbeams on the distant clouds
Which line the gorgeous west.

In the essay, "The Woman's Christian Temperance Union and the Colored Woman" (1888) Harper conveys her organizing activities, her ideological reasons for engaging this realm of social reform, and her historical relationship with the organization. Harper eloquently appeals to the audience to consider the temperance movement as a relevant aspect of part of the larger struggle for a higher, yet sober society.

A woman sat beneath the shadow of her home, while the dark waves of intemperance dashed against human hearts and hearth-stones, but there came an hour when she found that she could do something else besides wring her hands and weep over the ravages of the liquor traffic, which had darkened so many lives and desolated so many homes. Where the enemy spreads his snares for the feet of the unwary, inexperienced and tempted, she, too, could go and strive to stay the tide of ruin which was sending its floods of sorrow, shame and death to the habitations of men, and 1873 witnessed the strange and wondrous sight of the Woman's Crusade, when the mother-heart was roused up in defense of the home and all that the home held dearest. A divine impulse seemed to fan into sudden flame and touch with living fire earnest hearts, which rose up to meet the great occasion. Lips that had been silent in the prayer meeting were loosened to take part in the wonderful uprising. Saloons were visited, hardships encountered, insults, violence and even imprisonment endured by women, brave to suffer and strong to endure. Thousands of saloon visits were made, many were closed. Grand enthusiasms were aroused, moral earnestness awakened, and a fire kindled whose beacon lights still stream o'er the gloomy track of our monster evil. Victor Hugo has spoken of the nineteenth century as being woman's era, and among the most noticeable epochs in this era is the uprising of women against the twin evils of slavery and intemperance, which had foisted themselves like leeches upon the civilization of the present age. In the great anti-slavery conflict women had borne a part, but after the storm cloud of battle had rolled away, it was found that an enemy, old and strong and deceptive, was warring against the best interests of society; not simply an enemy to one race, but an enemy to all races—an enemy that had entrenched itself in the strongholds of appetite and avarice, and was upheld by fashion, custom and legislation. To dislodge this enemy, to put prohibition not simply on the statute book, but in the heart and conscience of a nation, embracing within itself such heterogeneous masses, is no child's play, nor the work of a few short moons. Men who were subjects in their own country and legislated for by others, become citizens here, with the power to help legislate for native born Americans. Hundreds of thousands of new citizens have been translated from the old oligarchy of slavery into the new commonwealth of freedom, and are numerically strong enough to hold the balance of power in a number of the States, and sway its legislators for good or evil. With all these conditions, something more is needed than grand enthusiasms lighting up a few consecrated lives with hallowed brightness. We need patient, persevering, Christly endeavor, a consecration of the moral earnestness, spiritual power and numerical strength of the nation to grapple with this evil and accomplish its overthrow.

After the knowledge and experience gained by the crusade, women, instead of letting all their pure enthusiasms become dissipated by expending in feeling what they should utilize in action, came together and formed the Woman's Christian Temperance Union. From Miss Willard we learn that women who had been crusading all winter called conventions for consultation in respective States, and that several organizations called Temperance

Leagues, were formed. Another step was the confederation of the States into the National Christian Temperance Union. A circular, aided by an extensive circulation through the press, was sent out to women in different parts of the country, and a convention was called, which met in Cleveland in November, 1874, to which sixteen States responded. A plan of work was adopted, financial arrangements made, and the publishing of an organ resolved upon. Mrs. Whittemyer, of Philadelphia, was elected President, and Miss Willard, of Illinois, Corresponding Secretary. This Union has increased in numbers and territory until at its last convention it embraced thirty-seven States and Territories. For years I knew very little of its proceedings, and was not sure that colored comradeship was very desirable, but having attended a local Union in Philadelphia, I was asked to join and acceded to the request, and was made city and afterwards State Superintendent of work among colored people. Since then, for several years I have held the position of National Superintendent of work among the colored people of the North. When I became National Superintendent there were no colored women on the Executive Committee or Board of Superintendents. Now there are two colored women on the Executive Committee and two on the Board of Superintendents. As a matter of course the colored question has come into this work as it has into the Sons of Temperance, Good Templars and elsewhere. Some of the members of different Unions have met the question in a liberal and Christian manner; others have not seemed to have so fully outgrown the old shards and shells of the past as to make the distinction between Christian affiliation and social equality, but still the leaven of more liberal sentiments has been at work in the Union and produced some hopeful results.

One of the pleasantest remembrances of my connection with the Woman's Christian Temperance Union was the kind and hospitable reception I met in the Missouri State Convention, and the memorable words of their President, Mrs. Hoffman, who declared that the color-line was eliminated. A Superintendent was chosen at that meeting for colored work in the State, at whose home in St. Louis the National Superintendent was for some time a Guest. The State Superintendent said in one of the meetings to the colored sisters, "You can come with us, or you can go by yourselves." There was self-reliance and ability enough among them to form a Union of their own, which was named after the National Superintendent. Our work is divided into about forty departments, and among them they chose several lines of work, and had departments for parlor meetings, juvenile and evangelistic work, all of which have been in working order. The Union held meetings in Methodist and Baptist churches, and opened in the African Methodist Episcopal Church an industrial school for children, which increased in size until from about a dozen children at the beginning, it closed with about one hundred and fifty, as I understand.

Some of the Unions, in their outlook upon society, found that there was no orphan asylum for colored children, except among the Catholics, and took the initiative for founding an asylum for colored children, and in a short time were successful in raising several hundred dollars for the purpose. This Union has, I have been informed, gathered into its association seventeen school teachers, and I think comprises some of the best brain and heart of the race in the city.

From West Virginia a lady informs the National Superintendent that her Union has invited the colored sisters to join with them, and adds, "Praise God, from whom all blessings flow." In a number of places where there are local Unions in the North the doors have been opened to colored women, but in the farther South separate State Unions have been formed. Southern white women, it may be, fail to make in their minds the discrimination between social equality and Christian affiliation. Social equality, if I rightly understand the term, is the outgrowth of social affinities and social conditions, and may be based on talent, ability, or wealth, on either or all of these conditions. Christian affiliation is the union of Christians to do Christly work, and to help build up the kingdom of Christ amid the sin and misery of the world, under the spiritual leadership of the Lord Jesus Christ. At our last National Convention two States were represented by colored representatives. The colored President of an Alabama Union represented a Union composed of white and colored people, and is called No. 2, instead of Colored Union, as it was not composed entirely of colored people, and in making its advent into the National Union brought, as I was informed, more than twice the amount of State dues which was paid by the white Alabama Union, No. 1.

The question of admission into the White Ribbon Army was brought before the National President, through a card sent from Atlanta. Twenty-three women had formed a Union, and had written to the National Superintendent of colored work in the North asking in reference to their admission, and if black sheep must climb up some other way to tell them how. I showed the card to Miss Willard, who gave it as her opinion "That the National could not make laws for a State. If the colored women of Georgia will meet and form a Woman's Christian Temperance Union for the State, it is my opinion that their officers and delegates will have the same representation in the National." The President of the Second Alabama was received and recognized in the National as a member of the Executive Committee, and had a place, as I was informed, on the Committee of Resolutions.

Believing, as I do, in human solidarity, I hold that the Woman's Christian Temperance Union has in its hands one of the grandest opportunities that God ever pressed into the hands of the womanhood of any country. Its conflict is not the contest of a social club, but a moral warfare for an imperiled civilization. Whether or not the members of the farther South will subordinate the spirit of caste to the spirit of Christ, time will show. Once between them and the Negro were vast disparities, which have been melting and disappearing. The war obliterated the disparity between freedom and slavery. The civil law blotted out the difference between disfranchisement and manhood suffrage. Schools have sprung up like wells in the desert dust, bringing the races nearer together on the intellectual plane, while as a participant in the wealth of society the colored man has, I believe, in some instances, left his former master behind the race for wealth. With these old landmarks going and gone, one relic remains from the dead past. "Our social customs."

In clinging to them let them remember that the most ignorant, vicious and degraded voter outranks, politically, the purest, best and most cultured woman in the South, and learn to look at the question of Christian affiliation on this subject, not in the shadow of the fashion of this world that fadeth away, but in the light of the face of Jesus Christ. And can any one despise the least of Christ's brethren without despising Him? Is there any path that the slave once trod that Jesus did not tread before him, and leave luminous with the light of His steps? Was the Negro bought and sold? Christ was sold for thirty pieces of silver. Has he been poor? "The birds had nests, the foxes had holes, but the Son of man had no where to lay His head." Were they beaten in the house of bondage? They took Jesus and scourged Him. Have they occupied a low social position? "He made himself of no reputation and was numbered with the transgressors." Despised and trodden under foot? He was despised and rejected of men; spit upon by the rabble, crucified between thieves, and died as died Rome's meanest criminal slave.

Oh, my brothers and sisters, if God chastens every son whom He receiveth, let your past history be a stimulus for the future. Join with the great army who are on the side of our God and His Christ. Let your homes be the best places where you may plant your batteries against the rum traffic. Teach your children to hate intoxicating drinks with a deadly hatred. Though scorn may curl her haughty lip, and fashion gather up her dainty robes from social contact, if your lives are in harmony with God and Christly sympathy with man, you belong to the highest nobility in God's universe. Learn to fight the battle for God and man as athletes armed for a glorious strife, encompassed about with a cloud of witnesses who are in sympathy with the highest and holiest endeavors.[2]

Even though Frances Harper supported the Fifteenth Amendment, after it was enacted she actively campaigned for the woman's vote. Harper sustained a racial consciousness for the overall women's movement, but she maintained emphatically that racial violence presented the most detrimental facet of American oppression. Her lectures and writings were consummate with the complexity of concerns that governed her politics. While she accentuated the interconnectedness of issues and the need to renounce racism and sexism, she reflected a strong classlessness in her vision of a democratic nation and an egalitarian lifestyle.

Without apologizing for the shortcomings of the black community, Harper's words qualify its unprecedented dilemma. While identifying the diabolical "democracy" which had not fulfilled its faithless promises, she inspired the radical community to persevere and to acquiesce to the challenge of the hour for independence and self-determination. Her appeals were not sequestered with lofty rhetoric, but were firmly grounded in the evidence of experience. In February 1891 in Washington, D.C. Harper spoke at the first triennial meeting of the National Council of Women of the United States. In one of her most celebrated speeches, "Duty to Dependent Races," Harper explains why the race issue is a women's issue. The council was founded for the advancement of women's work in education, philanthropy, reform, and social culture. Members Susan B. Anthony, Anna Julia Cooper, and Frances Welland (President of the WCTU) were present.

While presenting the educational needs of the freedmen and women, Harper advocated national education for all Americans. Her plea acknowledged the frustrated futility of the developing black population attempting human solidarity with the impoverished hostility of ignorant, poor whites; while political corruption benefited from racial and class conflicts, privileged racists prospered in governmental positions, abusing authority and undermining democracy. Speaking to an integrated audience, Harper's incisive depth identified the chilling horror of lynching and intensified the indifference of the republic conveniently turning its back on its dark citizens.

> *I deem it a privilege to present the negro, not as a mere dependent asking for Northern sympathy or Southern compassion, but as a member of the body politic who has a claim upon the nation for justice, simple justice, which is the right of every race, upon the government for protection, which is the rightful claim of every citizen, and upon our common Christianity for the best influences which can be exerted for peace on earth and good-will to man.*
>
> *Our first claim upon the nation and government is the claim for protection to human life. That claim should lie at the basis of our civilization, not simply in theory but in fact. Outside of America, I know of no other civilized country, Catholic, Protestant, or even Muhammadan, where men are still lynched, murdered, and even burned for real or supposed crimes. As long as there are such cases as moral irresponsibility, mental imbecility; as long as Potiphar's wife stands in the world's pillory of shame, no man should be deprived of life or liberty without due process of law. A government which has power to tax a man in peace and draft him in war, should have power to defend its citizens from wrong and outrage and does not is vicious. A government which would do it and cannot is weak; and where human life*

is insecure through either weakness or viciousness in the administration of law, there must be a lack of justice, and where this is wanting nothing can make up the deficiency.

The strongest nation on earth cannot afford to deal unjustly towards its weakest and feeblest members. A man might just as well attempt to play with the thunderbolts of heaven and expect to escape unscathed, as for a nation to trample on justice and right and evade the divine penalty. The reason our nation snapped asunder in 1861 was because it lacked the cohesion of justice: men poured out their blood like water, scattered their wealth like chaff, summoned to the field the largest armies the nation had ever seen, but they did not get their final victories which closed the rebellion till they clasped hands with the negro, and marched with him abreast to freedom and to victory. I claim for the negro protection in every right with which the government has invested him. Whether it was wise or unwise, the government has exchanged the fetters on his wrist for the ballot in his right hand, and men cannot vitiate his vote by fraud, or intimidate the voter by violence, without being untrue to the genius and spirit of our government, and bringing demoralization into their own political life and ranks. Am I here met with the objection that the negro is poor and ignorant, and the greatest amount of land, capital, and intelligence is possessed by the white race, and that in a number of States negro suffrage means negro supremacy? But is it not a fact that both North and South power naturally gravitates into the strongest hands, and is there any danger that a race who were deemed so inferior as to be only fitted for slavery, and social and political ostracism, has in less than one generation become so powerful that, if not hindered from exercising the right of suffrage, it will dominate over a people who have behind them ages of dominion, education, freedom, and civilization, a people who have had poured into their veins the blood of some of the strongest races on earth? More than a year since Mr. Grady said, I believe, "We do not directly fear the political domination of blacks, but that they are ignorant and easily deluded, impulsive and therefore easily led, strong of race instinct and therefore clannish, without information and therefore without political convictions, passionate and therefore easily excited, poor, irresponsible, and with no idea of the integrity of suffrage and therefore easily bought. The fear is that this vast swarm, ignorant, purchasable, will be impacted and controlled by desperate and unscrupulous white men and made to hold the balance of power when white men are divided." Admit for one moment that every word here is true, and that the whole race should be judged by its worst, and not its best members, does any civilized country legislate to punish a man before he commits a crime?

It is said the negro is ignorant. But why is he ignorant? It comes with ill grace from a man who has put out my eyes to make a parade of my blindness—to reproach me for my poverty when he has wronged me of my money. If the negro is ignorant, he has lived under the shadow of an institution which, at least in part of the country, made it a crime to teach him to read the name of the ever-blessed Christ. If he is poor, what has become of the money he has been earning for the last two hundred and fifty years? Years ago it was said cotton fights and cotton conquers for American slavery. The negro helped build up that great cotton power in the South, and in the North his sigh was in the whir of its machinery, and his blood and tears upon the warp and woof of its manufactures.

But there are some rights more precious than the rights of property or the claims of superior intelligence: they are the rights of life and liberty, and to these the poorest and humblest man has just as much right as the richest and most influential man in the country. Ignorance and poverty are conditions which men outgrow. Since the sealed volume was opened by the crimson hand of war, in spite of entailed ignorance, poverty, opposition, and a heritage of scorn, schools have sprung like wells in the desert dust. It has been estimated that about two millions have learned to read. Colored men and women have gone into journalism. Some of the first magazines in the country have received contributions from them. Learned professions have given them diplomas. Universities have granted them professorships. Colored women have combined to shelter orphaned children. Tens of thousands have been contributed by colored persons for the care of the aged and infirm. Instead of the old slave-pen of former days, imposing and commodious are edifices of prayer and praise. Millions of dollars have flowed into the pockets of the race, and freed people have not only been able to provide for themselves, but reach out their hands to impoverished owners.

Has the record of the slave been such as to warrant the belief that permitting him to share citizenship with others in the country is inimical to the welfare of the nation? Can it be said that he lacks patriotism, or a readiness to make common cause with the nation in the hour of peril? In the days of the American Revolution some of the first blood which was shed flowed from the veins of a colored man, and among the latest words that died upon his lips before they paled in death was, "Crush them underfoot," meaning the British guards. To him Boston has given a monument. In or after 1812 they received from General Jackson the plaudit, "I knew you would endure hunger and thirst and all the hardships of war. I knew that you loved the land of your nativity, and that, like ourselves, you had to defend all that is most dear; but you have surpassed my hopes. I have found in you, united to all these qualities, that noble enthusiasm which impels to great deeds." And in our late civil conflict colored men threw their lives into the struggle, rallied around the old flag when others were trampling it underfoot and riddling it with bullets. Colored people learned to regard that flag as a harbinger of freedom and bring their most reliable information to the Union army, to share their humble fare with the escaping prisoner; to be faithful when others were faithless and help turn the tide of battle in favor of the nation. While nearly two hundred thousand joined the Union army, others remained on the old plantations; widows, wives, aged men, and helpless children were left behind, when the master was at the front trying to put new rivets in their chains, and yet was there a single slave who took advantage of the master's absence to invade the privacy of his home, or wreck a summary vengeance on those whose "defenseless condition should have been their best defense?"

Instead of taking the ballot from his hands, teach him how to use it, and to add his quota to the progress, strength, and durability of the nation. Let the nation, which once consented to his abasement under a system which made it a crime to teach him to read his Bible, feel it a privilege as well as a duty to reverse the old processes of the past by supplanting his darkness with light, not simply by providing the negro, but the whole region in which he lives, with national education. No child can be blamed because he was born in the midst of squalor, poverty, and ignorance, but society is criminal if it permits him to grow up without proper efforts for ameliorating his condition.

Some months since, when I was in South Carolina, where I addressed a number of colored schools, I was informed that white children were in the factories, beginning from eight to ten years old, with working hours from six to seven o'clock; and one day, as a number of white children were wending their way apparently from the factory, I heard a colored man say, "I pity these children." It was a strange turning of the tables to hear a colored man in South Carolina bestowing pity on white children because of neglect in their education. Surely the world does move. When parents are too poor or selfish to spare the labor of their children from the factories, and the State too indifferent or short-sighted to enforce their education by law, then let the Government save its future citizens from the results of cupidity in the parents or short-sightedness in the State. If to-day there is a danger from a mass of ignorance voting, may there not be a danger even greater, and that is a mass of "ignorance that does not vote"? If there is danger that an ignorant mass might be compacted to hold the balance of power where white men are divided politically, might not the same mass, if kept ignorant and disfranchised, be used by wicked men, whose weapons may be bombs and dynamite, to dash themselves against the peace and order of society? To-day the hands of the negro are not dripping with dynamite. We do not read of his flaunting the red banners of anarchy in the face of the nation, nor plotting in beer-saloons to overthrow existing institutions, nor spitting on the American flag. Once that flag was to him an ensign of freedom. Let our Government resolve that as far as that flag extends every American-born child shall be able to read upon its folds liberty for all and chains for none.

And now permit me to make my final claim, and that is a claim upon our common Christianity. . . . It is the pride of Castle which opposes the spirit of Christ, and the great work to which American Christianity is called is a work of Christly reconciliation. God has heaved up your mountains with grandeur, flooded your rivers with majesty, crowned your vales with fertility, and enriched your mines with wealth. Excluding Alaska, you have, I think, nearly three hundred millions of square miles. Be reconciled to God for making a man black, permitting him to become part of your body politic, and sharing one roof or acre of our goodly heritage. Be reconciled to the Christ of Calvary, who said, "And I, if I be lifted up, will draw all men to me," and "It is better for a man that a millstone were hanged about his neck, and he were drowned in the depths of the sea, that he should offend one of these little ones that believe in me." Forgive the early adherents of Christianity who faced danger and difficulty and stood as victors by the side of Death, who would say, "I perceive that God is no respecter of persons." "If ye have respect of persons ye commit sin." "There is neither Greek nor Jew, circumcision nor uncircumcision, Scythian nor Barbarian, bond nor free, but Christ is all, and in all."

What I ask of American Christianity is not to show us more creeds, but more of Christ; not more rites and ceremonies, but more religion glowing with love and replete with life,—religion which will be to all weaker races an uplifting power, and not a degrading influence, Jesus Christ has given us a platform of love and duty from which all oppression and selfishness is necessarily excluded. While politicians may stumble on the barren mountains of fretful controversy and ask in strange bewilderment, "What shall we do with weaker races?" I hold that Jesus Christ answered that question nearly two thousand years since. "Whatsoever ye would that men should do to you, do you even so to them."[3]

Frances E. W. Harper and the Rise of Black Feminism

In higher walks of life too, the coloured women have made progress. The principal of the Coloured High School in Philadelphia was born a slave in the District of Columbia; but in early life she was taken North, and she resolved to get knowledge. When about fifteen years old, she obtained a situation as a house servant, with the privilege of going every other day to receive instruction. Poverty was in her way, but instead of making it a stumbling block, she converted it into a stepping stone. She lived in one place about six years, and received seven dollars a month. A coloured lady presented her a scholarship, and she entered Oberlin as a pupil. When she was sufficiently advanced, Oberlin was brave enough to accord her a place as a teacher in the preparatory department of the college, a position she was enabled to maintain with credit to herself and honour to her race. At present she is principal of the coloured High School of Philadelphia, a position which she has held for several years, graduating almost every year a number of pupils, a part of whom are scattered abroad as teachers in different parts of the country. Nearly all the coloured teachers in Washington are girls and women, a large percentage of whom were edu-

cated in the District of Columbia. Nor is it only in the ranks of teachers that coloured women are content to remain. Some years since, two coloured women were studying in the Law School of Howard University. One of them, Miss Charlotte Ray, a member of this body, has since graduated, being, I believe, the first coloured woman in the country who has ever gained the distinction of being a graduated lawyer. Others have gone into medicine and have been practising in different States of the Union. In the Woman's Medical College of Pennsylvania, two coloured women were last year pursuing their studies as Matriculants, while a young woman, the daughter of a former fugitive slave, has held the position of an assistant resident physician in one of the hospitals. Miss Cole, of Philadelphia, held for some time the position of physician in the State Orphan Asylum in South Carolina.

In literature and art we have not accomplished much, although we have a few among us who have tried literature. Miss Foster has written for the Atlantic Monthly, and Mrs. Mary Shadd Cary for years edited a paper called the Provincial Freeman, and another coloured woman has written several stories, poems, and sketches, which have appeared in different periodicals. In art, we have Miss Edmonia Lewis, who is, I believe, allied on one side to the negro race. She exhibited several pieces of statuary, among which is "Cleopatra, at the Centennial."

The coloured women have not been backward in promoting charities for their own sex and race. One of the most efficient helpers is Mrs. Madison, who, although living in a humble and unpretending home, had succeeded in getting up a home for aged coloured women. By organized effort, coloured women have been enabled to help each other in sickness, and provide respectable funerals for the dead. They have institutions under different names; one of the oldest, perhaps the oldest in the country, has been in existence, as I have been informed, about fifty years, and has been officered and managed almost solely by women for about half a century. There are also, in several States, homes for aged coloured women: the largest I know of being in Philadelphia. This home was in a measure built by Stephen and Harriet Smith, coloured citizens of the State of Pennsylvania. Into this home men are also admitted. The city of Philadelphia has also another home for the homeless, which, besides giving them a temporary shelter, provides a permanent home for a number of aged coloured women. In looking over the statistics of miscellaneous charities, out of a list of fifty-seven charitable institutions, I see only nine in which there is any record of coloured inmates. Out of twenty-six Industrial Schools, I counted four. Out of a list of one hundred and fifty-seven orphan asylums, miscellaneous charities, and industrial schools, I find fifteen asylums in where there is some mention of coloured inmates. More than half the reform schools in 1874, had admitted coloured girls. The coloured women of Philadelphia have formed a Christian Relief Association, which has opened sewing schools for coloured girls, and

*which has been enabled, year after year, to lend a hand to some of the more
needy of their race, and it also has, I understand, sustained an employment
office for some time.*[4]

The essay, "Coloured Women of America," was published in
England. It is preceded by the following introduction: "During the
recent Women's Congress an interesting paper was read by Mrs. Harper,
of Philadelphia, describing the present condition of some of the
coloured women of the Southern States, and the speedy advance which
they have made in civilization since independence. Their condition is
so little known in England, that we transcribe a portion of the essay for
our readers."[5]

The continental connections of the women's movement provided
an international visibility for Afroamerican women in the arts and in
politics. The political connections established during the abolitionist
movement continued after the war, and the educational and social affiliations determined a strong women's network. Harper congratulates the
strides and ambitions of Afroamerican women, describing overall
progress at large and citing the particular accomplishments of some,
such as Mary Shadd Cary and Edmonia Lewis. Harper met Cary, an
editor and activist, in Michigan in 1856 through abolitionist work,
and Harper became acquainted with Lewis, a black-Chippewa, as a fellow artist living in Philadelphia. Edmonia Lewis crafted the bust
of Bishop Daniel Payne of the A.M.E. church for the 1876 American
Centennial Celebration in Philadelphia, and when the bust was officially
unveiled and dedicated to his memory, Harper read her poem, "To
Bishop Payne."

More oblique references foreshadow future important personalities in the women's movement. "A colored lady, who was born a slave,"
and received a scholarship from Daniel Payne when she entered Oberlin
College, and became the principal of a colored high school in Philadelphia, appears to fit the profile of Fannie Jackson (Coppin), who was also
a classmate of Edmonia Lewis. Coppin was the class poet, and her studies at Oberlin included the more rigorous "gentlemen's course," including Latin, Greek, and higher mathematics.

Coppin, an exemplary teacher and prominent school administrator, was active in the A.M.E. church and in national and local educational
associations. Coppin fought against racial and gender discrimination in
the work place, was an advocate of industrial education, and established
one of the first industrial education curriculums. As the editor of the
A.M.E. Church Review, she published some of Harper's poetry and essays.

Hallie Q. Brown, another black feminist closely associated with Harper, was born in 1850 into a Pittsburgh family that aided the Underground Railroad. Brown's family moved to Canada in 1864, where they worked politically with Mary Shadd Cary, but returned to the U.S. in 1870 so Hallie could attend Wilberforce University. The Browns were active in the A.M.E. church, and Hallie taught in Reconstructionist schools in various regions of the South. In 1886, she graduated from elocutionary school and began lecturing throughout the country and in the British Isles on civil rights, women's suffrage, and the temperance cause. Her political activities placed her in organizational proximity to Harper. Brown was a member of the WCTU and one of the founding members of the National Association of Women's Clubs. She is the author of *Homespun Heroines and Other Women of Distinction* (1926), probably the first collection of biographies about outstanding black American women from all walks of life, spanning from Phillis Wheatley to Madame C. J. Walker, and including Harriet Tubman, Sojourner Truth, Fannie J. Coppin, Frances E. W. Harper, and others. Like the intellectual protagonist in "The Two Offers," Brown never married and lived to be one hundred years old.

Anna Julia Cooper, the first black woman to earn a Ph.D. (from the University of Paris), did marry, but like Harper was soon widowed (in two years). Cooper was a renowned educator and author of the first philosophical book written from the black feminist perspective, *A Voice from the South* (1892). Born in 1858 in Raleigh, North Carolina to an enslaved woman and her white slavemaster, Cooper's resistance to patriarchy could have been a logical extension of her maternal legacy. Cooper was admitted into St. Augustine Normal School in 1868 where she received a B.A., and in 1887 she received an M.A. from Oberlin. She became principal of a "colored" secondary school in Washington, D.C., which would later be named Dunbar High School.

Cooper advocated a strenuous liberal arts curriculum, and the school became famous for its output of successful graduates who obtained professional degrees from Ivy League universities and other "prestigious" institutions such as the University of Michigan. Like Coppin, Cooper's school provided both an industrial education and a liberal arts curriculum. Both Coppin and Cooper advanced industrial education before Booker T. Washington founded Tuskegee Institute in Alabama.

Cooper was active in national feminist and educational organizations. She worked with white feminists and advocated a racial consciousness in the women's movement. Her book, *A Voice from the South* (1892), was published by Aldine Publishers in Xenia, Ohio, four miles from Wilberforce's active political and educational community. Aldine was a noted publisher of books by black writers during the early twentieth century. Cooper's book was critical to the formation of black feminist thought, and like Harper's novel, *Iola Leroy*, published the same year by a Boston publisher, provided a tangible text for black feminist consciousness.

Cole, Foster, Shadd, Cooper, Coppin, Brown, Harper, and Lewis crossed paths in those key areas of intersection for the Underground Railroad, where not only intense political activity ensued but also where educational and cultural activities emerged. Chatham, Ontario; Boston, Massachusetts; Chicago, Illinois; Detroit, Michigan; Philadelphia, Pennsylvania; Oberlin, Ohio; New York, New York; Washington, D.C.; and Wilberforce, Ohio are places where these women lived and worked for change and where black feminist thought developed.

The needs of the emerging community weaved the woof and wool of thoughts and deeds, a perception and a vision that evolved from the extended family lifestyle that created a communal texture of values for survival during enslavement. During slavery, many mothers had no husband and too many children were shuffled from place to place. The concept of "brother" and "sister" was firmly related to the identity of a family constructed by the blood of Christ and the blood ties of the overseer's whip.

Many of these women pursued economic independence and professional careers. If married, they supported principled politics on the part of their spouses, and if single they assumed awesome tasks that exceeded the conventional expectations of blacks or women. Harper's political activity directed progressive actions of radical women, and her literature, widely read in national black periodicals, influenced the broader black community's position on women's rights and their social relationship to issues such as lynching, suffrage, temperance, and education. The poem, "John and Jacob—A Dialogue on Woman's Rights," reflects in conversation the gender values within the black community.

John and Jacob—A Dialogue on Woman's Rights

I don't believe a single bit
In those new-fangled ways
Of women running to the polls
And voting now adays.
I like the good old-fashioned times
When women used to spin,

And when you came from work you knew
Your wife was always in.
Now there's my Betsy, just as good
As any wife need be,
Who sits and tells me day by day
That women are not free;
And when I smile and say to her,
"You surely make me laff;
This talk about your rights and wrongs
Is nothing else but chaff."

    John
Now, Jacob, I don't think like you;
I think that Betsy Ann
Has just as good a right to vote
As you or any man.

    Jacob
Now, John, do you believe for true
In women running round,
And when you come to look for them
They are not to be found?
Pray, who would stay at home to nurse,
To cook, to wash, and sew,
While women marched unto the polls?
That's what I want to know.

    John
Who stays at home when Betsy Ann
Goes out day after day
To wash and iron, cook and sew,
Because she gets her pay?
I'm sure she wouldn't take quite so long
To vote and go her way,
As when she leaves her little ones
And works out day by day.

    Jacob
Well, I declare, that is the truth!
To vote, it don't take long;
But, then I kind of think somehow
That women's voting's wrong.

    John
The masters thought before the war

217

That slavery was right:
But we who felt the heavy yoke
Didn't see it in that light.
Some thought that it would never do
For us in Southern lands,
To change the fetters on our wrists
For the ballot in our hands.
Now if you don't believe 'twas right
To crowd us from the track.
How can you push your wife aside
And try to hold her back?

Jacob
But, John, I think for women's feet
The polls a dreadful place;
To vote with rough and brutal men
Seems like a deep disgrace.

John
But, Jacob, if the polls are vile,
Where women shouldn't be seen,
Why not invite them in to help
Us men to make them clean?

Jacob
Well, wrong is wrong, and right is right,
For women as for man;
I almost think that I will go
And vote with Betsy Ann.

John
I hope you will, and show the world
You can be brave and strong—
A noble man, who scorns to do
The feeblest woman wrong.[6]

Harper engages a very clever strategy in the poem, "John and Jacob—A Dialogue on Woman's Rights" (1885). This conversation between two men would more likely attract a reading by men who do not usually listen to women. Since many of the more hostile resistors to gender equality did not engage in political conversation with women, but would debate the issue with other men, the poem could ignite a broader male response and readership. The voice of John, the enlightened one, could be the position of Frederick Douglass or T. Thomas Fortune arguing the inherent contradictions of gender discrimination by comparing such thinking to racial discrimination. The poem reveals how humans do not necessarily arrive at a more tolerant or liberal view of others by virtue of their own suffering. Unfortunately, the issue of sexism in the Afroamerican community became more prevalent with liberation as the models for freedom were often more reflective of the Victorian patriarchs than of the radical abolitionists.

"Fancy Etchings" or "Fancy Sketches," a three-part serialized short story published under both titles in *The Christian Recorder* (April 24, May 1, 1873, and January 15, 1874) contains a feminist theme placed squarely in the black experience. The characters discuss intemperance, Christian character, and economic self-determination. Reflective of the social and political work of black feminists, the story develops around these concerns and the sexist resistance of black men to women's rights. Three women—an aunt and her two nieces—exchange their histories and pursuits and demonstrate sisterly support for each other with a progressive outlook. One of the nieces, Jane, is a poet. She explains that the power of writing has given her inner strength. Uncle Glumby glumly dismisses her poetry as frivolity with a sexist comment, "Can you cook a beef steak?" The aunt attempts to explain her husband's indifference as a consequence of his cultural ignorance and limited social experience.

As a forerunner in black literature, Harper often enlists writing as subject and symbol to promote literacy and to recruit blacks to become writers. The product and the production are used to change attitudes and to demonstrate the power of the pen. This short story explains the dynamics of the woman poet's dilemma while in evidence it supplants the conventions that ignore her voice. Harper reiterates her appeal to women to make their lives meaningful by contributing their creative powers to the development of a new culture.

Frances Harper's renowned presence in the black women's movement was as much attributable to her popularity as a writer as it was to her long-standing political stature. Likewise, the publication of her novel *Iola Leroy, or Shadows Uplifted* in 1892, regarded by her activist peers as a representative work of Afroamerican cultural experience, was particularly timely for the woman's era of the 1890s. Anna Julia Cooper's *A Voice From the South* (1892); Lucy A. Delaney's *From the Darkness Cometh the Light or Struggles for Freedom* (1891); Kate Drumgold's *A Slave Girl's Story* (1898); Emma Kelly's *Megda* (1891) (a novel published by the same Boston printer that published the first edition of *Iola Leroy*); and Harper's *Iola Leroy*, constituted a new era in black women's writing. These works and the periodicals edited and published by black women's organizations determined the beginning of a major literary movement.

Frances Harper, Ida B. Wells, and Iola Leroy

Ida B. Wells was one of the young women who did take up the pen in the struggle against injustice. In concert with Harper's radical writings, Ida B. Wells, a younger but nationally-noted activist, took a strong stand against lynching. Wells gained notoriety when she sued the Chesapeake & Ohio Railway in 1884 for its Jim Crow practices. After taking a seat in the "Ladies Coach," a conductor ordered her to sit in the smoking car. Refusing to do so, the conductor attempted to forcibly remove her. In response, Wells bit the conductor's hand. The conductor called for reinforcements, and three more conductors dragged the small woman out of the car.

"Wells was the first Afroamerican to challenge the 1883 nullification of the Civil Rights Bill passed during Reconstruction."[7] She became even more threatening to the advance of segregation, when her writings against lynching began to appear. She contended, "lynching was merely an excuse to get rid of Negroes who were acquiring wealth and prosperity and thus keep the race terrorized and 'keep the nigger down.' "[8] "Nobody in this sector of the country believes the threadbare lie that Negro men rape white women,"[9] Wells asserted.

When this editorial appeared in her Memphis newspaper, *Free Speech*, Wells, traveling across the country, was in Philadelphia visiting with Frances Harper and attending the 1892 National Conference of the A.M.E. church. During this stay, Wells also visited with Fannie Coppin and observed her school. Wells wrote in her autobiography:

> I had never been East or witnessed the deliberations of a general conference. Mrs. Frances Watkins Harper of that city had visited Memphis the winter before as my guest and invited me to be her guest in Philadelphia. Bishop H. M. Turner, who was over the Memphis district, had also urged me to go to the conference without fail. Mr. T. Thomas Fortune, the brilliant editor of the New York Age, who had often flattered me by copying my articles, had already written to say that he hoped I would give the East a lookover before I decided where I would cast my lot.[10]

When Wells reached New York City, Fortune informed her that an Associated Press release had reported that the *Free Speech* had been silenced by "a committee of leading citizens" who had "run the business manager, J. L. Fleming, out of town, destroyed the type and furnishings of the office, and left a note saying that anyone trying to publish the paper again would be punished with death."[11] The article further indicated the newspaper was owned by Ida B. Wells, "a former schoolteacher, who was traveling in the North."[12]

Harper and Wells were known for their aggressive, verbal assaults against lynching, which constituted a critical aspect of black feminist politics, the elder reinforcing the radicalism of the younger, extending the legacy. More than any other younger feminist, Wells represented ideological and activist politics similar to Harper. Harper symbolically embraced Wells when Harper endowed her novel's protagonist with Well's nom de plume, Iola.

Colored Women's Organizations

Afroamerican women's participation in the abolitionist movement was significant. Their presence was critical to the development of the feminist consciousness in the radical perspective and in the day-to-day struggles of the Underground Railroad. Frances Harper and other key figures like Harriet Tubman, Sojourner Truth, Mary Shadd, Charlotte Forten, and her daughters, Sarah and Harriet, were nationally renowned and respected in the radical community. They and lesser known black women gained membership in existing abolitionist and feminist organizations, and through their own efforts sustained a legacy of struggle. At the same time, the realization of racism in the women's movement and sexism in the Afroamerican community, made the organizing of black women necessary and inevitable.

Historical considerations of black women during these vital years has been slighted, despite their political presence during any era of Afroamerican struggle. The racist and sexist aggression directed against black women determined a resistance that could entertain little compromise, for there is little to negotiate on the bottom line. The advent of post-Reconstruction revisionism threatened the basic survival of people of color; while the federal government launched wars against the Plains Indians, the Ku Klux Klan launched terrorist attacks against Afroamericans.

Identified in the forefront of abolitionism and feminism, Frances Harper's vision interfaced and extended the transition of an old age into a new era. Representative of black feminist thought, she articulated and clarified the multi-faceted complexity of American repression as she guided the eager consciousness of young activists advancing into the twentieth century. By virtue of this stature she was positioned at the helm of black feminist politics, and from this position she reiterated the need to criticize racial policies and practices. Harper profoundly affected the ideological perspective of emerging national black feminist organizations. As the disappointments in the Reconstruction era and in the federal government determined stronger resistance on the part of women, Harper's words encouraged and guided them. At the same time, she cautioned them about corrupting dynamics of political ambition.

In 1893, as part of the World's Columbian Exposition, the World's Congress of Representative Women met in Chicago. Hallie Q. Brown, Anna Julia Cooper, Fannie Jackson Coppin and Frances Harper joined Sarah J. Early, Fannie Williams, and Frederick Douglass for this moment in feminist history.[13] "The Woman's Era," a term which symbolized the spirit of black feminism was first referenced by Harper while quoting Victor Hugo, in her essay, "The Woman's Christian Temperance Union and the Colored Woman." But the magnetism of the term characterized the movement captured by the momentous force of Harper's historic speech, "Woman's Political Future," delivered before this gathering. Her speech epitomizes the crystalline spirit of a perspective unspoiled and undaunted since her earliest years at the lectern in 1854. It could be considered Frances Ellen Watkins Harper's political manifesto.

> *If before sin had cast its deepest shadows or sorrow had distilled its bitterest tears, it was true that it was not good for man to be alone, it is no less true, since the shadows have deepened and life's sorrows have increased, that the world has need of all the spiritual aid that woman can give for the social advancement and moral development of the human race. The tendency of the present age, with its restlessness, religious upheavals, failures, blunders, and crimes, is toward broader freedom, an increase of knowledge, the emancipation of thought, and a recognition of the brotherhood of man; in this movement woman, as the companion of man, must be a sharer. So close is the bond between man and woman that you can not raise one without lifting the other. The world can not move without woman's sharing in the movement, and to help give a right impetus to that movement is woman's highest privilege.*
>
> *If the fifteenth century discovered America to the Old World, the nineteenth is discovering woman to herself. Little did Columbus imagine, when the New World broke upon his vision like a lovely gem in the coronet of the universe, the glorious possibilities of a land where the sun should be our engraver, the winged lightning our messenger, and steam our beast of burden. But as mind is more than matter, and the highest idea always the true real,*

so to woman comes the opportunity to strive for richer and grander discoveries than ever gladdened the eye of the Genovese mariner.

Not the opportunity of discovering new worlds, but that of filling this old world with fairer and higher aims than the greed of gold and the lust of power, is hers. Through weary, wasting years men have destroyed, dashed in pieces, and overthrown, but to-day we stand on the threshold of woman's era, and woman's work is grandly constructive. In her hand are possibilities whose use or abuse must tell upon the political life of the nation, and send their influence for good or evil across the track of unborn ages.

As the saffron tints and crimson flushes of morn herald the coming day, so the social and political advancement which woman has already gained bears the promise of the rising of the full-orbed sun of emancipation. The result will be not to make home less happy, but society more holy; yet I do not think the mere extension of the ballot a panacea for all the ills of our national life. What we need to-day is not simply more voters, but better voters. To-day there are red-handed men in our republic, who walk unwhipped of justice, who richly deserve to exchange the ballot of the freeman for the wristlets of the felon; brutal and cowardly men, who torture, burn, and lynch their fellow-men, men whose defenselessness should be their best defense and their weakness an ensign of protection. More than the changing of institutions we need the development of a national conscience, and the upbuilding of national character. Men may boast of the aristocracy of blood, may glory in the aristocracy of talent, and be proud of the aristocracy of wealth, but there is one aristocracy which must ever outrank them all, and that is the aristocracy of character; and it is the women of a country who help mold its character, and to influence if not determine its destiny; and in the political future of our nation woman will not have done what she could if she does not endeavor to have our republic stand foremost among the nations of the earth, wearing sobriety as a crown and righteousness as a garment and a girdle. In coming into her political estate woman will find a mass of illiteracy to be dispelled. If knowledge is power, ignorance is also power. The power that educates wickedness may manipulate and dash against the pillars of any state when they are undermined and honeycombed by injustice.

I envy neither the heart nor the head of any legislator who has been born to an inheritance of privileges, who has behind him ages of education, dominion, civilization, and Christianity, if he stands opposed to the passage of a national education bill, whose purpose is to secure education to the children of those who were born under the shadow of institutions which made it a crime to read.

To-day women hold in their hands influence and opportunity, and with these they have already opened doors which have been closed to others. By opening doors of labor woman has become a rival claimant for at least some of the wealth monopolized by her stronger brother. In the home she is the priestess, in society the queen, in literature she is a power, in legislative halls law-makers have responded to her appeals, and for her sake have humanized and liberalized their laws. The press has felt the impress of her hand. In the pews of the church she constitutes the majority; the pulpit has welcomed her, and in the schools she has the blessed privilege of teaching children and youth. To her is apparently coming the added responsibility of political power; and what she now possesses should only be the means of preparing her to use the coming power for the glory of God and the good of mankind for power without righteousness is one of the most dangerous forces in the world.

Political life in our country has plowed in muddy channels, and needs the infusion of clearer and cleaner waters. I am not sure that women are naturally so much better than men that they will clear the stream by the virtue of their womanhood; it is not through sex but through character than the best influence of women upon the life of the nation must be exerted.

I do not believe in unrestricted and universal suffrage for either men or women. I believe in moral and educational tests. I do not believe that the most ignorant and brutal man is better prepared to add value to the strength and durability of the government than the most cultured, upright, and intelligent woman. I do not think that willful ignorance should swamp earnest intelligence at the ballot-box, nor that educated wickedness, violence, and fraud should cancel the votes of honest men. The unsteady hands of a drunkard can not cast the ballot of a freeman. The hands of lynchers are too red with blood to determine the political character of the government for even four short years. The ballot in the hands of woman means power added to influence. How well she will use that power I can not foretell. Great evils stare us in the face that need to be throttled by the combined power of an upright manhood and an enlightened womanhood; and I know that no nation can gain its full measure of enlightenment and happiness if one-half of it is free and the other half is fettered. China compressed the feet of her women and thereby retarded the steps of her men. The elements of a nation's weakness must be ever found at the hearthstone.

More than the increase of wealth, the power of armies, and the strength of fleets is the need of good homes, of good fathers, and good mothers. . . .

Woman coming into her kingdom will find enthroned three great evils, for whose overthrow she should be as strong in a love of justice and humanity as the warrior is in his might. She will find intemperance sending its flood of shame, and death, and sorrow to the homes of men, a fretting leprosy in our politics, and a blighting curse in our social life; the social evil sending to our streets women whose laughter is sadder than their tears, who slide from the paths of sin and shame to the friendly shelter of the grave, and lawlessness enacting in our republic deeds over which angels might weep, if heaven knows sympathy. . . .

O women of America! into your hands God has pressed one of the sublimest opportunities that ever came into the hands of the women of any race or people. It is yours to create a healthy public sentiment; to demand justice, simple justice, as the right of every race; to brand with everlasting infamy the lawless and brutal cowardice that lynches, burns, and tortures your own countrymen.

To grapple with the evils which threaten to undermine the strength of the nation and to lay magazines of powder under the cribs of future generations is no child's play.

Let the hearts of the women of the world respond to the song of the herald angels of peace on earth and good will to men. Let them throb as one heart unified by the grand and holy purpose of uplifting the human race, and humanity will breathe freer, and the world grow brighter. With such a purpose Eden would spring up in our path, and Paradise be around our way.[14]

Shortly thereafter, a derivative women's club in Boston began publishing the journal, *The Woman's Era.* Inscribed by the speech Harper delivered before the Congress in Chicago, it became the voice of black feminism. Concurrently, in 1895, the First Congress of Colored Women convened in Boston, and by 1896, the National Association of Colored Women, led by Mary Church Terrell, became the largest black women's organization in the country upon the merger of the National League of Colored Women and the National Federation of Colored Women. Harriet Tubman, who had converted her house into the John Brown Home for the aged, was the featured speaker on a platform consisting of Fannie Coppin, Ida B. Wells, and Frances Harper.

Harper was elected vice-president of the National Association of Colored Women in 1897 at a meeting in Nashville, and at the second convention of the organization in Chicago, August 1899, she delivered an address, "Racial Literature." The organization addressed political issues, public and domestic, as well as historical and cultural concerns. In particular, these women investigated the whereabouts and welfare of Mary Brown, John Brown's widow, to assure her well-being.[15]

Conclusion

Together, the work and writings of black feminists constructively criticized the reserve of those white feminists who refused to identify white male terrorism as a feminist issue. Likewise, the black feminist reproached black men for their regressive patriarchal tendencies. But despite their ideological and programmatic efforts, these basic contradictions, which divided and defined the American social reality by race and gender, further diminished the possibility of a unified vanguard movement and the fulfillment of Harper's radical vision. However,

Harper maintained a distinctive presence in the movement and re-mained active until she was physically unable to do so.

Harper's work and writings on intemperance regularly appeared in the *A.M.E. Church Review*, wherein she encouraged the black community to recognize the enslavement of intemperance. Though the temperance movement will eventually be assessed as repressive during Prohibition, Harper's campaign against alcoholism cannot be summarily dismissed. Alcoholism and drug addiction are still disproportionately higher in communities of color in the United States, a degenerative condition that still refracts the dreaded imagery of "The Drunkard's Child" in de-pressed neighborhoods and reservations. Her name appeared on the WCTU honor roll in 1874 and posthumously in 1924.

Harper's editorial in *The Woman's Era* (1894), "How to Stop Lynch-ing," is one of her most powerful indictments of duplicity against the fed-eral government. Harper demands responsibility from the government to intervene and protect southern blacks from terrorist attacks. This voice is charged with the same eloquent passion that empowered her words against the hunting and kidnapping of fugitive slaves before the abolition of slavery. It also reflects the ongoing struggle for survival in a hostile na-tive land.

> *In his very admirable and searching address delivered in this city, April 16th, Judge Albion W. Tourgee proposed as a remedy to prevent the lynching of colored people at the South, that the county where lynchings oc-cur be compelled by law to pension the wife and children of the murdered man. This, he said would make murder costly and in self defense the local authorities would put a stop to it. At first blush, this is an attractive sug-gestion. But why not hang the murderers? Why make a distinction between the murderers of white men and the murderers of colored men? If the pun-ishment for murder is hanging why hang the murderer in one case and in the other let the murderer go free and exact of the county a fine? If an eye for an eye and a tooth for a tooth is the rule in one case why should it not be the rule in the other case? No, the truth is this, nothing is to be expected from the South. The colored people must look to the general government. It had a right to their services and lives in time of war. They have a right to its protection certainly in time of peace. It is idle to say that it must leave to state govern-ments the protection of the lives of its citizens. Why not leave to state gov-ernments the punishment of counterfeiters? If the United States government can protect money, the property of its citizens against destruction at the hands of the counterfeiter, it can protect the owners of the property against loss of life at the hands of the murderer. It is an astounding proposition that a great nation is powerful enough to stop white moonshiners from making*

whiskey but is unable to prevent the moonshiners or any one else from mur-
dering its citizens. It can protect corn but cannot protect life. It can prevent
the sale of tobacco unless the seller pays a revenue to the government but it
cannot protect its citizens at any price. It can go to war, spend millions of
dollars and sacrifice thousands of lives to avenge the death of a naturalized
white citizen slain by a foreign government on foreign soil, but cannot spend
a cent to protect a loyal, native-born colored American murdered without
provocation by native or alien in Alabama. Shame on such a government!
The administration in power is particeps criminis with the murderers. It can
stop lynching, and until it does, it has on its hands the innocent blood of its
murdered citizens.[16]

But to-day the traitor stands
With the crimson on his hands,
Scowling 'neath his brow of hate,
On our weak and desolate,
With the blood-rust on the knife
Aimed at the nation's life.

Asking you to weakly yield
All we won upon the field,
To ignore, on land and flood,
All the offerings of our blood,
And to write above our slain
"They have fought and died in vain."

To your manhood we appeal,
Lest the traitor's iron heel
Grind and trample in the dust
All our new-born hope and trust,
And the name of freedom be
Linked with bitter mockery.[17]

CHAPTER 8

Retrieval of a Legacy

A stricken heart may be aching beneath magnificent attire. A human heart may be starving, not for bread, but for heart support and Christly sympathy. A warm pressure of the hand, a word fitly spoken, may seem to be the giver a little thing, but to the receiver it may be as a well, springing up in the desert dust. . . .

Only a word—a loving word,
Sown 'mid prayers and tears,
  May bloom in time, and fruitage bear,
Throughout the eternal years.[1]

Reflections

In addition to Harper's feminist activism and her temperance campaign for the WCTU, in which she held organizational positions and for which she lectured, a generous portion of her later years was devoted to youth work. Defying the boundaries of denominations and sectarianism, she worked with a number of churches in the black community of north Philadelphia, where she lived. With Reverend Henry L. Phillips at the Church of the Crucifixion, she worked against juvenile delinquency while her daughter taught Sunday school. Harper was a member of the Sarah Allen Missionary Association, which fed the poor and children, and she taught Sunday school at Mother Bethel A.M.E. Church while still a member of the Unitarian Church on Chestnut Street.

During the 1876 Centennial Exhibition, the Philadelphia black community attempted to celebrate the occasion by installing a bust of Richard Allen, the founder of the A.M.E. church, on the Centennial grounds. Their request and their enthusiasm to participate in the Fourth of July festivities were denied. As their liberated identity as equal Americans was slighted by this rejection of Allen's bust, the sculpture by Edmonia Lewis was most timely by its late arrival. Placed on a tenuous mounting "on Nov. 8, one day before the Centennial Exhibition closed, the bust was erected on a temporary pedestal and dedicated in a cold and driving rain."[2] Frances Harper recited "We Are Rising," a poem written for the occasion.

The bust was later removed. Some believed it lost. Journalist Margaret Hope Bacon tracked the bust of Allen to Wilberforce University, but the absence of records leaves this claim to speculation and probability. The irony of Allen's tribute intersects with the pattern of strayed, misplaced, and discarded legacies. Harper, standing in the rain, would also be destined to a late and damp reception.

Let Me Make Songs for the People

Let me make songs for the people,
Songs for the old and young;
Songs to strike like a battle cry
Whenever they are sung.

Let me make the songs for the weary,
Amid life's fever and fret,
Till hearts shall relax their tension
And careworn brows forget.

I will sing for the poor and aged,
When shadows dim their sight,
Of the bright and restful mansions,
Where there shall be no right.

Our world, so worn and weary
Needs music, pure and strong
To hush the pangs and discords
Of sorrow, pain and wrong.[3]

In addition to her poetry and fiction, Harper's major literary contribution was the application of poetic techniques to rhetorical expression. Her subtle incorporation of alliteration and internal rhyme into essays and speeches exalted Afroamerican oral and written traditions reflecting a vital, creative culture. Her power transferred the improvisational ingenuity of one genre to enhance the delivery and impact of the other two, distinguishing a particular style and commanding a historical presence. Insofar as her poetic skill facilitated her oral delivery, conceptualized her prose, and ingrained her essays, the occasional interlacing of lyrical verse in all of these verbal experiences highlighted poetry as the focal point of Harper's imagination.

As a woman of color, the sheer presence of her person at public lecterns contradicted the rationale for racial, gender, and class prejudice and the institutional premise for discrimination. The poetry books she left in the hands of her audiences served as memory and magic for the artistry and tenacity of the cultural heritage she articulated, as her adeptness with technique and form produced innovative and impressive literature. Maintaining the vantage point of the downtrodden, Harper constructed the visionary perspective of a Christian woman warrior confronting injustice and *educated wickedness*. Her heroic style confounded her century and confused subsequent critics.

Poems on Miscellaneous Subjects issues a social critique that cuts to the heart of the undemocratic American reality. Her imagery infused American literature with voices silenced by social prejudice or muffled by cultural disadvantage. Subsequent poems extended her radical feminist vision in the relentless pursuit for the realization of the promised land and the American democratic ideal. Her other major works, including *Sketches of Southern Life* and *Moses: A Story of the Nile*, probably contributed more to the building of a literary tradition than most works written by other nineteenth-century black writers. But at the same time, the practical value of these stellar poems by Harper served a practical purpose as cultural texts in the freedmen's schools and Sunday schools. Her activist involvement with the A.M.E. church during the Reconstruction era, as lecturer and teacher, provided a distribution network and a pedagogical context for her literature. Her impact on the larger black community can be correlated with the eminence of Langston Hughes in the twentieth century. Taking into account the fifty thousand books that were in print by 1872, a projection that at least one hundred thousand books by Harper were in print by the end of the century is a modest estimate.

Harper's work, written and oral, exemplifies studied reflection balanced by common sense. This invaluable blend of studied knowledge, common sense, and a broad range of racial, gender, and class experience is a rare combination in Western literature. Harper's aesthetic retention of "mother wit" assures a class attitude that cannot be undermined by diction or deportment. Like Aunt Chloe and Aunt Linda, Harper's foremost concern is the integrity of the human spirit, and as she explained in "Our Greatest Want" in 1859, the emulation of a materialistic society and superficial values that enslave their white relatives threatens the substance of character and the spiritual values of country. She reiterates in 1898:

*Persons too ignorant to read a single sentence may be learned enough
in heart-love to translate the language of an eye that beams with sympathy,
or a countenance that glows with compassion. After the outbreak of rebellion, when the school was taking the place of the slave-pen, a number of my
acquaintances went South as teachers. Among them was a plain looking
woman with a limited education, and a young woman from the culture of
a New England school. One seemed to possess the warmer heart, the other the
riper intellect. Both from their standpoints may have done the best they knew.
I have heard of some of those people to whom they ministered saying of the
younger woman who attempted to advise them: "God knows she ain't white,
but she puts on mighty white airs." But of the other teacher: "She is low down,
but she feels for we." False politeness can cast a glamour over fashionable fol-
lies and popular vices and shrink from uttering unpalatable truths, when
truth is needed more than flattery. True politeness, tender as love and faithful as truth, vales intrinsic worth more than artificial surroundings. It will
stem the current of the world's disfavor, rather than float ignobly on the tide
of popular favor, with the implied disrespect to our common human nature,
that it is a flaccid thing to be won by sophistry, and satisfied with shams.*[4]

Harper's creative ingenuity invented a thematic strategy to confront the complexities of audience response to racial and gender issues.
Iola Leroy is first a "white" woman whose identity is radically altered by
economic circumstances; her epic demonstrates the necessity to obliter-
ate all categories of social discrimination. Like Iola, America must commit class suicide in order to acquire its full potential as a humane
democracy. As the severity and extremity of compounded repression are
nearly unimaginable for those outside this particular or combined class
experiences, Harper relegates a once-wealthy "white" woman to the status of slave in order to demonstrate distance and disparity between the
extremes in racial, gender, and class perspectives. This technique serves
to provide a contextual range for character interaction that is necessary,
yet unprecedented in American literature. The realization of the proletarian novel engages ascending aspirations of the oppressed, as it illuminates and subverts the dominant paradigm.

In the position of Ishmael, Harper arrived at uncompromising con-
clusions. No matter in which direction she pivoted, the affront to human
frailty attempted to deny or to disadvantage her black female existence.
Without the power of the ballot, which she fought for with abolitionists
and feminists, she enforced her voice and her text to remind and to insist
that the practice of democracy has to take precedence over privileged
protocol. As the achievements of the Fifteenth Amendment were only a

temporary victory, Harper crafted her rhetoric to accommodate the irony and the tyranny infecting white complacency and plaguing black destiny.

During the later years, Frances Harper self-published her last book, *Poems*, as reprintings and copyrights identify her Bainbridge address. Such a command over her work, and the poems therein, suggest a communal purpose for publication as well as the instability of community resources. Primarily servicing the literacy and biblical programs in churches, the direct themes and simple ballads are instructive and inspirational. Undoubtedly, her most diligent creative efforts in her later years were her novels.

Most of her later poetry attempted to facilitate the conflict and confusion that compounded and oppressed the vision of the young. Unlike the aesthetic of the leisure class, the thematic thrust of the lyric was to uplift the spirit and to untangle the intellect. These poems were offered as a source of comfort and direction during a time when the defeat of the Reconstruction and the advance of racial terrorism against people of color issued a future maimed by legal segregation and demeaned by economic subordination. The passion characteristic of her abolitionist poetry, once used to enlist the sentiments of sympathetic "free" Americans, black and white, was now employed to inspire generations of black Americans to overcome the adversities of bigotry and the advance of racial hatred.

Frances Harper's legacy was discarded because that which is valued as culture is more often than not determined by those in power. Mary Helen Washington explains: "What we have to recognize is that the creation of the fiction of tradition is a matter of power, not justice, and that that power has always been in the hands of men—mostly white but some black. Women are the disinherited."[5] Likewise, Paul Lauter reiterates this point in his essay, "Is Frances Ellen Watkins Harper Good Enough to Teach?", stating that the recent attempts of right wing academics to narrow the literary canon has been circumvented by progressive growth in the academy, "but that effort has been more than offset by the impact of affirmative action personnel and admissions policies on curricula: it oversimplifies the process, but the more women of color, for example, have entered the academy, the more their concerns for their own history and culture have had the effect of diversifying the range of academic study." Furthermore, "we are more inclined, Ann Fitzgerald has suggested to me, to let the work teach us, rather than imposing our needs upon it."[6]

Our thinking is changing because the world is changing. As the world expands our universal interactions transform into more complex patterns of thought, and these will replace intolerance with patience and ignorance with intelligence. The integral presence of black women in positions of power and influence will further stimulate inquiry into that history and the legacy of that particular vision. For that and many more reasons, France Ellen Watkins Harper has been retrieved from obscurity as black women claim their rightful inheritance.

Resurrection

In 1909, two years before Frances Harper's death, her daughter Mary died. The irony of death had orphaned Harper again. Her mother's early death three years after her birth; the sudden death of her husband after only four years of marriage; and the death of her daughter reflect a pattern of mournful isolation.

After a short illness and being confined to her room for two months, Harper died on February 22, 1911. Funeral services were held on February 26 at the Unitarian Church on Chestnut Street. Like Moses, she was buried in an unmarked grave. Her body was laid to rest in the John Brown section of Eden, the cemetery for blacks in Philadelphia. Like the Eden of her poetry, *'neath sheltering vines and stately palms* she was laid to rest.

> *'twas the land*
> *Of crystal fountains, love and beauty, joy*
> *And light, for the pearly gates flew open,*
> *And his ransomed soul went in.*[7]

But the inheritance of freedom we acquired through her activism did not even provide equality for her grave. And like Moses, who *led the children of Israel over the Red Sea but was not permitted to see them settled in Canaan,* Frances Harper's eighty-five years serviced a vision beyond her earthly years. The burial crypt, however, does not form the end of Harper's life poem, just as the imprints of her text did not dissipate with the disposal of her papers or through the critical dismissal of her literature. But the long solitude of her legacy, like disenfranchisement after slavery, was a cruel fate for someone who had so diligently served her community and her country.

Following the Harper path, I discovered the living commitment to her memory. While Frances Foster continues to mine Harper's literature from obscure resources, Reverend Daniel Aldridge, a Unitarian minister in Atlanta, organized a successful campaign to place an appropriate headstone on Harper's grave on September 27, 1992 during a convention for the Unitarian churches, one hundred years after the publication of *Iola Leroy*. The original headstone was retrieved, having sunk beneath the earth, and it revealed an 1824 birthdate. This date conflicts with the 1825 year generally given and further complicates Harper's origin. However, since 1825 was the date reported during her lifetime, it is the one that seems most reliable.

Harper's direct bloodline ended with the death of her daughter, Mary, who died childless. But Frances Harper's brother-in-law, Clarence Harper, a free black, and his wife Martha, the daughter of a runaway Indian slave, named their daughter Frances Ellen after this prominent relative. Two generations later, Louise Somers Brown named her daughter Frances Ellen. As the name was retained, the commitment of the tradition was preserved through maternal lineage.

Frances Ellen Brown (whose name change to Falaka Fattah reflects her choice of an African cultural frame of reference) is actively involved in youth work in Philadelphia. Her belief in family is the foundation and philosophy of the House of Umoja, where gang youths are given a renewed sense of purpose in today's society wherein juvenile delinquency has become too commonplace. Ironically, Falaka's son, Chaka Fattah, has reconnected the lineage by naming his daughter Frances Ellen Fattah. By this, Chaka (the name of a fearless nineteenth-century Zulu warrior) has reiterated the value of an Afroamerican heritage, whereby the meaning of naming is the carriage of action transcending the severing of orphanage and the limitations of blood as racial and cultural bonding. About Harper's home, Falaka Fattah said, "I have only been inside the house once. But the spiritual essence of my love for Philadelphia resides there."[8]

During the 1976 Bicentennial celebrations, 1006 Bainbridge was designated a historical site. While the television crew crowded the steps of the old Philadelphia row house, Rosa Cannistraci curiously noticed the excitement. She discovered Frances Harper and explored her history. Realizing the significance of this "modest and great woman," she decided to purchase, protect, and restore the house to its original demeanor. Without any outside financial support, other than her own business resources as an independent contractor, Cannistraci determined to distinguish this building as a fitting tribute to Frances Harper's legacy. Like Still, Cannistraci believes there needs to be a light in the front.

> There are so many others who the country praises who have done nothing. Frances Harper worked for the freedom of the colored people and for the rights of women. She was a great woman. I want to make this house the way it was when she lived in it. I know exactly

234

how it should look, with marble steps and a gas light. And on the front I'm gonna put a plaque with the poem "Bury Me In A Free Land" and Harper's name on it, so everybody can see it. I want some black people to live in it. Maybe another great poet will live there.[9]

Winding Out the Spiral

Walking south, in the direction of a one-way street toward Bainbridge, I travelled through the emergence of displacement. The neighborhood was once a secret harbor for runaway slaves, a labyrinth of passages through attics interconnecting pockets of secret rooms. The voices of black children playing basketball inside the steel checkered fence collide against the echo of iron hammers slamming lumber. The awkward overlap of eras frame the haggard, but sturdy door to 1006 Bainbridge. The windows, partially covered by yellowed newspaper, are secured by the consistency of ageless bricks.

Turning into the alley to circle the house, voices fall from an open balcony. Two men, speaking American-Italian with hands and Mediterranean rhythms, accentuate their exchange. I call up to them to confirm the address. Grateful for the interruption of the unusual, they openly smile and pose for my camera. As they transform this house into a respectable homage to Frances Ellen Watkins Harper, I frame them like abstract verbs. As I photograph them, I tell them some of her biography and the history of the property; their work is infused with renewed interest.

Climbing the back staircase into a re-wooded, modernized interior, an ethereal warmth surrounds me. The workers explain that the house bears little resemblance to its earliest years, only the intricate detailing around the marble fireplaces is reminiscent. But it does not matter. I did not come in search of a mausoleum, but to encounter Harper's home for a quiet moment.

I followed the path of this poet whose Underground Railroad commitment intersected with fiery personalities of John Brown, Frederick Douglass, Harriet Tubman, Susan B. Anthony, Elizabeth Stanton, and Ida B. Wells. Prepared by her uncle to generate a space in American cultural history, her magnificence, probably most appreciated by William Still, still emanates despite the dimming of distance and the obscuring of details. Tilling a tradition of resistance, her voice often grated the special interests of her comrades. She claimed and criticized black and white, male and female; embracing them all, but trusting only in God.

In the aftermath of a civil war won and subsequent struggles foiled, she told the freed,

Get land, everyone that can, and as fast as you can. A landless people must be dependent upon the landed people.

The present haunt of the homeless huddled on Philadelphia corners reflect this truth.

You have muscle power and brain power. You must utilize them or be content to remain forever the inferior race.

Our dissipating youth and our complicity with confusion suggest a frightening future.

Frances Ellen Watkins Harper's countenance was undaunted by hostility or incivility. Displaying the faith of Moses and the enlightenment of Christ, Harper focused on a vision. By action and articulation she cleared a path, redeemed and renewed, toward the retrieval of discarded humanity.

Let the hearts of the women of the world respond to the song of the herald angels of peace on earth and good will to men. Let them throb as one heart unified by the grand and holy purpose of uplifting the human race, and humanity will breathe freer, and the world grow brighter. With such a purpose Eden would spring up in our path, and Paradise be around our way.[10]

Harper's home before restoration

FRANCES E. W. HARPER
(1825-1911)

An author, lecturer, and social activist, Harper lived here and devoted her life to championing the rights of slaves and free Blacks. She advocated education as a way of advancement for Black Americans.

PENNSYLVANIA, HISTORICAL AND MUSEUM COMMISSION 1992

1006

Harper's home restored

Notes

Introduction

1. Maxwell Whitman, "Author, Lecturer and Abolitionist," Introduction to Frances Harper, *Poems on Miscellaneous Subjects* (1857; reprint, Philadelphia: Rhistoric Pub., 1969).
2. Bettina Aptheker, *Woman's Legacy.* (Amherst: University of Massachusetts Press, 1982), p. 2.
3. Ada, [Sarah Forten], "Lines, Suggested on Reading 'An Appeal to Christian Women of the South' by A. E. Grimke," *The Liberator* 6 (Oct. 29, 1836).
4. William Wells Brown, *The Black Man: His Antecedents, His Genius, and His Achievements* (1863; reprint, New York: Johnson Reprint Corporation, 1968), p. 525.
5. Frances Harper, *Minnie's Sacrifice. The Christian Recorder* (Sept. 25, 1869).
6. Harper, speech, "Woman's Political Future," in *World's Congress of Representative Women, 1893.* ed. May Wright Sewall (Chicago, n. p., 1894), p. 433.
7. I am defining this term as W. E. B. Du Bois explains it in *The Souls of Black Folk,* whereby an oppressed person responds with a dual thought system, one for the oppressor and the other for the cultural community of black people.
8. Benjamin Brawley, "Three Negro Poets: Horton, Mrs. Harper, and Whitman," *Journal of Negro History* 2 (1917): pp. 391–92.
9. Vernon Loggins, *The Negro Author: His Development in America to 1900* (New York: Columbia University Press, 1931), p. 247.
10. Ibid., p. vii.
11. Ibid., p. 343.
12. Jay Saunders Redding, *To Make a Poet Black* (Chapel Hill: University of North Carolina Press, 1939), p. 42.
13. Ibid., p. 41.
14. Mary Helen Washington, *Invented Lives* (New York: Doubleday, 1987), p. 84.
15. Maryemma Graham, ed., *Complete Poems of Frances E. W. Harper* (New York: Oxford University Press, 1988), p. xlvix.
16. Ibid., p. liii.
17. Robert Hayden, "America's Poet Laureate," *Detroit Black Journal,* a documentary by Ron Scott, WTVS, Channel 56, Detroit, Nov. 1978.
18. Dudley Randall, interview with author, Detroit, Mich., Apr. 2, 1989.

Chapter 1

1. Frances Harper, to William Still, 1858, in *The Underground Rail Road* by William Still (Philadelphia: Porter & Coates, 1872), p. 763.
2. Ibid.
3. Ibid., p. 755.
4. Harper, "Days of My Childhood," *Anti-Slavery Bugle* (Sept. 29, 1860).
5. Theodora Williams Daniel, "The Poems of Frances E. W. Harper" (M.A. thesis, Howard University, May 14, 1937) p. 5.
6. Ibid., p. 6.
7. James H. A. Johnston, "William Watkins," *A.M.E. Church Review* 3 (1886): pp. 11–12.
8. Ibid., p. 95.
9. Ibid., p. 94.
10. *Freedom's Journal* (July 6, 1827): p. 66. Quoted by Leroy Graham in *Baltimore: The Nineteenth Century Black Capital*, p. 101.
11. Ibid., pp. 102–3.
12. Ibid., p. 112.
13. Ibid.
14. Ibid., p. 127.
15. Ibid., p. 112.
16. William Watkins, editorial, *The Liberator* (Jan. 21, 1832): p. 1.
17. Still, *Underground Rail Road*, p. 756.
18. The publication date 1845 also appears in biographical information. Since no copies of *Forest Leaves* are available, the conflicting bibliographical information remains unresolved.
19. John M. Brown, "Report of the Principal of the Union Seminary to the Ohio Conference," *Minutes of the Ohio Conference of the African Methodist Episcopal Church*, 1844, p. 19.
20. Still, *Underground Rail Road*, p. 756.
21. In ibid., p. 757.
22. Harper, "The Colored People in America," *Poems on Miscellaneous Subjects.*
23. In Still, *Underground Rail Road*, p. 758.
24. In ibid.
25. In ibid., p. 757.
26. In ibid., p. 758.
27. Bert J. Loewenberg and Ruth Bogin, eds., *Black Women in Nineteenth-Century American Life: Their Words, Their Thoughts, Their Feelings* (University Park & London: Pennsylvania University Press, 1976), p. 243.

28. *Portland Daily Press*, in ibid., p. 760. The Miss Dickinson cited is probably the abolitionist feminist, Anna Dickinson.

29. *Portland Advertiser*, in Dorothy Sterling, *We Are Your Sisters* (New York: W. W. Norton, 1984), p. 161.

30. In Still, *Underground Rail Road*, pp. 779–80.

31. July 5, 1871, in ibid., p. 775.

32. Jack Forbes, *Black Africans and Native Americans: Color, Race, and Caste in the Evolution of Red and Black Peoples.* (New York: Basil Blackwell, 1988), p. 135.

33. In Still, *Underground Rail Road*, p. 757.

34. In Sterling, *We Are Your Sisters*, pp. 174–75.

35. In Samuel Sillen, *Women Against Slavery* (New York: Masses & Mainstream, 1955), p. 71.

36. In Still, *Underground Rail Road*, p. 760.

37. Harper to Still, Buckstown Centre, Mass., Sept. 28, 1854, in ibid., p. 758

38. Harper to Still, Temple, Mass., Oct. 20, 1854, in ibid., p. 759.

39. Harper to Still, Tiffin, Ohio, Oct. 20, 1854, in ibid., p. 759.

40. Harper to Still (no place, no date), in ibid., p. 761.

41. Harper to Still, Lewis Centre, Ohio (no date), in ibid., pp. 761–62.

42. Harper to Still (no place, no date), in ibid., p. 763.

43. Harper to editor, *National Anti-Slavery Standard* 9 (Apr. 1859): p. 3, col. 3.

44. Harper to Still, Niagara Falls, New York, Sept. 12, 1856, In Still, *Underground Rail Road*, p. 760. Also in 1857 edition of Harper, *Poems on Miscellaneous Subjects* and Lydia Maria Child, *The Freedman's Book* (Boston: Tucknor and Fields, 1865).

45. Harper to John Brown, "From a Woman of the Race He Died For," Kendalville, Ind., Nov. 25, 1859, in James Redpath, *Echoes of Harper's Ferry* (1860; reprint, Salem, N.H.: Ayer Co., 1969), p. 418.

46. Harper to Mary Brown, in Still, *Underground Rail Road*, p. 762.

47. Ibid.

48. In Sterling, *We Are Your Sisters*, p. 164.

49. Ibid.

50. Harper to Still, no date, in Still, *Underground Rail Road*, p. 765.

51. Ibid., p. 764.

52. Ibid.

53. Harper to Still, Grove City, Ohio (no date), in ibid., pp. 766–67.

54. *The Proceedings of the Eleventh National Woman's Rights Convention*, New York, May 10, 1866, p. 45, Frances Harper Collection, the Historical Society of Pennsylvania, Philadelphia, Pa.

55. Harper to Still, Boston, Apr. 19, 1865, in Still, *Underground Rail Road*, pp. 766–67.

Chapter 2

1. William Lloyd Garrison. Preface to Harper, *Poems on Miscellaneous Subjects*. 2d. ed. (Philadelphia: Merrihew & Thompson, 1857): pp. 3–4.
2. William Still, review, *The Provincial Freeman* (Sept. 2, 1854).
3. *Frederick Douglass' Paper*, vol. 2 no. 6 (Jan. 13, l854).
4. Ibid., (Feb. 3, 1854).
5. Harper, *Poems* (Philadelphia: George S. Ferguson, 1895).
6. Ibid., pp. 49–50.
7. Joseph Priest and Rev. W. S. Brown, *Bible Defense of Slavery* (Louisville, Ky.: P. F. Brennan, 1851), title page.
8. Harper, "Temperance," *A.M.E. Church Review* 7 (1891): p. 373.

Chapter 3

1. Harper, "Our Greatest Want," *Anglo-African Magazine* 1 (1859): p. 160.
2. David Walker, *An Appeal to the Coloured Citizens of the World*. (1829; reprint, New York: Hill and Wang, 1965), p. xiv.
3. Ibid., p. 11.
4. Henry Highland Garnett, Preface to Walker, *Appeal*.
5. Walker, *Appeal*, p. 12.
6. Harper, speech, *National Woman's Rights Convention*, pp. 47–48.
7. Reminiscences of J. M. Jones, in Hamilton, *John Brown in Canada*, pp. 14–15; in W. E. B. Du Bois, *John Brown* (1909; reprint, New York: International Publishers, 1962), p. 257.
8. Harper, "From a Woman of the Race He Died For."
9. Harper, "The Triumph of Freedom—A Dream," in Frances Foster, *A Brighter Coming Day: A Frances Ellen Watkins Harper Reader* (New York: Feminist Press, 1990), p. 22.
10. Harper, "From a Woman of the Race He Died For."
11. Harper, "The Triumph of Freedom—A Dream," in Foster, *A Brighter Coming Day*.
12. Ibid., p. 23.
13. Ibid.

14. Harper to Still, Boston, Apr. 19, 1865, in Still, *Underground Rail Road,* pp. 766–67.
15. Harper, "Christianity," in *Poems on Miscellaneous Subjects.*
16. *Zion Herald,* Boston, Mass., in Still, *Underground Rail Road,* p. 779.
17. *Galesburgh Register,* Galesburgh, Ill., in ibid.
18. Still, Underground Railroad, p. 761.
19. Num. 12:1.

Chapter 4

1. Harper, speech, in *National Woman's Rights Convention.*
2. Elizabeth Cady Stanton, speech, in ibid., p. 3.
3. Susan B. Anthony, speech, in ibid., p. 48.
4. Ibid.
5. Lucretia Mott, speech, in ibid., p. 49.
6. Harper, "Two Offers," *Anglo-African Magazine* 1 (1859): p. 91.
7. Still, "Mrs. F. E. Watkins Harper," *Broadside,* The Historical Society of Pennsylvania.
8. Falaka Fattah, interview with author, Philadelphia, Pa., Aug. 4, 1987. Fattah (Frances Ellen Brown) is a descendent of Fenton Harper.
9. "A Lecture," *Sumter News* (S.C.), reprinted in the *Philadelphia Press,* (Sept. 17, 1867); in Still, *Underground Rail Road,* pp. 775–76.
10. Harper to Still, Darlington, S.C., May 13, 1867, in ibid., pp. 767–68.
11. Harper to Still, Cheraw, S.C., June 17, 1867, in ibid., p. 768.
12. Ibid., p. 770.
13. Harper to Still, Florence, S.C., in ibid., pp. 768–69.
14. Harper to Still, in ibid., p. 769.
15. Still, ibid., p. 769.
16. Harper to Still, in ibid.
17. Harper to Colonel Hinton, Wilmington, Del., July 26, 1867. Published as "Mrs. Harper—Affairs in South Carolina," *National Anti-Slavery Standard,* (Aug. 10, 1867): p. 2, cols. 5 & 6.
18. Bettina Aptheker explains in *Woman's Legacy:* "Precisely because passage of the Fifteenth Amendment was intended to advance the Afro-American freedom, it inevitably would have rebounded to the benefit of women, but only a class-conscious element could have seen that point in 1869," p. 49.
19. Philip S. Foner, ed., *Frederick Douglass on Women's Rights* (Westport: Greenwood Press, 1976), p. 87.
20. Ibid.
21. Aptheker, *Woman's Legacy,* p. 31.

22. Ibid.
23. Foner, *Frederick Douglass*, pp. 152–53.
24. In ibid., p. 90.
25. In ibid.
26. Paula Giddings notes that "The feminist and abolitionist camps weren't so neatly divided" (according to color or sex). Lucy Stone and Julia Howe were not as threatened by the black male vote. And Robert Purvis and Harriet Forten Purvis favored the feminist vote "despite the political difficulty of accomplishing this goal." See Giddings, *When and Where I Enter* (N.Y.: William Morrow and Co., 1984) p. 68.
27. Harper, "Mission of the Flowers," *Moses: A Story of the Nile*, p. 47.
28. Ibid.
29. "The Pennsylvania Anti-Slavery Society, a Thing of the Past," *New Era*, (May 6, 1870): p. 2, col. 6.
30. Ibid.
31. Ibid.
32. In Loewenberg and Bogin, eds. *Black Women*, p. 243.
33. Harper, "An address Delivered at the Centennial Anniversary of the Pennsylvania Society for Promoting the Abolition of Slavery," in Alice Dunbar Nelson, ed. *Masterpieces of Negro Eloquence* (New York: Bookery Publishing Co.), pp. 101–6.
34. Still to Harper, the Historical Society of Pennsylvania, Philadelphia, Pa. The last two digits of the date are indiscernible.
35. Harper to Still, Feb. 1, 1869, Athens, Ga., in Still, *Underground Rail Road*, pp. 770–71.
36. Harper to Still, Dec. 9, 1870, in ibid., p. 771.
37. Harper to Still, Feb. 20, 1871, in ibid., p. 772.
38. Harper to Still, March 29, 1871, Greenville, Ga., in ibid., pp. 772–73.
39. Harper to Still, Dec. 29, 1871, Montgomery, Ala., in ibid., pp. 773–74.
40. Harper to Still, July 5, 1871, Mobile, Ala., in ibid., pp. 774–75.
41. Harper to Still, Mar. 1871, Demopolis, Ala., in ibid., pp. 776–77.
42. Harper to Still, in ibid., p. 777.

Chapter 5

1. Harper, "Coloured Women of America," *Englishwoman's Review* (Jan. 15, 1878): pp. 10–15.
2. Harper, *Iola Leroy, or Shadows Uplifted*. (1892; reprint, Boston: Beacon Press, 1987), p. 47.
3. Ibid., p. 178.
4. Ibid., p. 171.

Chapter 6

1. Harper, *Iola Leroy*, (Boston: Beacon Press, 1987), pp. 256–57. Following references will be to this edition unless noted.
2. Still, Introduction to Harper, *Iola Leroy*. (1892; reprint, (College Park, Md.: McGrath Publishing Co., 1969), p. 3.

Chapter 7

1. Harper, "Temperance," *A.M.E. Church Review* 7 (1891): pp. 372–75.
2. Harper, "The Woman's Christian Temperance Union and the Colored Woman," *A.M.E. Church Review* 4 (1888): pp. 313–16.
3. Harper, "Duty to Dependent Races," *Transactions from the National Council of Women in the United States*, Philadelphia, 1891. In *Black Women*, eds. Loewenberg and Bogin, pp. 251–54.
4. Harper, "Coloured Women of America," *Englishwoman's Review* (Jan. 15, 1878).
5. Ibid.
6. Harper, "John and Jacob—A Dialogue on Woman's Rights," *New York Freeman* (Nov. 28, 1885).
7. Giddings, *When and Where I Enter*, p. 23.
8. Ida B. Wells, *On Lynching*. (N.Y.: Arno Press, 1969), p. 234.
9. Ibid.
10. Ida B. Wells, *Crusade for Justice* (Chicago: University of Chicago Press, 1970), p. 58.
11. Ibid., pp. 60–61.
12. Ibid., p. 62.
13. Hazel V. Carby, "On the Threshold of Women's Era: Lynching, Empire, and Sexuality in Black Feminist Theory," *Critical Inquiry* 12 (Aug. 1985): p. 264.
14. Harper, speech, "Woman's Political Future," *World's Congress of Representative Women 1893 Proceedings*, ed. May Wright Sewall (Chicago: n.p. 1894), pp. 433–37.
15. Australia Henderson, lecture, "The Woman's Era," delivered at the Afro-American Studies 15th Anniversary Celebration, University of Iowa, Mar. 1987.
16. Harper, "How to Stop Lynching," *Women's Era*, vol. 1, no. 2 (1894), pp. 8–9.
17. Harper, "An Appeal to the American People," *Poems* (Philadelphia: Merrihew, 1871), p. 6.

Chapter 8

1. Harper, "True and False Politeness," *A.M.E. Church Review* 14 (1898): p. 343.
2. Margaret Hope Bacon, "Frances Ellen Watkins Harper," *Philadelphia Tribune*, Nov. 11, 1987.
3. Harper, "Songs for the People," *Poems*, p. 13.
4. Harper, "True and False Politeness," pp. 343–44.
5. Washington, *Invented Lives*, pp. xvii–xviii.
6. Paul Lauter, "Is Frances Ellen Watkins Harper Good Enough to Teach?" *Legacy: A Journal of Nineteenth-Century American Women Writers*, vol. 5, no. 1 (Spring 1988).
7. Harper, *Moses.*
8. Falaka Fattah, "Poetic Power," *The Philadelphia Inquirer Magazine* (Oct. 24, 1982): 17.
9. Rosa Cannistraci, in conversation with author and Verna Cole, Aug. 5, 1987, in Philadelphia, Pa.
10. Harper, "Woman's Political Future," p. 437.

Bibliography

Andrews, William L. *Six Women's Slave Narratives.* New York: Oxford University Press, 1988.

Aptheker, Bettina. *Woman's Legacy.* Amherst: University of Massachusetts Press, 1982.

Bacon, Margaret Hope. "Frances Ellen Watkins Harper" *Philadelphia Tribune* (Nov. 11, 1987).

———. " 'One Great Bundle of Humanity': Frances Ellen Watkins Harper." *The Pennsylvania Magazine of History & Biography*, vol. 113, no. 1 (Jan. 1989).

Baker, Houston. Workings of the Spirit. Chicago: University of Chicago Press, 1991.

Baraka, Amiri (Leroi Jones). *Blues People.* New York: William Morrow, 1963.

Baskin, Wade, and Runes, Richard N. *Dictionary of Black Culture.* New York: Philosophical Library, 1973.

Barrow, Logie. *Independent Spirits.* London: Routledge and Kegan Paul, 1986.

Bentley, Fannie C. L. "The Women of Our Race Worthy of Imitation." *A.M.E. Church Review* 6 (1890).

Bergman, Peter M. *The Chronological History of the Negro in America.* New York: Harper and Row, 1969.

Birney, Catherine H. *The Grimke Sisters: Sarah and Angelina Grimke, the First American Women Advocates of Abolition and Women's Rights*, 1885. Reprint. Westport, Conn.: Greenwood Press, 1969.

Boyd, Melba Joyce. "The Critical Mistreatment of Frances Harper," *Drumvoices: A Confluence of Literary, Cultural & Vision Arts*, vol. 3 nos. 1 & 2, (1993–94).

———. The Radical Vision of Frances Ellen Watkins Harper." In *The Garland Companion to Nineteenth Century Verse*, ed. Eric Haralson. New York: Garland Press. Forthcoming.

———. *Song for Maya.* Detroit: Broadside Press and Detroit River Press, 1983.

Bragg, George F. *Men of Maryland.* Baltimore: Church Advocate Press, 1914.

Brawley, Benjamin. *The Negro Genius.* New York: Dodd, Mead, and Co., 1937.

———. *Early Negro American Writers.* Chapel Hill: University of North Carolina Press, 1935.

———. *The Negro in Art and Literature.* New York: Duffield and Co., 1930.

———————. Three Negro Poets: Horton, Mrs. Harper, and Whitman." *Journal of Negro History* 2 (1917).

Brown, Hallie Q. *Homespun Heroines and Other Women of Distinction.* Xenia, Ohio: Aldine Publishing Co., 1926.

Brown, John M. "Report of the Principal of the Union Seminary to the Ohio Conference." *Minutes of the Ohio Conference of the African Methodist Episcopal Church,* 1844.

Brown, Sterling A. "Negro Character as Seen by White Authors." In *Dark Symphony: Negro Literature in America,* eds. James A. Emanuel and Theodore L. Gross. New York: Free Press, 1968.

Brown, William Wells. *The Black Man: His Antecedents, His Genius, and His Achievements.* New York: Thomas Hamilton, 1863. Reprint. New York: Johnson Reprint Corporation, 1968.

———————. *The Rising Son or, the Antecedents and Advancement of the Colored Race.* 1873. Reprint, Miami, Fla.: Mnemosyne Publishers, 1969.

Carby, Hazel V. "On the Threshold of Women's Era: Lynching, Empire, and Sexuality in Black Feminist Theory." *Critical Inquiry* 12 (Aug. 1985).

———————. *Reconstructing Womanhood: The Emergence of the Afro-American Woman Novelist.* New York: Oxford, 1987.

Child, Lydia Maria. *The Freedman's Book.* Boston: Tucknor and Fields, 1865.

Clark, Alice. "Frances Ellen Watkins Harper." *Negro History Bulletin,* vol. 5 (Jan. 1942).

Cooper, Anna Julia. *A Voice from the South.* Xenia, Ohio, 1892.

Daniel, Theodora Williams. "The Poems of Frances E. W. Harper." M.A. Thesis. Howard University, May 14, 1937.

Dannett, Sylvia. *Profiles of Negro Womanhood.* Yonkers: Negro Heritage Library, 1965.

Davis, Elizabeth Lindsay. *Lifting as They Climb.* National Association of Colored Women, 1933.

Davis, Marianne W. *The Contributions of Black Women to America,* vol. 1. Columbia, S.C.: Kenday Press, 1982.

Daykin, Walter L. "Race Consciousness in Negro Poetry." *Sociology and Social Research* 21 (1936).

Dillon, Merton. *Elijah P. Lovejoy, Abolitionist Editor.* Urbana: University of Illinois Press, 1961.

Doctorow, E. L. *Ragtime.* New York: Bantam, 1974.

Douglass, Frederick. *The Life and Times of Frederick Douglass.* 1892. Reprint. London: Collier Books, 1969.

Du Bois, W. E. B. *John Brown.* 1909. Reprint. New York: International Publishers, 1972.

———. "Writers." *The Crisis* 1 (Apr. 1911).

Dunbar, Alice Nelson. *Masterpieces of Negro Eloquence.* New York: Bookery Pub. Co., 1914.

———. *The Dunbar Speaker and Entertainer.* Naperville, Ill.: J. L. Nichols and Co., 1920.

Dunbar, Paul Laurence. "An Ante-Bellum Sermon" and "The Poet." In *The Black Poets*, ed. Dudley Randall. New York: Bantam, 1971.

Fattah, Falaka. Interview with author. Philadelphia, Pa., Aug. 4, 1987.

———. "Poetic Power." *Philadelphia Inquirer Magazine* (Oct. 24, 1982).

Foner, Philip S., ed. *Frederick Douglass on Women's Rights.* Westport: Greenwood Press, 1976.

———. *The Voice of Black America.* New York: Simon and Schuster, 1972.

Forbes, Jack. *Black Africans and Native Americans: Color, Race, and Caste in the Evolution of Red and Black Peoples.* New York: Basil Blackwell, 1988.

Foster, Frances. ed. *A Brighter Coming Day: A Frances Ellen Watkins Harper Reader.* New York: Feminist Press, 1990.

Frazier, Elizabeth S., "Some Afro-American Women of Mark," *A.M.E. Church Review* 8 (Apr. 1892).

French, William P.; Fabre, Michel J.; and Singh, Amritjit, eds. *Afro-American Poetry and Drama, 1760–1975*, vol. 17. Detroit: Gale Research Co., 1979.

Fuller, Thomas. "Frances E. Watkins Harper." In *Pictorial History of the American Negro.* Memphis, Tenn.: In Pictorial History, 1933.

Garnett, Henry Highland. Preface to *An Appeal to the Coloured Citizens of the World*, by David Walker. 1829. Reprint. New York: Hill and Wang, 1965.

Garrison, William Lloyd. Preface to Harper, *Poems on Miscellaneous Subjects.* 2d ed. Philadelphia: Merrihew & Thompson, 1857.

Giddings, Paula. *When and Where I Enter.* New York: William Morrow and Co., 1984.

Gloster, Hugh M. *Negro Voices in American Fiction.* Chapel Hill: University of North Carolina Press, 1948.

Gordon, Elizabeth P. *Women Torch-Bearers, The Story of the Woman's Christian Temperance Union.* 2d ed. Evanston, Ill.: National Woman's Christian Temperance Union Publishing House, n.d.

Graham, Leroy. "William Watkins, The Teacher." In *Baltimore: The Nineteenth Century Black Capital.* Washington, D.C.: University Press of America, 1982.

Graham, Maryemma. ed. *Complete Poems of Frances E. W. Harper.* New York: Oxford University Press, 1988.

Handy, James A. *Scraps of African Methodist Episcopal History.* Philadelphia: African Methodist Episcopal Book Concern, n.d.

Henderson, Australia. Lecture. "The Woman's Era," delivered at the Afro-American Studies 15th Anniversary Celebration, University of Iowa, Mar. 1987.

Hill, Patricia Liggins. "Frances Watkins Harper's *Moses: A Story of the Nile:* Apologue of the Emancipation Struggle." *A.M.E. Zion Quarterly Review* 95 (Jan. 1984).

Hooks, Bell. *Ain't I A Woman: Black Women and Feminism.* Boston: South End Press, 1981.

Hopkins, Pauline E. *Contending Forces.* Boston: Colored Co-operative Publishing Co., 1900.

————. "Famous Women of the Negro Race: V. Literary Workers." *Colored America Magazine* 4 (Apr. 1902).

Hyman, Harold M., ed. *The Radical Republicans and Reconstruction, 1861–1870.* New York: Bobbs-Merril, 1967.

Johnston, James H. A. "William Watkins." *A.M.E. Church Review* 3 (1886).

Katz, Bernard, ed. *The Social Implications of Early Negro Music in the United States.* New York: Arno Press, 1969.

Keating, P. J. *The Working Classes in Victorian Fiction.* New York: Barnes and Noble, 1972.

Kelly, Emma. *Megda.* Boston: James H. Earle, 1891.

Kerlin, Robert Thomas. *Negro Poets and Their Poems.* Washington, D.C.: Associated Publishers, 1923.

Lauter, Paul. "Is Frances Ellen Watkins Harper Good Enough to Teach?" *Legacy: A Journal of Nineteenth-Century American Women Writers* 5, no. 1 (Spring 1988): pp. 27–32.

Loewenberg, Bert J. and Bogin, Ruth, eds. *Black Women in Nineteenth-Century American Life: Their Words, Their Thoughts, Their Feelings.* University Park and London: Pennsylvania University Press, 1976.

Logan, Rayford W. and Winston, Michael. *Dictionary of American Negro Biography.* New York: W. W. Norton and Co., 1982.

Loggins, Vernon. *The Negro Author: His Development in America to 1900.* New York: Columbia University Press, 1931.

Low, W. Augustus and Clift, Virgil A. *Encyclopedia of Black America.* New York: McGraw-Hill, 1981.

Majors, Monroe. *Noted Negro Women: Their Triumphs and Activities.* Chicago: Donohue and Henneberry, 1893.

Miller, Ruth and Katopes, Peter J. "Modern Beginnings." In *Black American Writers: Bibliographic Essays*, vol 1, eds. Inge, Bryer, Duke. New York: St. Martin's Press, 1978.

Montagu, Ashley. *Man's Most Dangerous Myth: The Fallacy of Race.* New York: Meridian Books, 1965.

Morrison, Toni. *Beloved.* New York: Random House, 1988.

Mossell, M. F. *The Work of the Afro-American Woman.* Philadelphia: George S. Ferguson Co. 1880.

―――. "The Colored Women in Verse." *A.M.E. Church Review* 11 (1885): pp. 60–67.

Noble, Jeanne. *Beautiful Also Are the Souls of My Black Sisters: A History of the Black Woman in America.* Englewood Cliffs, N. J.: Prentice-Hall, 1978.

Payne, Daniel A. *History of the African Methodist Episcopal Church.* Nashville, Tenn., 1891.

Pendelton, Leila Amos. *A Narrative of the Negro.* Washington, D.C.: K. C. Pendleton, 1912.

"The Pennsylvania Anti-Slavery Society, a Thing of the Past." *New National Era.* (May 6, 1879): p. 2, col. 6.

Petry, Ann. *Harriet Tubman*, 1955. Reprint. New York: Pocket Books, 1971.

"Photographic Essay: Black Women Writers." *Sage: A Scholarly Journal on Black Women* 1 (Spring 1985).

Priest, Joseph and Brown, Rev. W. S. *Bible Defense of Slavery.* Louisville, Ky.: P. F. Brennan, 1851.

The Proceedings of the Eleventh National Woman's Rights Convention, New York, May 10, 1866. The Historical Society of Pennsylvania, Philadelphia, Penn.

Quarles, Benjamin. *Black Abolitionists.* New York: Oxford University Press, 1969.

―――. *Blacks on John Brown.* Urbana: University of Illinois Press, 1972.

―――. *Frederick Douglass.* Washington, D.C.: Associated Publishers, 1948.

Quick, W. H. *Negro Stars in All Ages of the World.* Richmond, Va.: S. B. Adkins and Co., 1989.

Randall, Dudley. Interview with author. Detroit, Mich., Apr. 2, 1989.

Redding, Jay Saunders. *To Make a Poet Black.* Chapel Hill: University of North Carolina Press, 1939.

Redmond, Eugene B., ed. *Drumvoices: The Mission of Afro-American Poetry.* Garden City, N.Y.: Anchor Press/Doubleday, 1976.

Redpath, James. *Echoes of Harper's Ferry.* 1860. Reprint. Westport, Conn.: Negro Universities Press, 1970.

Reese, W. L. *Dictionary of Philosophy and Religion.* Atlantic Highlands, N.J.: Humanities Press, 1980.

Richardson, Harry V. *Dark Salvation.* New York: Anchor Press/Doubleday, 1976.

Richardson, Marilyn, ed. *Maria W. Stewart, America's First Black Woman Political Writer.* Bloomington: Indiana University Press, 1987.

Richings, G. F. *Evidence of Progress Among Colored People.* Philadelphia: George S. Ferguson Co., 1896.

Riggins, Linda N. "The Works of Frances Harper." *Black World* 22 (Dec. 1972).

Robinson, Wilhelmina S. *Historical Negro Biographies.* New York: Publishers Co. Inc., 1967.

Rollins, Charlemae N. *They Showed the Way.* New York: Crowell, 1964.

Rush, Theressa Gunnels; Myers, Carol Fairbanks; and Arata, Esther Spring, eds. *Black American Writers Past and Present: A Biographical and Bibliographical Dictionary,* vol. A–I. Metuchen, N.J.: Scarecrow Press, 1975.

Scruggs, Larson A. *Women of Distinction.* Raleigh, N.C.: Larson A. Scruggs, 1893.

Sewall, May Wright, ed. *World's Congress of Representative Women.* Chicago: n.p., 1894.

Sherman, Joan R. *Invisible Poets.* Urbana: University of Illinois Press, 1974.

Shorter, Susie I. *The Heroines of African Methodism.* Xenia, Ohio: Chew, ca. 1891.

Sillen, Samuel. "Mrs. Chapman and Mrs. Harper." *Masses and Mainstream* 8 (Feb. 1955).

———. *Women Against Slavery.* New York: Masses & Mainstream, 1955.

Simon, Paul. *Lovejoy: Martyr to Freedom.* St. Louis: Concordia, 1964.

Smythe, Mabel M. *The Black American Reference Book.* Englewood Cliffs, N.J.: Prentice Hall, 1976.

Sterling, Dorothy. *We Are Your Sisters.* New York: W. W. Norton, 1984.

Stetson, Erlene. *Black Sister: Poetry by Black American Women, 1746–1980.* Bloomington: Indiana University Press, 1981.

Stevenson, Katharine L. *A Brief History of the Woman's Christian Temperance Union.* Evanston, Ill.: Union Signal, ca. 1917.

Still, William. Introduction to Harper, *Iola Leroy, or Shadows Uplifted,* 1892 (2d edition). Reprint. College Park, Md.: McGrath, 1969.

———. Review. *The Provincial Freeman,* Sept. 2, 1854.

———. *The Underground Rail Road.* Philadelphia: Porter & Coates, 1872.

Stowe, Harriet Beecher. *Uncle Tom's Cabin,* 1852. Reprint. New York: Washington Square Press, 1973.

Tillman, Katherine Davis. "Afro-American Women." *A.M.E. Church Review* 11 (1895): pp. 477–99.

Turner, Darwin T. "Paul Laurence Dunbar: The Poet and the Myths." *CLA Journal* 8, no. 2 (Dec. 1974).

———. "Paul Laurence Dunbar: The Rejected Symbol." *Journal of Negro History* 52 (1967).

———, ed. *The Wayward and the Seeking: A Collection of Writings by Jean Toomer.* Washington: Howard University Press, 1982.

Turner, Lorenzo Dow. *Anti-Slavery Sentiment in American Literature Prior to 1865.* Washington, D.C.: The Association of the Study of Negro Life and History, ca. 1929.

Upshaw, Ida. "The Women of the A.M.E. Church." *A.M.E. Church Review* 12 (1896): pp. 345–52.

Walker, David. *An Appeal to the Coloured Citizens of the World.* 1829. Reprint. New York: Hill and Wang, 1965.

Wall, Cheryl A. "Frances E. W. Harper." In *American Women Writers: A Critical Reference Guide from Colonial Times to the Present,* vol. 2, Lean Mainero, ed. New York: Frederick Ungar, 1979.

Washington, Mary Helen, ed. *Black-Eyed Susans: Classic Stories by and About Black Women.* New York: Doubleday, 1975.

———. *Invented Lives: Narratives of Black Women 1860–1960.* New York: Anchor Press/Doubleday, 1987.

Watkins, William. "Editorial," *Liberator,* Jan. 21, 1832.

Wells, Ida B. *On Lynchings.* New York: Arno Press, 1969.

———. *Crusade for Justice.* Chicago: University of Chicago Press, 1970.

Whitlow, Roger. *Black American Literature.* Chicago: Nelson Hall, 1973.

Williams, George W. *History of the Negro Race in America, from 1619 to 1880,* vol 2. New York: C. P. Putnam's Sons, 1883.

Woodson, Carter C. *The Mind of the Negro as Reflected in Letters Written during the Crisis, 1800–1860.* Washington, D.C.: Association for the Study of Negro Life and History, 1926.

Work, Monroe N. *Negro Year Book.* Tuskegee Institute, Ala.: Negro Year Book Publishing Co., 1925.

Wright, Richard. *White Man Listen.* New York: Doubleday, 1957.

Wright, R. R., Jr., ed. *The Philadelphia Colored Directory.* Philadelphia: Philadelphia Colored Directory Co., 1908.

Yellin, Jean Fagan. *Women & Sisters.* New Haven: Yale University Press, 1989.

———— and Bond, Cynthia D., comps. *The Pen Is Ours: A Listing of Writings by and about African-American Women before 1910 with Secondary Bibliography to the Present.* New York: Oxford University Press, 1991.

Bibliography:
Frances E. W. Harper

Forest Leaves. Baltimore, 1845.

Poems on Miscellaneous Subjects. Boston: J. B. Yerrinton and Son, 1854, 1855. 40 pp.

Poems on Miscellaneous Subjects. Philadelphia: Merrihew & Thompson, 1855.

Poems on Miscellaneous Subjects. 2d ed. Philadelphia: Merrihew & Thompson, 1857.

Poems on Miscellaneous Subjects. 1857; Reprint. Philadelphia: Rhistoric Publications, 1969.

Poems on Miscellaneous Subjects. Switzerland: Kraus-Thompson, 1971.

Moses: A Story of the Nile. Philadelphia: Merrihew and Son, 1869. 47 pp.; 2d edition, 1870.

Moses: A Story of the Nile. 3d edition. Philadelphia: Frances Harper, 1889.

Poems. Philadelphia: Merrihew and Son, 1871. 48 pp.

Poems. Providence, R.I.: A. Crawford Greene & Sons, 1880.

Poems. Philadelphia: G. S. Ferguson, 1895, 1896, 1898, 1900. Reprint. Freeport, N.Y.: Books for Libraries, 1970.

Sketches of Southern Life. Philadelphia: Merrihew and Son, 1872, 1873, 1887, 1888. 24 pp.

Sketches of Southern Life. Philadelphia: Ferguson Bros., 1888, 1891, 1893, 1896.

Iola Leroy, or Shadows Uplifted. Boston: James H. Earle, 1892, 1895.

Iola Leroy, or Shadows Uplifted, 1892 (2d edition). Reprint. College Park, Md.: McGrath, 1969; New York: AMS Press, 1971.

Iola Leroy, or Shadows Uplifted. New York: Panther House, 1968.

Iola Leroy, or Shadows Uplifted, 1892. Reprint. Boston: Beacon Press, 1987.

Iola Leroy, or Shadows Uplifted, 1892. Reprint. New York: Oxford University Press, 1988.

The Martyr of Alabama and Other Poems. ca. 1894.

Atlanta Offering Poems. Philadelphia: George S. Ferguson, 1895.

Atlanta Offering Poems. Philadelphia: 1006 Bainbridge Street, 1895. Reprint. Miami: Mnemosyne Publication, 1969.

Poems. Philadelphia: George S. Ferguson, 1895.

Poems. Philadelphia: 1006 Bainbridge Street, 1898.

Poems. Philadelphia: 1006 Bainbridge Street, 1900.

Idylls of the Bible. Philadelphia: 1006 Bainbridge Street, 1901.

Light Beyond the Darkness. Chicago: Donohue and Henneberry, n. d.

The Sparrow's Fall and Other Poems. Np., n.d.

Complete Poems of Frances E. W. Harper. New York: Oxford University Press, 1988.

A Brighter Coming Day: A Frances Ellen Watkins Harper Reader. New York: Feminist Press, 1990.

Index

INDEX

Books in the African American Life Series

Coleman Young and Detroit Politics: From Social Activist to Power Broker, by
Wilbur Rich, 1988

Great Black Russian: A Novel on the Life and Times of Alexander Pushkin, by
John Oliver Killens, 1989

Indignant Heart: A Black Worker's Journal, by Charles Denby, 1989
(reprint)

The Spook Who Sat by the Door, by Sam Greenlee, 1989 (reprint)

Roots of African American Drama: An Anthology of Early Plays, 1858–1938,
edited by Leo Hamalian and James V. Hatch, 1990

Walls: Essays, 1985–1990, by Kenneth McClane, 1991

Voices of the Self: A Study of Language Competence, by Keith Gilyard, 1991

*Say Amen, Brother! Old-Time Negro Preaching: A Study in American Frustra-
tion,* by William H. Pipes, 1991 (reprint)

*The Politics of Black Empowerment: The Transformation of Black Activism in
Urban America,* by James Jennings, 1992

Pan Africanism in the African Diaspora: The African-American Linkage, by
Ronald Walters, 1993

*Three Plays: The Broken Calabash, Parables for a Season, and the Reign of Wa-
zobia,* by Tess Akaeke Onwueme, 1993

*Untold Tales, Unsung Heroes: An Oral History of Detroit's African American
Community, 1918–1967,* by Elaine Latzman Moon, Detroit Urban
League, Inc., 1994

*Discarded Legacy: Politics and Poetics in the Life of Frances E.W. Harper,
1825–1911,* by Melba Joyce Boyd, 1994